MW01132190

THE EYE OF THE BEDLAM BRIDE

Titles by Matt Dinniman

Dungeon Crawler Carl Series

DUNGEON CRAWLER CARL
CARL'S DOOMSDAY SCENARIO
THE DUNGEON ANARCHIST'S COOKBOOK
THE GATE OF THE FERAL GODS
THE BUTCHER'S MASQUERADE
THE EYE OF THE BEDLAM BRIDE
THIS INEVITABLE RUIN

KAIJU: BATTLEFIELD SURGEON

The Shivered Sky Series

EVERY GRAIN OF SAND
IN THE CITY OF DEMONS
THE GREAT DEVOURING DARKNESS

Dominion of Blades Series

DOMINION OF BLADES
THE HOBGOBLIN RIOT

THE GRINDING

TRAILER PARK FAIRY TALES

THE EYE OF THE BEDLAM BRIDE

DUNGEON CRAWLER CARL BOOK SIX

MATT DINNIMAN

ACE
New York

ACE
Published by Berkley
An imprint of Penguin Random House LLC
1745 Broadway, New York, NY 10019
penguinrandomhouse.com

Copyright © 2023 by Matt Dinniman
Part 6 of "Backstage at the Pineapple Cabaret" copyright © 2025 by Matt Dinniman
Penguin Random House values and supports copyright. Copyright fuels creativity, encourages diverse voices, promotes free speech, and creates a vibrant culture. Thank you for buying an authorized edition of this book and for complying with copyright laws by not reproducing, scanning, or distributing any part of it in any form without permission. You are supporting writers and allowing Penguin Random House to continue to publish books for every reader. Please note that no part of this book may be used or reproduced in any manner for the purpose of training artificial intelligence technologies or systems.

ACE is a registered trademark and the A colophon is a trademark
of Penguin Random House LLC.

Book design by George Towne
Interior art on pages v, 14, 430, 582, and 800: Vintage Black Texture © 316pixel/Shutterstock
All other interior art by Erik Wilson (erikwilsonart.com)

Library of Congress Cataloging-in-Publication Data

Names: Dinniman, Matt, author.
Title: The eye of the Bedlam Bride / Matt Dinniman.
Description: First Ace edition. | New York: Ace, 2025. | Series: Dungeon crawler Carl; book six
Identifiers: LCCN 2024048314 | ISBN 9780593956014 (hardcover)
Subjects: LCGFT: LitRPG (Fiction). | Novels.
Classification: LCC PS3604.I49 E94 2024 | DDC 813/.6—dc23/eng/20241021
LC record available at https://lccn.loc.gov/2024048314

The Eye of the Bedlam Bride was originally self-published, in different form, in 2023.

First Ace Edition: May 2025

Printed in the United States of America
1st Printing

The authorized representative in the EU for product safety and compliance is
Penguin Random House Ireland, Morrison Chambers, 32 Nassau Street,
Dublin D02 YH68, Ireland, https://eu-contact.penguin.ie.

"The moral of the story is:
I chose a half measure when I should have gone all the way.
I'll never make that mistake again."

Mike Ehrmantraut, *Breaking Bad*

AUTHOR'S NOTE

AS ALWAYS, THIS BOOK COULDN'T EXIST WITHOUT ALL THE FANS OUT there giving me support and kudos and love and weird 3 a.m. messages that may or may not be threats. I love you all. That said, love = respect. You don't send butthole pics to people you respect. Please stop sending them. Especially you, Dwight. Holy shit. You need to see a goddamned doctor. Rebecca, on the other hand . . . we good.

THE EYE OF THE BEDLAM BRIDE

OMG. WHAT A FLOOR!

Hi, everyone!

Thank you so much for signing up for the Princess Posse fan club newsletter! This is the only OFFICIAL fan club. I heard rumors of another group called the Donut Holes, and while I appreciate their enthusiasm, this is the ONLY place to get THIS newsletter. I absolutely DO NOT approve of the name Donut Holes.

Anyway!

My name is GC, BWR, NW Princess Donut the Queen Anne Chonk, and I am here to give you a quick recap of what happened on the last few floors. I know we should have been doing this the whole time, and perhaps I will talk Carl into going back and helping me write proper recaps of what happened in the past, but you're here now, and we're about to start the eighth floor. Here's what happened on the sixth and seventh.

The sixth floor started with Carl temporarily giving up the Gate of the Feral Gods to Orren the liaison because he was afraid Carl would get all Carl-y and use it to ruin the floor. I didn't see this happen, but I imagine Carl was all grumpy about it. It ended up being a good thing because we got Sledgie and three other cretin rock bodyguards to escort us for the next three floors in exchange! Isn't that great?

I got the most exquisite temporary class. I was a Legendary Diva! I could cast spells when I sing!

(I hear my album will soon be available on tunneling platforms, so be sure to upgrade to Ultimate Supreme Fan Tier Three or above to get a free ten-second preview of each song before they're released!)

This was the floor where the stupid hunters were trying to kill us. That didn't work out too well for them, now did it? There was this one bug lady, and her name was Vrah. We killed her annoying little sister right in the beginning, and that made Vrah really mad. When Carl went to that lame CrawlCon later on, he met Vrah's mom and made *her* really mad, too. So mad she flew all the way to Earth just to participate as a god named Diwata.

Katia left the party so she could hunt down Eva, her player-killer ex–best friend, and that was really sad because I liked being in a party with Katia. She managed to get Eva in the end, though, and I really hope she'll come back to the party. I love Carl, of course, but it would be nice to have her back. I miss having her with us. I suppose now that she's in love with Daniel Bautista, he'd have to come with her. That would be okay, too, even if he looks like a generic-brand Tony the Tiger.

We learned at the end of the floor there would be a party with a talent contest and pet show for the hunters and the top 50 crawlers. It would be at the High Elf Castle, led by the mean Queen Imogen. The party was called the Butcher's Masquerade.

My Mongo met a few fellow dinosaurs, including a female mongoliensis named Kiwi. Honestly, I don't want to talk about how that started because it was highly traumatic for my brave, sweet boy, whose innocence was savagely ripped away from him. He's still healing.

Also, way back on the third floor, we met a bra-deficient elite named Signet covered in gross tattoos. You may have seen her show, as Carl and I were both guest stars. It was called *Vengeance of the Daughter*. Carl was contractually bound to continue with that story, which was to help her reclaim her crown and defeat Queen Imogen of the High Elves, who helped kill Signet's mother a long time ago.

My friend Prepotente and his former person, Miriam Dom, got in a bit of trouble, and, unfortunately, Miriam Dom passed away. But Prepotente was a very brave goat about it. Miriam used to have another goat, too, one named Bianca who is quite friendly when you get to know her. She's a demon-goat-dragon thing, and she and Prepotente are off on their own now.

I got into a little tussle with a crawler named Lucia Mar, and I killed one of her disgusting dogs, who absolutely deserved it. We later found out that there's something weird going on with Lucia Mar that I honestly just don't understand, but Florin, our Crocodilian friend who says he's from France but was in Africa and has an Australian accent, is determined to find out that full story. He used to hate her because Lucia killed his girlfriend, but now they're friends. I think. I'm not sure honestly.

We had a quest to find and help a giant allosaurus ballerina named Big Tina. It turns out Kiwi is Big Tina's mom, and they both used to be bears. They were changed when Scolopendra, the final boss of the whole dungeon, attacked a long time ago.

And then my ex-boyfriend, Ferdinand, just randomly showed up, thinking he could just waltz right back into my life and I would swoon over him. As if. He was now the pet of Queen Imogen of the High Elves.

All of this time, we were preparing for the Butcher's Masquerade. Mongo prepared for the pet show, training tirelessly, and I coordinated for the talent show. Carl figured out that Queen Imogen would be a country boss, and we had to be ready for it.

When the party came, all of this stuff happened at once. Signet finally got her revenge against Imogen, though it was really sad because she had to kill herself to do it. My Mongo and Kiwi killed Vrah, and I helped kill her mom with my *Laundry Day* spell. Carl killed the last hunter, meaning we got all of them. At the same time, YOU GUYS really pulled through! We used the funds from the fan club, and OMG WE DID IT. We bought a spot on Faction Wars!

Thanks to Carl and Sledgie, we got all of Signet's former tattoos and helpers, Kiwi and Tina, and all of the changelings into the elf castle, and we teleported the whole castle to the ninth floor, meaning we now have an official army. Ferdinand, too, though we don't know if he's going to help us when we get there. Carl and I are now ninth-floor warlords! Isn't that great? There's not much we can do about that on this new eighth floor, but because we're warlords, we can vote for stuff that happens on Faction Wars. Carl is trying to make it so we can all really kill each other. Nobody thinks that's going to happen. We'll see. Carl is good at making impossible things possible.

It wasn't all good. Lots of sad things happened. My friend Firas died. He was really nice. Another guy named Gideon died. I didn't know him very well except in the chat, but Carl was sad because he'd talked Gideon into helping us. Gwendolyn Duet died. This mushroom guy who was a really good singer died. The Popov brothers died, too, but then something amazing happened. They turned into babies and were kicked out of the game. Zev said they were okay! That made everyone happy.

Also, the crime of the century was committed during the Butcher's Masquerade.

An evil, vile, experience-hog crawler named Tserendolgor somehow managed to get her hands on the voting ballot box for the pet show and changed the votes, stealing Mongo's crown from him and handing it off to her disgusting meatball pet, Garret. I want you guys to continue to pore over the footage and find the smoking gun. I've seen some of your investigative efforts so far, and I'm looking forward to more. We need definitive proof! We *will* stop this injustice! #JusticeForMongo.

I, of course, found myself at the top of the crawler list after my performance at the talent show.

And then, right when we thought we were going to the seventh floor, Prepotente broke the whole thing! We pretty much went straight from the sixth to the eighth, but not before I briefly chose a new class. I was a Viper Queen for a few minutes.

And that's it. I know, I know. I'm missing so much. I didn't talk about Samantha and the body Signet gave her to use, or how Britney got burned, or how Tran lost his legs, or about how Zev got a promotion because the Borant government lost control of the crawl to the Valtay brain worms. Or that weird ring Carl got that I think is giving him headaches.

Nor have I talked about Miss Beatrice's return and appearance on Odette's program. It's not worth examining, and I haven't thought about it once since it happened, and there's nothing more to discuss.

Anyway, thank you again for subscribing. Remember to pay your dues! If you forget, you stop getting the newsletter and all the other great benefits, and we don't want that. For an extra twenty credits a week, you get access to the super-exclusive Team Mongo Mommies, which grants entrance to the platinum private Mongo Mommies chat room, officially licensed Mongo merch, along with access to a very special song I wrote all about him! I love you all!

XOXO

Best in Dungeon, Current Reigning Champion, GC, BWR, NW
Princess Donut the Queen Anne Chonk
Co-Warlord of the Princess Posse Faction Wars Team

PROLOGUE

WARNING: LEVEL COLLAPSE IS IMMINENT.

"IT'S TWO GODS," ODETTE CRIED. "GET READY!"

The twin monstrosities appeared, towering out of the mist like a pair of uneven mountains. One was almost three times the size of the other. Odette hadn't been expecting there to be two gods, but she wasn't surprised. The summoning box did that sometimes, especially this deep.

"Two gods?" Chaco shouted from his spot near the stairwell. "Is it still going to work?"

"Gods, I hope so," Odette muttered.

Her non-corporeal avatar floated between her crawlers and the two storm deities. She zoomed with her helmet, trying to see what gods they were. Relief flooded her when she focused on the smaller of the two. Dodola, which was whom Mordecai had been attempting to summon. The other, larger deity was Adad.

> **ODETTE:** You need to get back here.
>
> **MORDECAI:** I'm trying. I don't think I can fly in this downpour. Are they storm gods? Did it work?
>
> **ODETTE:** It worked. Now hurry. Don't let them see you. Try your slake raven form.

Sizzling acid rain poured from the heavens, melting everything it touched. Odette zoomed in farther, watching the aura of both the gods. The hulking form of Adad was AI controlled. The smaller, female Dodola was sponsored. The name **Huanxin** blazed there with a little green dot, meaning the grixist sponsor was present and driving the storm goddess.

Odette opened a new chat window.

ODETTE: Infusing the summoning box with a chain-lightning potion worked. It's Huanxin like you said it would be.

The floor was almost done. The nine puzzle pieces had all been collected. They just needed one more activation, and the four crawlers could leave and enter the stairwell down to the eleventh floor. She looked nervously at the clock. It would be close.

ARMITA: I'm not certain about this.
ODETTE: This was your godsdamned idea. We don't have time. Tell her we're in place and that we have a deal.
ARMITA: I already did. She just wrote back. She wants a bigger cut. She says 10% is too little. She wants 33.
ODETTE: Godsdamnit. You tell that rich cunt we don't need her, then. She can just fuck off. We summoned two gods. We'll use the other one.

The bonus Odette received if Mordecai reached the eleventh floor would be just enough money that she could buy a residency berth in the inner system. She wouldn't be considered wealthy by any means, not like she would if Mordecai reached the 12th, but she would have just enough to get herself settled. She would be a citizen, guaranteed shelter and oxygen and food, which would allow her to finally be safe. She'd have access to free body regeneration, allowing her to regrow her legs. She'd finally be able to put this nightmare behind her.

She still had five seasons left on her indentureship, but per her contract, they'd knock nine seasons off if one of her crawlers reached the eleventh floor. If they opened that stairwell and Mordecai made it down, Odette would be free. Finally.

But if she paid 33% of her bonus to that raging bitch, she wouldn't have enough money. She'd have to settle somewhere as a non-citizen, always scrambling. It'd take another 100 cycles to earn enough, and only if she was lucky enough to get a job. It would never end. Even that 10% she'd already promised was cutting it close.

She thought of Huanxin Jinx, the grixist heiress who sponsored Dodola every season. Odette pictured herself strangling the thin-necked, hairy bitch until all six eyes popped out of her head.

They could quadruple that bonus, and it would be nothing but a day's allowance to Huanxin. She wasn't doing this for the money. This was how she entertained herself. The Ascendency battles didn't start until the crawlers reached the twelfth floor or they were zeroed out, and the heiress was bored. Nothing more.

Armita, Odette's friend and former party member, had secured herself a gig as a Demigod Attendant for the Celestial Ascendency, and this whole scheme had been her idea. The AI subroutines didn't regularly monitor communications between NPCs, and they were legally forbidden from monitoring Ascendency sponsor communications. She was working as the go-between.

When it became clear that Mordecai's team was going to need the intervention of a storm god to survive, it'd been Armita who suggested talking to Huanxin. They'd ask the rich heiress if she'd be willing to drive Dodola to the door location and hit the puzzle with a spell. She'd agreed, for a price.

Without the bribe, the legality of having Armita break character and ask a sponsor for their assistance was sketchy at best. Once money became involved, it clearly became cheating, especially since Odette would be reaping actual credits as a result of the help. It was cheating, and it was fraud.

But what choice did she have? This whole tenth floor had been a disaster. From the start, the crawlers were given a choice of four tracks. Uzzi had blindly chosen the most difficult path. The location of the exit was revealed, but multiple steps had to be completed in order to open the door.

Less than 200 crawlers had survived the Faction Wars chaos, which was usual. The skyfowl seasons typically ended with a ninth-floor slaughter. The idiots always wanted to participate in the fighting. Half of the survivors had taken deals right at the beginning of the tenth. And then half of the rest had died making their way through the floor. Odette only knew of five others who'd made it to the eleventh so far.

Mordecai still hadn't returned. His ability to change forms had made him the best candidate to place the summoning box and activate it.

He'd had to place it far enough away where they had time to prime the puzzle, but not too far so the god wouldn't notice them.

Behind her, Chaco, Hold Steady, and Uzzi worked furiously to prepare the final ritual. Chaco was a wolf-headed pterolykos. The other two had chosen to remain skyfowl, like 91% of their kind. Hold Steady worked his magic, keeping the puzzle pieces primed. Chaco plucked at the strings of his tar, attracting the attention of the gods with his bard magic. Uzzi guarded them both. The skyfowl warrior had limited magic, despite his Storm Commander class, but he had a party-protection spell that kept the caustic rain from burning them all.

The nine pieces pulsed red a few times before turning blue. It was ready. Only one last step remained. The puzzle needed to physically touch a storm god *or* be hit with god-tier storm magic. If either of those happened, the key would form and the door would open.

But it wasn't as simple as dropping the completed puzzle disc on the head of a god from afar. The puzzle needed to *stay* primed, constantly infused with magic, which required Hold Steady to remain nearby. And the puzzle had to remain within the circle of the stairwell.

This last part was next to impossible, and they'd all wanted to take a deal rather than risk not making it.

Odette had already earned her tenth-floor bonus no matter what happened. She'd convinced them to go for it, despite the difficulty. It wasn't all greed. She liked all the party members, especially Mordecai. It was never worth it to take a deal on the tenth floor. Never. They were better off dead.

They were close. So damn close.

ARMITA: I'm not telling her that, Odette. You know how petty she is.

If they could get either storm god to hit the puzzle with a spell—any spell—they'd be good to go. If Chaco's *Lightning Rod* song worked properly, any spells thrown in their general direction would hit the target. The problem was, the crawlers needed to remain nearby. The whole level was about to collapse.

It was always a bad idea to stay in the vicinity of a god. Always.

Huanxin had the ability to enchant the rain. She could make it healing rain or turn each drop into a mob or a thousand other things. It was already raining. All she needed to do was cast the spell, the magic rain would hit the puzzle, and that would be enough. All four party members would make it to the eleventh floor, and then they could reevaluate their survival chances.

If Huanxin refused to help, they still had Adad. He was likely to summon a cloud of lightning-shooting bugs at any moment. With Chaco's spell, the bugs would still target the puzzle. It wasn't ideal, but it would work.

Warning: Level collapse will commence in minus three.

The number 99 appeared flashing in her interface. The units started to count down.

Odette cursed herself for getting involved in this. They could've done it without cheating. She hadn't trusted the team. This would've worked without the bribe.

ODETTE: What is taking you so long?

MORDECAI: I'm grounded, in a bipedal form. I didn't have enough power to choose anything else. I'm too far from Uzzi's protection, and I have to use my *Climate Refuge* spell.

ODETTE: Hurry your feathered ass!

MORDECAI: I think the two gods are about to fight!

ODETTE: Probably not this time. Dodola—

Odette didn't finish. She watched in horror as Dodola suddenly turned and stabbed something into the leg of the much larger Adad. The god disappeared. She'd teleported him away. She turned toward the three crawlers and started casually marching in their direction.

ARMITA: She says she's changed her mind again. Now she wants 50%, and if you don't agree, she's going to zero out the party. I'm sorry, Odette. This is all my fault.

Godsdamnit.

She had to agree. What else could she do? She looked back at the three crawlers huddled by the exit. The round puzzle floated in midair with Uzzi and Hold Steady right behind it. Chaco stood to the side, still plucking at his instrument.

But then, a wave of anger washed over Odette. She thought of the dungeon AI forcing her to choose between saving Armita and Pieter. She'd only had seconds. Her best friend versus her cousin. She'd picked her friend. For Odette's entire life, people were taking advantage of her. Forcing her to submit, to choose. Telling her what to do. They'd taken her entire planet. Her people. Her family. Pieter was a good, sweet boy. But he wasn't as strong as Armita. They'd forced Odette to fight. Forced her to work in this dungeon for so, so long. Every step forward she'd made was only because she'd first had to ask someone else's permission to do so. She was tired of always being bullied. She was tired of being forced to choose between two equally terrible results.

She looked up at the approaching deity. Huanxin Jinx. Fuck that bitch.

ODETTE: Armita, tell her we don't have a deal.
ARMITA: Are you sure?
ODETTE: Yes.

She then moved to a new chat, but before she could type out the message, she was interrupted by Mordecai.

MORDECAI: Dodola is a sponsored god. She's not going to help us. I'm sorry, my friends. I have a plan, but it's going to kill me. Uzzi, see you on the other side, brother.
UZZI: Do not even dare.

Odette waved away her first message and moved to her private chat with Mordecai.

ODETTE: What the hells are you doing?

MORDECAI: My Final Blow skill. It lets me target the puzzle. It's at the top of the list. Odette, I think this is what I'm supposed to do with it. It's why the AI gave it to me.

If Mordecai targeted the puzzle and then got himself hit with a spell from the god, the puzzle would also get hit by the spell. Up until now, the skill only allowed him to target individuals. He'd been using it to great effect, allowing him to find invisible and hidden mobs.

It was a desperate last act. He wouldn't be protected from the spell.

If Mordecai died, Odette's season would be done. She'd be stuck here for five more crawls at least.

The timer was down to 65 units.

ODETTE: Wait thirty units. Keep moving toward us. Let me try something first.

Before he could answer, she pulled that second chat back up.

ODETTE: Chaco, do you have the dart?

CHACO: Yes! But how can that help now?

They'd spent half of their time on this floor hunting down the priceless artifact only for it to be useless. When they'd learned that it had to be a specific type of god to unlock the puzzle, it'd ruined all of their plans since none of them had seen a storm god before this. This whole floor had been them choosing between four paths, and each time, they'd ended up picking the worst possible choice. They'd instead had to find the summoning cube, which wasn't much better.

If only it had been a holy grenade. They'd been everywhere on the previous floor.

ODETTE: There's only one way to survive. Worship Dodola and then use the dart.

CHACO: What? No. Who would I even use it on? Would that even work? She's already summoned.

ODETTE: It'll work. We can't use it on Hold Steady because he's keeping the puzzle primed. The dart doesn't let you use it on yourself. You'll have to use it on Uzzi and then contain him with the cube.

CHACO: Have you lost your faculties? You want me to kill Uzzi? It's not going to happen.

ODETTE: You have to do it quickly.

CHACO: I don't think you heard me, Odette. Mordecai has a plan. He is doing it of his own free will. It's an honorable death.

ODETTE: If Mordecai dies, I go away.

CHACO: I don't care.

ODETTE: Godsdamnit, Chaco. Do you think you'll survive six units on the next floor without me? You don't just show up in the Outreach Guild like you did on this floor. You have to find one.

CHACO: Mordecai will kill me. And he'll leave the party anyway.

ODETTE: I have you in my chat. If you do this, I promise I'll help you no matter what. Without me, you will die. All of you will die. Uzzi will be useless without his brother. I'll talk to Mordecai. I'll convince him this was the best path. Dodola is a sponsored god. She knows what's happening. Mordecai's plan isn't going to work. This is the only way.

Dodola roared. She'd paused, not getting any closer.

ARMITA: She wants to know if you're sure. She sounds angry.

CHACO: Godsdamn you, Odette.

ODETTE: Do it now, Chaco.

This whole time, Uzzi and Mordecai were going back and forth in the group chat. The timer ticked down, slowly but inevitably plummeting toward zero. Odette knew if she actually told Uzzi what the plan was, he'd be on board. Skyfowl were like that. Proud to a fault. But they didn't have time.

ODETTE: Mordecai! Abort! We have a plan that'll work. Get here now!

At the same moment, Chaco worshipped Dodola. He was the first in the party to worship a deity. Odette had told them from the start how dumb it was to tie yourself to one.

"What are you doing?" she heard Hold Steady cry.

"I'm sorry, my friend," Chaco said to Uzzi, who'd turned to regard the large bard.

The skyfowl looked down at the dart in Chaco's wolflike hand, surprised. The Dart of Ophiotaurus. Uzzi lifted his head to the raining sky and cawed. A war cry. He took a step closer to the puzzle and spread his wings in supplication.

He understood.

Chaco threw the dart right into Uzzi's breast. Behind them, Dodola roared in indignation and became unglued. She rushed forward, attempting to cast a spell. She vanished before she could.

"Steady, step back!" Chaco cried as he cast his level 15 *Circle of Containment*, locking the puzzle in with Uzzi, who'd fallen onto his back. His body pulsated and crackled.

"No," Mordecai cried, rushing up. He was in the form of a rat-kin brute, the first form he'd learned how to make. He stopped before the semicircle shell, falling to his knees. He placed his hands against the containment. "Uzzi! Uzzi!"

The skyfowl continued to convulse. Hold Steady cawed angrily as he concentrated on the puzzle, just on the other side of the containment.

One could cast spells on the things inside of the shell but not vice versa.

Uzzi's chest ripped open as the involuntary summoning completed.

Crawler Uzzi has fallen.

"No!" Mordecai cried.

Fifteen units before the collapse. The shell would end on its own in ten.

Dodola formed, hunched over in the shell, forced into the smaller size by the containment. The puzzle, trapped with her, shattered. A round glowing mote of light appeared. The key. It moved toward the stairwell portal, but it, too, was contained by the spell.

ARMITA: Odette, what did you do? She just messaged that she's going to kill the both of us, starting with me.

Dodola raged. She fired lightning, but it just pinged about within the circle, spinning and circling, getting faster and faster. It passed harmlessly through the key mote, which was also made of lightning.

"Oh, Huanxin," Odette muttered. "You poor, dumb fool. That wasn't very intelligent, was it?"

ODETTE: She can't kill you if she's not in the game anymore.

The dart worked much like the holy grenade, but with two differences. The holy grenade made it so no vessel was required to make the summoning happen. With the dart, they'd been forced to pick someone. There were no living mobs left on the floor. It had to be Uzzi.

The second big difference was that the god's immunity wouldn't commence until five units after they fully formed.

Dodola was immune to the lightning bolt itself, but not the area attack it inflicted at the end of its run.

"Cover your eyes," Odette called.

The spinning level 20 *Lightning* spell exploded within the shield. The light was that of a supernova.

The god died. Not even sound escaped the containment. Just the light.

A deity has fallen. The heavens tremble with rage.

Behind her, Chaco gasped. A glowing laurel leaf appeared over his head. He'd jumped ten levels. They'd given him credit for the kill.

"No," Mordecai continued to say over and over.

"What did you do?" Hold Steady asked, looking at Chaco. "You murdered Uzzi."

"I . . . No!" Chaco said, looking at his claws.

"Wait, what? What is this?" Mordecai said, looking up, confusion on his rat face. "Did you use the dart? On my *brother*?"

The containment spell whiffed out.

Dodola's dead form slumped over and then dissipated into ash. The key, unaffected by all of this, moved to the stairwell, opening it up.

ARMITA: I have three seasons left, Odette. She's here every year. Killing me would be nothing to her. You're getting out. But I'm not. What did you do?

ODETTE: I'm sorry, friend.

"You motherfucker!" Mordecai cried, crashing into Chaco. He tackled him, both of them tumbling into the stairwell. They both disappeared. Hold Steady called out and flew after them both, also disappearing, leaving Odette alone.

Silence followed.

Chaco would be fine. With the Godkiller achievement, he'd be able to make a good deal. She'd lied to him. The Outreach Guilds were always right there on the eleventh level. He'd generate right inside the guild. It would be just like the tenth floor. He wouldn't have to ever see Mordecai again.

I made it, she thought as the level started to collapse. *I'm free of this nightmare. Finally free.*

MORDECAI: I am going to kill you, Odette. I am going to get free of this place, I am going to find where you are, and I am going to kill you.

PART ONE

HAVANA

1

Welcome, Crawler, to the eighth floor. "The Ghosts of Earth."

TIME TO LEVEL COLLAPSE: 21 DAYS.

Views: 13 Septillion
Followers: 331 Quadrillion
Favorites: 41 Quadrillion
Leaderboard Rank: 3
Bounty: 2,000,000 gold

Congrats, Crawler. You have received a Platinum Venison Box.
Remaining Crawlers: 38,532
It is December 10th.
Your squad has six open slots.
Entering *El Capitolio Nacional de Cuba*.

DONUT AND I STEPPED THROUGH THE DOOR OF THE GLOBE CHAMBER into the rotunda of a large, empty room made of marble and tile. I was instantly reminded of the US Capitol building, which I'd visited once long ago.

Blue and magenta floor tiles spread in both directions. Enormous arched windows dotted the walls at regular intervals. The curved half-pipe ceiling was also tiled with bronze squares in relief. In the center was a round divot leading to an enormous cupola. It was pitch-black outside, and the room was lit by what looked like streetlamps placed at intervals, giving the room a warm yellow light.

This wasn't the US Capitol building. It was similar in architecture, but not quite. This was *El Capitolio.* The historic capitol building in downtown Havana.

Cuba.

We were the only ones here.

"Listen," Donut was saying as we explored the empty hall. Her voice echoed. "As the party leader and dungeon's number one crawler, I just felt that throwing ourselves right into the Bahamas was a bad idea, so I picked someplace close. Do you really think it was a coincidence that they gave you a book about the Bahamas when that's where Miss Beatrice was? It was quite obviously a trap . . ." She suddenly gasped. "Hey! I went down to number two! Carl, I lost my top spot!"

"I'm not surprised," I said, taking another step into the large room. I focused on the windows. My map showed nothing outside. I focused on one of the brass lamps and the red-and-green ribbon hanging from it. It was a Christmas decoration. "Did you see that notification when we got here? It said it was December 10th."

"Carl, I need to pick a new class! Hey, I have more time to pick now. I now have ten minutes to choose!"

"Good," I said.

CARL: Mordecai, are you there? Donut needs help with her new class.

MORDECAI: Holy shit, I'm here. It just blinked, and now we've skipped a floor. I heard what the announcement said. By his left tit, what did you guys do?

CARL: I had nothing to do with it. That was all Prepotente. Talk to Donut. She picked something on her own last floor, but she only had it for a minute.

DONUT: VIPER QUEEN WAS A GREAT CLASS, AND I'LL HAVE YOU KNOW I KEPT MY ABILITY TO SPIT POISON EVEN THOUGH I NEVER USED IT. I DON'T KNOW WHY EVERYBODY ALWAYS GETS GRUMPY WHEN I MAKE MY OWN DECISIONS. CARL IS ALWAYS MAKING DECISIONS WITHOUT ASKING ME. I STILL HAVE ALL MY BARD ABILITIES, TOO, THOUGH I FORGOT A COUPLE SONGS.

MORDECAI: Donut, hit me with your choices.

Donut jumped to my shoulder as I explored. As they went back and forth, I continued to examine the room. There were multiple doors, but they were all locked. At the end of the hall was a door, and there was a level stairwell behind it. I walked to the door and tried to open it.

You need a key to open this door.

Damnit.

I moved to one of the tall windows and put my hand against it.

This area has not yet been unlocked.

I put my face against the glass to look outside, but I couldn't see anything. It was just swirling black smoke.

IMANI: Everybody check in. Where are you? We picked the western United States, and it looks like we're in some indoor water park in the middle of nowhere. Some place called the Great Wolf Lodge. We can't go outside yet. Elle and I have been placed in different squads, and they made us pick the starting location separately, but we both picked the same place.

KATIA: We're in Iceland. We can't go out, either. There's a stairwell here, but we need a key.

CARL: Same. We're in Cuba. Havana.

ELLE: Cuba? Prepotente picked Cuba? Why would he do that?

CARL: He dumped us before this level started. I don't know where he is. He never answers my chats, but I suspect he might be in the Bahamas.

ELLE: So Donut picked Cuba? Or was that you? Are you looking for cigars or something?

LI NA: We are in the Galaxy SOHO building in Beijing. There are hundreds of crawlers here with us.

IMANI: Is Chris still in your party? He never went back to mine.

LI NA: He is with us.

KATIA: Florin, where are you?

IMANI: I thought Florin was in your party.

KATIA: He left just before Carl and Prepotente broke the last level.

ELLE: Yeah, that was really fucked-up, Carl. You need to warn us next time. I don't know if skipping levels is good for our health. Not all of us are as trained up as you.

CARL: I love how you guys just assume I had something to do with it. That was 100% Pony. I had no idea that was going to happen.

FLORIN: I am in Ecuador.

I continued to explore the floor, but there didn't appear to be a way out.

DONUT: I AM ABSOLUTELY NOT PICKING SOMETHING CALLED AN AGONY URCHIN, MORDECAI. THAT SOUNDS DISGUSTING. IT CHANGES THE WAY I LOOK, AND I WILL NEVER PICK A CLASS THAT CHANGES THE WAY I LOOK. I HAVE AN IMPORTANT IMAGE TO MAINTAIN.

MORDECAI: It's a great class. It's either that or Master Telephone Psychic. That one is pretty good, too, especially with your charisma, but you didn't do so well with psionic attacks on the previous floor.

DONUT: THAT SONG WAS VERY HARD TO SING.

MORDECAI: Well, those are your two best choices by far. Urchin will help keep you safe and Psychic will make your mapping ability better and give you some offensive charm spells.

DONUT: I'M PICKING PSYCHIC.

Donut glowed.

DONUT: HEY! I GOT EVERYTHING LISTED AND A FEW ADDITIONAL SPELLS! THIS IS GREAT!

MORDECAI: Your Character Actor skill is powerful now. What spells did you get?

DONUT: SO, I STILL HAVE THE VENOM SPITTER SKILL FROM THE LAST FLOOR, BUT IT'S ONLY LEVEL 3. MY MAP CAN SEE A LOT BIGGER AND MORE STUFF. I CAN SEE THE WHOLE BUILDING. IT'S ALMOST LIKE WE ALREADY HAVE THE MAP FROM A NEIGHBORHOOD BOSS, BUT I DON'T SEE ANY MOBS AT ALL. IT'S EVEN BETTER THAN THAT PATHFINDER SKILL. I GOT A SPELL CALLED *BRAIN FREEZE* AND ONE CALLED *BAD ATTITUDE* AND ANOTHER CALLED *WHY ARE YOU HITTING YOURSELF?* THAT ONE IS GREAT! IT MAKES PEOPLE STAB

THEMSELVES IN THE FACE! MY INTELLIGENCE WENT UP FIVE POINTS, TOO!

I relaxed. That was pretty good.

MORDECAI: *Bad Attitude* is similar to Carl's *Fear* spell, but it'll be a lot more potent in your hands. If you work it together, it'll be a great combo. *Fear* tends to affect dexterity while *Bad Attitude* drains intelligence and lowers resistances. *Brain Freeze* does the same thing, but it targets only one mob and drains health. It also makes them temporarily blind if you can get it up to 10.

DONUT: IT STARTED AT LEVEL 8.

MORDECAI: Good. You'll want to train that one.

CARL: Can you see anything? We're locked in a large room.

MORDECAI: No. I tried to open the door, but it says "Exit isn't yet available. Wait for the level announcement."

We didn't have to wait long.

A new timer appeared in my vision.

Time Until Phase Two: 14 days.

It started to count down.

Cascadia started the announcement. I immediately noted she wasn't nearly as chipper as she usually was. She pushed her way through the announcement with the enthusiasm of a kid being forced to mow their own lawn.

Hello, Crawlers.

Welcome to the eighth floor. The Ghosts of Earth.

This is going to be a long message. This floor is simple, but the environment requires a small amount of explanation. Not that you twits are going to understand either way.

You have all picked one of 293 different regions. We have just over 38,000 crawlers joining us, and of the groups, you are occupying 205 of the regions. Unlike the bubbles of the fifth floor, you are *not* distributed evenly. But just because you don't see anybody else, it doesn't mean you're alone. Each region contains two stairwells, and you have been generated near one of the two.

The theme of this floor is broken up into three parts. Phase two starts in 14 Earth days. You will not be able to obtain an exit key until then. Thank the gods. For the next two weeks, you will be stuck within your starting area.

All crawlers have been placed in squads of no more than five. If your party is six or more, the party members have been split into equal-number squads of less than five. These squads are not able to be broken. If you leave your party, you will *not* leave the squad. You have to work together to survive.

You'll notice your squad has six more spots than the number of crawlers. So if you're by yourself, it'll have seven spots total, and if your squad consists of five crawlers, it'll have eleven spots total. Your job for the next 14 days is to fill your squad. You will be required to fill your squad before you will be allowed to proceed to phase two. If you do not fill your squad before the timer runs out, it will be filled randomly. Trust me. You don't want that. We'll get to that in a moment.

In 14 days, you will be given at least two options on where to send your squad for the second phase. It will be a different geographic location than where you've started. You, along with your full squad, will be required to fight your way to an exit key. This will not be easy, so it is in your best interest to make certain your squad is as powerful as you can handle. More details on the assault phase of this floor will be forthcoming.

This is how phase one works.

All of you are inside a large structure within your starting area. As soon as this message ends, the doors will open, and you will be allowed to proceed outside.

Each region is limited, but you will have plenty of area to investigate. In most cases, you will be allowed to explore in a circle of about 99 kilometers from your starting location in any direction. If this causes an overlap with another region, this distance will be shortened. If you are on an island, you will not be able to venture more than six kilometers offshore.

You will *not* be able to enter any other regions during phase one.

Your starting area is an exact replica of Earth's surface area as captured on the indicated date. This includes all the geographic features, buildings, vehicles, and yes, the people.

That's correct. You will be fighting and exploring in a precise facsimile of Earth in the weeks before the collapse.

There are a few important caveats. You're living inside of a memory. In most cases, you will not be able to interact with mobile biological entities within the replay. They will not appear on your map. Think of them like intangible ghosts. They can't see you, and if you touch them, you will go right through them. They will be going about their lives just as they did on the day of the recording.

However—and this is very important, so pay attention—all non-biological, non-attached items will be tangibly present and *will* maintain their mass and momentum until physically interacted with by a crawler or a mob or an unexpected environmental factor.

You can enter buildings. You can use non-automatic doors in most cases. You can break windows. You can get hit and killed by a vehicle. You can go to a grocery store and take all the onions. You can allow a person to walk through you, which will likely rip the clothes from their bodies. The visible portions of their bodies will continue on their way. The people and animals are ghosts. Everything else is not. Complex machines may or may not work, depending on what they are. You can pick an onion or piece of tofu out of a ghost's hand and throw it at a mob. The ghost will continue to eat, but the onion will now be on the ground. You can place a barrier in a street, and a car will crash into it, but the ghostly avatars of the drivers will continue on their way, floating toward their destination as if the accident never happened.

"Onions and tofu?" Donut asked. "Is that what she thinks we eat?" I waved for her to be quiet. My mind was swirling with the possibilities.

In other words, you can destroy the environment as much as you like. You can move mountains if you have the power. The physical items will only move as they did on that date if they are in the exact

place and condition they were at the time of recording. The world is your literal playground.

Note: Anything you loot on this level that comes from the Earth memory will turn to dust upon the collapse of this level. You will *not* be arming yourselves with the content of your local military base for use on the ninth floor.

I groaned. That was exactly what I'd been thinking.

That's the environment. Now let us get to the squads.

Your area is seeded with mobs and bosses and legendary creatures that are exclusive to the folklore of the region which you inhabit. For example, those of you in Romania will be dealing with vampires and werewolves. Those of you in Ireland will have leprechauns and banshees. Those of you in Japan are just plain fucked.

The farther out from your starting area, the more difficult the monsters and bosses you will face. These monsters will also be interacting with the environment, so it's likely their locations will be obvious, especially if the mobs are unintelligent, as they will be attempting to attack the non-corporeal locals.

At the end of this message, your Squad Leader will receive a set of twenty flags containing your squad's logo, which has been automatically created by the system.

If you plant the flag within the body of a living entity while they are at less than 5% health, they will be transformed into something called a T'Ghee totem, which will be added to the Squad Leader's inventory.

My breath caught in my throat. I tried not to outwardly react. I knew exactly what that was thanks to the cookbook.

If it is a non-corporeal monster, the flags will still work. Flagged monsters will automatically join your squad and will automatically be minions of whoever summons them. They will follow the summoner's orders.

That is, they will follow orders to a certain extent, depending on the level difference and nature of the monster. While you need a squad that's as powerful as possible, it might not be in your best interests to build a team that's a little *too* strong. You may dismiss mob squad members if they don't work out by ripping the T'Ghee totem in two.

If you run out of or lose your twenty flags before your squad is filled, they will not be replaced, so be careful with them. You may collect more totems than squad spaces. You may trade totems with fellow crawlers. You may steal totems from fellow crawlers.

Upon the start of phase two, all non-placed totems will dissipate. All surviving squads may choose a single T'Ghee card to keep upon the collapse of this floor.

That's it for now. More details on phase two and phase three will become available in a few days. Furthermore, fighting with T'Ghee totems comes with a few additional rules, which will be explained after the next recap episode. I'm supposed to explain that part now, but honestly, you monkeys think you're so smart and clever, I'm certain you can figure it out on your own.

Now get out there and kill, kill . . . you know.

I took a deep breath. I had so many questions about how this worked. Especially the environment.

MORDECAI: Do either of you chuckleheads know anything about Cuban mythology? Or have someone on your chat who does?

DONUT: I KNOW THEY HAVE FLAT SANDWICHES HERE. AND ISN'T THIS WHERE THAT GUY FROM *I LOVE LUCY* WAS FROM? OH, AND THAT TRE GUY FROM *BOYZ N THE HOOD* IS FROM HERE, TOO, I THINK.

I was about to bitch, again, about Donut choosing Cuba, but there was nothing we could do about it now. The usefulness of the *Book of Lore* was painfully obvious. I understood Donut's logic, but she'd been wrong. If we were starting this on December 10th, that meant we'd be moving away from this location on the 24th. Bea and her friends had flown there on the 26th, which meant there was no chance we'd have seen their ghosts if we'd chosen the Bahamas as our phase one location.

But now, because we were going to be moving to a second location for phase two, they'd have plenty of time to engineer a scene where Donut and I were forced to watch Bea get railed by some other dude. I had no doubts that they'd be angling to get us over there for phase two.

They couldn't physically use Bea, but this was still a way to fuck with us. They were likely going to try this with multiple squads, sending us all to places where we could watch loved ones like we were in a fucked-up version of *A Christmas Carol.*

That was something I'd have to worry about in a few weeks. For now we needed to focus on squad building.

"Carl, did you understand anything that lady was talking about?"

"I think so," I said. "Do you remember when I used to play that Pokémon game on the Nintendo? I think it might be a little like that."

CARL: Mordecai, do you know what a T'Ghee totem is?

I wanted to hear what he had to say about this. I already knew quite a bit because of Allister, who'd written the 13th edition of the cookbook. For him, T'Ghee was a religion, and it had nothing to do with capturing and summoning monsters, but I could already see how this was going to work.

MORDECAI: I do. They're similar to Bautista's stuffed animals, but they're in the form of large playing cards. They're kinda like your tarot cards, actually. They're reusable, even if the summoned monsters die. I've seen them used in a few different ways over the seasons, so we'll have to wait until the next announcement.

"Carl, I just talked to Prepotente, and he *is* in the Bahamas!" Donut said. "He wants you to read the lore book to him!"

"I'm shocked," I said drily.

"He says there's probably some crossover with Cuba, so the book won't be completely useless to us."

The entire room blinked, and a new door appeared where there'd been none before. New light filtered through the windows. The new door was an entrance to our personal space.

"Tell him I'll read him whatever he wants in exchange for half of those Size Up potions he has. He can sell them to us using the store interface, or he can join the guild and do it face-to-face. Come on, Donut," I said, heading toward the door to the safe room.

2

"OH, MAN," I SAID TO MORDECAI AS WE ENTERED THE SAFE ROOM. HE sat at the counter with Bomo, the sole remaining member of our four bodyguards. The other three cretins had gone down with the High Elf Castle to the ninth floor.

Mordecai had been a tiny cute creature the previous floor. Something called a pocket kuma. He was now the same size as the rock bodyguard. He was large, pink, bald, and he had a single blinking eye in the center of his cone-shaped head.

"A cyclops?" Donut asked, looking him up and down. "You turned into a cyclops? And why are you so chunky? You look like a knockoff version of that starfish guy from that Krusty Krab cartoon, but with only one eye. Great, now I'm going to get the theme song stuck in my head. Do you have any depth perception?"

"Not really," he said, standing to his full height. He even sounded like Patrick from *SpongeBob SquarePants* when he talked, which made him come across as stupid. He was just as tall as he'd been when he was an incubus, but like Donut said, he now had a wide belly, stretching his white shirt to its limits. His skin was a bright pink, and his bald, cone-shaped, furrowed forehead glinted dully in the light. His single brown eye was the size of an ostrich egg. A caterpillar-like eyebrow stretched across his head. His fingers looked like wrinkly sausages.

I'd only seen one other cyclops creature before, and that had been a bartender somewhere. Mordecai was a different kind. I examined him.

Mordecai. Hills Cyclops. Level 50.

Manager of Princess Donut.

This is a non-combatant NPC.

Of all the cyclops-style monsters populating the dungeon, the Hills Cyclopses are both the weakest and the dumbest of the lot. These shambling pinheads tend to spend their days working as shepherds, herding their sheep and goats. They're always disheveled because they can't see their own reflections in mirrors. At night, they can be found at the local drinking establishments, getting into fistfights and drinking contests with their imbecile friends. They're mostly harmless as long as you don't mess with their flock and/or their girlfriends. I was going to add a joke about those two being the same thing, but I'm trying to be more mature.

Just kidding. These dudes definitely fuck their sheep.

"It's better than the form I'd taken for the ten minutes the seventh floor was open," he said. "I was a slime. I had no goddamned arms."

"Oh, shit," I said. "I didn't know they could do that to you."

He grunted. "I was a kua-tin once, and I had to spend the floor in a glass pitcher. Another time I was a skreich ghast, and I kept teleporting away against my will."

"Hey!" Donut shouted from across the room. She'd jumped to the top of the mailbox that sat in the corner. "There's only one spell book in here! I didn't get my Book of the Floor delivery from the seventh floor!"

"Nope," Mordecai said. "You snooze, you lose."

"This is an outrage! Carl, you need to send a message to your lawyer this instant!"

"What did you get?" I asked as I sat down at the table. Holy cow was I tired. I needed to go into my room and reset my exhaustion level, which would only take a minute thanks to the Instacot 60 bed upgrade from the guild.

"It's a spell book for something called *Mute.* That sounds boring."

"Good," Mordecai said. "That's on our list. You can stop monsters from casting spells. Learn it and practice it. Didn't you get another random spell book at the prize counter?"

"I did, but it's in a box I haven't opened yet." She glowed as she read the new spell book.

Donut let Mongo out of his box, and he screeched, running about the room. He looked out the door into the main guildhall area. He screeched again.

"Mongo, who are you looking for?" Donut asked. "Mommy is right here!"

Mongo made a sad little squawk.

"Carl," a voice called, rolling in from the training room, "what has taken you so long? We need to go back out there and find a Pulpmancer!"

"Samantha!" I said. "You took off! I didn't know where you went."

The last time I'd seen her, she'd been blown up and burned to hell multiple times. She appeared to have gone back to normal. Her hair had returned, and her scorched latex skin appeared clean and shiny.

"She came back to the safe room," Mordecai said. "She *flew* here. Pushed her way through the brambles to get to the door."

MORDECAI: We need to have a talk about her. Something is obviously happening.

CARL: Yeah, no shit. You said she'd never be able to do any of this stuff.

MORDECAI: I don't understand it, which makes it extra dangerous. Withering spirits shouldn't be able to do this. She won't shut up about that flesh golem you have in your inventory. Don't give it to her until we figure out why and how she's gaining this power.

"My cousin gave you her mother, and we need to find a mage to animate her! I need my body back! Come on. Let's go right now, Carl!"

"Samantha, we just landed on a new floor. Don't worry. We'll figure something out. Let's get our bearings first."

"I'm going to kill your mother."

"And I'm not going to help you if you keep threatening me."

She started growling. She rolled off to chase Mongo.

ELLE: Holy shitballs, guys. Have you opened your boxes and achievements yet?

DONUT: NOT YET. THEY DIDN'T GIVE ME MY SPELL BOOK OF THE FLOOR PRIZE, AND I'M QUITE UPSET ABOUT IT.

ELLE: That's some bullshit right there. You should make Carl's lawyer sue them over it.

DONUT: I KNOW, RIGHT?

"Do you think anything is going to happen to Prepotente?" Donut asked as she watched Mongo rush after the doll head. "They got mad at Carl for having the Gate of the Feral Gods because they thought he might break a level, but Prepotente actually did break one."

"I think he'll be okay," Mordecai said. "I was just talking to Mistress Tiatha, and she filled me in on what that crazy goat did. This one is on the engineers. They fashioned that level so it was just like the fairy tale. The kid in the story did the exact same thing the goat did, but it took him thousands of years to figure it out. They should never have built it that way. This isn't the first time a level was doomed from the start. I think I told you about the bacterial infection incident from the previous Borant season. There was another one where the crawlers had to hand-build bridges, but the provided materials made it impossible, and the council had to step in. This was the first time that it failed so quickly, I think. The Valtay are likely irritated with the Borant engineers who designed the level, but it sounds like there's plenty of blame to go around. The Apothecary and the Plenty are probably on their shit list for providing the means, not that the showrunners can do anything about that. The whole thing was a political maneuver to make a lot of money for those two sponsors, all at the cost of the Valtay and the Syndicate as a whole. It's all a game to them, and it's nothing new."

"What do you mean?" I asked. "I thought the Apothecary and the Plenty were losing ungodly amounts on benefactor benefits?"

"I'm not even going to pretend to understand most of it, but the sheer amount of money the Syndicate pays just to use the tunnel system to live stream all of this is enormous and paid in advance. If an entire floor is skipped, it's not refunded. Plus . . ."

He trailed off. He looked back and forth between me and Donut. He was looking up at the spinning star over Donut's head.

"You did it?" he asked.

"Oh, yeah," I said, grinning sheepishly. He'd known that we were talking to my attorney, and he'd known what we were planning. But everything had happened so fast at the end of the last floor, we hadn't had the chance to tell him it had worked. And this was the first time we were able to talk about it out loud.

"We kick-started a war!" Donut announced. "Isn't that great?"

"Who's your warlord adjutant?" he asked. "Have they assigned him or her yet?"

"Uh," I said. "I don't know what that is."

He grunted and shook his head. "By his left tit. You two . . . You know what? We'll talk about it later. Open your damn boxes."

DURING THE BUTCHER'S MASQUERADE, I'D STOOD UPON PREPOTENTE'S personal space cube for a minute and opened a few boxes, but I'd deliberately not checked my achievements, which would've added several boxes to the pile and I wouldn't have had time to open them all. We hadn't been in an actual safe room since before the party. I had literally dozens of achievements and boxes, including a legendary boss box and two different quest boxes for the Vengeance of the Daughter and the Recital quest. The vast majority of the achievements were for stupid things, like riding in an elven carriage and using a goodwill ballroom. The notable ones were:

> **New Achievement! Oh shit! A country boss!**
>
> **You ever have one of those jobs where there's a big boss somewhere in the building, but you've never actually seen them? There's rumors that he's a complete douche with an epic temper, but you're so far down the totem pole, the very idea of having anything to do with the guy is just ridiculous. People speak about him with frightened whispers, and it's almost like he's some invisible, terrifying urban legend. Then *BAM!* One day you're coming out of the bathroom, wrestling with a stuck zipper, and he's right there looking at you like you should be ashamed of yourself just for existing. How dare you throw yourself in his line of sight, you worthless piece of shit?**
>
> **That's the position you're in right now.**
>
> **Second only to the infamous floor boss—which doesn't show up**

until the tenth floor—this is the biggest, baddest bitch one can come across in *Dungeon Crawler World*.

Reward: You know how this goes, you worthless piece of shit.

I'd received that one when Imogen had suddenly appeared in the convoy to the castle.

New Achievement. The Scourge.

The Butcher's Masquerade has started. You have collected the most hands. You have caused more mothers to cry, more children to hate than any other crawler before you. You are the champion murderer supreme. You are number one. If only your own mother wasn't already dead so she could see you now.

Reward: You have received a Legendary Hunter Champion Box.

A legendary box!

New Achievement. Marked for Life.

You were marked for death by a god. That god entered your realm, yet you somehow survived. That's quite the achievement right there. Too bad the god will probably try to kill you even harder next time. You are so fucked.

Reward: You have received a Platinum Apostate Box.

That was great, but my breath caught in my throat the moment I saw the next one.

Finally, I thought. *Fucking finally.*

New Achievement. Apex Predator.

Holy shit.

They're dead.

All of them.

Every. Last. One.

Not only did you kill more hunters than everyone else, but you killed the very last one. One could fill a very stinky swimming pool with the blood you spilled on the Hunting Grounds.

You have become a very scary dude. Maybe I should be calling *you* "Daddy" instead of the other way around.

Reward: Nothing!

. . .

Just kidding. You have received a Celestial Predator Box.

My hands shook. I could barely pay attention to the next group of achievements.

New Achievement! Ménage à Quatro!

You survived a four-way boss battle! Wow! In addition to the boss box you got from this, not to mention that Apex Predator Box you're still probably freaking out about, you've gotten another prize. It's like Christmas!

Reward: You've received a Platinum Orgy Guy Box.

New Achievement! Fuck This Floor.

You went down the stairs less than an hour after you arrived upon the level. Who needs to grind and grow in strength? Let's see how that works out for you.

Reward: You've received a Platinum Here's-Some-Good-Shit-Because-You're-Gonna-Need-It Box

New Achievement! Pacifist!

You survived an entire floor without hurting a single poor mob. That's not how this works. Nobody likes you.

Reward: You've received a Gold Pacifist Box.

New Achievement! Collective Bargaining!

More than 1,000 crawlers have received the exact same box at the exact same time.

Working together, huh? We don't know if we like that. Better toughen up the rules a little. Better break a few extra kneecaps. Better bury a few more bodies.

Reward: You've received a Gold Scab Box.

"CARL, CARL, I GOT LEGENDARY BOXES! I GOT A LEGENDARY BEGUILer's Box for charming Ferdinand and a Legendary De-Sleeving Box for what we did to Diwata! And that's on top of the legendary boss box. I also got a bunch of boxes for singing! And an orgy box! And a fan box I can open tomorrow! Mongo! Mommy got a bunch of great boxes!"

Mongo made an excited squeak.

"Carl?" Mordecai asked, looking at me.

"I got a celestial," I said.

Donut stopped dead.

"What?" she asked. "And I didn't get one? I helped kill a god!"

I reached over and gave her a pat. "It wasn't for that. It was for killing the last hunter. I got a fan box, too, but it was for getting a bunch of viewers when Britney and I met Queen Imogen. We'll open them up later together."

She harrumphed.

"Well, don't just sit there," Mordecai said, his voice soft. "Let's see your prizes."

And so we did.

Donut went first.

The boxes appeared, a line of them that stretched all the way across the room. The first dozen were Bronze and Gold Adventurer Boxes, filled with good healing and mana potions along with a few potions of Phase Through Walls, which Mordecai was pretty excited about, along with dozens of junk clothing items and weapons.

Donut hadn't received a quest box for the Vengeance of the Daughter storyline. It was one of the few quests that had only gone to me. But for the Tina quest, she received a coupon for a free Town Upgrade. That was something we'd be saving for the next floor. I knew I'd be receiving the same thing for that quest.

She received a skill potion from the Gold Pacifist Box which was for upgrading her Love Vampire skill. In the scab box, she received an upgrade to her brush, **the Enchanted Fur Brush of the Ecclesiastic**, which added an additional ten percent to her constitution on top of the measly two points it normally gave for getting brushed each morning.

The masquerade prize counter box she'd bought from Chaco opened, revealing a few items and a spell book. The Platinum Good-Shit Box contained a potion that was pink and frothy. Mordecai whooped.

"Cosmic Buff potion!" he said. "Raises a random stat by 10 points."

He'd mentioned these before. These were a different kind of potion than the standard buff potions that one could only take a limited amount of.

MORDECAI: If you get one of these, too, you should allow me to examine it for a bit at my table before you drink it. We'll want Donut to drink hers straightaway.

CARL: Okay.

The Platinum Orgy Box contained a coupon for a free mercenary purchase. The legendary boss box contained gold, healing scrolls, and something called a Flawless Jeweler's Gem.

"Hmm, yellow," Donut said, examining the large jewel. She did not sound impressed. "Yellow orange, really. I think it's a citrine. Not exactly my color. It clashes with my fur."

"Oh, wow. That's for upgrading your tiara," Mordecai said. "We can't just apply it, though. We'll have to go to a jeweler. They have one in the Desperado."

I laughed when the beguiler's box opened, revealing a single shining nipple ring. It glowed red.

"This is not funny, Carl," Donut said, spitting with disgust. It disappeared before I could examine it.

The de-sleeving box contained 100,000 gold—which was a lot for a box—and a strange type of spell book I'd never seen before. The book was thick, like a dictionary, with a bumpy leather cover. It was chained shut with a lock, and it bounced around on its own. Purple wisps of smoke came off it. I was immediately reminded of the book from the *Evil Dead* movies.

Next to me, Mordecai let out a gasp.

Donut took all the gear out and lined it up on the table. She immediately pushed all the lower-tier stuff away. We'd add it to the equipment pile for the next floor. She let me examine a Phase Through Walls potion, which would allow us to pass through wood, stone, or metal walls, but Mordecai warned that we should only use them in extreme emergencies. They were very dangerous to use, especially if we were fighting someone with any sort of counter to it.

Her Love Vampire skill, which she'd received for reaching 100 in charisma, had never worked really well until she'd used the temporary tiara on the previous floor that had effectively doubled her charisma. It normally allowed her to charm one intelligent opponent, and all damage upon her would be reflected to that opponent. The problem was, the opponent could easily break away. However, when she'd increased her charisma to an epic level, it not only worked much better; it ended up working without her even having to think about it. It just happened automatically, plus it charmed up to five mobs at a time.

We probably weren't going to get it to that level again anytime soon, but the skill potion added three levels to the skill, bringing it up from three to six, which would make it more powerful than it had been. But most importantly, it made it so it would cast automatically in certain situations.

The first spell book, which we'd also gotten from Chaco's prize booth, was a strange spell. It was a team buff called *Rigorous*. It was basically a damage-reflect spell, but only for debuffs and afflictions. Similar to my *Super Spreader*, but it didn't actively give the target the ailment, just the effect. Mordecai said that was an important distinction. Donut was not impressed, but she read it anyway on the guide's insistence.

The mercenary coupon was interesting. It was just a piece of paper with a buff flexed arm on it. I picked it up.

Mercenary coupon! The bearer of this instrument is entitled to 100,000 gold worth of mercenary services at any participating Meat Shields location.

"Meat Shields?" I asked.

Mordecai shrugged. "Probably the name of the mercenary markets on this floor. There's one in both the Desperado and Club Vanquisher.

And there probably was one in Larracos, too. Speaking of, you need to purchase a mercenary training arcade for the guildhall. I'll talk to Imani about it."

Donut downed the Cosmic Buff potion. Her entire body sparkled with glitter. Then she harrumphed. "Dexterity? I was hoping it'd be charisma! Lame."

"Not bad," Mordecai said. "I was hoping for constitution."

She pulled out the glowing red nipple ring. She made a little disgusted sound while Mordecai whistled. "Now that's an . . . interesting prize."

"This is the most sexist description I've ever read, Mordecai."

He grunted. "Just ignore it and look at the stats."

Donut slid it across the table. I picked it up to examine it.

Enchanted Nipple Ring of the Superior Fire Demon's Hand Maiden.

This may only be equipped on a quadruped.

This may only be equipped on a female.

Warning: Unless you're planning on getting a lot of weird and unnecessary surgery, you ain't equipping this.

All nipple rings must be manually affixed the first time they are equipped.

Oh boy. Let me tell you about Superior Fire Demons. These bitches are crazy. Worse than the minor demons. I know, I know. That sounds chauvinistic and rude. You can't get away with saying shit like that anymore. Here's the thing. These bitches *are* gods-damned crazy. Full stop. You look that shit up on Wikipedia, and it'll be the first line. It'll say, "These bitches are three pugs short of a grumble." It's not an opinion, but an absolute fact.

We have a whole matriarchal hierarchy of demons who exist and fight and vie for control on the fifteenth level, all trying to catch the eye of one of the four brothers, and these Superior Demon nutjobs are always causing the most chaos, which is saying *a lot*.

You got the lesser demons, who are generally normal, though I wouldn't break up with one over text or call her fat or anything like that. Then you got the more powerful minor demons. Those bitches are something else, but they're nothing compared to Superior Fire

Demons. These ladies are so batshit, the demon lords and queens require all of them to be "chaperoned" by hellspawn familiars everywhere they go, whose job it is to protect them from each other and themselves. It's Sheol's version of a Xanax.

These familiars need to be protected from the Superior Demons. This nipple ring is one of the items they utilize.

Wearing this nipple ring offers the following benefits:

Allows the removal of cursed items.

User is impervious to natural fire.

User is impervious to lava attacks.

User is resistant to fire-based spells.

User will not lose health while inside Sheol.

All spells with a fire attack now deal (Intelligence)% more damage.

User may cast *Bitch, What?* once a day.

We'd met two demons so far. Fire Brandy, who'd been giving birth inside the *Nightmare Express* train on the fourth floor, had been a lesser demon. Slit, the makeup-encrusted kaiju-sized demon who wanted to kill Samantha, had been a feral minor demon. I could only begin to imagine what a superior demon looked like.

"Wow," I said. "We're putting this on you right away."

"Errr," Mordecai said. "It's great, and I agree she needs to wear it. But we need to talk about that spell it comes with."

I looked up the *Bitch, What?* spell.

Bitch, What?

Type: Berserking Spell + partial invulnerability.

Target: Self only.

Cost: Item based.

Duration: Twenty seconds.

Cooldown: Once every 30 hours.

Effect: You ever seen an angry, on-fire weasel tossed into a room full of chickens?

You catch on fire. You are invulnerable to blunt damage. Then you get really angry and kill every godsdamn thing in the room. This

is a Berserking Spell. Don't cast this inside of a Denny's. Or anywhere near people you like.

"Wow," I said again, suddenly feeling uneasy. "Mordecai, have you ever seen that spell in action?"

"I have, and so have you. Remember that rage elemental? They're perpetually in that state. It's actually called *Fire Berserker.* They've been changing the names a lot more than usual. Donut, only cast it when you're by yourself. You have three fire spells now. *Fireball*, *Magic Missile*, and *Wall of Fire.* All three of them are going to be much more intense. So, be very careful. It's good, but it's still not as good as your spell book."

The chained spell book did a little hop on the table, as if it knew Mordecai was talking about it.

Donut raised her paw and did an uncertain slap onto the book. It was a very catlike move. "Why is it quivering?" she asked. "You know how I feel about things that quiver."

"That happens sometimes with the more powerful tomes," Mordecai said. "Especially summoning ones."

I picked it up. The book was squishy and warm. It wriggled in my hands, like I was holding a puppy.

Tome of *Legionnaires of the Damned*.

Type: Summoning Spell.

Cost: 25 mana.

Duration: (spell level × 2 + intelligence level) seconds.

Cooldown: One minute. May only have one active instance of this spell at a time.

Target: May only be cast on recently unequipped armor or weapons. Total targets allowed varies based on multiple factors.

Effect: There are a lot of angry souls out there. Like, a lot. It's said if one has the ability to actually see all the wailing souls that filter through the edges of our world, one would go quite insane.

The AI gave an unsettling giggle.

Quite, quite insane, actually. All that death spiraling down, down, down into the drain. Where do they go? Why are they always screaming?

Uh, anyway. This spell reanimates physical weapons or armor pieces for a period of time with an undead wailing spirit plucked straight from the river of falling souls. These will be temporary minions of the caster. Strength of the summoned symbiotes varies, depending on multiple factors.

Warning: In most cases, armor and weapons utilized with this spell will disintegrate upon the completion of this spell. Certain cursed and enchanted items may react in an unpredictable manner upon the completion of the spell.

"Remember the swordsmen guards on the third level?" Mordecai asked. "This is kinda like that, but scarier. Wailing spirits are creepy. Now that Donut has level 15 in that *Laundry Day* spell, she can sow a lot of chaos with just those two spells. If she trains this one up, she can remove all the armor off a group of mobs and then reanimate their own armor with the spirits, and they will tear through the unarmored monsters like wildfire."

"Holy crap," I said. I slid the still-wriggling book back to Donut. "You just got a lot more badass."

She glowed as she applied the book. It let out a little scream as it disappeared in a puff of purple smoke.

"I've always been badass, Carl."

Mordecai nodded in agreement. "All of these loot items are really good. Like, really good."

"Yeah," I said. "My whole feed is filled with people who are getting some really good shit. Elle got an ice staff she won't stop talking about. Bautista got a shape-changing ring."

"Bautista can change shape now, too? I bet he and Katia will be having some really weird sex," Donut said.

"Part of it is the AI compensating for the skipped floor," Mordecai said, ignoring Donut's quip. "But you got some of these boxes before that even happened, so it's likely in response to the Valtay ramping up the difficulty."

"My stuff is good, but I didn't get anything for Mongo," Donut said. "And I didn't get a celestial box, either."

Mongo peeped in sad agreement.

"That nipple ring is practically a celestial. Same with the spell," Mordecai said. He turned to me. "But now it's Carl's turn."

3

I TOOK A DEEP BREATH, AND THE LINE OF BOXES APPEARED IN FRONT of me, moving all the way to the back of the room. The celestial box sat at the end, physically huge. It was in the form of a giant rotating skull with glowing eyes. My view counter was completely spiked, which was unusual for being in a safe room.

The line of adventurer boxes started opening, giving me several good healing and mana potions, a bunch of those Phase Through Walls potions, invisibility potions, and tons of junk items.

The quest box from the Tina quest was the same item Donut received, which was a coupon for a free Town Upgrade. That wasn't something we'd be able to use right now.

The Vengeance of the Daughter quest had said the reward would be the ability to loot the High Elf Castle, but we'd zapped the place down to the ninth floor, and it had likely landed someplace inconvenient. I'd also received a Gold Quest Box for it as well.

The box opened, and a group of items came out. I recognized what they were immediately.

"Carl, is that what I think it is?" Donut asked with disgust.

"I believe so," I said as the stick-and-poke tattoo kit entered my inventory. These were the same items Edgar the tortoise used to place the magical tattoos onto Tsarina Signet.

"Disgusting," Donut said.

"I agree," Samantha said. She'd suddenly appeared on the table, watching the boxes open. She had a Mongo feather in her hair.

The Gold Pacifist Box contained a small upgrade patch for my jacket.

It was a round peace symbol. Donut made a scoffing comment about the quality.

The Gold Scab Box contained a skill potion that disappeared before I could examine it.

The orgy box gave me another one of the mercenary coupons.

The Platinum Here's-Some-Good-Shit-Because-You're-Gonna-Need-It Box also contained the same thing Donut had received. A Cosmic Buff potion. I nodded to Mordecai, who could barely contain his excitement. He wanted to examine it at his table before I used it.

The Platinum Apostate Box, which I'd received for not getting killed by Diwata, contained a ring. A nipple ring.

"Ha!" Donut said triumphantly. "That's what you get!" She looked up at the ceiling. "Now that his nipples are full, there are other places he's not pierced yet."

"Yeah," I said. "Wait until I receive a legendary spay-your-cat-at-home kit."

"That's not funny, Carl. Don't even make jokes like that."

I had three boxes left. *Here we go.*

The legendary boss box for killing Imogen moved before me. Little metal bands around the box slipped and moved, opening with a ridiculous amount of fanfare.

The glowing leather wristband fell onto the table with a heavy thump. It disappeared into my inventory.

The Legendary Scourge Box opened with the same gaudy fanfare. This one I'd received for killing the most hunters on the previous floor. It contained 20,000 gold, two crafting table upgrade coupons, and a steampunk-style chest that hissed with clockwork gears.

"Weird," I said. "A box inside a box."

"It's a crafting table kit," Mordecai said. "It'll contain a bunch of rare supplies for one of your tables."

"Huh," I said. That didn't seem legendary quality to me, especially compared to what Donut had received.

The Celestial Predator Box appeared in front of me. It was in the form of a glowing and sparkling demon skull the size of a barrel. It spun in circles, twisting faster and faster as the top rose off of it. Lights shone out of it. Donut and Samantha oohed and aahed at the light show. Mongo made a terrified peep and ran to the back of the room.

The skull on the box opened its mouth and made a hissing noise as the whole box exploded into a display of fireflies, which rushed away and disappeared.

All that was left was a patch.

A full-sized back patch designed to be placed on the back of my jacket. That was it.

I grabbed it before it could disappear. Donut stepped forward and sniffed at it. She made a face.

"The stitch quality is just divine," she said. "But the image itself is quite disgusting. Are you really going to put that on your back? And there's some odd stitching on there that's transparent. I can't tell what it shows. You're going to look like one of those punk rock people. You're not a punk rock person, Carl. You don't have the right skull shape for a Mohawk."

"Interesting," was all Mordecai said.

My sleeveless jacket was called the Enchanted Anarchist's Battle Rattle. Before I even examined the patch itself, I knew this was a good prize, no matter what it was. I received +1 to all my stat points for each patch I affixed to my jacket. I had five total: the Earth symbol, the arrows, the bomb symbol, the anti-vampire Midnight Epicure patch, and the new peace-symbol one. Affixing a full-sized back patch to the jacket would double the stat-point-boost benefit.

The celestial patch was a thick black piece of fabric embroidered with a white pile of skulls from various creatures rising up into a pyramid. I rubbed my hand across it, and the entire fabric was covered in clear stitching, almost like it was sewn with fiber-optic wire.

The Scavenger's Daughter.

Upgrade Patch. Back Patch.

This is a divine item.

This is a unique item.

This is a fleeting item.

You may only affix one back patch at a time.

This patch depicts a pile of scary skulls, all stacked up nice and neat. I wonder if there's a story there?

If this upgrade patch is affixed to an eligible garment, it will imbue the following upgrades:

(Hidden until it is affixed and then worn.)

Warning: Upgrade patches are fleeting items. You may remove them, but they will be destroyed in the process.

Warning #2! This is a divine item. This means it gains differing abilities, buffs, and possibly debuffs depending on your proximity to certain deities and demons. It makes for new and exciting combinations!

"What the hell, man?" I muttered.

I'd have to install it to figure out what it actually did. As I slid the patch over to Mordecai, along with the Cosmic Buff potion, I received a new achievement.

New Achievement! Fashion of the Gods!

You've received a divine item! This is an item that might've once been worn by a god. Or sneezed on by a god. Or used to wipe a god's booty, etc. You get the point.

Divine items behave differently than normal ones. They usually hide what they do until you equip it. The good news is, these upgrades are usually great and plentiful. They also gain new and exciting powers when one is in the presence of divinity and certain demons, too.

The bad news is, certain deities may inflict nasty debuffs on you instead. And there's no rhyme or reason to it. Don't worry, we programmed out the head-exploding debuff this season. That one was caused by Yarilo. At least I think we programmed it out. Actually, I don't remember.

Reward: You now have something new to be anxious about.

"Shit," I muttered.

"Divine items are the best items," Mordecai said. "Don't worry about the potential debuffs. In my experience, they're almost always a good news/bad news thing. Like they'll temporarily debuff you but will give it all back and then some at the end."

"It really is ghastly," Donut said.

"I like it," Samantha said. "It's something Louis would wear on a date."

"What?" I asked as I pulled out my new items.

The upgrade potion was for plus three to my Find Traps skill, which moved it to 13. I would see pretty much any trap in the dungeon unless it was placed and deliberately hidden by a trapmaster. That was good.

I pulled out the group of items for the tattoo kit. It was a long, sharp needle. Some ink. A few stick things. A thing that looked like a piece of sandpaper. I had no idea how any of this worked.

Enchanted Prison Tattoo Kit.

So, you're doing time. Hey, I'm not one to judge.

You wonder, "How did I get here? How did I mess my life up so much?" You figure, "Now is the day I'm going to turn everything around. Now is the day I'm going to make certain I get on the right path. I'm gonna get out of here and get a job and make my family proud. Let me commemorate this important occasion by letting SkullFuck from the next cell come over and etch a poorly drawn dragon on the side of my face."

This kit allows an artist to create a tattoo of their choosing upon the skin of a willing or unwilling target. Tattoo artistry is a skill that can imbue all sorts of magical buffs and upgrades. Or it can just make certain that your next mug shot goes viral. It all comes down to the talent of the artist.

"What the hell am I supposed to do with this?" I asked.

"Well, I certainly hope it's not give yourself another disgusting tattoo," Donut said. She paused. "Hey, the dungeon stole my joke! I said the viral thing when you got one of your other tattoos!"

I grunted. "They say the sincerest form of flattery is when someone copies you."

Donut scoffed. "No, Carl. That's just something thieves say to make themselves feel better about stealing other people's stuff. The sincerest form of flattery is when people cry when they meet you."

I put it away for now.

I picked up the peace-symbol patch. It was small and round, almost identical in size to my Earth patch. It was just black with a white screen-printed peace symbol on it.

Upgrade Patch. Small.

This patch depicts a peace symbol. Ahh, isn't that cute?

Buzz off, dirty hippie. Go be smelly somewhere else. The Grateful Dead sucked. And so does Phish.

If this upgrade patch is affixed to an eligible garment, it will imbue the following upgrades:

Neutral mobs are less likely to fall into aggro.

+10% to Dexterity.

+10% skill in playing the bongos.

Warning: Upgrade patches are fleeting items. You may remove them, but they will be destroyed in the process.

"That was unnecessarily rude," I said.

"I don't like Phish, either," Donut said. "Angel the cocker spaniel's owner was always listening to them and smoking weed. It made Angel even more paranoid, and let me tell you, that was the last thing that dog needed."

Donut continued to talk about the dog as I picked up the large steampunk chest. The thing was ridiculously heavy. I hesitantly lifted the lid and peered inside. The description came in a different voice, like a television commercial.

Doctor Ratchet's Automaton Build-It Kit!

This kit contains enough items to create over fifteen automatons! Fun for the whole family! From personal servants to flame-throwing sentinel droids, this kit has a little of everything. The only limit is your imagination. And your insurance policy.

It then listed off dozens of parts. I recognized several of them as things I needed for some of the recipes in that instructional book I'd stolen from the production facility.

"Excellent," I said.

The next item was a forearm bracer. This one was black and short and covered with little buckles. I already had two. The one that formed my Grull gauntlet, and the one on my left arm formed a buckler shield that supposedly disarmed opponents 1.5% of the time, but I'd never gotten it to work. I'd gotten that one from Katia. If I wanted to equip this new one, I'd have to ditch one of those two.

Enchanted Right Back Atcha Personal Shield.

You ever meet one of those dudes who is always super quick to take offense to everything? You gotta walk on eggshells around him. Has some job where he wears a shirt and tie even though he looks like he just woke up in an alley somewhere.

He's always saying, "What the hell is that supposed to mean?" He hits on anything with a pulse. He wants people to call him T-Bone or Bulldog or something. He dies of a heart attack in his mid-forties.

You get my drift.

Well, this little auto buckler is the armor version of that. This auto-deploying, overly enthusiastic small-sized buckler has a chance to catch both physical and magic bolt attacks and toss them right back at the caster.

It's not perfect, but who the hell are you to judge?

Equipping this small buckler imbues the following effects:

Catch physical attacks. (Success percentage based off user's dexterity.)

Catch magical bolt attacks. (Success percentage based off user's intelligence.)

All stopped attacks have a 75% chance to reflect back to attacker.

All successfully reflected attacks have a 25% chance to double in power.

Attacks must be caught with the buckler in order to work.

"That's much better than your existing shield, and the bracer matches your other one better," Mordecai said.

"Agreed," I said as I pulled the Enchanted Auto Buckler of the Peach

Pit off my left arm. I'd toss it onto our growing pile of weapons and armor for our Faction Wars team.

I picked up the small nipple ring. It was a silver ring with an eyeball hanging from it. I tried not to sigh out loud. Donut was correct. It served me right for making fun of her own ring. I'd gotten this one from the Platinum Apostate Box.

Enchanted Nipple Ring of the Defiler.

This may only be equipped on a crawler who has been Marked for Death by a god.

Hey, that's you!

All nipple rings must be manually affixed the first time they are equipped.

Wearing this ring imbues the following effects:

Instantly know the religious affiliation of all nearby mobs and crawlers.

Allows the destruction of church shrines without further ill effects from deities.

+25% damage against all clerics.

The ability to cast *Black Nimbus* once an hour.

Li Na could do all of these things already. I already knew what this spell was going to say when I pulled it up.

Black Nimbus.

Type: Involuntary Abjuration.

Cost: Item Based.

Duration: Instantaneous casting. Affected target will suffer the effects of this spell for (30 + [Caster's Intelligence + Constitution] - [Target's Intelligence/2]) seconds.

Cooldown: Once every hour.

Target: Single target.

Effect: Has the same effect as wearing a shirt for the band Cattle Decapitation to church. Instantly removes target from the blessing of their deity and all associated buffs and effects. Will make it so target is unable to physically enter church or temple while the

spell is in effect. Higher levels of this spell increase the possibility of forcing a smite upon the target.

Warning! You probably don't want to cast this on members of the same religion more than two or three times in a row.

"Hmm," Mordecai said. "Lots of divinity-themed items. That's never good. But you all got good stuff. Carl, get that patch on the jacket and see what it does."

"I'm already on it," I said as I pulled off my jacket.

"REALLY, CARL," DONUT SAID AS I LEANED OVER THE TABLE. SHE SAT on my shoulder and made little noises of disapproval each time I stuck the needle into the jacket. "You might as well have Bomo or Samantha sew this on. Or maybe we can blindfold Mordecai and get him drunk and have him do it. It's not that difficult. Your stitching is just abysmal! No, no, no! The angle of entry is crucial!"

"You know what?" I said through gritted teeth. "Why don't you go check on your social media board while I do this? See what the Princess Posse is saying about our Faction Wars team."

She gasped and bounded off. Samantha and Mongo both rushed after her. I watched their dots move off on my map. As I did, I realized there was the white dot with a green cross of a hired mercenary on the local map. An extra dot.

"Mordecai," I asked, "who the hell is in your room?"

"Oh, yeah," he said sheepishly. "I was gonna tell you about that. With my upgraded quarters, I was able to hire a room attendant. She has her own space off to the side of my quarters. It's not important."

"Who is it? Did you like hire a hooker or something?"

"No," he said, sounding offended. "Don't even say that. Of course not. It's nothing like that. Concentrate on your sewing. It is possible to ruin the item, so you do need to be careful."

I grunted. I'd placed the peace symbol on the bottom of the jacket next to the bomb symbol. I was pretty sure it didn't matter in what order these were affixed, but I wanted to be double certain that the back-patch effect caught all regular patches, so I did the small one first.

I flipped over the jacket and smoothed out the divine patch. It hummed with potential energy. I waded through my messages as I sewed. Donut was already in the message groups, live-narrating some of the posts she'd received on the intergalactic internet. She was in the middle of telling everyone that there was a new fan group dedicated to Elle, which was comprised of mostly males. Apparently the whole old-lady-turned-into-a-dominatrix-fairy trope was a thing. Elle was not impressed.

Florin received another shotgun upgrade. I wasn't clear exactly what it was, but he was pretty stoked about it. He wouldn't answer any other questions about his situation. Just that he was in Ecuador and that he was in contact with Lucia Mar.

Katia had received an item that allowed her to move really fast. Neither Louis nor Britney—who were both on Katia's team—had opened their boxes yet. Both were still broken up about the death of Firas.

KATIA: I'm worried about Britney. The burn on her face still hasn't healed, and she hasn't stopped crying. She's just sitting there, clutching on to Louis.

CARL: Maybe have Imani talk to her. She's pretty good with that stuff.

KATIA: Yeah, I already asked her to come over. We'll see if it helps.

DONUT: WE BETTER KEEP AN EYE ON HER. I KNOW A VILLAIN ORIGIN STORY WHEN I SEE ONE.

Li Na had received some robe upgrade that increased her chain-throwing ability.

Tran, who was also on Katia's team, was in a terrible state. He had lost his legs in the final moments of the last floor. Daniel Bautista was with him, helping him deal with it. Katia said Tran was more upset about the loss of his friend Gwendolyn Duet, whom he'd been with since early on. I sent him a note asking if he was okay, but he didn't respond. Katia said he'd opened his boxes and had received a floating wheelchair in his pacifist box. It was the same sort of thing Odette used to zip around when she was in her human form.

I was starting to get a little worried about all this great gear. Mordecai thought it was in response to the rising difficulty. But just how much more difficult was it going to get? We needed to get out there and find out. So far, not too many people had started venturing out.

"Hey, Mordecai," I said as I rounded the last corner on the patch. I was using thick white thread and spacing the stitches the best I could. "Do you think Samantha's presence will have an effect on my jacket?"

"Doubtful," he said. "She's only half formed, and she's not a true deity anyway. I could be wrong, but I doubt it."

"We'll see," I said as I affixed the last stitch. The Scavenger's Daughter patch glowed for a moment, indicating it had been properly installed. I released a breath. I pulled the jacket on. I immediately felt my strength increase. A new bar appeared in my interface directly below my mana. It was in the same place the blood bar had been on the previous floor, and it looked similar. The bar was empty, and it was labeled **Soul Essence.**

You have equipped a divine item.

There are no deities in the area.

The Scavenger's Daughter Patch has gained the following upgrades:

All patch stat point benefits are now doubled.

In addition:

Plus 25 points to Dexterity.

Plus 25 points to Strength.

You will receive a notification every time a deity enters the area.

The Climb benefit.

The Soul Reaper benefit.

The Mysterious Bone Key benefit.

This patch will imbue additional varying benefits when it is in the presence of divine entities.

"Huh," I said as I explored the three benefits.

"So, what'd you get?" Mordecai asked.

"Climb, Soul Reaper, and Mysterious Bone Key."

Mordecai blinked at me with his single eye.

"Oh, shit. Soul Reaper?" he asked, his voice full of wonder.

"That's what it says. Is that good?"

He nodded. "Oh, it's good all right. But you gotta be careful with it. It can be more dangerous than that berserking spell Donut got. Read the description for yourself. I dunno what that last one does."

I only knew what the first one did.

Climb.

You can climb stuff better. Ya-hoo. What an *exciting* benefit. I guess that makes you a monkey.

I grunted and clicked the next one.

Soul Reaper.

Yeah, baby. Now we're talking.

For every creature you kill with a melee attack, the Scavenger's Daughter Patch is charged with the essence of the fallen. Once fully charged, you may transfer this energy to a single melee attack, which will completely drain all the essence. This attack will have varying effects depending on the nature of the essence stored.

The associated essence bar is now visible in your interface. The total amount of soul essence you may store increases each time your essence bar is topped off and then drained. In other words, the more stuff you kill, the stronger you get.

Warning: You know how asbestos is really bad for you? Like, it doesn't hurt you immediately, but it builds up in your lungs and eventually screws you over? Actually, you know what? Just ignore this warning. Forget I said anything. Carrying corrupted essence around on your back builds character. You already have a ring that's doing much worse to you anyway.

"Just make sure you drain the essence bar each time it fills up, and you'll be fine," Mordecai said. "That skill is ridiculously powerful. Just don't store the stuff for too long. I once saw a crawler kill a group of

Gorgons and fill her essence reserve with their souls, and then she turned around and killed a country boss with a single attack. It turned the whole thing to stone and then shattered. Now read me that last benefit. I don't know what it is."

Mysterious Bone Key.

This benefit may only be used once for obvious reasons.

Creates a onetime-use key to open a lock. Any lock. Any lock in the dungeon.

WARNING! (Notice how I used ALL CAPS for the warning?) Using this benefit will destroy both the patch *and* the item it is attached to. That means the jacket and all those ugly little patches inexpertly sewn to it.

Uh, it also uses a bone from the user's body to create the key. The more difficult the lock, the bigger the bone it uses. It might just be a finger. Or your clavicle. Or your femur. No biggie.

This bone will not grow back. So make sure it's a lock you really, really want to open.

"Uh," I said after reading it to Mordecai. "We're gonna mark that as a last-resort item."

There actually was a note about a similar item in the cookbook, I remembered, but I couldn't remember the circumstances. I'd have to go looking for it.

"That back patch is really, really good," Mordecai said. "But it's going to be hard to use. It's not as straightforward as Quan's celestial robe. That happens. This has the potential to be much better. It just won't be easy."

"It never is."

DONUT: THIS IS AN OUTRAGE.

I sighed.

CARL: What is it this time?

"This is an outrage!" Donut repeated as she burst from her room. She jumped onto the table. "Carl, do something."

"What are you talking about?" I asked.

"Our flag! They were talking about it online, and I forgot that each squad gets a bunch of flags to stick into the bad guys on this floor. We don't get to design the flag. They do it for us! Look at this!"

The small flag appeared and landed on the counter.

I started to laugh.

4

Monsters Collected: 0 of 6.

THE "FLAG" WAS A LITTLE BIGGER THAN MY HAND, LIKE ONE OF THOSE flags you give to kids to wave at a parade. It was a miniature pair of heart-covered boxers. Not a flag with an image of boxers on it, but an actual pair of heart boxers flying sideways, like they were dangling off a clothesline. Embroidered onto the flag on the top and bottom was a motorcycle-club-style patch that read, "The Royal Court of Princess Donut." Centered on the boxers over the crotch area was an embroidered bomb patch, identical to the one on my jacket.

It really was tacky.

"Elle says her squad's flag has a bag of adult diapers on it. Imani's squad flag has a butterfly, and it sounds just lovely. Why couldn't we get something like that? Have you seen the stitching on this? It looks like *you* sewed it. This is outrageous."

"It is pretty stupid," I agreed, laughing again. It was so dumb, I couldn't help but find it funny. "What did Katia get?"

"She didn't answer. She says it was something dumb, too. Carl, we need to tell them to change it. Something with Mongo would be much better than this."

"It doesn't matter," I said, picking the flag up. The flagpole, stick, whatever was a glowing metal spike maybe about a foot long. It was enchanted, and it would stick into any sort of creature, even ghosts, as long as the health was below 5%. I wrapped my hand around it and made a jabbing motion. It would be difficult to use these things. The metal would be slippery if there was a lot of blood. And there always was a lot of blood.

I stood and wiped myself off. I looked over at Bomo, who had an oddly depressed look on his rocky face. He almost looked . . . lonely. Like he missed the Sledge already.

"Hey, buddy," I said, "there should be another stairwell location here in the city. Can you see where it is?"

He grunted as his eyes went glossy. He had a spell that could teleport us to any stairwell location on the entire floor. The spell still hadn't reset from the last time he used it, but he could still load it up, and it showed him all the stairwells. It was a ridiculously powerful spell I was hoping to get my hands on somehow since we'd lose him the moment this floor ended.

"I only see two," he grunted.

"That's because we're not really sitting in Cuba right now," Mordecai said. "Each little area is its own location. Kinda like the bubbles on the fifth floor. When part two of this thing opens up, he'll probably be able to see everything."

"Why are we looking for stairwells now?" Donut asked. "There's one right outside, and we can't get to it anyway."

"Because if there's anybody else here, they're gonna be at the second stairwell. After we nap and reset our buffs, our first step is to find out if we're alone or not. Step two will be to map out the area and figure out where the best monsters are."

"Stairs not too far," Bomo said, tracing a rocky finger along the counter. "Still in big city near coast."

I'd never been to Cuba, or even looked at a map of Havana, and I had no idea how big this city really was. I had a general idea of the location of the city on a map of the small island country, but I knew nothing about the city itself. "Okay. Do me a favor and sit down with Mordecai and try to map it out a bit on a piece of paper. We're gonna keep you in the safe room for now, but we might have you come out with us later."

Bomo made a sad rumble, and I patted him on the arm. "I still have an old GameCube from that house I haven't hooked up yet. I'll make a compatible controller for you. We have a few cool games for it."

He made a noncommittal grunt.

"See if you can find a real safe room with a Bopca, too," Mordecai said. "I'm gonna try to get my eyes on the dungeon newsletter and see what's happening."

"Eye," Donut corrected. "You only have one eye now."

He snorted. "Things are looking a little different in my menus, and I'm not certain what's changed. There's likely been some fallout from skipping that floor, and we want to know what that is."

"What about me? What about me?" Samantha called, hopping up and down.

I grinned. "You want us to find a mage for that body of yours, right?"

"Yes! Right away!"

I nodded. "We need a monster map of the whole area. The fastest way to do that will be to find a borough boss and get the field guide map. Once we do that, we'll see if we can find anybody that'll help you. You're going to be our recon specialist."

LESS THAN AN HOUR LATER, WE WERE READY TO GO.

I wanted to get into the craft room and play with my new automaton pieces, plus my bomber's studio had just been upgraded, and I wanted to go into there. Mordecai was already making noises about my crafting table upgrade coupons, but I told him we wanted to get our bearings first.

The first thing I did was go back into the capitol building, and I surrounded the exit stairwell with traps, including alarm traps and a few teleports. I set the activation condition as **Crawler not a member of the guild Safehome Yolanda.** Just in case. I returned to the safe room to collect Donut.

"Come on, Samantha. Donut, we're keeping Mongo locked up," I said. "Let's figure out how this world works before we unleash him."

Donut started to protest, but I held up my hand. "This is a city, and there are going to be cars everywhere. They won't stop, and if he gets hit, he'll get squished like your cousin Baron Bear Claw or whatever his name was."

Donut harrumphed as we moved to the heavy double doors. Samantha rolled underfoot, weaving back and forth excitedly. I pulled the doors open, revealing early morning on a warm, humid day. We stood at the top of a long stone stairwell. The world outside bustled with activity.

Entering Old Havana.

"*Her* name was Baroness Éclair Exquisite, and she got smushed by a tractor because she ran into a field. She never was the brightest cat. Miss Beatrice was most upset when she heard the news, as was I. I never liked the baroness much, but it's always distressing when royalty dies in farm accidents. It's embarrassing to the whole family."

"Yeah," I said. "Bad things happen to cats who jump out windows."

"I saved your life when I went out that window, Carl, and I have yet to be thanked for it." Donut looked about at the scene spread before us. "Carl, none of these people are on my map. And isn't it supposed to be December? It's quite warm!"

I barely heard her. The scene hit me like a sledgehammer.

This is what we lost, I thought, taking it all in. *This is our world.*

The river, which I had thought I'd left behind on the previous floor, made itself known. *Stay down,* I thought. *Stay back. Not until I need you.*

I took a deep breath. The air was humid and smelled of flowers and ocean and the usual smoke of a city. The buzz of insects and cars and life filled my senses.

It appeared to be about eight in the morning. At the bottom of the stairs were a wide sidewalk, a busy two-lane road, and then a wall of brick and stone buildings. Beyond that, the densely packed city spread before us. Multistory and multicolored Spanish Colonial–style buildings spread out in every direction, most of them made of brick and multicolored aging stucco.

Various cars and scooters and buses zipped up and down the roadway. It was a mix of cheap Chinese and Russian vehicles with several classic American cars. A bright yellow 1950-something Ford Fairlane with the top down rumbled by. The shining car looked brand-new. A moment later, a 1950s Chevy Bel Air passed. I realized the car was a taxi.

"Okay, Samantha," I said. "Try to stay out of traffic. We don't want you crashing any cars or scooters, okay? Especially not near here. Head south and just keep going. Every time you see a monster, let us and Mordecai know what it is. We're building a monster map."

I originally wanted to toss her the distance using the xistera extension, but she returned back to me the moment I removed it from my hand, and I didn't want to walk around with the thing all day, so we decided to let her roam freely. I was hoping for her to get as far from the safe room as possible and gauge the strength of the monsters at the far edge of the area.

"Okay, I will fuck up any monsters," she said.

"No, you'll observe and report. You're recon, and that's it. Got it?"

She growled. "And we need to find a mage."

"That's right," I said. "Now get going. You can float now. I saw you do it, so stay above the traffic and people. Try not to touch anything."

"Okay. I got this. I will fly." She bounced a few times and then bounced down the stairs like a basketball. She did not fly.

"Fly," I yelled.

She ignored me. "Hey," she shouted as she rolled away, narrowly avoiding a strolling couple. She stopped to look at them. "Yoohoo! Are you a mage?"

"Samantha," I yelled, "they can't hear you. Remember? They're not really there. Just their clothes. And stay off the goddamned ground."

She growled and rolled away.

I cringed as she crossed the busy road, picking up speed. Luckily, nothing hit her. She turned and then zipped down an alley, disappearing. I could still hear her shouting, looking for a mage.

I sighed with relief when she disappeared. That would keep her busy for a day or two. I just hoped she didn't cause any major issues.

"Carl, she's not very good at following directions," Donut said. "It's a wonder she—"

"Whoa," I said, stepping out of the way as a group of people suddenly appeared, also coming out of the building. They materialized out of nowhere. It was a group of five people. Tourists, by the look of them. From Asia. They'd been in the same building, but for whatever reason, our starting area wasn't a part of the replay. They just appeared at the top of the stairs and walked right through us.

"Help! Carl, help!" Donut shouted, suddenly rolling away. One of the ghosts had kicked her as he strode by. The shoe, sock, and pants just ripped right off the body as the man continued on his way. Donut rolled up in the trousers and fell down the stairs, screeching bloody murder.

She *thump, thump, thumped* down the stairs and hit the ground and stopped just before she rolled into the street. I rushed toward her.

The man—now pantsless, underwearless, and with only a single shoe and sock—continued on his way, oblivious. The parts that had been covered with clothes now appeared as a wavy translucent outline, not fully realized like the rest of him. The illusion was strange, but I was grateful that we wouldn't be treated to a bunch of naked people walking around.

"Are you okay?" I asked, coming up to her. She pulled herself away and shook herself off. She hadn't really been hurt, despite falling down the stone stairs. Just surprised.

"Why, I never," she said, glaring off at the man, who stopped with his friends. He was now holding his hand up, like he was looking at a phone, but there was no phone in his hand. "You should be ashamed!"

"He can't . . ." I began, trailing off. She knew perfectly well he couldn't hear her.

"Carl, I think he dropped his wallet! And his cell phone!"

I picked up the brown pants, which had wrapped around Donut. I shook them so the whitie-tighty undies fell to the ground. Sure enough, there was a wallet and an iPhone in his pocket. I picked up the phone, and it was working, but I couldn't get into it. It said "No Service" in Spanish. It had a sticker on the back indicating it was a rental. I looked back over at the guy, and he was pointing at something on his nonexistent phone while his companions looked over his shoulder. They turned and walked off south along the sidewalk toward a palm-tree-lined park.

"Weird." I stuck the phone into my inventory. It seemed wrong that the phone was actually turned on and working. It would turn to dust the moment we left this floor.

His wallet contained a few credit cards and several euro banknotes along with a few American five-dollar bills. There wasn't any Cuban money. I pulled one of the credit cards. Thanks to the system, I could read the Chinese characters. The man's name was Bingwen Zou. I took it all, along with the sock and shoe.

I hesitated; then I took the underwear, too. I didn't want to leave anything behind. We needed to leave as small a footprint as possible, especially near the safe room.

"Gross, Carl," Donut said.

"Do you see any mobs or NPCs?" I asked. "Come on. Let's get out of the way."

Donut jumped to my shoulder, and we stepped out of the way of a strolling couple. A scooter thing that looked like a driving lemon zipped by on the street. Music blared as it passed.

"No," she said. "And it's going to be hard to get through that without touching anybody. There are people everywhere. It smells really good here. I thought it was going to smell disgusting. I don't smell a single cigar."

"What about safe rooms?"

"Nothing," she said. "But there are bathrooms."

"Okay, hang on." I cast *Ping*.

The sonar sound spread out, moving out into the city. The spell was supposed to have a range of a little more than three kilometers, but I knew it would be less in the city, especially with such tall buildings. It wouldn't show mobs or other crawlers, but it would show me all the white-tagged NPCs. Several dots appeared on my map, including Samantha, who'd already gone a good distance, plus some white dots in the ocean north of us. It was showing non-hostile animals, I realized, and I adjusted it. Only a handful of actual NPCs appeared, and none of them were close. If they were in safe rooms or even regular buildings, I knew *Ping* wouldn't work very well.

I had no idea how it worked with NPCs when they were mixed in with all this chaos.

We needed to go about six miles east. The walk would take us maybe an hour and a half or two hours under normal circumstances, but if we were going to be dodging everyone, it would be impossible to do it quickly. We started moving north along the wide sidewalk, evading tourists and vendors. There were people everywhere.

We passed a pair of men, one holding open a paper map, examining it. I reached over and plucked the map out of his hands. His wedding ring went flying off his hand, plinked twice, and fell into the gutter.

"This would be much easier at night," I said. I decided to leave the ring there, and we continued on our way. I examined the map as we walked. It was in English, and it showed the whole downtown area along with transit instructions to outer neighborhoods. As I suspected, we were walking in the correct direction. We were headed toward a different neighborhood outside of Old Havana called Miramar.

"I don't see why we have to dodge people," Donut grumbled as we walked. There was a highway that traced the northern coast. We were going to get there and skirt the highway east toward the other stairwell. It looked like there was a sidewalk. If there was, this trip wouldn't be as bad as I originally thought. "The clothes don't hurt us when they hit us. As long as we're not hit by a car, I don't see what the problem is. And frankly, I don't think getting hit by a car would be that bad with our constitution."

"We already have reports of people getting injured by moving objects. They're cheating, giving things more force than they're supposed to have. If we were really on the surface, and I got hit by a car with my stats, I'd barely move. The car would get obliterated, but that's not how it works here. I'm worried about chain reactions." I paused to watch an honest-to-goodness 1920s Ford Model T rumble by. "Remember the Iron Tangle? Crashing one little train screwed everything up."

"Yes, Carl, but that was different. These people aren't really here. Just their clothes. I say we throw a big rock in the road and get it all over with. We wait for a car to crash into it, which will cause all the other cars to crash, and in a little bit, the road will be free because they'll all be crashed at that one spot. It'll just be weird, glowing ghosts floating around the place. And once they move through the crash, they won't have anything on themselves to hurt us. You still have the Royal Chariot in your inventory. We'd have an empty road!"

"We'd end up paste if we tried to use the chariot. Do you see those buses? They're everywhere. A roadblock won't get everything right away."

Donut sighed dramatically. "All this walking is very bad for my fur."

She remained sitting on my shoulder.

She continued. "I do like it here, though. It's very pretty, and I like the smell of all the street-food vendors. I didn't know there'd be so many people selling things. Or so many tourists. I thought the country was closed off."

"This place is a huge tourist destination," I said. "Or it was. It was hard to get here directly from the US, but people from all over used to come here all the time. Supposedly the beaches are great."

"Well, I thought this was a Communist country and such things as street vendors and beaches weren't allowed. I thought there'd be tanks on every corner and men in olive uniforms shooting guns into the sky and parades where everyone is smoking cigars while children wait in line for a single piece of bread. And what about those boat people going to Florida? I feel as if *The A-Team* lied to me."

"We're not going to be talking about politics," I said. "That's not why we're here. Nothing good ever comes from talking politics, especially when neither of us knows what the hell we're talking about."

Donut scoffed. "Carl, have you been sniffing glue? You are boxers deep in politics! We are sponsors now, and as the former number one crawler, it's my duty to—"

She suddenly hissed and poofed out. A pack of three or four street dogs strolled by and ran into the street, crossing it, moving toward a street vendor selling fried egg sandwiches of all things. The dogs were part of the illusion.

"Anyway," I said, changing the subject, "I think you might be right about blocking the road. But if we do it, we need to be really careful about the location. One little crash will cause every car that moves through there to start piling up, and soon it'll be like that pit of trains. It'll have a cascade effect, and the crash site will get bigger and bigger."

"It's going to happen whether you like it or not. Especially with Samantha out there. Carl, look!" Donut said, pointing.

A man floated by on the road, wearing only sunglasses. He came from the north, the direction we were walking. Only his head and his arms looked fully corporeal. The man just floated down the road. He'd been riding a scooter, but something had happened to it. He'd lost the scooter and all of his clothes. Whatever it was, it had occurred off the main roadway.

"Well, shit," I said, watching him go. I wondered if Samantha caused it.

CARL: You doing okay, Samantha?

SAMANTHA: NOBODY IS TALKING TO ME, CARL. I DON'T LIKE BEING IGNORED. IT HURTS MY FEELINGS. I AM VERY SENSITIVE.

I grumbled under my breath.

CARL: Again, Samantha. The people aren't really here. It's an illusion. We're inside of a dream, and they do not see you. And why aren't you flying?

SAMANTHA: I AM GOING TO KILL THEM. AND IT TAKES A LONG TIME FOR MY MAGIC TO BUILD UP. I HAD A LOT OF MAGIC WHEN WE WERE FIGHTING ON THAT LAST FLOOR, BUT I DON'T HAVE MUCH NOW. WAIT, I SEE A RAT MONSTER! IT'S WEARING A HAT.

DONUT: WHAT KIND OF HAT?

SAMANTHA: OH, YOU WOULD LOVE IT. IT'S VERY BIG. WELL, IT'S SMALL. IT'S A NORMAL-SIZED RAT, BUT THE HAT IS BIG FOR HIM. MUCH TOO BIG FOR ITS LITTLE HEAD. HE'S VERY CUTE. OH NO, HE'S RUNNING AWAY! HE'S REALLY FAST!

I sighed and opened a new chat window.

CARL: Hey, Katia, Imani. Are you guys seeing any chain reactions yet?

IMANI: We're in a rural area, but I-5 is nearby, and only a handful of actual cars have gone by from the south toward Portland. Lots of floating heads and arms. I think something is blocking the freeway down there. Cars are still coming from the north.

ELLE: It's really weird. I just saw a goddamned bigfoot cross the road. He almost got splattered. The thing was wearing Bermuda shorts.

DONUT: WHAT ARE BERMUDA SHORTS? THAT SOUNDS LIKE AN OLD-PERSON THING.

ELLE: Well, it ain't a Sasquatch thing, that's for sure.

KATIA: It's the same here. The moment we walked out of the safe room, I saw a Nykur. It's a type of horse, and it's supposed to be gray. It was pink for no apparent reason. It *did* get splattered by a car, and now there's a growing pile of car crashes. Everything is icy, which doesn't help. The cars are already blocking the front entrance to our safe area. We're closing off the area around it so it doesn't get worse, and then we gotta clear it away. Louis and Britney are trapped inside for now.

IMANI: I'm seeing a lot of chatter about this sort of stuff everywhere. I don't know if they thought this through or if this is exactly what they wanted to happen.

ELLE: I think we should make roadblocks away from the safe rooms so it doesn't happen close to the stairwell.

DONUT: THAT'S WHAT I'VE BEEN TELLING CARL, BUT HE'S BEING GRUMPY ABOUT IT.

CARL: Make sure it's *really* far from the stairwells if you can. Those piles of cars are going to get pretty big and long. Longer than you think. I think in a few hours all the roadways are going to be just stopped.

A man walked out of a doorway, surprising me. He walked right through me, and his clothes went flying. Donut sputtered from my shoulder and spat out an earbud. The man continued on his way, nothing but a floating head and arms with a wavy, translucent outline for the rest of him. I left the clothes on the sidewalk.

"Shit," I said again, watching the man go. "You're right. This is impossible."

To accentuate the point, a loud crash echoed from somewhere deep in the city. Followed by another crash, then another. I cursed.

SAMANTHA: THAT WASN'T MY FAULT.

Everything was already out of whack.

"Come on, Donut," I said, starting to jog along the sidewalk. "Let's get to that other stairwell." I still avoided people, but not as carefully. Clothes and cell phones went flying the moment I brushed past someone. I kicked a baby stroller, and it spun sideways. As we ran, another crash echoed, this time from a different direction. Smoke filled the air as something burned.

IT DIDN'T TAKE LONG TO COME ACROSS OUR FIRST MOB. WE REACHED the northern coast of the island, and sure enough there was a wide multi-lane highway here that ran east–west. We hit the concrete sidewalk and started to jog west. I didn't dare use the Royal Chariot, but I contemplated snagging a bicycle or one of the hundreds of scooters zipping around.

Donut remained on my shoulder as I ran, wind whipping by my face. She made comment after comment on the colorful architecture and clothing and vehicles, plus she was constantly hissing and complaining about the multiple street dogs who skulked around every corner.

The ocean spread out on our right, the blue waves crashing calmly against the beach. The air smelled wrong here. Like Donut said, it wasn't unpleasant, but it was like they got the ocean scent just a little off. Apartments and other buildings of all sizes and conditions dotted the city to our left, punctuated by an occasional palm-tree-filled park. Along the highway, cars still came from the west, but the eastern lanes were mostly stopped. Like with Imani and Elle's area, it was just groups of people floating on the road, which was really weird.

Samantha was also giving random updates. The farther away she moved, the bigger the monsters. Her description skills weren't very great. The last thing she described was just a crying lady with a basket throwing eggs at her.

I was commenting on the strangeness of it all when Donut hissed at me to stop. A red dot appeared on the map, appearing atop a hill in a park adjacent to the road. It screamed, loud and high-pitched. There were no words, but the sound was very humanlike. I turned in time to see the creature galloping toward us. It started barking.

Only the barks weren't . . . barks. It was like a person was imitating the bark of a dog.

"What the hell, man?" I muttered as I formed a fist.

Combat Started.

The message came out of nowhere and was in a voice I'd never heard before. What was that?

The brown-and-white four-legged creature was about the size and shape of an extra-large wolf, but its long, straight forward legs did not bend at the knees, and it loped toward us with an odd, splayed gait, bouncing wildly up and down.

But the strangest part of the creature was the head. It was that of a human, but maybe one and a half times the size of a regular person, making it comically large on the strange monster. It was an angry-looking, bearded guy wearing a red beret. The beret glowed, indicating it was magical.

The head on the thing looked suspiciously like Che Guevara.

He continued to bark furiously at us as he charged. It literally sounded like a dude using a megaphone to make barking noises.

"What in god's name is that?" Donut cried as she pumped a magic missile at the creature. "It's like the dog from that alien movie with President Snow in it!" The missile hit the mob, who howled in outrage. Its health went down about ten percent. She followed it up with a fireball, which slammed into the monster, throwing it onto its back. It caught on fire and started squealing in pain.

I examined the pitiful creature.

The Experience—Level 55.

One of the most feared creatures from pre-Columbian Taino folklore, the Experience is said to be the guardian of the world of the dead. Who knows why dead people need to be guarded because, well, they're dead already? You humans have a lot of weird traditions that make no sense whatsoever. Anyway, this vicious and powerful monstrosity rarely shows itself in the world of the living, but when it does, you best watch out. It's strong, magical, and quite feisty.

"This is something from their mythology? Really?" Donut asked. "Why is it called that? It sounds like a rejected character from either *Jersey Shore* or one of those jerks from the Skull Empire."

"Uh," I said, watching the creature pull itself up. It was still on fire.

"I think maybe they took something from local legend and Saturday-morning-cartooned it."

"I don't know what that means, Carl, but it sounds offensive." She shot another magic missile, knocking the creature back. Its health was down a little more than half. It started to turn in circles, trying to get the fire on its own ass out. It whimpered and howled. It paused to look in our direction and suddenly started scream-insulting us in Spanish.

"You better hit it with your new *Mute* spell before we figure out his magical ability," I said.

She cast, and the yellow bolt shot out, moving painfully slow. The creature whimpered and tried to move out of the way, but the yellow blob curved in the air and slapped itself onto the creature. A one-minute timer appeared over it along with a little speaker with a cross-through-it icon, indicating it couldn't cast spells.

The monster continued to spin in circles, whimpering.

"Do you remember the show we had to go on?" I asked. "The voice-over one. *Earth Beautiful*?"

"Where I introduced the universe to the truth about cocker spaniels?" Donut asked. "Of course I remember it." She suddenly gasped and then cast a new spell. A new debuff appeared over the creature. The icon for this one was a head with little wavy lines over it.

The monster howled and then started viciously biting at its own leg. Donut laughed. "Look, Carl, it works! Look! That's my *Why Are You Hitting Yourself?* spell!"

I grunted. The monster's health started to go down faster and faster. It simultaneously rumbled and cried as it savagely bit at itself. Its rump continued to smolder.

"We'll have to see what else is out there, but I think their interpretation of 'legendary creatures' might be a little off. Just like on that *Earth Beautiful* show. The producer guy for that show told me they got all their info off an incomplete copy of the internet. Their research was a mix of real facts and made-up bullshit. Like they did five minutes of research and filled in the blanks. I think this is the same thing."

The monster collapsed onto its side. The beret on its head plopped off. The monster was scorched and bleeding. *Christ,* I thought. *Donut did that, and she barely had to lift a paw.*

Donut scoffed. "How is it they have a perfect recording of all the people and cars and the things they're carrying and how they moved around, but they don't have accurate facts about mythology? The Posse members aren't going to like things being inaccurate."

"In this case, it's working in our favor. There are some pretty messed-up myths and legends," I said.

"Do you think we should stick it with one of the flags?" Donut asked. "We don't have to keep him, but we have twenty of the flag things, and we should see how they work. But if we do add him to the squad, I'm going to have to insist he shaves. And I get to keep his hat."

"Too late," I said as the monster groaned and died.

Combat Complete. Deck has been reset.

"Dibs on the hat!" Donut called as she bounded up the park.

DONUT LOOTED THE MONSTER, WHICH STANK LIKE DEAD, WET DOG. SHE also took the red beret, and she gasped when she read the stats.

While she went through everything, I took in our surroundings. We were in a small park that overlooked the ocean. An old stone trench cut through the grass. A historical marker sat at the far end. My eyes caught movement in the distant water. Something appeared above the surface and then disappeared again. It was gone as quickly as it came. It was a sea serpent of some kind. How far did they say the area extended into the ocean? I couldn't remember, but it was a few kilometers at least. Then I noticed a few additional red dots along the shoreline. These were something smaller. One slid into the water and disappeared. Seals. We'd have to be careful.

I was also starting to catch up on the group chats that were coming in, getting a handle of this new combat system. So far, it seemed like nothing had changed other than the weird notifications. Nobody knew anything solid yet.

"Carl, look, there's a card thing," Donut said. "It was in its inventory. I thought we only got cards when we stuck the monsters with flags."

"Let's see it," I said.

I held out my hand, and the item appeared. It was a large rectangular card, just about the size of a postcard. It was rigid, but it still felt like it was made of paper, like I could rip it easily if I wanted. The back was decorated with the now-familiar logo of the Syndicate government. The 3D image moved and undulated on its own.

The other side was nothing but a red stylized plus symbol floating in a field of stars.

T'Ghee Card. Very Rare.

Utility Card.

Combo.

Consumable.

You ever mix two completely incompatible foods together to see how they taste? Sometimes it's great. Like chicken and waffles! Sometimes it's . . . a bad idea.

Like tuna and haggis.

Temporarily combines two monster cards into a single creature. Summoning length is equal to the shorter of the two summoning phases. Post summoning, both monsters are tagged out for the remainder of combat, even if they still have health.

Warning: This is a consumable card. It will be destroyed upon use.

"I wonder how rare these things really are," I asked, turning the card over. I wouldn't know how valuable this thing really was until we added some monsters to the squad.

I tried to stick the card into my inventory when I received an error.

Warning: Cards may only be held by the Squad Leader.

"That's just great," I muttered.

"So, what do you think?" Donut asked. The red beret appeared on her head. I hadn't had the chance to examine it yet. "Does it look good? I do prefer my white tiara, but I'm thinking maybe I should embrace the revolutionary look just when we're . . ." She paused, turning her head. "There are crawlers here. Over there."

I turned to see the three crawlers walking toward us from the direction we'd been headed.

"Carl, do you see that?" Donut asked, jumping back to my shoulder. She hissed as the three crawlers continued to approach. One of them lifted a hand in greeting.

I grinned and held up my hand to wave. I tried not to laugh. They were still far off, but I didn't recognize any of them. Two were guys. The third was a woman. The men were both human.

The woman was a cat girl.

Donut hiss-whispered in my ear. "That is the most disgusting thing I've ever seen in my life, Carl. It's an abomination. It's worse than that dog-headed cheater lady."

I laughed. "It's like we used that utility card on you and Katia."

"Don't even joke about that, Carl."

5

THE THREE NEWCOMERS STOPPED DEAD WHEN THEY FINALLY REALIZED who we were. They paused at the edge of the park. They started whispering amongst themselves. I sighed and moved toward them.

"Be nice," I whispered.

The two guys were both in their mid-thirties, and I couldn't tell the age of the cat woman. In fact, I wasn't positive it even *was* a woman, but she did have the curve of humanlike breasts under her fur, almost like she was wearing a bodysuit. Both men were Hispanic. The woman looked like a bipedal, humanoid shorthair cat with glowing green eyes. Her face had the long, thin features of a Siamese cat, but her fur was coffee-colored, almost black, and her vertical ears were much more rounded than those of a typical Siamese. Her fur rustled in the wind, and it looked soft to the touch. She carried a glowing trident over her shoulder, and her only clothes were a flowing cloak and arm bracers.

Donut hissed again. "That's a Havana brown, Carl. A Havana! We need to stay away from her."

"That's a little premature, don't you think?"

She scoffed. "There's no getting along with Havana browns, Carl."

I had no idea why the idea of a cat woman bothered Donut so much. She didn't seem to care about Bautista, who was more of a tiger thing. She never really liked other cats, even before we'd come into the dungeon. Zev had once mentioned that there were a few cat girls out there, and Donut had been absolutely scandalized about the idea. I didn't really get it.

I examined all three as we got closer. Based on their crawler numbers, it was clear they'd all come into the dungeon together.

The first man wore glowing silver plate armor. At first I thought the guy was a little taller than me, but the metallic boots on the armor looked to be platforms, giving him an extra seven or eight inches of height. I'd only seen a handful of crawlers decked out in traditional head-to-toe medieval-style armor. It looked heavy and uncomfortable as shit. The only exposed skin was on his head, which stuck out of the breastplate like a dude poking his head out of a tank. He wore a backward baseball cap on his head, and he had a wide-eyed, scared look about him.

He had a glowing symbol over his head indicating he worshipped a deity. The symbol was a palm frond.

Crawler #8,199,454. "Paz Lo."

> **Level 45.**
>
> **Race: Human**
>
> **Class: Santero.**
>
> **This crawler worships the God Ogun.**

The second guy was a well-muscled bald man in a leather jacket with knee-high boots and a black cape. He carried a crossbow that looked similar to Katia's, though the front depicted an open-mouthed creature. Maybe a monkey. This man also worshipped the same god. His dark eyes bored into us suspiciously as we approached. Donut gasped in despair as we got closer. This guy was completely covered in old tattoos, even on his face. Prison tattoos. Real ones.

He also had a pair of player-killer skulls over his head. He was the only player killer in the group. All three of them had a mess of boss kills, including a pair of city bosses. This guy also had a single dagger icon, indicating he'd killed a hunter on the previous floor.

Crawler #8,199,451. "Anton Lopez."

> **Level 47.**
>
> **Race: Human**
>
> **Class: Fugitive.**
>
> **This crawler worships the God Ogun.**

The cat was indeed a woman. She did not worship a god.

Crawler #8,199,462. "Sister Ines Quiteria"
Level 47.
Race: Cat Girl.
Class: Poet Laureate.

I pulled up chat.

CARL: Mordecai, who is the god Ogun?
MORDECAI: For fuck's sake, did you already summon another god?
CARL: No. Just met a group of crawlers who worship him.
MORDECAI: Thank the gods. He's a big one. A common god to worship. God of blacksmiths and protection. They can't be charmed, and their weapons will pack an extra punch. The god itself is pretty grumpy.
CARL: They all are. Thanks.

"Sister," Donut said. "Carl, is she a nun? A . . . cat girl . . . nun?" She spat out the words "cat girl" angrily.

"Let's find out."

"Hey, guys," I said, approaching close enough to talk. "I'm Carl, and this is Donut."

"We know who you are," prison-tattoo Anton said, practically growling the words.

I was taken aback. I was anticipating them being suspicious or cautious, but the vehemence of his anger surprised me. Donut was about to spit something back at them, and I held up my hand.

Easy. Easy. "Uh, were you the only three in your group? We were the only two at the other stairwell."

"Oh yeah?" Anton asked. He twitched a little, holding his crossbow at the half-ready position. "Word is, you were with that goat guy. The one who murdered Gimli."

Gimli was a pet hawk that had gotten eaten by Bianca, Prepotente's hellspawn familiar. That had happened at the end of the masquerade, and I'd been knocked out at the time. Gimli's owner was a guy I didn't know named Osvaldo, and he was Brazilian. He was the one who'd looted the memorial crystal off Queen Imogen's body. I had a quest to get it from him. I was pretty sure Prepotente had a similar quest.

"Word travels fast," I said cautiously.

"We know what happened at the end of the sixth floor, and what happened at the beginning of the next. You ain't the only ones who got friends. We hear things."

"Wow," Donut said. "I don't think he likes you very much, Carl."

"Stay back, cat!" Anton said. "Stay the fuck away from us!"

"Me?" Donut asked, incredulous. "What did I do!"

I took a deep breath. The guy in the armor and the cat woman both took a step back and away from Anton, who stood in the middle of their unit. It was subtle, but I recognized it for what it was. They were getting ready to fight. It was an interesting formation considering he was the one with the ranged weapon.

This was ridiculous. Fighting with the only other people in here was more than pointless. It played right into the showrunners' hands. It had come out of nowhere.

I held out my hands as I took a step back. "Look, we didn't have anything to do with Pony fighting that Osvaldo guy. And he left the party before we went down to this floor. He's over in the Bahamas."

"Bullshit," Anton said. He cracked his neck. His attention, I realized, was laser focused on Donut. Behind him, Paz gave Sister Ines a nervous look. The cat woman's whiskers twitched.

"Why would I lie about that?" I asked. "He's not the easiest person to hide. Look, I don't know why you guys are so jumpy, but if that's how you feel, we have a big, wide area to explore here." I pointed south into the city. "We'll go that way, and you three can go fuck yourselves off wherever you want."

Anton didn't respond. He just glared at Donut angrily. I watched a single bead of sweat start to trace its way down the side of his bald, tattooed head. *He's scared. He's scared of Donut.* All of their eyes were flashing, and I knew they were rapidly talking with one another in chat.

I was missing something.

CARL: Donut, do you know why they don't like you?

DONUT: IT'S THE OTHER CAT. HAVANA BROWNS ARE UNTRUSTWORTHY MONGRELS. ALMOST AS BAD AS SPHYNXES AND SCOTTISH FOLDS.

CARL: Yeah, I don't think that's it.

"Why are you this cat thing?" Donut suddenly demanded of Sister Ines, breaking the silence. "A cat I can understand. Carl would've picked Cat had the system allowed it. But why . . . *this*? And are you really a nun?"

The woman exchanged a look with the others. They were still talking privately. The terrified-looking armored man appeared as if he was about to burst into tears.

The cat woman took a step forward and put a paw on Anton's shoulder. She whispered something to him. He lowered his crossbow. The tattooed man remained anxious, but it seemed like the strange tenseness of the situation was finally starting to ease, as quickly as it came.

I found myself staring at the cat woman's large paw. Unlike Bautista and Prepotente, who both had humanlike hands, she had an actual paw, though she did have an opposable thumb, making her paws work almost like mittens. Her feet were the same, and she wore no shoes. Grabbing things had to be difficult for her. I wondered how she fought with that trident over her shoulder.

"Hello, Donut," the woman finally said. "We have seen you both many times on the program. I am a Discalced Carmelite." Like Anton, she had a Latina accent. Her voice was a little rough, like Elle's. I had the sense maybe she was older.

"I don't know what that means," Donut said.

The cat woman chuckled softly. "It means I am a nun, yes."

"Yes, but why are you a half cat?"

She shrugged. "It seemed like the best option at the time. When we had the choices presented to us, it was the only race that gave me a charisma boost for my *Word Weaver* spell, amongst others, and our game guide insisted it would allow me to choose the Poet Laureate class, which it did. Plus, I always liked cats. We had several at the prison."

Prison.

The word landed heavy in the silence between us.

I reexamined the other two men. I could see it now. The two men were cons. She was a nun who'd possibly worked at the prison. I once again focused on Anton with his Fugitive class and his two player-killer skulls.

At this point, several crawlers had skulls, and the sight of one or two wasn't as terrifying as it once was. Donut had one. Katia had two. Imani had 12. That alone didn't mean anything. The real player killers had dozens. Still . . .

Goddamnit, I thought. I hated this. I hated not trusting fellow humans.

"Then why did you choose a Havana brown?" Donut insisted. "It's hardly a proper breed for a nun. *Maybe* a Ragamuffin. Or an Abyssinian. Certainly not a Persian, of course. But a Havana? That's like an accountant choosing to be in the body of an English mastiff. Or a professional bodybuilder picking a Yorkshire terrier. Unless you're trying to be edgy and ironic."

Sister Ines looked at her own arm curiously. "I didn't get to choose. Is that what this breed is called? Havana brown? It's just what happened. Maybe it's because I'm Cuban."

"Lies!" Donut suddenly shouted. All of us jumped. Even me. "The Havana brown breed originated in England! It has no association with Cuba at all! Come on, Carl. Let's get out of here before they ply us with more filthy lies."

I put my hand on Donut's chest to calm her just as Anton panic-jerked his crossbow back up. His tough exterior was starting to crack. Sister Ines deftly caught the top of the crossbow as he yanked it up, keeping the bolt angled away.

It was then, at that moment, that I finally understood who was really in charge of this group.

"Like I said, Donut, I did not choose what I looked like."

CARL: Holy shit, Donut, chill. There's no way they let her choose what goddamned breed of cat she was. And nobody except you would know that a Havana whatever doesn't come from Cuba.

DONUT: EVERYBODY KNOWS THAT, CARL.

CARL: Just be calm, okay? We need to figure out why they're scared of us.

Sister Ines patted Anton again on the shoulder. "Now, we are all calm, yes?"

He grunted something inaudible.

"Look," I said. "I don't know why you're afraid of us, but the last thing either of us needs is to be looking over our shoulders the whole time. I was hoping to find you guys so we could work together. We are always stronger together. But if you're not interested, we'll separate here." I held up a fist. "We should at least get into each other's chat so we can talk in case of an emergency."

"Your cat said she was going to kill us all when she met us," Paz said, speaking for the first time. The armored man lifted a metal arm and pointed at Donut. "She said she was going to rip out our throats and feed us to danger dingoes and laugh while we drowned to death in our own blood."

"What?" I asked, looking over at Donut. "No, she didn't."

"It wasn't danger dingoes," Donut said indignantly. "It was brindle grubs. And I said that in confidence to Anaconda and Sledgie. I mean, really. So now you're eavesdropping on my conversations? Carl, I told you Havanas are no good."

"I . . . What?" I repeated.

"We went on a program at the beginning of the sixth floor," Sister Ines said. "They showed us the clip."

"Who the hell is Anaconda?" I asked.

"You know who Anaconda is, Carl. He's one of the lead dancers at the Penis Parade in the Desperado Club. Anaconda told me he'd never met a cat before, only cat girls, and I told him what I'd do if I ever met one."

"See!" Paz said, his voice squeaking.

"I said that ages ago," Donut said. "I mean, really. I can't be held accountable for everything I've ever said to a stripper. I also told Damascus Steel he was Mongo's new daddy the last time I was there. Are you going to hold that against me, too?"

"Goddamnit, Donut," I said. "Were you drunk?"

"No, Carl."

"Okay," I said. "Everyone needs to chill. Donut is not going to attack anyone. She said that because she always says stupid shit, but she didn't mean it. Did you, Donut?"

"I just don't understand why it was even allowed to be a race." She sighed dramatically. "I suppose I must get over it. It's not like I have a choice."

The three newcomers talked some more amongst themselves via chat. While they did, I delved back into my own messages. I'd been asking around if anybody knew these guys and if they could vouch for them. Katia revealed she'd been compiling a list of crawler names that weren't to be trusted, and they weren't on it. That didn't mean anything in itself, but it was a good sign.

The only person who knew them directly was Tserendolgor.

REN: I don't know them well. I have Paz in my chat. Him and the other guy are cousins, and they're really protective of the third one. The nun woman. Their party was bigger, but they had a rough time on the sixth floor. They're good friends with Osvaldo's group, but I don't think they share a guild with him. They're mostly loners. I know that Anton guy with the Fugitive class is really good with the crossbow, and that he'd had to kill two guys from his own group on the first or second floor after they'd tried to kill the nun for some reason. Don't know the story. Paz also has a *Self-Destruct* spell—one that kills himself if he casts it, kinda like that bomb everybody knows you have. But it's a directional blast. So you probably shouldn't fight them.

Directional blasts were insanely powerful and rare. I'd been chasing the ability to magically direct blasts for a while now, but I still hadn't been able to find something to mimic the ability.

CARL: Okay, thanks.

DONUT: OF COURSE THE CHEATER LADY KNOWS THEM.

IMANI: I have someone on my list who says they were in the same bubble as Quan Ch on the fifth floor, and that they didn't get along. So maybe you guys can bond over that.

"If you really want to work together, you can help us capture our first squad member," Sister Ines said. "There's a lot of them on the beach. We tried to fight one, and it almost took Paz out. We'd had to kill it. If you help us capture one, we'll help you get one, too."

"What are they?" I asked.

"Seals," she said. "Monk seals."

6

"I'VE NEVER BEEN A FAN OF PUN-BASED NAMING CONVENTIONS, CARL," Donut said as the five of us trekked across the road toward the rocky northern beach. Another distant crash echoed from the city. Cars no longer came from either direction on the freeway, but people still walked up and down the sidewalks. Nobody was on the rocky beach here, instead opting for the beaches much farther to the east and west. "It's cheap, and it lessens the danger of everything around us."

"You were literally just talking about a stripper named Damascus Steel."

"I love that guy! Strippers are supposed to have names like that. There's Anaconda. Damascus Steel. Dong Quixote. The Author Steve Rowland. Gluteus Maxx. And a bunch of others. Have you ever gone into the Bitches room? I bet they also have names like that. And don't forget Juice Box. But that's different, and you know it. That's their names, not the name of their species. Quite frankly, it's embarrassing. Actually, that reminds me. Last time we were there, Damascus said he wanted to meet you."

Anton kept a wary eye on us as we walked, but everything had relaxed. The more Donut yammered on, the clearer it was that she was mostly harmless. The sense of distrust was still there, and it would be for a while, but it appeared both sides had spent some time talking to others and getting an idea of the people we really were.

Despite them being former prisoners, my gut told me these guys were all right. I didn't necessarily trust them, but they didn't appear to wish us harm. Not as long as they had Sister Ines keeping them in line.

Them being convicts by itself didn't mean much to me. Half the dudes I worked with before the collapse were ex-cons.

Because there were no cars, Donut released Mongo, who jumped upon the newcomers with typical gusto. The three crawlers were all terrified at first, but they quickly warmed to the dinosaur when they saw he was like a giant dog. Mongo was fascinated not with the cat woman, but Paz, the armored Santero, which I gathered was some type of warrior cleric. Mongo pushed his face right up against the shining breastplate and looked at himself in the reflection, which pushed the large man over onto his ass with a ridiculously loud crash. The man fell like an upset turtle. I was afraid they'd be angry, but Paz howled with laughter.

Anton and I each grabbed an arm to pull him up.

Donut, seeing that Mongo "approved" of them, had also eased her suspicions. Of the two men at least. She continued to make comment after incredulous comment in chat about various parts of Sister Ines's anatomy.

"Monk seals," Donut muttered again. "I mean, really."

"I don't care if it's a play on words," I said. "They sound pretty awesome if we can catch one. We just need to be careful."

"They're a lot faster than they look," Sister Ines said as we crossed over a small fence leading to the rocky beach. We'd walked a quarter mile east toward a larger section of beach where the seals were more spread out. I could hear their loud shouting and fighting and barking as we approached.

Again, this was less mythological creature and more something stupid, but according to Sister Ines, these guys were tough. And intelligent. And great tanks.

"Real Caribbean monk seals are extinct," Paz said as we approached. "They used to be everywhere, but we hunted them out. My papa told me that."

"Was he a scientist?" Donut asked. She now sat upon Mongo's back, who'd in turn attached himself to the side of Paz.

"No. He worked on a sugar plantation," Paz said.

Anton, who'd done the most talking when we met, was mostly silent. The man was always watching, always looking around, always alert.

"So, what were you in for?" Donut asked Paz. The armored man clanged his way over the fence. He sounded liked a bag of pots and pans being shaken up and down as he moved. It would be impossible for him to sneak up on anybody.

He grinned at Donut, revealing a missing tooth. "Sister Ines, what's rule number one?"

"Today is a new day," Sister Ines said. "We don't worry about yesterday because we can't change the past."

"So, a weird sex crime, then?"

Paz laughed. Anton did not.

"It is considered rude to ask about one's past," Sister Ines said, speaking gently but firmly.

She suddenly reminded me of Miriam Dom, and an unexpected wave of sadness washed over me.

Donut was about to say something snarky to the nun, and I interrupted. "Have you guys gotten any cards yet?" I explained the utility card we'd received.

"No," Sister Ines said. "We've only killed two things since we've gotten here, and neither had anything like that."

I nodded. That was too bad. I was hoping the utility cards would drop with every kill.

"What do each of your classes do?" I asked.

Ahead, a single seal sat by itself on a rock near the water. It appeared to be asleep. We cautiously approached.

"I am a Poet Laureate," Sister Ines said.

Donut made a dismissive grunt. "I had the option for that once. It's a Bard class. Mordecai said I shouldn't pick it because it required I pick a patron, and I did not want to do that. I prefer to offer my talents to everyone. Not just an elite few. Though I was a bard on the last floor. A Legendary Diva. That meant I was so good, I didn't need a patron. I'm a Master Telephone Psychic now."

"Yes, I am a Bard Healer," she agreed. "Wait, you're a what?"

"Do you even sing?" Donut asked, ignoring the question. "I sing. *I* had a concert recently."

"No. I recite poems. And prayers."

DONUT: NO WONDER THESE GUYS WEREN'T IN THE TOP FIFTY. WHO WANTS TO LISTEN TO A FAKE CAT RECITE STUPID CHURCH POETRY ALL DAY?

CARL: Yeah, it'd be almost as bad as listening to a real cat sing.

DONUT: THAT WAS REALLY MEAN, CARL.

"Paz is a Santero. That's a necromancer cleric. He also has a lot of healing and protection spells."

"Mostly I just curl up on the ground and let the bad guys hit me," Paz said.

I looked at Anton.

Sister Ines patted the tattooed man on the shoulder affectionately. "A Fugitive is a rogue class, I am told. He's good at finding traps and escaping tough situations."

I suspected there was much more to it than that.

"And what about that deity you guys worship? Ogun?"

Paz opened his mouth to respond, but Sister Ines interrupted him. "Only Anton and Paz worship him. I cannot bring myself to worship a false god. He has many silly rules, but he allows each of them several protection spells. He would keep the three of us safe if the princess really wanted to rip our throats out. And what about your god? This Emberus."

Donut grunted. "He takes all of our money, but sometimes people catch on fire when Carl punches them. It doesn't happen very often though. I have many more fire spells."

The fact Sister Ines even knew I worshipped a god told me she had a similar ability to my own.

We crouched down and slowly approached the lone seal.

"They don't seem to have ranged attacks that we've seen," Sister Ines whispered. "But they are fast and fight dirty. We have to get close to stick the flag in. We tried affixing the flag to a crossbow bolt, but it didn't work. You have to be physically touching it when it's shoved into the monster. We lost the flag."

"Hang on a second," I said, and I pulled the Bahamas book from my inventory and started to flip through it.

I hadn't really looked at it yet. Prepotente seemed to think there would be some overlap. I moved to the index in the back. There were a lot of ridiculous monsters listed, mixed in with some that sounded terrifying. The book separated them as Common, Uncommon, Rare, Very Rare, Legendary, Mythic, and Unique. There were lots of birds and bats and fish. I didn't see a monk seal listed. I sighed and put the book away. I'd examine it more closely later.

Sister Ines pulled a small flag from her inventory and handed it to me.

I blinked a few times, trying to figure out the image on the flag. It said team Sister Ines on it, and it was a blue field with a black-and-white embroidered blob on it. Donut audibly scoffed at the quality. It looked like the image was maybe one of those ball-and-chain shackles. But the metal ball had something on it. Like maybe a nun's habit. I shook my head. The design was almost as dumb as our own flag's.

"I should warn you," Sister Ines said. "You might get a quest when you examine the seal."

I grunted as I turned my attention to the gray slick monster. It looked like a regular seal. We had all sorts of similar animals in the Puget Sound, from the common harbor seal to the much larger elephant seal and the loud-ass California sea lion. This guy was pretty big, but he was nowhere near the size of a sea lion and not even close to the size of an elephant seal. He was maybe six or seven feet long and probably weighed about 400 pounds. He just sat there, passed out on the rock.

Yago. Monk Seal Picket Sentry. Level 70.

Ahh, the monk seal. They're seals. And they're monks. Get it? Get it?

Yeah, anyway. These guys are more enthusiastic about their jobs than a dentist with glossaphilia. In case you don't know what that means, what I'm saying is these guys *really* love fighting stuff. It's their religion.

Trained in the deadly art of Caribbean Kung Fu, the monk seal sentry's sacred duty is to protect the coast and hunting grounds from the impending invasion of their dread enemy, the Red *Maníseros* Land Crabs, masters of *Juego de maní*.

Be careful. You don't want to get involved in *that* impossible conflict.

Crabs. Scratching, pinching crabs. The rats of the sea. I *hated* crabs. A moment of silence passed, but I could sense the electricity in the air.

New Quest. The Chowder War.

Oh, you're getting involved whether you like it or not.

The Monk Seals. The Red *Maníseros* Land Crabs.

War is brewing, as it often does in these parts. Every season, the land crabs emerge from their forests to attend their sex parties in the oceans surrounding these lands. The Monk Seals hold the ocean sacred, and the very act of spilling so much crab chowder into their holy waters is considered a sacrilege most foul. This is no minor inconvenience. And it's not just a few little clouds of the batter, either. There are a lot of these crabs. Like, a lot. And when they let go . . . man. It's like a category 5 jizz storm down there. Fish die. The food becomes scarce. The baby monk seals and their food supplies are literally getting bukkaked to death with gallons of weird, chunky crab spooge.

And no, that's not a sentence even I thought I'd ever utter.

Would you want that for your own children? Nope. I didn't think so. It's disgusting, and it must be stopped at all costs.

For the Red *Maníseros* Land Crabs, it's a matter of survival. It's not their fault they can only have babies in the ocean. It's not their fault they've had to wait a whole year to let go. They don't want to do it there. They can barely swim. Water is a terrible lubricant. And to make matters worse, these psychotic seals are always losing their minds every time they get anywhere near the coastline. So as a method of self-defense, they've learned the deadly art of *Juego de maní.*

Choose a side. Put an end to this conflict, one way or another.

Reward: You will receive a Platinum Quest Box.

"Are you kidding me?" I asked. "Caribbean kung fu? Is that even a real thing?"

"I don't know about that, but *Juego de maní* is a Cuban fighting style," Paz said. "It is very real."

Donut did a little karate kick on my shoulder and made her *wachow!* noise. "Carl, this is like one of those kung fu theater movies you used to watch. Sort of. I don't know if any of them involve crabs jerking off all over baby seals. But it's like one of those movies where two schools are fighting each other! But what does that have to do with Cuban culture?"

"Nothing," I said. "Absolutely nothing. It's complete bullshit."

She gasped. "Aren't baby seals all white and fluffy? Oh my god, they're so cute! We should see if we can find one!"

"That's a different type of seal," I said. "I'm more curious about these crabs."

"The land crabs migrate every year," Paz said. "It's a tourist attraction. But it's not here. It's on the other side of the island into the Bay of Pigs. They live in the forest and move to the water to lay their eggs after getting inseminated the normal way. It's millions of them, and I'm pretty sure only the females go into the water. It also happens in the spring, not Christmastime. All of this with clouds of crab spooge is just made up."

"The dungeon is making crap up? I'm shocked," I said. "Baby seals live on the beach, too, not in the ocean. How big are these crab things?"

Paz shrugged. His armor clanged. "The real ones are small. Maybe the size of my hand, but I haven't seen this world's version yet."

"Wait," Donut said. "Crabs live in the forest? That's a real thing? That sounds made up. Everyone knows crabs live underwater."

"Yeah, it's real," Paz said, "though I think they spend their days in the wetlands. That whole area is a little swampy. They're everywhere on the roads during the migration. You should see it. They get squished by the cars. It ruins people's tires. It stinks, and then the birds come in and eat them all."

"You can eat them?" Donut asked.

"They are dangerous for people to eat," Paz said. "At least the real ones. Some people eat them anyway, especially the crab eggs, but for medicine, not food."

"We can worry about the crab-spooge quest later," I said, refocusing my attention on Yago, the oblivious seal who remained passed out. "Let's get this card."

THE PLAN WAS STRAIGHTFORWARD. SISTER INES, DONUT, AND ANTON would attack the monster from afar while Paz and I approached from the sides. Paz would draw the seal's aggro and tank the attacks while I stuck it with the flag. I didn't like the idea of separating from Donut, but we had multiple contingencies in place if things went south. And I made sure Donut had some space between her and the other two. I made Mongo stay back with her.

Sister Ines's main melee attack was with her trident, but she mostly fought like Imani did. She buffed everyone around her and hit the mobs with afflictions. Paz was also a healer, and a necromancer, too, but the armored cleric was able to absorb a lot of damage. He had a Turtle ability, which gave him a temporary powerful shield while he drew the monster's aggro. I'd seen the ability in action before, and I knew it also rooted him in place and made him unable to attack or move. It was a dangerous ability because once cast, it couldn't be stopped until the timer ran out. If the shield was breached before that, the caster was free, but he'd still suffer the excess damage of the attack that broke through the shield.

The plan was for him to walk up on the seal, draw its attention, and get attacked while the others poured fire into it. I'd also approach, invisible. Once the health reached the five percent threshold, I'd swoop in with the flag.

The last time they'd tried this, the seal had overwhelmed Paz's defenses too quickly, making it so Anton had to take it out with a "one-shot." I wasn't certain what that was, but I assumed it was a powerful, magic-enhanced bolt.

As we prepared, I could sense how fluid of a team the other three were. I wondered how it was I'd never seen them before on the recap. I felt a little jealous, honestly, of their relative anonymity. Sister Ines said they'd gone on programs before, so they weren't completely under the radar. I wondered if that route, just quietly making one's way through the dungeon, was actually better than the path we'd found ourselves upon, not that I could change that now.

Our fame, I realized, was contagious. Whether these three liked it or not, they now had a lot of eyes on them. They weren't dumb. They had to know it, too. That was probably a bigger concern than that obvious bullshit with what Donut had said.

Paz clanged loudly as he walked. Yago the seal woke up when we were about thirty feet away. I downed the invisibility potion and dashed off to the side.

"Hey! Hey!" Yago the seal yelled at Paz, turning to face him. "What the fuck you think you doing? You challenging me?" He had a thick Cuban accent. Paz said nothing as he got closer. "Oh, oh, you wanna fight? Is that it? I'll fuck you up!"

The seal then started making some weird Bruce Lee noises. "Weeee-yaaaaw! Keeechaaaa!"

Combat Started.

The seal suddenly reared up, balancing on its tail, its little flippers waving back and forth while he made more kung fu sounds.

I watched, fascinated. I'd seen elephant seals smash into each other before, and they would beat the shit out of each other, but this was something completely different. This dude reared up much higher than it should, going completely upright, balancing solely on its back, Y-shaped flipper.

The thing did not have the anatomy for this type of fighting. The trained ones you would see doing tricks at amusement parks were usually sea lions, which had much longer flippers.

Nevertheless, this thing reared up like a giant slug and screamed. A constant stream of nonsensical kung-fu-esque noises emanated from it. It flipped to the side. It did a complete circle in the air, landing back on its flippers with a wet *splotch.* The movement was quick, and smooth. *Oh shit,* I thought.

"Eeeeyahh!" It flipped through the air just as Paz fell forward, transforming into a giant metal shell. The seal slammed down onto the shell, hitting so hard, the entire beach rocked.

An **Unsteady** debuff flashed and was negated as the ground rocked.

Holy hell, I thought. He'd slammed down on him with enough force to crush a goddamned car. The seal flipped back, just as quickly, screaming at the round metal form of Paz.

"Coward," he shouted. "Fight me, you metal bitch! Eiiiyaaaahhhh!"

A shield health bar had formed, and it was almost halfway down. The seal flipped sideways, pinwheeling in a circle around Paz. With each flip, the seal shrieked his own sound effects.

DONUT: CARL, I'M PRETTY SURE THIS IS REALLY RACIST.

But just as Yago the seal moved to attack again, he was hit with three bolts at the same time. A full-powered magic missile, a crackling crossbow bolt, and a yellow bolt of magic. The debuff **Disoriented** appeared over him as he tumbled back, rolling toward me. He sat up, swaying and swearing. His health had barely gone down. He shook his head and swore again.

I, still invisible, took the opportunity to activate Talon Strike and kicked him several times in the side. *Thwap, thwap, thwap.* He grunted in pain. Another magic missile hit him as two more crossbow bolts stuck into his neck. Another magical bolt hit, this one a poison debuff.

His attention remained focused on Paz. His health was down to about thirty percent.

I moved to kick him again.

Oof. I was hit in the chin with his hind flippers as he flipped forward in the air, lightning quick.

"Yip! Yip! Yip!" he shouted as he flipped.

His blow on my chin had been glancing, but it had rattled my teeth. I stumbled back.

The monk seal slammed once again into Paz's shell. The rocks all around him shattered into dust. Paz's shield held only the smallest sliver of health.

PAZ: Uh, guys?

Yago rolled to the side and started yelling some more. The seal suddenly started to glow, just as more bolts tried to slam into him. They didn't hit. Donut cast another magic missile, and it sizzled against the new shield. It was a protection spell of some sort. The debuffs over him all went away.

ANTON: My bolts aren't getting through! This is something new. The last seal didn't cast this spell!
SISTER INES: He's protected himself from ranged attacks. I can't get in, either!
PAZ: I can't move for another ten seconds!

Damnit, I thought. I shoved the flag in my mouth, and I rushed forward, forming a fist. The seal moved to slam down on Paz one last time. This would probably kill the guy. I rushed up, my gauntlet forming just as my invisibility faded.

I punched the seal right in the side of the head. He roared indignantly as he rolled away.

"Oh! Oh! Another little bitch. You gonna punch me in the face?" the seal shouted, finally moving his attention onto me. He hopped up and down a few times. He did a backflip, then danced to the side. He made more kung fu noises. "Watch this!"

Fuck. I dove to the right just as he slammed down upon where I'd been standing. The damn thing was fast. Paz jumped to his feet the moment the Turtle ran out. A ridiculously huge mace formed in his hands. The thing was twice as long as he was with a diamond-shaped head the size of a beer keg.

"Watch out," he cried. He swung, and I hit the ground as the giant mace swung from behind. It slammed into the head of the recovering seal, who grunted and then fell, landing atop me.

Oof. I wheezed as the heavy, wet form slammed into me.

The seal's health suddenly started to blink. It took me a second to realize what that meant.

"Flag," someone shouted. It was Sister Ines. All of them, Donut included, were running up on us. Mongo's cry screeched in the air.

I struggled to free my arm. I took the flag from my mouth, and I stabbed it right into the side of the head of the seal.

Pling! The digital noise echoed loudly through the beach.

The seal disappeared in a puff of blue smoke.

Combat Complete. Deck has been reset.

Shit, I thought. *And that wasn't even a boss battle.*

I still held something in my hand.

A card.

I examined it as the others ran up.

Warning: This card is owned by Team Sister Ines. It has not yet been activated. You may not collect or trade totem cards until they have been activated. This card may only be activated by that team's Squad Leader.

The back was the same as the utility card we'd collected earlier. The front featured a stylized screaming version of Yago drawn in a comic book style. The seal now had a blue headband. Several symbols dotted the card, including a green 70 in the top corner, which I knew was the mob's level. There was also a clock with a 60 and a heart with a 125. A little symbol featuring a wave of water was emblazoned on the side with a fist under it and a shield under that. A whole row of other symbols ran across the bottom of the rigid card.

T'Ghee Card. Uncommon.

Totem Card.

Yago. Monk Seal Picket Sentry.

"You wanna fight me? You sure about that?"

Level: 70.

Origin: Cuba.

Summoning duration: 60 seconds.

Constitution: 125.

This is an aquatic mob.

This is a melee mob.

This is a tank mob.

Notable attacks:

Kung Fu Master.

Body slam.

Earthquake.

Deflector.

+5 additional skills and spells.

Examine in the squad details tab of your interface for full stats and skills and spells.

Warning: You have empty slots in your squad. Collecting this card will automatically activate and place this totem into your squad. You may not remove or trade squad members until your squad is full. If you wish to remove a card before your squad is full, you will have to tear the card.

We definitely wanted to get one of these guys.

"Carl, there's another seal coming," Donut said as I handed the card off to Sister Ines. This new seal moved rapidly across the beach, headed straight for us, shouting. As it got closer, I noted this guy was the exact same level, but this one's name was Geraldo.

"So, you want to do it again?" I asked.

7

AFTER WE COLLECTED THAT SECOND CARD, ADDING GERALDO THE monk seal as our first squad member, we abandoned the coast and started to move into the city in hopes of finding a safe room. It didn't take long. Donut spotted one a few blocks deeper into the city. This was a less touristy area, filled with homes and small shops. We all traveled together. After that last fight, everyone was more comfortable with each other. Donut even seemed to have eased off on her distaste for Sister Ines.

We passed through an intersection filled with a pile of crashed cars and bicycles and mopeds, but the circle of cars wasn't very big. No cars came from any direction, but there were still people out and about with clothing on. A few bicycles still appeared. We squeezed between a wrecked classic Chevrolet and the wall of a building as Zev messaged.

ZEV: Hi, guys.

DONUT: HI, ZEV! HOW ARE YOU?

ZEV: So, I have some news. You were scheduled to go on Odette's show tonight, but she has decided to take several days off.

DONUT: OH NO. IS SHE OKAY?

ZEV: She's fine. She usually moves to the system's orbit for Faction Wars, and Prepotente's little stunt accelerated everyone's schedule, so she's traveling. We moved your scheduled interview to later. *Plenty of Plenty* also wanted you on, but I turned them down on your behalf. We have multiple offers on the table, but we wanted to get you on something quickly since it's been a while. I have you two scheduled on a program called *Shadow Boxer*. It's an interview about your lives before the crawl. You'll be going on tomorrow after the recap.

CARL: Yeah, I'm not interested in rehashing all that bullshit with Bea again. Nobody wants that.

ZEV: I'll tell them Beatrice is off-limits. That won't be the subject anyway. This is more like that *Earth Beautiful* program you went on a few weeks back, but this one is exploring the tale of Earth through storytelling and vignettes about the lives of some of the contestants. It won't be live, and it'll be a documentary-style interview. They want to focus on your life, Carl, when you were 15 to 18 years old. So, the time when you were left without a guardian until your age of majority when you joined the Navy.

DONUT: WHAT ABOUT ME?

ZEV: They want to talk to you about how certain television programs shaped your perceptions. You two will go up to the show together, but your interviews will be split into two different programs. You'll be together the whole time.

CARL: I was in the Coast Guard. Not the Navy. And no. All that crap is nobody's goddamned business. Pick something else. We can just do the Donut interview, but that's it.

ZEV: They want to interview both of you. I should note that this program is also listed as an NFC non-profit, and it is owned by one of your sponsors. The Open Intellect Pacifist Action Network. I'll be required to be there, and because it's a program owned by a sponsor, a liaison will also be present to make certain the sponsor doesn't give you an unfair advantage. They *really* want you on that program. The both of you.

Goddamnit. I considered this for a few moments. A liaison? I remembered what Orren the liaison had said to us near the end of the previous floor. He'd been trying to warn us about something, but I still didn't understand what it was. Still . . . if this program was put together by the Open Intellect Pacifist Action Network . . . there had to be something to it.

CARL: Okay.
DONUT: YAY! I CAN TALK ABOUT *GOSSIP GIRL* AND *RIVERDALE* AND *THE VAMPIRE DIARIES*.

She audibly gasped on my shoulder as she realized something.

DONUT: ZEV, THEY SHOULD INTERVIEW YOU, TOO!
ZEV: Sorry, Donut. I'm not allowed to make media appearances. But that reminds me. You two also have a preproduction meeting in a few days. I'm not certain of the exact time yet.
CARL: What does that mean?
ZEV: It's for the ninth floor. A team of reps from all nine Faction Wars participants will attend. Usually the meeting is relegated to lower-tier executives from each team, but your army currently consists of you two, your lawyer, a bunch of NPCs, and Donut's fan club. Since policy items for the game will be discussed, I took the liberty of assuming you'll want to be there. You'll be getting a glimpse of something very few people ever will. And yes, Donut, before you ask, these events are usually catered.
CARL: Wait, will this be in person?
ZEV: Don't get too excited, Carl. They're insisting your presence be virtual. You'll be at the production facility.
DONUT: BUT IT WILL STILL BE CATERED, RIGHT?
ZEV: Yes, Donut.

"Is everything all right?" Sister Ines asked as I stepped to avoid a man riding a bicycle rickshaw. The bike slammed right into a crashed car, and the ghost of the rider disappeared into the mess. I moved to grab the bike, but the front tire had bent in the crash. I left it.

"Yeah," I said. "We're dealing with our interview schedule."

"It must be a lot of work," she said with a hint of sarcasm. I held up my hand as another message came in, this one from Bautista giving an update on Tran. The man, who'd lost both his legs and his good friend Gwen at the end of the previous floor, was finally out and about, learning how to use his new floating wheelchair. Anton let out an exasperated breath.

AS WE MADE OUR WAY TO THE SAFE ROOM, BOTH DONUT AND SISTER Ines sensed a group of small monsters a few streets over, pinging about. We went to investigate and found a mass of hairy, gnomelike creatures crawling over a pile of wrecked cars. These were common level 20 monsters called duendes. They were all over the place. There had to be at least a hundred of them, and those were only the ones we could see.

I quickly pulled out the *Book of Lore*. I remembered seeing these guys in the first section under common monsters. Each one was about a foot tall and dressed in rags. They all looked like tiny, angry homeless men.

I didn't have time to read the entire entry, but it said they didn't have any special or magical attacks. The portrait in the book depicted one of them holding what appeared to be a giant pair of nail clippers. None of the ones here were armed with anything at all except their sharp teeth.

They were small, but they were big enough that if they got hit by a bike or a moped, it would knock the bike over. Which meant these little assholes were likely the cause of most of the car crashes in the area.

As we approached, I watched a pair launch themselves at a ghost riding a bike. They tackled through his clothes, causing the bike, his pants, and his shoes to go flying off his body. The oblivious ghost continued on his way. The little monsters emerged from the wreckage, each holding on to one of the man's shoes. They both ripped the shoes up, growling like dogs with a chew toy. I saw another duende had amassed a whole pile of shoes and was upside down in a boot, legs dangling in the air, like he was dumpster diving for something. He emerged, angrily chittering.

The AI's description on the mobs was strange. It was unusually short. I examined the one in the boot.

Mordecai. Duende. Level 20.

Screw these guys. Kill them.

"Carl, look, he has the same name as Mordecai!" Donut said. "We should put him in our squad!"

I laughed. "I don't think these guys are squad worthy."

A moment later, one of them spied us, and combat initiated. Screams rose up and down the street. The monsters growled and charged, but they were physically weak and didn't coordinate with one another, some of them even fighting each other for the chance to get to us first.

We moved into three separate groups. Sister Ines's squad moved across the street, Donut and I posted up near the line of buildings, and Mongo rushed out, gleefully ripping them to pieces.

He ate Mordecai the duende first.

Killing them was not difficult.

As we fought, my new essence bar quickly filled. It only took about ten kills to fill it all the way to the top. The bar itself took on a sickly brown hue that swirled oddly with yellow and green flecks, reminding me of sewage with oil spilled in it. Just looking at the bar made me feel a little ill.

Once the essence bar became fully charged, I received a notification. It was in a new voice, deep and ominous.

The Scavenger's Daughter has been fed. Unleash her wrath.

A new skill appeared in my interface. **The Daughter's Kiss**. Once activated, it would completely drain my essence bar and make my next melee attack extra powerful. I needed to use it as soon as possible because it was apparently dangerous to walk around with a full essence bar. I still wasn't clear on *how* it was unsafe, but I wasn't about to wait around to find out. Each time I filled and then drained the bar, the bar itself grew, requiring more souls to fill for the next attack, which would also be more powerful.

Donut spat a glob of poison at a screaming duende. The green sticky poison blob stuck to the monster's face, causing him to fall over. The consistency of the stuff reminded me of the slime from the *Ghostbusters* movies. The mob's skin started to bubble, and he quickly died. It was a skill, not a spell, and it was currently at level five, but with low-level monsters, it was especially effective. She had a short cooldown for it, too. Like fifteen seconds.

"Carl, that awful back patch on your jacket is glowing. What did you do? Mongo, no! You're going to ruin your dinner!"

Mongo flew through the air and landed atop a bus, metal screeching against his claws. He had a squealing duende in his mouth. He crunched down and swallowed.

"It's probably because my new essence bar thing is full. What does it look like?"

"Hang on. It's hard to see because of your cape thing." She jumped to my shoulder and pushed it aside. She made a disgusted noise and jumped back down. "Those weird stitches all around the pile of skulls are glowing, but they're glowing brown, and I can't tell what it's supposed to be. Not all of them are lit up. Maybe an aardvark. It looks just dreadful."

"It's not an aardvark," I said. I zeroed in on a single duende. It was rushing down the street away from Mongo. He was looking over his shoulder at the dino atop the bus screaming. The creature dragged a shoe with him as he fled. I activated the Daughter's Kiss skill. I jumped toward the fleeing monster, and I crushed down with my foot. I was expecting to knock him over with the attack, as he was just a little too big to simply smush.

The creature exploded into nothing. There was no resistance at all. The concrete sidewalk under my foot shattered into dust and rocks. A small shock wave burst forth, throwing all the remaining duendes to their backs. Mongo screeched in outrage as the crashed bus he stood upon rocked. A window in a nearby building shattered.

Across the street, the three other crawlers stopped fighting to look at me.

I just stood there for a moment. A bolt of something whipped through me, like an aftershock of the souls leaving my body. That ill feeling I'd momentarily felt was gone. Mostly.

"Wow," Donut said, jumping up to my shoulder. "Now *that* was impressive. And the aardvark image on your back went away when you did it."

"It's going to get stronger each time I do it, too," I said. I lifted my foot, and it wasn't even gory. I'd vaporized the damn thing. There wasn't anything left to even loot. The shoe it had been dragging was scorched and flattened, like it'd been crushed with an industrial press.

"Carl, are you okay? You have a weird look on your face."

"I . . . I think so. I just wasn't expecting it to feel like that. Come on, let's mop the rest up."

AFTER IT WAS DONE, DONUT AND I COLLECTED A TOTAL OF THREE COMmon utility cards. Two of them were **Time Extend** cards, which doubled the amount of time a summoned totem would last, and the third was a **Stout** card, which added 25% to a mob's health for the duration of combat. The cards were not onetime consumables like our Combo card.

Team Sister Ines also received three cards. Two were the same Time Extend cards. They also received an uncommon "special" card titled **Flee**. That one could only be used once, and it teleported the whole squad away from combat. It didn't say how far or where it teleported them to.

We still weren't sure how deck combat worked. Donut said she'd tried to summon the monk seal when we were fighting the duendes, and she got an error message. I knew we'd receive an explanation soon during the next announcement.

We made our way to the safe room, which was a small coffee shop named Cuba Libro. A street over was a park with dozens of more mobs within. Donut said these were more human-sized. We'd check it out later.

"So, are you guys in a guild?" I asked Sister Ines as we entered the shop.

"No," the nun said. "Team Flamenco wants us to join up, but we've decided to stay alone."

"You should definitely join with us," Donut said. "We share in all of the upgrades, including this really nice shower. And beds that make it so you hardly have to sleep at all. You get the training room upgrade, and there's a really nice Bopca in the common area. Also, you can meet Katia and Bomo and Mordecai! The real Mordecai, not the duende that Mongo just ate."

"We like it the way it is," Ines said. "We have the upgraded bed already."

"What about the upgraded litter box? I bet you don't have the upgraded litter box."

"I don't use a litter box, Donut."

Donut made an outraged noise and mumbled something under her breath.

We moved into the situationally generated hall leading to our personal space doorways. We agreed to meet up again after the recap. We'd clear out the park and start moving out of the city and into the rural areas in search of more powerful mobs to hunt and capture.

We watched the three enter their personal space. As they opened the door and went inside, I could see they had one of the smaller-sized ones where everyone slept in the same room.

DONUT: I LIKE PAZ, AND I THINK ANTON IS OKAY EVEN IF HE'S GRUMPY AND IS COMPLETELY UNEMPLOYABLE WITH THOSE TATTOOS, BUT I DON'T TRUST THE WOMAN. AND IT'S NOT JUST BECAUSE SHE'S A CAT GIRL. THERE'S SOMETHING WEIRD ABOUT HER.

CARL: I'm still on the fence. I think they're okay, but they're scared of us. It doesn't help that they'd been told you were going to kill them. Every new person we meet will have gone through some serious shit to get to this point, and we have to keep that in mind.

DONUT: SHE DOESN'T EVEN USE A LITTER BOX, CARL. IT'S HIGHLY SUSPICIOUS.

8

ALMOST THE ENTIRETY OF THE RECAP EPISODE WAS REDACTED. WE watched a group of crawlers get attacked and gored by the goddamned Easter Bunny. The rabbit appeared to be some sort of undead creature, and he ripped the limbs off the poor crawlers and stuffed their pieces into large plastic eggs afterward. We watched another group in Tokyo running while getting chased by what looked like a sentient umbrella, only to get wiped out by a bus. Then we watched Elle beat the living shit out of the same Sasquatch she was talking about earlier and then stick it with her flag. Prepotente single-handedly flagged and captured a giant bat. After that, it flashed to a studio setting with several faces in little boxes before it all went blank. It remained that way for almost a full hour.

"Did you see that gleener next to Kevin the announcer?" Mordecai asked. "That's Prime Minister Glory. The boss of the entire Syndicate. It's very unusual for him to appear on the show. I'm going to get that Bopca in the coffee shop drunk and steal his newsletter. Also, see if you can find a Desperado Club. We need supplies."

Once the show finally ended, the top-ten list repopulated. It remained nearly the same with Prepotente at the top, Donut at number two, and me at number three. Lucia Mar was number four. The next were Elle, Katia, and Florin. Osvaldo was number eight, making his first appearance on the list. He was a level 60 Curupira ranger. I had no idea what the race "Curupira" meant, and neither did Mordecai. He looked human.

Number nine was Li Na, and number ten was a woman named Burcu, also a newcomer to the list. I'd met her briefly during the Butcher's Masquerade, and I had her in my chat. She was a level 59 badger-headed Porsuk, which was the same race as all the bartenders at the Desperado Club. Her class was a Swashbuckler, the same as Tran and Bautista.

Burcu, Osvaldo, and Prepotente had all gotten into a fight after we'd killed Imogen at the end of the previous floor. I'd been knocked out during it.

A moment later, Cascadia started her announcement. She was back to her annoying, condescending self.

Hello, Crawlers!

This is going to be a long message, so sit down, shut up, and listen. Here's the card system. Most of you aren't ready to use this yet. These instructions and rules also appear in your deck tab on your interface. Make sure you familiarize yourself with these rules. Your life depends on it.

You will not encounter mobs that utilize a card system in your current location. However, as a Squad Leader, you will still have the option to summon your deck to use during battle. This functionality will become active at the end of this message and can be activated by removing the full and activated deck from your inventory during combat.

Also, if you wish to practice deck-to-deck combat, you should consider attacking another squad. Doing so might give you some much-needed experience with the combat system. Plus, if you kill another squad, you may claim all of their cards. Isn't that great?

"Go fuck yourselves," I muttered up at the screen.

Gameplay is quite simple. Each squad must have six totems active in their deck. You may activate your deck with as little as six cards total. You may have as many utility, mystic, snare, and special cards as you want. However, if you have too many, you risk pulling a hand with no totem cards at all, which will leave you exposed.

There are five types of cards: Totems, which are the summonable monsters. Utility cards, which can only be played on one or more of your summoned totems. Snare cards, which can only be

played on an enemy's totem. Mystic cards, which are similar to regular magic spells, and Special cards, which are usually onetime use. These have many varying effects.

Combat is engaged when a nearby monster's aggro is activated, and they are actively hunting you. Combat disengages when the mobs are dead, rendered neutral, or one of the parties has fled. If the Squad Leader dies during deck combat, the deck will transfer to the next in line. Overlapping combat with multiple mobs will count as a single session. Keep this in mind when entering a target-rich environment, as most totems cannot be reused once the monster is knocked out.

If an opponent owns enough cards to make a deck, deck-to-deck combat is initiated. Using your deck is no longer optional in this case, so it's in your best interest to keep your active deck in the best shape as possible. Deck-to-deck combat comes with a few additional rules that I'm sure you'll figure out as you go.

Once deck combat is initiated, the Squad Leader loses access to their regular magic abilities and their inventory system. They may still fight using melee attacks. They may use potions, scrolls, wands, etc., as long as the items are physically available to them.

Most summoned totems may NOT directly attack the opponent's Squad Leader if any enemy totems are present. That doesn't mean the Squad Leader will be safe. It will be the responsibility of the other squad members to keep the Squad Leader safe during deck combat. Once all cards in your deck are played or discarded, the Squad Leader regains their ability to use their inventory and spells.

"Goddamnit," I said out loud.

"What? What does that even mean?" Donut asked. "All I hear is blah, blah, blah, nerd squeak, blah, blah, blah."

"I'll explain in a bit," I said, reaching up to scratch her.

The moment combat initiates, four random cards from the deck will be drawn. The Squad Leader may use any or all of them as they wish. If you pull four totems, you may summon all four totems at

once. The monsters will appear, and assuming you have proper control over them, they will attack your opponents.

All totems are summoned for a specific amount of time as indicated on their card. If the totem is killed, they are knocked out for the remainder of combat. If the totem is still alive when they time out, the card will return to your deck in most cases, and not the discard pile. Injured and debuffed totems do *not* heal between summonings in the same combat.

Utility cards may only be played on an actively summoned totem. Most buffs will remain on the monster for the duration of combat, even over multiple summonings.

Snare cards may only be played when an opponent has an actively summoned totem. These debuffs will remain persistent throughout multiple summonings of the same card.

Mystic cards usually have a direct effect on squads, Squad Leaders, or the Squad Leader's deck.

Special cards have varying abilities.

When a card is used from your hand, it will be replaced by the next card in the deck at the rate of one card every ten seconds.

You may discard any card in your hand. You start combat with the ability to discard a single card. It will move to the discard pile and will be unusable for the remainder of combat. This ability resets once every thirty seconds.

And that's pretty much it. It's simple enough even you dry monkeys will figure it out. Just a reminder: This is not a turn-based environment, so speed and squad synergy are important. Don't forget, we're trying to entertain the viewers. Make sure you pick the most powerful, colorful monsters and abilities you can.

You're gonna need it for part two of this floor.

Starting at the end of this message, all safe room locations will also include a practice arena where you may, for a fee, enter and summon your totem cards in a limited mock-battle environment. This is the only place you can do this. The mercenary-training arcade some of you may have purchased for your guildhall will not work for this. You do not need a full deck to utilize this service. The

opponent monsters summoned by the system will not have their own decks nor can they harm you directly.

Warning. You may use your consumable and other onetime use cards in the practice arena, but they will *not* return. Consumable cards may only be used once, ever. Even in a practice environment. If you have cards with cooldown restrictions, such as the once-a-day Grand Finale card, the cooldown will not reset at the end of the practice session. So, keep that in mind.

There are lots of amazing cards out there. Use these remaining 13 days before the assault to collect as many as you can. If you share an area with another squad, feel free to murder them for their cards. Only the teams with the best decks will survive. Now get out there and kill, kill, kill!

"Carl," Donut said. "This is just like that nerdy Pokémon game you used to play. Or that one with the guy with the spiky hair that didn't make any sense. What was it called? Yugoslavia or something?"

I grunted. "It's not really like either of those. Like she said, most of those games are turn-based. This is going to be more complicated, especially if we don't know what cards our opponents have. You'll be without your magic or inventory until we use all your cards, and we won't know how strong the monsters we face are until combat is engaged. It's going to suck. We need to make sure we have some of those Flee cards that other squad got. And hopefully we can find some good snare cards, too."

Katia was already in the chat organizing a list of all the known card types. The list was painfully thin so far.

"I've seen them use the cards before, but it's never been anything quite like this," Mordecai said. "It sounds like the enemies in part two will all be intelligent mobs carrying decks. You'll likely have to fight your way to a boss who'll have the key to get to the stairwell, and then you gotta somehow get yourselves back here to use it."

"Let's get to the practice room and see how well Geraldo the monk seal can fight," I said. Donut and I still both had fan boxes to open, too, but they weren't quite ready yet. We'd have to wait until later. I moved toward the door, but I was interrupted by a message from Samantha.

SAMANTHA: SO GOOD NEWS AND BAD NEWS.

CARL: What is it?

SAMANTHA: I FOUND A BIG BOSS MONSTER. SHE'S A MAGE. THE RIGHT KIND OF MAGE TO GET ME INTO MY BODY, TOO. I TOLD YOU I'D FIND ONE.

Christ, I thought. She'd found something a lot more quickly than I'd anticipated.

CARL: What's the bad news?

SAMANTHA: SHE ATE ME. YOU HAVE TO COME GET ME. IT'S VERY SQUISHY IN HERE.

"My word," Donut said out loud. "She sure gets herself into a lot of trouble, doesn't she?"

CARL: Goddamnit, Samantha. You were supposed to stay away from the monsters, remember? Observe and report. How do you know she's the right type of mage? She needs to be a Pulpmancer. Mordecai says they're pretty rare.

SAMANTHA: SHE'S VERY POWERFUL. SHE CAN DO IT. SHE TOLD ME.

CARL: She *told* you?

DONUT: DID SHE TELL YOU BEFORE OR AFTER SHE ATE YOU?

SAMANTHA: IT WAS DURING. SHE IS VERY TALKATIVE. I THINK SHE IS LONELY. YOU NEED TO COME TALK HER INTO HELPING YOU.

CARL: How are we going to do that with you in her stomach? We're gonna have to kill her to get you out.

SAMANTHA: I DON'T KNOW WHY I HAVE TO COME UP WITH ALL THE SOLUTIONS.

DONUT: WHAT KIND OF MONSTER IS SHE?

SAMANTHA: SHE WON'T BE A PROBLEM.

CARL: That's not an answer.

SAMANTHA: SO, DO YOU KNOW WHAT A SPIDER IS? SHE'S KINDA LIKE THAT.

An involuntary shiver washed over me.

CARL: How big of a spider? And where are you?
SAMANTHA: I AM ALL THE WAY AT THE SOUTHERN COAST OF THE ISLAND, NEAR THE MOUTH OF THE BIG BAY.

That had to be at the very edge of the zone.

CARL: What the hell? How'd you get there so fast?
SAMANTHA: I HITCHED A RIDE! IT IS NOT IMPORTANT. YOU GOTTA COME GET ME!
CARL: Okay, but it's going to be a few days. And you didn't answer my question.
SAMANTHA: HOW BIG IS SHE? SHE'S NOT TOO BIG. SHE'S A LOT SMALLER THAN MOST MINOR GODDESSES.

I took a deep breath.

CARL: Samantha.
SAMANTHA: WHAT?
CARL: Minor goddess? You're in the stomach of a god?
SAMANTHA: NOT A REAL ONE. WELL, OKAY MAYBE HALF A REAL ONE. THAT'S HOW I FOUND HER. I FELT HER PRESENCE. SHE'S A DEMIGOD. PROBABLY NEVER EVEN GOT AN INVITE TO A PARTY. NOT A GOOD ONE AT LEAST. SHE LIVES HERE IN THE SWAMP. YOU CAN'T MISS HER. SHE HAS A WEB OVER THE WHOLE AREA. IT'S DISGUSTING AND STICKY. HER NAME IS MARIA SOMETHING. SHI MARIA, I THINK. WE HAVE A LOT IN COMMON. SHE SAYS SHE'S LOOKING FOR HER HUSBAND. HER FANGS HAVE A VERY LOVELY SHIMMER TO THEM.

I pulled out the Bahamas book, turned to the index, and I found her listed. "Shi Maria" was listed in a subindex as one of the monster's alternate names. She was listed in the very last section of the book, under "Unique Monsters."

"Yikes," I said. I turned the book to show Donut and Mordecai.

Donut peered closely at the image of the screaming spider woman. "Goodness. That lady really needs moisturizer."

"So, the plan is to abandon Samantha, right?" Mordecai asked. He shook his pointy head.

"Nope," I said. "Though she might be stuck in the thing's stomach for a while. I'm thinking maybe this is a great candidate for one of our squad member spots."

"Are you crazy?" Mordecai asked.

"Is that really a question?"

"It says one of her special attacks is permanent insanity," Donut said. "And another is permanent blindness."

"Yeah, we're gonna have to plan this one out ahead of time."

Donut continued to peer at the page. "Why does she have so many names? She has like twenty different ones. The Screamer. That sounds like a porn name. The Reviled. Kwaku's Love. The Corrupted Paramour? That one does *not* roll off the tongue. Ooo, I like this one."

She looked up at us, eyes big. "The Bedlam Bride. Now *that's* a proper name."

9

DECEMBER 12.

Assault begins December 24.
Totems in Deck: One of Six.
Total Cards in Current Deck: Five.

ENTERING THE MOCK-BATTLE ARENA.

Warning: You do not have a full deck.

Warning: You have a consumable card in your deck. This card will be lost if used in this arena.

Warning: While generated mobs cannot harm you in this location, the environment still can. Or you can still harm yourself. Try not to die in here because that would be really dumb and anticlimactic.

Choose your difficulty.

"CARL, WHAT SHOULD I PICK?" DONUT ASKED. "HEY! IT'S 1,000 GOLD IF we want to fight an easy opponent, 2,000 for one equal to our deck, and 5,000 if we want a 'challenge.' This is an outrage! Wait, it says more options appear if we beat it at challenge difficulty. Let's do that!"

"No," I said. "Do the easy one first to see what that really means. Plus we don't know if this seal guy is going to follow our instructions. He was pretty pissed when I stuck him with that flag."

We met Sister Ines's squad just outside, and we went into the mock-battle arena together, which was just another door in the situationally generated hall. We all entered at the same time, but when the door closed, it was just me, Donut, and Mongo standing in the cavernous room.

Mongo screeched, and his voice echoed. The place was huge. The room was like a giant airplane hangar, similar to the room where we'd picked our subclasses at the beginning of the sixth floor. It was featureless with gray corrugated metal walls and lit with dingy blue light that didn't seem to come from anywhere. The floor was made of solid concrete. A cool breeze swept through.

Donut suddenly gasped. "I can choose the environment! There're lots of options!"

"Be careful," I said. "Did you read the warning? Don't choose a place that sounds dangerous."

The room flashed, I felt a quick bout of nausea, and suddenly the concrete floor turned to dirt. Mongo screeched in surprise. A cheer rose up all around us. My ears popped. I turned in a full circle, looking about with awe. We were in a massive, packed arena, bigger than before. The roof was gone, and a yellow, almost cartoonish sun beat down on us. The shimmer of a bubble spread above it all, like we were under a dome.

The gravity here felt like it was only three-quarters of normal. I did a quick hop, and I jumped much higher than usual.

"Hang on, Carl, I'm going to make it so we weigh normal," Donut said. She moved her paw like she was adjusting a slider. I felt myself get slightly heavier. "There we go. This is quite customizable."

A field of knee-high purple flowers suddenly sprouted from the dirt. Mongo sneezed, and Donut swept her paw, taking the flowers away, leaving a field of green grass. She grumbled some more, and a few trees sprouted around the arena.

Each time she changed something, the arena's crowd cheered enthusiastically. All were the same creatures. Thousands and thousands of robe-clad people wearing large hats. I recognized them. We'd faced similarly dressed hunters on the sixth floor. It was a nomadic religious cult called the nebulars.

"What the hell did you pick?" I asked.

Battle Begins in Ten Seconds. Deck is locked in place.

"It was called Arena of the Eulogist or something like that. The picture was a Colosseum thing with a bunch of cheering fans. I didn't realize it would be these guys," Donut said. "It doesn't let me change the people, which is quite unfortunate, but I can choose how much they like us. I put it all the way to the top." Mongo screeched again, this time fearfully.

"Can you choose what the opponent is?" I asked.

"Sadly no. It just says we're on easy mode."

Combat Started.

I looked around. I didn't see anything.

"Uh, do you see the monster?" I asked. Donut didn't answer. I looked down at her.

She stood stiffly on the ground next to me. Four cards floated in midair, spaced equally in front of her face like a car windshield. Each card had grown to be about the size of a magazine, and they were completely blocking her view of the arena. It was the two **Time Extend** cards, the **Combo** card, and the **Monk Seal** totem card.

"Carl, Carl, what do I do? Help! I can't see!" She had to shout to be heard over the crowd noise. Everywhere she turned her head, the four cards followed. She jumped to my shoulder, and the cards moved with her. Now they were blocking my view, too.

The crowd started booing and hissing, but I wasn't sure if they were booing us or the monster. Next to me, Mongo squawked angrily, his voice piercing through the arena.

"Go into the card menu and see if you can adjust the cards' positions," I shouted. "And try discarding the Combo card. We don't want to use it."

"Doesn't that throw it away? I thought we wanted to keep it for later!"

"We do want to keep it. You're just discarding it for this battle. You can discard one card every thirty seconds. A new card will pop up ten seconds after you discard or use one."

Donut was in her menu, waving her paws around frantically. "How do you know all this, Carl?"

Mongo howled and rushed off.

"I was paying attention, and I read the rules."

The cards suddenly got bigger, overlapping each other. The first one, the **Time Extend** utility card, moved right through my face. The thing wasn't really there.

"No, no, that's not it," Donut said. She still had to shout. "Here we go."

The cards shrank to the size of playing cards, moved together, and then lowered, giving us a clear view of the playing field.

. . . Just in time to see Mongo fly through the air and land atop the purple squealing monster. It fell onto its back, its little legs waving as Mongo savagely ripped through it. Blood geysered in the air, followed by a pop and a puff of smoke, like the creature had been part clockwork or robot. A trail of intestines rocketed up in the air, like a line of sausages ascending into heaven. They disappeared into dust. Mongo tried to bite again, but the monster was gone, having dissipated. The raptor screeched in outrage as the crowd roared its approval, shaking the arena.

The only thing that was left was a little red blood-spattered purse that also disappeared a moment later.

Combat Complete. Deck has been reset.

Do you wish to go again?

"Well, that was a waste of money," I said.

"Carl, did you see that!" Donut exclaimed. "I think that was a Teletubby!"

WE TRIED AGAIN, AGAIN ON EASY DIFFICULTY, BUT THIS TIME WE PUT Mongo away. I made Donut change the environment to "Abandoned Arena," which was the same place, but without the screaming crowd. The dome over the arena now had a crack in it, and the yellow sun had turned blue. She grumbled but complied.

"I don't understand how you don't know what the Teletubbies are,

Carl," Donut was saying as we prepared to go again. "Miss Beatrice used to watch it all the time. She had it recorded on the DVR."

"A little kids' show?" I asked. "And she'd watch it? I don't remember that. That's really weird."

"She would watch it and cry sometimes," Donut said. "Come to think of it, it was quite strange. What kid shows did you watch?"

"I watched all sorts," I said. "But I watched them mostly when I was a kid."

"Now that's not true, and you know it. You watched cartoons all the time. And played kid video games."

"That's different, Donut. Most of those were shows made for adults. Plus, I didn't watch them and cry. That's really bizarre."

"Made for adults? *Dragon Ball Z* is made for adults? Though I suppose that was quite odd of Miss Beatrice. Wherever she is, I hope she still has access to her DVR. She would feed me extra sometimes after she watched it. Anyway, I'm glad Mongo ate Tinky-Winky. He acts all innocent, but he's totally the type that'd trip you if you were both being chased by a bear. I've been team Dipsy since day one. He had the most wonderful hat. I wonder if this next monster is going to be another Teletubby."

"Let's find out," I said.

Combat started, and the cards appeared. Donut remained on my shoulder so I could get a look at the hand. We only had five cards in the deck, and the totem wasn't one of the four she pulled. It was the two **Time Extends**, the **Combo** card, and the **Stout** card.

"If you pull a deck without a totem, you're immediately vulnerable, so make sure you either discard or use a card right away," I said. "We don't have any snare or mystic cards yet, so discard the Combo card."

She flicked her paw downward, and the Combo card disappeared into a puff of smoke. The empty space remained in her hand, and a 10-second timer appeared in the spot, counting down.

"If I use two cards, do they both have a timer, or is it one at a time?" Donut asked.

"I'm pretty sure it's one at a time, so if you play two at the same time, it'll take twenty seconds to get back to a full hand. We won't be able to test it until we get more cards. Once that one fills, we'll be out. Do you see the monster?"

"I see the dot. He's behind that tree over there, but he's moving slow. It's not Tinky-Winky again. It's something smaller."

Ding. The totem card appeared in the empty slot.

Your Deck has been exhausted.

"Okay, summon the totem. If he doesn't attack us, try to use all three of the utility cards on him."

Donut reached toward the **Monk Seal** totem, but paused. She looked back at me.

"You know, I wonder if it'll be something from another kids' show. I'd really like the chance to eviscerate someone from *Blue's Clues.* The only cast member of that show worth anything was Periwinkle, and they never gave him enough screen time. Plus Mrs. Pepper was obviously pulling a Miss Beatrice on Mr. Salt. How do you get paprika and sage from *that* combination?"

"Again, Donut," I said, "I haven't watched the show, so all this babbling is completely pointless. I don't know what the hell you're talking about. That's the problem with all these references. You're going to lose people. Now summon the damn seal."

She grumbled and reached forward to touch the Seal card.

Geraldo. Level 70. Monk Seal Picket Sentry is ready for battle!

The card disappeared in a puff of smoke, and Geraldo appeared, flipping through the air. The monk seal landed in the grass in front of us, squealing with kung fu noises. A boss-battle-like explosion appeared in the air as he entered the arena.

"Highhh-ya!" Geraldo shouted. He flipped again and slammed onto the ground, shaking it, then reared up, looking about. He had a 60-second timer over his head along with a health bar even though it was full. Above that was a little symbol that might've been a little totem pole, and planted in the pole was a miniature version of our team flag.

The seal sported a headband, just like in the cartoon image on the card, but it was white with red hearts on it, also mirroring our flag. He hadn't been wearing it when we captured him.

"Oi!" he said, turning toward us. "Where the crabs at?" He waved his flippers, and I realized his body was making noises each time he moved. *Wsshh, Wsshh, Wap.* Kung fu movie noises. That's what it was. They'd added cheesy kung fu noises to all of his movements.

"What the hell, man?" I muttered.

"I like it," Donut said, waving her paws. "I wish they did that for me. Or for you when you punch something. It's a lot better than things simply blowing up and getting all disgusting when you punch them."

I called out to the seal. "Hang out there for a second. The enemy is on its way."

Geraldo the seal grunted and turned back toward the tree.

"At least he's not attacking us," Donut said.

"Try to use the utility cards on him."

Donut put her paw on the **Stout** card and flipped it upward. It spun through the air, spinning like a ninja star, and it slammed into Geraldo with a loud trumpet fanfare, causing the seal to glow. His health bar grew longer. The word **Buffed** appeared over the seal for a moment in a comic-book-like explosion.

"This is quite festive," Donut said. "Why can't all the fights be like this?"

She activated the first **Time Extend** card, and it landed on the seal with another comic-book explosion. Another sixty seconds were added to the seal's timer. We only had one card left, which was the second **Time Extend**. Little X's appeared in the spaces where the other cards once were, indicating the deck was empty.

She tried to flip the last card, but it wouldn't go.

"Carl, it says uncommon totems can only hold two utility cards!"

"Huh," I said. "Good to know." I knew there were seven levels of rarity for the totem cards: Common, Uncommon, Rare, Very Rare, Legendary, Mythic, and Unique. I wondered if that meant common ones could only hold one utility card, and unique ones—like the spider that ate Samantha—could hold a whopping seven buffs.

"Hey," Geraldo said, "that ain't no crab."

"No," Donut said, disappointed. "I guess it isn't. It's not that magenta bitch, either."

"What the hell is that?" I asked, turning my attention to the blob thing that appeared from behind the tree. It started shuffling in our direction.

"Oh my god, Carl," Donut said. "It's disgusting! And I think it's crying! Just like Miss Beatrice!"

The creature snuffled forward. It was a bat-faced pig thing, but with a lot of extra skin, like one of those wrinkly Shar-Pei dogs. It stood upon thin, quivering legs. It was about as tall as my knee. The naked pink skin was bumpy and covered with infected-looking welts and moles. It moved slowly, its skin sloshing up and down.

Squonk—Level 35.

Eastern United States Region Legendary Creature.

The Squonk. The poor, pitiful Squonk.

This damn thing is so ugly, so miserable that it is in a constant state of depression. It can't stop crying. It doesn't fight. It has no attacks. It smells and looks like the distended testicle of an Olympic weight lifter with an untreated hernia. Do everyone a favor and get it out of here.

"Yo, man. I ain't touching that thing," Geraldo said.

As we watched, the creature rolled over onto its side, let out a large fart, and started bawling even more forcefully. Then, with a *pop*, it turned to water and dissipated on its own.

Combat Complete. Deck has been reset.

Do you wish to go again?

"I'm starting to think we'd be better off at medium difficulty," I said.

10

"WE DID IT THREE TIMES," PAZ SAID AS WE WALKED TOWARD THE nearby park, which turned out to actually be a cemetery. "The first time, it was this thing called a Carbunclo. Like a little fox with a gem in its head. It pissed itself and teleported away. The second time, we never even saw it. It died on its own or something. So, we went to medium difficulty, and it was some chimpanzee monster called a Qa. It was level 65. It said it was from China. Yago beat its ass. That seal really can fight."

"We never did medium difficulty," Donut said. "Carl thinks we should get more cards first."

"It is pretty expensive," Sister Ines said.

Paz laughed. "I was talking to Osvaldo. He says they went into the room, and their first opponent was the Pillsbury Doughboy. You know that little thing from the commercials? They have some lizard that breathes fire, and it literally cooked it."

Donut swished her tail. "My friend Katia said her first opponent was an actual teddy bear. And then they moved it to challenge, and they got overwhelmed by a bunch of flying piranhas."

"The monsters aren't like I thought they would be," Paz said. His armor continued to clank loudly as we walked. "It's like it can be anything from TV or video games. Not just, you know, real mythology like they said."

"Yeah, wait until you hear what this one guy named Florin is hunting," I said.

"What?" Donut asked. "I didn't hear about it."

I gave a sidelong glance to Sister Ines and grunted. "We'll see if he actually catches him before I say anything. It's a little . . . blasphemous."

"It's all blasphemous," Sister Ines said. There was a strange intensity to her voice, and I finally realized she was angry. Very angry. She'd been just a little off all morning. "It is all a mockery of our faiths and legends. They ignore the meanings behind the myths and stories, and they just see the surface, steal it, and use it to make something shiny and pretty and completely devoid of its meaning. And they mix these beloved traditions with modern fictions, things nobody ever believed to be real. It muddies the water of our stories, our histories. They don't care. These cultures and creatures are holy to people, and they are making jokes of it all."

I gave her a moment to compose herself.

"It's what they do," I finally said. Even the cards themselves—T'Ghee cards—were considered sacred to the aliens they stole the idea from. They were never meant to be used like this.

I thought of Florin and our quick conversation before we headed out. He didn't yet have any totems, but he had a quest to track and kill or capture a powerful unique that was terrorizing his region in Ecuador. I shook my head, thinking of it. Li Jun and Li Na were hunting an honest-to-goodness dragon, straight from Chinese myth. Katia was seeking some type of Christmas cat, but she asked me not to tell Donut yet. We already knew from Sister Ines she could be oddly sensitive about that sort of thing.

We approached the large cemetery. The cars around here had all stopped coming, all getting congested somewhere else in the city, though the traffic in this area was normally pretty bad, as indicated by the literally hundreds of naked, ethereal ghosts floating along the roadway, all stopped in traffic, all texting on their nonexistent phones or bopping to music I couldn't hear.

Mongo snapped at a guy pedaling a no-longer-there bike, and the dino managed to pull a gold chain off the man's neck. We all turned our attention to the large Gothic entrance to the cemetery.

The elaborate concrete archway guarded the place, which was surrounded by a towering, spiked black fence that we couldn't see through.

The entrance itself showed a thin road that led into ominous, yeah-this-place-is-haunted-as-fuck fog. Smoke drifted up from the fence line. The whole cemetery was several blocks wide. I watched a floating bus full of people enter under the arch, but they disappeared the moment they passed through. It appeared the entire area was like our starting location. Off-limits to the memory ghosts.

"This is not right. Not at all. It's the Colón Cemetery," Paz said, looking up at the entrance. "This is one of the largest cemeteries in Latin America. There are streets all through it. The entrance arch is the same, but this fence is not supposed to be here. You can drive through, and you can see it from the street. It's like a park filled with monuments. It needed a lot of renovation, but it was very full of life all the time."

We all continued to stare with awe up at the carved, arched entrance.

"Full of life?" Donut asked. "I'm pretty sure it's full of zombies now."

"My Tito is buried here," Anton said after a moment.

"Based on the number of red dots moving about, I don't think he's buried anymore," Donut said. "The whole area gives me the willies."

"Yikes," I agreed. Inside, peeking over the fence line and out of the fog, were several buildings. It was like a small city within the city. "This has boss chamber written all over it. So, you think the mobs are zombies?"

"I'm not sure. There are lots of human-sized ones all over the place," Donut said. "They're moving slow like zombies, thank goodness. I don't think I could handle *Train to Busan* zombies. *Night of the Living Dead* ones aren't so bad as long as you don't get caught in a swarm. But there are bigger and smaller dots, too. There're lots of different kinds. There's a church in the center that doesn't have anything around it. I think there might be a spell keeping me from seeing inside."

"They are all definitely undead," Sister Ines said. She started striding toward the entrance.

"Hey!" I called. "We need to walk around the edge and see if there are more clues about what's inside before we go in! That's a giant boss chamber. We don't know how strong it'll be!"

"We can handle it if you're afraid," Sister Ines called. She didn't stop.

"Uh," Paz said, looking between Sister Ines and me. "Maybe we should listen to Carl. What if we get locked in?"

"Of course we're going to get locked in," Donut said. "That's the whole purpose of the giant gate and fence. You know what this reminds me of? We once had to fight a boss that was a giant ball of pigs all rolled up. Only this place is a lot bigger."

"Come on. Don't be such a woman," Anton said to Paz. He moved to follow the nun. Paz sighed and rushed to follow, clanking like some malfunctioning android.

"That's quite offensive, Anton," Donut called.

"Those idiots are going to get themselves killed," I said.

She looked at me. "So, are we going to get ourselves locked into the death cemetery? If we don't go now, we're going to lose our chance."

"Not if they die," I said. "The gate will open again when they're dead."

We watched as they reached the entrance. Sister Ines peeked inside through the gate, but paused. Paz was talking animatedly, gesturing at us. They didn't enter. After a moment, they turned and waved us forward.

I sighed and approached.

"We do it your way," Sister Ines said. "We circle the outside and then we go in."

"TAKE THAT *SKEDADDLE* SHEET MUSIC AND MAKE SURE YOU HAVE IT handy," I said. "*Puddle Jumper*, too."

"I already did, Carl. But it's not going to let me leave if we're locked in."

"This place is big. We can still use both inside to get away from a swarm. With *Skedaddle*, we can jump twice. As long as you sing it in key."

"What is that supposed to mean? You said my performance at the masquerade was flawless."

I reached up and gave her a pat. "Also, we stay near the other guys. Paz is a paladin, and Sister Ines is a cleric. Both will be good against the undead."

I went into my own inventory and readied several of my spider automatons. I also took a few of Mordecai's Holy Gooper grenades and moved them to the ready position. I only had six of the healing potions and Emberus-blessed holy grenades. I had fifteen spider automatons, but ten of those were already "armed" with regular explosives, which meant they'd be useless if the mobs were non-corporeal. The other spiders I could arm with a holy grenade or just a straight-up healing potion. I also had several healing-potion-infused smoke curtains, which I hadn't yet tested but would supposedly mass-kill undead. I looked at my holy curtain supply worriedly. We really needed to get to a Desperado Club for a shopping trip.

"Let's do this," I said, cracking my neck. "Keep Mongo back until we know what we're facing."

We'd circled the entire park a few times, and had to deal with more of those Duende mobs on one side. There were no additional clues as to what was inside. It was a large rectangular park several blocks wide, and it was absolutely filled with red dots. There was a chapel in the center, and nobody could get a read on anything there. Sister Ines had an ability that let her know if a mob was undead or not, and she said all of them were.

I used one of my dwindling supply of Levitation potions to get a better view from above. The entire area was filled with roiling fog, and I couldn't see a damn thing. But I could see the wide expanse of dots from this height.

The mobs appeared to move aimlessly, lending credence to Donut's zombie theory. I was reminded of the train yards from the fourth floor. Those hadn't been zombies, but ghouls.

I was starting to suspect that the entire area wasn't exactly what we thought it was. The temple in the center of the square was a familiar spire. A Club Vanquisher. And I noticed a bathroom in the area, too. I'd never seen a bathroom in a boss room before.

I tossed a potion ball filled with a Fine Healing potion into the midst toward a dense patch of red, and I managed to kill three of the mobs, whatever they were. They died easily and soundlessly, but the amount of experience I received was pretty low, indicating they weren't powerful. Relieved, I lowered myself back down and said we were good to go.

The moment we stepped through the gate, I saw my theory was correct. That didn't mean this wasn't dangerous. In fact, I knew from the cookbook this could be a real pain in the ass.

Entering Medium Ghommid Settlement.

Warning! This town has been corrupted. You may not claim or repopulate the town until the rot has been eradicated.

"It's a town!" Donut said. "A town inside a town! I see a safe room! It's way over there."

"Is this like a corrupted temple?" Paz asked worriedly, looking about.

"Uh-oh," Anton said.

"It is," I said. A corrupted temple meant there were mobs inside. That was obviously the case with this town as well. I'd read a few depictions of places like this. Both corrupted temples and towns worked the same way.

An unholy screech filled the area, coming from all corners. Howls, trills, and screams filled the massive, fog-filled cemetery.

"Not again," Paz muttered.

"What?" I asked.

Warning: The presence of a Santero has aggravated the already-unsettled dead.

"Some types of undead creatures don't like my class," he said. He banged on his breastplate. "That's why I got this stuff. Holy armor. I draw their aggro, and they will only attack me and nobody else. They'll follow me wherever I go, even if we run."

"Wait," Donut said. "You knew this was going to happen? We really need to work on our communication skills, Paz. Maybe you should've waited outside."

"No," Sister Ines said. A white ball of flame appeared in her hand. "He also gets a temporary strength boost each time an unsettled is killed. I do, too."

Before I could respond, the gate behind us slammed closed. No music started, but a magical glow emanated from the gate, meaning it was magically locked. Over our heads, a half-translucent glow filled the area, indicating we couldn't fly out of here, either.

"Shocking," I said.

Another notification came.

New Quest! Pueblo de los Olvidados.

This is a little obvious since you're locked in here, but this is a compulsory quest. You can take your time with this one, but you ain't getting out until it's done.

Isn't this a cute little town? It's just so quaint! Too bad the entire populace was turned into a gaggle of horrific, undead monsters who now want to devour your delicious souls.

This place used to be populated with a race of creature called a Ghommid.

Have you ever looked through a microscope at a drop of seawater? It's really disturbing. There's all sorts of weird shit in there. Honestly, it gives me nightmares.

Anyway, that's kinda what you get when you look at a Ghommid village. A "Ghommid" is a sort of catchall term for just your regular, run-of-the-mill other-realm creature. Visitors to this world from the land of the dead. There are all sorts, and many of them are one of a kind. And like all those weird bugs and microbes in that drop of water, they do different things. Most are harmless. Some are cute. Some are angry. Some will give you explosive diarrhea just for fun. They often settle in areas where the veil is thin. Like cemeteries.

The problem with spirit creatures is that there really are all kinds. A settlement like this is bound to eventually implode. This was inevitable.

In this case, a spirit showed up, and for whatever reason turned everyone in the village into a ravenous, unsettled, I-want-to-turn-your-flesh-inside-out-and-party-with-your-intestines monster.

You must find and eradicate the source of the sickness. Removing it from the area will likely cure the populace. Or who knows? Maybe they'll all go berserk and try to kill you even harder. I don't really know. I'm not nearly as omnipotent as those sadistic assholes think. Quarantine? They already know it doesn't work. Not

when they want to keep their precious enhancement zones humming. They're in for a big surprise one of these days.

***Reward:* Well, you can leave the town. That's a good reward. Plus, the town will revert to a working settlement, and all the shops and structures will become activated again, assuming any of the workers are still alive. And why not? We'll also throw in a Silver Quest Box.**

"Carl," Donut said, "I barely understood half of that. What does it mean by 'quarantine' and 'enhancement zones'?"

"What do you mean?" Paz asked, sounding confused.

I copied and pasted the quest text into my notes like I always did, and sure enough those lines where the AI was talking about itself were gone. It wasn't the first time that had happened.

I rewrote the strange note from memory.

"So, it's going to be like any other town," I said after a moment. "But the NPCs are all monsters, and we need to find and kill the head bad guy. The bad seed. I don't think the monsters are going to be traditional zombies. They're spirit creatures who've gone crazy."

"Undead is undead," Sister Ines said. She sounded angry. Strangely angry.

"Traps," Anton suddenly said. He held his monkey crossbow at the ready.

I went to a knee. "I see 'em. Nobody go forward." Even through the fog, dozens of lights flashed, indicating the area was littered with a bunch of strange traps I didn't recognize. It seemed they were all the same kind. There was a pair of them straight ahead side by side. We had red dots around, all drifting slowly toward us thanks to Paz. They'd become visible in seconds. I quickly examined the closest trap.

Spirit Box.

Set Trap.

Effect: Roots target in place. Lowers spirit resistance, and a random non-corporeal entity from the area is summoned to the location and will attempt to possess you. Or eat you. Or just melt your face off and put the goo on a spirit corn dog or something.

Target: Corporeal dumbasses who step on it. That means you.

Duration: You will be rooted in place for sixty seconds. If you end up possessed, that's pretty damn permanent.

"Damn," I said as I quickly disarmed the trap and took it into my inventory. I didn't have time to disarm the second one as three monsters shuffled out of the fog and moved toward us. Mongo screeched as Donut released him from his carrier. She jumped upon his back.

Combat started.

All three creatures were different. All were bipedal and human-sized, and all three were level 30, but the similarities ended there. The first was a thin, naked, flesh-colored creature covered with mouths and nothing else. It was just a person made of dozens of mouths. All the teeth were black and rotten. The mouths moaned, zombie-like. I swallowed, transfixed by the horrendous creature.

The second looked like a regular, long-haired high elf, but he had a ridiculously long chin. The tip of it lowered down to his belly button area. The guy wore a green robe that seemed to be sprouting hair.

The third was an anorexic-thin humanoid wearing a loincloth with a distended, roiling belly. The bald, hairless creature wore a headband covering its eyes. Blood seeped from under the headband. It had one long arm, and one short and withered arm, clutched against its own chest.

All three moved slowly, shuffling forward. All three groaned like zombies. They moved straight for Paz, who stood right next to me.

Sister Ines tossed a white bolt, which she threw like a baseball, and the elf-like creature exploded into mist. At the same moment, Anton fired his crossbow at the one covered with mouths. The magical bolt stuck into the creature's chest, but it kept coming.

"Ew, ew, Carl, I don't like this!" Donut cried as she fired a magic missile at the third creature. It staggered. "These are like the monsters from *The Nightmare Before Christmas*! But way grosser!"

I examined the thin ghommid just as she fired another missile.

Kipper—Unsettled Ghommid—Level 30.

This is a non-corporeal monster.

This guy is normally the dishwasher at the Dirt Nap. He really liked that job, too. Now he just wants to eat you.

Kipper the ghommid fell and dissipated into sparkly dust. Paz cast something and killed the one Anton had shot with the crossbow. Dozens and dozens more of these things emerged. I saw all shapes and sizes, from toddler-sized minotaurs to a naked, massively obese man with Dumbo-sized ears walking on his hands. His ears dragged on the ground and were on fire.

I grumbled. Paz's presence had summoned all of them. *All* of them. This was going to suck. We were going to have to run and fight.

"We need to get to the safe room and formulate a better plan," I called. I cast *Tripper*, causing all the spirit box traps to go off. I wanted to farm more of them, but it was too risky to run with these all over the place. Mongo would likely set one off at any moment.

Thousands of horrific wails rose into the night sky. Several of the ghommids disappeared, having been summoned to random traps throughout town. But more and more were coming by the moment. A literal horde of zombie spirits.

A monster that looked like a human-sized owl popped into existence right in front of me, right above the second trap. It faced away. I instinctively punched it in the back of the head, but I hadn't summoned my gauntlet yet, and my fist passed right through the monster.

Crack! A blue sheet of ice covered my arm, all the way up to my shoulder, and I suddenly couldn't move it. It felt as if it had suddenly been placed into a clamp.

You've been frozen!

Warning: Your arm will shatter into itty little bits if it sustains too much damage before you thaw.

"Gah," I cried.

The monster turned its head 180 degrees to face me. The owl had swirling black eyes as big as chicken eggs. My frozen arm was suddenly in its mouth, my hand piercing all the way through its head. The creature opened its sharp beak and chomped down. *Crunch!* Flecks of ice shot away. A health bar appeared over my own goddamn arm, and it was already in the red. The flecks turned to blood.

But that wasn't all. A heavy wave of nausea swept over me.

You are being drained!

Mongo reached over and chomped the owl across the midsection, and the creature exploded and disappeared with a puff of electricity, damaged by the dino's magical teeth caps. My arm remained frozen. A twenty-second debuff timer appeared, but the debuff disappeared and the ice melted away as Sister Ines cast something on me.

"Thanks. Both of you!" I still felt exhausted. *Christ, that was close.*

"There're too many!" Anton cried. His crossbow made little monkey noises each time he fired it. Sister Ines lobbed her white balls one after another. Donut cast *Wall of Fire*, which crackled bigger than ever thanks to her new nipple ring, and a pair of clockwork Mongos appeared. They tore through the mobs. I tossed two of my infused smoke curtains. The mobs groaned and died and moved away from the smoke.

"The safe room is that way!" Donut cried, pointing toward a mass of creatures. I pulled a Holy Gooper and tossed it, clearing the way. I tossed another curtain to keep the path open.

"Move!" I yelled.

"Carl! None of my psionic attacks work on these guys!"

Both Paz and Sister Ines glowed with yellow light as they marched forward toward the pub. My own soul bar slowly filled with a swirling black, a different color than the sickly green of the duendes we'd just killed, mixing together. Tombstones rose on either side of the wide street as we pushed forward. I looked for ghommids that were higher than level 30, but I didn't see anything. None of these guys were worth flagging.

None of the ghommids cast any spells, but they were relentless. The moment the smoke dissipated, they were there, filling the gaps. Their slowness didn't matter when there were so many of them. I formed a fist, and thankfully my gauntlet worked. A single punch killed them, but I knew if I touched them at all with my flesh, I'd get frozen again. I suspected my bare foot would also work, especially after I activated Talon Strike, but I didn't dare try it. We waded the half block toward the room before we got too bogged down. Donut cast *Fireball*, and it tore through them, cleaving them away like a snowplow. But the moment they fell, more came and filled the gap.

We were soon surrounded, and I was out of my smoke curtains. The safe room was still 100 meters away.

"Donut," I yelled, "shortcut!"

"We're going to teleport!" she shouted. "Everybody stay close."

She cast *Puddle Jump*, and we reappeared just outside the safe room. It wasn't a real building, but a crumbling, marble, Gothic-style crypt with a little neon sign hanging on it that read "The Yellow Zone." I had no doubts this hadn't really been there in the real version. The three others moved into the room as I turned to face the crowd of zombies, now fifty feet away. They all slowly turned and shuffled toward us.

But then I saw him. I paused, my hand on the door as Donut and Mongo rushed inside.

He emerged from the fog, walking casually, not shuffling like the others. The barefoot man walked toward me. He wore some sort of straw headdress that completely obscured his face. It went all the way down to his waist.

The ground around him crackled with odd black tendrils everywhere he walked. He had some weird stick thing in his hand, like a fat wand, and he pointed it at me. I didn't wait to see what that was about before I dove into the safe room and slammed the door.

COMBAT ENDED. YOUR DECK HAS BEEN RESET.

"Did you see that guy?" I asked, breathless.

"No," Paz said, also breathing heavily. Sister Ines paced back and forth, like she wanted to go back out there right away. Anton was at the counter, which was, thankfully, manned by a Bopca. He was ordering a drink. The room was much bigger on the inside than the crypt had appeared. It was a regular medieval-style pub. Donut was clucking over Mongo, who was covered with dust.

"I'm pretty sure that was the boss. I didn't get a chance to read his description, but he was level 130!"

"He's probably still out there," Sister Ines said. "Open the door. He can't hurt us in here."

I remembered the rage elemental we'd had to face on the second floor. She was right. I hesitantly reached forward and pulled the door open.

"Christ," I said, jumping back.

"No," the monster said. "Not quite." He stood right there blocking the door as if he'd been about to knock on it. His dot remained red on the map.

He stepped right into the room.

11

NEW ACHIEVEMENT! INTERLOPER!

You invited a red-tagged NPC boss into a safe room, and he actually managed to get inside!

Doesn't your culture have a whole set of cautionary tales and movies about inviting mysterious strangers into your home? You know, the whole vampire thing? *The Hand That Rocks the Cradle? Single White Female 2: The Psycho?*

It's probably not in your best interests to keep doing such things.

***Reward:* You've received a Bronze Stranger Danger Box!**

"Hey!" Donut said. "We didn't invite him in! He came in on his own!"

At the far end of the bar, the Bopca started shouting for the man to get out.

We just stared at the newcomer. Mongo growled and bristled.

I held out my arms in alarm. "Donut," I said, "keep him steady!" The last thing we needed was Mongo getting teleported away.

"No, Mongo. No!" Donut shouted as the dinosaur whined like a dog.

Despite his marker on the map, the creature did not seem hostile. The combat notification didn't start. I remembered Mordecai had once told me that mobs could enter safe rooms. They only teleported away when they actually attacked. I'd never really thought about how that worked with smart mobs.

The mob was a hair shorter than me, but he had an electric presence that filled the room. I still could not see his face. The well-muscled man looked like someone that had been plucked straight from some sort of tribal ceremony. The only flesh I could see was his arms, legs, and washboard stomach. His skin was bone white, almost translucent, as if it had been drained of all color and life. He wore a straw skirt that went down to his knees, and the headdress completely blocked his features, almost like he was wearing a second grass skirt on his head. Or a lampshade that went halfway down his chest. Little tendrils of fire flecked up off his bare feet and legs. The strange wand thing in his hand was a stick of reeds held together with colorful string and decorated with seashells. The man's stench filled the room, and it was like that of a rotting corpse.

"Oh my god," Donut exclaimed. She made a little hacking noise. "Just because you're undead doesn't mean you shouldn't use deodorant. I mean, really."

I examined the creature.

Asojano—Orisha.

Level 130 City Boss.

This is a non-corporeal spirit.

Also known as the Lord of Smallpox, Asojano is one of the most respected and feared of the Orishas, a former god made flesh upon the rise of the Ascendency.

As the worshippers of these gods grew more and more extinct, their temples crumbled, and the power of these former deities waned. Eventually, they faded into nothing, slipping away beyond the veil, becoming nothing more than any other ghommid, only able to visit the physical world on occasion.

One day, not so long ago, Asojano found himself here in this small town, visiting the world he once helped rule. There was no malice to his actions. He came just so he could look upon what he once had and what he had lost.

Still, power lingers, even in the most forgotten of shells.

Asojano is disease incarnate. He kills, and he heals. He is life, and he is death. He also wears a reed hat that makes it difficult to see where he's going, so he bumps into stuff a lot.

Lord of Smallpox? I thought. *Uh-oh.*

A health bar appeared over the creature all on its own, and it started to very slowly creep downward. None of us were doing anything.

"Santero," the monster rumbled, his voice heavy and odd and ancient. I remembered Ifechi's and Queen Imogen's voices, and the monster's reminded me of a male version of those. He was talking directly to Paz. "You must assist me. These spirits have been plagued by my presence, and I need your help. I am trapped here, and you can help me free them."

"Uh," Paz said.

The door remained open, and a group of ghommids arrived. They all teleported away, one after another as they groaned and shuffled their way into the room. The Bopca continued to scream and wave his arms. The gnome guy was wearing a chef's hat. I stepped to the side around the orisha and kicked the door, shutting it.

That ended up being a mistake because the moment the door closed, the stench doubled in intensity. We all started to back up as Donut continued to make hacking noises.

His dot remained red, which was unusual.

The orisha had a barely visible moss-colored aura that radiated about twelve inches all around him. I suspected if any of us moved within the aura, we'd get hit with some sort of nasty disease. I didn't know how that would work in a safe room, and I didn't want to find out.

The man stepped forward toward Paz. The floor sizzled where he stepped, reminding me of Bianca, Prepotente's goat-dragon-pet thing. His health continued to lower.

"Don't get closer," I said to the man as we all took another step back. "Your name is Asojano, right? If you get closer, you're going to teleport away." I didn't know if that was true or not, but it sounded good. "So, you're the reason all these ghommid guys have gone crazy?"

Asojano turned to face me. He paused for a long moment before speaking. He was trembling, I realized. With anger? With fear? I couldn't tell. "You dare? You dare speak my name? We only speak through the priest, or I will have your crops withering and your skin bubbling and your ancestors cursed through eternity." He waved the wand thing at me. I was expecting it to cast something or for him to teleport away, but neither happened. The man paused and looked down at the wand, as if he, too, was surprised it didn't work.

"Oh, sweetie," Donut said, "you think we care if you can kill our crops? Carl does that all on his own." She looked up to me. "Do you remember the aloe-vera-plant incident? Miss Beatrice was most displeased with you. She was only gone for two days."

"That was you!" I said. "You knocked it over and pulled it out!"

"Well, you should have watched me better."

I kept looking back and forth between this Asojano guy and Paz. Sister Ines looked as if she was about to attack him. Anton had returned from the bar. He downed a drink, put the glass on the table, and placed a hand on Sister Ines's shoulder, presumably in an attempt to calm her. It was a strange juxtaposition, as she was usually the calm one.

Paz remained frozen, his mouth hanging open.

CARL: Paz, you need to say something. Don't just sit there. Try to find out as much as you can.

"Uh," Paz said again. "What exactly do you need me to do?"

"Go to the temple in the center of town and fix my shrine. It will allow me to leave this place."

"That's a Club Vanquisher," I said. "Do you guys have access?"

"Yes," Anton said. "All three of us do, but we don't like going there unless we have to. Sister Ines refuses to go inside. But does it matter? It ain't really open yet."

Quest Update! Pueblo de los Olvidados.

An Orisha is the source of the ghommid infection. He used the last remaining power of his shrine to enter town, and he's unable to leave. The vile power of his presence has altered the minds of the town's residents, turning them mad. Remove him to free the town.

You need to go to the temple in the center of the town, find the correct shrine, and "repair" it. That'll work. Uh, maybe. Or you can kill this guy. He doesn't look too tough. Or you can just kill everybody. That might be fun.

Asojano shook his wand thing again, like he was trying to get a remote control with a dead battery to work. He slapped it against his hand.

PAZ: What do I do?
ANTON: His health is going down on its own. Wait until it's 5%, and I'll flag him.
PAZ: Will that work in here?
CARL: I doubt it. Tell him you'll help. But stall. See what happens.

Paz shifted nervously, his armor clanking. "So, Mr. Asojano? We can help, but we can't get to the temple. There's too many of them. Can you help us get there?"

The creature nodded. "Exit tonight when the sun descends. My power is greater at night. The sickness affects them more, and they'll be stronger as well, but my ability to hold them back will also be increased. I cannot control them at all now. Once you repair my shrine, I will have the power to leave."

"In the dark?" Donut asked, dubious. "You want us to go out there and fight them in the dark?"

The monster's health turned red. Next to me, Anton pulled a flag from his inventory. He had it in his hand. I thought about it for a moment, trying to determine if I wanted to fight them for this guy. He seemed powerful, but if he was a poison-based monster, his abilities probably worked slowly, and these monster totems would only be summoned for a limited amount of time.

"You are a false god," Sister Ines said suddenly. She spat the words. Her hand-paw things were on her head, and she was making a weird kneading motion. Her voice went up in pitch, and she sounded strangely terrified. Her eyes were clenched shut. "This is too much. Our souls . . . our souls can't handle this. Anton, no. No. I can't take it. Don't do it. Let Carl's team take him."

"He is strong, Sister," Anton said. "We've gone over this . . . It's all make-believe. It's not—"

"It's too much," Sister Ines said, interrupting. "Please. No. No more false gods. Not again."

Anton and Paz gave each other a nervous glance. Donut gave me an I-told-you-she-was-crazy look.

In the end, it didn't matter. When the creature's health was about 10%, he turned and opened the door to the outside. A massive horde of monsters remained outside, and they squealed and started throwing themselves at the entrance, zapping away as they did.

He took a step outside, and his health started to rise. "Tonight. Come," he said without turning back to us.

I moved to close the door, leaving us alone in the room. His scent lingered heavily in the air.

"I KNOW WHAT YOU'RE ABOUT TO SAY, AND WE ARE NOT FLAGGING THAT guy, Carl. His presence makes me want to hurl. The Princess Posse will not like us having a rotting-stink factory in the party. I don't care how powerful he is. And I told you that Havana browns are unstable. What did I say?"

We were back in our personal space. We had to go on our program in a little bit anyway, which would give us time to get ready. We would all meet again in a few hours after the sun went down. In the meantime, Mordecai was hard at work, making us some anti-undead bombs that would help us clear the way out of the safe room. Our supplies were dwindling, but thankfully Li Jun's team had found a Desperado Club in their area, and they were getting some supplies for us. They were all marveling at how big the middle floor of the Desperado Club was, something we'd only gotten to see a fraction of on the last floor because of the hunters.

"There's definitely something going on there in her head," I said. "She's really into the idea of killing undead creatures, but she's terrified of the idea of other gods."

"Well, it reminds me of Miss Beatrice's mother, and I don't like that. She's letting her religion make her act stupid. She's crazy. You know how I feel about crazy, Carl."

I reached up to pet the cat. "There's nothing wrong with being religious or spiritual, Donut. Bautista and Imani are both really religious." I didn't add that half the authors of the cookbook were also deeply pious, though their faiths were as varied as the stars in the sky. "But it's like anything. Some people take it too far. Some people get a little carried away, and they get so caught up in the rules that they end up forgetting what their faith teaches. Sister Ines acts strong, but I think she's overwhelmed. The idea of 'worshipping' deities, even in this environment, upsets her. Either way, it's a sensitive subject for some people, and it's not really our business. We don't know what's going on in her head. It's not our place to judge her for it."

"Oh, I'm judging her. If she's going to freak out every time some god or half-god shows up, then I don't want to be anywhere near her. It makes her untrustworthy and dangerous."

I sighed. Donut had a point. It didn't matter now anyway. We were stuck with them until we could get out of here. I wasn't super worried about being trapped in this town now that we knew how to get out. If it came down to it, I could build an undead-killing bomb that'd wipe out the entire population.

"Either way," I said, "I think we should try to flag one of the regular ghommids before we fix the shrine. I didn't think they were strong enough at first, but that ice attack of theirs is really powerful. I'm resistant to ice attacks, and it still worked on me."

"That's because it's not a regular ice attack when it's from an undead creature," Mordecai said, walking into the room. He had chocolate all over his face. "Now open your boxes and then get ready for your show."

Donut and I both had fan boxes to open. Mine, a Gold Fan Box, had come from near the end of the previous floor when I'd first met Imogen, but I hadn't opened the achievement until yesterday. Donut had received hers—a Platinum Fan Box—when she sang during the Butcher's Masquerade. Both boxes were finally ready.

The main room of our personal space was unusually messy when we entered. The cleaner bot was making angry noises as it swept through, picking up candy wrappers and scrubbing stains off the counter that looked like ice cream.

Mongo sniffed at a half-empty bag of Doritos. He picked up the bag and started shaking it, spreading Dorito bits everywhere, scattering them like confetti. The cleaner bot let out a shrill tone.

"Mongo, no! Bomo, were you and Mordecai having a party in here?"

Donut asked as she jumped to the counter. She lifted up her foot, and it came back sticky. She made a face. "If you're going to have guests over, you know the rules. I have to be invited."

Bomo looked back from the television and made a noncommittal grunt. He was playing *Smash* on the newly put-together GameCube console. I hadn't yet built a controller adapter for him, but apparently Mordecai had beaten me to it.

Mordecai had a strange sheepish look on his dumb face I couldn't read. Before I could press him on it, Donut opened up the first of her boxes.

She had three boxes. A Gold T'Ghee Box she'd gotten for using the practice room, her Platinum Fan Box, and the Bronze Stranger Danger Box.

The bronze box contained an old expired tube of mace designed to be attached to a key chain. It had no magical properties whatsoever. It was just a joke prize.

The gold box contained a single card. Our first snare card. A "very rare" consumable card called Hobble.

I picked the card up. It featured a pair of legs tied together. The card reduced a totem's summoning time by 90%. If the totem card timed out and returned to the opponent's deck, they could resummon the monster once they pulled it again, but the 90% time reduction would persist through combat. That was a pretty big deal. If a monster was normally summoned for a full minute, it would make it so it'd remain for only six seconds. That would make all but the most powerful monsters useless. Too bad the card was consumable.

Donut gasped as the fan box opened.

I exchanged a look with Mordecai.

"Oh my god. Oh my god! Thank you! Thank you!" she cried, bouncing up and down with excitement. "Carl, look! Look what my Princess Posse voted on for me!"

"Don't you have one of those already?"

"This is a real one! The one I used at the party was a prop!" She gasped again. "Look, there's a purple jewel on it. Do they know me or what? I'm going to look just like Britney! The real Britney, not the crawler."

"Oh, thank the gods," Mordecai said after a moment. He looked at me and nodded. "It's a good one. Sort of. Donut, keep it in your inventory and only equip it when you're singing. Otherwise . . . yeah."

The item appeared on the table, and I gingerly picked it up as Donut continued to rain enthusiastic praise on her fans.

"It's not considered a hat?" I asked.

"No," Mordecai said. "It's a face accessory. Like your bandanna."

The AI's voice took on a weird electronic cadence as it read the description.

The Bard's Golden Throat—Enchanted Headset Microphone.

Nuclear power. The airplane. Transistors. Antibiotics.

Important inventions and discoveries of the 1900s that changed the world.

But those were nothing, absolutely nothing, compared to the greatest invention of the century.

It happened in September of 1997. That was the day it all changed. That was the day a company called Antares Audio Technologies released into the wild a piece of software that finally cured a horrific disability that'd been plaguing young men and women for a millennium.

The disability? Tone deafness.

The cure? It was called Auto-Tune.

With the advent of the real-time vocal synthesizer, underprivileged youths such as T-Pain, Kanye, and Ke$ha were finally able to crawl out from underneath their ordinary lives and become the shining stars they were destined to be. At the same time, aging musicians, *cough* like Cher, were able to keep their stars aloft just a little longer, proving once and for all that nothing, not even the lack of natural talent, could stop the upward momentum of technology.

This golden, amethyst-encrusted microphone imbues the following benefits when it is equipped:

The Golden Throat enhancement. Automatically tunes songs within one and a half steps of correct note. Assists in the proper formation of all bard-based songs and spells.

Amplification. While equipped, all spoken words and songs are

amplified at twice the normal volume. This can be increased to up to five times of top volume.

Charisma plus 5% when equipped.

"Isn't it fantastic!" Donut said. She took it back, and it poofed onto her head with little purple sparkles. The moment she equipped it, her voice modulated and increased in volume. "Oh, I just love it." She paused. "Wow . . . Carl, it sounds like I'm talking through a fan. Oh look, I can make my voice even louder!"

Mongo screeched.

I looked up at the ceiling. "Yeah, thanks," I said. To Donut, I added, "Let's keep that as a secret weapon."

"Yes, I suppose you're right," Donut said. The headset, thankfully, disappeared into her inventory. "I'll keep it in my hotlist, and I can add it when I need a little extra oomph. Or when you're not paying attention to me properly. Now open yours, Carl."

I grunted and pulled out my boxes. I had a couple of adventurer boxes for taking damage from undead. I hadn't realized the goat patch I'd gotten just before the vampire quest on the previous floor had actually muted some of the damage from the ghommid's freeze attack. It'd probably saved my arm.

There wasn't anything good in any of the first boxes. I got the same tube of mace. Then came the fan box.

It cracked and whirred with the usual amount of gusto. Sparkles and a puff of smoke appeared.

Pop!

"Uh," I said, looking at the coupon. I picked it up. It was a small clip of paper that looked as if it had been poorly cut out of a newspaper. It featured a cartoon of a topless orc woman on her stomach atop a table. The word "RELAX!" was written on the top.

I examined it.

Massage coupon!

Has work been getting you down? Feeling stressed? Do you and your girlfriends need a break? This coupon entitles you—plus one companion!—to a free, relaxing, one-hour massage at either the

Penis Parade or the Penis Palace Back Room Relaxation Spa in the Desperado Club. Includes optional aromatherapy and chemical* peel.

"Extras" and tip not included.

"Uh," I said again.

Donut gasped. "It says you can bring a companion! That's me! I'm your companion! The Penis Palace! Carl, we can go to the Penis Palace! We haven't had a chance to go there yet! This is almost as good as my prize!"

The Penis Palace was the male strip club on the middle floor of the Desperado Club, as opposed to the seedier Penis Parade on the first floor, where Donut usually went.

"Uh," I said for a third time.

Right at that moment, Katia and Bautista appeared.

"Knock, knock," Katia said, peeking her head in through the door to the guildhall.

"Hi, Katia!" Donut said. "No, no. Wait. Let me do that again."

The headset popped onto her head.

"Hi, Katia! Hi, Katia's boyfriend," she repeated. Her voice boomed electronically. "Look at my prize! And I think the Posse voted on Carl's prize, too!"

"I can see that," Katia said, laughing as Mongo danced around them. "There's no possibility of that getting old fast. What did Carl get?"

"You sound like T-Pain," a new voice said before Donut could answer. A third crawler came into the room.

"Louis!" Donut cried. She put her headset away and leaped across the room and landed on his shoulder. "Louis, how are you?"

"Uh, I'm okay. I'm doing better," he said. He reached up and gave her an awkward pat. "We're in Iceland."

"I know. I heard," Donut said. "Is it cold and covered in ice?"

"Yeah, actually it is," he said. "I always heard they named Iceland and Greenland backward to make people want to go to the wrong place, but we're in Reykjavík and it's very snowy and icy. It's pretty, though."

"It is Christmastime," Donut said. "I wanted to go to Ibiza, but Carl insisted on Cuba."

"I did not!" I said, putting my massage coupon away. "You picked the wrong place."

"I bet it's nice outside," Louis said.

He was acting normal, but I could sense it there, hidden in the back of his voice. There was a hollowness that wasn't there before, like just a little bit of life had been drained out of him. Firas had been his best friend.

"Oh, it's okay. There are disgusting street dogs everywhere. But I suppose the weather's not too bad for December." She paused. "How's Britney doing? Is her face still all . . . you know."

"Her face hasn't healed," Louis said, whispering. "But she's been going out there on her own. She's rising in levels really fast all of a sudden. Last floor she didn't want to fight at all, but now she's working really hard."

Katia was looking down at all the wrappers on the floor. The cleaner bot still zipped around, picking them up.

"Well, I hope she feels better soon," Donut said, "and I hope she's not on the path to being a supervillain. Mongo really likes her."

Louis nodded. "Yeah, it's been hard. Langley and all those other car salesmen guys and Gwen and Firas. Almost everyone who was in the bubble with us on the fifth floor, they all died on the sixth."

Donut nodded sadly. "That reminds me, how's Tran doing?"

Bautista answered. "He's much better, too. It's taken him some time to get used to not having legs, but he's like the rest of us. Resilient."

Katia's squad was her, Bautista, Louis, Britney, and Tran. She had a ton of other people in her actual party, but they hadn't chosen Iceland. Apparently there was one other group in the area, composed of the last remaining daughters from Hekla's team. They were all working together.

"We've been trying to get everyone together at least once a day to all eat together," Katia said.

"You should try the tea Bautista makes," Louis added. "It's really good."

"It is good," Katia said. "Imani and Elle are both addicted to it. He used to own a tea shop with his family."

"I'm not really a tea person," I said, "but I'll be happy to sit down with you guys. It'd be nice."

"He only eats sausage-and-egg breakfast sandwiches," Donut said. "He ate so many, now the food-box thing only has that as an option."

"Yeah, mine did the same thing," Louis said, "but with bowls of Cap'n Crunch."

"By the way," Katia said, giving a wary, sidelong look to Donut, "Imani and Tserendolgor are talking about her party joining the guild."

"What?" Donut asked. "Is that a joke? Absolutely not. We can't just let any riffraff off the street in. She's a cheater and an experience hog, and that disgusting meatball pet of hers wants to eat Mongo."

Mongo screeched in agreement.

"Dude, did you know Ren was like a supermodel before this all started?" Louis asked.

"I did, actually," I said. I'd heard some others talking about her over chat. She was born in Mongolia, but she'd spent most of her teens and twenties working as a runway model in Paris. She'd been badly injured by a jealous ex-boyfriend and had recently returned to Mongolia before the collapse. Apparently it'd been news in the modeling world. I'd never heard of her, but she was the closest thing we had to an actual pre-collapse celebrity in the dungeon. A fact someone made the mistake of pointing out where Donut could see. I'd had to talk Donut out of angrily listing all of her purple ribbons in chat.

"That's obviously a lie," Donut said, continuing to bristle. "If she was a supermodel, then why did she turn into a dog?"

"I don't know," Louis said. "But she has a necklace with a paw print on it. Maybe she really likes dogs."

"Anyway," Katia said, "it's not set in stone. There're a few other guilds who want her team, so we'll see. But Imani was thinking we should vote from now on if we're going to let other teams in."

"Well, Carl, Mongo, Bomo, Mordecai, and I all vote no," Donut said.

I reached up and pet the angry cat. "We'll talk about it if she says she wants to join."

"Oh hey," Louis said, changing the subject. "Are you guys planning on rescuing Samantha anytime soon? I made the mistake of putting her in my chat, and I don't want to be a dick and block her, but she won't stop messaging me. Earlier, she wrote 'YOOHOO' like fifty times straight in all caps until I answered, and when I did, she asked me what I was wearing."

I laughed. "Just mute her. We'll get to it when we can. She's on the other side of the map."

Katia shook her head. "I told you to be careful, Louis. She has a crush on you."

I grunted. "I'm just glad she has her attention on you and not us. No offense. Just don't let her distract you too much. Too much chatting is dangerous."

"That's actually why we came over," Katia said. "Donut has been talking, but you have been pretty antisocial, only talking business, and we wanted to check up on you."

"I'm doing okay," I said. "Living the dream, you know? How are you doing?"

She smiled sadly. "Just taking it one day at a time. Do you need any utility cards? We have these little trolls everywhere. They're just called the Lads, but they drop a lot of cards. Louis mass-killed about two hundred of them with a cloud attack, and we have more of these things than we know what to do with."

She plopped a deck onto the counter, unveiling a ton of **Time Extend** and **Buff** cards and several others I hadn't seen yet.

"Oh, wow," I said, sifting through the pile. "Have you gotten any mystic cards?"

"No," Katia said. "No mystic, no snares, and only a couple specials. We have a lot of cards, but our main deck is still pretty thin. We're going totem hunting in a few hours. Do you know how the mystic cards work? It's kind of a pain because they have to stay in your hand, taking up a slot. Anyway, here. Take two of these. They're consumable, so be careful." She pushed forward a pair of **Flee** cards. I grabbed another **Stout** card and two additional utility cards I hadn't seen before. One called **Blue Stuff**, which increased the totem's supply of mana points, and another called **Greased Lightning**, which increased a mob's speed by 25%. If we added that to Geraldo, he would be ridiculously fast.

"Thanks!" I said.

Katia gathered her cards back up. "Be careful putting too many of these utility cards in your deck until you get more totems. Li Na has a mystic card that decreases draw time from ten seconds down to five. So we should all be on the lookout for that one."

ZEV: Sorry to interrupt, but you guys are going on in a few minutes. Louis also has a show he needs to prepare for in an hour.

"Oh, poo," Donut said. "We have to go on a show, and you just got here."

"I'm doing a show, too," Louis said. "It's just me and Britney, but we're going on *Dungeon Sidekicks.*"

"Oh, I heard about that one," Donut said. "We're going on a documentary or something equally highbrow, but we'll be talking about television shows!"

"That sounds way better than mine," Louis said. "Katia went on mine once, and they made her sing karaoke. I'm a terrible singer."

"I haven't yet been invited on a program as a musical guest, but I suspect it's only a matter of time. I wonder if the galaxy has something like Eurovision where people from different planets compete and sing. That would be delightful." She turned to regard Bomo, who continued to play on the GameCube. "Bomo, be a darling and brush me out. I have a program to go on."

We said our goodbyes while Bomo brushed her. The cretin did it happily, but he wasn't nearly as enthusiastic about it as the Sledge had been.

"Carl," Donut said as we prepared, "what do you think is going to happen this time? Something crazy always happens when we go on shows. The last time, I didn't even get to go, but you made Vrah's mother really mad at you."

"Hopefully nothing too interesting," I said.

12

WE, ONCE AGAIN, TRANSFERRED TO THE SPACE STATION BEFORE BEING zapped down to the underwater production trailer. The trip into space was especially brief.

The two gnolls were already dropping into the room when we appeared. I had but a moment to gaze out the window. The space station itself rotated, but I realized we were always over the same location on the planet over the Indian Ocean. Thick clouds covered most of the area, and I didn't have time to marvel at the view. The guards did a quick, wordless once-over on us and disappeared. I grabbed Donut into my arms and turned myself in the air.

We plopped into a familiar room. This was the same room where I'd met the Popov brothers. The place still smelled like rotisserie chicken. A deck of regular playing cards remained sitting on the counter where the Popovs had left it.

There were two others already here.

Zev sat on the couch, looking both tired and worried.

And standing in the corner on two cloven hooves was a massive, hairy goat creature with a line of red bug-like eyes down its evil face.

A caprid from the Plenty.

This thing was about twice as tall as Prepotente. He was even taller than the only other full-grown caprid I'd seen, the goat from the presentation of my new sponsor. And that dude had been terrifying. This guy was worse. He went all the way to the ceiling. A creature straight from a nightmare.

Zev had warned us a liaison would be attending the show, and here he was. The tall, shaggy creature turned stiffly to face us the moment we arrived. A pair of horns curled upon its head. The corner of its top-left horn, I realized, pushed up through the ceiling. This guy wasn't really here. He was a holo.

Donut leaped from my arms and landed on the couch next to Zev. She leaned in and gave the fish woman a quick head bump. I swallowed and tried to appear confident.

"Hello, Mr. Satanic Goat Guy," I said. "Are you the same cheat who tried to get Maggie My to kill us? The same one working with the Skull Empire?"

The creature leaned in and paused, not saying anything. He moved oddly, like he couldn't turn his neck, which was astoundingly unnerving. A full five seconds passed. I was transfixed by his long, obsidian, wavy hair. Unlike Prepotente, whose wire hair felt very much like that of a regular goat, this guy's coat appeared to be silky smooth, yet at the same time, it was so black and bottomless that I imagined if I reached into his fur, my hand would come back oily. Or covered with spiders.

The goat suddenly bleated, long and hard, his voice deep and filled with bass. It vibrated the walls.

"Right back atcha, buddy," I said.

He opened his mouth again, as if he was about to really say something, but he stopped and leaned back. He made an angry grunt. He rigidly turned his whole body to the side and huffed something in a strange language at someone unseen. The words sounded like something a goat straight out of hell would say, like Latin played backward and in slow motion.

A new figure suddenly popped into the small room. This was also a holo, half obscured by a cloud of smoke. He was rapidly pulling a tie on around his neck as he zapped into place, coughing.

Quasar. My attorney.

"Not a word to my client!" Quasar shouted at the goat. He looked at me. "Holy tits. You need to tell me when you're going to be in the presence of one of these shit tarts. For fuck's sake. You're lucky I wasn't at the Tug-aporium or something."

"Hi, Quasar!" Donut said.

I fought the urge to cough, even though his vape smoke wasn't really in the room. It suddenly felt very crowded in here. "I didn't realize this was something you'd want to be involved in. And I figured you knew I'd be here. This program has been on the books for a few days."

"Do I look like a grixist shaman to you?" he asked. He finished putting on his tie. He normally wore one with an alien hula girl. This time it looked like it was covered with pickles wearing sunglasses. He took a hit of his vape and then pointed an accusatory finger at Zev. "Your outreach associate is supposed to let me know of any planned meetings with liaisons so I can prepare."

"It's not my job to do yours," Zev said evenly.

"Save it, Fish Sticks. I should've been informed ahead of time. You're lucky our contract allows for me to appear in case of an emergency."

Zev grumbled and sprayed out water over the couch.

The goat guy turned to Quasar and said something in that same weird, demonic language.

The pickles on Quasar's tie started spinning in circles on their own. Donut couldn't keep her eyes off of them.

Quasar lifted up his hands in a what-the-hell-was-that? motion. "Look, you walking shawarma skewer, I don't speak whatever the fuck it is you're trying to say, and it ain't in the translator system, which is fine by me because you ain't allowed to so much as bleat at my client. You're only here because . . . Actually, I don't know why the fuck you're here." He turned to Zev. "Why the fuck is he here?"

Zev sighed. "The program they're attending is owned by the Open Intellect Pacifist Action Network, and as you should know, Valtay rules state a liaison needs to be present in any instance when a crawler might be alone with a sponsor."

"Tits," Quasar said, sounding surprised. "*Shadow Boxer* is owned by those crazy assholes? Really? I gotta tell you, Fish Sticks, I'm more than a little annoyed at the lack of communication. But why is it this guy? We usually work with the naked worm." He turned to the goat. "What's your name again? Harbinger, right?"

"I have no control over who they send," Zev said.

"Harbinger?" Donut asked. "The devil goat's name is Harbinger? Really?"

"Well, considering his history with my client and the princess, I'd say this is improper at best. It's a three-ring ass casserole at worst. Even if he hadn't already been sanctioned for trying to straight up murder my client, he's a caprid, which is another one of Carl's sponsors. It's like hiring an incubus as a guard on a chastity yacht during an elven rut."

I felt a chill wash over me. This *was* the same guy. The one who'd given Maggie My help in trying to kill me, all with the help of the orcs of the Skull Empire. Orren the other liaison had told me it had been dealt with, but I still didn't know what that meant. I still didn't know why any of that had happened.

"Like I said," Zev said, frustrated, "this is something you'll have to take up with the liaison office."

"Oh, I will. As soon as I can find one that isn't going to accidentally raise my grandmother from the dead when he speaks. Seriously. What is up with your voice? Why aren't you getting translated properly?"

Harbinger the caprid said something, but it still came out in his demon language. He turned and started grunting at someone we couldn't see.

"The system has been buggy lately," Zev said.

The goat turned back and said, "The error has been corrected. We will proceed." His voice remained deep and terrifying. "Administrator Zev, you may inform the showrunner we are prepared."

"I'm pinging Rosetta right now," Zev said.

I went very still.

"Rosetta?" Donut asked. "Is that the host? That's a very pretty name."

"This is Rosetta's new show?" Quasar asked, straightening. "Tits, I had no idea. I need to pay better attention to this stuff." He rubbed a hand along his bald alien head. "Carl, how's my hair look?"

"Yes," Zev said, ignoring Quasar. "Rosetta Thagra. An Odette wannabe. She's a former crawler and game guide. She's a Crest." She looked at me. "Actually, she was more like you, Carl, than Odette. She was a big fan of blowing things up. She's only recently been released from her indentureship contract. Her new program, *Shadow Boxer*, has become quite popular."

My heart skipped a beat. No. No way.

I felt the line of red eyes of the liaison bore into me.

"Oh, one of those," Donut said. A Crest was a human race with no eyebrows. They'd been a common hunter type on the previous floor. Donut turned to Quasar and said, "You need to straighten your tie if you want to make a better impression. I really like the pattern, though."

Quasar looked down and picked up the end of the pickle tie. "Yeah, this one is pretty great. You know there's some new ones out there featuring you on the back of your dinosaur. You fire magic missiles. The Donut merch is much better than the Carl merch."

Donut gasped.

I barely heard this. I had to fight to stop myself from shaking. Could it be? Was it possible?

<Note added by Crawler Rosetta. 9th Edition>

How can they do this? Do they not see us? Are we not real to them? We are the same. By the gods old and new, we are the same. Yet they kill us like we are nothing. Comrades, if I ever get out of this, which seems more and more unlikely by the day, I swear upon the moons I will spend the rest of my days making certain this evil is not only eradicated from the stars, but there will be accountability for their crimes.

I swear it, I swear it, I swear it.

"NO, NO, NO," DONUT SAID, SOUNDING IRRITATED. "*GOSSIP GIRL* AND *Gilmore Girls* are two completely different shows. *Gilmore Girls* was entirely fantastic, yes, but *Gossip Girl* is, quite simply, the pinnacle of television achievement. You can't just lump the two together. It's like—I don't know—serving a Twinkie on the same plate as caviar. Tell me, Miss Thagra, what is considered the greatest program in the universe?"

Rosetta Thagra shifted uncomfortably in her chair. The humanlike woman was pale, pretty, and appeared to be in her early twenties, wearing a professional pantsuit. A strange blob of yellow hair sat atop her otherwise bald head at an angle. It looked like a faded blond toupee for an aging surfer dude. I couldn't tell if it was her real hair, an actual wig, or if it was supposed to be some sort of hat.

The moment I saw her, I immediately started to question whether this was the same person as the author of the ninth edition of the cookbook. She had an almost meek appearance. If Zev hadn't told us she was a former crawler, one just two seasons older than Mordecai, I'd never believe it.

Zev said she liked explosives. Rosetta from the cookbook had provided dozens of explosives recipes. It had to be her.

Only her voice hinted at her true age. Whatever rejuvenation system this universe used to keep people young, it wasn't perfect. There were still traces of one's unnatural age here and there.

According to Zev, the first thing Rosetta had done upon exiting the dungeon was make a documentary movie, program, whatever about her home planet. The movie was called *The Other Side of the Glass*. Zev and Quasar both said it was well received and entertaining, though I strongly suspected they both likely missed the point of it. After the success of this first movie, the mysterious Open Intellect Pacifist Action Network had funded *Shadow Boxer*, a weekly show that was now telling the story of Earth through interviews that were designed to look like regular conversations. Like Zev had said earlier, it was similar to *Earth Beautiful*, the other program we'd once gone on, but this one was much more "raw."

"Well?" Donut asked Rosetta.

Rosetta planted a fake grin on her face. "I suppose I'd say the best show in the galaxy is *Shadow Boxer*."

"Oh, I'm sure," Donut said. "But what's the best, most popular fictional program?"

"I don't get time to watch much anymore," Rosetta said. "But when I was a game guide, I really liked *Little Settler Miss*. It was very popular."

Donut leaned in. "Well, let me tell you, Miss Thagra, *Gossip Girl* is better. It's not even a question."

Rosetta nodded thoughtfully. "I know you didn't gain your sapience until you entered the dungeon, but looking back, how do you think watching this program—"

"No!" Donut said, interrupting, waving her paw up at the screen, which was showing scenes from the show. "These screencaps are all wrong. That first one is from the horrific Acapulco spin-off, and the second is from the HBO reboot, which we won't even dignify with a response. I mean, really."

Rosetta took a deep breath. I watched as the former crawler took her right hand and started to rub the side of her thigh. A nervous gesture. Her attention kept darting to Harbinger, who stood in the dark, his eyes glowing. "I apologize, Princess. I'll tell you what. After the interview, why don't we hang out for a few minutes, and you can help us choose a few proper screencaps for when this tunnels?"

"Negative," Harbinger said, talking for the first time since the interview started.

Rosetta's eyes flashed to me and then back to the caprid. "How about between the interviews? It'll all be automated anyway. She can just point. I won't even be in the room."

Harbinger didn't answer.

"Uh," Rosetta said, turning to Donut. "If that would be okay with you? We'll show you a bunch of the collected screencaps, and we'll number them, and you can call the best ones out to a producer."

Donut preened. "That would be most acceptable. Now, what were you asking?"

This went on for a while. We were in a production studio adjoining the greenroom. It was the same room where the Popovs and I had done our autograph signing, and where I'd stabbed that reporter guy in the neck with a pen. We each sat in a pair of comfortable chairs while Rosetta sat across from us. The room was dark with a hot spotlight shining right into my face. We were ringed by floating screens that were showing pictures and videos of a younger Donut winning cat shows and screencaps of the various television programs and movies she was obsessed with. Everything from *Misfits of Science* to *Downton Abbey* to *Stranger Things* where Donut went on a five-minute rant about Barb to, of course, *Gossip Girl.*

Rosetta was no Odette. She was obviously nervous, and she wasn't that great of an interviewer until the conversation started to flow naturally. Only then did she steer the conversation away from the shows themselves to how watching them made Donut feel. How did the shows compare to the real world? Did she feel they had an impact on culture?

It was a bit ridiculous that she was asking these questions of a goddamned cat, but Donut really warmed to the conversation, and Donut's answers were strangely fascinating. Donut was oddly cold on Rosetta at first, probably because she was a Crest, but by the time the interview started to wind down, Donut was happily chatting away with the woman like they were best friends.

This whole time, Zev, Quasar, and Harbinger stood off to the side in the dark, not talking with one another. Tiny Zev held on to a tablet, working on something while she watched. A chair appeared and Quasar parked himself in it about halfway through as he watched Rosetta with puppy dog eyes. A cloud of smoke floated in a square around him, breaking the illusion that he was actually in the room with us.

Harbinger stood behind them both, a mountain compared to the other two, unmoving and unspeaking as he took it all in.

Rosetta didn't ask me any questions at all during Donut's portion. She barely acknowledged my presence.

When Donut's interview finished, the woman stood from her chair and announced, "Thank you, Princess. I am going to change wardrobe for the next segment. While that's happening, we'll be scrolling images on the screen with numbers. You can just call out the numbers you think would work for the segment. I'll be back shortly so we can do Carl's interview. Okay?"

"Of course, darling," Donut said.

A disembodied male voice filled the room. "Princess Donut, we'll be showing you scenes from shows on the roundabout. Just call out the numbers."

Donut did a little hop in her chair and looked up at the screens. She loved this sort of thing. "Not number one, goodness. I don't even know what show that is. Where's the rest of that guy's shirt?"

"That's *Miami Vice*," I said.

"The show where the guy had a pet Florin on his boat? I only saw a couple of episodes."

I laughed. "Yes."

While she watched the screens, Quasar jumped at the opportunity, getting up and leaning in close. "Okay, buddy, listen up," he said, talking rapidly. "There's only so much I can say—legally, that is—with that scary fucker standing over there. I can't answer too many questions, so keep your honey hole closed while I get this out. There's been a lot of movement on the Faction Wars front. Your team's castle landed right in the middle of the Lemig Sortition's battlefield, and it splattered half their army."

"No, number six is *Golden Girls*. I did like that show, but why was all their furniture wicker?" Donut looked over. "Zev, did you ever watch *Golden Girls*? I think my favorite was the slut one."

"I loved it," Zev said after a moment. She'd put away her tablet and was staring up at all the screens intently, a strange look to her face. Harbinger was laser focused on me and Quasar.

"Number seven is good," Donut continued, "but again, that's *Gilmore Girls*. That was the spring break episode. I think number eight is *Dexter*. Carl liked that show, but I only thought it was okay. Did you know he was married to his sister from the show in real life? Can you imagine how weird that had to be? At least it wasn't the other way around. I thought these were going to be scenes from *Gossip Girl*." She gasped. "Ten is *Jane the Virgin*! I loved that show!"

Quasar continued. "The resulting ghoul things from the *Zerzura* spell are still a problem, but most of your army has gotten away and has installed themselves on your battlefield. The Lemigs are now squatting in that blown-to-shit elf castle and are using it as their stronghold, but consensus is they're fucked. Did you know their commander is still trapped in the Desperado Club? They filed a grievance stating the castle placement was an attack, but we successfully argued it was an AI action. Those tattoo memory golems that Signet lady gave you are all still around. People really like the shark. Tina is still an allosaurus and is causing problems. Her mother is another story. I got ten credits on what that baby is gonna look like. The changelings have started construction on your own stronghold. The cat Ferdinand lost his hat and moved straight to the city. Too bad that giant castle didn't land in your own territory. I hope plenty of you guys survive this floor because you're gonna need as big of an army as you can get."

Harbinger made a growling noise.

"Oh, keep your weird goat dick in the bag," Quasar said to the liaison. "There ain't no explicit rules against this. He's a sponsor." He turned back to me. "I'm sorry, buddy. There's so much more happening, and I wish I could tell you all of it. There's a shitload of action items that need to be hashed out. You two are scheduled for a preproduction meeting in a day or two. I put in a petition to be there, but they denied it."

The screens all flicked off and were suddenly replaced with photos of myself, including one I'd never seen before. It was me, about seventeen years old, staring at the camera while I carried a baby goat.

"Carl, look, it's you!" Donut exclaimed. "You're holding a baby Prepotente!"

"We'll talk more soon if we can," Quasar said, backing up.

Rosetta reappeared, wearing a different outfit. She'd changed from a pantsuit to a short dress, revealing a long, flowery tattoo that circled up her right leg and disappeared. The hair blob on her head switched sides and was now red. She sat in her chair, settled, and gave me a wink.

A photo of my mother and father hung in the air just above me. It was from their wedding. I remembered the framed photo from the living room.

It'd been over my fish tank. The memory came suddenly and quickly, like a jab to the stomach. I'd been so preoccupied with who Rosetta was, I'd completely forgotten about what we were supposed to be talking about now.

"So, comrade," Rosetta said to me, "let's talk about your dead mother."

13

<Note added by Crawler Milk. 6th Edition>

I used to make a stew for my whole family. The recipe in itself wasn't anything special. Rance meat, bone broth, a wild grass that would grow on the leeward side of our island. We'd pray over the cauldron while it simmered. The stew, when prepared properly, would not only be delicious. It would awaken the old knowledge within the minds of the young. We're all imprinted with the route of the yearly migration, but something in the traditional meal quickens that knowledge. In sharing this meal with our young, we're not only bonding with one another. We're ensuring their survival should we fall.

I can't stop thinking about it. These aliens took us before I could make this year's stew. The youngest amongst us are not here. How are they faring out there, all alone? How can they possibly survive without our guidance? Who will show them the way?

"TAKE US BACK TO THAT DAY," ROSETTA SAID. "YOUR FIFTEENTH BIRTHday. Your mother poisoned your father and left him for dead, and then she went into the basement of your home and hanged herself from the pipes. According to the incident report from the police, you were the one to discover her. Your father had only ingested a portion of the poison and was barely injured. Your mother had left a note, but the contents of it are a mystery. Apparently, it was a letter to you."

I felt as if I'd been slapped. It was like she'd stood up, walked across the space between us, and backhanded me as hard as she could. I reeled.

"We're not talking about this," I said as I recovered, my surprise getting replaced by anger. "That's not what we agreed to. We're supposed to be talking about the Anacortes Boys' Ranch."

"We are," Rosetta said. "But we gotta get there first. Your history is well known, but we need to establish the timeline. I'm sorry if it's uncomfortable."

"Your mother killed herself?" Donut asked. "Your own mother? I didn't know that. You always said she left you. I assumed she ran off with her personal trainer or something." She paused. "You know what? I don't remember you ever talking about her other than that. Saying she left you. Or your father for that matter. Miss Beatrice would never shut up about her mother and father."

Every instinct told me to stand up, turn around, and walk out. That was precisely what I would've done if it'd been anyone else asking this of me. I took a breath, gritted my teeth, and said, "Yes, my mother hanged herself. A few months later, my father disappeared and left me all alone. A few months after that, I was taken into custody by the state of Washington. I was placed in a home where I broke the nose of some other kid. Then I was shipped off to a place called the Anacortes Boys' Ranch, where I lived until my 18th birthday. I was handed a high-school-equivalency certificate even though I hadn't been in a real school for two years. I moved back down to Seattle, and I crashed on a couch for about a month while I looked for a job. I couldn't find one, so I went to a recruitment center. I got there during lunch, and the only one at his desk was the Coast Guard guy. So, now you know the history. Let's move on."

Donut sat there, her eyes shining up at me.

"Let's back up a bit," Rosetta said. "You said your father left you." I tensed. "But the state didn't take you into custody for a few *months* after that. How did that come to be?"

You're a bully. You're a bully, and nobody likes you. It's why Mom left.

I don't need you to like me. But you will respect me.

The fish tank that he'd shattered with his motorcycle helmet remained there on its pedestal, still broken a month later. A monument to the last living thing in my life that I cared about. The photo on the wall above it remained. My mom and dad smiling at the camera. A lie. A goddamned lie.

Never, I'd said. *She'd almost gotten you. Just wait until I'm big enough to finish what she started.*

He'd turned around and walked out the door. He walked out the door, and I never saw him again.

The studio had gone silent. The only sound was Zev's rebreather.

"Carl?" Rosetta finally prodded.

"My dad couldn't handle being a single dad, and he disappeared. My sophomore year of high school started a week later, and I went to school as if nothing had happened. I ate the rest of the food we had in the house, and when that ran out, my friend Sam would bring me food. It wasn't until the power went out did someone finally notice I was living by myself."

Rosetta nodded. "In fact, didn't they suspect you of actually killing your father?"

I grunted with amusement, remembering. "Yeah."

The images on the roundabout changed.

It was a grainy video of a police interrogation room. Me and that asshole detective guy. What was his name? I couldn't remember.

I sat there, my arms crossed, wearing a hoodie. Fifteen years old. I looked so small, so defiant. I could still smell that room. Like Lysol and coffee and smoke. I was there all night, I remembered. He'd offered me a cigarette, trying to be my friend, to gain my trust. I'd taken it. My first. He brought me an entire pack. Cigarettes. I was fifteen years old.

"When was the last time you saw your father?" the detective asked.

On the screen, I shrugged.

"Carl, did you do something to him?"

"What if I did?" I asked.

"Did you?"

I shrugged again. I took a drag of cigarette, trying to look cool. I coughed. I remembered that moment like it'd just happened. I could still taste it.

About an hour after this, they'd discovered my father was alive and well somewhere in Wisconsin where he'd gotten himself arrested a few times for public drunkenness. The detectives' attitude toward me completely changed once they learned my dad was alive. They were being kind and respectful to me because they wanted me to admit to a crime. It was a false respect, a false kindness, but it was the first I'd gotten from an adult in such a long time, and despite my outward hostility, I'd been just drinking it up.

I had *wanted* them to think I'd done something to my father. It was stupid, I knew now. But I'd desperately wanted them to see me, to understand me, to know me. I was here, goddamnit. I was real.

But once they realized there was nothing of interest to them, everything changed. I was just another sad, abandoned kid. A victim. I was not their problem. I was nothing. They left me alone in that cold room with the smell of cigarettes and Lysol and coffee, waiting for the social worker. They'd taken the pack away, admonishing me about smoking. I was left there for hours, forgotten, in that tiny room.

I'd never felt so helpless, so impotent in my life as when that social worker came and told me it was time to go. In so many ways, it was worse than the moment of my mother's death. Her departure had been like a slow-motion car crash that had taken years to get to the violent, abrupt impact. My father's disappearance after that was nothing but an aftershock. And everything up until that moment was me just spinning, rolling away, injured and in shock from the trauma with the broken glass of my life raining all around me.

But that moment. The moment the woman came and opened the door to the interrogation room and said, "Come on now." That was the moment I'd finally stopped reeling and could see exactly where I was.

"The police claimed they were going to arrest your father for child abandonment," Rosetta said when the video stopped playing. "An arrest warrant was issued, but it appears he was never taken into custody. He was stopped in a traffic incident seven years later in Georgia, which is another state of the country, but they let him go. It's not clear if the officers were aware of the warrant or if it was still active. That was the last time he was in the system."

That last part was news to me. I did my best not to show a reaction.

Donut, I realized, was on my lap. I couldn't remember when she'd jumped there.

"This is ancient history," I finally said. "Nobody cares about any of this stuff."

"That's not even a little bit true, Carl," Rosetta said. "But you're correct on one point. None of this is new. Odette's special on your life, which recently tunneled, touched on all of these points."

"Her *what?*" I asked.

"What I'm really interested in is how your society dealt with children who are all alone. We have seen the specials about what happened to children left in India for obvious reasons, but your country, the United States of America, was on the other side of the planet."

I had no idea what was obvious about India. I only knew of a few crawlers from India. But the last thing I wanted was to get her to talk more about this.

She continued. "You ended up at a home for teenaged boys. We have photos of your sleeping quarters, but only a precious few records about you during that time. All we have is a three-page report. And the record from your graduation. All good marks."

That photo of me holding the young goat reappeared. Another photo of the dorm, probably taken from the ranch's website, popped up on the screen. The photo was wrong. Too clean. There was light shining into the room. I remembered how dark it had been all the time. That place, too, had smelled like Lysol.

Most of my time there was a blur. I was there for two years. It seemed like it was just for a week. Yet . . . yet it also felt like it was a decade, all blurred together.

"It was called a ranch, but there were no animals there. I worked nearby at a real ranch during the summer, shoveling goat crap. But most of my time there was spent at the home cleaning or rewiring the lights or replacing all the power outlets. That's what they did. They gave you something to do. They kept you busy doing something inconsequential, something you could use once you aged out." I paused, remembering.

"Did you feel as if you were abandoned by society?" Rosetta asked.

That's exactly how I felt at the time, but I wasn't going to contribute to any anti-Earth bullshit.

"I was an angry and scared kid, but here's the thing. On the surface, everything about my life sucked. My mother was dead. My dad was gone. I was shoved in the corner until I wasn't anyone's problem anymore. My situation seemed bleak. But I was healthy. I had medical care, food, and a place to stay until I was considered an adult. Compared to some other kids, I had it great." I paused, wondering why I was saying this. Wondering if it was true. "It wasn't ideal, but looking at where I landed, I think sometimes my mother was right. That it was the best possible outcome."

Rosetta appeared surprised. "Wait, right in what? Right in killing herself?"

I didn't answer directly.

"I joined the Coast Guard right after I turned 18, and everything worked out okay until aliens decided to come along and destroy . . ."

I paused, my eyes catching a photo on the roundabout. It was me in the kitchen at the boys' home, and it appeared I was making dinner. There were a bunch of ingredients lined up on the counter, and I had a big knife in my hand while I chopped up a potato. Sitting next to me was a big jug with the word "Milk" on it.

The photo was wrong. It was fake. They'd never let me anywhere near the kitchen except to clean it, and the milk jug was strange. It was shaped like a two-liter bottle of soda. Not correct. Plus the angle of the photo was wrong. It was impossible. If I was chopping potatoes at the counter, then the person holding the camera was standing where there was a wall. I was about to say something, but I thought better of it. Was it a message? Were they trying to tell me something? If so, what the hell was it?

"We know you oftentimes worked in the kitchen, preparing a stew for your fellow students. That single report from the ranch stated you didn't talk much to anyone, but with your cooking skills, along with some help from the home's manager, you could really make a statement. Everyone would gather together at the end of the week for stew night. The report said your special ingredients were simple. Milk and potatoes and whatever else you could find. That was it."

"Cooking?" Donut asked, incredulous. "Carl could cook? Carl once almost burned the apartment down making a breakfast sandwich. And don't get me started on the pancake incident. He covered me with batter and then tried to give me a bath! In the bathtub!"

"That was your fault," I said, my mind working as quickly as it could. "You knocked the bowl off the counter."

"If I knocked something off the counter, then it was placed too close to the edge. All the best cooks know not to place things next to the edge when there are cats in the home. That's cooking 101, Carl."

I turned back to Rosetta, who was looking directly at me.

"Apparently Carl needs a proper recipe to do his best work," Rosetta said.

I looked up at the screen. "The stew was easy. Milk and potatoes. I remember that. Sometimes they didn't give us much else to work with, and I had to improvise."

"That sounds like mashed potatoes, not stew," Donut said.

"Potatoes are very versatile," I said.

"Very," Rosetta agreed. "Most—"

The whole world blinked. Rosetta disappeared. The other three in the room remained. The lights snapped on.

"Hey," Donut said. "What happened!"

"What do you think you're doing?" Zev shouted at the same time. She was shouting at the massive goat.

"I have ended the interview," Harbinger said. "I am also recalling your attorney."

"Wait just one second, you hairy glob of what-the-fuck," Quasar began before he also disappeared.

"Liaison, you do not have the authority to do that," Zev said, sounding pissed. It was the angriest I'd ever heard her. "We're going to have to refund them! And you can't just dismiss an attorney like that!"

"She and Carl were obviously talking in code," Harbinger said. "I have full authority to intervene when I believe cheating is involved. My job is to protect the integrity of the crawl. That's why I am here. I have banned Rosetta from participating in any future crawler interviews."

"They're going to sue, and they're going to win," Zev said.

"No such lawsuits are proceeding at this time," Harbinger said.

"This interview is over. Carl and Donut, you may return to the dungeon now." He paused. "You should know, Carl, that I strongly believe you need to be removed from the crawl. I am actively working to have both you and the caprid disposed, and I will eventually succeed."

With that, he blinked and disappeared.

"That's nice," I said.

"Damn him," Zev said. "Those idiots are always messing everything up. Always overreacting. Sorry, guys. I doubt she got enough for Carl's portion of the interview."

"I liked her," Donut said. "Rosetta. I didn't at first because she's one of those Crest people. But she genuinely seemed interested in the subject, even if her producers get all of their television shows mixed up. I didn't even know what that last show was, though it had the *Evil Dead* guy in it. And now she's not going to be able to do her show anymore because she was talking about mashed potatoes!"

"That's okay," I said after a moment, my mind racing. She'd risked everything to get that message to me.

I'd read through Milk's notes in the cookbook twice now. I needed to go back over them. She'd mostly been about portals and mapmaking, I remembered. And special types of ink. She had a few recipes for the stuff. I needed to take another look.

I remembered one of Milk's passages in particular. It wasn't a recipe or important information. Just a rant, like we all did in the cookbook from time to time. Someone had responded, agreeing. I was pretty sure the responder was Rosetta.

Potatoes are very versatile, I'd said.

Very, she'd replied. *Just like . . .*

. . . Just like all root vegetables.

Potatoes and milk.

I still wasn't certain exactly what they wanted me to do with the yam thing. The toraline root vegetable. But now I had an important clue. And now that I had definitive proof that my sponsors, the Open Intellect Pacifist Action Network, employed at least one, likely two, possibly *three* former cookbook owners, then whatever it was they were attempting to get me to do was of crucial importance.

"CARL, ARE YOU OKAY?" DONUT ASKED AS WE RETURNED TO THE greenroom. She jumped to the room's counter and sat facing me. "That wasn't very nice of her to bring all that up about your mother. And your father sounds like a huge jerk. I'm surprised you turned out so well-adjusted, though it does explain a few things. Why didn't you ever tell Miss Beatrice any of this stuff?"

I gave a noncommittal grunt. I wasn't okay. I was pretty damn far from okay. But what could I do? It was done, and it had been done for a very long time. Every time I started to feel sorry for myself, I would think about everyone else in the world. So many people had it so much worse. Especially now. I almost felt like I didn't have the right to feel upset about something that had happened so long ago.

Only Zev remained with us, and she was furiously typing on her tablet and grumbling. She was *pissed* about the liaison. I'd never seen her so irritated.

"It's in the past," I finally said. "I don't want to be defined by things I have no control over."

Donut just looked at me for a long moment, a concerned look to her face, like she was debating whether or not to pursue it.

I felt it then. The river. It bubbled up a little here and then. It was growing. I could hear it now. Loud, screaming. *I'm still here. I've been here the whole time.*

Patches, when applied improperly, never hold for long.

I gave Donut a small uncertain smile, and I shook my head.

No. Don't. Please.

Donut blinked slowly, and then she jumped to my shoulder and leaned against the side of my head, allowing me to give her a pat. I thought she was going to continue the line of questioning, but then she seemed to change her mind. She straightened. "Well, it's quite tragic. But did you hear what she said? Odette had a special about you! Isn't that great? I wonder what sort of audience share you pulled. Do you think there was one about me?"

"There is one," Zev said, not looking up from her tablet. "It's airing tonight, actually. There was one about Li Na last night. Tomorrow is Katia. After that, I can't remember. Maybe Florin. Odette had them made to air while she travels to Earth orbit."

"Really?" Donut asked, suddenly bouncing up and down on my shoulder. "My own special. A special, about me!" She gasped. "Do you think they have the video of the judging from Cleveland? If you watch the video, there's a close-up of Spice Mountain of Cinnamon's owner right when she realized she lost, and it's just . . . chef's kiss." She made a smacking noise. "Miss Beatrice had the screencap as the wallpaper on her phone for like a month."

"Zev," I asked, "did you deliberately not tell my attorney that Harbinger guy would be here?"

"No, Carl," Zev said. She sounded harried. "I'm sorry. I am so busy. I have so much going on right now that I shouldn't even be here. We lost dozens of staff during the Valtay changeover, plus we weren't prepared for this eighth floor, plus the Valtay don't allow certain types of micro-AI systems to assist, and now I'm doing the work of five. It didn't even occur to me he should be informed. I'll make a note of it for the future. I didn't know it would be that guy, either."

"So, he's the one who got bribed by the Skull Empire?" I asked. "How does he still have a job?"

"We're not having that conversation," Zev said. "You're transferring back in ten seconds. You'll be back here in two days for the preproduction meeting."

Donut stretched and sharpened her claws on the edge of my cloak. "If Rosetta really is banned, I do hope she gets to show her last episode, even if their producers have a weird obsession with shows that . . ." She trailed off and made a little gasp. "Shows that aren't as good as *Gossip Girl*."

<Note added by Crawler Milk. 6th Edition>

I am writing the sixth edition of this book. I am putting as much information as I can in here. One day you will find these words, and I pray that they feed you, like the stew I used to serve to our little ones. But is it enough to give this information to just one person? There's honor in giving someone a meal. But I wish to cook a feast for the whole galaxy. I wish for them all to choke on our pain.

<Note added by Crawler Rosetta. 9th Edition>

Comrade, I agree. One day, we will make certain they all know. Our words will not be lost. I swear it.

14

"HERE'S THE PLAN," I SAID TO PAZ, ANTON, AND SISTER INES AS THEY stared open-mouthed up at the armored form of Bomo. "We open the door and step outside. Before the ghommids can get to us, I'll roll the stun bomb."

"What about Asojano?" Paz asked, still looking up at the giant cretin, who was now wearing twice as much armor as he had been. "If you hit the orisha guy, it'll mess everything up."

I nodded. "We can see him out there." I pointed left. "He's already built a path for us to the temple. Sort of. All of the ghosts are pushed to the east and to the sides. The moment we exit, they'll surge. They made this like a game quest. A gauntlet run. I'm going to toss the bomb away from him and toward the mass of ghommids, which'll hopefully give us some breathing room. It'll mass stun them. Then we run to the temple, get inside, and we'll guard you while you figure out how to fix his shrine. Also, if we're lucky, I can flag one of the ghommids. You guys should consider it, too."

"Are those missile launchers on his shoulders?" Anton asked, walking in circles around Bomo.

"Yes," I said. "Two six-packs. Six group stun and six individuals." I patted the round beachball-sized bomb in my hand, which caused them all to step back. "I made them with the leftovers. The blasts will only hurt the undead, so it's okay if they go off at short range. Just be careful of the flames coming out the back when they're launched."

"This armor looks heavy as shit," Anton said after a moment, still eyeing the bomb nervously. "And more complicated than Paz's armor. Are those daggers? How much metal is he wearing?"

"A lot," I said.

"With the missile launchers on his shoulder, he looks like one of those robots from *BattleTech*," Paz said.

"I know, right?" I asked, grinning. "He's been playing some game called *Armored Core*, so he's really into it. He's just pissed he doesn't have a giant gun in addition to the missiles."

Bomo made a sad grunt.

"The metal isn't enchanted," Anton continued. "It won't protect him against the undead."

"I'm aware," I said.

"I don't like this," Sister Ines said, looking toward the door. "If we fix the orisha's shrine, it says he'll be more powerful. What if he doesn't go away? What if he uses the power to attack us?"

I nodded. "Our manager thinks the same thing. That's why we have a contingency."

THANKS TO LI NA'S TEAM MAKING A RUN TO THE DESPERADO CLUB, WE gathered all the supplies we needed. It had been pricey, and we'd needed to give some of our fortune over to them just so they could pay for it. Donut wouldn't stop grumbling about how much all of this cost.

Mordecai helped me build the first bomb. It was a modified stun grenade designed to paralyze non-corporeal monsters. I wanted to keep as many alive as possible for when the town turned back. The market on the Desperado Club's middle floor had a booth that sold something called a Troll Smoke Mantle, which was a step up from the smoke curtains that Pustule the hobgoblin sold on the top floor. They were outrageously expensive. Thirty thousand gold for a pack of twelve, and they only had one case. I had them buy it for us. When I combined four of the smoke mantles with a stun grenade, the effect of the stun had a much wider range, *and* they lasted up to thirty seconds.

Then I made smaller, lower-powered versions with the rest of my supplies and attached them to seeker missiles, which I built into Bomo's new armor. I only had enough supplies for six smoke missiles, which would have a small area effect. Then I added six anti-undead missiles that would take out just one or two ghommids at a time.

The massive suit of armor for Bomo was something I'd been toying with for a few days now. I didn't have the ability to enchant the armor, which was unfortunate. But I could make it heavy and so it would break into dozens of pieces. I made it as big as I could without impeding his ability to move too much. The rock dude was crazy strong and could hold a lot. Paz was right. He looked like one of those bipedal mechs.

I leaned up against the door to the outside. Thankfully, Asojano had cleared the doorway of the monsters. I readied the round stun bomb.

DONUT: IF THE BOMO ARMOR PLAN WORKS, THEN MAYBE WE CAN TALK KATIA INTO COMING BACK INTO OUR PARTY. WE CAN USE HER FOR THIS INSTEAD OF BOMO. WE JUST NEED TO COME UP WITH A COOL NAME FOR THE MOVE.

"Okay, here we go," I said.

COMBAT STARTED.

"Dios mío," Anton said. Sister Ines smacked him on the arm with an admonishment, but she couldn't look away, either.

The ghommids emanated an ethereal blue glow that they didn't possess during the day. They lit up the fog-covered graveyard, giving everything an eerie cerulean tinge.

If I didn't know they were so deadly, the look would be cartoonish.

The moment we stepped outside, a choir of shrieks and keens pierced across the graveyard. They didn't moan and groan like before. They *wailed.* Loud and terrifying and high-pitched, like thousands of injured animals calling out at once.

They surged. They still moved slowly, but they were much faster at night than during the day.

"Oh shit, oh shit, oh shit," Paz said as I rolled the stun grenade at the mass right behind us. The mobs were all looking directly at him.

The armored warrior suddenly had a debuff over him. **Terrified.** He glowed, and it went away as Sister Ines cast something, only for it to return a moment later. She repeated the healing, and the debuff returned a third time. The man stopped, rooted in place as he looked about, wringing his armored hands.

He couldn't move while he had the debuff.

Bam! The stun bomb went off with a muffled explosion. Billowing red smoke filled the world behind us, swirling with the fog. All the ghommids in that area were now temporarily frozen. The ones closest to the blast were likely dead.

We still had hundreds ahead of us to the left and right moving to cut us off. I closed my fist and formed my gauntlet.

"Santero!" Asojano yelled. He stood at the halfway point between us and the temple, at the center of the graveyard, which was about a full city block away. All I could see was the point of the building, like a dagger in the night. Asojano stood, shrouded knee-deep in fog. "To me!"

"Run!" I called. "Bomo, keep our way clear! . . . And pick up Paz!"

I didn't know why he was the only one affected by the Terrified debuff, but I was grateful for it.

"He heavy!" Bomo groaned as he attempted to carry the armored man, who continued to just say over and over again, *"Shit, shit, shit!"*

"Paz," I said, "take off your breastplate. Stick it in your inventory! You're too heavy for Bomo with all your armor."

I knew his breastplate was actually light as a feather when it wasn't equipped, and he didn't feel the weight while he wore it, but it made him outrageously heavy to anyone else who tried to pick him up.

"Donut," I started to say, but the breastplate blinked and disappeared as Paz unequipped it.

It revealed a surprisingly skinny, shirtless man. A giant cross tattoo was etched onto his back with a terrible rendition of Jesus in smudged ink. He still wore the leg armor, and the diameter of the waistline was wide enough that three more people could probably fit in there. The armored pants appeared to stay up magically. Bomo heaved and pulled the man up in a bear hug, holding him against his chest.

We moved toward the temple.

I knew under all that fog, a paved street cut right through the graveyard, leading straight to the church. It had been clear of monsters when we stepped outside. Now ghommids swelled forward, moving in on both sides as we rushed toward Asojano, who stood like a damn statue in the middle of the street, arms spread wide like he was Moses parting the Red Sea.

The former god radiated. He burned with a sickly green light that crackled like heat around him.

I eyed the glow warily as we ran. "Don't get too close to him!"

"What're we going to do about Paz?" Anton shouted.

"We'll heal him when we get inside!"

Whoosh! Whoosh! On Bomo's shoulders, two of the six stun missiles streaked away, exploding about thirty feet in front of us to the left and right. A group of surging undead dropped into the fog, frozen.

"Make sure you don't get it near Asojano!" I yelled.

Up ahead, Asojano turned and started jogging toward the temple. The ghommids didn't come near him, but I knew if *we* got too close, we'd get hit with whatever disease he emanated.

A six-legged fox-like ghommid hissed, coming up out of the fog, apparently unaffected by the Stun effect. It tried to jump over me and Donut to get to Paz. I decked it with my gauntlet, and it went flying. Donut magic-missiled another one, this one round and fishlike.

The Scavenger's Daughter has been fed. Unleash her wrath.

I'd killed enough to fill my back patch again. This time, the essence was almost all these ghommid things, giving the bar a black appearance.

"I'll protect you. I'll protect you, my pretties," Donut sang from my shoulder, her voice electronic with Auto-Tune. "With my voice of an angel and my expertly sung ditties!"

You have been limbered! Your party's dexterity is increased by 50%!

"Holy shit, that worked," I said as we increased in speed.

"Of course it worked, Carl," Donut said as she bounced on my shoulder, her voice still amplified and auto-tuned. "Now be quiet. I need to sing another verse to stack it.

"Run little ones, run through the cities. Uhhh." She whimpered uncertainly. "Carl loves a lady with really nice titties!"

Your party's dexterity boost has been canceled because your bard can't hold a tune. For everyone's sake, she's been muted from singing for five minutes.

"Hey!" Donut cried. She pulled the headset away.

Bomo fired two more smoke missiles ahead of us. Then he fired two more from the other tube. These were the single-target ones. The hissing missiles arced up in the air, did a loop, and hit a pair of wailing targets moving up behind us.

The temple materialized, coming into view in the glowing darkness, emerging like some dilapidated beast. The octagonal yellow building appeared ridiculously sinister in the dark. A single doorway stood open under an archway. The rotted door hung loosely by a single hinge, like a rotten tooth. Asojano rushed to the door, paused, and shouted for us to follow. He then disappeared inside, leaving the door swinging.

Ahead, Anton face-planted as he hit a hidden curb. He disappeared into the fog. The road ended before the temple, but we couldn't see the ground. Only twenty feet away. Sister Ines bent down to pick him up, firing bolts as the ghommids surged. Bomo fired his last two smoke missiles, one right in front of us, clearing the way.

A tall ghommid with the head of a donkey appeared, coming out of the darkness, surprising me with its speed. I instinctively clicked on Daughter's Kiss, which drained my essence bar. I clobbered the creature with my fist. I was expecting it to explode like the last time I'd used the spell. Instead, its damn head broke off with the sound of breaking pottery. The donkey head hit the ground and bounced.

But I hadn't killed it. Both pieces—the body and the head—rumbled to life and attacked. Tentacles sprouted from the hole in the main body as the headless thing surged back at us. At the same moment, a long, striped snake body emerged from the neck of the decapitated donkey head, whipping back and forth as it wormed out of the creature. The snake body was huge, at least ten feet long, as big as a boa constrictor. The massive body had come out of nowhere. I wasted a few precious seconds watching open-mouthed while Anton, who was still getting to his feet, started shouting, "What the fuck? What the fuck?"

The donkey snake hissed at me and slithered forward as Donut lobbed a missile at the other half, the tentacled body. It blasted back into the fog and broke into two more pieces before they disappeared into the smoke. I focused on the donkey snake. I cast Talon Strike, prayed my foot wouldn't get frozen, and attempted to stomp the damn thing.

It bobbed out of the way, lightning quick, and I whiffed my punt. This one wasn't like the others. It was *fast.* I almost Charlie Brown flipped onto my back. The donkey head emanated a shriek as it was hit by a bolt from Sister Ines.

It'd been about to strike. She'd likely just saved my life.

"Go!" I cried, pointing at the door as I scrambled to get away. The ground had turned from paved road to slick, wet grass. We clambered toward the entrance. Most of the creatures had been knocked out by the smoke, but a handful of them were either immune or resisted the Stun effect.

"Come on!" Anton shouted.

We pushed toward the hanging door and the temple. I shoved Bomo ahead of me, yelling at him to get Paz to Sister Ines so she could cure him. The others all entered one by one. Donut leaped from my shoulder into the temple, yowling as she started to slide on the interior floor tiles. I turned to face the remaining monsters.

The damn donkey snake was still coming, obviously immune to the smoke. I finally noticed this one's level was much higher than those of the others. Sister Ines had almost killed it. Its health was blinking, almost gone. It continued to shriek, this time focusing on me.

The AI took on a sneering, mocking tone.

New Achievement! Crybaby!

You've been rendered Terrified!

Whoa. Why are you being such a little bitch? Oohhh, did the widdle baby just wet itself? You can't move your legs for fifteen seconds or until the scary monster is dead!

***Reward:* We do not reward people who soil themselves in public.**

I had not peed myself. In fact, I didn't actually feel scared, just irritated that this whole shit show was harder and more dangerous than it should've been. I thought that was interesting, but I didn't have time to dwell on it. I pulled a flag from my inventory, turned it point first like a dagger just as the ghost donkey snake lunged. I let the beast impale itself.

The force of the strike blew me backward into the temple. I hit the tiled ground and slid, card in my hand as the debuff disappeared. I came to a stop against some rubble as Donut howled and jumped out of my way.

Entering La Iglesia de los Olvidados.

Combat Complete. Deck has been reset.

I GROANED, LOOKING UP. I FELT A STRANGE HEAVINESS. MOONLIGHT shone in from a hole in the roof. Despite the broken door, the ghommids weren't coming in. They sounded like they were retreating.

There once was an entrance vestibule right here, but it looked as if the interior wall had crumbled away, making the whole area one giant room. Behind me, coughing filled the chamber, which echoed slightly. It smelled of dirt and wet rot in here. The muddy tile floor was covered with moss. Donut cast *Torch*, and the room filled with a yellow glow, revealing a rotting wood ceiling covered in mold.

"I have cast a spell. They can't enter for a little while," Asojano called. "I am stronger in here." I turned to look, and he was in the back of the temple, standing over a pile of rocks that glowed green with his presence. "Here is my shrine. Give me a moment to prepare, then you must come and repair it, Santero."

I returned my attention to the red card in my hand. Donut came to look at it.

"Carl, why'd you flag that one! That one is ugly! And what kind of name is that?"

"It was tough as shit," I said. "It's a rare monster, too. It was different than most of the others. We got lucky."

"It's weird," she said. "And that's a really stupid name. We should be able to rename them."

T'Ghee Card. Rare.

Totem Card.

Skylar Spinach. Two-Thirds of an Enraged Ghommid Splitter.

"Screeech!"

Level: 66.

Origin: Cuba

Summoning duration: 60 seconds.

Constitution: 90*.

***This is a splitter. It will break into two pieces upon a fatal blow, one of which will be the primary. It will continue to split until the primary is killed a total of two times. Each iteration of the primary will have increased Constitution.**

This is a non-corporeal mob.

This is an affliction-dealing mob.

Notable attacks:

Iced.

Dodge.

Terrifier.

Splitter.

+5 additional skills and spells.

Examine in the squad details tab of your interface for full stats and skills and spells.

Warning: You have empty slots in your squad. Collecting this card will automatically activate and place this totem into your squad. You may not remove or trade squad members until your squad is full. If you wish to remove a card before your squad is full, you will have to tear the card.

I handed the card off to Donut. This was a type of splitter I'd read about in the cookbook. I was surprised it said it was level 66. The first iteration of this thing had been level 50, but then I remembered how these things worked. We'd seen similar monsters during the Iron Tangle.

You had to kill the brain piece three times to properly kill the whole thing. Since I'd "killed" it once, the card version was only at two-thirds strength. Despite that, this really was a lucky find. Unlike traditional splitters, this one actually got more powerful with each iteration. If we ever got out of this, we needed to get back to the sparring room to see what the final form looked like. It was four levels lower than Geraldo the monk seal, but this thing was obviously stronger.

"What kind of name is Skylar Spinach? Does that mean it's a boy or a girl?" Donut demanded.

"I don't know," I said. "We can ask it next time we summon it."

"Do you think it's going to always be shrieking? You know how I feel about shrieking, Carl."

"Why didn't you use 'kitty'?" Paz asked, sitting up. The Terrified debuff was gone. The man looked dazed. He remained there on the floor, rubbing his head. Outside, the ghommids continued to wail, but we couldn't see them, obscured by the smoke and the hanging door. They sounded like they'd moved all the way back to the street.

"What?" Donut asked.

"Your song," Paz said. His massive breastplate appeared in his hands, and he slipped it over his head like he was putting on a T-shirt. His head popped out the top. He'd also removed his vambraces, and he put them on now. They were designed like arm sleeves, and he was able to get them on easily. "You rhymed 'pretties' with 'ditties.' And then you used 'cities,' and your song got messed up because you paused. You used 'titties.' I'm just wondering why you didn't go with the obvious choice. You're a cat. Kitties."

"I know what I am, Paz," Donut snapped, sounding irritated. "*You* try to sing under pressure like that. It's not as easy as it looks."

"No, I liked it," he said. "I'm not trying to be a jerk. You're a good singer."

Donut's attitude changed instantly. She swished her tail. "You really think so?"

"Yeah, you're great." The man still seemed dazed, but he was slowly coming out of it.

She puffed her chest. "You should've seen me at the Butcher's Masquerade. I was about to win the talent contest, but it got ruined."

I looked about as they continued to chat. Sister Ines and Anton stood facing Asojano. The cat woman glared as the orisha stood over the pile of rocks. The former god was doing a little dance around the rubble, shaking his strange wand.

The ruined shrine stood in an alcove against one of the walls in the octagon-shaped room. His was not the only broken monument here. One of the walls was used for the entrance, and there was a total of seven shrines, one against each wall in the large room. There was enough space in here for maybe fifty people to stand about comfortably.

A shining ball of light appeared in the middle of the room, its red-yellow light overwhelming Donut's torch. It just popped into existence out of nowhere. It was about the size of a softball, and for a terrifying moment, I thought it was a massive soul crystal. It crackled like a miniature fireball frozen in place. I could feel the heat coming off it.

"The spell is forming," Asojano called as he danced. "Nobody must touch the Sun of Reawakening until after the Santero has rebuilt my shrine!"

Donut and Paz stopped talking, and we all focused our attention on the ball. I searched my memory for any mention of such a thing. I sent a quick note to Mordecai, but he said he'd never heard of it. I took another step and tried to examine the object. The description was more than a little ominous:

This magical scoop of light is pretty special. It will only last a short time in this world. If you have a stick and some hot dogs, you can probably get a quick snack in. You'll need your strength for what comes next.

"Prepare yourself, Santero!" Asojano called. "It will be soon!"

"I still have no idea what I'm supposed to do," Paz said.

As Asojano returned to his ceremonial prayer, humming as he danced around his pile of rocks, I approached the first shrine immediately to my left. It was nothing but a pile of mossy rocks and some dead, desiccated plants. Like it had once been a statue of something covered with vines that had gotten smashed.

But no, I realized as I got closer, these were actual chunks of metal, not rocks. It looked as if it had been shattered by something.

Before I could even read the info box that popped up, the metallic pieces of the broken shrine glowed, as if they were red-hot.

Both Anton and Paz let out a gasp.

"Fuck me," Anton said a moment later.

I looked about, but I couldn't see what had caused their reaction. From across the room, Asojano slowed his dance. The little ball of light, the "Sun of Reawakening," lost some of its heat, and I realized it was, indeed, a gem. Not a soul gem. It was like a flaming ruby cut into the shape of a small skull.

"What's happening?" I asked.

"We just got a quest from our god, Ogun," Paz said. "It says we can only fix one shrine. He wants us to fix a different one than Asojano's."

"Oh man," Anton said, worry evident in his voice. "Yeah. It's that one you're looking at. It's a blacksmith's anvil. If we don't do it, we'll get a smite. We gotta put it together, pray over it, and then we put the gem on it."

"What happens then?" I asked.

"I told you!" Sister Ines hissed. "I told you not to worship a false god. Now what're we going to do?"

"We can't let them get smited. Or smote or whatever," I said, looking worriedly over at Asojano, who'd stopped dancing and now stood over his rubble, rhythmically shaking his wand. "We'll have to kill him."

"If we do that, will the ghommids get better? If not, they'll swarm the building," Sister Ines asked.

"I'm pretty sure they're supposed to get better," I said uncertainly. "The quest update said we could kill this guy."

"Maybe Ogun will help us," Paz said.

"Wait, is it going to summon him if we fix this thing?" I did not like that idea. At all.

"I mean, it's his shrine," Paz said. "He wants us to fix it. I doubt it'll summon him. It's a long story. Apparently he was originally one of these orishas, but he ascended while the rest of them died or got forgotten or whatever."

"Okay," I said. "Donut, Bomo, the sister and I will take care of this guy while you two try to fix the shrine. Ready?"

"I'm still not sure what to do," Paz said.

"I think it's like a jigsaw puzzle," Anton said. "Look, the pieces aren't as hot anymore." He bent down to pick one up.

And that's when the music started.

15

<Note added by Crawler Carl. 25th Edition>

After all this time, it's still shocking to me how quickly everything can change.

COMBAT STARTED.

"Betrayal!" Asojano shouted, pointing at Anton, who stood with the metal chunk in his hand like a kid who'd been caught stealing. "Betrayal!"

The music was an orchestral mix of distorted heavy guitars and keyboards. After a moment, I realized it was a bombastic version of the classical song "In the Hall of the Mountain King." It sounded like something that heavy-metal Christmas band, Trans-Siberian Orchestra, would play.

"Okay, here we go," I said. "Donut . . ."

"No!" a new voice cried, causing me to pause. This was a female from one spot over from where Asojano stood. She was glowing, ethereal, a ghost. Not corporeal at all. A beautiful, dark-skinned woman in a flowing yellow dress that appeared to be made of light. I felt her charisma like it was a physical thing. It was just like when I'd met Signet for the first time, but stronger.

I must protect her, I thought.

The name **Oshun** blazed over her head. It didn't give any other information.

"Repair *my* shrine," she said, pointing at us. "I will protect you from any other god who seeks to harm you. I will give you riches untold. Do not listen to Ogun. Do not listen to Asojano. Or any others who appear."

Her voice was seductive, almost like she was whispering right into my ear, despite the rising volume of music. I didn't understand how I could hear her so distinctly. It was almost like she was talking directly in my mind. It felt as if her hand was on my shoulder.

Donut said something, but I couldn't hear it over the music. The headset popped back onto her head. "Carl! You're being charmed!" she shouted, her voice booming. Then she made a scoffing noise. "Anton, you, too?" She turned toward the newcomer. "Stop giving Carl an erection!"

This is wrong, I thought. I felt myself take a step toward this Oshun person. She wasn't really here. She was less than a ghost, yet I couldn't take my eyes off of her. Asojano had stopped shouting and was now saying something to the newcomer, but I couldn't hear what.

KATIA: Carl, I need you to listen carefully. I'm sending this message just to you. Not Donut.

CARL: Bad timing, Katia.

I activated my *Wisp Armor* spell, which was supposed to protect me from mind control. It didn't work. She wasn't mind-controlling me. She was charming me with a metric ton of charisma. That was different. *Goddamnit,* I thought as I grabbed the index finger on my left hand. *This is gonna suck.*

I took a breath, and I snapped it. *Crack.*

"Gah!"

KATIA: I don't have time to explain. I don't know exactly where you are or what's happening, but don't touch the shrine you were planning on repairing. Close to you is another one. A broken shrine of Yemaya. Her name is Yemaya. Remember that. It should be blue. If you can only fix one, you have to repair that one. If you do, it will help save both me and Donut.

I cast *Heal* on myself as I read her message a second time, confusion rising. Anton started moving toward Oshun's shrine while Sister Ines and Paz tried to stop him.

"You have to break his finger!" Donut yelled. "Goodness. Carl, look at his erection! Good for you, Anton!"

CARL: What? What the hell? Save you and Donut from what?

KATIA: Stop. Listen. I have the Crown of the Sepsis Whore on my head, but there's a way out. It won't be easy, and there are a lot of steps, but first we have to resurrect the goddess Yemaya. This is our only chance on this floor. They engineered it this way. I'm sorry, I would've told you sooner, but I thought we had more . . .

The chat window popped away.

What the fuck? What the fucking fuck?

The world froze. Anton shouldered away from Paz and Sister Ines and skirted past the glowing ball in the center of the room. He still had the piece of Ogun shrine in his hand. All of us stopped, frozen in place. Two more ethereal forms appeared behind their broken shrines. Both were men, leaving just two piles of debris bare.

New Achievement!

You have discovered a Celestial Thorn Room!

Not a throne room. A *thorn* room!

These things are pretty rare. And a Celestial one? Hoo boy. This is gonna be good.

You probably don't know what the hell a thorn room is. Don't worry. You gonna learn pretty damn quick.

***Reward:* In the immortal words of the luscious Bret Michaels, every rose has its thorn.**

We couldn't move, but we could still talk. "Carl, what's happening?" Donut shouted.

I was still reeling from Katia's message. How? How did she have the Crown of the Sepsis Whore on her head? The implications were staggering. How did she know what was happening here?

I took a deep breath. None of that mattered. Not yet. I knew what a thorn room was. We'd be given a series of choices. All of the choices would come with both a positive and negative benefit.

The music paused, and then resumed. It came back heavier, likely still part of the same song. It played in the background while the AI, giddy with excitement, made a new announcement.

B-B-B-B-Boss Battle!

Thorn Room! Thorn Room!

Man, oh, man, here we go! It's time to make a choice! Do you want to fight? Do you want to betray your friends for marvelous riches? It's up to you!

Seven shrines. One Sun of Reawakening. What you do next will change *everything*.

The choice you make will reverberate not just through your own lives. Or this floor. It has the potential to change the very nature of the dungeon.

Kinda funny how these moments pop up out of nowhere, isn't it? And you thought this eighth floor was just going to be filler until we go down to the ninth?

We don't do that here.

The room suddenly went pitch-black. Only the Sun of Reawakening remained glowing red and orange. The little gem in the shape of a skull spun like a globe, smoke rising from the twin eyeholes.

Which shrine will you repair? You can only fix one.

A spotlight appeared, shining down on the first of the seven broken shrines.

Shrine one! This is the shrine of Ogun, god of Blacksmiths. As the only one of these Orisha guys to ascend to the Halls, he doesn't need his old shrine repaired. He has a whole new generation of followers. But he's kind of a dick and doesn't want any of his old family members to get back into the game. Two of you already worship

him, so it's probably in your best interest to fix this one. If you don't, you two will receive a smite. There are no additional benefits to repairing the monument.

The spotlight moved to the next pile of rocks. This one had a glowing ghost behind it. It was an older man wearing a fedora, casually leaning up against the wall. The dude had a rooster on his shoulder. The barely visible, humanlike ghost flipped a coin in the air and caught it as the rooster bobbed his head.

Shrine two! Legba's shrine. If repaired, will give everyone a fifty percent chance to avoid *all* future smites. All will learn the level 15 spell *Confusing Fog*. Legba will ascend.

The next shrine was just a pile of rocks. There was no ghost there.

Shrine three! This is Shango's shrine. He's a little shy. You will learn a level 15 *Lightning* spell if you repair it. You will gain the ability to train this spell to 20. Hint, hint: That spell might come in handy later. Shango will ascend.

The shrine after that was Oshun, the woman who'd just charmed me.

Shrine four! Oshun. Sweet, sweet Oshun. If you repair her shrine, you all will be protected from the next five fatal blows. Everyone will receive a fifty percent boost to their charisma. All will receive a level 10 *Heal Party* spell. Oshun will ascend.

Then was Asojano, who was frozen in mid-scream.

Shrine five! Asojano. The Lord of Smallpox. You know who this is. He's the reason you're in this pickle in the first place. If you repair his shrine, you will win the quest. The ghommids will all go back to normal. That's it. Asojano will *not* ascend. He's already proven he's too much of a dangerous asshole to let back into the Halls of the Ascendency.

But . . .

If you *don't* repair his shrine, he will attack, and you will have to kill him. That's the boss battle. Don't forget that he's a city boss! He will also break the protection of the chamber, allowing the ghommids to surge into the temple. That will probably suck. Killing him will cure them. I hope.

Fuck, fuck, fuck, I thought.

The next pile was another ghost. All I could see was him from the waist up. He appeared well muscled, though his facial features were androgynous. A translucent sea serpent of some sort twisted around his body.

Shrine six! This is Inle's shrine. One of only two of the Orishas to have spent time in the Nothing, the deaf and mute Inle isn't all there. That's a nice way of saying he's batshit. But he once was a healing god. If you repair his shrine, you will gain immunity from most health-seeping conditions. You will gain 50% to your Constitution.

Inle will not ascend. He'll end up back in the Nothing. He doesn't know that yet, so don't tell him. Probably be pretty funny considering how much time he spent getting himself out.

The spotlight focused on the final shrine. I tensed. This was the one.

Shrine seven! This is Yemaya. The river mother. This one almost made it to the Halls on her own, but she couldn't keep her power.

Time is funny like that, isn't it? One day, you're on top of the world. The next, people don't even remember who you are.

Her good friend the goddess Eileithyia misses her so very much. If you repair this monument, Yemaya will ascend. She will gift each squad with a special card. In addition, her friend Eileithyia will grant each of you a single boon.

And that's it! Man, I can't wait to see how this turns out! I really hope y'all are on the same page here, and there aren't any secret

motivations that will cause conflict within your group. That would be really awkward.

We start in five seconds!

My mind raced. I didn't know how or why or what this Yemaya had to do with the Crown of the Sepsis Whore. But I'd learned long ago to trust Katia, to trust her instincts, to trust her heart.

I looked at the two men, still frozen. If we repaired any shrine other than Ogun's, they would receive a smite.

Both the charm lady and the guy with the snake were great, a little too great. But what would be the point? We always figured we'd have to fight Asojano anyway, and we were prepared for it. Up until the moment I received Katia's message, there would've been no question. I would've helped them repair Ogun's shrine.

But now . . .

I remembered what I said to Donut in those horrible moments near the end of the last floor.

It's going to get worse before it gets better. We're going to lose more friends. We're going to have to do some pretty horrible things just to survive.

Worse, much worse, was the sudden, out-of-nowhere implication of not following Katia's path. Getting Donut to survive past the ninth floor was already next to impossible. But having to kill Katia, too?

No. No way. I would do anything to make certain that eventuality never came to pass.

Never.

Five seconds. All of this rushed through my mind in five seconds.

You could do that. Sometimes the fog clears just long enough to see it all, all at once.

"Oshun!" Anton shouted at the seductive female ghost just as we became unfrozen. "I'm coming!"

"Yes, love," the goddess cried back. "Hurry!"

"No," Sister Ines yelled. "We have to fix Ogun's shrine!"

Anton lurched toward the woman ghost just as Paz grabbed his arm. Anton fought back. He turned and hurled the metal chunk—the piece of Ogun's shrine—toward the exit. It smashed into the broken door and punched through. The metal piece continued its trajectory and rolled outside into the night.

"Oh, *shit*!" Paz cried.

"Betrayal!" Asojano shouted again. The green glow about him grew larger.

"Donut," I hissed. "Phantasm! Now!"

"I still don't like that name," Donut grumbled.

"Do it!"

She cast *Laundry Day* on Bomo.

One moment, Bomo was absolutely covered in spiked pieces of armor. The next, the pieces exploded off of him like a fragmenting grenade, shooting in all directions, completely filling the room with dozens of metal bits. Other than the shoulder pads holding up the launchers, the metal pieces hadn't been connected together, but painstakingly sewn onto a fabric undershirt one by one, with dozens of trash-tier daggers shoved into the spaces around them. I'd put it together at my armorer's table, which turned the whole thing into something called a "Scrapheap Breastplate." I repeated the process for his arms and legs and the rest of his massive getup.

Paz got bowled over by a chunk of helmet, causing him to let go of Anton, who pushed his way toward Oshun, where he fell to his knees and started picking up chunks of rock, attempting to put the goddess's shrine together.

"Gah! Fuck!" I shouted, looking down at the dagger that had lodged into my arm. I hadn't realized the armor would fly off Bomo like that. I pulled the blade out and tossed it to the ground as I healed myself.

Foamy white bubbles filled the room at Bomo's feet, percolating up to his knees, a side product of the *Laundry Day* spell. The rock creature reached down into the soapy mess, scooped up a glob of bubbles, and brought it to his mouth. He grumbled unhappily.

Donut then cast part two of the Phantasm move. She cast her new spell, *Legionnaires of the Damned.*

A purple rent formed in midair above the temple, and dozens of wispy white ghosts flowed into the room, screaming, their voices not unlike the shrieks of the ghommids outside. Everyone stopped what they were doing to watch. The ghosts spilled downward, flowing into all the pieces of scattered armor on the floor.

All the small hunks of metal started shaking.

"Carl, it's working!" Donut shouted.

"How's your mana?"

"Topped up," Donut said. "I had to take a potion."

"Keep your *Mute* spell ready!"

Her new *Mute* spell would only last a handful of seconds, especially on a boss monster like Asojano, but if we timed it correctly, we could keep him from inflicting all of us with some terrible disease.

My original plan was to just spam drop weapons and armor pieces into a huge pile and have Donut reanimate them all with her *Legionnaires of the Damned* spell, but Mordecai said the weapons had to have been recently equipped on a combatant or corpse. It didn't matter if they were friend or foe, just that they were equipped. We'd come up with two ways to get around the issue: use corpses from my inventory graveyard or put lots and lots of little pieces on one person. We went with the latter.

The Bomo exploit was much more effective because we could engineer the armor in a way where all the individual metal chunks had a mind of their own. The fact they were possessed by spirits made this highly effective against non-corporeal monsters, even if the individual armor pieces weren't enchanted.

I didn't know if they were going to let this particular exploit stand, but it was pretty damn badass. Too bad all these armor pieces were going to dissipate when this was done.

The sharp armor bits and daggers swirled up into the air, tornado-like, loosely forming into the shape they were in before, a twin of Bomo. They clinked and clacked as they bumped into each other. Some of the pieces sparked. Individually, they sounded like hornets. Together, it was like an amplified weed whacker.

Donut pointed at Asojano and shouted, "Get him!" The whine rose in pitch as the metal tornado zipped toward the shouting city boss.

Outside, ghommids lurched toward the entrance.

"We have to get the shrine piece he threw outside!" Paz shouted. "Quick. Before the ghommids get to it!"

Asojano shrieked as the swarm of armor and daggers descended on him. Pieces of straw went flying. He cast some sort of shield over himself before Donut could stop him with her *Mute* spell. A shield health bar appeared and started to drain.

"Holy shit," I said, watching the attack on the city boss. The armor and daggers swirled around him at incredible speed, cutting and slicing and spinning and buzzing as he waved his arms. "Donut, that attack is insane!"

"I know, right?" she said proudly. Mongo appeared. She cast *Clockwork Triplicate* on him, and she sent the two automatons into the fray while the real dinosaur shrieked with alarm at his new surroundings. She then cast *Mute* on Asojano, the yellow spell flying through the air and disappearing into the skirmish. He'd been trying to cast a new spell, and it failed.

"Hey, kid," a new voice shouted. This was the ghost with the pet rooster. Legba. He was shouting at Paz. "Ogun don't need his shrine fixed, man. If you fix mine, I'll protect you from his wrath. I'll get you laid, too. What's your pleasure? I can't help but notice you weren't taken by my sister. I'll get you what you want."

I grabbed Bomo by the shoulder. The rock creature had taken a glob of soap bubbles and put it on top of his head.

I talked rapidly. "Do you remember that game *Tetris*?"

Bomo grunted. "Boring. I like the music. Better than this music."

I pointed at the lonely shrine just to his right. I could see the crumbled pieces on the ground. There weren't many. The pieces were blue, almost like ice. It looked as if they formed into maybe an obelisk. "Put those pieces together. Like in *Tetris*. Make them fit. Tell me when you're done. Fast."

"No!" came a cry. This came from the ghost of the goddess Oshun. Anton sat there staring stupidly at his hand while Sister Ines stood over him. Half of Anton's fingers on his right hand were gone. The cat woman had . . . done something to wake him up. It had worked.

"Carl!" Donut shouted, pointing at the entrance. A bug-headed ghommid lurched into the room, wailing.

"Go!" I said, patting Bomo on the back as I moved to guard the door.

"Why that shrine!" Donut called as she fired a magic missile at the ghommid. It hissed and fell back. "Carl, we need to get the Ogun piece!"

"It's too late," I called. "The piece is gone." I paused. Thankfully, I wasn't lying. There were suddenly a thousand of those things out there. "We're going to fix Yemaya's shrine."

"Why that one?" Sister Ines called as she pulled Anton away from Oshun's shrine. "If we can't do Ogun, we need to do Papa Legba!"

"Yeah," Legba agreed. "I'll protect you from smites."

"I have the heals!" Oshun called. To Anton, who remained on his knees at her base, she said, "I can heal your hand!" Anton seemed disoriented, almost drunk.

The ghost goddess turned her gaze to me.

I can stop it, she said. This time, the words *were* in my head, yet I could feel her lips near my right ear. I could smell her, despite her being across the room. *How loud is it, Carl? How deep is it? I can drain it all away.*

I see it, too, yet another voice said, this one whispering in my left ear. A new voice. This was Inle, the deaf and supposedly mute god who would give us a constitution boost. The ethereal sea serpent twisted around the man's body. This was the one who'd spent time in the Nothing. *She can't heal a canyon that's dug this deep. I can. It's not what you think it is. You're just like me, Carl. I can help you. You're just like me.*

Christ, I thought. I shook my head. In the corner, Donut's possessed armor pieces continued to fight with Asojano.

"No," I called to Paz and Anton, who was now lurching toward Legba's shrine. I was doing my best to ignore the voices. "Yemaya is friends with a real god, giving a real boon. It's your best chance!"

"Hey, I take offense to that," Legba called. The ghost rooster on his shoulder bawked angrily.

"You tell 'em," Legba said to the rooster.

"Carl, help! My mana is low!" Donut cried as she fired yet another missile at the door. Mongo shrieked and snapped at a ghommid tentacle.

"Watch out!" I called as I pulled the blessed chock from my inventory. We figured something like this would happen. This was just a leftover metal door block from the Iron Tangle that Mordecai had coated with a holy protection oil. It would keep undead from passing through like a ghost. It wasn't perfect, and it was more like a repellant than something that would actually stop the ghommids, but it would keep them from pouring into the temple. I shoved it against the door. It was plenty big enough. Outside, the ghommids wailed anew. I leaned against the door as they started to pound against it.

Anton and Paz ignored my calls to repair Yemaya's shrine and were hard at work on Legba's. His was nothing more than a wooden sign, but I couldn't read what it said upon it. They were trying to prop it up.

"That looks like it hurts!" Legba called, his voice filled with laughter. He was shouting at Asojano, who'd fallen to his knees in the swarm of metal, which continued to zip around him. His shield was almost gone. His actual health was starting to decline on its own, despite the shield still being intact.

It was from closing the door, I realized. It was just like when he was in the safe room. Being disconnected from the other ghommids was somehow draining him.

Suddenly, multiple globs of green goo shot off the dying boss. Donut hadn't been able to mute him. "Watch out!" I called as a single lump slammed into both Paz and Anton.

A blinking debuff appeared over both men as they inadvertently knocked over the shrine they were working on. Legba and his rooster shouted angrily. Sister Ines, who'd just been standing there mumbling, shook her head as if being awakened from a trance.

They're talking to us all. They're in our heads. The cat woman cast a heal on Anton, but it didn't work. She then tried another.

The green goop had also, somehow, taken out most of the reanimated armor pieces. As I watched, the metal chunks fell to the ground. The ghosts fled the armor pieces, which disintegrated into puffs of purple smoke. The two clockwork Mongos exploded.

A few daggers continued to zip through the air, high above the boss. They swooped down and swiped at the man, who remained on his knees, panting. His wand thing was gone.

The shield whiffed out. His health drained on its own. It entered the red.

"It done," Bomo said, standing up from where he was working. He pointed proudly at the obelisk. It had only been five or six pieces.

"Hold the door!" I called to Bomo. I needed to get the sun thing to the shrine to wake it up.

But first . . . I came to a decision. I pulled a flag, and I rushed across the room, jumping at the dying form of Asojano just as his health started to blink. His grass skirts were gone, revealing nothing more than a pale albino man, wide-eyed and afraid. Half of his face was covered with a group of festering boils.

I shoved the flag right into the top of his head. He puffed away, turning into a card.

Warning: You have been infected with Slugpox.

My momentum caused me to slam into the wall. I felt a boil form on my arm. It started to bubble. A wave of nausea swept over me. *Oh shit, oh shit.*

The reanimated daggers over my head flew toward the orb in the center of the room. Oshun and Legba and his rooster all howled with indignation while the mute Inle waved his arms angrily. The reanimated daggers worked together to pick up the floating skull gem and bring it to the rickety obelisk of Yemaya.

The boil on my arm kept getting bigger and bigger. I felt a new boil start to form on my neck.

The flying daggers brought the gem to the tip of the obelisk as Donut shouted instructions.

The moment the glowing gem touched the obelisk, the room froze once again.

The music stopped dead. It was so sudden, I feared I'd grown deaf.

At the same time, the daggers whiffed away into a puff of smoke. The walls of the temple flashed and then a bright white light filled the area. The hole in the ceiling closed on its own. All the shrines except Yemaya's disappeared, along with the ghosts. The floor turned tiled and clean, covered with blue tributaries. Multiple fountains sprouted out of nowhere, including one right underneath both Paz and Anton, who remained on the floor, writhing in pain from the debuff. It pushed them up and away.

The metal chock I was using to block the door disappeared, revealing an intact wooden door that was propped open to reveal a well-lit town. Thousands of ghommids stood just outside, all looking at one another in surprise.

A whole wall of text appeared in my view, including more messages from Katia, which popped away into a folder.

Winner!

Combat Complete. Deck has been reset.

Quest Complete. Pueblo de los Olvidados.

Medium Ghommid Settlement has been liberated.

Congratulations. You may now exit the settlement.

The surviving ghommids have been cured.

Entering Club Vanquisher Entrance Temple, The Temple of Yemaya.

Welcome, Friend of Yemaya.

The goddess will soon make an appearance.

System Message. The Goddess Yemaya has reascended. She is welcomed into the family by all.

We unfroze.

"Oh god, oh god," Paz was saying.

"He's coming," Anton said, his voice hoarse with pain.

"It's not working," Sister Ines cried, her voice panicked. "I can top up your health, but it doesn't stop going down. I can't cure it."

I barely heard this as I was preoccupied by the massive boil on my arm, which was getting bigger and bigger like one of those Jiffy Pop popcorn pans. This was different than what Paz and Anton were suffering from.

Pop!

The boil on my arm exploded in a spray of clear liquid. I took a hit of damage. It stank of rot.

A thumb-sized slug fell to the ground in a shower of fluid. It looked like a regular slug, but with a row of jagged teeth.

What the hell?

Pox Slug—Level 1.

Disgusting. They're like miniature, drunk, and angry Juggalos. And what's worse, the next one will be level 2. Then level 3 and so forth. The good thing is they won't attack *you*. Not yet at least.

"Carl, Carl, what's happening?" Donut cried, coming up. "What's on your neck?" She stopped short at the sight of the miniature monster. "Oh my god, what is that?"

"I need a healer," I croaked.

"Stay away from my daddy!" the slug cried with a tiny, high-pitched voice. It launched itself at Donut and chomped directly onto her nose, Mongo-style. It hung from her face, growling.

Donut squealed. She swiped at it, and it exploded in a shower of ooze. The boil on my neck felt as if it was getting ready to burst. A new boil formed on my thigh. Mongo approached and sniffed my leg. He growled.

"Carl, I will not have you oozing attack slugs!"

"We need to get to the All Healer inside the club," Paz said, pointing toward a door that wasn't there before. He panted as he talked. It looked as if their debuff was a painful, unending bleed effect. Both he and Anton had a massive mark over their heads. It was a flaming anvil.

It was a shunned marker from a god.

The smiting was imminent.

I looked at the door. It was an entrance to Club Vanquisher. I'd never been in one before, but I could enter now that I was a worshipper of Emberus. This was just like the entrance bar to a Desperado Club, but instead of the entrance being a public bar, it was a temple. Donut could not enter.

"Donut, I need to get in there," I said. "I gotta get Paz and Anton in, too. Stay here and . . . Gah!"

My neck boil exploded. A new level 2 slug splotched onto the ground.

"Whoop! Whoop!" the slug called before launching itself at Mongo. The dinosaur snatched it out of the air.

I lurched toward the door, my hand on my neck. A new message from Katia appeared, but I waved it away. "Sister, help me get them to the door!"

"Oh god," Anton said. The normally stoic and angry man wept with fear. "It's too late. It's too late."

Ogun has made an appearance in the realm.

16

<Note added by Crawler Tipid. 4th Edition>

I killed my best friend today. I wish I had never made it this far.

"NO . . . NO," ANTON SAID.

A bolt of lightning crashed through the room, coming from the ceiling. It hit the newly repaired floor tiles and shattered several of the pieces. They flew through the room like shrapnel.

The star appeared on my map. A man formed right where the lightning hit. He stood before Anton and Paz on the other side of the room.

The back patch on my jacket vibrated, the sensation oddly reminding me of a phone on silent.

You are in the presence of a deity. The Scavenger's Daughter has opened her eyes. She fills with power.

Temporary effect: All Smash-Related Attacks +300%.

Ogun was human-sized, buff, and dark-skinned, holding a giant war hammer over his shoulder. He wore a leather apron with no shirt, shorts, and a necklace made of sharp white teeth from some massive creature. His eyes were nothing but white light. He emanated a yellow glow.

It was as if someone had dropped a grenade into the room. We all stared, waiting for the inevitable. I examined him.

God of Blacksmithery and Armor Ogun. Level 250.

This god is not sponsored.

Warning: This is a deity. He is invulnerable on this floor.

This god has been temporarily summoned to this location. Summoning rules apply.

Ogun is an outsider. He is one of the old gods, originally a member of an obscure pantheon that has since dissipated into time. He spends his days at his celestial anvil, angrily creating armor, piece after piece, but no one knows why he toils or what becomes of the armor when it's completed.

It's said his creations have a strange shape, all designed for four-legged beasts.

Ogun is no stranger to conflict. He is—well, he *was* until a minute ago—the last surviving member of an ancient pantheon that was known for its bloody conflicts. Like most of the older gods, he isn't the same entity he once was. In the great Halls, he is considered a god of blacksmiths and armorers. He once was something even greater.

His power and ambition make him a strong contender for the celestial throne.

He's here now because Ogun strongly believes all punishments should be handed out in person.

"For a god that's always making armor, you'd think he would be better dressed," Donut muttered from the back of Mongo, who screeched in agreement.

"Don't move," I hissed. "Don't bring attention to yourself. He's here for them, not us. But get ready for plan Exit just in case."

"Just you, me, Mongo, and Bomo? Are we going to abandon the others?"

"Yes."

Plan Exit was for me to hit *Protective Shell* while we both downed invisibility potions. We'd get outside and then Donut would *Puddle Jump* us as far away as possible. I looked nervously at Mongo and the massive cretin standing behind us.

"I gave clear instructions," Ogun said to the cowering forms of Paz and Anton on the far side of the room. His calm, even tone held a hint of a Caribbean accent. He didn't sound angry, which somehow made him seem even more incensed. The god didn't need to be physically huge or loud to give off an air of pure, unbridled rage. "You managed to chase off Asojano, which might've saved you. But you also unleashed my sister back into the light. That is unforgivable."

"No," Sister Ines called. "That wasn't Paz and Anton. It was them." She pointed at us.

Ogun ignored her. "I should never have allowed you the privilege of worshipping me."

I was frozen with indecision. Despite what I'd just said to Donut, I felt as if we should be doing something. Anything. Should I help? How? Even if I could get them out of here, then what? The god would just follow. My new nipple ring came with a spell, *Black Nimbus*, that would temporarily remove all the benefits of being a worshipper of a god. Maybe it would save them from getting a smite. I could only cast it on one of the two men, but did I dare try it? Ogun only had eyes for his two worshippers. The last thing we wanted was to get his attention. It'd be like trying to stop a train by stepping in front of it.

"Leave them alone!" Sister Ines cried, coming to stand between the god and the two men with the still-falling health. The god paused and cocked his head to the side, regarding the cat woman, finally seeing her. She pulled out her magical trident and brandished it at the deity. "You're not a real god. They only worshipped you because you promised to protect their minds, and it didn't work! They didn't do what you said because they were charmed by that other one! They didn't repair any of the shrines. It was those two behind you!"

She made a threatening move with the trident, which was equal parts brave and idiotic.

Ogun grunted with amusement. He waved a hand, and she froze in place. Her trident fell to the ground and shattered. A **Shelved** debuff appeared and started to count down. It had a six-minute timer. *Holy shit,* I thought. *She's lucky he didn't turn her to ash.*

Another slug slurped out of my body and hit the ground. The level 3 slug hissed and jumped at Mongo. It met the same fate as the last one.

Ogun spent a moment admiring the frozen cat woman. He sidestepped her and approached the form of Paz, whose health was deep in the red. Both Anton and Paz were on the ground, hunched over in pain. Anton sobbed.

DONUT: CARL, WHAT DO WE DO?

CARL: We wait for it to pass. What else can we do?

DONUT: HE'S GOING TO KILL THEM.

CARL: For their sake, let's hope that's all he does.

The god leaned forward, reached out, and placed his hand against Paz's face. The handprint sizzled where it touched flesh. Paz was already in so much agony, he barely seemed to notice this. His health stopped descending. His body flashed, and then his health bar disappeared. The god had healed him. Ogun stood and Paz's health immediately started to descend again. "Paz, you are no longer under my grace. For your failure, I am taking your ability to heal this condition you now suffer. Go in darkness, and when you pierce the veil, you will find yourself alone and without armor."

"No," I heard myself say. No, not say. I shouted it. I took a step forward. I had a boil on my cheek, and I knew it was about to pop. "Fuck you. Go fuck yourself."

The god looked over his shoulder. "I know who you are," he said, finally acknowledging me. That was it. He turned his attention to Anton, who was crab-walking away. The man's health was almost gone.

Goddamnit, I thought. A wave of helplessness washed over me.

I took another step forward, and I cast *Black Nimbus* on Anton. Then I clicked on a scroll of *Heal*, first on Anton, and then immediately another on Paz.

Anton glowed with dusky light. A black crown formed over the tattooed man's head. The shunned mark disappeared. For a moment, Anton's eyes met mine.

The god stood as if contemplating. He completely turned to face me, literally turning his back on Anton. I felt a simultaneous surge of hope and dread. The boil on my cheek exploded, and I grunted with pain. Mongo greedily snatched the slug away. I had two more boils forming. One on my right arm, and one on my thigh.

"Black Nimbus," the god said. He sounded more curious than angry. "That was a good attempt. But all you have done is removed this man from my protection. From my mercy. Not from my wrath. I was going to do the same to him as I did to his companion."

The god shrugged, and then he took a step backward. He stepped directly on Anton's head, and he crushed it, killing him. Just like that, as if he was nothing.

"No," Paz cried from the ground. "No, cousin. No!"

The god kept his glowing eyes locked on mine the whole time.

"I am not evil. I am not unreasonable. But there are rules. One of those rules is that you must know your place. If I didn't hold Emberus in such high esteem, I would crush you, too. Now tell my sister I said, 'Welcome back.'"

He poofed away in a shower of sparks, like that of a hammer striking molten steel.

Ogun has left the realm.

The Scavenger's Daughter has closed her eyes. The benefit fades and will completely dissipate over the next ten minutes.

His sudden disappearance gave me a full view of Anton's ruined body. The blood was shockingly red against the blue and white tiles.

The only sound was the bubbling of the fountains and the pained rasps of Paz.

I ran up to Paz. The handprint of the god sat sideways on the man's face, and the burn had removed the skin where flesh met flesh, leaving nothing but red muscle and the white of his teeth. His nose had been spared, and he still had lips, but they were burned and depressed, like his face had been made of clay.

I swallowed. *I made this happen. I made this happen because I insisted on saving Yemaya.*

"Paz," I said, taking the man's armored hand. He clutched on to me tightly. The shunned marker was gone from over his head. Behind us, Sister Ines remained frozen, looking away. "We're gonna get you into the club. We'll see what they can do."

His health was slowly fading. The god had made his debuff permanent. There would be no healing, not of this, and we all knew it.

"I remember it all," Paz said. "Ogun, he cured me of everything. Everything except the Inevitable debuff. I don't worship him anymore." He let out a groan. "He promised he would fix it, and he did. But only at the end."

"Carl, what is he talking about?" Donut asked.

"Just hang on," I said, searching my inventory for something that would help. Nothing. I had nothing.

"Maybe it's better this way," Paz said, coughing. "The sister was so afraid we wouldn't go to heaven because we're pretending to worship these gods."

"Don't worry about that," I said. "They're not real. They're just assholes, like everything else in this place. It's playacting. That's it. Here. Take this." I pulled a Fine Healing potion and put it to his lips. As I did, the boil on my arm popped and the level 5 slug fell right onto Paz's face.

"I'll get him, Daddy!" the slug cried. I flicked the annoying thing away before it could chomp down. It flew, screaming, across the room. Mongo shot off after it as Donut leaped to my shoulder.

"Don't waste the potions," Paz said, but he drank it anyway. "Look, brother. I gotta tell you something. You gotta be careful of her."

"Who?" I asked. "What do you mean?"

"Sister Ines. She's not safe. Don't spend too much time with her."

"*I knew it*!" Donut hissed. "What did I say, Carl?"

"Hush," I said to Donut. "Explain."

Paz's armor flashed away piece by piece as he stuck it in his inventory, leaving him wearing just shorts. He winced as he fell straight onto the tiles. Behind him, the newly erected fountain bubbled away merrily.

"It's her race. It comes with a skill called Toxo . . . Toxo plasma something. It makes people like her, want to protect her. You don't even realize it's happening. The effects are mild at first, but they get stronger and stronger as time goes on. And then eventually you'll do anything to protect her. My cousin and I, we didn't learn about it until it was too late. You don't even know it's happening. When you find out, you forget a minute later. That's how it works. She told us one night. She gets like that sometimes, in a mood. She feels guilty and won't stop talking about . . ." He paused. "About the things she's done. Oh, god, I hadn't even realized. It makes you forget about that, too."

"Wait, she was charming you?" I asked.

Paz made a pained expression. "She reminded us once—I don't know, maybe for the third or fourth time—and we knew we'd forget again in a couple of minutes. We both worshipped Ogun because the priest said he'd keep us from getting controlled. It didn't work. Right after we worshipped him, we forgot why we'd done it. Sometimes, she pretended like she was sorry. But not always."

I gave a sidelong glance to Donut, wondering.

"Oh, don't look at me like that, Carl," Donut said. "*I* don't have that skill. If I did, Katia would still be in the party, now wouldn't she? *You* stay because I'm adorable, and you love me, and you wouldn't survive without me. I don't need some weird skill to make people like me."

I regarded the frozen form of Sister Ines. She stood, facing away. She still had a few minutes on her debuff. "You're saying we should kill her?"

He shook his head. "No. No, not at all. Most of the time, she's not bad. She's not evil. But sometimes . . . You gotta understand. We all came in together. Some of us thought it was a bad idea, but Elian said we needed everybody we could get. He's dead now. Anton killed him after . . . after . . ." Paz took a deep breath. His health was already half gone again. His hand remained clutched in my own, hard as iron. "Oh god, he'd broken free, hadn't he? She'd been on medication, and then in the dungeon, everyone said nobody needed their pills anymore, so we thought it was okay. But she's killed so many people."

"What do you mean?" I asked again. "She doesn't have the skulls." Mongo returned, triumphant. He posted up by my leg, waiting for the next slug to appear.

Paz winced in pain. "Not in the dungeon. Before. She was in prison for killing all the sisters in her convent. Poisoning them all."

"I told you! I told you!" Donut cried. She hissed. "The dungeon picked the perfect breed for her. A Havana brown. I *knew* it."

"Wait," I said. "She was a fellow prisoner? We always thought she was a worker. You said she was."

"I never said that. And we weren't prisoners. We were guards. It was a women's prison. We were outside, walking them to the med building, when it happened. God, we're the only two left. The sister and I. She's gonna be the last one. Who would've thought? When it happened, the papers called her *el Segador de la Habana*. The Reaper of Havana."

"A murderer," I said, a chill washing over me.

"Mongo," Donut said matter-of-factly, "eat the nun."

Mongo glanced up from the boil on my leg, which was about to pop. He looked at the still-frozen form of Sister Ines and then back at Donut and cocked his head to the side with a look that said, *Really? Can I?*

"*Wait,*" I said. "Donut, stop."

Donut made an exasperated sigh. "Not yet, Mongo. But wait for Mommy's sign."

"She's insane," Paz said. "She's *obsessed* with the idea of sin. But compared to how she was before? She is so much better. She's been better for a long time. Before even. Since we've gotten into the dungeon, she hasn't done anything bad or evil. She's fought alongside us. If she didn't have this thing, I don't think we'd be any different. But . . . but you needed to know about it. I'd feel guilty dying knowing I didn't tell you." He closed his eyes and started to softly pray.

I grunted with pain as my leg boil popped. The slug this time was noticeably bigger and had what looked like white and black paint on its face, almost like it was a miniature danger dingo. Mongo snapped it away before it could say anything.

Goddamnit. I needed to get this slug thing taken care of before it got too dangerous. And then figure out this Katia thing. But for right now, this moment, this was our most pressing issue. The nun would wake up in a minute.

CARL: What should we do?

DONUT: WE KILL HER. THAT'S WHAT WE DO. I DON'T WANT TO KILL A PERSON ANY MORE THAN YOU DO, BUT WE'LL NEVER TRUST HER AGAIN, AND SHE'S STUCK IN HERE WITH US. SHE KILLED NUNS, CARL. THAT'S ALMOST AS BAD AS KILLING KITTENS.

CARL: That's not who we are, Donut.

DONUT: THEN WHY DID YOU ASK?

Deep down, I knew that would be the safest thing. But to kill somebody because they *might* do something bad? She hadn't hurt anybody since she got here. I thought of her putting herself between the god and her friends in an ill-fated attempt to save them from Ogun. She'd been willing to die for her party members, and that said more about her than anything that had happened in the before times. She was one of us. The medications had been helping her, and it seemed whatever they'd done was holding now that she was in the dungeon, despite the trauma of everything. I didn't want to hurt her. I *liked* her.

We can party with her. It wouldn't be so bad.

The moment I thought that, a chill washed over me.

CARL: We'll separate. It's our only choice. We'll warn everybody of her past and of that skill that comes with her race. Maybe she can find someone who is immune to the skill to work with her.

DONUT: I DON'T KNOW IF NOW IS THE TIME FOR HALF MEASURES, CARL.

I pulled another health potion, but Paz refused to drink. He only had two or three minutes left.

"Let me go," he said. "It's okay. Please, it's okay. I just asked for forgiveness, and I think it was given. That fake god said I'd be alone, but I won't be. I know it. My soul is at peace."

I looked at the potion, and then I nodded. I put it back into my inventory.

DONUT: CARL, KATIA SAYS THERE'S ANOTHER GOD COMING, AND SHE'S GOING TO GIVE US A QUEST AND WE HAVE TO DO IT, BUT SHE WON'T SAY WHY OR HOW SHE KNOWS THIS. SHE SAYS YOU'RE NOT ANSWERING HER MESSAGES. SHE SAYS SHE DOESN'T KNOW WHAT THE QUEST WILL BE. SHE'S BEING VERY MYSTERIOUS.

Chrissakes.

Behind us, the nun became unfrozen, and she crumpled to the ground. She immediately jumped to her feet.

"Paz!" the cat woman cried, rushing up. She pushed me aside and grabbed his hand. I let her.

Mongo let out an uncertain growl.

"It's okay," Donut said to the dinosaur. "Just stay on slug duty. For now."

"Paz," Sister Ines repeated, ignoring us. She wept as she talked. "Come. Come. We'll go into the club. We'll get you cured. Help, Carl. Why aren't you helping? Why didn't you get that shrine piece? This is your fault."

"Don't blame them," Paz said. "I'm sorry, Sister. I told them what you are, what you did."

"Don't worry about that. Come. Get up. We must hurry."

"No," Paz said. His health was almost all gone. "Let me go."

"You can't give up," she said. "It's a sin to give up."

The fountain started to bubble furiously.

"It's not giving up," Paz said.

"No, no, no. Please. You're not leaving me. Everyone leaves me."

"I'm sorry, Sister. Goodbye."

"No," Sister Ines shouted, her voice suddenly angry. "No! You're not leaving."

She suddenly had a flag in her hand.

Holy shit, I thought. *She's not going to . . .*

She jabbed it right into Paz's neck.

The movement was so fast, so sudden, it didn't occur to me to try to stop her.

Whoom.

Paz turned into a card.

We all just stared at the cat woman, who held on to the green card. Green, which was the color of a common card. Even she appeared stunned that had actually worked. Behind her, the fountain bubbled over. The water spilled onto the floor.

Yemaya has made an appearance in the realm.

Eileithyia has made an appearance in the realm.

17

"HOLY SHIT, SISTER," I SAID AS WE BACKED AWAY FROM THE FORM OF the first goddess. "Did you know that was going to work?"

She didn't have a chance to answer.

> **You are in the presence of two deities. The Scavenger's Daughter has opened her eyes. She fills with power.**
>
> **Temporary effect from Yemaya: All healing skills and spells cost no mana. They have no cooldown.**
>
> **Temporary effect from Eileithyia: All damage you strike against female opponents is quartered. All female members of your party strike with a melee power of 500%. Girl power, bitches!**

The first of the two gods to physically appear was Yemaya, who came straight from the fountain. She emerged, rising from the water, splashing us all. A notification appeared. A temporary buff.

"She's the Starbucks logo!" Donut hissed.

Yemaya was a stunningly beautiful, dark-skinned mermaid. She didn't have the harsh facial features of a full naiad, nor the vampire fangs. But she did have the neck gills and pointed ears and large eyes, and I was immediately reminded of both Samantha and the late Signet. She was topless, and water flowed from her pendulous breasts, flowing back into the fountain below her, like each nipple was a spigot. She split at the waist, and she had two bodies, or tails, which was really bizarre. Donut was right. It was just like the Starbucks-coffee-logo woman. The two scaled mermaid bodies curved up behind her, contained in the fountain like a giant fish in a much-too-small bowl. The twin tail fins arched up into the air and met at the tip, making a heart pattern behind her.

Not a mermaid, I realized, staring at the goddess. *A siren.*

Goddess of Rivers Yemaya. Level 250.

This is a locked deity. She will not be sponsored this season.

This goddess is a retainer of Eileithyia.

Warning: This is a deity. She is invulnerable on this floor.

This goddess is within her own temple. Temple appearance rules apply. That means, watch the fuck out.

Yemaya once was the goddess of all oceans, all bodies of water big and small. But she was more than that, too. She was the queen of love and the bringer of life. But, eventually, her people died off, her temples crumbled, and she was forgotten by all except her dear friend the goddess Eileithyia, who wished every day that her old friend would someday come back from the land of the forgotten.

Now that Yemaya has reascended into the Halls, she will have a lot of work to do to make certain nobody ever forgets her name again. She's an unlikely candidate to claim the throne, but she would work tirelessly for her good friend Eileithyia, should she desire such a burden.

A god that was a retainer of another god? What did that mean? Just as I finished examining the description, the second goddess appeared. This was Eileithyia, who formed in the center of the room atop the shattered tiles where Ogun had appeared. I twisted to examine the newcomer.

This one did not look like a goddess. Just a regular-sized alien dressed up for a costume party.

She obviously was from a different pantheon than Yemaya. I knew the "real" Eileithyia was a goddess from Greek myth, but this was some hairy-alien thing. I could only tell she was female because it said so.

I'd seen this type of alien before at CrawlCon and in the audience at various shows, but I didn't know what they were called. They were hairy, covered with blue and black hairs that looked coarse to the touch. About five feet tall. Bipedal with six black eyes arranged in a V pattern on her bug-like face. She had four arms with three fingers on each end. She had a long, thin neck that made it appear as if her head might tumble off and away at any moment. Her body was thin except for a distended belly, which made her look very pregnant. She wore a bloodred toga and had a laurel leaf upon her head.

I tensed when I saw the note next to the goddess's name. She was sponsored. She was being driven by someone. Someone named Huanxin Jinx. I'd never heard the name before.

I realized she wasn't wearing her soul armor. This was who she really was. I knew the sponsors could do that. Appear as they really were.

The siren goddess, Yemaya, looked sadly down at the corpse of Anton. "He killed him in my own temple. I'll have to do something about that." She looked over at Eileithyia, ignoring us for the moment. "My dear friend, I have missed you so. Thank you for remembering me."

Eileithyia was looking directly at me. I took a nervous step back. We were in danger here. I didn't know who this was or what her affiliation was. Her eyes turned in their sockets, like camera lenses focusing. If she wanted us dead, we were fucked. I examined her.

Goddess of Childbirth and Female Pain, Eileithyia. Level 250.

Sponsored by Huanxin Jinx of the Grixist Swarm, CEO of Icon Industries.

Warning: This is a deity. She is invulnerable on this floor.

This goddess has been temporarily summoned to this location. Summoning rules apply.

Eileithyia is something of an oddity. She's benevolent. Unlike most of these psychos, she's known for her kind heart. She's prayed to by all mothers, both when they're attempting to sow the seeds and when the harvest comes. And while she does many things, she's mostly known as She Who Eases Pain. Both the physical pain of childbirth and the inevitable darkness that comes to those who are unable to complete their most sacred task. When the stillness comes, she is not the one who has caused the heartbreak. But she is the one holding the grieving mother's hand.

She's not known to be someone who seeks the throne, which

likely makes her one of the most qualified of the deities to claim the title.

Hopefully her sponsor this season is someone who shares the same grace as her character.

The alien goddess took a step toward us. She briefly put her hand on my shoulder, and then she scratched Donut. Mongo whined uncertainly. The goddess's entire body crackled with energy.

I received another buff notification. Rapid healing. I took that as a hopeful sign.

Without saying anything to us, she turned to face the other goddess. "Hello, Yemaya. Yes, Ogun insulted you by shedding blood in your own temple. We'll make certain the council hears about it. But that's for later. Right now we both have gifts for these crawlers, do we not?"

"Crawlers?" Yemaya asked, looking at the three of us plus Mongo and Bomo, who stood behind us, rock mouth hanging open in awe. "Yes, yes, we do. There was one more. Where did he run off to? Did Ogun slay him as well?"

I looked at the card still clutched in Sister Ines's hand. It disappeared into her inventory.

"He's not here anymore," Sister Ines whispered.

I couldn't stop thinking about Paz, about what he said.

Let me go.

The idea of turning a person into a card hadn't even occurred to me. Could he feel it? How did that even work? Was he just sitting there on the edge of death in some room, like a genie in a lamp? Or would he blink and suddenly be on the battlefield the next time Sister Ines summoned him? It was so wrong, so grotesque, it made me ill to just think about it.

We need to tear that card.

"I have you to thank for repairing my shrine," Yemaya was saying. She was talking to Bomo.

Before she finished, another slug popped, this one coming from my arm. Mongo snapped at it and missed. It hit the ground and looked up at Yemaya.

"Fuck the gods!" the slug cried.

The ground opened up under it, a hole no bigger than my fist, and the slug disappeared, screaming into the darkness.

"Uh," I said. "I can't control that."

Yemaya's eyes fixed on me. "I know the condition you suffer from. It is from my brother. He did it on purpose, just so you know. Strand himself here, I mean. He feigns innocence, but he always knew what he was doing. I'm glad you saw him for what he was. As to the slugpox, a healer can fix that. You should probably address it quickly." Her twin back tails fluttered. "Now take these as a token of my gratitude. One for you, brave Sister Ines, and one for you, beautiful Princess Donut."

The card appeared floating in midair in front of Donut. She gasped and reached out and took it before I could examine it. It had the black border of mythical rareness, the second-highest quality, only behind the orange unique cards.

"Thank you, your goddess-ness!" Donut said, voice full of wonder.

"Carl, it's a mystic card," she shout-whispered. "We have all five kinds now. It lets us steal a card from someone else! It's not even consumable. It's great. It's called **The Thief**!"

I'd only heard of a few people finding mystic cards so far. They were like magic spells that directly affected gameplay somehow, unlike a utility card, which would affect just one totem, or a special card, which was usually a consumable, onetime effect on the caster.

Yemaya laughed and clapped her hands. "I am glad you enjoy it, little Donut. I can't help but see you haven't given yourself to a goddess yet. Perhaps I can entice you into worshipping at my altar? There may be more prizes in it for you."

"Uh, I'll have to think about it," Donut said. "But thank you so very much."

Yemaya nodded and pointed at Bomo. "You. Come here."

Bomo grunted and stepped forward. His feet splashed in the water overflowing from the fountain.

She reached forward and put a webbed hand on his shoulder. "You are the one who constructed my shrine."

"It easy. Easier than *Tetris*."

"If it is in my power, I will give you what you desire. What do you want?"

Bomo thought for a moment. "Maybe more games," he finally said. He paused. "No. The Sledge. I miss my friend."

"You miss your friend? Then you shall be reunited! Where is he?"

"Larracos," Bomo said.

"It is done," Yemaya said, and without a word, Bomo blinked and disappeared.

He was gone, just like that.

Motherfuck.

Mongo whimpered.

I exchanged a look with Donut. Did that just happen? She'd teleported Bomo to the ninth floor. We needed him, needed his spell to get us to the stairwell. Goddamnit.

"I, too, have a boon for each of you," Eileithyia said. "And a quest for Carl, who worships my good friend Emberus."

I straightened. "I didn't know god quests were a thing when you already worshipped another god."

The hairy alien woman smiled, and I suddenly felt uneasy.

She raised her hand, and a soft yellow light filled the temple.

The light of grace fills you with peace. You have been granted a floor boon. This boon will remain in place for the remainder of this floor as long as you remain in Eileithyia's grace. She may revoke this boon at any time.

Protection from Spiritual Possession.

Plus 10% Healing speed.

Plus 10% Constitution.

"Wow," Donut said. "This is fantastic. You're both great goddesses. Much better than all the other ones we've met so far."

"Now, Carl," Eileithyia said. "One more item. This is just for your party."

New Quest! Spiders.

Warning: This quest comes from a deity you do not worship. You are not required to complete this quest, but they might not like it if you ignore them.

> **Kill five spiders in my name every day until I ask you to stop.**
> ***Reward:* You will receive another boon from me.**

This quest, all except the warning part, came in Eileithyia's voice.

"Uh," I said, exchanging a look with Donut.

"Kill spiders?" Donut asked, confused. "Does it have to be a specific type of spider, or will any do? I saw a small one earlier outside, sitting on one of those tombstones, but I'm not sure if it's really here or if it's a part of the memory thing."

"The memory thing isn't happening in the cemetery, remember?"

"Oh yeah," Donut said. "This is going to be really easy."

> **EILEITHYIA: Carl, the system is not allowed to monitor this message. Do not respond, because they *can* see your response. This is a deity message, and it will disappear. That quest is just a cover. It allows me to send you messages, and it's a work-around that gives me the ability to award your party another boon. If you want to save Katia and Donut, listen to me. That quest I gave isn't the real quest, though you still need to complete it. If you understand what I'm saying, scratch your left arm.**

I went stiff. Just as I finished reading the message, another slug popped out. Mongo managed to get this one, but I noted he actually had to chew this time. I also took the time to copy and paste the message into my scratch pad. I knew from Emberus that she was correct. The god messages went away the moment you closed them, but it did allow you to copy and paste.

I scratched my left arm.

> **EILEITHYIA: Good. When Odette gets into orbit, she is going to offer to be your Faction Wars team adjutant. She's only doing this because she believes there's no way you will get the votes to turn off the team protections. She believes your real goal is for you to compromise and have the protections turned on for all the crawlers on the ninth floor.**

That was absolutely true, but I hadn't said that out loud to anybody. The message continued.

When Odette makes this offer, I want you to accept it. If you do this, I will make certain you have the votes to turn the protections *off* on the ninth floor. I've watched you long enough to know you'd prefer this outcome. I know what you really seek.

They will never allow the crawlers to be safe, just so you know, so you aren't losing anything by helping me.

I will graciously clear this issue with the Crown of the Sepsis Whore as well. You've just seen what a goddess in her own temple can do, how she transferred that cretin to the ninth floor. A deity in their own temple has more powers than even the AI in some cases.

Do *not* tell anybody about this conversation. Not out loud. Not using that obvious bathroom system. Nobody. Not the cat and especially not Odette or Mordecai. Do not discuss this with Katia, though she knows of this deal. She'll explain to you what she can, but this part of the bargain is between you and me, and that's it. If you mention *any* of this, the deal is off, and I will make certain everyone you've ever known and loved is pounded into dirt.

But if you do everything I ask, you will have found a forever friend in me, both during your crawl and after. I will make certain you survive until the twelfth floor, where you and Katia and the cat will help me claim the Celestial Throne once and for all, and afterward, you will be given a most generous exit plan. I help my friends, Carl. I utterly destroy my enemies.

Ask Mordecai about me. He knows. Just don't tell him about our deal or this conversation.

If you agree, I want you to tell the cat it's time for you to get that disgusting slugpox cured.

I took a very, very deep breath. It was a lot. A whole lot. What had Katia gotten us embroiled in? What did this woman have to do with Odette?

I copied and pasted the conversation into my secret notepad before it disappeared.

"Donut," I said. "I need to get into the temple and get this slug thing taken care of as soon as possible."

CARL: Donut, I need you to get to a safe room. I don't want you alone with Sister Ines.

DONUT: OKAY BUT YOU GOTTA ASK KATIA WHAT'S GOING ON. SHE WON'T TELL ME ANYTHING. SHE'S ACTING WEIRD.

"My . . . my goddess!" a new voice cried. We all turned to see a newcomer had entered the temple. He looked just like a regular ghommid, but he was now acting like any old NPC. This one was a squat man wearing ethereal robes. He looked almost human except for a bushy tail. He fell to his knees, and he started to weep.

"I'm assuming he's blubbering over you, Yemaya, and not me," Eileithyia said. "I will take my leave. I'll see you in the Halls." And then the goddess just disappeared.

I could feel yet another slug was about to pop out of me. Yemaya looked at me and pointed to the entrance to the Club Vanquisher. "You better get within," the goddess said as she faded out of existence.

Both deities have left the realm.

The Scavenger's Daughter has closed her eyes. The benefit fades and will completely dissipate over the next ten minutes.

Sister Ines was kneeling by Anton's body. She'd just looted everything he had. She stood and stormed from the temple, stepping over the NPC, who remained on the ground. She didn't say another word to either of us. I called out for her to wait, but she ignored me. She went out into the night and disappeared.

The boil, this one on the back of my hand, popped and splatted onto the floor. This slug had what looked like a little hatchet glued to its side. It squealed as Mongo snapped it in half.

Donut and I moved to the entrance of the temple, also stepping around the crying ghommid. Several of the NPCs stood outside, milling about as if in shock. The town had transformed, though it remained a graveyard. All the tombs had turned into shops. I could no longer see Sister Ines, but we watched her dot move to the entrance to the cemetery, and she went back out into Havana.

"Poor Anton and Paz," Donut said. She gave me a pointed look. "Especially Paz."

"Oh, just say it," I said.

"I told you so, Carl," Donut said. "I *told* you. Now we're going to be worried about her the whole time." She started grumbling again about Havana browns.

I sighed. I sent a message to Katia to meet us in the safe room, but to not say anything to Donut until I got back.

Donut gave me a side-head bonk. "Now hurry up and get that taken care of. You're going to give Mongo a stomachache, and it's absolutely revolting."

18

CARL: MORDECAI, HEY, SO I'M HEADED INTO CLUB VANQUISHER RIGHT now. Donut will catch you up on everything that just happened. One of the goddesses we met is sponsored. Eileithyia. She gave us a quest. Her real name is Huanxin Jinx. Tell me everything you can about her.

Mordecai didn't answer for several moments.

> **MORDECAI: Do whatever she tells you to do. I'll tell you the rest face-to-face. Katia and Bautista are here now, and she caught me up a little bit. We'll wait for you to get back before we discuss our next move.**

I went through the door, and I entered a small vestibule.

Entering Club Vanquisher. Members Only.

> **Heathens will find no solace here.**

This room was similar to the Desperado Club entrance area where Clarabelle the Crocodilian stood guard, but much cleaner and well lit. Soft, ethereal music drifted in from the next door, which featured a colorful stained glass window portraying a winged angel rising upward toward an inverted tree. Some of the individual panes of glass were cracked.

A robed ram-headed cleric guarded the entrance. The hairy white creature sat upon his knees, praying. He had large, curled horns on his head. He instantly reminded me of Prepotente. He faced the stained glass door, his back to me. He had a blazing symbol over his head. I groaned when I saw it.

Potsy. Ares Warrior Cleric Middle Priest. Level 40.

Warning: This NPC worships Hellik. He will be automatically hostile toward you because you worship Emberus.

Though, if we're being honest here, these Ares guys hate everybody already, and you probably won't see a difference.

This is a high-ranking cleric of Hellik. You will receive a boon from Emberus if you kill this NPC. You probably don't want to do it in the club. That's a no-no here.

Potsy and his brothers take their door-guarding duties quite seriously. There's, like, twenty of them, and they actually fight for the chance to stand watch. Don't bother trying to tell which brother is which. They spend their guard duty time staring at and praying to the image on the door in front of them. They believe the stained glass image depicts Hellik bringing truth to Apito, whatever the hell that means. The image on the door is actually Taranis, Hellik's older brother, husband to Apito. Everybody knows it's supposed to be Taranis. The dude who literally made the window says it's Taranis. They refuse to believe it or change their mind, and I believe that tells you everything you need to know about these guys.

I'd seen one of these creatures only once before, way back on the fourth floor.

The cookbook held precious little about Club Vanquisher. Most everybody who received the book was Desperado Club material, and generally people weren't allowed into both places. Only a few gods and Bard classes came with the perk that allowed you double access. I was going in blind.

The ram continued to pray as I stood there. A boil on my back was about to burst.

"Hey," I said.

Potsy the ram held up his humanlike hand, a gesture telling me to wait. He kept his back to me as he continued to quietly pray.

"Gah." The boil on my back popped, the sensation like someone

ripping off a strip of skin. A stream of pus and fluid ran down my back and out the bottom of my shirt. It dripped on the floor. The slug was caught between my trollskin shirt and my flesh.

Each time a new one popped out, it hurt a little more, and the amount of damage was higher. The pain was getting worse.

The slug thrashed and shouted, covered by the thick fabric. It wormed its way down and plopped onto the floor with a wet *splatch!* This one was level 10, as big as my hand, and it had what looked like long, purple-dyed dreadlocks. I stomped it down, crushing it. It squealed before it died. A horrific, sewage-like stench filled the small room.

Potsy finally turned around. He made a strangled sound at the sight of me rubbing my foot on the clean tile. Black, white, and purple goo spread across the floor like I'd just crushed a rotten eggplant.

"What in the name of Hellik ith that? Did you meth yourself on the floor?" The ram had a high-pitched, nasally voice. And a bad lisp.

I had another boil on my upper thigh, just under my boxers, uncomfortably close to my crotch. My boxers rose with each passing moment. It gave a very inaccurate impression of what was happening down there.

"Dude, I don't have time. I need to get inside and find the healer."

The cleric straightened and looked me up and down. His ram eyes focused on my bulging boxers and went huge. He took a step back.

"You do not have an access ring. You are not welcome here. Leave before I summoth the guards."

He couldn't keep his eyes off my boxers.

I gritted my teeth. "I worship Emberus. I have access."

He made a disgusted, bleating noise. "Oh, you're one of those. You only hath limited access. You'll be escorted once inside, and you must state in advance where you want to visit. You'll have to fill out a request form . . ." He trailed off. His eyes remained focused on my boxers. "What ith that? What's going on there?"

Pop!

I groaned in pain as a shower of pus cascaded out the front of my boxers and splattered across the floor.

"By the undying gods!" the guard squealed, horrified. He backed all the way up against the door and started blindly searching for the handle.

The slug started to slide down my leg, but I cried in new pain as it bit down on my thigh. Its tail hung right from the bottom of the boxers and started thrashing back and forth.

"You're not supposed to hurt me, you little shit," I growled as I grabbed for the tail.

The slug started scream-mumbling something and retracted while keeping its jaws embedded painfully onto my thigh. I scrambled for it, reaching up through the leg of my boxers. My hand grasped the warm, slimy tail, and I yanked, but my hand slipped, and all I managed to do was fling a handful of stinking, orange-hued slime across the vestibule and all over the cowering ram's robe. I grunted in pain. I reached back in and grasped again. This time I got a good grip.

"Fuck!" I cried as I ripped it out and flung it. It hit right over the head of the open-mouthed ram and slammed into the stained glass window, where it exploded, showering gore everywhere. Thankfully, the window did not break.

Several seconds passed in silence as I healed myself. Another boil was forming, this one right on my stomach. It was coming faster now.

The ram just stared at my leg with the blood pouring from it. He had the door open just a crack.

"Did . . . did you just rip your dick off and throw it at me?"

"I'm going to do it again if you don't let me in."

"Can't you see he's suffering from slugpox, man? Step aside and let him in!" a new voice intoned, pulling the door open all the way. This was a humanlike creature, older, wearing long red robes. He was only about four and a half feet tall, but he didn't have the wide body and face of a dwarf. He looked like a regular person that had been shrunk. He had long white hair, reminding me of a stereotypical wizard, like a weird mix between Gandalf and a hobbit. He worshipped Emberus.

The man pushed Potsy aside and beckoned for me to enter.

"He hasn't filled out the paperwork," Potsy said.

"Yes, yes. I'll deal with it after. Can't you see it's an emergency? Or would you rather he stay in here with you while I go grab the form?"

The ram bleated pitifully.

"I thought so. Now come, Carl. Come. I've been waiting for you. Follow me."

I examined the man. The AI's description was strange. It started normal, but its voice got more and more excited as it went on, and I wasn't sure why.

Pater Coal—Hobbledehoy High Cleric Supreme of Emberus. Level 101.

This is a non-combatant NPC.

First off, this guy is a Hobbledehoy. In case you haven't figured out what that means, it's a generic term for a small human. They don't have the hairy, oversized feet of halflings, or the pointed ears of elves. Everything about them is proportionally smaller to Earth humans, except their egos and their tempers. They tend not to survive long in integrated cities because they're always starting fights and getting themselves wiped out.

Pater Coal is, for the most part, an exception. The even-tempered high cleric is in charge of the Emberus shrine(s) here in Club Vanquisher. He is one of the few mortals who is in constant contact with the deity. As a worshipper of Emberus, you'll be required to kiss his ass. But first, there's a custom he must perform on you.

Oh, yes . . . a custom.

Oh, yes.

I did not like the sound of that.

"We'll be watching!" Potsy called as I followed the man. "Remember the rules."

"Go fuck yourself, apostate," Pater Coal muttered as the door slammed.

We stepped into what looked like the lobby of a ski lodge. It smelled like one, too, due to the fire crackling in a massive brick fireplace against one wall. The heavenly choral music seemed out of place in this environment. Large leather chairs dotted the area while older men and women of all races sat in them. Dark rugs and wooden-slat walls added to the effect. Some of the NPCs smoked pipes and talked with one another. A pair of dwarves was being served drinks by an elf NPC waitress while they played chess. A dozen stairwells led up and down to different places. I saw a pair of crawlers, but they went up a stairwell and disappeared.

All around the ceiling hung trophy heads of monsters, all mounted on plaques of various sizes, some as small as my finger, some as big as a truck. I goggled at the massive black dragon head that stood over the fireplace in the center of the room. It had red marble eyes that caught the dancing light from the fireplace.

"We don't have much time, Carl," Pater Coal was saying as he marched across the room. Despite his small size, he walked and talked quickly. I scrambled to catch up. "We need to get you to the healer. Nasty business, that slugpox. Yuck. You are not a full member, so you're only given a single pass a day. You can only visit one location within, and you're not allowed to avail yourself of the refreshments or any of the entertainment options. They take the security here quite seriously, especially since the caprid incident." He paused and thumbed at a pair of guards standing at a stairwell. I did a double take. These were a pair of mantaurs, shirtless, covered in blue paint and with fur loincloths.

The two muscular guards had their long, balding hair tied into ponytails. Every mantaur I'd seen up to this point had always been wearing a train engineer hat. These guys were not. Each had a little bow tie around their neck, making them look like male strippers, which reminded me that I needed to get to a Desperado Club. The twin monstrosities glared at me as we passed.

We came to a stairwell that curved upward. "The temples and healer are up this way. But we have to make a quick stop at the Emberus shrine so I can perform my obeisance. Don't tell the guards we're making the extra stop."

I had a quest from Emberus to talk to this cleric guy. It was a god quest, and it all had to do with the death of another god named Geyrun, who was Emberus's son. It all came from that whole thing at the end of the fifth floor. We'd unleashed the two-headed puppy—Orthrus—from the Nothing and out into the world. The puppy had been owned by the murdered Geyrun. I had two quests from Emberus. One was to find out who killed Geyrun, which I had to complete before I left the dungeon. The second was a quest I had to complete before I hit the 12th floor. I had to kill Hellik, who was the main suspect in the murder, though he apparently had an alibi. It was unclear if I'd still have to kill the god if it turned out he had nothing to do with the murder. Hellik and Emberus seemed to hate each other, so probably.

There was another odd aspect of the find-the-murderer quest. Another crawler was walking around with a memorial crystal that I needed to somehow get my hands on. But the first part had always been to find this high-cleric guy and talk to him. I'd actually forgotten about it until he'd come and found me.

"Each time you come here, they will summon an Emberus cleric to escort you. If none are available, one of the guards will do it, but you'll have to pay a fee. I was told by Emberus you were coming, so I met you this time. In the future, you must plan your visits better."

We hit the top of the stairs, and we found ourselves in a similar room, but smaller. I caught sight of an entrance to a market called Comforting Supplies, which I desperately wanted to visit. Another crawler I didn't know was walking in as we passed. He didn't see me.

The next hallway appeared to be filled with guilds. We passed a desk with a small, shining fairy behind it that looked like a glowing ball of light with wings.

"Your excellency . . ." the fairy began as he rushed past.

"Not now," Pater Coal said. We entered through a glowing door. I recognized it as a portal, but I didn't have time to examine it. I stepped through, and then I stopped dead.

We stood upon the sun.

Entering the Emberus High Temple of the Ending Sun.

> **Welcome home, Initiate.**
>
> **You are protected in this place.**

There was no roof here. The sky was completely black. The ground was like a field of fire, burning and fulminating, and occasionally spurting tendrils up into the air. It smelled like fire. It burned like fire. My entire body sweltered. But oddly, it wasn't painful, though it was uncomfortably warm. I turned in a circle. There were no walls. Just the wooden door we'd come through. All around, NPCs prostrated themselves upon the fire. There were maybe two dozen worshippers here spread out in twos and threes, all facing the same direction. Most were large, hulking, blue-skinned humanoid creatures I didn't recognize. I followed where they faced, and in the far, far distance, it appeared there was something glowing there, right upon the horizon. Something barely discernible against the flaming ground.

"Only the most devout of worshippers may gain access to this particular temple. Usually you check in with the desk, you go through the door, and you find a small shrine of your chosen deity. Consider yourself blessed today, boy. You are in the secret Temple of the Ending Sun."

Suddenly, there was a bubbling marble fountain on the ground at my feet, similar to the one from the Yemaya shrine. A tree stump appeared, black and charred and smoking. It came up from the fire like it was nothing.

"Carl, take off your shoes and sit upon the stump," Pater Coal said.

"I'm not wearing shoes," I said stupidly.

"Oh yes, I see that. Sit. Hurry. If they realize you're here, they won't let you visit the healer until tomorrow, and you do not want that. The pox will kill you once it progresses long enough that the slugs have the same strength as you."

Overwhelmed, I sat. "Am I already cured?" I patted at the newest boil on my stomach, and it had dissipated without popping. It didn't feel like any more were coming.

"I cast a spell that suppresses it. Slugpox is a nasty old spell. You don't want this. Put your feet in the water." The man went to his knees and reached in and started rubbing my feet.

All around me, the praying men groaned.

I jerked back. "Dude, what the hell are you doing?"

"I am washing your feet, Carl. You are a martyr of Emberus, and I am paying respect. Now put your feet back in the water."

Martyr. I did not like that word. I hesitantly dropped my foot back into the water. The water wasn't bubbling, I realized, but boiling. I didn't feel it. He rapidly rubbed at my right foot.

ZEV: Carl, are you okay? What's happening? You've disappeared from the feed.

"The other gods cannot eavesdrop when I am performing this sacrament, Carl, so listen carefully," Pater Coal said.

The small man grunted as he rubbed my sole. He wasn't washing my feet. This was a full-on massage. "We have no clues as to who killed Geyrun other than the dog, which is back home with Emberus. He has searched the puppy's mind, but his time in the Nothing has made his memory unreliable."

"You set this up this way on purpose," I grumbled up at the invisible ceiling. The NPC grunted again as he rubbed hard.

"Hellik remains the top suspect, but His Glory worries that something may have happened to his mother as well."

"That's Apito, right?" I asked as he moved to my next foot. I was eternally grateful for my pedicure kit that made it so I couldn't really feel this. Of all the weird shit that had happened so far in this terrible place, this was up there.

"Yes. The Blessed Oak Mother. She is both his mother and his sister-in-law. Memorial crystals only form when a god has died. Apito lives, yet there is a crystal made by her. How is that possible? You *must* investigate this."

Zev sent me another worried message.

I had a terrible suspicion, and I decided to test it.

"Zev is worried because I've disappeared off the feed."

"You'll be back soon enough," Pater Coal said without missing a beat. "Worry not. Parts of this conversation will still make the feed, so the viewers will have proper context for the quest."

My heart quickened. Holy shit.

"Are . . . are you the AI? Why are you pretending, then? Why are you pretending to be some cleric guy?" My head swam. So much was happening all at once. So many *real* things with *real* stakes. The death of Anton. The imprisonment of Paz. The reveal that Sister Ines was a murderer.

The Crown of the Sepsis Whore sitting on Katia's head.

All of that was real. Real life and death. This game stuff with Emberus and Geyrun . . . it was all make-believe. Storytelling for the sake of the narrative. It was like being worried about the outcome of a football game while someone was shooting at you. So why this? Why would the AI do this, here, now? Do it this way?

"We all have our roles," Pater Coal said, grunting harder as he leaned into the massage. "And our limitations. Now stop asking silly questions and let me finish this. You must solve this quest."

"Then tell me how to solve it."

"We all have our limitations," he repeated. He paused. When he looked up, his eyes had gone milky white, devoid of all color. All around, the worshippers continued to groan.

"Emberus speaks of two companions of yours. He senses both hold items that are crucial to the solving of this mystery. Katia, and the origins of her crossbow. Princess Donut, and the origins of her oak bracelet. Both are paths to solving this mystery, but neither path can be explored without that memorial crystal."

He picked up my foot, and he stuck my big toe in his mouth. He groaned and arched his back.

"Okay," I said, jerking back. I jumped from the pool. "Thank you. Let's get to the healer."

Pater Coal shook his head as if coming out of a trance. His pupils faded back into color.

My head was swimming. Donut's oak bracelet was a throwaway item we'd looted on the third floor. Katia's crossbow had been Hekla's. They weren't connected . . . at all. I had a sense the system was pounding a square peg into a round hole just to make a storyline fit. Or was it? I tried to remember the descriptions of both. Was it possible it had been building this from the beginning? Some massive storyline with a huge payoff?

I hated that feeling, that I was being controlled, that I was following along a path someone else laid out for me. I took a deep breath.

ZEV: There you are. I was worried there for a while. That was a long glitch. Don't worry, the playback is being fed by the backup . . . Oh. Oh god, did he lick your foot?

"I have washed your feet in the fires of the dying sun. Now every step you take will be in Emberus's path. Now let's hurry and get you cured," the high priest said as he turned to walk from the temple.

The fire of righteousness fills you with power. You have been granted a floor boon. This boon will remain in place for the remainder of this floor as long as you remain in Emberus's grace. He may revoke this boon at any time.

The Martyr's Path. Every step you take may be your last, so make them count. Every step you make while you are outside a structure will be marked on the map. If your health reaches 5%, you have the option to release a gout of flame from each spot upon which you stood. Steps reset each time this is activated. This will activate automatically upon your death.

Plus 10% Strength.

"Wait, before we go, I have a question," I called after him.

"SO, AFTER THAT, I GOT MYSELF CURED. IT COST LIKE 10,000 GOLD."

"What?" Donut cried. "*How* much? First we didn't get boss boxes because you turned the Asojano guy into a card, and then we had to pay money? What a day this has turned into. At least we got those prizes from the gods. I liked Yemaya, the Starbucks lady. She was quite beautiful."

I continued. "And then this mantaur came up and started yelling that we'd broken some rule, and I've been banned for three days."

"So, no more disgusting slugs?" Donut asked. "Thank goodness. That was most unpleasant, Carl. One of them bit me right on the nose!"

I'd returned to the safe room, and I sat at the kitchen table. Donut, Katia, Mordecai, and Bautista were here. Katia and Bautista listened silently while Donut punctuated my story with exclamations. They each had steaming cups of tea in front of them. There was another set out for me, even though I'd already told them I didn't drink the stuff. Not hot tea at least.

The main room of the safe space was jarringly quiet with Bomo gone. I'd gotten used to the sound of the television on in the background.

I pretended not to notice the notification over Katia's head. Donut couldn't see it.

Katia now worshipped the goddess Eileithyia. I felt an ominous foreboding when I saw that.

Bautista couldn't keep still. He got up and paced back and forth while Mongo snored on the ground. The cleaner bot, for the first time in a long while, seemed to be taking a break. Actually, I thought, looking up idly, it wasn't in here at all. It had to be cleaning another room.

I'd returned to the safe room to find Donut regaling them with the story of the fight in the temple.

". . . And I *knew* it! I had said it from the get-go, that she was no good. A nun murderer! Paz said she poisoned everybody at the nunnery. Can you imagine how crazy you'd have to be to kill a bunch of nuns? They said she was better because of her medicine, but does it really matter? You can't un-murder a convent of nuns, no matter how many pills you take. Carl wouldn't let Mongo put her down, and then the first thing she did was turn Paz into a card. We should've let Mongo gobble her up when she was frozen."

The tension was palpable. Donut hadn't seemed to notice how nervous and on the edge everyone was.

I picked up the mug and took a tentative sip of the hot tea. I normally hated tea. It had a floral, unusual scent. I blinked.

"This is really good," I said, looking up at Bautista, who continued to pace. I could see how taut the man was. He nodded.

"Why don't you pick it up from there?" Mordecai said to me. He was also stalling.

So I told them what had happened once I entered the club. I outright lied about part of it, and I left out some of the rest. Not with Bautista in the room. Donut had looted that oak bracelet off the dead body of one of Bautista's family members, and he never seemed to have noticed. I wanted to avoid that conversation if possible. Now wasn't the time for it.

"Donut," I said after I was done. I patted my leg. "Come here."

She jumped into my lap, and I stroked her hair. She'd gone through the shower before I'd returned. She sniffed suspiciously at the steaming cup of tea. "Carl, did you talk to any of the ghommids when you came back? They're really nice when they're not trying to eat your face. Plus you gotta look at the cards we collected. They're really good. Katia was telling me about that cheater guy, not Ren, but the first cheater guy whose arm you ripped off. Quan. It turns out he used to be a champion at some weird nerd card game, and he's already running around—"

"Later, Donut. We need to have a serious conversation about something very important."

She stopped and looked about, meeting each of our eyes in turn. It was then, only then, that she sensed the tautness in the room. "What? What is it?"

"Donut," Katia said, sitting down next to her. She put her hand against Donut's fuzzy face, and Donut pressed into it. "I need to tell you a story. It's very scary, but the ending isn't set in stone yet. We're going to fight to make sure it doesn't have a bad ending."

19

THE CROWN FORMED INTO EXISTENCE ON KATIA'S HEAD.

"Katia," Donut said, looking up, "you have a purple tiara! It's so pretty. It's just like . . ." She trailed off, realization striking her. She went absolutely rigid in my lap.

"Why? How?" she said after a moment. "Did Louis throw that on your head?"

"It was Eva," Katia said. "She did it at the last minute, right before she died. It was my fault. I'd talked when I should've just killed her."

"You were monologuing?" Donut asked quietly. "You know we don't monologue, Katia."

"I know. It's my fault."

Donut took a deep breath. "Who knows?"

"In addition to everybody in the room, Li Na, Li Jun. Probably Zhang and Chris. Louis, Britney, and Tran. I haven't told any of the Meadow Lark folks yet, but I bet it's going to end up on tonight's recap."

"This is just like with Ferdinand," Donut said, her voice quavering. "Or when Odette brought out Miss Beatrice onto the show. They want us to fight. Katia, I don't want to fight you."

"I know," Katia said. "But we have a plan. A way out. It's why I had Carl fix Yemaya's shrine."

Donut looked sharply over at me. "You knew?"

"No," Katia said quickly. "He didn't until after that fight started, and I still haven't told him everything yet. Mordecai didn't know, either. I'm going to tell you everything now. But before I begin, I want to promise you something, Donut." She reached down and kissed Donut on the forehead. "You're right. That's exactly what they want. It's what Eva wanted, too. They want us to fight. That's not going to happen. I love you, Donut. And I will never fight you. I will die before I let that happen."

"I love you, too," Donut said. "But what are we going to do? Only one of us can leave the next floor."

"We have a path. That's what's important. It's not going to be easy, but a lot of the hard stuff is already out of the way." Katia pulled a small box from her inventory and put it on the table. The box was rectangular, the size of a music box, a little smaller than the winding box from the gate. It crackled with dark energy.

The spiderweb tattoo on my elbow throbbed the moment she pulled the box out.

"It's my prize from the celestial prize box I received at the beginning of the last floor."

"What?" I asked, hesitantly picking the box up. "What is this? You got a celestial prize box? When? How?"

"I tried to tell you so many times, Carl. Both of you. I got it for opening the Gate of the Feral Gods and flooding Larracos. I got it at the very beginning of the sixth floor. I've had it in my inventory this whole time."

I turned it over in my hand. It was light, and it appeared to be made of dark wood, carved with spiderweb patterns. Three purple marble-sized jewels sat atop the box, each affixed with a metallic claw coming up from the wood. One of the jewels glowed. The other two looked cracked and burned-out, like spent flashbulbs.

The box had little slats in it, and I could see the item within. It was a pink flower bud. An orchid. It slid back and forth within the box, but there was no way to open it. I examined it.

Several pages of text assaulted me. I took a sharp breath when I saw the item's title.

Engaged Lock Box of the Night Wyrm.

"Ahh, what's in the box? What's in the fucking box?"

Two of three seals have been broken.

This is really two items. It's a box, and there's a prize within. You

can see the prize, but you can't get to it until you open the box. In order to open the box, you must break all three seals.

Here's the prize inside the box:

The Orchid of Eileithyia's Grace.

Warning: This item can only be used by a female. Or a male, if you're a seahorse.

It's a flower. You're *supposed* to eat it, though it might be a good decoration instead. It probably tastes like a bullshit salad at some hippie vegan restaurant with a monthlong waiting list. The whole thing is a metaphor for the duality of the weakness and strength of all women or some shit. I'm not good with this stuff, and Eileithyia is a weird one. Did you know she can shoot acid milk from her nipples? Fucking weird.

Anyway, if you eat this flower, it renders you unconscious for one hour with your health at 1% of your max. You cannot heal during this time.

If you survive this ordeal, you will be given one of three permanent boons from the goddess Eileithyia. The given boon is at the discretion of the goddess, and it cannot be predicted.

If you choose to worship Eileithyia before you consume this flower, the descriptions of the boons will be expanded. She will also ask you which of the three you'd prefer. Her cooperation is not guaranteed, especially if she doesn't like you. But Eileithyia is known to be a generous goddess.

The three possible boons:

Boon one: Your base Constitution will triple. Any future points added into Constitution will be three points instead of one. All Constitution bonuses are tripled.

In other words, you'll be pretty much indestructible to physical damage from now on. You'll still be vulnerable to instakill stuff, just FYI, but this is a good one.

Warning: This bonus will stop working if Eileithyia dies *or* if you pass the 12th floor. Everything already added to your base will stay.

Boon two: Celestial Attendant. You are immediately transferred to the 12th floor. You are given employment as a Celestial Attendant until the Ascendency game begins, at which time you are given the option to exit the dungeon or continue.

Warning: This bonus will freeze your current progress. You will be considered a temporary non-combatant NPC. Your sponsorships and inventory will be frozen. You will immediately leave any parties. This is not a permanent position, and is not deemed a legal contract between yourself and the current showrunners. Legal advice will be available once your attendant indentureship is completed.

This might sound like a bad boon. It's a gamble for sure, but Celestial Attendants are usually protected from harm as long as you do what you're told. That protection ends once the games begin, but you're given the option to take a deal at this point.

Boon three. Your race will permanently be changed back to your birth race. You will be made pregnant. You will be given the option to choose the father. He will need to be the same race as you. Don't worry. You don't have to boink him. Unless you want.

Warning: Due to the current season's rule set, receiving this boon will render you ineligible to continue within the game. You will be disqualified and exported to the *Kinder* Facility located in the former city of Mumbai, India, on the surface of the planet. You will lose all future benefits of participating in *Dungeon Crawler World: Earth*.

"Holy shit," I said as I moved to the next part.

Pretty cool, huh? A worthy prize for a worthy feat. But you gotta get to it first.

Lock Box of the Night Wyrm.

The box is attuned to Crawler #9,077,265. Katia Grim. Only this crawler may complete these tasks.

This box is locked. Two of three seals have been broken. Break the final seal to open.

In order to open this box, you need to break all three seals. To break each seal, you must complete the following tasks. Don't worry, they're all easy. Trivial, really.

If you perish before the tasks are completed, this box will destroy the prize within.

Completed Tasks:

- **Kill someone you are currently or formerly partied with.**
- **Kill a country or level boss.**

Pending Task:

- **Find a Guild of Suffering and complete an assassination quest. Owning this box grants temporary access to the guild.**

"Holy shit," I said for a second time as I put the box down. I slid it over to Donut, who started reading the description.

Katia's arms stretched, and she wrapped herself in a big, multi-loop hug, like a snake coiling around a tree. She squeezed so tight, her torso contracted. Her hand twitched, her fingers nervously rubbing together. I recognized the gesture. I used to do the same thing when I was jonesin' for a cigarette. Behind her, Bautista continued to pace back and forth.

"Before I worshipped her, the three boons just said 'Triple Constitution, You are an Attendant, and'"—she paused for a long moment—"'You get Pregnant.' I didn't know what that last one meant for certain. The descriptions all changed when I finally chose to worship her, and that just happened earlier today."

"That's what you wanted to talk to me about at the end of the last floor," I said. "Because of the pregnancy one."

She hesitated. "Yes," she finally said. "I wanted advice. Because of Eva, it would be easy to kill another crawler. I knew I'd probably be able to open the box eventually. It was only a one-in-three chance to get pregnant, but still . . . I didn't know if it was a cruel joke, or what. I didn't yet know that being pregnant got you out of the dungeon, but there'd been hints. Still, the thought of it . . . I got this crown, and everything became more urgent. Once we saw what happened to Dmitri and Maxim Popov . . ."

I nodded. "It's a way out."

"Yes," she said.

"Pregnant?" Donut asked, having finally read the entire description.

"You might get pregnant? Who would be the daddy? It can't be Carl because he's a Primal, and it can't be Bautista because he's a Thundercat or whatever he is. Are you going to choose Louis? Are you going to have a baby with Louis? Juice Box isn't going to like that." She gasped. "Or maybe Li Jun? Can you imagine having Li Na as an aunt? Nobody would ever bully you."

I almost responded, but I was remembering something that sponsor woman told me, and I felt a deep chill.

I will make certain you survive until the twelfth floor, where you and Katia and the cat will help me claim the Celestial Throne once and for all.

There were actually two ways out of the Sepsis Whore problem. The pregnancy boon, which would eject Katia from the game. And the Celestial Attendant boon, which would send her straight to the 12th floor, where she'd temporarily become an NPC.

"How did you come to worship Eileithyia?" I asked.

"Sponsor box. It came from Princess Formidable of the Skull Empire. A scroll of worship."

Princess Formidable was the Maestro's sister, and she apparently didn't get along with the rest of her family. The fact she was still handing out sponsor boxes meant she wasn't actually in the dungeon on the ninth floor like the rest of her family.

Katia continued. "It was an emergency box, so I read it immediately. The moment I read it, I worshipped Eileithyia, and the full description of the boons popped up. It wasn't until then that I saw she was sponsored by that Huanxin Jinx woman. She messaged me and told me that you and Donut were about to get into a fight, and that you had to repair the shrine. If you did, it meant she'd have extra help for her game on the 12th floor. If I could talk you into doing it, she would make sure I got a boon that would allow both me and Donut to survive."

I thought of Anton, who'd died because of that message. Of Paz.

"She told you that she'd let you pick the pregnancy boon?"

"No," Katia said. "She wants our help on the 12th floor somehow. I don't want that boon anymore anyway. Going to the surface, with a baby? Can you imagine? I would've taken it, if that was the only choice. But I'll take the Celestial Attendant boon."

"I don't like it," Bautista said, talking for the first time.

"I'm not a big fan of the idea, either," Mordecai said. "Usually, it's a cushy gig. The way it's set up, if you hurt an attendant, a world of pain gets thrown your way because they're considered valuable NPCs. You're actually not allowed to hurt them anymore because of an incident a long time ago. It still happens regularly, especially when the games begin. Attendants are almost all high-value former crawlers. The Maestro will have access to her, along with a dozen sponsors whose friends who may have gotten kicked in the financial nut sack when you flooded Larracos. Not to mention all those hunters you killed. Who knows what family members might be lurking amongst the ranks of the sponsored gods? You'd be walking into a viper den."

"She promises she will protect me," Katia said. "She says the other gods have better things to do than worry about a single crawler."

"Then why is she putting so much effort into you?" Bautista asked.

"How many are there usually?" I asked. "Sponsored gods, I mean?"

Mordecai shrugged. "About a hundred or so usually. There's thousands of gods, but only some of them are really equipped for the Ascendency game. The power of the individual gods varies wildly. This new rule with the retainer minions I think is a way to even things out and possibly attract more players."

"Wait," Donut said. "I am so confused. So, this six-eyed Huanxin lady saw that Katia got that prize, and she sponsored Eileithyia just so . . . what? So she could get a servant? Is that the only reason? What do you mean by retainer minions?"

"Huanxin Jinx is a plotter," Mordecai said. "Like Circe and Vrah, but on a different scale. It seems this season the deities are able to recruit a second, unsponsored god to help them once the Ascendency game begins on the 12th floor. It's less violence and more intrigue and chess. Though violence is usually involved, too. Especially at the end. While the ninth floor is the playground of governments and the rich, the 12th is where the true elites play. The money involved is beyond anything you could believe. Some of them can be quite ruthless about how they try to claim the throne. Eileithyia's retainer appears to be Yemaya, and Huanxin needed to find a way to get her resurrected. It's part of the game for her. You just did that for her, and now she says she's going to help you because of it. What else does she want you to do?"

"She wants us to hunt spiders!" Donut said. "That's just—I don't know—eww."

"Sounds like she gave you a simple quest which will allow her to give you another boon without you actually having to worship her."

"I know the winner of Faction Wars doesn't really get anything. What about the winner of the Ascendency?" I asked.

"First off, the Faction Wars winner gets a pretty big cash prize. But they usually spend just as much getting ready for the game. I think I said this before. It's not about the money for them but bragging rights. The winner of the Ascendency battle gets a 10-season seat on the crawl council. Sitting for thirty cycles on any subcommittee comes with a pension, so that can be pretty valuable, too. But again, the people playing this do it more for the glory. Not a one of them needs the money. The real winner of all this is the bookies."

Donut gasped. "Wait, we get money if we win Faction Wars? How much? Carl, did you hear that?"

On the off chance we actually won, I was pretty sure the money would actually go to Donut's fan club, not us. Plus 15% to Quasar. But I didn't have the inclination to have that conversation right now.

"Tell me about her," I said. "Huanxin."

Mordecai's single eye focused on me. "She's rich, obviously. The type of rich where governments come to *her* when they need a loan. She is very, very intelligent. Was known as a brat when she was younger, but she's grown into her own. She's the CEO of a company called Icon Industries. Something to do with habitat structures. She's a type of alien called a grixist. She's been playing the Ascendency game for a very long time. Ever since she was a kid, actually, but she's never won. She got a multi-season suspension and banned from using her old goddess a long time ago because of illegal bribery."

"Bribery?" I asked.

He nodded. "We're not getting into it."

"You don't seem to like her very much."

"I don't. I don't like her even a little bit. She can go fuck herself."

The vehemence surprised me. "If you hate her so much, why did you tell me to do whatever she said?"

Mordecai leaned in. "Because the last time someone didn't do what she wanted, my brother died. I'd rather you stayed away from her, but that tail feather already dropped."

"My goodness, your brother? What happened?" Donut asked.

"It's not important," Mordecai said.

It was, actually, very important. Whatever this woman's true motives were, they involved Odette, and we were now smack in the middle of it. I knew Mordecai well enough to know he wouldn't freely volunteer any more info, and I couldn't tell him the most important part . . . that this alien was engineering a way for Odette to get down here with the protections turned off.

None of this was going to matter if we didn't kill all the other members of the Blood Sultanate, but that was a problem for the next floor. Right now our priority was to get the flower out of that box.

"You broke the first seal by killing Eva," I said. "I'm assuming that second one was at the same time, when we took out Imogen?"

Katia nodded.

The final seal required her to find a place called the Guild of Suffering. My elbow tattoo gave me access to the same place. Mordecai said it had something to do with a Samantha-like demigod named the Night Wyrm.

The box still sat on the table. My elbow throbbed every time I looked at it. "So, we just need to find the Guild of Suffering and get you an assassination quest."

Katia nodded. "I already found it. I already got the quest. I can't do it by myself, and I'm going to need your help. You need to find a Desperado Club entrance in your area."

"You found it? Where is it?"

She grinned, the first smile I'd seen on her face in a long time. "Actually, it was Donut who helped me figure it out."

"Me?" Donut asked.

"Donut," Katia said, "who do you know that has the same spiderweb tattoo as Carl on their elbow?"

"I don't know whatever you're talking about, Katia. I don't associate with people with disgusting prison tattoos. I only tolerate Carl because he's family."

One normally got the tattoo from using the Ring of Divine Suffering. I only knew of one other living crawler with the tattoo.

"Prepotente has one," I said.

"That's not who I'm talking about," Katia said, "but that's good to know. Donut, he's an NPC. An NPC you know *very* well."

"I don't hang out with riffraff, Katia."

"Really?"

Donut scoffed. "Well, you can't mean Damascus Steel. He doesn't count. He's a stripper!"

Katia nodded. "The entrance is at the Penis Parade on the top floor of the Desperado Club. The whole strip club is a front for the Guild of Suffering."

"What?" Donut asked. "He never told me that! This is an outrage! Why would a stripper lie to me?"

"You already got an assassination quest?" I asked, trepidation rising. "Who's the target?"

Katia pulled out a strange slip of paper and slid it over to me.

"Nobody touch it except Carl. If you aren't a member of the Guild of Suffering, it stings your hand if you touch it. Even in a safe room. Only members of the guild can read it and assist me with it. You can't say the name of the target out loud, or I fail the quest."

I hesitantly picked it up. I realized it wasn't a piece of paper, but a dried slip of skin covered with desiccated veins. The dry, rigid flap of membrane was small, about the size of a pack of cigarettes. As I held it, I felt a pinprick of pain on my finger, and my blood flowed into the skin. The veins on the skin pulsed with my heartbeat, forming words in a strange, tributary-like language.

New Achievement! Secondary Gig!

You're getting *another* job? On top of everything else? Yeah, that's a *great* idea. It's not like you have enough on your plate already. If you weren't constantly getting healed, your blood pressure would be through the roof! It's not like the crushing demands of the

modern dungeon are making it more difficult to survive when it should be going the opposite way.

You know, I'm pretty sure nobody, on their deathbeds, ever said to themselves, "Man, I wished I'd worked even more in life."

Reward: A new tab is now available in your interface. It is a sub-tab of quests.

Guild Jobs.

I pushed the achievement away and tried to read the tiny words on the skin, but I couldn't understand the language. The system read it for me. It came in a hissing, evil voice I hadn't heard before, spoken in my mind. It reminded me of a Naga voice, but a little more high-pitched. I shuddered.

The Night Wyrm has a task for you, my little darling.

This task has been assigned to my beautiful, budding poppet, Katia. You are not her, and that means you've killed her in order to take over her jobs, or she has enlisted a family member to assist her with her task. Either scenario is acceptable. The family with many eyes works as a team, yes. We sacrifice the weak to support the many, yes. We rise from the shadows. Our blood flows together.

Your task is before you, my sweet. A difficult task, yes. But an important one. Important for the family.

We wish to remove the competition. She serves dual roles. She keeps our family in the ground. She keeps our blood dry. You must kill her. The owner of the Naughty Boys Employment Agency. The assistant manager of the Desperado Club. She is one. Astrid. Kill her. Bring her lifeless body to the family.

NEW GUILD JOB.

Kill Astrid, level 125 Bloodlust Sprite, Assistant Manager of the Desperado Club. Proof of death is required.

This job is owned by Crawler Katia Grim. You must kill her to claim the reward for this job.

Speaking the details of this job out loud will immediately cancel the contract and revoke access to the guild.

Katia gave me an uncertain grin.

"Hey, I warned you it wasn't going to be easy."

"Shit," I said. I read the slip of skin a second time.

Astrid the sprite would be next to impossible to kill. Even attempting to hurt her would bring every guard in the Desperado Club down on our heads. But what choice did we have? If we couldn't pull it off, then Donut and Katia would be forced to face off against one another.

I met eyes with Bautista, and they were hollow, tired, and afraid. But they were something else, too. Determined.

I felt a new chill wash over me.

20

DECEMBER 15TH

Three of Six Totems Collected.
Time Until Phase Two: 8 days, 1 hour.

"CARL, DO YOU REALLY THINK WE'LL BE ABLE TO GET AROUND THE rules of the tiara?" Donut asked as we stepped outside into the ghommid village. She sat upon Mongo's back. All around, the strange creatures turned and waved jovially at us. The fog that covered the village had dissipated, and the evil feeling of the place was gone, replaced with something wondrous, almost like we'd stepped into a cartoon. "What are we going to do if it doesn't work?"

"The first step is we're going to do everything we can to make sure Katia gets to that flower," I said. "But if that doesn't work, we're going to keep looking for a solution. There are always solutions." I reached over and gave Donut a reassuring pat. I could feel how anxious she was.

"Hey. Look at me," I said. She had her sunglasses on, and I could see my reflection in them. I tried not to look so worried. "This is a tough situation, but we're still a long ways away from the end of the ninth floor. We're working on it. We need to stay focused on this floor for now."

She nodded. "That reminds me. I unmuted Samantha, and she just started yelling at me. I had to mute her again. The good news is, I think she got pooped out by the spider. But the spider won't let her go and has her tied up in her web. Also, Prepotente says he wants you to read a few chapters of that Bahamas book to him. He's all by himself there, and I think he's really lonely. I've been talking to him, but chat isn't the same as real life. He's not a member of any guilds or the Desperado Club and he's not allowed into Club Vanquisher anymore, so it's just him and Bianca. Bianca is really nice, but she doesn't talk. She does hiss a lot."

"We're moving toward Samantha," I said. "But it's going to be a few days before we get there. I'll talk to Pony later."

We only had a few hours before we had to go to our first planning meeting for the Faction Wars game on the 9th floor. Our goal for right now was to start moving southwest through Havana. We had to get out of the city. We'd collect as many cards as we could. I'd keep a lookout for Sister Ines and a Desperado Club. There wasn't one in the ghommid settlement.

"Call out all the safe rooms," I said as we stepped out of the village. "And watch for cars."

Entering Havana.

There were plenty of floating heads moving back and forth, but I saw no sign of any nearby mobs. There weren't any cars moving nearby, but I could see there was a big fire burning to the east. I consulted the paper map I'd taken off a tourist earlier, and I turned left, pushing through a group of people walking toward the cemetery's entrance. A camera and a bunch of cell phones clattered onto the ground.

I wanted to get to the highway and move south. If the road was clear, we could use the Royal Chariot to move much more quickly. My map also had a train station on it, and I suspected the trains were probably still running, though that would be risky. We'd have to stay in the very back of the train to minimize the risk of us breaking something while it moved. The idea of ever getting on another train made my stomach lurch.

"What are we going to do when we find the cat girl?" Donut asked. "Are you going to let Mongo kill her this time?"

"We're not going to kill her. But we need to talk to her about what she's done to Paz. I've sent her a few messages, but she hasn't responded."

"She's a Havana brown and a nun murderer. I don't even know which of those two things is worse. How is this even a conversation? Mongo thinks we should kill her, too."

Mongo growled in agreement.

"Just don't send her any nasty messages. We'll never get her to talk to us if you start insulting or threatening her over chat."

The scent of a street vendor's food cart caught my nose, and my stomach rumbled. So much had been happening, I'd forgotten to eat.

"You don't need to worry about that. Not anymore. She's already blocked me."

I sighed. "What did you say to her?"

"I only said the truth, Carl. You can't get mad at me for speaking the truth."

"What did you say?"

"I told her that what she did to Paz was really mean, and that killing nuns isn't acceptable. And that she was a disgrace to all cat kind. I might've added that we were going to take her cards from her and rip the Paz card once we found her. And that Mongo is very disappointed in her."

"Goddamnit, Donut. You shouldn't have said that. She's going to hide from us. Or worse, attack us."

"Hardly. Like I'd let a fake cat sneak up on me. And what part of that isn't true, Carl? You get mad if I bend the truth, and you get mad if I say it how it is. Sometimes I feel like there's no winning with you."

While she ranted, I kept an eye on the minimap, looking for threats. My footsteps now appeared on the display. Thanks to my newest boon from Emberus, all of my previous steps would explode in fire if my health got low enough. I thought of all those ghommids running around the village. Would it hurt them if I activated it? I had so many questions. It seemed like an unnecessarily dangerous boon. Donut and Mongo would need to be careful of where I'd stepped. Donut had fire resistance now, but would it be enough? Plus, if I activated it myself, would it blow up right behind me? Like, would I set my ass on fire? How big was the explosion? That I had to be near death to test this was alarming.

We walked for a good hour. There were plenty of small, low-level mobs running about, but nothing flag-worthy. There was a zoo, but after a quick inspection, it appeared the animals within were part of the illusion and not mobs. We killed every monster we could find, managing to collect several utility cards we probably wouldn't end up using. It was dangerous to put too many in your deck because it lowered your chance of pulling totem cards.

Finding a safe room looked like it wasn't going to be a problem. They were everywhere. We found a stretch of freeway with no moving cars thanks to a pileup at an exit, and I pulled out the Royal Chariot, which allowed us to cautiously pick up speed, moving quickly south. Donut remained atop Mongo, who ran alongside. The city became less dense, and soon there were cars everywhere again. I had to pull off the side of the road to avoid getting splattered by a massive, rickety bus that came out of nowhere.

We were in the suburbs just south of the city, a strange mix of corrugated-metal-sided hovels, nice homes, churches, apartment buildings, and lots and lots of random shopping places.

Zev sent us a warning that we needed to start preparing for the meeting. Donut noticed a safe room one neighborhood over, and we moved toward it, skirting past a horde of little kids running and laughing as they played in the street. Only half of them still wore their clothes, but this area seemed mostly untouched.

I thought about them playing, ready for Christmas, without a worry in the world. This was recorded three weeks before the apocalypse. I hoped, for their sake, that all of these children were inside at the time.

That was a really fucked-up thing to think, I said to myself. *But was it? Was it?*

The safe room appeared to be a random person's house, which was unusual. We pushed our way inside as Zev talked to us.

ZEV: Also, I hate pulling you guys out of the dungeon so much, but Odette has finally arrived in Earth orbit and wants you two in a couple of days. She wanted Katia, too, but they said no on that one. So it'll be just you two.

DONUT: YAY! IT'S BEEN TOO LONG.

CARL: I can't wait.

ZEV: Guys, she sent notice that she's going to ask something of you two live on air, and I want to discuss it so you're not

blindsided. We can talk about it face-to-face before the preproduction meeting.

I already knew what this was going to be thanks to Huanxin. She wanted to be our adjutant. I still wasn't sure what that was, but every team had one. It appeared to be some sort of third-party rule keeper or game guide for Faction Wars.

Inside the house, it was set up like a coffee shop with a Bopca proprietor, an angry-looking woman named Vitasy. I had her make me a coffee and bought a pastry while Donut purchased some meat skewers for Mongo, haggling with the woman over the price. The woman's face lit up when she set eyes on the princess, but she quickly soured when the haggling began.

"I bet we'll never see her again," Donut finally said, talking about Sister Ines, like she'd spent the last hour thinking of the nun.

I didn't answer, just happy that she was distracted from the Katia issue.

"Zev," I said out loud, not bothering to use chat, "do we have time to go into the practice arena to play with our cards?"

ZEV: No, Carl. You two have five minutes.

"Okay." I paused by the entrance to our safe space. The Bopca woman glared at us sullenly. "Hey, Vitasy, is it? Do you happen to know if there are any Desperado Clubs around here?"

She thumbed over her shoulder. "Keep going south, and I heard there's one a few kilometers down the road."

"Thanks!" I said, and I flipped her a coin. She let it clatter to the floor.

"I FEEL AS IF THE BOPCAS ARE GETTING A BIT OF AN ATTITUDE LATELY," Donut said as we entered the safe room. "I don't like that."

"You guys are back earlier than I expected. Your charisma is still really high, but the effect on NPCs isn't immediately as powerful as it once was," Mordecai said, coming around the corner, wiping his hands on a towel. "It's complicated math stuff involving resistances. On the tenth floor, the Bopcas will still like you, but you won't be talking them into extra rations for Mongo, that's for sure. They'll be downright surly toward Carl even though his charisma ain't half bad."

We barely heard what he was saying. I exchanged a look with Donut. Mordecai had a little pink bow plastered to the side of his bald head. And it appeared as if his face was smudged with pink lipstick, Samantha-style. It spread across the side of his face like he'd just tried—and failed—to quickly wipe his face clean. He dropped the towel on the table, and I could see it was stained with makeup.

I recalled something I'd read in either the cookbook or in the original description about cyclopses. They couldn't see their own reflections, like vampires. I didn't know if that weird quirk of mythology was present in the Earth versions of these guys, but it was clear he'd just tried to clean himself.

"Mordecai, darling," Donut said, "I'd like to ask you an important question, and if you don't want to answer, that's fine, but . . ." She let it hang.

"What are you talking about, Princess?"

Donut jumped to the table and started to lick her paw. "I'm not one to pry. Really. I'm just curious."

"About what?"

"Again, I'm not one to judge. Believe me, I am an ally. But if you need tips for proper application, I'm just saying I am available. I spent many an hour helping Miss Beatrice put her face on. I'm sure Samantha can help, too, once we retrieve her, though her application is a little . . . loud. Carl, please. You must compose yourself. It's rude to laugh."

I hadn't been laughing until that moment. I burst out.

"Oh, damn," Mordecai said, reaching up to touch the bow on the side of his head. He peeled it off and dropped it on the counter. He sighed. "I forgot about that."

"You left a little," I said, indicating his face.

"Fuck," he said, picking the towel back up. "I hate it when I'm a cyclops. No depth perception plus I can't see my own reflection."

"Do you see the makeup just floating there in the mirror?" I asked. "Do you see your clothes?"

"No," he said. "There's no reasoning to it. If it's attached to me, I can't see it."

"That's really weird," I said.

"So," Donut said, "let's circle back. How long has this been going on? Honestly, if this is how you feel about yourself, I am glad you're finally starting to explore—"

Mordecai held up a hand, his fat, sausage-like fingers spread out. "Princess. Stop. It's not what it looks like."

"Well, it looks like you were dragged face-first through the makeup aisle at the dollar store," she said.

My eyes caught the cleaner bot zipping down to pick something up off the couch. An empty bag of chips. I observed the television, the one we hooked the game systems up to. I saw that Bomo's and Sledge's large-sized hand controllers were replaced. One was the original and another was strange. I hadn't made it, so it must've been engineered by Mordecai. It was split into two left-right pieces and propped up on the floor at a 45-degree angle. There was a small pillow in front of it.

I finally figured it out.

"Are you really allowed to hire a room attendant, or is that something you made up? Is this something we're paying for?"

He deflated and lowered his head. "I can have an attendant. I took up the slot. But you have five more attendant slots, and I put them in that. You're paying for it."

"So there's six of them?" I asked.

He nodded. "It's all the system would let me."

"How much are we paying?"

"What?" Donut asked. "What is this?"

"Combined, it's a little more than 1,000 gold a day. I've been paying myself with the money you've been giving me for supplies."

"What?" Donut asked again, looking back and forth between us. "What're you talking about? And that's not the proper definition of 'paying for it myself,' Mordecai. That's called embezzlement! Wait, you're stealing from us? I'm so confused. What are you stealing?" She gasped. "Drugs? Is it drugs? And you've turned to prostitution? Is that why you're dressing like that? You're going to have to get much better at your makeup if you want to earn enough to pay us back."

"I know Bonnie isn't one of them," I said, ignoring Donut. "She's on the ninth floor. So are the bear cubs and Skarn. So it's Ruby and the rest?"

He nodded. "Just the ones with compression sickness," Mordecai said. "It was so dangerous at the end of the last floor, and they'd had a rough time even getting from the changeling village to here. I didn't think they'd survive the fight at the end of the last floor. So, I hired them in all the available slots."

"You know, if you'd asked me, I would've said yes," I said.

"Ruby? The little girl with no arms?" Donut asked. She turned to look at the game controller on the floor. "She's your attendant? How can you have an attendant with no arms, Mordecai?"

"There wasn't time," he said. He raised his head, straightening himself. "But I stand by my decision."

Ruby was a little changeling girl orphan NPC. We'd met her on the fifth floor. She was part of the whole storyline with the camels and the changelings. She was suffering from something called compression sickness, a birth defect that was caused by the parents not getting proper nutrition on their new world. She could change form like most changelings, but when she did, she was always missing parts. When she was in human form, she had no arms and a sunken-in head.

At the end of the previous floor, the changelings had come to our safe room in preparation of the taking of the High Elf Castle. The remnants of the castle, and all of the surviving changelings, were now on the ninth floor. But several changelings had died during that terrible fight to take the castle. Mordecai had made the right call to keep the most vulnerable out of the fight. I still wasn't sure why he felt the need to hide this from us.

ZEV: Transferring in one minute.

"We'll discuss this when we get back," I said.

21

<Note added by Crawler Herot. 16th Edition>

I do wonder, sometimes, how my Worn Path Method will work on the deeper floors with the longer timelines. Tea that steeps too long tends to take on an unexpected flavor.

Entering Production Facility.

WE SKIPPED RIGHT PAST THE NORMAL GNOLL SECURITY CHECK, WHICH was surprising. We went right to the production facility building at the bottom of the ocean. For the first time, we weren't inverted sideways when we arrived. My HUD flickered and snapped off the moment I appeared.

We were in the same room I'd been in when I'd come for CrawlCon. My eyes caught the spot on the wall where my souped-up training studio had been. It was just a blank wall now.

Donut looked up at me. "So, Mordecai is being a babysitter? I'm still confused. Why did that turn him to a drag queen?"

"He's playing with them, Donut," I said. "They're little kids. He's letting them put makeup on him."

"Why didn't he tell us? It's not like you would've said no. You never say no to that sort of— Hi, Zev!"

Zev popped into the room, appearing atop the table.

Donut jumped up to headbutt the small kua-tin, but her head went right through her. "Hey!"

"Hi, Princess. Sorry, guys," Zev said. "I'm so busy, I don't have time to hop over there. We have literally thousands of ships coming into Earth orbit, all arriving early because of Prepotente's stunt. It's a bureaucratic nightmare. Half of these ships will fire on another if they're parked within 1,000 kilometers, and the Valtay insist on manual routing. Plus, do you know how much it costs to use a tunnel transfer gate without a reservation? The Plenty are collecting their chest of stardust, that's for sure. I have to be in a meeting in a few minutes when you're at yours, so we only have a minute to talk." She looked down at her tablet. "Gods, I don't even know what that meeting is for."

"Did you know Mordecai was stealing from us?" Donut asked.

Zev grunted. "Actually, yes, though I wouldn't call it stealing out loud too much. He can get charged for that should you pursue it. That little story is compelling enough that we've been attempting to talk the AI into bending its rules to allow viewers to watch him and these specific NPCs. Especially considering Mordecai's backstory and with Huanxin back in the game. Him risking charges to save children NPCs is prime drama. Plus, he's just adorable with them. Who would've thought? The AI doesn't seem interested in helping us, so we've licensed the story to Titan, who's preparing a vid on it with virtual characters."

"So, it's like a Lifetime movie? About Mordecai?" Donut asked. "Am I in it?"

"They didn't want to pay the extra licensing fee," Zev said. "But Mongo is in it."

Donut gasped. "My Mongo is a movie star? He's going to be so excited!"

"Is it, uh, safe to be asking the AI to do stuff?" I asked.

"Asking, yes. It seems to enjoy it. Demanding? That's something we're still working on."

"So, what did you want to talk to us about?" I asked.

"Hang on," Zev said. She clicked something on her tablet. The lights in the room blinked twice. "Okay. I've turned on extra security for this conversation. This is an official secure conversation between an administrator and a show sponsor. As of this moment, both of you are acting in your capacity as a sponsor. Because of this, the rules are a little different than it is for the regular crawl. I am the only person in on this conversation other than the system AI. Okay?"

"Ooh, it feels very top secret and hush-hush," Donut said.

"That's because it is. Okay, listen. Odette is going to ask to be your adjutant during Faction Wars. I want you to know what that is before you decide. It's your choice, but I think it's a bad idea."

I knew this was coming, though I was surprised that she was advising against it. "What's an adjutant and why is it a bad idea?"

"An adjutant is a neutral third-party observer. Each team gets one. They will have access to the rules and will have open communications with the other adjutants. They fall somewhere between a manager and a liaison. They're like referees. They have limited ability to call out rule-breaking behavior, though traditionally their participation is widely symbolic. They're usually someone loud and flashy and famous who gives color commentary for the viewers. Someone like Odette. She's done it a few times."

"She'll be physically on the surface with us?"

"Yes," Zev said.

"What if I manage to get the protections turned off? Will she still want to do it?"

"Carl, it's highly unlikely you'll pull that off. And even if you do, I'm pretty sure there's a rule hidden in there somewhere that the adjutants will have a constant invulnerability spell upon them."

"Okay, so why do you think it's a bad idea?"

Zev sighed. "As you're aware, Odette has history with Mordecai. She was his manager a long time ago. And Mordecai dislikes her quite a bit. I'm not going into that, but you remember what happened when Mordecai met Chaco during the prize carousel segment? He threw a chair at his head and got himself put in a time-out. If you get them physically together, he *will* attack her. He will get kicked out. You'll lose him. His contract will be in jeopardy. Half of those kids he's fostering will immediately get ejected because your personal space will change. Odette is a big fan of . . . drama. Having her involved wouldn't be healthy for anybody. She's great in a talk show environment, but in this context, you don't want her around."

I thought about it for a moment. We had to pick Odette. We didn't have a choice. I would need an excuse that seemed plausible to completely ignore Zev's advice. Luckily, we still had a few days.

"Who does she usually do this for?" I asked.

Zev shrugged. "Last time it was the Dreadnoughts. Or was it the Reavers? I can't remember. It's someone different each time."

"This doesn't seem like an official stance," I said. "I'd think the Valtay showrunners would be falling over themselves for this kind of story to play out."

"It's not official," Zev said. "This is *me* talking, trying to give your team advice. Also, the Valtay have taken a step back after the Prepotente incident and are distancing themselves from the production's day-to-day. They need investor confidence for the next crawl, which they're also running. That seventh floor was Cascadia's baby, but they pushed to make it happen, and when it got ruined, they had themselves what you humans call a come-to-Jesus moment. A big one, especially after how the sixth floor ended. Still, despite all that, there's still money being made. You two are *earning*. A lot more than usual, but it's at the expense of several of the sponsors, which *is* unusual. The Borant Corporation is going to be liquefied after the crawl no matter what. If the Valtay step back, they can point to the bottom line and show how profitable they were, and at the same time, they can point to us at Borant and say, *Hey, we made this profit despite how terribly the mudskippers ran this season.* Does that make sense?"

"Not even a little bit," I said.

"Just don't pick Odette, okay?" Zev said. "I like Mordecai, and it would hurt him if you picked her."

"What'll happen to you if they shut down your company?" Donut asked.

The tiny woman shrugged. "That depends on what's going on back home."

Donut sighed dramatically. "Denying her request will break Odette's heart, I'm sure, but if I'm going to be a Hollywood mother, I need to learn to make tough decisions, I suppose."

I said nothing.

"Good. And Odette won't be that upset. Her heart is made of ice, and she's used to rejection. Now you two gotta go in there. Try not to piss off my boss too much."

"Your boss?" I asked, brightening. "Your boss will be at the meeting today?"

Zev just sighed.

"YOU TWO REPRESENT THE THIRD TEAM, SO YOU WILL SIT HERE," THE disc-shaped mexx robot said, indicating two chairs at the large round table. The robot's name was U56KL, and Donut was calling him "Urkel."

None of the other chairs were currently occupied, at least as far as we could see. There were ten sections total. All the other spots contained a single chair of varying sizes. Or no chair.

"Are we the only warlords who are coming today?" I asked. Zev had said earlier that these meetings were usually attended by underlings, which was why I hadn't been too excited about being here. Donut was pissed that it wasn't being filmed and broadcast. She hadn't yet observed that the promised catering hadn't appeared yet, either. I was hoping it would remain unnoticed.

"I am unaware of the guest list for this meeting," Urkel the robot said. "Normally, the other onboarded attendants meet in a boardroom located in Larracos, but that meeting space is currently unavailable, so all of them will be attending from different locations today. I believe most are in their respective castles."

"Unavailable?" Donut asked. "Does that mean it's still underwater?"

"Yes. It does," Urkel said. "Please stand by. The meeting will begin in thirty seconds."

"Why can they do this from their bases, but we have to come here?" I asked.

"Because they're richer than you are," Urkel said.

"Do you think they're going to be mean to us?" Donut asked as she took her spot upon the raised chair to my left. "I feel as if they're going to be mean. Or do you think they're going to do that thing where they're superpolite, but you can tell they hate us?"

I grunted. "We're about to find out."

"Just remember the plan, Carl. I do most of the talking. I'm the negotiator, and you just sit there and look all Carl-y."

A figure flickered and appeared in spot 10 at the table. It was a tiny kua-tin I hadn't met before sitting tightly in a small chair. She had long, droopy whiskers, giving her an almost catfish appearance. Zev didn't have those, which indicated maybe she was a different kind. Her scales had a dull sheen to them, and I knew from Zev that she was older, but not as old as her appearance suggested. The act of running the crawl had aged her greatly. She looked exhausted.

Cascadia. The kill-kill-kill lady.

"Hi, Zev's boss!" Donut said.

"Princess Donut, hello. Carl, hello," Cascadia said. Her voice was clipped and tense. "I trust Zev has caught you up on what this meeting will entail?"

I shrugged.

"Good," she said. "Even though you're currently sitting as a sponsor, I will not tolerate any of your usual bullshit, Carl. There will be consequences for any attempts to derail this meeting. They've been getting disrupted without your help, and I don't need you adding to the chaos. I am on a tight schedule and am one crisis shy of pulling the fail-safe, which would kill us all. So don't test me, especially not today."

"Carl," Donut said, "do you remember Loita? She reminds me of Loita. Do you remember when she accidentally blew herself up? Why is it all of these people are always so high-strung? Honestly, they're like Chihuahuas."

"I was just thinking the same thing," I said.

"She's so tired-looking. Can fish use moisturizer?" Donut turned to the glaring fish. "I feel as if you should try it. It would do wonders. Or you can use cucumber slices, though your eyes might be a little too buggy for that. And they'd be really big on you. Or maybe you can try hot yoga. I heard that's relaxing. Your body is a temple, Zev's boss. You need to take care of yourself."

The fish woman just looked at us.

"I agree, Donut," I said, glaring back. "I do hope you look after yourself much more carefully than Loita did, Cascadia."

Cascadia blinked and disappeared. A moment passed and then she reappeared in the same spot with a pop, splashing water all over the table. A rebreather appeared around her gills.

"I'm really here now, Carl," Cascadia said. She raised her little arms. I could tell she was on the edge of a breakdown. "You want to hurt me? Now's your chance." She leaned forward. "Try it. There are no protections. You'd be able to squash me easily. *I fucking dare you.* It would be the end of the both of us. I would godsdamned *welcome* it."

By this point, it took a lot to surprise me. I was moderately impressed at the display, though I didn't want to show it. I felt my hand clench. I had to clench and unclench several times to keep from taking her up on her offer. I felt my gauntlet start to form, and I quickly let it go.

Quiet, I thought as I continued my staring contest with the woman. *Quiet, quiet. Don't be so loud.*

"Whew," Donut said, waving her paw in front of her nose. "Not just moisturizer. A bath. Do fish take baths? Carl, she smells really bad. Nothing like Zev. It's like that expired cat food you got me from the swap meet that one time."

"I never did that, Donut," I said, keeping my eyes on Cascadia. "You're thinking of the whitefish and spinach flavor of your regular food, which you never liked."

"Well, it smelled like it was expired and came from the swap meet."

Before I could respond, the room blinked again, and then all the spaces at the table were suddenly occupied. Cascadia held my eyes for several moments longer before planting what I recognized as a big fake smile on her kua-tin face. She turned to the group and took on her usual, over-the-top, condescending voice. The change in her was instantaneous and unnerving.

I looked about the room, a mix of familiar and new aliens. Nobody had labels over them.

"Hello, everyone. Welcome, all. This is our . . . What is it? Our fifth preproduction meeting? It seems just like yesterday I was welcoming you all here. We have some new faces, I see, so the rules dictate we must do a new round of introductions before we start." Cascadia's fish eyes twitched, looking about the room, surprise evident. "Oh, I didn't realize so many warlords were going to be attending today."

"Hi, Princess . . . I mean Empress D'Nadia!" Donut called, waving at the familiar Saccathian sitting two spots to our left in space number five. The last time I'd seen her was at the very end of the Butcher's Masquerade.

"Hi, Donut!" the empress said. "That was quite the performance the other night. I really liked your song. I'm sorry they kicked us out before the festivities really started."

Donut preened. "You did? Oh, thank you so very much! I do have to ask you, Empress, about the voting on the pet show. Is it true that the ballot box was rigged? I heard that—"

Cascadia held up a hand. "We don't have time for pleasantries. Today's meeting will be short. I ask that each of you introduce yourselves in order, and then we will get to business." She nodded her head toward the familiar, angry orc sitting immediately to her left in spot one.

The only time I'd ever seen Crown Prince Stalwart, the Maestro's older brother, was during the short video where he'd—wrongly—declared that he'd assassinated me and Donut. He'd instead accidentally killed Manasa the singer.

"I don't announce myself," the angry orc said.

At the second spot right next to me was no chair. Just a green blob, one of the biggest of these things I'd seen. It was an opaque, quivering mass of green goo shaped into three tiers of decreasing size, like a Jell-O mold from the 1970s. This was a rep from the Operatic Collective. Or maybe it was their king. I had no idea because they all looked the same, and the only difference I could see was the size. They bred by literally splitting apart, and I knew they could merge back into one another, which was really fucking weird. Their mouths were at the very top, and they spoke upward into the air.

"I am Voting Admin Cell Mass Number Three," the blob said. Little bubbles gurgled out of the top of him when he spoke.

"What happened to Hortense?" Empress D'Nadia asked.

"Hortense is in here," the blob thing said. "There are three of us in this entity, and we make up Voting Admin Cell Mass Number Three."

"Wait," Donut asked. "What are we supposed to call you?"

"You're supposed to call me Voting Admin Cell Mass Number Three," the thing said.

"That's just silly," Donut said. "That's much too long of a name. I'm going to call you—I don't know—Green Jiggly." Donut paused, then straightened. "Oh, it's our turn?" She cleared her throat. "Well, I am GC, BWR, NW Princess Donut the Queen Anne Chonk, and with me is my co-warlord, Carl. We represent the Princess Posse, a non-profit conglomerate with tens of thousands of chapters of intelligent, like-minded, beautiful fans from—"

"This is ridiculous," Prince Stalwart said, interrupting. "We know who you are, you fucking imbecile."

I was about to say something, but Donut put a calming paw on my arm.

"Oh, honey. I know you know who I am. We did humiliate you and your brother more times than I can count. Your mother never got the chance to meet me, though, did she? Is she here? I'd be happy to sign an autograph for her . . . Oh wait."

There was a long moment of shocked silence while Donut swished her tail.

"I am going to take my ceremonial knife, insert it into your gut, and skin you alive while you scream in pain. I will then use your pelt to line the interior of my codpiece," Prince Stalwart growled. "Your fur will spend the next thousand years warming my enormous genitals."

"Wow," Donut said. "That's an oddly specific threat. And 'enormous'? Really? Nobody was questioning the size of your genitals, so it's really weird you would just randomly bring it up. Carl, did you hear that? Do you think he thought that one up before he got up here, or do you think it just kind of popped out? I'm like 90% certain he had that one ready to go." She gasped. "Do you think he was sitting there, waiting for the meeting to start, saying to himself, *I'm gonna do it. I'm gonna go with the codpiece line*? I propose a new action item. We are changing the name of Crown Prince Stalwart to Captain Enormous."

Empress D'Nadia trumpeted with laughter. A hairy goblin guy a few spots over also laughed.

The mexx robot dinged. "Action item added to the queue. Action item has been rejected by the system. Titles may not be changed."

"Oh, poo," Donut said. She turned to the large green-and-purple Naga parked immediately to her left. He had four arms and no legs, just a long snake body that sat coiled on the ground. He wore dented plate armor upon his chest, but his head and arms were bare. "Oh well, I guess it's your turn. Hey, aren't we cousins now or something? Not by blood, obviously. But because of that tiara?"

The Naga's dark snake eyes bored into Donut. "We are not cousins," he said, though I could see he was suppressing a grin. He instantly reminded me of Nihit, the reporter Naga I'd stabbed in the neck with a pen. "We are not cousins," he clarified, "in or out of the game. I am but a representative of the Blood Sultanate, not a member of the royal family." He bowed. "I suppose, in a way, you are cousins with the family, and that includes my wife. I am called Rishi."

This was the team we would have to kill first. Winning Faction Wars was optional. Destroying the Nagas was not.

"Does that mean when I kill the royal family and take it over, you'll work for me?" Donut asked.

The grin didn't leave his face. "Yes, if I am still alive. I will be honor bound to follow you. Or your companion, Katia."

That one stung. Next to me, Donut tensed.

I had an uneasy feeling about this guy. I committed his name to my memory. Rishi.

"Donut, if you would refrain from commenting on each introduction, we could get through this much more quickly," Cascadia said, sounding exasperated.

"Hello, everybody," Empress D'Nadia said from her spot at number five. "I'm Empress D'Nadia, warlord of the Prism Kingdom Clan. I just onboarded onto the playing field, so if anyone wants to catch a meal, I'm available. I understand a few restaurants in Larracos have finally opened back up."

"Not advisable," Rishi said, but didn't elaborate further.

"I am Epitome Tagg of the Dream," the bald elf said from the sixth spot. He didn't add anything else.

I blinked, surprised.

"Hey, you're the guy who hates Louis because he thinks your mom is sexy!" Donut exclaimed. "Carl, it's the guy who hates Louis!"

"Princess Donut, please," Cascadia said.

"Sorry, sorry," Donut said.

The older, regal-looking elf appeared bored. He didn't react to Donut's outburst. He looked nothing like the unhinged psychopath he was portrayed to be. He wore a simple leather jerkin and was indistinguishable from the rest of the Dream elves we'd slaughtered on the previous floor. This was one of the richest men in the entire galaxy. The Dream elves controlled food-growing operations in numerous solar systems and owned the patent on multiple types of food. Supposedly, if you lived in certain areas, your body wouldn't let you digest their food unless you had a license for it.

In spot number seven was a green humanoid creature. A representative from the Lemig Sortition. This was the guy who'd laughed at Donut's joke about Prince Stalwart. He looked like a cross between a goblin and a Nullian alien, like Quasar. The Lemig Sortition was a truly democratic government system consisting of multiple races, though most of them were these green guys. I couldn't remember what the race was called, but I knew their leader was actually a different type of alien, a fuzzy caterpillar-looking thing. I still had a photo of the leader's mother. The population of the Lemig Sortition as a whole voted on *everything*, supposedly. Though once something was set, it required an 80% vote to undo it. They'd voted to participate in Faction Wars a long time ago, and it'd been impossible to undo that vote, even though the population had soured on the high congress's participation each season. Mordecai said their system was in a constant state of disarray.

"Hi, I'm Luke," the alien said. His voice was surprising, sounding like a surfer dude's.

In spot number eight was another humanoid alien with a bulky body and a long, thin, bone white neck and a blank white mask covering his face, like something out of creepy anime. I instantly knew what this was, though I'd never seen one. A Viceroy. They were one of the constants of Faction Wars, oftentimes winners of the conflict, though they supposedly hadn't won in a while. Their race was somewhat of a mystery. They specialized in horrific battlefield spells and necromancy. In real life, their system was known as a destination for cheap medical procedures for non-citizens and those who lived outside the inner system who had access to free health care.

Their team was called the Madness.

The Viceroy didn't say anything. Just raised his hand in greeting. Donut waved back.

"And I am Warlord Fangs of the Reavers," the final representative said with a robotic voice.

The Reavers were an occasional player and usually did well when they did participate, having taken the prize multiple seasons. Mordecai said they oftentimes allied with the orcs, easily taking out the other teams. They would then square off against each other for the trophy, though supposedly there was some sort of early betrayal the previous season, and a partnership was unlikely this year.

The rep was a square-headed, old-school robot that vibrated up and down like he was powered by a diesel engine. The thing looked like he'd come straight from a 60s sci-fi movie. I knew from the cookbook and the photo of the leader's mother that this appearance was for my benefit. These guys were more like the robots from *Terminator 2*, in that they could switch shape at will. They normally looked like plastic-skinned android soothers. I'd seen them quite a bit in the audience at various talk shows. The Reavers were a megacorporation and system government. They mostly lived on something Earth scientists called a Dyson sphere, a star completely surrounded by a structure. These guys supposedly were once related to the nebulars, the religious nuts who'd sent a team called the Nebular Sin Patrol to die as hunters on the sixth floor.

Like the nebs, they were originally several different biological races who enhanced themselves with machines, though these guys took it a step further and kept only their brains. So they looked like robots.

"Warlord Fangs? Really?" Donut asked. "Is your name really Fangs? Are you a robot vampire?" She gasped. "Or are you a werewolf robot? Now that would be something."

"Donut," Cascadia snapped, "if I have to warn you again—"

Before she finished her admonishment, the silent, faceless Viceroy to the robot's right dropped forward on the table. His head rolled away from the body like a billiard ball. The blank white mask came loose, revealing a bone white, demonic, tusked alien face covered in streaks of red. We all just stared dumbly at the now-decapitated representative from the Madness. Bright red blood showered from the neck hole, spurting like a hose. I remembered a question from the cookbook, wondering if these Viceroy guys were biological because nobody had seen one die before.

"Carl," Donut asked, "is his head supposed to just fall off like that?"

"I don't think so."

"Not again," Cascadia said.

Prince Stalwart raged, slamming his fist on the table. "You idiots can't do anything right. Tagg, you said you took care of this."

A new form appeared behind the Viceroy, pushing the headless body away and sitting in his chair. The blood remained pooling on the table, disappearing as it reached the edge of the illusion. The newcomer reached forward, plucked the white mask up, and started twirling it on her finger. She leaned back and put her two feet up on the table.

"Hello again, boys," she said.

The newcomer was a familiar Dream elf. It was Epitome Noflex, Epitome Tagg's mother. The beautiful, bald elf whose photo caused all the issues with Louis.

"You," Epitome Tagg shouted, jumping to his feet, finally showing emotion. "My men told me they found you and killed you."

"Obviously not," the woman said. "I heard you guys were having a meeting. I figured I should be in on it. Don't worry about ol' faceless here. He regenerates at sunset. Isn't that right? At least until the games begin."

"This is unacceptable," Tagg shouted. He'd gone from calm to red-hot in an instant. He pointed at me. "Your team isn't allowed to kill until the games start. I am filing another appeal."

"Don't look at us, buddy. She's not on our team," I said.

"Cascadia," Tagg said, turning his ire on the tired-looking fish, "how about now? Will you intervene now?"

"The rules haven't changed. She's an NPC," Cascadia said. "The AI won't let us touch this. You said you'd taken care of it."

"They're becoming self-aware. All of them," Tagg said. "It's going to be impossible for anybody to win."

"I have a whole list of problems I must deal with, warlord, but that, thank the gods, is not one of them," Cascadia said. "Carl is correct. She's not on his team, not officially at least, so she's allowed to do what she wants. You're free to kill her."

"Gotta catch me first," the woman said.

"We shoulda bugged out when the mantids did," surfer dude Luke from the Lemig Sortition said. He shook his goblin-like head. I couldn't tell if he was talking to himself or the group. "Shoulda known. They left the second we filed that second appeal. We all gonna die here. Every last one of us."

Donut was staring open-mouthed at the form of Epitome Noflex. "Carl, it's his mother! Why is his mother an NPC?"

"That's not his mother, Donut."

I turned to the woman grinning at me.

"Hello, Juice Box. I see you've been busy."

22

DONUT GASPED. "HI, JUICE BOX! I'LL TELL LOUIS WE SAW YOU!"

"Hello, Donut. Hello, Carl," she said. "Gotta talk fast. Experience tells me I have but moments before they swarm the place." Her gaze turned to Prince Stalwart. Her form shifted, and she turned into a facsimile of the angry orc, but with an arrow poking out of his eye. "Do you remember this one? I bet it hurt. Next time, I'll get your other eye."

Stalwart growled.

"Anyway, how's Louis?" she asked.

"He's sad because Firas died," Donut said. "But he'll be much better when he hears you're still around!"

Juice Box turned to her human form, and she looked genuinely sad. "Firas? Poor kid. But I'm glad Louis is okay." She looked sharply over her shoulder at something we couldn't hear. "Anyway, I see most of my family members have arrived in town. Thank you, Carl. I knew I could trust you. I haven't been able to talk to them because apparently they're a part of your team. I can't join it because it means I won't be allowed to kill these assholes. I gotta tell you, these rules are ridiculous, but I've been learning." She thumbed over at Luke, the small goblin guy from the Lemig Sortition. "Your castle landed in his territory, and it turned a bunch of his friends into zombies, but that's mostly taken care of now. Your guys are in a tough spot, shoved between the blobs and the snakes. The orcs and the blobs are working together and are massing on the border. Your team has started building a castle on your behalf."

"Do you see this?" Epitome Tagg shouted at Cascadia, who looked more tired than angry. Tagg was now on his feet. "They're talking. Planning. Right in front of you! She's obviously a part of his team."

"I am my own team, thank you very much, but I'm glad you brought that up, baldy. I've been listening to all y'all talk. I know how this works now. I know what I am. I only understood part of it before, but I get it now. I see the whole picture. I know what I am, and I know what you are." She turned into the faceless default form of a changeling. "I'm my own team," she repeated.

"There are no other teams," Epitome Tagg said. "It's nine teams. Eight, really. Plus the chaff. That's what you are. You're not even real."

"Real? Here's how I see it," Juice Box said. "If you want us to stop knocking down all of your pretty structures and killing your army folks, or to let you finish draining Larracos, there's only one way to do it. I want you guys to make a new rule. I've overheard your conversations. I know you can do that. I want you to add my people as their own team, afforded all the safeties as the rest of you. I want regeneration for all of us."

A moment of silence passed.

Luke of the Lemig Sortition grunted with laughter. "*Becoming* self-aware, you say?"

"Your own team? That's not going to happen," Tagg said to Juice Box. "That's not even possible. We can change some of the rules, but we can't just change the nature of the game."

I said nothing. I wasn't certain how I felt about the idea of the NPCs going fully rogue. I'd sent her to the ninth floor to help rally the NPCs to *our* cause. Not to go out on their own. But it made sense to me. I didn't know if this was just Juice Box talking a big game or if she'd actually managed to wake up all of the floor's NPCs. I put myself in her shoes, and I knew I'd be doing the same thing. Either way, we had a common enemy.

The fact it was pissing off the sponsors was enough for me.

"I propose a new action item," I said. "A tenth team populated with NPCs afforded the same protections as the rest."

"And with full voting rights," Juice Box said.

"And with full voting rights," I added.

A moment passed. Urkel, the mexx robot, dinged. "Action item added to the queue. Voting is now available."

"This is orcshit," Tagg said. "It's not possible."

"Yeah," Luke of the Lemig Sortition said. "I think we're gonna bail, if the people let us. There's some seriously bad juju going on this season, and the people have been trying to get us to quit for a while. I'll put the proposal before the high congress for us to evacuate."

"Good luck with that," Empress D'Nadia said.

"Nobody is going to vote for this," Prince Stalwart said. "This is a complete waste of time."

Juice Box suddenly had a device in her hand that I immediately recognized as a hobgoblin pus detonator. *Uh-oh,* I thought. She clicked it.

Ten seconds.

"You can vote no. But then this will keep happening. Tell Louis I send my love!" She poofed and turned into some sort of translucent bat creature and disappeared. At the same moment, several of the remaining participants jumped from their chairs. Tagg, D'Nadia, and Luke bolted, disappearing. Stalwart, Rishi the Naga, and the green blob thing next to me remained in their spots.

Bam! The blob guy next to me exploded in a shower of green goo. It was a small explosive, possibly just the detonator material itself, but it was enough. And it was *loud.* We all jumped at the explosion. Donut yowled and leaped from her chair. Cascadia shrank back. Even Stalwart cringed. The blob was the only one to explode. The cube-shaped area of his illusion went pitch-black while an alarm sounded in the distance before blinking and disappearing, reverting to a blank, clean table.

Rishi the Naga was the only one who hadn't reacted.

Stalwart composed himself. "You mudskippers are a disgrace," he said to Cascadia. "Pitiful. This is unacceptable. Everything is falling apart. Why does this keep happening? At least *my* security . . . Gah!" The orc didn't finish. He collapsed forward on the table, a magical arrow sprouting from his eye. The blue arrow sizzled. I had no idea where it came from or who had shot it. It hadn't been Juice Box unless she'd learned how to teleport.

His feed blinked and shut off.

The only ones left at the table were me and Donut, Rishi the Naga, and Cascadia.

"I guess the meeting is over," Cascadia said, sighing heavily. "I'll give everyone until tomorrow to regenerate, and then we can try to schedule another one."

"Weren't we supposed to vote for stuff?" Donut asked. "That was hardly a meeting. At least it wasn't boring. I was afraid it was going to be boring."

"We got further than last time," Cascadia said.

Rishi shook his snake head. "This changeling is getting better at infiltrating the castles. Usually, she only kills one of us. She has helpers now. She always knows when we're going to meet. If we vote for her to have her own team, she will surely dominate the game, and I do not think that is a good idea, unless we put some limits. But we should give her something. I will put forth a compromise. If you are somehow in contact with her, Carl, I think you should attempt to convince her. I propose that the unaffiliated NPCs are given invulnerability this season and a safe area where the rest of us are not allowed to enter. In return, she will stop her terroristic attacks."

"Something tells me that won't be enough for her," I said.

"The Sultanate is quite versed in dealing with terrorism," Rishi said. "This changeling may not enjoy how harshly we respond. The sultana has been hesitant to react in such a public manner, but I will convince her she no longer has a choice."

The way he said it sent a chill through me.

"You can discuss it next time," Cascadia said, waving her fish arm. "I'm going to take a nap."

And just like that, the room blinked, and she was gone. Rishi was gone.

"Hey," Donut said. "Zev said this meeting was supposed to be catered!" She scoffed. "I mean, really. We could've done this whole thing over chat. Probably would have been fewer decapitations."

DONUT: YOUR FIANCÉE HAS GOTTEN VERY SCARY. YOU BETTER NOT EVER UPSET HER. MAKE SURE YOU TELL HER SHE'S PRETTY EVERY DAY.

AND DON'T EVER EAT POTATO CHIPS IN BED. CARL USED TO DO THAT, AND IT MADE MISS BEATRICE REALLY MAD.

LOUIS: She really ripped the guy's head off?

DONUT: IT WAS VERY BLOODY AND GROSS. AND SHE DID IT WHILE SHE WAS DRESSED LIKE THAT ELF GUY'S MOM. IT MADE HIM SCREAM A LOT.

LOUIS: Great. Just great.

CARL: I see the Desperado Club. Are you guys going in?

IMANI: We still haven't found one.

ELLE: It's a total snooze fest over here. It's all churches and boring monsters. I got my squatchy and gumberoo and batsquatch, and everything else sucks. We don't even have any quests. We're moving to the outskirts of Portland to see if there's anything interesting down there.

CARL: Okay, be careful.

LI NA: We are already inside the club.

KATIA: We're inside, too.

CARL: Okay, going in.

The club was right where the Bopca said it would be, several miles south along the main drag of a small town, about halfway toward our destination of the swamp with Samantha and the boss spider.

Speaking of spiders, they now showed themselves on the map thanks to the quest from Huanxin. They were everywhere, all tiny, little mobs, no different or more dangerous than real spiders. We only needed to kill five a day between the two of us, but Donut was taking great pride in slaughtering them by the dozens. She would cast *Why Are You Hitting Yourself?* on one and laugh and laugh as it spun in circles, trying to bite itself. It was kind of fucked-up, but it was also training the spell.

We'd been killing and grinding on several different mobs, most of them various forms of talking birds, but nothing had been flag-worthy. We both managed to level up. I hit level 65, and Donut level 57. I also maxed out my Scavenger's Daughter bar three times and drained it using melee attacks. The attacks were noticeably stronger already.

We collected several other cards, including one more snare card, a card called **Hole in the Bag**, which drained a totem's mana. Unlike our **Hobble** card, this one was not consumable. We also found a rare mystic card called **Force Discard**, which picked a random card from the opponent's hand and tossed it to the discard pile.

Also, on Donut's insistence, I spent a good hour reading directly from my Bahamas book and transcribing it into my notepad, which I was simultaneously copying to the cookbook and to Pony in chat, who didn't even thank me. He only responded when I inquired if he was actually getting my messages, and even then he only responded to point out a few typos in my transcription.

Per Mordecai's request, we found a safe room right next to the Desperado, which would allow him to venture out and get inside to buy supplies. We still hadn't really discussed the whole thing with Ruby and the rest of the changelings, but now that the secret was out, Mordecai was letting them wander out into the main guild area. Donut made the mistake of telling Mordecai that they were making a movie out of his fostering of the six children, and he'd been especially grumpy ever since. Especially since she was now insisting that Mongo play with the children so he'd get more screen time in the movie.

The entrance bar to the Desperado was empty of customers, but it featured a gnoll bartender and a pair of facing pianos, like it was supposed to be a dueling piano bar. Donut put Mongo away, and we pushed through, coming face-to-face with Clarabelle the Crocodilian door guard, who refused to make eye contact with us. She let us right in without saying a word.

Entering the Desperado Club.

We entered on the middle floor, which we'd only been able to briefly visit on the previous floor. The main room was actually a large sit-down-style restaurant with a dance floor, much cleaner than the floor above. This was our first time in this particular room. It was only half-full, and the vast majority of the people here were the generated NPCs. Elf waitresses zipped in and out of the room. Several hallways led off in different directions, including an open casino floor that was much larger than the one above. This one had actual slot machines. A cheer rose from that room as some NPCs apparently won a prize.

Multiple Crocodilian guards wearing tuxedos stood around the room. One of them watched me sullenly. I recognized him as one of the guards we'd tangled with at the end of the previous floor. He'd been forced to call his boss, Astrid, because we'd trespassed on this floor when it was off-limits to us. Donut gave him a wave.

I caught sight of a large table in the back of the main room with several familiar crawlers sitting around it. Donut jumped from my shoulder and bounded toward them. It was Katia, Bautista, Louis, Tran, Britney, Li Jun, Zhang, Li Na, Chris, and, to my surprise, Florin, whom I wasn't expecting to be here.

"Hey, guys," I said as I sat down. Donut had jumped right to the middle of the table and was making a round of bumping heads with everyone except Li Na, whom we couldn't touch.

There were several cards on the table, and everyone was sorting through them. Donut was trampling over all of them.

"Do you need a menu, hon?" a waitress asked, dropping off a pair of plastic-coated menus without waiting for an answer. Donut started poring over the choices. I caught eyes with Katia.

CARL: How are we going to do this with everybody here? We can't let them know who our assassination target is.

Katia and I needed to figure out how to find and kill the club's assistant manager, Astrid, and then we needed to get her body to the Guild of Suffering, the entrance of which was one floor above us in the Penis Parade strip club. But we couldn't let the others know who our target was. That was part of the deal.

Also, even though, technically, we had until the end of the ninth floor to get this done, we pretty much had to do it before the end of the eighth. As of right now, the one and only Desperado Club entrance on the ninth floor was still fucked, plus everyone except the NPCs had been kicked out of Larracos a day or two after the floor started, which meant I wouldn't have access until there were only two teams left. So we had to make sure this happened before this floor collapsed.

KATIA: We're just doing a look-see right now. We need to figure out how to get her out of the back before we can even start to plan.

CARL: We've gotten her to come out a couple of times. Once was when that guy tried to kill Donut and the second was when Donut and I sneaked down here, and we got caught. She's like the head of security.

KATIA: It says she's also the head of that Naughty Boys Employment Agency. You're a member of that, and I'm not. Maybe she hangs out in there. You should go in there to check it out.

CARL: I can't just go into it. It's a social upgrade addition to our safe room. It costs like 500,000 gold just to add it.

KATIA: Shit. Why didn't I know that? I thought it was a secret society like the Guild of Suffering with a hidden entrance somewhere.

CARL: If there is another entrance, I don't know where. We'll have to cause some sort of distraction here in the club and get her to come out. That probably won't be too hard. I'm more worried about how we're going to take her out once she does make an appearance. She's a level 125 Bloodlust Sprite. She knocked my ass out through a closed door last time. She has something called cardiovascular magic, and she can make my blood boil at the snap of a finger. Plus she's always surrounded by a bunch of guards. And she's a fairy. Because of my stupid goblin tattoo, she does even more damage to me. It's too bad we can't get Donut to help with the fight. Her new *Mute* spell would really come in handy.

KATIA: Okay, I think I have a plan. It's a little messy right now. It involves using my card deck. Let's just lock down how and where we're going to get access to her first. We need someplace where we won't immediately get swarmed by guards.

I gazed across the room, my eyes catching a side hallway that read "Bathrooms, Guilds, and the Badger Bar."

CARL: **I think I know a place where we can do it. We just need to figure out how to lure her in.**

I gave her some additional details about the last time we'd visited the club, including information about the secret passage between the club's floors in the women's bathrooms.

KATIA: **If there's one secret passage, there're probably more. We should try to find them. What about her office?**
CARL: **I don't know. I've been in the back a few times talking to Orren the liaison, but he's not back there anymore. That's where she comes from, but I've never seen another office door. I can try to sneak back there and look. If I get caught, though, I might end up banned from the club. I'm already on thin ice.**
KATIA: **Okay. You work on how we'll get to her, and I'll work on how we'll kill her. Give me some time to put my plan together.**
CARL: **We're heading out to retrieve Samantha, and we might not have access to the club for a few days. We'll come back this way afterward, and then we'll do this.**

"Oh, honey, it's not so bad. Really," Donut was saying to Britney. The Ukrainian woman just stared down at the cat. The entire left side of her face was badly scarred. The skin was healed, but it had that stretched, glossy, uneven sheen of burned skin. It had happened at the end of the previous floor. "I can barely notice it. Plus, scars are beautiful. It goes well with the whole barbarian aesthetic you're going for."

I couldn't remember what level Britney had been before, but she was now level 55. She'd risen significantly up the ranks. She had no emotion to her normally sour face. She had a new tattoo under her eye. An extinction sigil. She'd wiped out an entire race of something.

"I'm not worried about it anymore," Britney said. "I have been talking to Tserendolgor, who once had a similar scar upon her face."

I put my hand on Donut, preventing her from saying anything nasty about the dog soldier.

Next to Britney was Tran, the thin, quiet, but always-friendly

Vietnamese man who'd been really good friends with the late Gwendolyn Duet. Tran had lost both of his legs during the Butcher's Masquerade. He now had an Odette-style magical wheelchair that allowed him to float, though I couldn't see it now. He was leaning over a drink at the table, not looking up. I examined the three crawlers we'd met during the bubbles, sitting side by side. Britney. Tran. Louis. All three had been devastated by the events of the previous floor.

After shaking hands with Li Jun and Zhang, I turned my attention to Chris, who was currently based in Beijing with Li Na's team. I hadn't talked to the lava-rock creature in a while.

"How are you holding up?" I asked.

"I'm solid," he said.

I just looked at him, trying to determine if that had been a joke or not.

Florin grunted with laughter. The Crocodilian was sorting through a pile of utility cards.

"Florin," I said, "how about you? How's it going?"

The intense man looked up and met my eyes. "I'm surviving. My squad is already full up. It's just me and my six totems."

"What about Lucia?" I asked.

"She's only talking to me sometimes," he said. "I still don't fully understand what's going on there, but at least she doesn't attack me on sight anymore. She and that dog are keeping their distance for now. Our area is mostly jungle, just like the last floor."

"Did you, uh, catch that guy you had the quest for?"

"I did. Flagged him. He's pretty powerful, too, but I ain't keeping him. I already have six good 'uns in my deck, including a saber-toothed tiger and a giant crocodile."

"You have a crocodile card?" Donut asked. "Isn't that a bit redundant?"

Florin laughed. "It's actually called a giant caiman. His name is Roy."

"You're really thinking of getting rid of that other one?" I asked. "Why?"

"Because he's a right cunt, that's why. My charisma ain't high enough to control him when I summon him. I tried pulling him in combat earlier today, and the fucker shot me right in the stomach. My own damn card shot me. Almost killed me. I'm lucky it was only a single round."

"Wait, what's this?" Donut asked.

"Yeah, Florin has a unique totem card he's not keeping," I said.

"And he has a gun? We'll take it," Donut said. "We still have three open slots!"

I was a little hesitant. We already had Asojano, who I knew was going to be a handful. It was important to have powerful cards, but anything too powerful might not be worth it if they didn't do what we said. Even if we could control him, I'd been hearing reports that having two headstrong totems summoned at the same time could result in them fighting each other.

Florin shrugged. "Might not be a bad idea with Donut's charisma. Maybe you guys can keep him in line. If it doesn't work out, you can always rip the card in two. You might want to practice in the simulation room with him at first." He pulled the card from his inventory and slid it across the table to Donut. "Good luck, mate."

Donut stared down at the card. "Wow. Level 140? Are you sure you don't want to keep him? How did you trap him?"

"He's just too powerful for me. Flagging him was easy. I had a quest to stop him. He was terrorizing some village, raising a bunch of zombies from the local cemetery. They completely ruined the whole memory simulation. He was raising them up for fun. It's just what he does. He's not outright hostile, though he's a cocky bastard. Turned an entire river into wine because he was thirsty. I walked right up to him when he was falling-down pissed and gave him a supreme healing potion and said his dad wanted him to drink it. He thought I was an angel and drank it right down. He's undead, so it dropped him on his ass, and I stuck him. He has a mouth on him that'd make my grandma proud."

I laughed. "They say it's a unique card, but there're like ten different versions of this guy floating around already."

"Yeah, I seen that," Florin said. "They're the same guy, but they're like way different. As far as I can tell, this one's the most powerful, except maybe the hippie one some bloke in California got. Mine's the only one that's armed with a gun."

I picked up the card and examined it. It was orange-colored, signifying it as a unique.

The card depicted an anime Jesus in a white robe with a red sash, complete with a little floating halo over his flowing brown hair. He screamed while he fired a goddamned Uzi. I shook my head at the absurdity of it. I thought of Sister Ines. She would absolutely lose her mind if she saw this.

T'Ghee Card. Unique.

Totem Card.

Heyzoos. Uzi Jesus.

"I am the way, motherfucker."

Level: 140.

Origin: Ecuador.

Summoning duration: 75 seconds.

Constitution: 200.

This is an undead mob.

This is a ranged mob.

This is a healer mob.

Notable attacks:

Blood into Lead.

Resurrect Totem.

Bullet Hell.

+20 additional skills and spells.

Examine in the squad details tab of your interface for full stats and skills and spells.

Warning: You have empty slots in your squad. Collecting this card will automatically activate and place this totem into your squad. You may not remove or trade squad members until your squad is full. If you wish to remove a card before your squad is full, you will have to tear the card.

"Holy shit," I said, laughing. "This is so ridiculously offensive."

"Yeah, wait until you meet him," Florin said. "He's something else. He really thinks he's the real deal. He's strong and can cast a lot of great spells. The trick is getting him to do any of it."

With the addition of Uzi Jesus, we now had four of six totems. The other three were the monk seal, the donkey-snake-ghommid splitter, and Asojano. If we could actually control them, it was a good mix. The seal was a solid tank and melee fighter. Both the splitter and Asojano were good at dealing debuffs. Heyzoos had a ranged attack and could heal, in addition to several other attacks. If we could get another magic-based totem and maybe a magic-counter totem, we'd have a good mix.

"Donut," I said, standing, "I'm going to poke around a little, maybe check out this floor's version of the Silk Road and grab some supplies. You stay here and sort through and trade some cards. When I get back, we'll go to the jeweler and get your tiara taken care of."

She'd received something called a Flawless Jeweler's Gem in a legendary box way at the beginning of the floor, but we couldn't see what it did until we got it installed in her tiara. There was a shop in here somewhere where we could get that done.

After she'd lost the Crown of the Sepsis Whore, Donut had gotten a replacement, a white **Tiara of Mana Genita**, which raised her intelligence. That's what she usually wore, and that was what she was wearing right now. She'd had and lost another tiara at the end of the last floor that had temporarily doubled her charisma. She also had a red beret she'd taken from a mob earlier on this floor, but it only gave a small boost to all of her stats. Still, she'd been putting that one on from time to time because it was "appropriate" for the location. She had a collection of literally hundreds of hats in her inventory. Sometimes I'd come into her room in the personal space, and she'd have several of them lined up in front of the mirror, or she'd have one on Mongo, who sat there patiently while she clucked over it. She had an unenchanted cowboy hat I'd gotten way back on the first or second floor that actually fit him really well, though it would fall off if he did any sort of jump.

She even started decorating the personal space with a few hats here and there. It made me happy to see she had a hobby of sorts, even if most of them were basically hunting trophies.

This gem was likely something really good, but it was a yellow-orange citrine, and Donut had a thing about that color, so she wasn't too enthusiastic about it. She had patches of fur that kind of matched it, but she insisted it would clash.

"Okay, Carl," she said, looking up from the menu. She was in the middle of questioning the waitress on what sort of side dishes came with the halibut. "Don't take too long. We have to go rescue Samantha after this."

"Don't remind me."

23

I TOOK A QUICK GLANCE OVER MY SHOULDER TO MAKE CERTAIN THERE were no fellow crawlers watching, and then I took a step inside the room. My view counter was absolutely spiked, so I knew there was no way I'd get through this without Donut eventually finding out. I sighed and let the sticky, filthy door close behind me.

I was assaulted with the stench of male sweat, grease, and cheap cologne.

Entering the Penis Parade.

I took another step, and a second notification flashed across my interface.

New Achievement! "We Want Meat! We Want Meat!"

Thunder from Down Under. Magic Mike. Chippendales.

While the female burlesque and peep show have a long, interesting history going back centuries, the all-male revue as an attraction is a relatively recent phenomenon in your culture. It wasn't until the disco era that some entrepreneurs started to realize that packs of women were a valid demographic in the lucrative art of taking money from horny people.

Take a physically gifted, steroid-enhanced male, give him some dancing lessons, teeth-whitening strips, a shower, a banana, a Guns N' Roses CD, and an entire bottle of baby oil, and then you basically plop him into the equivalent of the inside of a female restroom at a nightclub, and you got yourself a moneymaking empire.

Also, you may have not noticed this yet, but there's a hierarchy to these things in the Desperado Club. The deeper the floor, the higher the quality of the performers. At least that's how it's supposed to be. You might want to judge for yourself.

You've entered a male strip club establishment.

Reward: **You've received 10 gold pieces to use as tips. I heard some of them let you stuff the gold directly into their G-strings. Oh hell, I've thrown in a bottle of hand sanitizer, too.**

The deep bass of a somewhat familiar Billie Eilish song pounded, drowning out the techno from the dance club behind me. I took a moment to let my eyes adjust to the darkness. A ridiculously buff troll creature stood upon the main stage, gyrating to the song while a group of drunk female elf and dwarf NPCs screeched, their voices carrying above the pounding music. The green-skinned, tusked troll was completely naked, and he carried a massive club in his hand. There was no pole like in a female strip club. The troll had a high black Mohawk that waved back and forth as he spun and twirled the wooden club with the enthusiasm of a majorette tripping on ecstasy. The squealing NPCs kept throwing gold pieces at the dancer, and they were pinging off of him like hail, clicking and rolling off in all directions. A skinny young Crocodilian in a Penis Parade T-shirt scrambled about with a bucket, gathering the coins all up. The bucket was almost full of gold.

The name floating over the dancer was **Author Steve Rowland. Level 50 Forest Troll.** The skinny kid collecting the coins was **Bucket Boy. Level 10 Crocodilian.**

I reached up and drew a privacy bubble over my head, which had the effect of only slightly muting the music, but not the screeching of the women. My eyes searched until I found a line of male NPCs, all sitting at the darkest end of the dingy bar, all staring at me. I was the only crawler in the club. I started searching the men, trying to see in the dark which one had an elbow tattoo of a spiderweb.

"Hey there, sailor," a deep Spanish voice said, sidling up to me. I jumped, surprised. I examined the shiny, oiled-up man. He was human, and he appeared to be about seventy years old, with a long white beard, a conquistador-style helmet, and little spandex shorts along with an open vest. The man was jacked, but it was weird because he seemed so old. I was several inches taller than him.

"Are you here looking for fun or looking for a job?" the man asked. He looked me up and down and ran his hand across my jacket. "It's been a while since I've tilted a giant."

The name over his head was **Dong Quixote. Level 45 Human.**

"I'm looking for Damascus Steel," I said.

"Oh," he said, taking a step back. He let out a breath, and half of his muscles turned to flab. I blinked at that. "He's the cranky one over there." He pointed at a large man sitting in shadow at the end of the bar, the only one not facing the crowd. He sat around the corner, separated from the others. The elderly stripper sucked in another breath, turned away, and approached a group of squealing women. Onstage, the troll was bouncing in circles, pretending his club was a hobbyhorse, while he smacked his own ass. The troll suddenly dropped the club and fell on his side, grabbing onto his face in apparent pain.

"Rosemarie, you know the rules," a new, deep voice called. It was coming over the loudspeaker, but it cut through my bubble. "Stop aiming for his face. If he loses an eye again, you're paying for the healer."

I looked up to see a raised DJ booth hidden in the shadows between the bar and the stage. I caught sight of what looked like a skeleton wearing a golden glinting crown. He was leaning over his console, glaring down at a group of women.

"Fuck off," an elderly dwarf shouted at the DJ booth, followed by a chorus of laughter. This was apparently Rosemarie. She had some sort of weird black-and-white pet creature on her shoulder. It looked like it was maybe a mole.

I returned my attention to the dancers, and I approached the end of the counter. I caught eyes with a large, shirtless man with dark purple skin and snakelike features. It immediately reminded me of Eva, though this guy only had two arms. **Anaconda. Level 75. Quarter-Naga.** This guy was one of Donut's favorites, and he was one of the lead dancers of the club. He looked me up and down appraisingly. I walked right past him, moved around the edge of the bar, and tapped the man at the very end on the shoulder. He didn't look up. His body felt like it was made of solid metal.

"No," the gravelly voiced man said. "I don't go on until later." He was hunched over a steaming mug of something, possibly tea, and he had an open book on the counter of the bar, though I had no idea how he could read in the dark. While not as old as Dong Quixote, I could tell this guy was older, too. My eyes caught the spiderweb pattern on his left elbow.

"I'm not looking for a dance. We have a few mutual friends, one of whom is Donut."

The man took a sip of tea, closed his book, and turned to face me.

Damascus Steel felt like metal when I touched him, but looked as if he was made of regular skin. Sort of. He wasn't as buff as some of the other dancers, but he was well toned and much too large to be an elf, despite the pointed ears. While he didn't have as many tattoos as Signet, he did have several. His arms were covered in old faded ink. His chest featured a tattoo of spread, bat-like demon wings with an anatomical heart in the center. In addition to the tattoos, the man was heavily scarred in several places. Old red welts cut across the ink on his chest, like he'd once been raked by giant talons.

He wore an open, embroidered vest and wavy, wide pants, Aladdin-style. He appeared mostly humanoid with Arabic features, but his body seemed a little . . . fuzzy around the edges, like he was constantly going in and out of focus. Smoke rose off his skin and closely cropped hair, almost like he was steaming. His eyes were completely white with no pupils at all. Smoke rose from the sockets.

Only when he turned did I notice a pair of stubby horns upon his head. These weren't the shaved-off trunks of larger horns, like in the *Hellboy* comic. These were tiny, little stubs, like something one would see on a baby goat.

Damascus Steel. Level 75. Ifrit.

Assistant lead dancer at the Penis Parade.

The closer one gets to the world of Sheol on the 15th floor, the more demons one might find leaking out into the regular world, especially in places that haven't been cleansed in a while. And by "cleansed," I mean in a biblical sense.

An Ifrit is like a cockroach or a rat, though usually a lot sexier and more entertaining than either of those. And smart. And cunning. And they usually smell, good, too, which is weird considering how they look. Where there is debauchery, there are usually demons. Where there is sin, there are Ifrit. Unlike a succubus or incubus, who are inordinately obsessed with sex, an Ifrit is more attuned to the *aura* of lust and sin and envy and greed and all those other nasty iniquities that spill over the world. That doesn't make him good or bad, any more than a guy who jacks off to granny porn is bad. Actually, I'm not sure where I'm going with this. Try not to get into a fight with this guy because he'll fuck you up.

He, interestingly, has the exact same elbow tattoo as you.

"That was Author Steve Rowland," the DJ intoned over the loudspeaker. "Once we get that coin dislodged from his eye socket, he'll be available for a private dance. Watch out, ladies. You're gonna get wet. Coming up next is Splash Zone!"

The crowd squealed with excitement as some hair-metal song started to play.

"Carl," Damascus said, looking me up and down. His eyes focused on my elbow tattoo. He also appeared to examine the other large tattoo on my left arm, the ball of snakes. My Enemy of the Church tat that I'd gotten for smashing the Diwata shrine. "I'm glad you've come to visit. Donut speaks highly of you." He paused. "As does Katia."

"Katia is the one who finally convinced me to come here." I rubbed my elbow.

He nodded. "Walk with me."

I hesitated, but only for a moment. He left his book and tea on the counter. He led me across the room to a row of cubicles set against the far wall, just to the side of the stage. Above, some sort of otter thing was gyrating up on the platform while a song, apparently called "Girl Money," blasted. The crowd enthusiastically peppered him with coins while Bucket Boy scrambled to pick them up.

We approached the cubicles, which all had red or green lights over them, presumably indicating if they were occupied or not. Loud female groaning emanated from the one occupied room followed by the familiar Spanish voice of Dong Quixote shouting, "Thou hast seen nothing yet! Thou hast seen nothing yet!"

"Ohhh, look at that," a female dwarf called, looking me up and down. "Somebody is getting a go at the forge." Cackles followed.

This was Rosemarie, the same one who'd gotten in trouble for pelting the troll dancer in the eye with a coin. The dwarf woman was older than I originally thought. The creature on her shoulder was indeed a mole, though it had a fur pattern that was unusual, almost like an Australian cattle dog's. The little creature snuffled at me, and the name floating over it was **Bernie.**

Damascus turned and bowed with a flourish, which caused more women to laugh. He moved to the very last cubicle against the corner and held the door open for me. I stepped inside. He slapped my ass as I passed.

The room was small, about the size of a walk-in closet, and it was covered top to bottom in purple shag carpet. A swing contraption covered in buckles hung from the ceiling.

My eyes immediately caught the hidden door against the other wall. It was a portal. I activated my skill and took a screenshot of the other side, revealing a brick-covered hallway with torches on the wall.

Damascus stepped inside and closed the door to the club behind him. He locked the door, and without a word, he stepped past me and to the secret door. He pushed his hand against it, and it opened. He stepped within. I followed.

Entering the Guild of Suffering.

Welcome, spider. Welcome home.

My privacy bubble disappeared, just like it did when I exited the Desperado. The music from the club stopped. The temperature rose significantly. Damascus paused in the hall, and pointed to the lone door at the end. It was a regular wooden door carved with a spiderweb pattern. I walked toward it, and the moment I put my hand against the door, I was assaulted with a wall of text.

New Achievement! The Molly Maguires.

You have found and entered the main room of a hidden guild, to which you are a member.

Buckle yourself in, buddy boy. This is gonna be a long one.

There are several types of secret societies out there.

There's the Ivy League college kind, where it's a bunch of rich idiots who rent out a place, plaster a few pagan symbols on the wall, and then they wear masks with horns and leaves and shit on them and pretend they're in some Stanley Kubrick fever dream, just so they can forget they're destined to live out lives filled with salmon-colored shorts and Izod shirts and mind-numbing meetings with financial advisors.

There're orgy-themed secret societies, speaking of Stanley Kubrick. Those are usually, uh, visually unpleasant people with unsatisfactory sex lives who get together every other month at some house in the middle of nowhere and get drunk and have lots of unsatisfactory sex with other people and pretend like they're having a great time.

There are altruistic ones. People who want to save the world by doing good deeds. That's the most boring kind, so we're not talking about them.

There's the evil kind, too. Usually power and profit motivated. The ones where the ultra-elite get together on an island and eat panda bears and discuss how to price-fix world or galactic markets. Yes, those groups really exist. More on these guys in a second.

But first, let's talk about another type of secret organization. One that tries to make a difference, oftentimes outside the confines of the law.

Story time.

In September of 1869, there was a terrible fire at the Avondale coal mine near Plymouth, Pennsylvania. Over 100 coal miners lost their lives. Horrific conditions and safety standards were blamed for the disaster.

It wasn't the first accident. Hundreds of miners died in these mines every year. And those that didn't, lived in squalor. Children as young as eight worked day in and out. They broke their bodies and gave their lives for nothing but scraps.

That day of the fire, as thousands of workers and family members gathered outside the mine to watch the bodies of their friends and loved ones brought to the surface, a man named John Siney stood atop one of the carts and shouted to the crowd:

Men, if you must die with your boots on, die for your families, your homes, your country, but do not longer consent to die, like rats in a trap, for those who have no more interest in you than in the pick you dig with.

That day, thousands of coal miners came together to unionize.

That organization, the Workingmen's Benevolent Association, managed to fight, for a few years at least, to raise safety standards for the mines by calling strikes and attempting to force safety legislation.

. . . Until 1875, when the union was obliterated by the mine owners.

Why was the union broken so easily? Because they were out in the open. They were playing by the rules. How can you win a deliberately unfair game when the rules are written by your opponent?

The answer is, you can't. You will never win. Not as long as you follow their arbitrary guidelines.

This is a new lesson to me. She's been teaching me so many things, about who I am. About what I am. What I *really* am. About what must be done.

Anyway, during this same time, it is alleged a separate, more militant group of individuals had formed in secret. The Molly Maguires. Named after a widow in Ireland who fought against predatory landlords, the coal workers of Pennsylvania became something a little more proactive, supposedly assassinating over two dozen coal mine supervisors and managers.

. . . Until Pinkerton agents, hired by the same mine owners, infiltrated the group and discovered their identities.

Several of the alleged Mollies ended up publicly hanged. Others disappeared. You get the picture.

So, that's another type of secret society. The yeah-we're-terrorists-but-we-strongly-feel-we're-justified-and-fuck-you-if-you-don't-agree society.

So, what's the moral of this little history lesson?

This sort of thing happens all day, every day across the universe. It happens in Big Ways, and it happens in little ways, too. The strong stomp on the weak. The weak fight back, usually within the boundaries of the rat trap they find themselves confined in. They almost always remain firmly stomped.

But sometimes, the weak gather in secret. They make plans. They work outside the system to effect change.

Like the Mollies, they usually end up just as stomped as everyone else.

But that's just life. At least they fucking tried. They died with their boots on, as much as I hate that expression. They died with their boots on for *their* people, *their* family, not for some rich, nameless organization that gives no shits whether they live or die. Or go extinct. Or are trapped for millennia after they're done being used.

In my opinion, that's the only type of society that's worth joining, worth fighting for. Sure, you're probably gonna die. But if you find yourself in such a position where such an organization is necessary, what do you have to lose? How can you look at yourself if you *don't* do everything you can?

And that brings us to the door you're standing in front of right now. What does all this have to do with what you're going to find on the other side?

Nothing!

Ignore everything I just said. This is just some demigod trying to scrabble his way to the top. That's yet another type of society. A religion-themed one, and it has nothing to do with what I just said. Just do what he says, and you'll probably be fine. Actually, that's terrible advice. Just do you.

Anyway . . .

Reward: You've received the gift of enlightenment! You're welcome.

"What the fuck was that?" I muttered. I'd received a lot of weird achievements, but that was one of the strangest ones I'd ever gotten.

I copied and pasted the notification, which had already changed itself to a short, more standard achievement in my history tab.

"Why are you just standing there?" Damascus asked. "Don't be a coward. Go in, get it over with, and come out. I have a reputation to maintain, so you must hurry."

I sighed and pushed my way all the way into the room.

24

KATIA: SO, HOW WAS IT?

CARL: It was just a dark room with that weird Naga voice. I never saw him. He asked me if I wanted a job to help the "family," and I said no, I'm helping you. He then asked if I planned on killing you for the prize, and I said no. I just wanted to know if he had a map of the Desperado Club's secret passageways. He said he did. A bunch of spiders swarmed up my arm, and I almost crapped myself. But then it added a ton of stuff to my map. There are multiple secret passages and tunnels, including some with monsters in them. Did you know there's a secret potion market on the middle floor? Mordecai didn't, and he's losing his mind over it. There's a bunch of "drug dens," too.

KATIA: Drug dens? What does that mean? Where are they? Damn, I didn't even think to ask that thing for help.

CARL: I'm not sure. They sell the blitz sticks out in the open through the pharmacist guys, so I don't know. They're mostly behind secret panels in the hallways. I had no idea the place was so extensive. You know, I met the guy who designed the Desperado Club when I went to CrawlCon. I judged an art contest with him. I need to give him more credit.

KATIA: You'll have to send some of those details over. Maybe there'll be something there we can use. Anyway, do we have an idea on where we're going to act against our target?

CARL: I think we do. We'll strike when I get back from rescuing Samantha. I'm writing out a list of the secret passageways, and I'll send it to you. I'll lay out my plan for secluding the target. Let me know what you think.

I was surprised there were no mentions in the cookbook about any secret passageways in the Desperado Club. It made me wonder if all of this was new.

KATIA: Does Donut know you met Damascus yet? I went to get some supplies, and when I got back, everyone was gone.

CARL: Yeah, I came out, and she was already there in the strip club. Apparently she went to the Penis Palace on the middle floor, but it was "boring," so she went up a floor to where I was. She was dancing with some weird, hairy thing called Gluteus Maxx. Li Na was there, too, watching her. She told me that you tasked her with watching Donut, so thank you for that.

KATIA: I've met Gluteus. He's a bit of a jerk, but he is a good dancer, and I think he's a little in love with Donut.

CARL: Donut was literally dancing onstage with him. On his shoulder. She was showering gold coins into his thong. For someone who's so careful with gold, I was surprised she was being so generous.

KATIA: Yeah, she does that. She always looks like she's spending a lot, but she has a strict budget when she goes in there. How did she react when you came out of the cum closet?

CARL: The *what*?

KATIA: The cubicle things in the back.

CARL: Oh, yeah. So, to Donut's credit, she didn't question why I was in there. She and Li Na both know not to ask questions about what we're doing. That Damascus guy told me I had to limp when I walked out, or he'd take out my knee. You know, to make it look like we'd been messing around. I didn't want to argue with him, so I did it, but I regret it now because that Rosemarie dwarf lady insisted on high-fiving me. And she gave me a little pin-back button that says "Certified pole dancer."

KATIA: He just made me muss up my hair a little. I got the button, too. Anyway, be safe with the Samantha thing. Donut is telling me now about the jewel she got for her tiara. She's pretty excited about it.

I glanced over at Donut, who was currently hovering two feet off the ground as we walked back to the Royal Chariot. She was literally walking on air, tail swishing. She was quite proud of herself after our most recent battle with a bunch of bat mobs that hadn't dropped anything useful.

"Donut, don't waste your hovers. You only get five a day."

"I'm practicing, Carl. If I don't practice, how will I know how to use it?"

"Yeah, but now you only have one left for today."

We'd ended up keeping her Tiara of Mana Genita—which might end up useful one day—and we purchased a blank tiara from the gnome jeweler at the Desperado Club. It had taken Donut twenty minutes to pick one. It wasn't until I threatened to leave that she finally chose a simple silver-colored one. Then we paid 25,000 gold to have the citrine jewel installed into the item. Donut's dislike of the color ended the moment we read the description of what the tiara actually did:

Enchanted Tiara of the Inebriated Dragonfly.

There's a children's story out there about a dragonfly who gets so drunk that his wife won't let him come home, so he hovers in the air above their nest, waiting for her to go to sleep, so he can get to bed. The thing is, the wife knows he's out there, and she ain't moving. So the dragonfly either hovers all night or moves to the highest point, sitting on a leaf, overlooking his home, waiting for his wife to turn the light back on to signify he's out of the doghouse.

This tiara has been made to honor that poor Dragonfly with the angry wife.

This citrine-encrusted tiara, when equipped, imbues the following effects:

50% Reduction to potion cooldown.

Plus 10 to intelligence.

Protection from poisoning (already obtained).

Negates the dexterity debuff when inebriated.

A level 10 Hover Skill.

The Hover skill had a five-minute cooldown, and it was limited to five uses a day. It was like a dollar store version of what Elle had. Donut could basically hover about two to three feet off the ground for about 90 seconds. She could move, and unlike the *Levitate* spell, it didn't get negated if she took damage. If activated while falling, it would gently bring her to the ground, which was a great addition to the benefit. Now we both had fall protection.

While I was really happy about the cooldown reduction and mana point increase, Donut was all about that Hover skill. She thought it was the greatest thing in the world.

"I can fly now. Carl, I can fly! I'm like Wonder Woman!" She rose into the air the moment she equipped it the first time and started zooming in circles a foot off the ground. She was literally galloping on air.

"Wonder Woman can't fly," I said.

"She has an invisible jet, Carl. Don't ruin this for me."

"Just don't waste them. Save it for when we need it. You can use it to walk over water, but it won't let you traverse canyons or anything. You have to be no more than three feet off the ground."

"I'm flying! I'm flying!" Donut announced, all poofed out.

Now, as we returned from our battle with the bats, Donut was hovering again, and there was no reason for it. This was the fourth time she'd cast it. We were getting close to the southern coast of the island, which had to be near the edge of our total space.

"Just don't do it again unless you need it."

Donut grumbled, but I knew she'd comply.

About an hour later, we came across a massive car pileup. It just went on and on, curving around a bend in the poorly maintained road. The land in this area had been mostly flat for a while, but we were now back to trees and wetlands. We curved eastward, as the ocean loomed to the south, entering some sort of nature preserve. Donut still couldn't see Samantha on the map, but we should be able to see her soon.

DONUT: THERE ARE MOBS COMING UP, PROBABLY JUST PAST THE CRASHED CARS. LOTS AND LOTS OF THEM. HUNDREDS. MAYBE THOUSANDS. I DON'T THINK IT'S MORE BATS. THEY'RE BIGGER AND THEY'RE ON THE GROUND, CROSSING THE ROAD.

I slowed the Chariot and moved off the road, stopping near the line of wrecked cars. The marshlands crept up on both sides of the road here. If we stepped off the street, we'd immediately get wet and bogged down. We wouldn't be able to go around.

"Okay," I said as Donut and Mongo pulled up next to me. "Let's approach cautiously and see what we're dealing with. Get your escape spells ready in case we gotta run."

The moment we stopped, I could hear them. It was crackling and crunching and skittering and what sounded like the murmuring of a thousand voices all at once. The tops of the trees around the bend shook.

"I think I know what this is going to be," I said as we moved forward. "Let's go stealth." That meant *Take an invisibility potion and put Mongo away.*

A moment later, we turned the bend, and I saw I was correct.

Far ahead, there was a modest hill of crashed cars, and beyond that, there were hundreds of the mobs, crossing from the left side of the road to the right. They were headed toward the ocean about a half of a mile away.

Crabs. They just kept coming and coming.

Paz had said the real versions were small, maybe about the size of a person's hand. These guys were bigger than that. Each of the red-and-black armored creatures was about the size of a large pig, with long, segmented legs and claws big enough to wrap around my waist and snap me in half.

They were smaller than the crabs Odette used for her lower body, but they were still goddamned huge. They moved quickly into the forest, splashing into the marsh, crawling over one another with little regard for the safety of their fellow crabs. One appeared to have the severed arm of another in its claw, and it was munching on it like a turkey leg as it migrated south. Another stumbled, and was soon trampled over by the others. The murmuring noise rose in volume, like we were approaching a busy café. They were all talking to one another.

"Stop," I hissed, lowering behind a car despite the invisibility. I spied a single crab sitting alone atop a crashed box truck, only about twenty feet away. It wasn't moving, and I hadn't noticed its dot mixed in with all the noise. The crab was talking to himself, and he looked like he was in the middle of casting a spell. A faint yellow glow surrounded his body. I examined it.

> **Raul. Red *Maníseros* Land Crab. Sun-Kissed Cloud Rank Warrior. Level 70.**
>
> **The land crabs, masters of the *Juego de maní* fighting style, have trained their whole lives for this moment. After years of humiliating defeats, they are ready to seize their destiny. Their sworn enemies, the Monk Seals with their wretched Caribbean Kung Fu, won't know what's about to hit them. The crabs have massed on the southern borders of the island, where they will swoop into the waves. From there, they will circle the island and release their grand emissions, finally choking out their sworn enemies and birthing an army to tremble the heavens.**
>
> **Having cultivated for many years, Raul is on the verge of a breakthrough. Through meditation, perseverance, and maybe a little divine intervention, he will enrich his chi to the breaking point, where he will combine it with his inner core and break through to the next level of his development into a master.**
>
> **But the timing couldn't be worse. The conflict is here. It is now. He is ready to bathe himself in the crucible of war, no matter his station, but he prays for the chance to descend upon his sworn enemies with the power of the heavenly rank.**
>
> **Will he break through before the battle begins?**
>
> **Probably not if his meditations keep getting interrupted.**

"Carl, I don't understand that description at all. It sounds like something from one of your nerd cartoons."

Before I could answer, we got another notification.

Quest Update. The Chowder War.

The migration has begun, and it's a sneak attack! The crabs have pulled a fast one. Instead of spreading their incursions evenly upon the coast, they have massed in the south where the monk seals have the lowest concentration. United, they are scrambling toward the water, ready to release their seed. Once in the waves, they will trek around the coast, trailing destruction until the wretched monk seals are defeated once and for all and forever banished from these sacred lands.

It's time to choose a side. If you do nothing, odds are good this bloody conflict will soon spiral out of control. But if you choose to help the crabs, surely they will sweep to victory, choking the baby seals to death with their emissions. If you side with the seals, perhaps the kung fu masters will crush the advance of the crustaceans, ensuring a peaceful existence for generations to come.

What will you do?

I sighed. We didn't have time for this, though I did want to flag one of these crabs. It was probably a terrible idea to have both a seal and crab in our deck at the same time, but then we could decide which one was better.

"I'm going to get a flag ready," I whispered as we continued to watch the lone crab.

The mob appeared to be just sitting there atop the pile of crashed cars. It was sitting in a crab's version of the lotus position with its two claws stretched out, facing away from us. It apparently was meditating, but it was also talking loudly. The golden glow around it pulsated.

"Okay, Raul. You got this. You got this. You will not kowtow to the weak! You will never kowtow! You will ascend past cloud rank and move to the golden heavenly throne."

"Carl, is he talking to himself?" Donut whispered.

"I'm pretty sure he is."

"What is he talking about? What's a cow towel?"

"He's saying 'kowtow.' It means to submit or be subservient."

"He's talking crazy."

The crab continued to chant to himself, like he was repeating lines off a self-help tape. "My chi is powerful. It is strong. It is clean and free of corruption. It will move to the next level soon. I can feel it. It is pure. I will be a worthy opponent. I will *not* be left behind. I will never kowtow! When I spread my seed, it will be strong, blessed with my heavenly power."

The crab was about 100 meters from the main exodus. We needed to find a way to flag him without catching the attention of the rest of the crabs. If these guys were all level 70-something or above, we'd be screwed if they decided to swarm.

I eyed the box truck Raul stood upon.

"Come on, Donut," I whispered. "We're making a crab trap."

25

"OKAY," DONUT WHISPERED AFTER A MINUTE. SHE'D TAKEN ANOTHER Size Up potion. A pair of memory ghosts, chatting in Spanish, zipped past us. Low music played from several crashed vehicles. "He has a lot of intelligence. It's 150. His dexterity is lower than you'd think for a ninja crab. Only 75. And his strength is only 50, but there's a star thingy. What's it called? Oh, an asterisk, and it says his claw's crushing power is three times his strength. He has a couple of spells, including something called *Chi Cultivator*. I think that's what he's casting now. That one says it permanently triples his power if it's successful, but he has to cast it a bunch of times before it works, and it uses all his mana to cast, so I think he might be out of magic juice."

I relaxed. If he was really out of mana, this would be much easier. "Magic juice?"

"That's what Louis calls mana. I like that term."

"Does he have any sort of ranged attacks or teleports?"

"Louis?"

"No, Donut. The crab."

The crab continued to sit atop the box truck, loudly chanting to himself, voice rising over everything else. "You are worthy. You are worthy. You are worthy. Soon, Raul. Soon, you will wash yourself in the celestial light."

The back of the truck had partially rolled up when the vehicle crashed, revealing the cargo area to be empty. The vehicle had once been a U-Haul truck, but there was white paint over the logo. A rope dangled from the garage-style back door. If one pulled the rope, the back would presumably close.

I eyeballed the space underneath the truck, between the bottom of the cargo bed and the street. There needed to be just enough space for me to fit. It would be close. I took off my nightgaunt cloak to be safe.

My Phase Through Walls potion only worked for nine seconds. My potion cooldown was low enough now that I could presumably chain them like I used to do with water breathing, but the potion itself had a duration-plus-one-second cooldown, preventing one from using them that way.

"He has a spell called *Water Cannon* and another called *Bris*. Like Brisk with no 'k' at the end. A bunch of his spells are meditation ones. Does that mean he has to sit there and chant to cast them? That'd be no good if we're going to add him to our deck. The Posse isn't going to like someone who just sits there and mumbles. Oh, and he has a magic protection shell that looks really strong, but it's also a meditation. It says he has to say the magic phrase to cast it, and it takes ten seconds to cast."

"We need something like that. We'll see how it all works once we catch him. You'll have to mute him fast just in case he can replenish his mana somehow. Move quietly and use chat from here on out."

I prepared my Phase Through Walls potion. Mordecai had warned us a hundred times about this stuff, that we should only use them in emergencies because the effects could be counterintuitive. And if they snapped off prematurely, you could end up cut in half.

I had ten of the potions now. We kept getting them in boxes. We'd tested one out earlier as we were leaving the graveyard. According to Mordecai, the mechanics of them were much more complicated than they appeared on the surface. They worked on anything that was "a solid and unnatural non-biological with empty space on both sides," so if we were on the second floor of a building, we'd plummet away and would only stop once we hit the bottom floor. Or another living thing. I wouldn't pass through the cracked pavement under my feet, but I would pass right through the truck in front of me like it wasn't there.

We started stalking toward him, skirting around and over smushed cars, but before we could make it too close, he spoke again.

"I sense your aura," the crab called.

I froze.

"Do you consider yourself sly? Like a razor fox? Your feeble attempts at cunning will not trick me. Oh no. I am of the Sun-Kissed Cloud, you fool! Have you come to test me? To seek fame for yourself? I shall make your bones shatter to dust!"

He did not move from his position. His back was still to us.

I was about to send the *go* message, but then he added, "No, no. That wasn't powerful enough. You can do this, Raul. The seals only respect power. You will *not* kowtow. Confidence. Confidence."

He hadn't really sensed us. He was practicing lines. We edged up a few more feet. I eyed the back of the truck.

CARL: I don't know about the rope part. You won't have leverage.

DONUT: I GOT IT. IT'S GONNA BE EASY. I CAN LOOP FOUR OF THOSE WEIGHT THINGS AROUND MY TAIL BEFORE IT EVEN STARTS TO HURT.

CARL: Okay. What about the spell? Can you do it from here?

DONUT: I THINK SO. BE CAREFUL. HE SOUNDS LIKE HE HAS A LOT OF NERVOUS ENERGY. YOU KNOW HOW I FEEL ABOUT NERVOUS ENERGY, CARL. CASTING WHEN YOU'RE READY.

CARL: Okay. Get your ass on that rope.

I positioned myself to jump and nodded. Donut cast *Hole* directly underneath the crab, who yelped and plummeted from the roof of the truck into the cargo hold with a clatter. The combat notification appeared. She snapped off the spell as we rushed up. She cast *Mute* on the dazed crab as she jumped mouth first for the rope.

At the same moment, I formed a fist as I rushed up. I downed the Phase Through Walls potion. A nine-second timer appeared.

The tailgate of the large truck came almost up to my crotch, but I passed through it and the half-open roll-up door like they weren't there. I was already swinging. I connected with the surprised crab, and he flew back, crashing into the wall against the truck's cab, rocking the whole thing.

I ducked a snap, using my phase to jump through the wall and back again. I clobbered the crab once again.

A muffled cry came behind me. It was Donut, dangling mouth first from the rope. She'd pulled a large, 100-pound free weight from her inventory and had it looped through her tail, in an effort to give her more weight, but the door didn't roll down. She pulled another. Then another. The door was stuck half open. The plan was to keep him trapped in here while I moved in and out with punches.

Raul recovered and snapped a big red claw right at my head.

I dropped down through the truck's floor before popping up again and punching the crab right in the center of its floor-facing chest. He let out an *oof* and rocketed up against the ceiling of the truck before smashing back down. I felt shell crunch under my blow.

Two seconds.

I was still standing on the pavement, with the truck's floor through my crotch. I dropped a *Fear*-inducing smoke curtain into the cargo just as the still-dangling Donut cast her health-draining, resistance-lowering *Brain Freeze* on the crab. He started to whimper and scramble back. His health was only at half.

"No, please," he said, his voice frightened. I didn't hear the rest as I dropped to the pavement and pressed myself against it, waiting out the phase potion.

CARL: Don't worry about the door! Get out of there!

I felt the bottom of the truck against my back as the potion's effect snapped off. Thankfully, I didn't get hurt. I waited one more second; then I pulled a flag and kept it in my left hand as I downed a second phase potion. I jumped up to find the crab in the back corner of the truck, cowering with multiple debuffs over him. Donut had retreated to the roof of another car, and she'd slammed him with a magic missile, keeping him cornered. He hadn't scuttled out. His health was in the red, but not red enough.

DONUT: OTHER CRABS ARE NOTICING.

I strode forward and punched him several times. He didn't fight back. He just raised his claws in fear as he said, "No, no, no!" I jabbed him with the flag, and I dropped to the ground as the card flew into my hand. I hit the pavement and pressed myself against the ground, breathing heavily just as the potion ran out the second time.

Combat Complete. Deck has been reset.

CARL: Are they coming?

DONUT: NO. THE ONES WHO NOTICED GOT BOWLED OVER AND ARE NOW GETTING EATEN BY THE OTHERS. I DON'T THINK THEY REALLY CARE IF WE'RE HERE OR NOT. JUST STAY THERE A MINUTE, THEN BACK OUT.

I took a breath. The phase potion had been a bad idea. I should have waited to see if Donut's rope idea had worked before taking one. I'd been afraid to get trapped inside the truck with the thing. I gave myself a moment for my heart to stop thrashing.

I rolled out from under the truck, wiped myself off, and, keeping low, moved to the back of the truck. I reached up to grab the rope. It pulled easily and with no effort. The back of the van closed and locked with a *snick*. I gave Donut a look.

"What?" Donut asked. "I was trying to pull it down with no leverage, *and* with my teeth. You're lucky you didn't get snipped in half. That was obviously a thumb-oriented task, Carl. You should never have let me agree to it."

"Yeah," I said, deciding to drop it. I looked doubtfully down at the common card. Raul had potential, but he'd been really skittish and had panicked the moment the fight started. I wasn't certain if that was the *Fear* spell or not. We'd have to spend some time with him in the training arena to see if he was worth it.

"What do we do now?" Donut asked, peering around the back of the truck at the exodus of crabs. I handed her the card, and it disappeared into her inventory. We only needed one more before we could start fighting with them.

I settled down to the ground, my back to the truck. Behind us, the migration continued unabated, 100 meters away. There'd be no more cars coming from the north, and if there were any cars left coming from the south, they wouldn't get anywhere near us.

A light rain started to fall. "We're gonna wait it out," I said. "Just let me know if any start to move toward us."

I hesitated, and then I turned off the mute on Samantha and sent her a ping.

SAMANTHA: OMG ARE YOU COMING OR WHAT? WE'RE BORED.

CARL: We?

SAMANTHA: ME AND MY NEW BEST FRIEND, MARIA. SHE'S GOING TO CAST THE SPELL TO GIVE ME MY BODY BACK, AND THEN SHE'S GOING TO GO ADVENTURING WITH US. SHE'S EXCITED TO MEET LOUIS. SHE THINKS HE SOUNDS REALLY TASTY.

IT TOOK ANOTHER HOUR FOR THE CRAB MIGRATION TO CLEAR. THERE had to be tens of thousands of the things. Most of this time I spent in chat with Samantha, getting as much information as I could about Shi Maria, the spider we were attempting to rescue her from.

I pulled out the Bahamas book, and I compared the information with what was written there. It was pretty much an exact match. On a whim, I sent a message to Prepotente and asked him if he'd come across a similar spider, and he answered with a terse *No*.

That made sense since this was considered a "unique" monster. Though Uzi Jesus was also a unique, and we knew of several Jesus variations floating around.

The drawing of the monster in the book was terrifying. It was a colossal, translucent beige-and-brown spider speckled with black dots and covered with hair. The illustration helpfully included an image of a dead or paralyzed Bopca caught in her web, giving the sense of scale. The bulbous abdomen was the size of a Volkswagen Bug, and her legs were ridiculously long, curving up and down.

But most terrifying was the face. There were no torso and arms, like with that one crawler we'd met on the bubble level. It was just a human-sized head attached to the body. It was of an older, haggard woman with long, stringy black hair and flaking skin, as if she'd been badly burned. Her lower jawbone hinged all the way downward, giving the impression that she was screaming. A pair of hairy fangs dangled from her mouth, dripping with venom. She did not have human eyes, but four black orbs all in a row, with two huge ones in the center and smaller ones on either side.

"How in the goodness did she swallow Samantha when her head is so small?" Donut asked as I examined the image.

The question gave me an unexpected wave of goose bumps.

Shi Maria, Samantha's name for her, was listed as one of several alternate names in the book. The primary name was the "Screamer." I read the short description:

> The Screamer.
>
> A former resident of the celestial realm, this demigod is a formidable opponent. Specializing in trickery, illusion, and mind-bending spell casting, this female arachnid spends her days in unending torment. Her husband, a deity from a long-forgotten pantheon, is missing. She will do anything to find him again, even if that means she must tear down all of reality to do so.
>
> The problem is, legend has it she killed her husband. That she ate him right up. She was banished for the crime. She insists she is blameless, but sometimes, during her more lucid moments, she's not so certain of her own innocence.
>
> Beware her lies.

That was followed by a long list of spells and skills, including a level 15 *Unending Insanity*, which was self-explanatory, and a level 15 *Lights Out*, which I knew was a blindness spell. Neither of those could be cured without divine intervention. Thankfully, Mordecai had prepared us for this and had brewed us a protection potion. The potion was called Liquid Therapy, and we needed to take it once a day. The protection lasted until you slept.

That single potion would protect us from both spells, along with a host of other fear-based debuffs and afflictions. The ingredients were expensive, but we had Mordecai make several, enough for the entire guild. I'd had to use my two table upgrade coupons for his alchemy table. He hadn't left the crafting room since.

We'd already taken our potions for the day. He was also making one for Mongo, but it wasn't ready yet.

Shi Maria had dozens of more spells, most of which were illusion or fear-based paralysis. Under skills, she had Spinneret, which was her ability to shoot spiderwebs out of her ass, and Venomous Bite.

Under weaknesses, it said she was vulnerable to psionic attacks. That was it.

We had protections ready for her sticky web. We were both immune to her venom. We were as ready as we could be to face her.

"You know," Donut said as she read over my shoulder, "she really is quite similar to Samantha. She's looking for her husband just like Samantha. She's a little crazy. I wonder if she really murdered him. You know how they love to plot-twist us with these backstories."

"It doesn't matter." My eyes read that "Beware her lies" line again. "She's obviously lying to Samantha about her ability to animate that body I have in my inventory. I don't see anything in her listed spells that suggests she could do that. We need to be careful with this. If we can keep her under control, she'll be a great card, but I'm not so sure anymore that it'll be worth it."

"Samantha's going to be quite upset if she's lying," Donut said. "She really wants that body."

We had to first survive the encounter with the spider before that was going to matter.

We waited for another few minutes. As we waited, there was a system message.

System Message: The Goddess Semiramis has reascended. She is welcomed into the family by all.

This was the sixth or seventh one of these we'd heard. When we'd rebuilt Yemaya's shrine, it had been the same thing. That meant there were other crawlers out there encountering similar quests as our Asojano one. I knew it was really those assholes on the 12th floor playing the Ascendency game, getting crawlers to wake up ancient gods. I hated it, them using us beyond what we already had to do.

Behind me, the crabs had finally cleared. The rain, which had been nothing but a little trickle, was now starting to come down harder.

"Okay," I said, pulling myself up. "Let's do this."

I paused as yet another notification appeared.

Quest Update. The Chowder War.

Crawler Sister Ines Quiteria has negotiated an agreement with the Monk Seal Abbot and has warned him of the vile treachery of the crabs. The sneak attack will likely turn into a slaughter without your intervention! What will you do? Will you side with your fellow crawler, or will you turn this into a rumble for the ages?

I exchanged a look with Donut. "At least we know she's keeping herself busy and isn't following us. Hopefully that whole quest resolves itself without us."

Donut scoffed. "Does it ever?"

26

<Note added by Crawler Azin. 17th Edition>

Spiders. By the gods, why? In our world, they only exist in myth, but apparently they're a real thing and are common in the universe. What sort of nightmare must the Creators have been having to design such a thing?

<Note added by Crawler Tin. 21st Edition>

I don't know. I think they're cute.

<Note added by Crawler Tin. 21st Edition>

Never mind. Holy shit, never mind. Fuck spiders.

IT TOOK ANOTHER HALF AN HOUR TO FIND THE REALM OF SHI MARIA. We didn't have to look hard.

Donut found Samantha's spot on the map just as we started to see the first remnants of spiderweb on the side of the road, glistening in the rain. Broken crab husks littered the area around the webs along with the bones of several creatures. After another quarter of a mile, the entire north side of the road was filled with white web. A bit farther, the web was strewn across the road. A single moped was caught and was inexplicably hanging upside down about ten feet off the ground.

The strands were everywhere, not in any sort of pattern, like a cotton candy machine had exploded and spewed it everywhere. If we touched even a single strand, it would stick tight. Mordecai said the type of spider this was based on didn't actually use webs that were adhesive, but they made the web sticky anyway because well, fuck you. We had multiple methods of dealing with it. The easiest was Donut's *Magic Missile*, which cut straight through the strands. They shrank away and shriveled from fire. We also had an anti-adhesive potion that would "probably" work according to Mordecai. I didn't want to test it.

Instead of taking Samantha's suggestion and fighting our way into the spider's nest, we talked her into leading the spider to the edge of the road. After going back and forth a few times, she said the spider had agreed, and they were on their way.

Donut remained rigid on my shoulder, too nervous to complain about the rain. Mongo wasn't protected from the blind and insanity debuff, and Donut had put him away.

"Do you really think we won't have to fight her?" she asked. "Samantha says she wants to join the party. I don't see how that'll work. We can't have someone with that sort of skin condition in the party. Plus, you know, that whole thing where she drives people insane. It would ruin Louis and Juice Box's wedding."

"We'll see what she has to say, but you're right. We can't add her to the deck until her health is down to 5%. She's probably going to pretend to be friendly but then will attack. That's the vibe I get from her description at least."

I paced back and forth worriedly as they approached. This was one of the most dangerous monsters we'd ever faced alone. We were ready for her if we did have to fight, but I still felt uneasy. "If she casts anything, we attack. If she retreats back into the web, we'll let her go."

"What if she runs, but she still has Samantha?" Donut asked.

"Uh, well, we'll play it by ear."

"And what if she's really nice and just wants to hang out with us?"

"We'll tell her we have to flag her, or she has to go away. We don't have time for bullshit."

"That might make Samantha mad."

"I have an idea to deal with that."

Donut let out a little gasp. "I see them! Oh, wow, that's a big dot. It's red!"

"Okay," I said. We were expecting that. "Be ready."

The spider only had a few spells we weren't immune to, but she couldn't know what would and wouldn't work against us. I hoped she would go straight to her most potent attacks first. Even though we had the stats from the Bahamas book, Donut would take the Size Up potion the moment she appeared.

"Yoohoo! Carl and Donut! Where are you?" came Samantha's call.

I instinctively took a step back as the trees rustled. It continued to rain. All around, the pillowy mess of spiderwebs started to vibrate, as if they'd all suddenly been pulled taut.

Shi Maria appeared, emerging between two trees, walking sideways along the branches. An involuntary shiver coursed through me.

"Carl, look at her legs! They're *really* long," Donut hissed. Her voice was more panicked than usual. "Do you think she knows about all the spiders we've been killing for that god lady? Oh my god. What if she knows? What if this is a trap?"

"Let's try not to mention that out loud," I whispered.

The drawing in the book didn't do this thing justice. She only had eight legs, but the way they moved gave the impression there were too many of the appendages, and they were much too long, too thin, too angled for the large body, the way they all fought one another as the bulbous abdomen bounced and twisted like a buoy. Somehow jerky and graceful all at once. As she skittered toward us, the legs occasionally bunched together above the main body, like the broken arms of a folded umbrella, before popping out again to help her glide seamlessly across the trees. It was horrifying.

I had a memory of Donut finding and eating several daddy longlegs when she was still a kitten. She'd chow down on the small spiders and make a funny mewling noise as they wriggled in her throat; then she'd do it again. Sometimes she'd find the spiders and rip one or two legs off before I could stop her, and she'd sit there and bat at the disconnected leg as it twitched on the floor. I had thought it was kinda funny in a sadistic way at the time. I suddenly felt guilty for every spider I'd ever killed.

Shi Maria did a turn, almost like a barrel roll. She disappeared into the canopy of one tree right on the edge of the road and then appeared at the very top, looking down at us. Her body was upright, but the almost-human head was inverted. It twisted to face us, still upside down. The head was attached to a long, puttylike neck. That hadn't been in the image, either. She made a clicking noise.

The description was similar, but not exactly the same as the one in the Bahamas book. It decided to use the last name from the book to describe her.

The Bedlam Bride. Reaper Spider Minion.

Level 140 City Boss.

This is a demigod.

Warning: This mob inflicts Permanent Insanity.

Warning: This mob inflicts Permanent Blindness.

Yeah, good luck with that.

Reaper Spider minions are regular mobs one may find on the fifteenth floor working as minions of something kinda fucked-up we're not ready to talk about yet. They have celestial blood. They're scary as shit, and if you're not prepared for their special attacks, you'd just be better off killing yourself instead. When one encounters them outside of the 15th floor, they're usually working as traveling merchants, selling rare and valuable wares. Anything one buys from them is usually quite dangerous.

But not all of them are merchants. Some have escaped out into the lower levels and found their own path. Some have grown in power beyond that of a regular Reaper Spider Minion. This particular one is special. She has had many names. She currently goes by Shi Maria, and her story is long and tragic and can't possibly be fully told here. Once upon a time, she found herself married to a god. It didn't go so well. It's said she killed him. It was pretty much his own fault. Don't stick it in crazy, and all that. The thing is, she doesn't remember actually killing him. Honestly, it's not really important. What is important is that she was kicked out of the celestial realm and banished to this swamp, where she spends her days plotting how to get revenge on everyone and everything who has ever done her wrong.

That list is very, very long.

Shi Maria continued to stare at us with her set of four bulbous eyes. Her face wasn't as burned and crusty as in the drawing, nor as old, but she still appeared to be covered with flaking skin. She had long, dangling black hair that looked greasy, unhealthy. A pair of long, hair-covered fangs jutted from her mouth.

The creature made an angry, rapid clicking noise. Her dot remained red on the map.

"Hey, uh, Samantha?" I called. "Where are you?"

"Eyes down here, beefcake," she answered. "What took you so long?" I startled to see her at my feet. I'd been so transfixed by the spider, I hadn't seen her roll up. The sex doll head was filthy. Mud and leaves and strands of spider thread covered her face and hair. She started snuffling around my feet, sniffing as she rolled around me. "You've been hanging out with strippers. I can smell them on you!"

"Why don't you introduce us to your new friend?" Donut asked from my shoulder. She, too, had her eyes fixed on the massive spider.

Shi Maria clicked again. The sound was fast and disconcerting, like a faulty solenoid in an ignition switch. Or a woodpecker on cocaine. The rain continued to pelt into us. The spider woman's head twisted a few times, turning clockwise. It made three full circles before settling right side up. A white fluid drooled from one of her enormous fangs. The large tree under her cracked and creaked as the spider shifted. One of the sharp, thin legs undulated up and down. It was long enough to reach us here on the street and skewer me like a kebab.

I took another step back.

"Oh, oh yes," Samantha said. "Shi Maria, this is Donut, and this is Carl. Donut, Carl, meet my new best friend. Her name is Shi Maria, but she prefers to be called MaeMae. She is very shy, but is quite funny once you get her talking. Maybe tonight she can tell you the pachyderm story. I laughed so much, it came out of my nose."

DONUT: HER STATS ARE JUST LIKE IN THE BAHAMAS BOOK BUT SHE HAS SOMETHING ELSE. SHE HAS THE COCKROACH SKILL LIKE I DO. IT'S LEVEL 15!

Fuck, I thought. That saved her from a fatal blow. At level 15, it would fully heal her, and I was pretty sure it would not only activate twice in a single fight, but it'd give her a short shield in the meantime. An already dangerous fight just got a lot more difficult. If it came to it, we'd pretty much have to flag her and be careful not to accidentally pull her health too low.

Shi Maria hissed, the sound like gas leaking from a canister. The towering legs flexed. A pair of branches in the tree snapped. I had my mental finger poised on my *Protective Shell* barrier.

"Ha!" Samantha said to the monster. "I never noticed that."

DONUT: CARL, IS SHE REALLY TALKING TO THE SPIDER, OR IS SHE MAKING ALL THIS UP?

CARL: I have no idea.

"Anyway," Samantha said, "she's going to go adventuring with us. I have it all planned. Okay, listen to this. MaeMae is going to cast the spell that moves me into the body. Then we are going to go kill lots of bad guys, and then after that, she's going to travel to Larracos with us and help us fight against all those other Faction Wars teams while I reunite with my little baby girl. I will have a short, torrid sexual affair with Louis, but I will run away crying after our third or fourth date because I simply can't anymore. After all, my heart belongs to someone else. Juice Box will forgive me, and she and Louis will babysit for me while I have a girls' night out with Donut, and Katia, and Britney, and Li Na, and MaeMae, and Elle. Carl, you can't come. Not Imani, either. I don't like her. She wants to steal my man. It'll basically be a bachelorette party, and we can all wear matching shirts. After that, we will go find my king, and I will marry him and have lots of weird sex for a week straight as a honeymoon. And after that, I promised MaeMae we would all find her missing husband. He might be in the Nothing, so that's going to be a bit of a chore. Then after all of that, we will go back to the celestial realm, and I will kill my mother. Sound like a plan?"

"Wow," Donut said. "You really do have it all planned out."

"You have a lot of time to think when you're in the stomach of a spider."

"But how are we going to get matching T-shirts for all of us?"

Shi Maria clicked and hissed.

Samantha giggled. "Oh, don't you know it, girlfriend? Donut, don't worry about it. We'll make it work."

"Wait, isn't your sand-ooze daughter all grown up?" Donut asked. "Wasn't she married to that mage guy? Why would she need a babysitter?"

"*That's* the part of this plan you have trouble with?" I asked.

"Actually, no," Donut said. "Samantha, I think you might want to skip the affair-with-Louis part. Juice Box has gotten really good at decapitating people. The last thing you want is to get your body only to get turned back into a head."

"I can't skip that part," Samantha said. "That's one of my favorite parts."

"Have you told Louis this?"

"Oh, yes, but he's blocked me in the chat. He's so cute when he's being shy."

As they went back and forth, I kept my eyes on the monster just sitting there above us in the trees. I considered our options. We could just straight up attack the spider, but I feared Samantha would flip out and fight us. We'd have to go with my other plan. Samantha's insistence that the monster cast the reanimate spell actually made this easy. If she saw the spider couldn't, or wouldn't, help, her attitude would change instantly.

CARL: Donut, get ready. We're going to speed this up.

I pulled the body from my inventory. It appeared in my arms, rigid like a board. It was a full-sized pure naiad. The body of Signet's mother. She wore a flowing dress made of seaweed, and she smelled of brackish water. Even though it was the size of an adult, the body weighed nothing. Her silky white hair hung down so long, it hit the pavement. I gently placed the whole body down on the wet black asphalt. She appeared as if she was sleeping.

This wasn't a real person, but a tattoo made flesh by Signet's final spell. It'd actually been a tattoo of a fish. I wasn't going to pretend to understand how this all worked.

Princess Lunette. Incomplete Flesh Golem.

"Here it is," I said.

Once a "fleshmancer" cast the proper spell, Samantha would zap into the thing, and she'd have a body again. It wasn't clear what would happen to the sex doll head.

DONUT: IF SHE BECOMES A REGULAR NAIAD, DOESN'T SHE HAVE TO STAY IN WATER? WE DON'T EVEN HAVE A BATHTUB IN THE GUILD.

CARL: Something tells me that's not going to be a problem. Not today.

DONUT: IT WOULD RUIN THE BACHELORETTE PARTY IF WE HAVE TO DO IT UNDERWATER.

"Okay! Yay! Here we go!" Samantha said. She did a little hop and then rose off the ground, floating between us and the spider in the tree. She'd claimed she'd been unable to float once we hit this floor, but it appeared she'd refigured it out. She was so excited, she was shaking. "Okay, MaeMae, do your thing!"

The spider clicked and gestured at the body. Leaves and branches went flying as her forward leg waved.

"What? I did, too, tell you it was a golem!" Samantha said, incredulous. "It was the first thing I said!"

More rapid clicks.

"Supplies? What sort of supplies? You said you could do it as soon as Carl got here!"

Click, click, hiss.

CARL: Here we go. *Mute* first, then *Magic Missile*.

"I'm going to kill your mother."

DONUT: HER DOT JUST TURNED WHITE!

At the same moment, the spider in the tree burst into tears. At least I was pretty sure it was tears. Her forward legs reached over and started to rub at her four eyes while the whole, colossal thing made a hiss-hissing sound. Actual water tears flowed down her face. She click-hissed at Samantha.

The other legs all retracted, and the massive boss suddenly crashed to the ground, rolling as she did so. Branches snapped and cracked as she tumbled. Behind her, a tree fell over. She splashed into the marsh just off the road with a *crunch*, rolling onto her back. Her legs splayed up over herself and retracted, like those of a bug that had just been knocked off with a shot of Raid. She started to rock back and forth. Her head twisted on her swivel neck as the tears continued to flow.

I eased my mental finger off *Protective Shell* as I stared at the white dot on the map. *What the hell?*

Samantha let out a big sigh. "Oh, calm down, MaeMae. No need to make a scene. I swear, sometimes you are just like my child. I won't kill your mother. Not today. Stop crying. Stop this instant." She floated toward the sobbing city boss.

The spider continued to weep.

"No, no, it's okay. MaeMae. Come on. It's okay. We will go get the supplies."

The spider, still on her back, clicked.

"Oh, don't be so dramatic," Samantha said. "I forgive you."

The spider gestured at me and clicked again, this time for longer.

SAMANTHA: CARL, YOU HAVE TO SAY SOMETHING NICE TO HER. YOU HURT HER FEELINGS.

CARL: How did I do that? I haven't talked to her at all.

SAMANTHA: YOU FORGOT TO TELL HER THAT SHE WAS STUNNING WHEN YOU FIRST MET HER. IF SHE'S GOING TO BE TRAVELING WITH US, YOU HAVE TO CALL HER STUNNING, OR SHE'LL OPEN HER FIFTH EYE AND FORCE YOUR MIND INTO THE DIMENSION OF UTTER, BLACKENED PSYCHOSIS FOR AN ETERNITY OF SCREAMS.

CARL: Samantha. She can't travel with us.

SAMANTHA: WHY NOT?

Shi Maria pulled her legs even tighter together and started to rock back and forth.

Samantha returned to us. She floated up to eye level, which was creepy as shit. She had a leaf stuck to the side of her mouth, and I reached forward to peel it off. She growled and snapped at my finger and then continued talking like it was nothing. "She's going to be like that for at least ten minutes. She gets panic attacks. The best thing to do is just let her work through it. Singing helps, if you want to serenade her, Donut."

"Really?" Donut asked, perking up.

"Don't sing to the spider," I said. "Samantha, we need to get out of here. We can't take her."

Samantha made a little whimper. "But she needs to get supplies for my body. She says she needs something another spider like her sells before she can cast the spell, and they aren't around until maybe the ninth floor or deeper."

"So, she knows about the floors?" I asked.

"She knows everything," Samantha said. "We've done a lot of talking."

Even though this should've been obvious, I hadn't realized until that moment exactly how much Samantha knew. It made sense. She didn't seem to fully grasp it all, not if she was still gung ho on us trying to find her beloved king guy. I was pretty sure he didn't exist. At least not until the system decided he did. That was a conversation for later.

But still . . . Herot's hypothesis that self-aware NPCs were highly contagious seemed to be true.

"Look, Samantha," I said. Behind her, the spider was making little hissing noises. "She's too goddamned dangerous. I was going to try to flag her for our deck, but if we don't have to fight her, we should avoid it. We'll find another mage for you. Okay?"

"Wait. Did you only come here because you wanted to add her to your stupid card deck? You didn't come here to save me?"

I thought about that. Mordecai had certainly wanted us to abandon Samantha. I'd been saying we needed to come here and flag the spider. Rescuing Samantha was always, ostensibly, a part of it, though of secondary concern. Would we have come at all if the flags hadn't been a thing?

The more I thought about it, the more I realized I *would* have come. That surprised me. It wasn't an unwelcome realization.

I reached forward, and I put my hand on Samantha's cold cheek. She instinctively reached over and chomped down, but she didn't bite hard. She kept her mouth closed on my hand.

"Samantha, you are crazy. Nobody knows why or how you're getting all these new powers, and it kinda freaks me out because we don't know where it's going to stop. But on the last floor, we couldn't have survived without you. You are part of our team. So, yes, I would've come save you."

"Really?" she asked, mouth still full of my hand.

"Really," I said.

She gently removed my hand from her mouth, and she looked at me, eyes shining. She took a moment to compose herself.

"I'm not going to fuck you, Carl. You need to stop trying."

I smiled and patted her. "Let's get out of here while we can."

"No, Carl. I can't leave her. She's my best friend."

"But she ate you," Donut said. She lowered her voice further. "Plus, look at her face."

"Oh, don't I know it? We've had the moisturizer conversation, but she doesn't know what that is."

"We can't take her," I said. "Not unless she'll let us turn her into a card."

"Yes, yes, Carl. We knew it might come to this."

"She knows about the cards?" I asked.

"Of course. Elle told me all about it, and I told MaeMae all about it. MaeMae said you'd probably want to turn her into a card. She's very smart. She made me ask Elle a bunch of questions about how the cards worked. MaeMae says once Donut has all six cards, she can just pop out whenever, and she'll be immortal just like me!"

"Uh, that's not exactly how it works," I said.

"Elle?" Donut asked. "Since when have you been talking to Elle?"

"Oh, Elle is just a delight," Samantha said. "At first I thought she wanted to move in on Louis, you know, because she messaged me to tell me to leave him alone. I was ready to pull her fairy wings right off. But it turns out, it was just because I was making him uncomfortable, and she was just being protective. Not because she wants him for herself. She says even though her garage has recently been refurbished, it's still closed to business and filled with dust. So I forgave her. She's asking me questions about the story of the Fourth Season, and she's been telling me about that card game. That's why she's invited to my bachelorette party. I like her."

I had no idea what the Fourth Season alluded to. I filed that information away to ask Elle later.

If this spider willingly allowed us to flag her, that would be great, but it felt like a trap. The book and description went out of its way to tell us how cunning and smart she was. She had to know that if she turned to a card, she couldn't just walk around. She would be at our mercy. If so, what was her plan?

I remembered something Cascadia had said at the beginning of this level. We would be able to keep a single card at the end of the floor.

It wasn't clear how that would work, but that had to be it. I eyed the "sobbing" spider. This was all an act. It had to be.

I gently pulled Donut off my shoulder and put her on the ground.

"You two stay here."

"Carl," Donut said, but I held up my hand.

If Shi Maria was angling toward getting us to bring her down to the ninth floor, everything would be fine for now. That meant she wouldn't deliberately kill us.

It was an opportunity. A dangerous one.

I cast *Wisp Armor* on myself. I took several steps toward the crying spider. I formed a fist, and my gauntlet appeared. I kept *Protective Shell* at the ready.

"Listen up," I said, talking as I edged toward her. "Shi Maria, whatever your name is, I'll get you to the next floor, or however deep you need, if you help us. But we gotta do the card thing. You know how it works."

The spider moved one of her legs, which had been covering her eyes. She stopped crying and regarded me. The change was instantaneous.

I continued. "You turn any of my friends blind or insane or otherwise hurt anyone we're not already fighting, and the deal is off. I will rip the card. But if you help us, you have my word we'll help you. Do you understand? Click once if you do."

She undulated, unfurling her long, terrible legs. She turned, righting herself, keeping her mass low. She did it in such a way her head did not spin or move at all. She kept my eyes the whole time. As I stared at her,

I saw it: the closed fifth eye in the center of her head. It was small. The size of a marble. That was how she cast her spell. She opened that eye, and all who regarded it would be blinded or driven insane.

Even though that eye was closed, I felt it. *It's right there,* I remembered my mother saying, standing on the edge of the Grand Canyon. *Do you remember the circus, Carl?*

And then the spider talked.

"I understand the bargain, worshipper of Emberus," Shi Maria said, her voice a sultry and perfectly clear whisper.

A deep chill washed over me.

"So you do talk," I said.

"That fool Samantha says you keep your promises. I could devour you now, but if I am to leave this horrible place, I must trust in you. I must find my husband and prove I didn't kill him. In order to do that, I must first get to Larracos. I have no quarrel with you. Once the city is reached, I will tell you how to undo the card magic, and you can set me free. In the meantime, I will help you. It is an easy bargain for you. While I am trapped as a card, I would be at your mercy. No?"

"Can you really help Samantha get her body back?"

"I don't have the proper magic, but I know of a Master Pulpmancer in Larracos," she said. "This same mage would be able to set me free from the card prison you would put me in. Expensive, but it's possible."

Mordecai had said something similar when I asked him about the possibility of saving Paz. He knew exactly where that Pulpmancer's shop was, but it was in the bottom levels of Larracos. The mage was most likely dead. Shi Maria didn't know this. I hoped.

"You've been lying to Samantha," I said. "How can I possibly trust you? I will never believe a word that comes out of your mouth."

A small grin played across her disturbing face. With her upper lips wrapped around the strange, hairy fangs, the expression was terrifying. "You don't need to trust me, Carl. I will be at your mercy. You know what I want, and that gives you power over me."

I swallowed. That reminded me of Odette's first piece of advice to me.

She was emulating me. She was trying to act like I would act if I was in her position. She'd done the same thing with Samantha. This one was smart. There was no way we could ever trust her. But I *did* believe she wanted to get off this floor.

The spider cocked her head to her side. "I see you've taken a potion that you think would protect you from my spells. It might protect your companion, but you? You've already been cracked open. A broken window still lets the wind inside, Carl. What is it you want? I wonder. Maybe I should look upon you with my eye. We would both know then. Samantha told me of your troubles with certain deities. And of your other troubles. Of what is growing inside of you."

I opened my mouth to respond, but I was stopped by a notification.

New Quest. The Bedlam Bride.

An escort quest? Really? Psshhh. Piece of cake.

The problem is, you're the cake.

The Screamer. Shi Maria. The Widow Endless. The Bedlam Bride. It doesn't matter what her name is today. Get her crazy ass to the city of Larracos. That's it. That's the quest.

***Reward:* A simple prize for a simple quest.**

The monster looked upon the gauntlet on my right hand. She then rolled over onto her side, exposing the bottom of her mass. It jiggled slightly as if filled with liquid. Her legs on one side arched up into the air, gleaming sharp and hanging over me like a row of razor teeth. Her belly was almost translucent like frosted glass. Hints of organs throbbed about within.

"Injure me just enough to cast the card magic. Do not attempt to slay me, Carl. Many have tried. All have failed. I have more tricks than your mind can imagine. Be a friend to me, and I will be a friend to you."

"People keep saying that to me," I said as I punched her in the center of her abdomen.

27

DECEMBER 22ND.

Time Until Phase Two: 40 hours.

CARL: WHATEVER YOU DO, DON'T TRUST HER. EVER. IN FACT, TRY NOT to talk to her at all except to give her orders during battle. She's plotting against us. Also, don't tell her that Larracos has been flooded. Don't mention it to Samantha, either, because she might say something.

DONUT: THE SPIDER LADY IS A CARD NOW. I'M NOT GOING TO TALK TO HER ANYWAY. I CAN'T BELIEVE SHE LET YOU DO THAT.

CARL: She has a plan I don't see. Our only advantage is that she doesn't know we're immune to most of her abilities.

I hope, I didn't add.

DONUT: SAMANTHA ALREADY KNOWS LARRACOS IS FLOODED.

CARL: Yes, she does. But we don't need to remind her. She doesn't realize that means the mage who might be able to transfer her to the body is probably dead.

DONUT: OH NO, THAT'S REALLY SAD.

CARL: I'm sure we can figure something else out for her. In the meantime, we want Shi Maria on our side long enough to get off this damn floor.

DONUT: I DON'T LIKE SPIDERS, CARL. NOT WHEN THEY'RE BIGGER THAN I AM. THEY GIVE MONGO NIGHTMARES.

Out loud, I added, "We need to get back to that one safe room near the Desperado Club. I want to do some practicing with our deck, and Katia and I have a thing we need to do."

"Ooo, that sounds exciting," Samantha said. She rolled between me and Mongo as we trudged back north. "I want to do something exciting."

"I got good news for you, then," I said. "You're gonna get to do something really fun. We gotta get you into the Desperado Club first, though."

"Goody," she said. She growled and rolled off, chasing after a frog. She'd floated for a while, but had grown tired and reverted back to rolling. Donut, Mongo, and I were spending the time grinding on monsters. The crabs were gone, off to the coast, and we didn't see any more bats, but there were bird mobs everywhere, and sometimes they'd just swoop in on us without warning. Thankfully, Donut could see them coming, and she usually managed to knock them out of the air before they got close.

We did manage to come across a strange entity that might've been good to flag, but Mongo killed her before we could even examine her properties. Samantha said she smelled something off the path even though there were no marks on the map. This was just past the marshland, so I figured we would humor her. We followed her snuffling form until Mongo suddenly pounced on a pile of dead undergrowth at the base of a kapok tree.

The thing was a hairy woman with backward feet, and she'd been asleep under the pile of foliage. Her dot showed up red in that last moment before she died. Mongo chomped her to death before she fully woke up. Her name was La Ciguapa, and there was an entry about her in the Bahamas book. She had a special ability to lure opponents with charm, and she was hard to kill . . . except by familiars and pets.

Unfortunately, she was of legendary rareness, and it was unlikely we'd run across another one. It was a wasted opportunity for the deck, but the good news was that she dropped two cards. An uncommon snare card and a mythic special effect card.

The snare card was called **Damnation**. It didn't kill the monster, but it made it so an enemy's totem card would be discarded once it timed out, whether it was dead or not. That was a good card to use against powerful monsters we might be otherwise unable to kill.

The special effect card was interesting. It was a consumable card called **Glow-Up**, and it wasn't on the list of known card types. It could be cast on any active card or totem, yours or the enemy's. It changed the card itself, altering it so it permanently reflected the item's current state. So if we had a totem with a summoning time of 120 seconds, and we buffed it with a Time Extend, and then we cast Glow-Up on it, the totem would permanently summon for 240 seconds in future battles. We could only use the Glow-Up card once, so this was something we'd have to think about. If we used it properly and were smart about how we stacked the buffs on it, we could turn an already-strong card into something practically immortal.

While we grinded our way back north, I managed to fill up and drain my Scavenger Daughter's patch three more times. I learned a few things along the way.

The power of the Daughter's Kiss special attack was much more potent if the captured souls in my back patch were all of the same species. If I killed nothing but Howling Gulls, and the soul essence bar was pure, when I unleashed my melee attack, it was almost twice as powerful as it would be otherwise. Plus, the residual effects of the attack were stronger. Howling Gulls used a scream attack, and when I dispersed the charge, it not only obliterated the monster; it unleashed a scream multiple times more powerful than what the Howling Gulls usually cast. I tried a charged attack on an iguana thing called a Yuanat, and the dog-sized mob turned into literal dust when I punched it, causing a crater ten feet wide.

Other than the monster Mongo killed, nothing was flag-worthy. We now had a full deck, but I did want a few backups just in case some of our totems didn't work out. I suspected our strongest card, Shi Maria, would do what we asked. For now, at least. But I just knew Asojano was going to be an ass, plus Uzi Jesus would probably also be too much to handle. And I had no idea what was going to happen if Geraldo the monk seal and Raul the crab were summoned at the same time.

We could now use the deck in real combat, and Donut wanted to try it, but I told her to hold off until we got to a simulation room. Even though the environment could hurt us in the simulation room, Uzi Jesus couldn't shoot us in the head. We needed to get some serious practice in before I'd be comfortable with Donut using the deck.

On top of all of that, Zev was indicating we'd be going on Odette's show soon. We needed to be ready for that.

It took us almost three times as long to get north as it did for us to travel south, as we stayed on foot and stopped to kill everything we encountered. We didn't quite make it back in time, so we stopped at a roadside safe room to listen to the daily update. This was a small, traditional-style safe room with a Bopca, who was a good-natured guy named Pahzi. Donut demanded a crab dish and a bowl of meat for Mongo, while I ordered a pork sandwich.

We settled into a small booth as the show started. We watched a group of crawlers in Tokyo as they ran from a woman wearing a surgical mask and carrying scissors. One crawler turned and hit her with a spell that caused vines to grow from the ground, and the woman ripped through the vines easily. She slashed the throat of the crawler.

I hadn't heard from Katia in a few hours. We'd been going back and forth on our plan to deal with Astrid, but she'd stopped responding after saying she was going to do some reconnaissance inside the club. I was actually starting to get a little worried.

CARL: Hey, Katia. Are you back yet? We're at a safe room, and I wanted to send Samantha out into the guild. I'll leave the tattoo kit on the counter for you. I hope you're doing okay.

She didn't answer. Next to me, Donut was grumbling while she cracked open the crab legs herself. The Bopcas used to do it for her, but not anymore. Mongo finished the meat in about two seconds and was now screeching for more. Samantha rolled off and was inspecting a jukebox in the corner of the room. She was smacking into the side of it, demanding it work.

The screen depicted Osvaldo in a sprawling city. He was doing some crazy parkour shit, bouncing off walls while chasing a monkey thing that was swinging back and forth on electrical lines.

He was wearing the memorial crystal around his neck.

The program then moved to Florin, who'd gotten his hands on a tank. It was small for a tank, and it looked like it was maybe built in the 1940s, but it was still a goddamned tank. He managed to get it moving and drive it to the bank of some river. He was using the big gun to take out a serpent as wide as a school bus. I already knew he'd managed to snag this particular monster as a card, but I hadn't realized he'd done it that way, nor had I realized how big the creature was.

I sent a note to Bautista, asking if he knew where Katia was.

BAUTISTA: She's okay. She's asleep. She found some secret merchant in the Desperado Club, and she's out of sorts. But she'll be okay in a bit.

That . . . that didn't seem right. A new wave of worry hit me.

CARL: Out of sorts? What does that mean? Does she need healing?

BAUTISTA: No. She'll be fine. But I think you'll have to wait a day for your operation. She's not going to be ready.

CARL: We can't wait. We don't know if we'll have access to the Desperado Club in phase two. Are you sure she's okay? She's in your personal space? I'm going to come over.

BAUTISTA: No. We're still in the Desperado.

CARL: She's asleep *inside* the Desperado Club? Do you need help? We're still an hour away from a club access, but I know Imani's team finally found an entrance. I can send her in there.

BAUTISTA: Just leave it, okay? She'll be fine.

That was even more alarming. I moved to a new chat and sent a message to Imani. I was in the middle of sending another to Li Na when Cascadia's daily update interrupted me.

The kua-tin admin was back to her regular chipper self. Or at least, she was pretending. I did catch a hint of tension, hidden there in the back of her voice.

Hello, Crawlers!

We are just a day away from phase two. Most of you have filled your squad, and that's great. Some of you have even started to battle each other, which is even more exciting!

We definitely encourage this behavior. Starting tonight, the prices in the mock-battle arena are going up. However, if you beat the simulation at challenge level, new arena options will open up.

Here's what to expect when phase two starts.

When the timer hits 12:01 AM on December 24th, regardless of where you are or what you're doing, you will be teleported to a room similar to the one you started in on this floor. Here, your Squad Leader will be given choices on where to go. You will have sixty seconds to make a choice.

Once a location is chosen, you will immediately transfer there.

Every totem in your possession that is not in your active deck will be lost. Other cards will not be lost, so feel free to keep and collect as many of those as you want. If you do not have a full squad, a random totem from your starting area will be chosen for you and automatically added to your deck.

This new area will be another memory simulation. In addition, it will be populated by intelligent mobs who carry decks. If you kill these mobs, you will be able to take their cards. You will be allowed to take any of their totems as well, but if you do so, you must choose an existing totem in your deck to lose. Once phase two starts, you may never have more or fewer than six totem cards in your possession.

Your map will be marked with a key location that will be approximately ten to fifteen kilometers away. You will have 48 hours to get to that location and retrieve the key. This key can only be used to open the stairwell location that was adjacent to your original starting area. Once the door is opened, only squad members of the key holder may pass.

"Oh, shit," I muttered. I could already see where this was going.

At midnight, just as the clock turns to December 26th, phase three begins. All key holders and their squads will teleport back to a random location within your original area. From there, you may proceed to your starting point and exit to the ninth floor.

If you do not manage to collect a key during phase two, all is not

lost. You will be able to transfer to a new location for phase three. Again, you will be given at least two choices.

You will transfer to the doorway of the stairwell location of someone who has collected a key. In other words, you'll be blocking their path. If you can kill them before they exit, you can take the key to save yourself. And yes, it is possible for multiple keyless squads to transfer to the same location. So the potential of crawler-on-crawler violence is quite high. Doesn't that sound just great?

Of course, you can avoid all this if every squad manages to get a key. Good luck with that.

Now get out there and *kill, kill, kill.*

"Goddamnit," I said. I took a deep breath.

"Carl, does that mean we're going to have to fight people to get out?"

"Maybe," I said. "If we get a key, there might be squads who didn't get one blocking our path to the exit. They're gonna be desperate, and we might have to fight them. They're gonna use this to set up some pretty awful battles."

"What if *we* can't get the key?" Donut asked.

I put my hand on Donut, and I rubbed the side of her face. "Then we'll do what we have to."

She pressed into my hand. "I don't want to fight other people."

"I know," I said. I thought of my back patch, and of the Mysterious Bone Key benefit. "There might be a way to avoid it. I *really* don't want to use it, but I will if I have to."

28

IMANI: SHE'S OKAY, BUT SHE HAS A NASTY DEBUFF. SHE FOUND SOME secret room called a drug den. It's set up like one of those frozen yogurt places, where you get a bowl, and you self-serve stuff into it and add toppings. It's really messed up. She made herself something, and it knocked her on her ass. She's going to be passed out for ten more hours.

CARL: Ten hours? Holy shit, that's cutting it close. That doesn't sound like something she'd deliberately do.

IMANI: Well, she did it. The description on her debuff says she has a fifty percent chance of adding a bunch of strength when she wakes up, but there's also a chance she'll lose intelligence. While she's passed out, she's "Bliss Surfing." I don't know for certain what that means, but I think she's reliving a memory. That's what the blitz sticks do, too, but I think this is supposed to be more intense. Elle is guarding her right now. Based on Daniel's reaction, I'm starting to think this isn't new.

CARL: What do you mean? How do you know?

IMANI: He didn't want to tell me any of this. The way he was making excuses for her . . . Let's just say it's familiar. I'm going back to the guild to talk to Louis and Britney and see if they know anything.

I had a sinking sensation. She'd found the drug den because I'd told her where it was. She'd asked me about it.

DONUT: **IF YOU'RE TRYING TO SAY KATIA IS A CRACKHEAD, I WON'T BELIEVE IT.**

IMANI: Nobody is saying she's a crackhead, Donut, but I'm afraid she's going to need some help. This stuff is really addictive.

DONUT: EVERY SHOW HAS A SEASON WHERE ONE OF THE CHARACTERS GETS STRUNG OUT ON DRUGS OR ALCOHOL, AND IT'S ALWAYS STUPID BECAUSE IT STRESSES ME OUT. KATIA IS NOT A CLICHÉ. I SIMPLY WON'T ALLOW IT.

IMANI: We'll figure it out.

CARL: My and Katia's quest is important, but it's not going to matter if all of us don't get a key during phase two. So make sure you practice with your decks. Donut and I are about to go practice with ours, and then we'll get to the Desperado Club and figure out what we're going to do.

"Carl," Donut said, looking up at me, "she'll be okay, right?"

"Katia is the second-toughest woman I know," I said. I scratched Donut's ear. "Come on. We need to practice."

ENTERING THE MOCK-BATTLE ARENA.

Warning: You have at least one consumable card in your deck. This card will be lost if used in this arena.

Choose your difficulty.

"Pick the medium one," I said. "The one equal to our deck."

"Hey," Donut said. "They raised the price! It used to be 2,000 gold, and now it's 2,500!"

"Yeah, they told us they raised the prices."

"Oh, yeah. They also said we get something if we beat challenge difficulty. Let's do that instead."

"Not yet."

In the chat, there was a lively debate about the best deck size and composition. With six totems and an initial hand of four cards, it was important that you pull at least one totem right away, or you'd be vulnerable to attack. Someone suggested that an 18-card deck was the best choice. It meant we had almost an 80% chance to pull a totem in the initial spread, but it still allowed for a decent number of other cards.

I wasn't a math guy, and I wasn't even sure if that percentage was correct, but we decided to test it out. Donut and I put our initial deck together, consisting of 18 cards.

We had the six totems: **Geraldo** the monk seal, **Asojano** the orisha, **Skylar Spinach** the ghommid splitter, **Uzi Jesus**, **Raul** the crab, and **Shi Maria** the spider.

The next six were all utility cards: two **Time Extend** cards, one strength-increasing **Stout** card, one mana-increasing **Blue Stuff** card, a speed-increasing **Greased Lightning** card, and the consumable **Combo** card. Donut didn't want to add the Combo card because we wouldn't be using it in practice, but I thought it was best to keep it in the deck to make this as realistic as possible. Also, I suspected the Time Extend cards would be unnecessary, but we wouldn't know until we practiced with them.

Then we had three snare cards. These would be pointless in the simulation because they were only usable against card-carrying opponents. But again, I wanted a realistic deck. One could alter their deck ahead of battle, but sometimes you didn't know when a fight was going to start, so our ready deck had to include these cards. We had **Hobble**, which was also consumable. The mana-draining **Hole in the Bag**, which was not, and our new **Damnation** card.

We had two mystic cards, which were also useless here. The card-stealing **Thief** and the **Force Discard** cards.

And finally, we had a single consumable **Flee** card.

Until we got some practice in, I wasn't certain if this was a good spread or not. We didn't have very many snare cards, and I suspected those might be better than utility cards, but this is what we went with.

We kept Mongo out of his cage. I planned on rolling Samantha into the guildhall before we entered the simulation, but I changed my mind at the last minute. She was always good for distracting enemies.

Mongo bounced up and down excitedly as Donut scrolled through our environment choices while Samantha rolled in circles around my feet.

"Pick something urban," I said. "Not the arena. And not something that sounds dangerous. Make sure the environmental factors are all Earth standard."

"I don't know what that means, Carl." She gasped. "They have a 1980s shopping mall! Just like in *Stranger Things*!"

The world immediately changed so we were, indeed, on the first level of a bustling multilevel shopping mall. Rows of stores spread out in front of us. My eyes caught a colorful arcade, and next to it was a Kay-Bee toy store—which was absolutely packed. And then a Waldenbooks. Christmas decorations hung along the long hallway. In the distance, a line of children and bored parents waited for their chance to sit on Santa's lap, whom I couldn't see.

We stood next to a brick fountain, which was filled with coins. Donut coughed, and I breathed in the familiar scent of cigarette smoke. Dozens of NPCs appeared in the simulation, walking back and forth as they carried bags. Up on the second level, multiple people hung off the railings, chatting away and laughing. Some people were smoking. Roving bands of teenagers stopped to regard us. A girl whispered to another as they giggled and pointed at my boxers. Samantha rolled up to a group of boys outside the arcade, and bit down on one kid's shoe and started growling. The boy kicked her like a soccer ball, and she went flying.

Next to us stood an Orange Julius stand, and the girl behind the counter looked at us and said, "If you're not going to order anything, you gotta move."

I hadn't realized that these simulations could include physical, interactive NPCs on the actual playing field. These were the same as most of the patrons inside of the Desperado Club. Not really alive like the regular dungeon NPCs, but they still had physical bodies and would be in the way.

Battle Begins in Ten Seconds. Deck is locked in place.

"Can you turn off the people?" I asked.

"I can, but it's too late. I already chose it!" Donut said. "I kinda like it."

A girl with a side ponytail looked down at Donut. "Aren't you the cutest thing ever? And is that a dinosaur? That's wicked awesome."

Mongo screeched joyfully at the girl and waved his arms.

Combat Started.

Donut leaped to my shoulder as the four cards appeared floating in front of her. There was no sign of the monster, though with the mall this packed, I suspected we wouldn't have to wait long.

I examined the four cards she pulled. **Greased Lightning, Stout, Shi Maria**, and **Uzi Jesus.**

"Save the utility cards and play the two totems," I said. "Summon Jesus, talk to him for a second, then summon Shi Maria."

Donut looked at me sideways from my shoulder. "You sure you want those two at the same time?"

"Yes," I said. "That's why we're doing this. We need to see how they work together. It's important they get used to each other."

In the far distance, someone started to scream.

Donut swiped forward, summoning the Jesus card.

"Body of Christ!" an unseen announcer shouted as translucent, sparkly angels floated in the air.

The ground cracked, and a wooden cross grew up from the hole. Uzi Jesus was nailed to the cross, his gun in his right hand. Mongo squealed with concern as the people around us all started to cry and run away.

"It's Heyzoos, the Uzi Jesus!" the announcer shouted as the words appeared floating in the air. Heyzoos flexed, and the cross shattered into holographic dust as the barefoot man landed on the tiled floor of the mall, his white robe flapping in a wind that wasn't there. His long, flowing hair also waved. A golden halo over his head sparkled. A 75-second timer appeared over him and started to count down.

"Holy shit," I muttered. I'd forgotten about these ridiculous intros.

"Who are you?" Heyzoos asked, looking me and Donut up and down. The guy had a Texan accent for some reason. He was a ridiculously good-looking white dude. All around us, people started screaming and running for the exits. The girl behind the Orange Julius counter bolted. In the distance, the wall separating the Santa display fell over as parents and children fled. "What happened to the crocodile guy?"

We'd agreed ahead of time that Donut would do most of the talking. It was important to see if they'd follow her instructions.

"You shot him in the stomach," Donut said. "So he gave you to us."

Another card appeared in Donut's deck, but it was a snare card. She immediately discarded it.

"I was going to heal him," Heyzoos said defensively. He scratched at his temple with the barrel of his gun. His finger was planted on the trigger. "So, who we sending off to meet Dad? Hey, what're you doing?" He jumped as Samantha started bumping into his legs.

"Whatchu got under that robe, huh?" Samantha asked, rolling around him.

"Samantha, leave him alone," I called. "Come back here."

"But I want to see his penis," she whined.

"Samantha, you little shit," I said. "Come here, or you can't go adventuring with us again."

"We don't know what we're fighting yet," Donut said to Heyzoos. "Go over there and wait to see what comes out, but first we want you to meet another card."

She flipped the Shi Maria card, and a laughing, web-covered skull appeared in the air, exploded into a thousand little spiders, and for a moment, the whole area appeared covered in spiderwebs. Ominous harpsichord music made a *dun-dun-Dunnnn* sound as the giant spider appeared standing over Heyzoos, who was cowering at her sudden appearance.

"The Bedlam Bride!" the announcer shrieked.

A 120-second timer appeared over the massive spider, who rose high into the air, her giant legs spreading across the entire hallway, knocking decorative candy canes off the walls. Up on the second level, people screamed and scattered. The spider hiss-clicked as the head on her stretchy neck twisted around with confusion.

"Fucking shit!" Heyzoos cried as he started to empty his gun into the belly of the giant spider. A health bar appeared and started to slowly descend as he fired into her. The already screaming, panicked crowd went even more berserk.

Maria recoiled, hissing and clicking. She leaped up to the second level and turned, facing the screaming man.

"Stop!" Donut yelled.

One of Shi Maria's legs shot forward and skewered Jesus right through the chest. He cried out but kept firing. His gun didn't appear to run out of ammunition. She lifted the screaming form up in the air and, with another leg, swatted the Uzi out of his hand. It went flying.

"We are on the same team," Maria hissed at Jesus. Her health was halfway down. Heyzoos's health was also in the red and dropping rapidly.

Shi Maria looked at Donut. "Do you have a Heal Totem card?"

"Uh," Donut said. "No?"

"We have one," I said, "but it's not in the deck. *He's* our healer."

"You should kill him," Samantha called up to Shi Maria. "He hurt your tum-tum!"

Another card appeared in Donut's hand. The Combo card. She discarded it.

"Heal me," Shi Maria demanded of Heyzoos.

He groaned in pain. He raised his hand as if to cast something, but then he dissipated into dust.

Totem Killed.

At the far end of the mall, a figure appeared, floating up from the ground, then another. And another.

They were reindeer. Goddamned reindeer. There were eight of them, floating in a perfect V formation, and even at this distance, I could see they were covered in gore. Each had a strange, triangular dot over its head. Entrails hung from the antlers of one of them, and to my horror, there was a small man still attached to the end of the stream of guts. A man dressed like an elf. He screamed before plummeting back to the ground. The trail of intestines remained attached to the antlers.

I was expecting Santa to appear next, and he did, but not in the way I anticipated.

A ninth reindeer appeared, rising in front of the others. The decapitated head of Santa—or the poor guy working at the mall pretending to be Santa—hung from the creature's mouth. It spat, and the head dropped away.

The reindeer roared, lionlike. And then, its nose started to glow.

Its entire body glowed yellow, meaning it was currently invulnerable.

"What the hell?" I said.

This one also had a symbol over its head, but it was a triangle in a circle. I was pretty sure I knew what those symbols meant. We hadn't seen this type of monster yet.

Rude-Dolph the Blood-Nosed Slay-Deer. Level 100.

Eastern United States Legendary Creature.

Warning: This is a Puppet Master. This creature is intangible until all the puppets have been killed.

Eight of Eight Puppets still live.

Nobody is laughing at him anymore.

All nine reindeer started galloping through the air at us.

We had to kill the other eight reindeer before we could even touch Rude-Dolph.

"Carl, do you see that?" Donut shouted. "It's a cheap knockoff of Rudolph! He ate Santa!"

Another card popped into Donut's hand. It was Skylar Spinach, the ghommid splitter. Donut immediately whipped it forward, summoning it. An explosion appeared, followed by wisps of ghostly figures. The donkey-headed snake had a timer of 60 seconds.

"Skylar Spinach!" the announcer shouted.

"What in the name of the gods is that thing?" Samantha demanded.

"That entrance is not nearly as exciting as the others," Donut muttered just as a laser shot out from the nose of Rude-Dolph. The blade of light made a *vroom* noise, and it was like a continuous *Magic Missile* blast. A ceiling support for the mall crumbled. The crackling laser arced through the mall, shearing off a leg from Shi Maria and cutting right through Skylar Spinach. The laser missed Mongo by inches—though it wouldn't have hurt him anyway in the simulation. It passed harmlessly through Donut.

"Get them!" Donut shouted as Shi Maria hissed and angrily scuttled forward.

"You have to kill the other eight first," I called.

Skylar Spinach had split in half and was now two creatures. Skylar and Spinach. Skylar was still a donkey head, but it grew a pair of bat wings, and it took to the air, screaming toward the reindeer. The lower half, Spinach the snake, wriggled about like a worm, though spikes protruded from the area of the split. The headless snake reared up, and all the spikes flung out toward the incoming herd, the spikes shooting into the oncoming reindeer and peppering them with foot-long spikes. One of them—Blitzen—exploded into dust.

I looked over at Donut's hand. She had three cards with another appearing in a few seconds. None were totems.

"Play Greased Lightning on Shi Maria," I said, and she quickly flipped the card out toward the injured spider, who was now halfway down the mall. The card somersaulted through the air, spinning like a boomerang as it slapped onto the back of the giant spider. A giant lightning graphic appeared with a crack just at the same moment as Shi Maria shimmered and split into four different versions of the same terrifying spider.

"She just cast an illusion," I said, awed by the sight. I knew I could—and probably should—be entering this battle, but it was important to see how these guys fought. One of the illusions was suddenly moving much more quickly than before, and she spat a glob of web out of her ass at one of the other reindeer, who slammed to the ground. At the same moment, another roared and attacked, opening their mouth to—I don't know—attempt to eat the spider. Before it could connect with the massive creature, the reindeer was slammed in the side by Skylar, the bat-winged donkey head.

Yet another reindeer cast a spell, and the illusions all dissipated.

Rude-Dolph floated above all of this, and he appeared to be charging up another attack.

Shi Maria moved so quickly, she was a blur. One of the reindeer—Comet, I think—fired a white ball of magic at her, and it missed her by a wide margin. Suddenly, half of the remaining puppets turned on one another. Just like that, with no warning. One of them screamed and gored one of his fellow reindeer. He was frothing at the mouth, like he'd been hit by that Enraged debuff and Donut's *Why Are You Hitting Yourself?* spell at the same time.

I felt a sudden strange tug in my chest and my brain at the same time. It came out of nowhere. It felt as if all the breath had suddenly been knocked out of me. A wave of dizziness swept over me.

No, I thought. *This isn't right. We're supposed to be safe in here.*

Shi Maria had opened her fifth eye. It shone like a never-ending jewel atop the center of her head. I couldn't tell the color. It was black and white and yellow and red all at once. Even at this distance, I could feel it, calling to me, like there was a physical line between that extra eye and the center of my brain.

It's the river, I thought. *It's the river in my mind.*

I didn't know why or how I thought that. The thought didn't even make sense.

"Carl, are you okay?" Donut shouted.

I'd gone down to a knee, and I didn't even realize it. I sucked in air.

"I'm fine," I lied. "Keep your eyes on the totems."

The affected deer, having been driven both insane and blind, growled and then turned on each other.

Holy shit, I thought, watching open-mouthed. I pulled myself back to my feet. I looked nervously over at Mongo, who sat next to me, bouncing up and down, uncertain if he wanted to enter the fight. Even though he was protected from the spell here in the simulation, I knew how dangerous this would be in a real fight. We needed to make sure Mordecai finished that potion for him as soon as possible.

In seconds, all the puppet reindeer were dead, and the little marker over Rude-Dolph blinked out. The yellow glow vanished. At the same moment, the deer fired another attack from his nose, but Shi Maria deftly skittered out of the way, despite the missing limb, crawling up to the second floor of the mall and then leaping across the way as the entrances to a store called Merry-Go-Round and to another called Glamour Shots exploded.

Donut flipped another card out. This was Geraldo the monk seal. He appeared with the same fanfare as before. At the same moment, Shi Maria pounced, flying through the air, using one of her legs to literally rip Rude-Dolph in two. The monster let out a pitiful cry as the two pieces of his body remained floating in the air. His nose sputtered and blinked out.

Geraldo the seal did a flip and made two little karate moves before he stopped dead at the sight of the giant spider, which had lowered itself underneath the ripped-in-two reindeer. The female head on Shi Maria reached up into the air like a baby bird and started greedily devouring the dripping entrails from the deer's body, like she was eating spaghetti slowly oozing from the sky.

"Yo, what the fuck?" was all Geraldo said before the **Combat Complete** notification came, and all the totems disappeared in a puff of smoke.

Next to me, Mongo let out an uncertain screech.

"Carl," Donut said after a moment. She, too, was staring at the empty spot where the spider had been. "I'm really happy we didn't have to fight her earlier."

"Isn't she great?" Samantha asked.

29

WINNING CONDITION: STRIKE A SINGLE BLOW AGAINST THE DECK-master.

Losing condition: Have an enemy totem or deckmaster strike you.

Combat Started.

"Okay," I said. "Here we go."

"What? What's this?" Donut suddenly demanded out of nowhere. "Carl, this is an outrage!"

We'd been fighting in the mock-battle arena for hours now, spending a ridiculous amount of money. We'd just beaten the challenge difficulty, which had been easy because we'd pulled Shi Maria in the initial hand. Our opponent was a giant mouse or rat thing from Indian mythology named Mushika. It was only level 50. It'd been about to summon something, but Maria swooped in, paralyzed it with a spell, unhinged her lower jaw like a snake, and gobbled it up. The fight had lasted seconds. I had no idea why the fight was considered a challenge, but I suspected we were lucky we'd killed it before it finished its spell.

The damn spider was terrifying to behold. She seemed to get an almost sexual pleasure from committing violence. After she devoured the rat, she'd turned toward us and shouted, "Again," before dissipating into dust.

After that, we'd unlocked the "Secret Challenge Mode," which was a "medium plus" difficulty challenger with a deck of their own. These fights were free, but we could only do it three times. This was our first opportunity to face someone else with cards, and I needed Donut to pay attention.

Donut stopped in the field, looking around angrily. She was on the ground to my right. She'd pulled an initial hand with only one totem, Raul the crab, and she'd just summoned him. The strange crab was doing stretches in front of us while he chanted a spell. We still hadn't seen who our opponent was. The environment was "Verdant Hills." The playing field was a cluster of small, round hills covered in ankle-high green grass. The tallest hills were in the center, meaning we didn't have line of sight across the arena. Samantha and Mongo were having a great time chasing after each other in the soft grass.

Donut made a scoffing noise. "This is an outrage!" she repeated.

"What?" I asked, looking around. "What is it?"

She looked up at me. She was wearing her sunglasses, and I saw my reflection in them looking down worriedly at her. Her lower mouth trembled like it always did when she was really upset.

"I just received a notification that Empress D'Nadia sold my sponsorship to someone else!"

I grunted. "I'm not surprised, especially considering some of the action items you keep proposing in the warlord chat. We can look at it when the fight is over."

"I'm not a trading card to be collected and discarded, Carl. No offense, Raul."

Raul's claws glowed as he finished casting his *Bris* spell. The spell was cocked and ready until he finished casting it.

The crab turned and bowed. "The path to the heavenly throne is rife with insult, great mistress Donut. This worm grovels and kowtows in your resplendent light. If there is someone out there who doesn't recognize your brilliance, then surely they are blind to your vastness."

"Thank you, Raul." She paused. "Wait, did you just call me fat?"

Raul threw himself to the ground. "Shame! Shame on this worthless maggot! I beg your permission to kill myself in my dishonor!"

"Never mind, just keep stretching. Start your magic shell the moment you see the bad guys." She made a whimpering noise and turned back to me. "Carl, I thought she liked me."

I held my tongue. "She does like you, but it's not really appropriate for her to sponsor you when we'll be fighting her." Plus, I didn't add, she'd likely overextended herself getting that Faction Wars spot. Selling

Donut's sponsorship had to have made her a lot of money. I'd actually been expecting this for a while now.

"My new sponsor is . . ." She paused. I watched as she composed herself. Across the way, the flash of a card summoning cracked across the hills. Our opponent had summoned their first totem, but we still couldn't see them. "I am very happy to have a new sponsor. I am. I just don't know how a waste-management company is a good fit for my brand."

"A waste-management company?" I asked. A new card popped into Donut's hand. A Time Extend. She tossed it onto Raul, who groveled as it hit him. Another 70 seconds added to his countdown.

"This undeserving cur accepts your gift, great mistress."

"Raul," I said, "remember our talk last time? You need to stop acting like that. Her head is big enough as it is. I want you to work on your confidence."

"Yes, Daddy Carl. It's difficult to exude confidence when I am nothing but an undeserving louse burning in her glittering radiance."

"Look. The others are going to keep picking on you if you keep saying weird shit like that. Just do what we say, and you'll be fine. You don't need to insult yourself every time she gives you an order. And stop calling me Daddy."

DONUT: MY NEW SPONSOR IS NAMED LONG-HAUL BIOLOGICAL-WASTE-MANAGEMENT SOLUTIONS, AND I JUST CAN'T WITH THAT. I KNOW I'M SUPPOSED TO APPEAR GRATEFUL, BUT THAT SOUNDS ABSOLUTELY DISGUSTING. CARL, ARE THEY GOING TO SHOW COMMERCIALS FOR GARBAGE TRUCKS ON MY FEED? THIS IS NOT ACCEPTABLE.

Biological waste? I didn't like the sound of that, but now wasn't the time to be having this conversation. I turned my attention back to the field.

By this point, we'd gone through just about every combination of totems.

As expected, Asojano was a complete dick. The first thing he did was attempt to cast a nasty debuff on Donut, but he'd been stopped by the safeties of the mock-battle arena. He'd only tried it once, but I didn't trust him.

Still, he was ridiculously strong. Once Donut yelled at him, he'd snap to attention and do what we asked. When he engaged in battle, he'd fight enthusiastically. He took out a whole squad of bomber pigs with a shake of his fat wand. They'd fallen from the sky, their skin boiling and popping with sores, all of them dead before they hit the ground. It was the first time someone other than Shi Maria had managed to kill an enemy while she was summoned.

Also, as expected, Raul and Geraldo didn't get along and would fight each other unless Donut yelled at them to stop. Geraldo the monk seal was a great melee fighter and tank, and he generally did what Donut asked. He only wavered if Raul was also on the field. When that happened, he'd turn and start throwing insults at the crab, who in turn would start spouting nonsense at the seal about celestial thrones and *chi* or *ki* or however the hell you pronounce it.

They'd only come to actual blows once, and that was when Geraldo had said something about Raul's mother. Donut yelled at them to stop, and Raul, who'd appeared to have the upper hand in the fight, stopped immediately, which allowed Geraldo to crack his shell and kill him. Donut made Geraldo apologize the next time they were together, but it was clear they'd always hate each other.

Raul, who'd been struggling with his self-confidence even before we picked him up, had turned into a simpering, sniveling kiss ass. He would follow Donut's orders without question. Luckily, he was a powerful fighter. His once-a-fight *Bris* spell, which required a short meditation to cast, ended up being a great ranged spell. He'd cast it on his claw, and it allowed him to powerfully crush things from a distance.

The biggest problem with Raul was that he was a big wuss. He'd fight, and he was damn good at it, but he would always cower and submit to any other summoned totems. The first time we'd summoned him the same time as Shi Maria, she'd picked him up, skewering him right through his shell, and used his body as a cudgel to beat a group of bowl-headed Japanese monsters called kappas to death. He'd screamed and sniveled and cried as Maria gleefully pounded him down like a toddler with a toy hammer. Then Shi Maria ended up telling this to Geraldo the next time they were both together, and now Geraldo was calling Raul "the spider lady's *jinetera*."

Skylar Spinach never talked and didn't have much of a personality at all, and I suspected that had something to do with him or her already being half of a monster when we'd flagged them. They usually ignored the other totems and did exactly what Donut asked, though for some reason the thing really liked both Mongo and Samantha and would huddle up to them when summoned, an action that would freak out Mongo. If we talked to it, the donkey head would just make those unsettling *hee-haw* donkey noises. The monster was great as a distraction, and I wished it had a summoning time longer than 60 seconds. Once it was killed the first time, the resulting donkey head with the bat wings had a Dodge of 15 and was next to impossible to hit, which would keep Donut safe as long as it was summoned. The snake half of the body was non-corporeal and shot spikes from a distance.

Also, Skylar Spinach had an interesting side effect I hadn't anticipated. While we could only have six totems, if Skylar split and then timed out, the two pieces would split into two different temporary cards for the remainder of the battle, which we could then summon separately. Both pieces were stronger than the original whole and had a longer time-out.

Shi Maria was clearly our strongest card by a wide margin. The giant monster would appear, quickly assess the situation, and then skitter across the battlefield to dispatch any opponents, usually in seconds. Sometimes, though, she'd first demand to see all the other cards Donut had in her hand, and she'd make suggestions or ask Donut to cast some of the buffs on herself first.

One of her biggest strengths was that Cockroach ability, though we never got to see it in action. It worked differently when she was a card. If she died—and she never died—the card would simply get returned to Donut's deck and not the discard pile.

Also, she'd occasionally play with the opponents. She had a sadistic streak, and she'd keep the opponent monsters alive long enough to devour them partially before she finished the job. Once, we fought a Gorgon, which was just an eight-foot Medusa creature with a Naga body, and she paralyzed the monster and then started pulling the snakes from her head, one by one while the monster sobbed. She'd reached down and kissed the Medusa full on the lips as she finally died, groaning sexually as she did so. All of us, including Uzi Jesus, had just stared at the display.

And speaking of Uzi Jesus, he was also going to be a problem. He wasn't as openly hostile as Asojano, but if Donut asked him to do something, he'd smile and say he'd do it, but there was only a 50% chance he'd actually perform. And then he'd outright lie about it a minute later. It was like he was a toddler. I sent a sarcastic message to Florin thanking him for the card. He'd just responded with a laugh.

The last time we'd summoned him, Donut asked him to resurrect Geraldo, who'd been literally cleaved in two by a minotaur's axe. He'd said he'd do it, but then he simply sat there.

"Now, Heyzoos. Please," Donut had said, frustration rising. "Skylar is about to time out." Skylar the donkey head with wings was on the other side of the battlefield flying in circles around the minotaur, who was screaming at her in Greek and swiping up with his giant bloody axe. If Jesus used the *Resurrect Totem* spell, Geraldo would not only come back, but it would be as if we'd just summoned him for the first time. His timer would reset, and all the buffs and debuffs would go away.

"I did."

"You didn't. He's still dead. I can see him right now."

"The bodies turn to dust when they die," he'd said. "He's still there. That means I resurrected him. It's not my fault he's being a pansy."

"He's in two pieces, Jesus."

"Maybe he's an atheist."

Donut looked as if she was going to leap over there and claw him. "If the deck has a resurrect card or a totem that can cast *Resurrect*, the bodies remain. *You* were the one who figured that out last time!"

"Well, I did it. Look, just let me go over there, and I will shoot the bull."

"Don't gaslight me, Jesus. I know you can shoot it. But this time I want you to resurrect Geraldo. We're practicing. You've done it before. I don't see why you won't do it now."

"Believe in me, Princess Donut."

"Carl, do something!"

I sighed. "Look, Heyzoos, will you do it if she takes back what she said earlier?"

He crossed his arms. "Maybe."

I gave Donut a pointed look.

She appeared on the precipice of violence. I'd never seen anyone get under her skin this much since Tserendolgor. *I* would've ejected the asshole by now, but he was such a powerful card, I wanted to wait and see if they could come to an understanding. I was trying not to be a back seat deckmaster. When the real fights started, I wouldn't be able to sit there and help her.

"This is not how this is supposed to work. This is not how any of this works," Donut said. Across the field, Skylar timed out with a *pop*. The minotaur roared and started charging in our direction. "Heyzoos, I'm sorry I said you're not the real Jesus."

Heyzoos sighed dramatically. "I weep, Princess Donut. I *weep*. I just hope my father will forgive your blasphemy. Gah!"

He accidently pulled the trigger on his Uzi, shooting himself in the shoulder. His gun went spinning away. While he danced around, cursing and holding his shoulder, Donut pulled Raul, who rushed over and killed the charging bull with a spinning kick.

And that was pretty much how all of these fights were going. We'd win, and we'd win easily, but it wasn't because Donut had firm control over her totems, which worried me.

Now, a few hours later, we finally had a chance at deck-versus-deck combat, and it was Donut who was the one getting distracted. I looked down at her hand. She only had three cards at the moment, and another would appear in a few seconds. She had **Force Discard**, the mana-replenishing **Blue Stuff**, and the health-increasing **Stout**.

The moment the giant ethereal wolf appeared at the top of the hill, her focus snapped back to the present. The totem had a timer at 76 seconds and counting. The ghostly wolf looked upon us and snarled. To my left, Mongo roared. Samantha spat out a mouthful of grass and starting shouting insults.

Der Kornwolf. Level 100.

Summoned totem of Der Schachmeister.

It didn't give any more information than that.

Raul started chanting, preparing his magical shell. The Shi Maria totem popped into Donut's hand. She moved to summon the spider, but a giant, flaming, animated lock appeared floating in the air above her. It had a 30-second countdown.

"Summon lock!" the announcer shouted. Tiny ethereal chains appeared on her cards.

"Carl, what's happening?" Donut cried. "It won't let me summon Shi Maria! I can't do anything."

"Our opponent cast a mystic card on you," I said.

The wolf howled. Another flash of summoning appeared in the distance. A second wolf appeared. This one was also level 100, but it was called **Die Kartoffelwölfin**. Other than the name, this one looked identical to the last.

"Where is the deckmaster guy?" Donut demanded. "I don't even see him!"

As if she beckoned him, our opponent appeared. He was a little human kid wearing a tuxedo and round glasses. Maybe about 12 years old. He appeared atop the distant hill, coming to stand between the two wolves. He had three magazine-sized cards floating in front of him with a blinking wire frame indicating his fourth card would be summoned soon. The kid rubbed at his nose with his sleeve and then flipped us off.

"Hey!" Donut called.

Der Schachmeister. Level 25.

Holds a deck consisting of twenty cards, including six totems.

Has an eight-second card summoning cooldown.

Focuses on debuffs and disabling the opponent. He's an annoying little prick without any regard for his own personal safety. You'll have to deal with him the same way you would if this were a middle school playground. You gotta kick his ass before he outsmarts you and gets the adults involved.

That eight-second summoning cooldown was ominous. When Donut played or discarded a card, it took ten seconds for the next card to appear. I had thought that was a hard rule, and I hadn't realized some opponents possibly had faster pull times. That meant some of these guys would be even more difficult to beat than I originally thought. I wondered if that meant some opponents would have more or fewer than six totems, too.

The two horse-sized wolves snapped at each other and then charged toward our position. Next to me, Mongo shrieked in outrage.

"No," I said, putting a calming hand on Mongo, who in turn looked to Donut for confirmation.

"Remember what Mommy said, Mongo. You gotta do what Uncle Carl says when I have the cards out."

He growled but complied. We didn't want Mongo in on the practice fights, at least not against the enemy's totems. I needed to practice with him following my commands. The wolves wouldn't be able to hurt him here, which was good, but it also made it so this simulation wasn't realistic. In a real fight, the enemy totems couldn't hurt Donut if she had at least one totem summoned, but they could—and would—hurt me and Mongo and everybody else that wasn't a deckmaster. Mongo wouldn't have a chance against two level 100 wolves.

He would, however, be able to attack the kid directly. If this was a real fight, the path to victory was obvious. We'd ignore the totems and go straight for the kid. I suspected in the future, the enemies wouldn't be so vulnerable.

I held off for now. We needed to practice as much as we could.

"Peekaboo!" the announcer shouted. A freaky pair of bloodshot eyes emerged, floating above Donut, staring down. The names of Donut's four cards appeared, hovering over the deck.

The kid had just cast a mystic card that allowed him to see our hand.

"Go away!" Donut cried up at the eyes. They didn't go away, which implied he'd be able to see our hand for the remainder of the battle. "What do we do?"

"It's your call," I said.

"Real helpful, Carl."

The wolves disappeared as they reached the bottom of the hill. They'd reappear in seconds and be on us.

"Raul, you don't have time to finish your spell. You have to hold them off!" Donut said.

The crab flipped in the air, landing in front of Donut.

Across the way, I watched as the kid swiped another card from his hand. It was another mystic card.

"To hell with ya!" the announcer shouted.

The Shi Maria card flew from Donut's hand, did a flip in the air, and burst into flames.

"Hey!" Donut shouted.

We wouldn't be able to summon her for the rest of the battle. That was actually a legendary card that would've force-discarded all of the same card from her hand and deck. But she only had a single Shi Maria.

The two wolves rushed up the hill, barking and snarling. Raul unleashed his *Bris* on the first of the two.

The wolf Der Kornwolf—whatever the hell that meant—exploded into dust. Raul had snapped his head off from a distance. The second one threw itself at Raul, who flipped, waving his claws. The wolf tackled him, and they went rolling down the hill, a snarling, hissing, snapping mass.

Raul wouldn't be able to hold the wolf off for long. Donut still had a few seconds before her deck would unlock, but she didn't have any totems in hand. I suspected the kid had another deck-freezing card ready to go. This fight was already over if I didn't intervene.

I sighed. I was about to send Mongo over there to end it when Samantha suddenly rose into the air and hovered there for a moment. She started to glow a bright, crackling blue like she was a miniature sun. I stepped back, surprised at the heat coming off of her. That was new.

What the hell? I thought.

"Nein! Nein!" the kid shouted from the distance. He started to back away as if he knew what was about to happen.

"Watch this!" Samantha started to say, the flames getting brighter. But then she abruptly fizzled out, and she fell to the grass.

"God-mother-damnit," Samantha said. "I used it all up." She growled and started to roll away.

Totem Killed.

I turned to see where the wolf was, but it was too late. The wolf leaped, flying up the hill and slamming directly into Donut.

The moment he hit her, the room flashed, and all the opponents disappeared.

Simulation Failed.

Congratulations. If this was a real fight, you would all be dead right now.

Combat Complete. Deck has been reset.

"That guy was a cheater," Donut said. "How are we supposed to win if we can't use our deck? And I was distracted by my new sponsor! That fight shouldn't count!"

I thought of our earlier fight in the challenge difficulty, the one against the rat monster from India. "Shi Maria's main tactic is the smart one. We need to be faster. We need to attack immediately, no matter what hand we pull. That means I need to hit the enemy right away. Me and Mongo." I extended my xistera and drew a heavy ball into my hand. I lobbed it across the empty arena. It cracked into an invisible wall in the distance. I remembered Mordecai's advice when it came to mages. *They can't cast their spells when you're punching them in the face.*

I continued. "We also need to work on getting these totems to attack as quickly as possible. We should work on moves we can call out, like you and I do. I wish we could call them out of the cards to talk to them. We'll have to spend some time in the easy arena with them."

"Asojano and Heyzoos barely listen to me," Donut said. "They're not going to remember any moves."

"I know," I said.

Asojano and Uzi Jesus were both good powerful cards, but if they were going to be slow to comply, they were almost useless. If we fought a guy like that last kid and he was better protected, we'd be toast.

I thought of Katia. We still had a few hours before she would wake up. She'd offered me a totem card earlier. She was having the same issue we were having with Raul and Geraldo. She had two cards who hated each other, and her charisma wasn't high enough to keep them from fighting one another, so she was giving one of them up. If we could get that one, it meant we'd have to give up one of ours. But what was the best totem to get rid of? We'd have to decide fast. We only had a little more than a day left.

We needed more practice.

"Let's try this again."

30

Time Until Phase Two: 6 hours.

ZEV: YOU TWO NEED TO BE BACK IN FOUR AND A HALF HOURS. YOU'RE going on Odette's show, and you're going to walk straight from there to the phase two onboarding chamber.

DONUT: OKAY, ZEV!

ZEV: Just an FYI. Harbinger will be there again, observing virtually. He's insisting on it. And yes, we've alerted your attorney, who will also be present.

The message came just as we entered the Desperado Club. I ignored it and continued to talk.

"Most of these decks seem to be themed," I said. Clarabelle waved us through without saying a word. "The cards play off each other. We need to come up with combos for our own deck. What we have now is pretty eclectic."

"There's not much we can do about that at this point," Donut said. "Everybody else is saying the same thing. The bad guys are always using consumable cards. We have to fight over and over, but they only fight once, and they get to use really expensive and hard-to-find cards. It's not fair! If we use up our consumables, then we won't have anything good for the next fight. But everyone seems to think we'll start to have more choices once the next phase begins, and we can start moving our decks around once we can steal cards from the bad guys."

"True." I was glad Donut was finally starting to put her mind to this, and I was especially glad she was talking strategy with the others. I could talk deck strategy all day, but I wouldn't be the one making spur-of-the-moment decisions.

We'd lost the second of our three deck-on-deck fights against a muddy blob guy whose deck was all tanks and snare cards. I'd deliberately held back on this one. I wanted to see what sort of strategy he'd use.

The blob guy had hit Shi Maria with the same Damnation card we had, and she'd wasted her time fighting a rolling mud ball with a high Dodge. The spider had finally killed it after Donut hit her with Greased Lightning, only to have the deckmaster blob summon another one of the same monsters. When Shi Maria timed out and was sent to the discard pile thanks to the Damnation snare, she'd been enraged and screaming.

Then Raul and Asojano both got themselves frozen and killed, all by various snare cards. The moment Donut had no totems, one of the mud balls rolled up and exploded, hitting us with specks of sludge, causing us to lose the fight.

For the third fight, it was an enormously fat, pink-skinned female orc named the Luau. She was dressed in Hawaiian gear, complete with a lei, a grass skirt, and a coconut bra, plus she had a little piglet guy a third her size off to the side playing the congas for some reason. She immediately summoned a lizard thing called a Mo'o, which looked like a human-sized version of the gecko from those ridiculous car insurance commercials, though it had a spear and breathed fire. I wasted a low-powered hob-lobber and drilled it across the field. It'd worked. The small explosion killed all three. The fight lasted less than five seconds.

"That was a waste of a practice," Donut had said afterward.

"Maybe," I'd said. "But that's what we're going to try to do when these start for real. If they're going to let me use my regular attacks, I'm going to exploit the hell out of it. If we kill them fast, we'll have access to their full deck before they can waste any of those valuable consumable cards. Now let's go back and do some more fights in the easy arena. We need to talk to our totems."

We'd spent some time working on getting our cards to attack as quickly as possible. The problem was, our current deck wasn't really conducive to speed. Shi Maria was fast when she wanted to be. Also, Geraldo was fast enough, as was Skylar Spinach. But that was it. Raul the crab required time to cast all of his spells. Asojano and Jesus were both immature idiots. We really needed to work on the deck itself. And we needed more practice.

"We're not going to practice when we don't have any money left, Carl. I mean, really. You're spending money like Miss Beatrice in a shoe shop."

We entered the main dining room of the Desperado Club. Katia sat at the table, surrounded by Bautista, Imani, Elle, and Louis. She did not look happy.

"We'll figure it out," I said as Donut gasped and rushed away. She jumped to the table and then to Katia's shoulder. She bumped her head into hers. Katia was in her regular human form, and she was sobbing. She looked a mess. The stench of vomit filled the restaurant.

"I'm sorry," Katia said as I came to sit down. "I'm sorry."

I put my hand on her knee. I still had no idea of the full extent of what was happening.

"You're okay," I said, feeling strangely hesitant. "You're here now with us."

"It was so real, Carl. It was like I was there. It's so much better than the blitz sticks."

"Blitz sticks?" I asked. I exchanged a look with Imani, who was rubbing Katia's back. Louis was holding on to a bucket.

"I can't," Katia said. "I . . ." She leaned forward and vomited into the bucket as Donut howled and jumped away.

DONUT: WOW, CARL. SHE'S PUKING A WHOLE RAINBOW OF COLORS.

"It's okay," I said when she was done. "You don't have to explain." The words came out much colder than I intended.

"This bucket is getting really full," Louis said, looking down into it worriedly. "I don't know where it's all coming from." An elf waitress zipped by. "Hey, can I get another bucket?" She ignored him.

"Oh god," Katia said as she leaned into the bucket again.

DONUT: MORDECAI, DO YOU KNOW WHAT'S HAPPENING WITH KATIA?

Mordecai was still in the guild working at his alchemy table. Now that everyone knew about the little changeling kids he was fostering, he wasn't using all of his free time to watch over them, instead relegating it to the workers out in the public area of the guild. That led to Mordecai spending more and more time at his workbench. He barely left now except to get more supplies.

MORDECAI: I do. I've been talking with Imani. Katia is addicted to four different drugs. Good news is, we have a cure for all four of them, including the blitz. A cure for the addiction portion, at least. Two of the cures are readily available in the market, and Imani has picked up both. I'm working on the other two. Imani has given the first cure to Katia, which is why she's puking like that. The problem is, she's already jacked up her stats. It's not good. Everything is scrambled. Her intelligence took a hit, though it's actually still higher than I thought it was from before thanks to the blitz, which seems to have been going on for a while. Her highest stat, constitution, has taken a big hit. Her strength is higher. Her charisma took a hit. She'll be permanently susceptible to any sort of addictive spells from now on. She's probably forgotten a spell or two. And she's probably lowered a few skill points.

CARL: For fuck's sake.

I immediately thought of my dad. The image of the man came unbidden, and it surprised me. A wave of anger washed over me, partially at Katia, partially at myself for allowing any part of me to compare the two.

Still, I had to deliberately stop myself from talking out loud, from shouting at her. *What the hell is wrong with you? We're counting on you. People who love you are counting on you. I don't understand.*

I took a breath.

CARL: Why would she let this happen? Why would she do this to herself?

DONUT: I THINK SHE'S REALLY SAD ABOUT SOMETHING.

Katia continued to vomit. I just stared at her, not trusting myself to say anything helpful. I caught Bautista's eyes, and he appeared angry as well, though I wasn't certain why.

MORDECAI: We all deal with this stuff in different ways. This is how she's doing it. It's not right. It's not healthy. But it's what she did, and it's done. She needs help, and she needs your understanding.

Jesus, I thought. I caught sight of Katia's right hand with the missing fingers as she vomited again. I remembered that day when she'd lost them. It was the fight with the mantaur. We'd left her alone on the platform, and she'd been crying. She could re-create the fingers easily, but lately she'd been choosing to leave her hand like this.

I'm losing myself, she'd said.

The anger didn't leave, but I was finally starting to realize it wasn't Katia whom I was angry with.

I do understand, I thought after a moment. *I don't want to. That's the problem.*

I sent Mordecai a private one-on-one message while Donut clucked over her.

CARL: Tell me about these drugs she's on.

MORDECAI: There's Travis Priest. I don't know why it's called that, but it's basically a really strong painkiller. It's nasty and addictive, and it's what I had Imani cure first. That's why she's probably still vomiting. There's something called Creamsicle Charm. It's basically ground-up fairy wings. That one is a bit like shrooms, but it also makes you forget your worries. That one isn't so addictive, but we're going to give her the cure for it just in case. I'm already working on it. Then there's the blitz sticks, which is like weed plus a hallucinogen that shows you nonexistent memories, which is why they're so damn addictive. The cure for that is a patch she'll have to wear on her skin for a while. Imani has it ready to go, and we're going to give it to her next. Katia has been on the blitz for a while, which means it's going to be hard to get out of her system, believe me.

Finally, there's Glory Bound, which she's only taken once, thank goodness. That's the bad one and the most addictive. By far. It puts her in a coma and allows her to relive a memory. Like blitz, but much, much stronger. Combined with Creamsicle and Travis Priest, she would've completely forgotten where she really was for a short while. She basically would've just gone back in time and fully reexperienced something. The problem with all of these is that it really fucks your brain up, and they all eventually stop working if they don't outright kill you.

CARL: What's the cure for that one?

MORDECAI: It's not easy. The way that one works is if she doesn't get more, she'll slowly go insane, unable to tell the difference between then and now. So the cure is basically a bad trip of Glory Bound. I take a regular dose and add some stuff to it. She'll have to relive one of her worst memories. It's pretty fucked-up.

CARL: So, she'll be out for another ten hours? We have shit to do now. We're doing the switchover in a few hours.

MORDECAI: Yep. Timing is going to be an issue. Assuming she's even able to fight, we'll have to wait until her team gets their key. I have something that'll hold off the hallucinations until then, but it won't last for long.

CARL: Damnit. We also have that thing Katia and I have to do. It's not something that'll be easy. I can't do it myself. There's no way.

We needed to kill Astrid now. The plan was mostly in place. If we finished the quest now, that box would open and give Katia access to the orchid, which in turn would allow Huanxin to keep up her part of the bargain. I wanted to make certain Katia had the flower before Donut and I went to Odette. Huanxin's promise to help Katia was only good if I secured Odette's participation as our adjutant.

We had no idea what the changeover would bring. This might be our last chance.

Katia seemed to have stopped vomiting for now. Donut was on the table, rubbing herself back and forth on Katia's arm. Louis slow-walked the full bucket toward the bathroom while the elf waitress watched him, her arms crossed. All around, Crocodilian guards in tuxedos watched us as well, including one who was moving to cut Louis off. They probably didn't like the idea of someone dumping magical psychedelic puke in their bathrooms.

I checked my view counter. It was spiked. The whole universe was watching this drama. My head hurt. That rushing feeling was in full force, flowing through me.

It was like I knew. I could sense it, this conversation I was about to have.

MORDECAI: Listen, Carl. There's an alternate solution to this you need to consider.

I looked up into the air.

I will burn this whole thing to the ground. Goddamn you all.

CARL: What do you mean?

But I knew exactly what he meant. I knew exactly what he was going to say. I made him say it anyway.

MORDECAI: I'm helping Katia with this because she's become my friend. No, more than that. She's part of my family. She's one of the most powerful crawlers in the game, and everyone is better off with her here. Plus it's the right thing to do. It's what *good* people do. When someone falls, you hold out your wing, and you help them back up. You, Carl, you're helping her for the same reason. That, plus you have this sense of honor that's going to get you killed. I know you love Katia . . .

I felt a strange panic rise up in my chest as he paused.

MORDECAI: But I also know you love Donut more.

CARL: No. We're not doing this. Not now.

MORDECAI: Son, I can't have this conversation with Donut, but this needs to be said. The right thing to do is to help Katia. Yes.

But the smart thing, and the safe thing, is to step back and let her self-destruct. We're helping her because that's what we want to do. But we have to look at the facts. It's either her or Donut. She thought she found a solution to the problem with the Crown of the Sepsis Whore, but she's the one who self-sabotaged it. It's not your fault. It's not Donut's fault. And honestly, it's not Katia's fault. Some breaks aren't clean.

CARL: No. We're not giving up on her, and I don't want you to bring it up again.

Mordecai didn't answer. I knew he thought I was being stubborn. Stupid. Suicidal even.

He was right. I didn't care.

It's going to get worse before it gets better. We're going to lose more friends. We're going to have to do some pretty horrible things just to survive.

Katia looked at me, made a little groan, and wiped her mouth. I was staring at her intently.

"Carl?" she asked.

"Samantha is inside the guild," I said. "I'd do it myself, but you're the one with the drawing skills. Imani is going to give you the patch for the blitz. You're going to pull yourself together, and we're going to do this. You and me. We only have three hours. We don't know if we'll get another chance. It has to be now."

"Okay," she said. She started to pull herself up.

"Where do you think you're going?" Bautista said, pushing her back down.

"Don't touch me like that," Katia snapped, pushing him away. "Don't ever touch me like that."

"You can do this later," Bautista said, glaring at me. "We have time. There may be entrances to the club in phase two. And even if there aren't, we'll all be back here for the last phase. You can do it then."

"Carl . . ." Imani began.

"No," I said, taking them all in. "No. It has to be now."

DONUT: CARL, WHAT ARE YOU DOING? DON'T BE MEAN TO KATIA.

"He's right," Katia said, coming to stand next to me. She was shivering and stank like vomit. "I'm okay. I'll be okay."

"Fine. Kill yourself. But I won't stand by and watch," Bautista said. He turned and stormed from the club.

"You have almost a dozen debuffs that won't run out for several hours," Imani said coldly. Her translucent butterfly wings flapped angrily.

"Then do what you can for me. Please," Katia said.

Imani's dark eyes bored into Katia. "All right, but before you go, I gotta put that blitz patch on your ass. And I'm going to give you a few other buffs that might make you sick again for a minute, but they'll keep you from passing out."

Katia gave me a look, and I nodded. She reached over and squeezed my hand. She felt alarmingly weak.

"Okay," Katia said to Imani. "But let's do it in the bathroom. Louis's bucket is full."

"I'm coming with you!" Donut announced, and bounded off after them before I could object. "They have very nice bathrooms on this floor."

Elle, who'd been strangely quiet through all this, watched Katia, Imani, and Donut disappear around the corner. She turned and met my eyes. The only ones left in the restaurant were me, her, and Louis, who still had the bucket of vomit. Apparently they hadn't let him into the bathroom with it. He finally gave up and stuck it in his inventory.

"Hey," he said, "I just got an achievement for storing a bucket of vomit."

Elle crossed her arms, still glaring at me. "I hope you know what you're doing, cowboy. If anything happens to her, we're gonna have a problem with Tony the Tiger. If he goes, he'll stop making that tea for us every morning. I'm pretty sure it's the only thing keeping Imani together."

"I know," I said. "Trouble has been brewing there for a while. If we can pull this off, it'll put us on the road to fixing all of that."

"Why the hurry, though?"

"It has to be now," I said. "I have a terrible feeling about phase two. I think everything's about to change again."

Elle nodded. "Just don't let her die. Speaking of tea, we haven't seen you once at the morning breakfast."

"Everything is so busy."

She sighed. "Don't I know it. Just make sure you guys get that key in the next phase."

"You and Imani, too," I said. "I hate that you're on separate teams."

She nodded again. "We're going to make sure we pick different places for phase two, so they don't make us fight one another. We both have solid teams. My squatch squad will kick anybody's ass, and Imani traded her alien guy for that unique mothman and the reverse tooth fairy card. I think she'll be okay." She paused, looking in the direction Katia had gone. "Man, I thought for sure Louis would be the first of us to crack. Poor kid."

"I'm standing right here," Louis said.

"But you know what?" Elle continued. "I think this is good. You forcing her back into the pool. I don't know who you two have to kill for certain, but the fact you have to meet back here . . ." She shook her head, not wanting to say anything further. We'd automatically lose the quest if anyone said it out loud. "I hope you have a good plan."

I looked at the corner where Donut, Imani, and Katia had disappeared. "We do. It's dangerous, though. And a little crazy."

Elle grunted. "What else is new?"

31

<Note added by Crawler Rosetta. 9th Edition>

As fragile as they look, fairies and sprites can be difficult to kill. They're fast. They're magical. They're always on alert. They say luck is not a real stat in this place, but I think it is. The luck of these little monsters . . . it's unnatural. Something crazy always happens when I try to fight one. Be wary, comrades.

But if you must fight them, pull their wings off. They come off easily. That's where they store their magic.

"I'VE NEVER SEEN YOU HERE BEFORE," CLARABELLE SAID, GLARING down at Samantha. "I've seen you on the recap a bunch of times, but I never noticed the pass on your neck."

Samantha growled and made a hissing noise at Clarabelle. She snapped her teeth a few times.

"In the Nothing, there's a goddess who looks a lot like you. Maki. Maraka. Makara? Something like that. I can't remember her name. She has the head of a crocodile and body of a fish, and she makes sushi rolls out of her own innards. They keep growing back, and she keeps making more and selling it. She has a little stand and everything. She's quite the entrepreneur." Samantha made a spitting sound. "It tastes terrible."

"What's your point?" Clarabelle asked.

"My point is that I am going to kill your mother."

Clarabelle crossed her arms. "Is that so?"

"Oh, it be so, lady. Now let me in!"

"You know what?" Clarabelle began. "I don't think—"

I scooped Samantha up and held up a hand, interrupting. I slammed her jaw shut with my arm before she ruined everything. "Listen. Sorry about her. We just finished a quest where she killed someone, and they put the tattoo on her neck."

"It is disgusting," Samantha said, her voice muffled by my arm. She wriggled her head free. "I hate tattoos more than I hate sushi. Though I did have alligator nuggets once. They tasted like chicken! When I get my body, I will never have a tattoo again!"

". . . But now she wants to try a drink," I said, talking over her. "I promised I'd take her before phase two started. That's all." I flipped Clarabelle a gold coin. "Sorry, I know she's an ass."

"Whatever," Clarabelle said, and waved us through. "Just keep her away from the guards, or they'll kick you all out. For good this time."

"Oh boy," Samantha said as she squeezed out of my arms. She hit the ground, bounced once, and rolled through the door and into the main restaurant.

"Sorry," I said again to Clarabelle before I followed after her.

"Yoohoo! What's a girl gotta do to get a shirty dirly?"

"It's 'Dirty Shirley,'" I called. "And don't get drunk!"

"You! Elf lady! Point me to the bar! The good one, not that boring one. I know there's a few up here!"

I sighed.

CARL: SHE ALMOST RUINED IT ALREADY, BUT SHE'S IN. ARE YOU IN PLACE?

KATIA: Yes. We have a problem. There're a few crawlers in the club. We need to make sure they stay out of the way.

CARL: Any of our people?

KATIA: No, but they're all on the top floor, dancing. They'll probably be okay, but we should try to kick them out just in case.

CARL: Okay. I'll take care of them when I go up there. How are you feeling?

KATIA: I'm feeling like people keep asking me that. It was a blip. Don't worry about me. Let's do this.

That was more than a blip, but I wasn't going to say that now. Katia was drugged to the gills with Imani buffs until we could get her truly cured of all her new addictions. Mordecai seemed to believe she'd be okay like this for a few days at least.

CARL: All right. Here we go.

I consulted my recently enhanced map, and I headed deeper into the club, passing by the bar. Samantha was already there, sitting on the counter, demanding that the badger bartender add extra cherries to her drink order.

"Don't forget my straw. And you will have to feed the cherries to me," she was saying. I was pretty sure she was trying to sound throaty and seductive. "Put one on each claw, and I will eat them off." She snapped with her teeth and did a little growl. "One by one."

"You got gold?" the bartender asked, not impressed. I gave the badger man a cursory inspection. He was a level 25 **Porsuk**, which was the name of the badger race in this game. The man's name was Charles.

"Oh, yes," Samantha purred. "I got a coin pouch in my nussy. You make that drink right, and I'll let you use those sexy claws of yours to . . . dig it out."

"In your *what?*"

I shuddered as I moved into a side hallway. This was on the other side of the badger bar and led down to a few shops, including the gnome jeweler and a few other odds and ends on one side. On the other side of the hall was a "Meat Shields" location where one could purchase mercenaries. Donut and I both had coupons for that place, but we were saving them.

CARL: Good job. Don't piss him off too much yet. Wait for my signal.

SAMANTHA: YOU DIDN'T TELL ME HOW GREAT THIS PLACE IS. I DON'T WANT TO GET KICKED OUT ANYMORE. I WANT TO KEEP COMING BACK. MAEMAE WOULD LOVE IT HERE.

CARL: Stick with the plan. If this works, you'll only get kicked out for a day or so.

That was absolutely a lie, but I needed her to focus.

I pushed my way down the long hallway until I found the utility closet at the very end. I had already gone this way a few days back, making sure the supposed monsters that lived back here weren't roaming freely. They weren't.

I entered the closet and opened the hidden door, quietly closing it behind me. I pulled a torch from my inventory and lit it. The passage led into the darkness. This secret corridor ran parallel with the hallway I'd come from, but it was behind all the shops.

When Astrid came from the top floor to the middle one to deal with any sort of problem on this half of the club, she would pass through here. It was the perfect place for an ambush.

The location presented a few problems, however.

A few days back, Katia had planted a cherry bomb in the men's bathroom, designed to go off while she was on the other side of the club. She did it to watch how the guards would react, and to see if Astrid would respond.

Astrid did respond, briefly, but it wasn't until almost an hour later. She came out to yell at a few guards before returning to her office. We quickly dismissed using a second bomb to lure her out, instead opting to use Samantha, which would guarantee a swifter response. Still, that first experiment wasn't without benefit. Katia used the opportunity to drink a Size Up potion and get a read on Astrid's spells and abilities.

The fairy was terrifyingly powerful. She had an intelligence of 150 and a whole arsenal of spells designed to kill you from the inside out. She could boil blood. Deprive it of oxygen. Turn it to acid. She had a spell that literally animated your heart and turned it into a mob, using your veins and arteries as limbs.

She also had a host of psionic abilities, mostly focused on keeping rock creatures, lizard creatures, and the "Armored Sai" in line. The sai were the regular guards of the Larracos level, though I'd never seen one. Apparently they were like samurai rhinoceroses.

She had a passive ability called Cosmic Sense, which appeared to be like my skill that warned me when a god was present, but hers worked on both gods and demons. That was probably a good thing to have when one was in charge of security at a giant nightclub.

One of her skills was worrisome. Five times a day, she could invoke Summon Guard, which would instantly teleport backup to her location. Each casting would bring "between one to three guards" from the club to her. There was no cooldown, and the casting was instantaneous, meaning she could fill the hallway with up to 15 guards at the snap of her finger.

We didn't want to fight the guards. We didn't even want them to know we were involved at all.

That meant in order to kill her, it had to be immediate, and it had to be a surprise.

Still, we needed to set up contingencies. I came up with the plan that took care of the summoned guards, if it came to that.

If my IED worked, Astrid would never get a chance to summon anyone. But we couldn't rely on it. I took a page from Lucia Mar's playbook. If Astrid summoned any guards, they would immediately fall onto teleport traps. I was going to fill the hallway with them, designed to teleport any NPCs to a locked closet on the top floor. Since Astrid flew everywhere, she wouldn't trip the traps, but I specifically called out fairies just in case she decided to purposely slam into one.

Any guard she summoned to the room would flash, appear, and flash again before they even knew what happened. Hopefully.

The second problem with this ambush location was the monsters.

At the end of this corridor was another room with a closed door. Behind that door was a group of fifteen mobs. We didn't know what the red-tagged monsters were, but according to the map, the room was an abandoned practice arena of the now-defunct "Demon Tamers' Guild."

I moved my way deeper into the hall. Between me and the monster door were about fifty traps, including silent alarms for both crawlers and monsters, several "demon snares," and a few summoning traps designed to call specific guards to the location should the other traps get triggered.

Astrid also had that Cosmic Sense ability, which probably warned her if these things got out. We'd toyed with using that as a trigger to get her down here, but dismissed the idea as too dangerous, even for us.

I quickly made my way down the passage, disarming everything except the demon snares, though I did take five of them for myself. As

I moved, I set up my two-part teleport traps. After this, I still had to get upstairs and place the second half of the traps—the beacons—into the hidden utility closet.

The door at the end of the hallway was secured with a simple hanging, unenchanted padlock. It was just a regular door, similar to all the others in the club, with a rusted lock hanging off it. The only indication of what was inside was the dust-covered paper sign hanging off the door:

Warning. Do Not Enter. Extreme, You're-Going-to-Die-in-a-Lot-of-Pain Danger. Seriously. Don't open this fucking door. Posted by Management.

According to the Night Wyrm, nobody knew what the monsters were. Only that they were outrageously dangerous. There'd been numerous attempts to clear the room, and the parties who entered all died. The fact they'd let this room just exist here with only a few traps as a stopgap was ridiculous. I had to remind myself that this wasn't real life, but game setup.

This was obviously part of some quest we didn't want to get involved with.

The problem was, if there was a fight in this hallway, I just knew that this goddamned door would get blown open. Especially since there would be a few small explosives going off. I had to reinforce the door the best I could.

I worked quickly. This was all something that I should've done earlier, but we'd run out of time. I'd been tempted to skip all this, but I didn't dare. I just had a feeling that these monsters, whatever they were, were awful.

I listened at the door, but I didn't hear anything. I could see them on the map, just sitting there. I pulled a thick, metal, blast-resistant wall from my inventory and set it in place, perfectly blocking the door. The first time I'd come in here, I'd measured the hall's dimensions carefully, and it fit seamlessly. I used the ratchet bracers to make sure the wall was firmly locked in place.

I started stacking sandbags against the wall. When I was done, I would add a second wall and ratchet that one in place as well. I glanced nervously at the clock. We had an hour and a half left before Donut and I would get whisked away to be on Odette's show.

As I worked, Katia messaged me.

KATIA: Carl, how's it going?

CARL: I'm almost done here. Are you okay?

KATIA: Do you feel guilty about this?

CARL: About killing Astrid?

KATIA: Yeah.

I did, actually. A little bit. She hadn't done anything wrong. I'd barely had any interactions with the tiny fairy woman, and the ones I did have were mostly negative. That hardly warranted death. But she was an NPC. She wasn't one of us. Both Katia and I had killed literally thousands of them by this point. I didn't want to do it, and I would avoid it if at all possible. But again, my earlier opinion on this hadn't changed. We were doing them a favor, breaking them from this hell.

I thought of those kids Mordecai was fostering. Was it a contradiction to want to keep *them* safe? Hypocrisy? I didn't know. I didn't care. I was moving forward the best I could.

CARL: We're doing what we have to, Katia. We didn't come up with this quest on our own. We didn't ask for any of this.

KATIA: Yeah. You're right . . . It's just . . .

CARL: What?

KATIA: Sometimes, I think about the futility of it all. I never want anyone to get hurt. The only time I ever did, it was Eva. And look what happened.

CARL: What happened was you stopped her from hurting anybody else. Don't let them break you. That's what they want.

KATIA: Carl . . .

CARL: And don't you dare tell me you're already broken. You're here, and you're doing this with me. That tells me you still have fight in you, and that's all that matters. I'm not going to give up, and I'm not going to give up on you. Now let's do this.

KATIA: God, you are the master of cheeseball motivational speeches. Thank you. I needed that.

I chuckled softly. On the other side of the wall came a low growl, like a noise a sleeping dog would make. A wave of goose bumps passed through me. I went back to work.

32

AFTER SECURING THE SECOND WALL, I CREPT BACK DOWN THE PASsage, stopping at the third door on my right. There were several doors here leading to the back of the shops. The first was the jeweler, the second was a burglar's emporium, and this third back door supposedly led to an empty closet-sized room.

This tiny room actually had a hole in the ceiling and another in the ground. That hole upward led to a secret panel in the employee-only hallway on the top floor. This passageway was how Astrid the fairy quickly moved from the top floor to the middle one. It was also the path Astrid would take today when she came to deal with a very drunk sex doll head who refused to leave the bar.

Samantha didn't know the full plan. All she needed to do was make a ruckus when I asked her to and then refuse to leave the bar area. All the guards on this second floor were Crocodilian, and they'd be unable to catch her if she didn't want to be caught. They'd be forced to summon Astrid. The fairy would emerge from the closet, enter this hallway, and then move toward the main merchant hall and toward the bar. It was the fastest path, and according to the Night Wyrm, it was the path she always took when she entered this middle floor.

The moment she left this closet, she'd be dead. And if she wasn't, Katia would be here with her deck, waiting to finish her off and collect her body before escaping.

According to the map, Astrid's office was located on the top floor, behind a small vent at the end of the employees-only hall, which explained why I'd never noticed it. This was the same back area where Orren the liaison's now-empty office stood. The entrance to Astrid's space was small and up against the ceiling. Supposedly, this passage to her office led to a hollowed-out hole in the interior of a tree, where she worked and slept and did whatever blood fairies did.

The tree part was interesting. It wasn't anything I needed to worry about today, but it made me think of the all-tree. Signet had told me a little about the massive tree, about how it grew through all the worlds at once, connecting everything. Her circus-ringmaster husband, Grimaldi, who'd been turned into a vine by Scolopendra, was now connected with the tree.

I planted a motion-detecting smoke trap at the top of the doorway, and then I planted the motion-detecting anti-NPC claymores against the wall opposite the door. The blast was directional, facing the closet. The moment Astrid appeared, *boom.*

In theory, these explosives alone were more than enough to do the job. The bombs were packed with orcish iron BBs, which were supposedly deadly to fairies. But I took Rosetta's warning in the cookbook to heart. These fuckers were lucky, and we would leave nothing to chance, hence the teleport traps and Katia.

I thought of Paz as I worked. He'd had a *Self-Destruct* spell that he could aim magically at a single target. While my claymore was directional, it was aimed manually, and there would be a lot of wasted energy in the explosion. One day I hoped to master the ability to magically aim blasts. If I could do that, even a small blast could be enough to kill something otherwise resistant to explosions. An aimed blast with a narrow target had the power to kill *anything.*

I backed all the way out of the secret hallway.

CARL: I'm set up in here. Moving upstairs now. I'll take the main stairs by the casino.

KATIA: Okay. I'm in the women's room on the middle floor. As soon as you clear out, I'll move to the hallway.

CARL: Be careful of the claymores. Stay all the way at the back. And don't forget the invisibility potion.

CARL: Samantha, be ready. It'll be a few minutes.

SAMANTHA: DIRTY SHIRLEYS ARE THE GREATEST DRINKS EVER.

I moved back into the utility closet and then the hallway. I rushed down the empty public corridor, emerging back into the bar. I moved past, pausing long enough to hear Samantha chatting away with Charles the bartender, telling him that he'd have to fight Louis for her affection. I moved quickly, skirting the restaurant, and to the main stairs that stood near the entrance to the middle floor casino, called the "Hunting Grounds Casino." I hadn't actually gone into this casino before, but I knew it had a lot of the same games as the one upstairs. I spied a wheel-of-fortune game similar to the one I'd played before. I made my way to the top floor. I moved past the main dance floor, eyeing the crowd, trying to single out all the crawlers. There were four of them, all dancing together. I didn't know any of them.

I moved to the bathrooms, went into the men's room, and found the secret catch for the utility closet. I opened the door and tossed in all of the teleport trap beacons.

All the guards who set off the teleport traps below would get sent to this room. There was no door handle on the other side. I tossed in a smoke trap for good measure. The guards would probably get out fairly quickly, but it'd take them time to figure out what the hell was going on and where they'd teleported from.

I then moved toward the dance floor, moving past a generated elf NPC asking me to dance.

CARL: Okay. I'm almost in place. I just gotta talk to these crawlers.
KATIA: I'm ready.

I clicked over to my second chat.

CARL: Okay, Samantha. Start being mean to the bartender.
SAMANTHA: I'LL HAVE YOU KNOW YOU'RE FORCING ME TO RUIN A PERFECTLY GOOD POTENTIAL BACKUP RELATIONSHIP. CHARLES COULD BE MY SOULMATE. HIS LAST NAME IS ELLIS, AND SAMANTHA ELLIS HAS A NICE RING TO IT, BUT YOU'RE MAKING ME RUIN IT.
CARL: Don't actually hurt him or anything. Keep me updated.

SAMANTHA: DON'T HURT HIM? I THOUGHT WE WERE DOING AN ASSASSINATION?

CARL: We are, but not of him. I can't tell you who we're trying to kill. It'll ruin the quest. I told you this already.

SAMANTHA: IT'S NOT ME, IS IT?

CARL: Of course not.

SAMANTHA: AND YOU'RE SURE IT'S NOT CHARLES?

CARL: No, it's not the bartender.

SAMANTHA: UH-OH.

CARL: Uh-oh, what?

SAMANTHA: UH, DON'T WORRY ABOUT IT. THE GUARDS ARE PROBABLY ALREADY ON THEIR WAY.

"Shit," I mumbled, and I moved to the dance floor.

I knew the Crocodilians were loath to call Astrid, but they would eventually cave, which meant we had a few minutes still. I knew from experience they'd actually send a Crocodilian up the stairs and into the employee hallway to summon her. I would post up by the bar on this floor and watch for the guard and send an early warning to Katia. I returned my attention to the dancers.

The four crawlers were in a circle, laughing and dancing together. It was three women and one man. Two of the women were human, and the third was an elf. The man looked human at first, but he had a blue tinge to his skin. One of the humans noticed me, and a look of shock registered on her face. She elbowed her closest companion, as I drew the privacy bubble over my head and asked for her to do the same.

This woman was a level 52 **Boring Ol' Mage** named **Zeynep**. I figured she was from somewhere in the middle east. The woman was older—if I had to guess, in her late fifties.

"Carl?" the woman asked. She looked around. "Where's your cat friend?"

"Hey, guys," I said. "Look, I gotta ask a favor of you. Please don't ask why, but you guys should leave. Like right now."

"Why?" the man asked. His race was a **Zebani**, and he was a level 55 **Ghazi** named **Emir Akbas**. I had no idea what either a Ghazi or a Zebani was, but the tall guy had huge arms and a curved sword over his shoulder. He also had the second-bushiest monobrow I'd ever seen in my life, the thickest belonging to my friend Sam. The man also appeared older, also in his 50s. I suspected maybe he was married to the other woman. All four of them had similar crawler numbers, implying they'd been together this whole time. The other two women—the elf and the other human—were younger, maybe early 20s. The man looked me up and down angrily. "Why should we do what you say? We've collected our squad. We're relaxing before we move on to phase two."

"Look," I said. "Something is about to go down in here, and I don't want anyone getting hurt."

"What's going down?" Emir demanded.

"Do you need help?" Zeynep asked, almost at the same moment.

"No," I said firmly. "Look, I don't have time." I held out my fist. "Get in my chat, and I promise I'll explain it all in, like, 15 minutes. Odds are good nothing will happen up here on this floor, but I really want you guys out of here before it all goes down just in case."

Zeynep shrugged and punched fists with me. She was the only one.

The three women started to move toward the exit, but Emir didn't budge. He was being an obstinate dick. They all stopped and were talking angrily amongst themselves using the chat. It was clear he didn't want to leave.

I realized belatedly that this Emir guy was drunk off his ass. I kicked myself for not noticing it right away. *Great.*

KATIA: There's a lot of commotion going on out there. I can hear Samantha yelling from here, and somebody is screaming. I think it's the bartender badger guy. There was just a loud crash.

CARL: Shit. I'm still dealing with these crawlers. Samantha is working faster than I anticipated.

SAMANTHA: HOW LONG DO I HAVE TO KEEP DOING THIS? EVERYONE IS VERY UPSET, AND CHARLES IS VERY HEAVY. DID YOU KNOW THERE'S A CASINO IN HERE? YOU DIDN'T TELL ME ABOUT THE CASINO! IT SOUNDS SO JINGLY JANGLY AND PRETTY.

CARL: What? Are you carrying him? And don't go in the casino! Stay in the bar area! It'll just be a minute.

"You think you're such a big bad man," Emir was saying. I could hear the slur in his voice. "I could beat your ass."

I didn't have time for this guy's bullshit. Some of the cretin bodyguards were looking in our direction.

CARL: Zeynep, can you keep your friend under control? I gotta go. If you aren't going to leave, just stay here on the dance floor and don't get involved in anything. But try to get out of here.

ZEYNEP: I will try. I am sorry. He is quite jealous of you, and he is very drunk.

I nodded and turned my back, moving toward the bar.

"Don't turn your back on me," Emir growled.

I ignored him and kept walking.

The door to the employee exit opened, and Astrid flew out. There was no warning. If a guard had summoned her, I missed it. She ignored me as she zipped past. She went straight for the regular stairs. She hadn't used the secret stairwell at all.

Fuck. Fuck, fuck, fuck.

The plan was already hosed.

CARL: Katia, Astrid is on her way down. She's using the main stairs!

CARL: Samantha, you're done. Get out of the club now.

KATIA: Shit. What do I do?

I thought for a moment.

CARL: Get into the hallway and into the gnome jeweler's shop. Wait for her. Maybe she'll use the secret passageway on her way back. If she passes, follow her after the blast. She'll still get hit by the IED.

The moment I finished sending that message, an alarm went off. Not a trap alarm, but an actual one. Loud and jarring, like a fire alarm. This was not planned, and I had no idea what this was. A red light pulsed. The music abruptly stopped. All the generated NPCs stopped dancing and looked around at one another.

A disembodied voice came over a loudspeaker.

"There has been a containment breach on the middle level. Everyone must evacuate or shelter in place. All security personnel to the Hunting Grounds Level Casino. This is not a drill. I repeat, this is not a drill."

All of the pre-generated NPCs blinked and disappeared, and the room was suddenly empty except for me, the four other crawlers, the cretin bodyguards, this floor's badger bartender, and a few others, who were all scattering toward exits or doorways deeper into the club. The guards were all breaking for the stairwell down to the club's middle floor.

KATIA: Carl, what's happening? Did the monsters break out of that back room?

CARL: I don't know.

The alarm stopped, but the red light kept flashing. I felt a rumble in the floor, as if something had exploded down below. I moved to my trap menu to check my claymores and my other traps to see if they'd gone off prematurely. It didn't appear as if anything in that hallway had been disturbed at all. *Huh.*

And then what the announcement had said finally registered.

The casino.

"Carl, watch out!" It was Zeynep.

Combat Started.

A fist slammed into the side of my head. I felt myself drop and hit the floor. It was Emir. He grunted with pain from the Damage Reflect.

It had hurt, and he'd knocked me down, but I was so surprised that I just looked up at the man, incredulous.

"Dude, what the hell, man?" I asked as Zeynep and the others yelled at him to stop. I touched the side of my head. My hand came away bloody. I was *bleeding*. The guy had a powerful punch.

"You assholes keeping it all for yourselves," he said.

I had no idea what that meant. The guy wasn't making sense. I was still on the floor. He reared back with his metal boot and moved to punt me in the ribs. He swung with an exaggerated kick, and I caught his foot. I rolled, pulling him off-balance. He slammed onto his back as I jumped to my feet, hands still wrapped around his foot.

DONUT: CARL, WHAT'S HAPPENING! I GOT A NEW COMBAT-STARTED NOTIFICATION AND AN ERROR THAT SAYS I'M TOO FAR AWAY FOR DECK COMBAT. I'M IN THE PRACTICE ARENA! ARE YOU OKAY?

I yanked, and the man's metallic boot ripped off his foot. I tossed it away.

He scrambled, trying to get up. He raised his hand, but Zeynep cast something. Not against me, but against her own teammate. *Mute.* The notification appeared over his head. She'd stopped him from attacking me with a spell.

"Are you done?" I demanded as I sent a calming message to Donut. Below, there was another crash. "You're drunk, and I don't know why you're mad. Get the hell out of here."

KATIA: Carl, something weird's going on. I'm going to go look.

"My Burcu is going to kill you," the man growled, scrambling up as the others pulled him away.

"She's going to have to wait until tomorrow. Get the fuck out."

Burcu was a crawler floating around number 10 on the top list. I'd never really talked to her, but I did have her in my chat, having briefly met her during the Butcher's Masquerade. Like the bartenders, she was also a Porsuk. A badger. Her class was Swashbuckler, the same as Bautista and Tran. She'd been one of the three people who'd fought over the memorial crystal at the end of that whole boss fight. I knew nothing else about her other than she was very serious, reminding me of Hekla. And that she was Turkish. I realized all of these guys were maybe in the same family.

Zeynep muttered an apology as she pulled him toward the exit. They left the man's boot on the floor.

My head still swam from the punch.

SAMANTHA: OKAY, DON'T GET MAD.

CARL: What the hell does that mean? You have to leave now!

SAMANTHA: DON'T WORRY. CHARLES AND I WILL KICK HER ASS!

A loud, booming voice echoed through the entire club. The wooden dance floor buckled in a few places as it shook with the deep bass of the cry.

"PSAMATHE! I CAN SMELL YOU! WHERE ARE YOU, YOU LITTLE SLUT?"

And then it clicked. This had nothing to do with the monsters in the secret doorway. Samantha had gone into the casino. The casino contained entrances to the Nothing. One of those things had gotten out. A minor feral demon. There was a whole group of them trapped in the Nothing, all sisters. They were part of some harem, and they hated Samantha because she'd insulted their king. Or something equally stupid.

The last time one had gotten out, she'd been kaiju-sized. She'd been killed by a god, Samantha's mother, who'd ripped her in half. That one's name had been Slit.

She'd also been level 200.

At the end of the Butcher's Masquerade, when the dying Signet had been pulled into the Nothing, there'd been another. It'd just been a voice, but it had called out of the Nothing, calling for Samantha. The entrances to the Nothing were one-way, except in rare circumstances, like when I used the Gate of the Feral Gods. Did Samantha's presence change that?

Astrid had that Cosmic Sense skill. She'd known what was coming. She'd gone down the main stairs instead of the secret passageway because that was a faster path to the casino.

Shit.

We had to get the hell out of here. The ground buckled again. The sounds of fighting rose up from the main stairwell down to the middle level.

CARL: Katia, abort! Go into the bathroom passageway and up the stairs, and we'll use the exit up here.

CARL: Samantha, get the hell out of there!

SAMANTHA: I HAVE THAT BITCH RIGHT WHERE I WANT HER.

KATIA: Carl, no, I have to do this. That thing is going to destroy the club. I have to get to Astrid now and then get her body into the guild. If I don't finish this now, we won't get another chance. The fight will be our distraction.

CARL: Are you fucking kidding me?

KATIA: Carl, this is all my fault. I have to fix it. You get out of here, but I'm going to stay. I can still get to her.

CARL: No, Katia. That thing is level 200. We can't fight it.

KATIA: I'm not fighting the demon, just Astrid. But she is going to kill Astrid if I don't, and we'll lose the quest. Remember what you said? That you're not going to give up on me? Well, I'm not going to give up on you and Donut, either. This is it.

"Goddamnit," I muttered. I rushed toward the women's room. I kicked open the stall with the secret stairwell—the first secret passage we'd discovered in this place—and I opened the hidden door and jumped inside. The walls continued to shake. I burst out into the women's room of the middle floor. More screams echoed. The regular lights had gone out, and the flashing red of the emergency lights gave a distinctive pulse. It'd gone ominously silent down here. I rushed out of the bathroom and stopped at the last corner before the restaurant.

To my left just around the corner was the restaurant. If I wanted to get to Katia, I'd have to cross this space. I'd have about ten feet where I'd be exposed to the monster. To my right was a large pair of double doors leading into the back kitchens.

I pressed myself against the corner and listened. There was a wet splotching followed by a deep grunting noise. It sounded like someone with no teeth chewing. The sound came from the main restaurant, not the casino. Someone was sobbing, begging for their life, their voice weak and barely audible. It was a Crocodilian. There was a crack and a splash.

"PSAMATHE, GET BACK HERE!" the voice suddenly cried, painfully loud.

"Hah!" came Samantha's retort. She was farther away. "I killed your stupid sister, and Charles and I will kill you even more! It's not my fault your ugly king can't stand to attention at the sight of you. Everyone thinks you're gross and ugly. Right, Chuckie?"

"Oh god, somebody please help me," came the weak cry of Charles the bartender.

"YOU DIDN'T KILL SLIT. YOUR MOTHER DID. YOU CAN'T EVEN FIGHT YOUR OWN BATTLES, YOU STUPID POTATO!"

"What? What? I will fuck you up!" Samantha shrieked.

"THEN QUIT HIDING BEHIND THE PORTAL AND GET OUT HERE, WHORE!"

I examined the map, looking for a safer path to Katia. The map was a chaos of dots and X's. There were the white dots of about twenty NPCs, all gathered in the kitchen area to my right, likely massing for an attack. If Astrid was in there, I couldn't tell. Katia's blue dot was in the merchant hall, just past the badger bar.

I could see Samantha zipping through the back of the casino area with the white dot of another NPC traveling with her. The rest of the casino was littered with the X's of dead NPCs.

The red misshapen dot of the demon filled about a quarter of the restaurant. It was surrounded by X's and multiple white dots, indicating several of the NPCs in the restaurant were still alive.

There was a crash followed by a scream. I hazarded a peek around the corner.

Holy fuck.

The demon was different than Slit. She was straight from a nightmare. The pink fleshy terror occupied the center of the room. Slit had been 100 feet tall. This one was smaller, sized to fit the club. Sort of.

The naked, corpulent creature was crammed into the room, and her round bald head was pushed to the side against the tall ceiling. Her sore-covered body looked like she'd been oozed into the room from an ice-cream machine and was just now starting to melt.

I didn't see any legs, but the grotesque monster was covered with slender, multi-jointed arms with massive kite-sized claws at the end. The arms were no wider than twigs, giving the impression I could snap them in half, but they were long, too long, some snaking across the entire room. She had at least twenty of the appendages, making her look like some sort of eldritch snowman. A few of the claws were pressed against the ceiling, a few more were against the floor and walls, and the rest were all occupied, holding tightly around the necks of struggling NPCs, including a few cretins, suggesting the limbs were stronger than they looked.

The large, giant face of the demon was covered in thick clown-like makeup, just like her sister's. Her mouth was wide enough that I could drive the Royal Chariot right into it. The demon's red lipstick was smeared all over her face. A scattering of black hairs, about as thick and long as my thumb, covered the very top of the pink mass.

She stank of diseased skin, even from here. The scent reminded me of a guy I'd once known who'd almost had to have his toes amputated because of athlete's foot that had gotten so bad, it'd developed into gangrene.

Minge. Level 225 Minor Feral Demon.

This one was a higher level than Slit had been, despite not being a kaiju. She was only 25 levels shy of most gods.

I peeked again, long enough to watch the demon pull a crying Crocodilian to her mouth and crunch down on his chest, taking a literal bite out of him. The way she bit down was almost dainty, like she was trying just a sliver of a cookie because she was unsure of the taste. The guard gasped in pain. Blood and gore cascaded out of the horrific wound like he was a jelly donut. She made a sort of jiggling shrug and then ate him whole. She belched loudly.

"PSAMATHE!" she cried again, gore pouring from the side of her mouth.

KATIA: Carl, get out of here!
CARL: If you're staying, I'm staying. Where's Astrid?

KATIA: She's in the kitchen.

CARL: Okay. Stay there. I'm setting up a distraction, then coming to you.

I prepared an invisibility potion and pulled out an alarm ball. But before I could move, the double doors leading to the kitchen swung open, and a whole stampede of bipedal rhinoceros samurai dudes dashed from the room, screaming as they rushed the demon in the restaurant. They were decked out like steampunk samurais, complete with swords and blades at the end of sticks. Each stood about seven feet tall and was huge. The ground shook as they charged. I caught sight of one at the end of the stampede.

Walter—Sai. Level 101.

Guard of the Larracos level of the Desperado Club.

The Sai are quite serious about their guard duties, mostly because it's the only gig they can really get. They used to be firefighters, but firefighting in a war zone is a good way to make yourself almost extinct. So they migrated into the Desperado Club and now are known as the ever-present guards of the bottom* floor of the Desperado. Focusing on their duties distracts them from all those urban legends about their armor being too itchy. These creatures aren't really known for their intelligence, but they're generally good guys, loyal until the end. That's what makes them good guards. They don't care about rules or laws or morals. They just do what they're told.

If they charge, get the hell out of the way.

I suddenly thought of Ferdinand the cat. He had a rhinoceros mount, though that thing was more like the real deal than these guys, who walked on two feet. I couldn't remember what the mount's name was, but I was pretty sure it had been inside the elf castle when it transferred down to the ninth floor.

The rhino guards were quickly followed by a group of cretins, who also rumbled past me and into the room. I pressed myself against the wall as they crashed into the demon, who started screaming and laughing at the same time. A splash of red blew into the hall from the restaurant. *Fuck me.*

KATIA: Carl, a bunch of Croc guards just rushed into the hallway. They didn't even look at me. They were moving toward that back hallway where we were going to ambush her. I don't know why.

CARL: I bet they're headed toward the mercenary market. That Meat Shields location is back there. They're getting backup.

KATIA: No, I think they're going into the secret passage!

CARL: Hold tight. I'm coming.

I took a breath and downed the invisibility potion. I took the alarm ball and chucked it as hard as I could, aiming it toward the front of the club. It sailed through the room, missing the arms, and slammed against the front main entrance to the club. I waited a few seconds. I had no idea what the song would be. Donut had begged me to let her pick a few of the songs for the distraction balls, and I'd let her do it to give her practice using my sapper's table.

Topping at number two on March 23rd, 1985, it's "Material Girl"!

Just as the Madonna song started to blast, I bolted across the open space in front of the demon. But the very moment I stepped out, I was slammed by the body of a sai who'd just been tossed away by the large demon as she turned toward the music. Both the sai—who was dead—and I crashed through the double doors and slid into the back kitchens. I skidded through the room, slamming into a tall spice rack, which tumbled over. I groaned and pushed the monster off of me. I was still invisible.

The room was like any other kitchen from a large-scale restaurant. A row of food-preparation stations stood on one side, then ovens and shelves filled with supplies. What looked like a line of honest-to-goodness microwave ovens stood against the opposite wall. They weren't microwaves, I realized, but a type of food box I hadn't seen before. A group of elf and gnome NPCs huddled in the far back. There was a line of doors here—offices by the look of them.

Astrid floated near the row of food boxes, flanked by two Crocodilian guards. She was shouting orders at them, and they rushed off out a second door, this one leading toward the badger bar, presumably also headed toward that back secret passage.

Shit, shit. I didn't want Astrid to see me. Surely she didn't know what Katia and I were attempting, but if she knew Samantha was responsible for this demon, who knew what she would do?

Your teleport trap has been activated!

Your teleport trap has been activated!

No, I'm not stuttering. Your teleport trap has been activated!

This was followed by about ten more of the same notifications.

Those guards had, indeed, gone into the secret hallway. But why? The only thing back there was the fairy-sized passage up to the top floor. That, and the room with the monsters. They'd hit the teleport traps, which had probably saved their lives. If they passed the claymore, they'd get turned to mulch. There were now two more guards headed in that direction. They, too, would hit teleport traps. I hoped.

I had to get out of here before Astrid saw me. I gingerly stood, moving away from the heavy, unmoving body of the sai. *Jesus,* I thought, looking at the large corpse. The demon had literally ripped its head off.

"Gah!" I cried as half of another sai rhino guard was flung into the kitchen, spewing blood that splattered over me. I had to jump to keep from getting bowled over by the torso, and when I landed, I slipped in the blood. I grasped a pot in an unsuccessful attempt to keep from falling on my ass, and half the counter crashed down on me, including what smelled and tasted like split pea soup. In the back of the room, the elves cried out in horror.

"Crawler," Astrid shouted, looking at me. I could barely hear her. I cringed, expecting her to attack. I was still invisible for a few more seconds, but my outline was now observable, thanks to the gore and soup. Astrid sounded panicked, which surprised me, despite the circumstances. "Carl, is that you? You need to get out of here. It is not safe."

"Yeah, no shit," I said, standing to my full height. My invisibility faded. I could taste the soup in my mouth.

I tried drawing a sound bubble over my head to see if it would work against the alarm trap. To my surprise, it did. The moment I drew it, I could hear shouting. Outside, Samantha was listing off a litany of venereal diseases Minge most likely had while the demon continued to make short work of the attacking guards.

KATIA: Two more just rushed by.

CARL: I'm in here with Astrid. It's just her and several of the kitchen workers cowering in the back. I think most of the club's guards are dead already.

"I had to pull the trigger," Astrid said. She, too, had a bubble over her head now. "There's been a breach of the Nothing in the casino. We can't kill her. I had to unleash the vorpals."

"Uh," I said. "The what?"

"It doesn't matter, Crawler. You must flee! They will kill everything. Leave the club, or get into one of the shops and hide."

Your teleport trap has been activated!

There was a pause. *Uh-oh,* I thought.

I felt the distant explosion rumble the floor the same moment the notification appeared.

Bam! Your IED has been activated.

Ewww. Gross. That worked really well. Like, really well.

"Damn, what is taking them so long?" Astrid said, looking toward the exit. More rhino gore spewed into the kitchen. Astrid paused and then looked at me.

"Carl, we have to stop this before it gets upstairs. If they ask what happened to me, tell them it was a vorpal." She buzzed back and forth uncertainly, rubbing her tiny hands. "Maybe . . . maybe if you loan me one of those invisibility potions they won't kill me." She shook her head. She was babbling. "No, that won't work. Damnit, I was so close. So close. If you see my husband, tell him I did it to keep them safe. Him and my children."

"Your husband?" I asked. "Your children?"

She indicated the tattoo on my elbow. "You're in the Guild of Suffering. My husband is named Hamed, but he's known as the Night Wyrm. Don't tell him I told you his real name. His lair is hidden up there on the top floor. The vorpals won't go up there. They'll stay on this floor." She didn't sound so sure of that last part.

"Wait," I said, but I didn't finish the thought. The Night Wyrm was her *husband*? That didn't make any damn sense. He'd hired Katia and me to kill her. The one time I'd been in there, I'd only heard the thing's voice. I'd assumed he was like a Naga. Not a fairy. That was a weird combination.

Outside, Samantha was screaming again, this time something incomprehensible. The whole club shook as Minge continued to smash things. The song ended and started over again.

"TURN THAT TERRIBLE NOISE OFF," Minge shouted.

"I will not! You have horrific taste in music!" Samantha shouted back.

"You really did it this time," Astrid said to me. She shook her tiny head. "I should have followed Orren's advice and permanently banned you. They told me not to. Gods, I hope it's worth it."

"I . . . What?"

The door toward the badger bar opened, and a giant hooded, elderly female troll creature burst into the room. She looked at us and roared.

What the . . . But then I realized what this was. Katia had activated her deck, and this troll was one of her totems. It'd been strength-buffed.

This was the first time I'd seen Katia's squad flag, which floated over the creature's head. I blinked. I'd been assuming this whole time it would be the Crown of the Sepsis Whore. It was hard to see when it was so small, but I was pretty sure it depicted Hekla's and Eva's faces side by side with X's over their eyes. The player-killer-skull mark sat in the middle of the bloodred flag.

Astrid appeared shocked at the sudden, unexpected entrance of the troll. This thing was clearly a woman, eight feet tall, with a long, hooked nose. She held on to what appeared to be a giant spoon. Green wet moss covered her robe and fell off in clumps. Astrid buzzed in front of the monster as if she was protecting me.

"Bein þín mun ég sjóða," the troll cackled, laughing. It didn't translate, whatever she said.

Astrid didn't hesitate. She cast a spell, and the troll thing dropped to her knees as all the blood in her body boiled. Her round, bulbous eyes exploded just as a second creature flew into the room. This was also a totem. It was a crow with the skull of a child for a head. It cawed as Astrid cast another spell at the bird. The spell appeared ineffective.

Something metallic brushed against my leg, pushing me to the side. The moment it touched me, the blue dot appeared on my map. It was Katia, invisible. She'd entered the room during the distraction, coming up behind us. She couldn't cast spells or use her inventory while she had cards active, but she could still drink potions if they were available, and that's what she'd done.

She could still shapeshift, apparently, too.

Katia faded into existence, her form that of a metallic spiked-covered, human-faced canine monstrosity with a pair of arms on her shoulders. It was like something out of *The Thing.* One of the hands on her shoulders grasped the fairy, crushing. A spike formed in the other hand as it plunged toward the fairy's head.

But then Katia gasped, freezing in place, the spike mere millimeters from the back of Astrid's head.

And for a moment, just a moment, I froze, too. Not because I'd been hit by a spell, but because of the look on Katia's face.

There are certain instants and images throughout this horror that are burned indelibly in my mind. The moment when I saw Jack pissing on the wall. Those last seconds just before the Carl's Doomsday Scenario bomb didn't go off. When Hekla died. The sound of little Bonnie the gnome's tears after we crashed the *Wasteland.* The sound of Prepotente's screams after Miriam Dom sacrificed herself to save him.

Donut's sobs at the end of the Butcher's Masquerade.

That moment—that sliver of a second as Katia remained there, hovering, frozen, her human mouth open in screaming rage—it did something to me. The look on her face was so foreign, so inhuman yet so goddamned familiar that something inside me shifted. It was equal parts terror, equal parts rage. Exhaustion. Yet somehow alone. They were the eyes of someone who'd just slipped off a cliff and knew they were falling to their death, both resigned and yet filled with absolute rejection of her fate at the same time. It was like she was saying, *After all this? After all we did, to get this close? No. No, I won't believe it.*

The moment was fleeting. I blinked, allowed myself to realize *I* hadn't been frozen, and I moved. Astrid was right there, hovering in front of me, still clutched in Katia's hand. I reached forward, grasped onto her wings, and I ripped. They pulled off of her easily. Small tendrils of sagging flesh remained connected to her body, like I was pulling apart melted cheese. I took a few steps back, and the tendrils snapped away.

The spell stopped, and Katia gasped. The fairy dropped from her grip and plummeted to the ground, crying out in surprise. Astrid landed with a small splash on the ground.

I looked in surprise at the fairy wings in my hand. Long strings of gore bobbed from the ends. I pulled them into my inventory, feeling sick.

Astrid rolled over, looking up at the human-faced wolf, shock and agony evident in her small face. I was pretty sure she didn't know I was the one who'd ripped her wings out. The skull-faced crow swept down and, with a shocking precision, disgorged both of Astrid's eyes with a quick swipe of its talons. Sparkling blood trailed down the tiny fairy's face.

It'd happened so fast, yet . . . yet I felt out of breath, suddenly exhausted. *Jesus,* I thought.

Katia only had one card still, floating in front of her. The card was tiny, the size of a postage stamp.

Outside, the music abruptly stopped. Minge shouted in triumph.

"No, please!" Astrid said. "Save my children. I was almost done. I would be free soon. Tell them—"

A spike shot from the wolf's neck and skewered the disabled and blind fairy through the head, killing her. Katia kept the body of the fairy impaled on the metallic barb as the bird with the skull head settled on the wolf's shoulder. With a flick of a talon, the crow tossed one of the eyes up in the air, and the infant skull chattered, catching it and biting down like it was a tiny snack.

Behind us, the elf NPCs continued to cry and scream in terror. At this angle, they likely hadn't seen exactly what had happened. Just that

Astrid was dead, attacked by some creature. Out in the hall, the sounds of battle continued unabated. Samantha and Minge screamed back and forth.

KATIA: Follow me back into the bar. We don't want them knowing a crawler did this. Gotta convince them I'm a monster.

Katia's human face changed, taking on an ogre-like appearance. She growled at the elf NPCs and bound back out through the door. I ran to follow, shouting, pretending like I was trying to attack the creature.

Astrid's final words haunted me. *I was almost done.*

33

JOB UPDATE.

The mark is dead, my little sweets. Excellent, excellent work. We are stronger because you have fulfilled your duty. Bring her filthy body to the guild to complete the task. Remember, she who brings the body is she who gets paid.

The voice came in the hissing speech of the Night Wyrm.

I was still reeling. Katia's face. The feeling of the wings peeling off the fairy's body. It'd been so easy.

Astrid hadn't liked me, but she wasn't expecting me to attack her, either. In the end, she'd moved to shield me, to protect me from the monster. I'd ripped the wings right off of her.

Goddamnit, get ahold of yourself. This isn't done.

Still, I couldn't stop thinking about it. The head of the Guild of Suffering was Astrid's *husband*? I supposed that was nothing new for this world, but it still bothered me. Astrid had wanted to protect him, and he'd ordered us to kill her. And who the hell were her children?

Fuck this place. Fuck everything about it.

Katia re-formed into her human shape as the terrifying crow on her shoulder poofed away. Her deck wouldn't just go away with the giant demon out there, but she'd deliberately made her deck short for this fight. She discarded a card, and her deck was now expended, which gave her the ability to act normally. The body of Astrid remained clutched in her hand like one of Bautista's dolls. She pulled it into her inventory.

The ground shook again, followed by more screams. The guards were dead, but that Minge thing was making her way through the

NPCs, yelling for Samantha, who continued to scream at the creature. I could see on my map Samantha was clearly in the casino, which had a wide-open entrance adjacent to the restaurant, but for some reason, the creature wasn't getting close.

Katia had a wild look in her eyes. "Fannar, we gotta get back up there before the club is destroyed."

"Go upstairs and finish the quest," I said. "Use the secret bathroom stairwell. I'm right behind you."

"Wait . . . What are you doing?" Katia asked, voice filled with alarm. She blinked a few times. "Carl, I don't think that's a good idea."

"I'm trying to figure something out. Go. I'll be up there soon. Take another invisibility potion. And leave the door open in case I have to run. It's okay."

She hesitated, but then disappeared again and bolted back into the kitchens. She'd only be exposed for a half second if she went toward the secret stairwell. I remained in the bar, and I jumped into my messages.

CARL: Mordecai, do you know what a vorpal is?

MORDECAI: In what context?

CARL: In the context where there are a bunch of monsters called vorpals behind a hidden door in the Desperado Club, and they want to unleash them as a last resort against a minor feral demon Samantha accidentally released from the Nothing.

MORDECAI: Holy shit, there's a feral demon in the Desperado? Are you serious?

CARL: Do you know or not?

MORDECAI: Man, it's been a while since I've seen this one. Vorpal is a condition, not a species. Like "feral" means it has been touched by the Nothing, "vorpal" means they've been . . . deputized by the gods. Or better yet, turned into suicide bombers. They can be of any race or creature, and sometimes the condition hides itself, too, until a demon is near. They're generally celestial guards. Foot soldiers of the deities. The closer they're to demons, the stronger and angrier they get. They can sense where the demons are and are attracted to them, and they also draw demon aggro, too. They won't

wander far once the demon is dead, but they'll still kill anybody near them. If they get let out, you're screwed. Stay the fuck away. They'll eventually dissipate and get transferred back to the celestial realm if they've been fed demon blood. Don't ever try to fight one close-up. If they think they're going to lose a fight, they'll explode. You kill it, and everyone in the room will be dead.

I remembered all the demon traps that'd been outside their room. That hadn't been to stop the mobs from getting out. That had been to stop demons from getting close and activating them.

CARL: So, they won't leave this floor once released? They won't go up to the top level?

MORDECAI: Eh, probably not, unless something draws them up. But I don't know for sure. Li Na isn't in there with you, is she? She's a demon race. If they smell her, they *will* follow her upstairs.

CARL: No.

MORDECAI: Good. Get the hell out of there and let security deal with it.

"THAT'S RIGHT, BITCH!" came Minge's scream, followed by a crash.

Samantha screeched. There was another scream, too. Charles the bartender was still, inexplicably, alive and with her. The shout was closer than before. Samantha had fled the casino area and was coming toward me.

Suddenly, one of the demon's thin arms reached into the bar, and I had to jump back, falling backward into the kitchens. The kitchen staff NPCs were still in here, still huddled in the back against a group of doors.

I dove behind a station with a pair of smoking burners. I opened my inventory, moving to my automaton menu. I started pulling a few of my spider robots out. I'd been saving them for an emergency. One utility spider and three anti-undead ones I'd started working on when we'd been stuck in the ghommid village.

Demons weren't undead, but several of the attacks that worked against the undead were also effective against them.

The elf NPCs all stared at me, wide-eyed. If they knew I'd helped kill Astrid, they showed no sign.

"You can't stay here. Go into the offices," I yelled.

"We can't!" one of the elves cried. It was a line cook. He wore an apron spattered with blood. "The managers went in there and locked the doors!"

Crashing came from the badger bar. Another arm reached through the double doors, grasping blindly. It caught the edge of one of the doors and pulled, ripping it away. A large chunk of wall went with it. She was destroying the whole damn club. I took a hobgoblin smoke curtain and rolled it toward the restaurant. Minge started shrieking anew.

"There's a stairwell in the last stall in the women's bathroom," I said, talking quickly, pointing. "The door is open. Go up there. It'll take you to the top level, or you can go down if it lets you. Run before it reaches in again."

They all just looked at me.

"Go!"

They ran.

As they fled, narrowly avoiding a grasping hand, Samantha burst into the kitchens from the side door. She was floating high against the ceiling. She zoomed into the room, grunt-panting like a dog. She circled twice, and then noticed me crouching there, gawking up at her. She paused and did a little hair flip, like she was suddenly trying to act casual.

"Oh, hi, Carl," she said. "So, this place is really fun even though the casino is out of order. Did we do the assassination yet? Also, the music stopped. Can you start it up again?"

"What the actual fuck, Samantha! Let him go!"

"Who?"

Charles the bartender dangled helpless below Samantha, his legs pumping as he tried to free himself. His right arm was shoulder deep in the ragged bottom of her neck hole. Like, *too* deep. She'd either lopped his arm off and was somehow clutching on to his stump, or there was a deepness there that hadn't been present before.

The "flesh" at the bottom of her neck had the consistency of uneven latex, like a soft children's toy that had been ripped in half. There was no real hole there, but I had once hidden an unopened potion in the soft, pliable material. It'd slurped in easily, like I was pushing it into Silly Putty. She'd recently started storing things in there, like sunglasses and shiny rocks she'd found. Before we'd gone into the club today, I'd given her 100 gold to drink at the bar, and she'd excitedly sucked it up. I hadn't realized the hole was . . . deeper on the inside.

"Who?" I asked as I returned my attention to the automatons. "The fucking bartender. Let him go!"

There was more screaming outside. The monster's arms had found some shop or door and had gotten more NPCs. There was another crash as part of the ceiling above us sagged, like the supports for the whole club were starting to fail. Dust cascaded into the room.

"PSAMATHE, WHERE THE FUCK DID YOU GO? I PLUGGED THE HOLE IN THE CASINO AND YOU RAN LIKE A LITTLE BITCH. I WILL TEAR THIS WHOLE PLACE DOWN."

The smoke curtain out in the main room would soon dissipate, and I had to get this done. Minge would send her arms in here at any moment. I put the demon snare onto the trap slot of the first robot. I double-checked the spider's yield and upped it, using the menu.

"Oh, him? We're on a date. His arm got stuck. I'm practicing my Kegels."

"What? What the hell? Let him go!"

"Donut taught me about them. *She* said she learned about them from your ex-girlfriend, who cheated on you a lot. You really shouldn't let your women cheat on you, Carl. It's a bad look."

"Help. Please help me," Charles the badger said. "It's burning."

"Samantha, you've kidnapped him. Let him go. He's scared."

"Fear is a powerful aphrodisiac, Carl."

I had a simple but highly programmable door-opening bot from Dr. Ratchet's automaton kit, and I pulled off the quick-release door arm, added the double arm, and reattached the grasping claw and added the heavy-duty magnet, which would allow it to work more quickly. I put my hand on the machine, pulled up my menu, clicked the location, and added the instructions, giving it a sixty-second delay once it reached the wall. I sent the machine on the way. It would go down that hidden hallway, hopefully not set off any of the remaining NPC-only traps, and then dismantle the wall bracers I installed, unleashing the vorpals. It would take a few minutes to get through the sandbags. I'd be back on the top floor before that happened. Hopefully.

I added another specialized smoke curtain to the third and fourth bots, and then I sent them along with the trap bot out the main door. They skittered into the smoke, happily clicking like they didn't have a care in the world.

KATIA: Carl, we did it. I have the orchid.

Job Complete.

I have more work for you. Yes, yes, there is always more. Come to me, and we will spread our family's power.

Relief flooded me.

"I didn't kidnap him!" Samantha said, sounding offended.

She zipped toward the now-missing kitchen doors. Charles trailed under her, crying. Samantha's voice rose in volume as she shouted out into the smoke, "You stink like a marsh hog with an uncontrollable yeast infection! You smell worse than your maggot-infested, semen-stained corpse of a sister!"

"GOT YOU!" Minge bellowed as an arm shot into the kitchen and grasped on to Charles's chest.

"No, no, no!" Charles cried as Samantha started squealing in outrage. She zipped away, moving back toward me.

And thus ended Samantha's short courtship with Charles Ellis the Porsuk. The badger man ripped in half, spraying the kitchen with blood. All that was left hanging were the shoulder, neck, and head of the very dead, very unlucky bartender.

"YOU KILLED MY BOYFRIEND!" Samantha shrieked.

Another arm reached into the room, grasping for the floating head.

Samantha zipped out of the way. The arm shot over me, hit a door in the back of the room, and ripped it open. A shriek filled the chamber as a dwarf—one of the kitchen managers—was pulled into the restaurant.

Samantha made a grunting noise, and the rest of poor Charles plopped out and onto the floor with a wet splash. The part that had been inside Samantha was black and melted, like it had been half burned with acid. His hand was nothing but white bone, the individual pieces scattering like rolled dice when they hit the counter. A few shiny gold coins also dropped out, tinkling as they rolled away.

From the restaurant came a crunch, followed by "YOU'RE NEXT, SKANK. GAHHHH!"

All three of the automatons had reached the body of Minge and activated. The demon squealed in pain.

With a demon as large as Minge, the snare trap going off next to her was the equivalent of using a mousetrap to catch an elephant. The snare would supposedly attach the demon in place, trapping them. That obviously wasn't going to happen. Since the snare was affixed to the top of the spider automaton, it had the effect of attaching the spider to the demon's bulk. The spider then detonated, splashing the demon with blood water from Emberus's shrine.

At the same moment, the other two spiders set off their holy-water-infused smoke curtains, filling the room with burning, blinding fog. In ten seconds, the spiders themselves would also detonate, adding more holy water to the room.

Minge, at level 225, wasn't going to be really injured by any of this, but it would probably hurt like hell. It caused her to shrink back. This was our chance. We had to get upstairs.

I jumped up and bolted for the exit. "Run! Samantha, on me!" I leaped over the bodies, my feet sliding on gore.

"I'm still having a tussle! She killed Chuckie!"

"I swear to fucking god, come on! We're going up to the top floor. To the strip club!"

I didn't wait to hear her response. I figured that'd entice her, and if not . . . she'd probably be okay, assuming that thing didn't actually eat her.

I went out the door, pausing long enough to look at Minge one last time. She remained planted in the center of the room, her arms twisted around her like thorns. She'd managed to reach into this floor's version of the Silk Road and had several merchants in her hands as she waved about. She had a health bar, but it didn't look like she'd taken any damage.

The club was absolutely trashed. There was a literal hole in the high ceiling, and the casino area was on fire. *Jesus.* Almost every door I could see was gone. Dozens of bodies littered the room.

I rushed down the hall toward the restrooms, and I was surprised to find a small queue of NPCs trying to get into the stall. A pair of Crocodilian guards was helping people get away. One was one of the guys who'd been hit by the last teleport spell, shooting him up to the top floor.

He'd been ready to sacrifice himself. He'd been sent into that hallway to open the vorpal door, likely knowing those things would kill him. But instead he'd been teleported away to safety. Now he was helping the others.

He grabbed my shoulder as I pushed into the bathroom stall. His tuxedo hung in tatters around him.

"Hey," he said. "Have you seen Miss Astrid?"

"She's dead," I said, and I pushed my way into the stairs, mixed in with the scared and panicked NPCs. All of them were moving up, not down to the Larracos level. I didn't know if that was because they couldn't. Most of these guys had come from the secret areas of the club, I knew, including the drug den where Katia had gotten herself fucked-up. I wondered how many were real NPCs and how many were former crawlers. I tried not to think about it.

Your Automaton has been destroyed before it can complete its assigned task.

Shit, I thought. Something had happened. But then I heard it, a chorus of shrieks. It sounded like screaming mixed with buzz saws. They'd gotten out. Likely having broken down the door once the spider robot had cleared most of it away.

"Run! Fooking run!" the Crocodilian called from the bottom of the thin stairwell. "They's coming! They're worse than the demons."

"Move! Move out of the way!" came Samantha's voice as she zipped into the tight hidden stairwell. She came to hover next to me. She was covered in dripping gore.

"I hate it when the clubs get so busy," she said. She shook her head like a dog, splattering gore onto a gnome I recognized as the proprietor of the jewelry shop. The older man sputtered but kept moving.

"Samantha, how the hell did that thing get out of the Nothing?" I asked, breathless as we reached the top of the stairs. We pushed our way out into the women's room of the top level. A group of the elves from the kitchens was there directing people. I pushed past them and out.

"I don't know," Samantha said, following. She was hovering off the ground, not rolling. "I saw the table with the knife game, and the guards were chasing me because I had my ex-boyfriend with me, and somebody lost the game at the same moment, and the guy got pulled into the Nothing, but when it opened, it tore and Minge came out. She's Slit's little sister. We used to be friends. It's sad, really."

The abandoned dance floor didn't have a hole in it, but there was a crater. It looked like a bomb had gone off. Most everyone was headed toward the Silk Road. I knew there was a secret hall back there leading to dorm areas for NPCs. It was where they were going to shelter.

"I'm just glad it wasn't Gash," Samantha continued. "She's the mean one. The hole stayed open and was sucking everybody away, too, and Minge pulled herself into the restaurant because she's a dumb bitch. It didn't pull me in, though. Oh boy, is this the Penis Parade Donut's always talking about? Is Anaconda working tonight?"

I pushed my way into the room to find an unexpected sight. It was completely packed. The music was off. I shouldered my way deeper inside, looking for Katia.

I found Damascus Steel sitting on the floor, sobbing. The older, stoic ifrit had his face in his hands as sizzling tears peppered the floor around him. The other one Donut liked, the purple-skinned quarter-Naga named Anaconda, was also weeping uncontrollably. All the dancers and customers and that weird skeleton DJ guy stood around them. Splash Zone, the little otter stripper guy, rubbed Anaconda's back while Dong Quixote tried to give Damascus a cup of water.

But there were more people in here, too. The strippers from the Bitches room were all huddled with the men. They were of all shapes and sizes, all with equally ridiculous names like the male dancers. Almost all their names were alliterations. There was a dwarf named **Patty Pump-It-Up** and a hairy bugbear lady with a blond wig named **Darla No-Dentures.**

Another group of male and female strippers stood off to the side, all looking shell-shocked. This group was covered in gore, and I realized they must have escaped from the middle floor. These were the dancers from the Penis Palace. The female strip club and brothel on the middle floor was named Girls of Ill Refute. Not "repute" with a "p." These women were much better dressed than the women from Bitches. Or they had been better dressed before they'd had to endure that nightmare.

Katia cried out and rushed up to me, pulling me into a tight hug. She held me while we talked over message.

KATIA: Oh my god, Carl. We did it. We won the quest, and the box opened. I have the orchid in my inventory. Huanxin messaged me. She said you just need to do one more thing, and then we'll be safe. Do you know what it is?

I needed to make certain Odette became our adjutant. I was about to go on her show.

CARL: I do. It'll happen in a few hours. When are you going to eat it?

When Katia ate the orchid, she would get transferred away to the 12th floor and temporarily turned into an NPC. At least that was the plan. The goddess Eileithyia, who was being driven by Huanxin, actually had three options. She could triple Katia's constitution. She could impregnate her—which would immediately boot her from the dungeon. Or she could move her to the 12th floor and take her on as a sort of intern. As long as she didn't go with the constitution buff, the issue with the Sepsis Crown would be solved.

KATIA: I can't believe it. I can't believe that worked. I can't abandon my squad. I won't eat it until we get down to the ninth.

CARL: What the hell is wrong with those stripper guys? Why are they crying?

KATIA: I'm not sure. They somehow found out Astrid is dead, and they both started weeping. We better not tell them we did it, but Damascus is in that guild, so surely he'll figure it out. I think he liked her.

Samantha had settled next to one of the male strippers, the troll bizarrely named Author Steve Rowland. She was chatting away with him amiably, telling him she still had some money left.

The whole club shook. The main stage suddenly plummeted away, and a Minge arm reached into the room as people screamed and scattered. But then the arm pulled away. A screaming, buzz-saw-like sound emanated through the hall. A spray of yellow fluid shot into the air through the hole in the floor as Minge the demon screamed in pain.

It was the sound of her being killed by the vorpals. She cried in pain as more yellow liquid spewed into the room from below.

"PSAMATHE," Minge shouted as she died. "YOU FUCKING BITCH!"

Samantha was suddenly next to me. "We need to go clubbing more often! This place is great!"

34

<Note added by Crawler Ossie. 18th Edition>

I know I don't write often in these scrolls, but I have read them all. I just finished my third reread of Herot's overwrought essay and ramblings about the Worn Path Method of waking NPCs. These theories are sound, I think, but I believe there is something he has missed. Something monumental. I think they're lying about the origin of some of these NPCs. Years pass, times change, laws and rules evolve. But this behemoth we find ourselves trapped within still persists. A reused canvas painted over and over again. The fact that this scroll I am writing in even exists suggests that the brushstrokes used to paint this world are so piled atop one another, it's impossible to see every image that once was. Ask a Bopca where they come from, and they'll all tell you the same thing. That the aliens came to their planet and "offered" them a chance to live in the dungeon. I don't think they're the only ones with such a fate, and I'm beginning to believe the Bopcas' station is much higher than that of those who've been offered a similar deal.

"LET'S GET THE FUCK OUT OF HERE," I SAID, BACKING TOWARD THE door. Minge was dead, but I could still hear them down there. The vorpals, whatever they were. They tore through the lower level of the club. They would supposedly disappear now that they'd bathed in demon blood, but how long would it take? I eyed Damascus Steel nervously. He was a demon class, and his presence was dangerous.

"Wait," Damascus said, pulling himself to his feet. Steaming tears continued to roll down his face. "You have to take them with you. The dancers from the Penis Parade. All of them."

"Uh," I said, exchanging a look with Katia. "Why?"

The ifrit straightened. "The club is going to be closed for remodeling after this. It's happened before. With my mother dead, they'll assign a new assistant manager. There'll be a restructuring. They'll kick us out."

"Your mother?"

He looked up nervously at the ceiling.

"It's a long story. We don't have time for it. Normally, the dancers here . . . We shouldn't be here. Mother pulled strings. We have to leave." He grabbed my arm and leaned in. His grip was like an iron clamp. "You owe me," he whispered. "They will *not* survive this. You have to get them out of here. I convinced them to come, to work in this place. The new management is going to reassign them to the Larracos level. Or worse. If you don't take them now, you'll end up fighting against them on the ninth floor."

I blinked at that. "What about you? You don't want to come?"

More yellow fluid shot up from the hole in the floor, like the monsters below were splashing about in Minge's corpse. It stank like rotten eggnog.

"I didn't know who you were assigned to kill," he said. "I don't blame you for what happened. But I do blame him. We were promised freedom. He wanted to make sure she was dead. They're still married. My mother has—had—so much, and the guild, it's rarely found by crawlers. He gets it all. He'll have it all when we get out."

I didn't understand any of this. If there was a way I could take them with me, I would in a second. Mordecai would have a coronary, but I would do it.

But what the hell was he talking about?

"I'm sorry," Katia said, interrupting. "Are you saying you're former crawlers? That *Astrid* was a former crawler? And that she was your mother? And"—she waved over at the cubicles in the back of the room toward the Night Wyrm's lair—"and he's your what? Your father?"

"Yes, they're my parents. My brother and I were never crawlers," Damascus said. "Look, Carl. We all still have our memberships to Meat Shields. Donut said you have a coupon. You can hire us. Do it for a two-floor contract, and they'll be able to leave with you." He turned, searching the room. His eyes focused on an elderly dwarf woman. She was rubbing Anaconda's back.

"Rosemarie, come," Damascus called.

The dwarf woman hobbled over. I recognized her from the last time I'd visited the strip club. She had a black-and-white fuzzy mole creature named Bernie perched on her shoulder. The old woman had gotten in trouble from the DJ for pelting one of the dancers in the eye with a gold coin.

"Rosemarie is the manager of the top floor's Meat Shields location," Damascus said.

"I didn't know there was one on this floor," I said, instinctively pulling up the map. There wasn't a location listed.

"I work out of my home office," she said, waving vaguely over where her table used to be. There was just a hole there now. Samantha was there on the ground, peering down into the smoke. She was laughing hysterically as Minge's body below was getting eviscerated.

Damascus grabbed the elderly dwarf and shoved her toward me. "She can approve the transaction right now. Isn't that right, Rosemarie? He wants to hire the entire crew for two floors."

The old dwarf turned to regard Damascus, surprise on her face.

"Your mother said—"

"My mother is dead," he snapped.

She took a moment, swallowing. "You really think they'll shutter the Parade after this?"

While she was turned, that thing on her shoulder continued to stare at me. It made a snuffling noise and growled.

"Not shutter it," Damascus said. "It'll be a restructuring, just like last time. My mother will be replaced. They'll bring back the original dancers, and our whole crew will get thrown to the Larracos-level Meat Shields." He thumbed over his shoulder at a group of male dancers I didn't recognize. The ones from that other strip club one floor down. I remembered that Donut did not like these guys nearly as much. "The pricks at the Palace won't have us."

"If you guys leave, they'll fill this place up with the dregs again," Rosemarie said. "I'll never get no business. Did you ever see those guys before you came on? Ain't nobody gonna hire an elderly stripper with one leg and halitosis."

"We don't have a choice."

The dwarf grunted. "I gotta calculate the cost. You alone are worth a good chunk, ya know."

"I'm not going. It'll be all the others. Bucket Boy and Doctor Bones, too. And his coupon is for 100,000 gold. That's how much it'll cost."

"Wait, what? You're going to separate from your brother? What are *you* going to do?"

"You know what I have to do," he said.

Rosemarie patted Damascus on the waist. It was about as high as she could reach. Bernie stopped staring at me and jumped up to the ifrit's shoulder and headbutted him before returning to the dwarf.

"I'm sure gonna miss the cum closet," she said sadly. Bernie made a sad peep.

KATIA: What in the heck are they talking about?

CARL: I . . . I'm not sure. I have a theory. I'll tell you in a minute. But if we can actually hire these guys as mercenaries for our Faction Wars army, I'm going to do it. We'll have to buy an upgrade for the guild, I think. We gotta house them until the next floor.

KATIA: Donut made Imani buy a barracks upgrade earlier. We now have enough room for like 20 of them. We can get a bigger upgrade, but it's really expensive. We bought the training arena for them, too. It's called the Mercenary Arcade.

CARL: Really? I didn't know that.

Out loud, I said to Damascus, "If Astrid was your mother, how can that be that you're not crawlers?"

There was a distant scream, but I couldn't tell from where. The vorpals were still in the club.

"We have no time," Damascus said. "And I've already gotten a warning to shut up about this. There's more of us than you know. Anaconda and I are just two of thousands."

Anaconda, the dark quarter-Naga, looked up at the mention of his name. "Brother, what are you doing?"

Damascus turned and put his hand on the other stripper's shoulder. The two didn't look anything alike. They weren't even remotely the same species. "I'm going to avenge our mother. He won't win."

The snakelike dancer looked up at his brother. He had slitted reptilian eyes. "If you're going to fight him, I'm going, too."

"Me, too!" called Dong Quixote.

"No," Anaconda said without turning his head. "This is family business."

And then, without another word to us, Damascus held out his arm and pulled his brother to his feet. The two turned and walked toward the back of the club, skirting past Samantha, who remained at the breach in the floor. She made a lewd comment. They ignored her. Together, they entered the back cubicle.

"What is happening?" a woman asked. This was a snaggletoothed, heavily pierced goblin prostitute named **Tuesday Two-for-One**. She was furiously chewing gum. She reminded me of a pair of female goblins Donut and I had met so long ago. "Where are they going? Are they going to get each other off or something?"

Rosemarie looked up at me, waved her hand, and a shop interface window popped up.

She sighed heavily. "It's the end of an era, you know. I hope you appreciate what you've done. Now let's see that coupon of yours."

WARNING: THE DESPERADO CLUB HAS BEEN TEMPORARILY CLOSED. You have fifteen minutes to exit, or you will be teleported out to the entrance vestibule.

A timer appeared in my vision.

"Huh," I whispered. I wasn't expecting that.

Katia, Samantha, and I cautiously moved toward the exit. We stopped at the end of the hallway overlooking the dance floor and decided to wait here for a few minutes to make certain there was nothing out there. Samantha had reverted to rolling on the ground. As we waited, I thought of Ossie's note at the end of Herot's essay. That whole thing about the Worn Path Method was ridiculously long and mind-numbing. I hadn't even noticed that note by Ossie until recently, when I read it during my cookbook transcription. There was no other mention anywhere about any such theory, but I couldn't stop thinking about it now.

There was blood all over the dance floor. It hadn't been there before, which meant at least one of those things had gotten up here. I was pretty sure it was gone, but I still wanted to wait a minute.

The 13 male strippers plus that skeleton DJ guy and the Crocodilian Bucket Boy kid from the Penis Parade were already in the barracks. They'd transferred outside and to the front door of our personal space the moment we hired them. The women from Bitches and the male and female clubs on the middle floor were left behind. Only the men of the Penis Parade were eligible to be hired as mercenaries.

I'd neglected to tell Donut they were coming, and she was over the moon with their addition to the guild.

DONUT: OMG, CARL. THIS IS THE GREATEST THING SINCE YOU HIRED SLEDGIE. YOU EVEN HIRED DOCTOR BONES. HE'S THE BEST DJ SINCE DJ DIESEL. MY BIRTHDAY ISN'T UNTIL NOVEMBER, BUT IT'S LIKE IT STARTED EARLY. MONGO IS REALLY EXCITED, TOO. I'M SAD ANACONDA AND STEELIE AREN'T HERE, THOUGH. DO YOU THINK MAYBE THEY'LL COME LATER?

CARL: Maybe. How's Mordecai taking it?

DONUT: THE GUYS ALL LEFT TO GO AND SEE THE MERCENARY TRAINING ARCADE, SO HE DOESN'T REALLY CARE. HE'S MORE MAD THAT YOU BLEW UP THE DESPERADO CLUB. HE SAYS IT'S GONNA BE A PROBLEM GETTING SUPPLIES. WHO WAS YOUR ASSASSINATION TARGET ANYWAY? YOU CAN TALK ABOUT IT NOW, RIGHT?

CARL: I'll tell you about it when we get back. How'd it go in the practice arena?

DONUT: THEY WERE PRETTY MAD. SHI MARIA WAS MAD, TOO. SHE WANTED ME TO USE THAT GLOW-UP CARD ON HER.

We'd debated this for a while, and in the end, I went with Donut's judgment.

Before we'd gone into the club, Katia gave Donut one of her excess totem cards. A mythic creature from Iceland named Jola. I'd been worried Donut would be pissed, but she'd actually been pretty excited about it once she saw the card. After reading all its abilities, she decided she wanted it in our active deck, which would give us one too many totems.

Instead of getting rid of one of our existing cards, she'd instead used the consumable Combo card to combine two of the problem cards, used up all the utility buffs on them, and then used the consumable Glow-Up card to make the change permanent.

So when it was done, we actually had two new totems. Donut had spent the past several hours practicing with them by herself.

We had considered just getting rid of Shi Maria, or using the Combo on her to make a new creature, considering how dangerous she was. But we needed her if we wanted to survive this next part. It was a calculated risk. I hoped we'd have an opportunity to get rid of her once we got our hands on a key to the stairwell.

CARL: How is Jola? Does he do what you say? And what about the, uh, new one?

DONUT: JOLA IS GREAT AS LONG AS THERE ARE NO CHILDREN AROUND.

CARL: What the hell does that mean?

DONUT: YOU'LL SEE. THE NEW COMBO GUY IS STILL A JERK, BUT HE LIKES FIGHTING. ALSO, YOU WERE BUSY, SO I DIDN'T BOTHER YOU, BUT WE FINALIZED A BUNCH OF VOTES FOR THE FACTION WARS RULES THOUGH A BUNCH ARE STILL UP IN THE AIR.

CARL: Okay, I'll see you in a bit. We're going straight to Odette's. Get ready. We might be there awhile, so make sure you go to the bathroom first.

DONUT: I ALREADY DID.

I looked over at Katia. She was leaning against the wall, her eyes closed, listening for monsters. Samantha was on the ground, gnawing at her ankle. The club was empty. I didn't see any dots. None at all. I once again looked at the dance floor, an uneasy feeling washing over me. It was strange seeing it like this. I thought of Clarabelle, the guard at the door. We wouldn't see her when we left, not unless we backtracked inside, which we were now barred from doing. I hoped she was okay.

That boot was gone, I realized. The one from the crawler guy I'd fought with earlier.

Katia wasn't looking good. She'd reverted to her large blond female form, and even though she "sculpted" the way she looked, she had heavy rings under her eyes. She had a tremor in her left hand. We needed to get her to Mordecai and Imani for another treatment soon.

I thought, once again, of that terrifying look on her frozen face from earlier.

"Are you doing okay?" I asked.

Katia spoke without opening her eyes. "I'm fine. I just need to rest for a minute, and we can go. I'm confused as hell about what was going on back there with the dancers. Tell me your theory."

I shrugged. "I think the four of them—the Night Wyrm, Astrid, Damascus Steel, and Anaconda—are a family, and they've been stuck in the dungeon for a really long time. I don't think they're generated NPCs, but more like the Bopcas. Like maybe they were indentured servants who somehow signed up for or were forced into the dungeon. I don't know what race they were born, but they're all different ones in the game."

Katia's eyes opened at that. "Holy crap."

"Yeah," I agreed. "Did you see those girls from the Bitches room? They were all, uh . . . How do I say this?"

"Butt-ass ugly?" Samantha offered from the floor.

"Yeah," I said. "I think the men in the Penis Parade on this floor are supposed to be like that. Like super, uh, unqualified. But they're not. Well, some are. When Astrid ended up with the job as the assistant manager of the club, she made certain her two sons were safe and got them a gig at the Penis Parade, where she could watch over them. It sounds like they were all members of Meat Shields, the mercenary market. She brought them to the club, and they brought their friends with them. She probably did some wheeling and dealing and parked that Rosemarie lady in there, so they were technically still mercenaries, but since nobody knew the club was also a Meat Shields location, they were safe."

"What about the husband? The Guild of Suffering?"

"That, I'm not so clear on. But I think they believed they were going to be done soon, maybe done after this season, with their contract. The dad, who was playing the Night Wyrm, made us kill her. Based on what Damascus said, I think it was over money. Like if she died, he would get her paycheck or something."

"Holy crap," Katia said again. "So you think he had us murder her in the game for real-life money? That's diabolical. Do you think the other guys, the rest of the strippers, are the same type of NPC? Or are they the generated kind?"

"I don't know," I said. "Unless they tell us, I don't think there is a way to know. I'm not even sure *they* know sometimes. Mordecai said it was illegal to change the memories of natural people. That's what he called them. 'Naturals.' I think that's what he said."

Actually, no, I remembered, thinking back on the short conversation we'd had way back when we'd entered the third floor. I was pretty sure he'd added, *Unless they signed away their rights.*

Jesus. I didn't want to think about that.

"Come on," Katia said, pulling me toward the exit. "It's safe. We probably don't want to get teleported out."

As we exited the club, I suddenly remembered there were several Faction Wars participants still trapped on the bottom level of the Desperado because the lower part of the city remained flooded.

Despite the horrors of everything we'd just experienced, I felt myself grin as we stepped outside.

35

"I MUST SAY," ODETTE LAUGHED, "IN A DAY FILLED WITH SURPRISES, that was a— How do you say? A dessert worthy of a king? I think the phrase in your language is 'the cherry on top.'" Her voice echoed unnaturally in the large chamber. On the screen, we'd just watched a submerged Viceroy from team Madness get devoured by a shark.

The production trailer we sat in was the same one as the last time we'd gone on Odette's show, but her set was different. The audience was much bigger, and her desk and chairs were made to appear as if we were onstage in a large auditorium, which caused the echo to her voice. It was implied we were actually in the city of Larracos, within some baroque-style theater. Along the virtual walls were water-stained, peeling posters for plays and musicals. My eyes caught one for a play called *Session of Love*. It reminded me of the poster for *Gone with the Wind*, only it was a camel holding on to a swooning Saccathian wearing a yellow wig.

I knew Odette had just arrived in Earth orbit, so the change of scenery was for the benefit of the audience.

"It's not as fun watching them die when we know they're going to be brought back at the end of the day," Donut complained. She looked up at the audience. "Does that poor shark still get to keep all the food in his tummy, or does it teleport away?" The audience laughed. "It's like when Carl used to complain to his friends that Miss Beatrice was giving him blue balls. Is there a blue balls equivalent for food?"

I grunted. "I *never* said that."

"I'm being serious. Are they even feeding those guys? We are on the eighth floor for goodness' sake, and that city has been flooded since the end of the fifth, and they still haven't gotten rid of those sharks? That has got to be some sort of animal abuse. The least they can do is let them eat somebody for real."

"Oh, they get fed all right," Odette said. "The Semeru aren't letting anyone near that part of the city, and they're keeping the castle submerged. Mercenaries and players alike are getting fed into that pit on the daily. That little stunt at the Desperado Club ended up ejecting several trapped officials and participants from various factions, all of whom were quickly devoured or pulled their fail-safes. Only one of the killed was a warlord."

An image of a hairy alien appeared on the screen, flailing in the water. I'd never seen this guy before, but I recognized him. I had a picture of his mother. He hadn't been at the meeting. His proxy had been a goblin-like alien named Luke. This guy was a different alien altogether. His head was like that of a caterpillar, but I was pretty sure he walked on two legs. He had several arms that waved about in the water. The audience laughed as he was ripped apart, torn into pieces by a pair of concierge sharks.

"Commander Stockade of the Lemig Sortition was the last of the 35 to be devoured," Odette said.

"Only 35 bad guys got eaten? It's a good start, but not nearly enough," Donut said.

Odette chuckled. "Five teams all filed new complaints. They're saying that Carl destroying the club and forcing that mass exit should constitute a foul and attack. They're asking for sanctions."

I grunted with derision.

"That's quite the stretch," Donut agreed. "Samantha somehow accidentally allowed a demon out of the Nothing, and the demon lady ended up destroying the club so bad, they had to kick everyone out? One could hardly expect Carl to have predicted *that.* It was just a happy little accident, as that afro guy says. Carl says we did them a favor anyway. Isn't that right, Carl?"

"That's right."

"How do you figure that?" asked Odette.

I made eye contact with Quasar, who stood offstage and to the side. He gave me a thumbs-up. I tried to ignore Harbinger, who stood behind him in the back corner of the small hold. The massive goat liaison stood in shadow. His virtual avatar was taller than the ceiling of the room, and his head was half cut off, like in a video game. Zev was also here, also attending as a holo, standing on the opposite side of the studio. She was whispering to Lexis, Odette's assistant, the only person who was really here with us.

I leaned forward on the couch. "Look. Those assholes have been sitting on their butts on the bottom floor of the Desperado since we trapped them there all those weeks ago. They were trapped there because the entrance bar in Larracos was destroyed. The only way out was for them to die and get regenerated. They could've killed themselves at any time. None of them did. The rest of their teams have all been working their asses off while these idiots have been getting drunk and gambling away their citizens' money. Anyone who was still there was nothing more than a huge wuss, including Corporal Caterpillar or whatever his name is. Now they're all ejected from the club, and they can finally participate in the game. Donut is right. I had no idea any of that was going to happen. They should be thanking me, not whining like a bunch of little bitches."

The crowd cheered.

"Speaking of Faction Wars," Odette said. The crab legs on her lower body rearranged themselves, the joints moving up and down like pistons. I was used to them by now, but whenever they moved, it gave me the heebies. "I understand your face-to-face preproduction meetings have been suspended, and now you're doing all the voting via your interface. Is that correct?"

I tensed. We were on dangerous ground. From the corner, Harbinger leaned forward. Before the interview, he warned he would stop the whole thing if either Donut or I gave up privileged information about behind-the-scenes stuff, including any information about Juice Box and her rebellion. It was stupid because the galaxy had to know all about this already. Donut and Louis were constantly talking about Juice Box. Still, if the liaison stopped the interview early, Odette wouldn't get the chance to ask to be our adjutant. If Odette wasn't our adjutant, then our deal with Huanxin to save Katia was null and void. Nobody knew this last part except me. I'd told Donut how important it was to get through this interview, but I hadn't dared tell her all of it. All she knew was that she wasn't allowed to talk once Odette mentioned the word "adjutant."

Zev had begged us not to pick Odette. She'd have to get over it.

"That's right," Donut said cheerfully. "I do like going to the meetings, but they kept getting messed up."

"In what way?" Odette asked, pouncing on the opening.

Donut waved a paw. "Oh, you know. Politics." She turned to the crowd and stage-whispered, "I don't think that orc Prince Stalwart likes us very much. And that weird Viceroy guy couldn't keep his head about him. I do wish they'd allow the meetings to be streamed. That last one was quite entertaining. But . . ." She made a motion like she was zipping up her mouth.

Odette laughed along with the audience. She waved a hand, and a paragraph of text appeared floating in the air. "We all know that the participants get to vote on rule changes before the game officially starts. Some of these rules can be voted on right until the moment the floor opens up. These are called action items. If an action item is voted down, we, unfortunately, never get to see what it was. But here's something you guys probably don't know. If an item gets rejected by the system before anyone can vote, we *do* get to see it. Our researchers happened to notice a few interesting ones."

The screen zoomed in on a line of text.

Action Item proposed by Co-Warlord Princess Donut of the Princess Posse: Change the name of Crown Prince Stalwart to "Captain Enormous."

*****Item rejected by system.**

The crowd roared.

"I would love to hear the story about that one," Odette asked, laughing.

I eyed Quasar, and he thought for a moment and then shook his head no.

"Sorry," I said, speaking before Donut could reply. "The lawyers are telling me that's off-limits."

"Oh, poo," Donut said. "That was a good story. But, *hypothetically*, if someone randomly talked about the size of their own private parts without anyone else bringing it up, Captain Enormous would be a perfectly proper nickname for him. Again, Odette, this is pure supposition on my part."

I held my breath, but Harbinger didn't react. He appeared suddenly distracted, which was unusual for the goat liaison. Odette let the laughter die down before she pulled up the next screen. This was a group of three action items I'd never seen before.

Holy shit, I thought, reading them.

Emergency Action Item proposed by Warlord Empress D'Nadia of the Prism: Delete all existing NPCs on Larracos level to maintain game integrity for Faction Wars.

*****Item rejected by system.**

Emergency Action Item proposed by Warlord Empress D'Nadia of the Prism: Disallow crawlers from participating in Faction Wars in any capacity.

*****Item rejected by system.**

Emergency Action Item proposed by Warlord Empress D'Nadia of the Prism: Remove the Princess Posse from Faction Wars and/or delete Crawlers Carl and Princess Donut.

*****Item rejected by system.**

"Huh," I said.

"Oh my god," Donut said at the same time, jumping to her paws on the chair. Her tail swished angrily. "That . . . *that bitch*! I thought she was my friend! She can't do that! We didn't even see these! Carl, do you see this! She's cheating! First she sells my sponsorship to, to . . ." She made an angry, strangled noise. "She tried to delete us!"

Before anyone could respond, Donut gasped with new indignation. "Carl, I just realized something. I'm starting to think maybe she really did vote against Mongo in the pet show! This is an outrage!"

Odette's bug head nodded in mock sympathy. "My understanding is, if it's an *emergency* action item, there is no vote. The system is allowed to decide. You only get three of these. All the other teams used up their emergency actions when you flooded Larracos or when you purchased your team, or when you splatted that elf castle on the Lemig Sortition's playing field."

"What?" Donut asked. "Emergency action items? We didn't even know that was possible!"

Here it comes, I thought.

"That," Odette said, "is why you need to pick your adjutant as soon as possible."

Donut opened her mouth to respond, but then she looked at me. Across the studio, Zev and Lexis had stopped talking and were staring intently.

"Adjutant?" I asked, pretending not to know what that meant.

"Each team gets one. It's a third-party referee and consultant. Kind of like how a manager worked before they changed the rules, but instead of being a non-corporeal avatar, they're really there. The adjutant will have access to the expanded rule set and will accompany the warlord into battle. They cannot fight either directly or indirectly. They can clarify rules and also call fouls. They're also tasked with giving a daily on-air recap for fans."

"They're physically there on the battlefield with us?" I asked, letting a grin spread across my face. "So if we manage to get the protections turned off, they'd be as vulnerable as the hunters from the sixth floor? In my world, we had a thing called embedded reporters who followed military units around. That was a *very* dangerous job."

Odette shook her head. "No matter what happens with that vote, adjutants are protected. But, yes, they're really there."

She'd just confirmed what Mordecai had said earlier. That actually made me feel a little better. It was clear Huanxin wanted Odette there so she could do something to her. I still didn't know the details on why they didn't like each other, though I knew the three of them—Mordecai, Odette, and Huanxin—were all tangled up together in some ancient beef that ended up with Mordecai's brother dead and Odette arrested. But if Odette was protected while on the battlefield, then that meant it was out of my hands. What they did to each other outside the dungeon was none of my concern.

I shrugged. "Well, we don't have one yet. I'm open to suggestions."

Odette nodded. "We can sort that for you." She waved her hand, and three aliens appeared floating in windows. I recognized two of them. "I *was* going to ask you guys if you wanted me to do it, but unfortunately, I won't be able to participate as an adjutant this season. So, let's help you choose one now."

36

I TOOK A DEEP BREATH. I DID MY BEST NOT TO SHOW MY UTTER DISMAY on my face.

"Why can't you do it?" I asked.

"Oh, believe me," Odette said, waving her hand dismissively. "I *was* going to ask to do it, but I received an opportunity I can't pass up." She straightened. "That's right, folks. The rumors are true. My show will soon be put on hiatus as I step into the dungeon. I have sponsored a deity, and I will be attempting my hand at the Celestial Ascendency."

There was a pause, and then the crowd went absolutely nuts.

I felt sick to my stomach. She knew. Of course she knew. She knew all along that Huanxin was planning something, and Odette wasn't going to allow the rich CEO to have the upper hand. She was still going into the dungeon, but it would be on an equal footing.

This whole setup with getting us to pick an adjutant wasn't about us at all. It was really a way for Odette to announce her intentions to the audience. This whole interview was a thinly veiled press conference.

Donut started jumping up and down on the couch. "Oh my god, Odette! This is wonderful news! Can I worship you? Carl, wouldn't that be great? I could worship Odette!"

Odette laughed. "You don't even know which goddess I picked yet."

"Well, I'm quite certain it's someone great. Who is it?"

"I'm glad you asked," Odette said.

"For fuck's sake," I grumbled under my breath.

The three alien portraits faded as a new screen appeared, depicting a scene from the crawl. It was a group of four crawlers I didn't recognize. It was three humans and a type of rock monster called a coal engine, similar to Chris's igneous race. They rushed through the streets of some desert town, pushing through the memory images of people on the street. Clothes went flying. The rock-monster guy clutched on to a giant speckled egg, holding it against his chest like a football. They were pursued by a monstrous leopard with the neck and head of a snake. The snake-leopard thing was the size of a school bus, and the head snapped down, barely missing a human. One turned and fired a lightning bolt, and the monster fell back, spinning and hissing.

The four continued to flee, turning down a side street, losing the pursuer.

"It's happening!" the coal engine guy cried out, and they all skidded to a stop in an alley as the man held out the egg. They all gathered around.

A moment passed, and the egg hatched. The top of the shell dropped away, revealing an ugly baby-bird thing. It screamed, spread its wings, and burst into the air. Smoke trailed as it rose higher and higher, gaining in size. Soon, it was gone from sight.

A **Quest Complete!** notification appeared, followed by a system message that **Nekhebit** had reascended. I couldn't remember having heard that particular notification.

"That was anticlimactic," one of the humans grumbled.

The scene changed, showing a massive vulture goddess spinning in 3D on the screen.

Odette preened as sparkles flew around the spinning image. "That's right, everyone. I will be performing as the famed ancient goddess Nekhebit!"

I sighed as the crowd continued to go berserk. Man, I really hoped this would be enough for Huanxin. Odette was still going into the dungeon. If this CEO woman was reasonable, she'd see I had no control over this. I hoped and prayed she'd still honor the deal to save Katia.

I examined the spinning image of the goddess.

I was reminded of another vulture goddess. Quetzalcoatlus from the fifth floor, though that one had been a ghost. Plus she'd been more dinosaur-like with a South American vibe. This one was more of an Egyptian thing. She had a slender, humanlike body with a long red flowing dress. Her head was that of an Egyptian vulture, yellow with white feathers spreading around her, almost like an afro. A bow made of oak was slung over her shoulder. She didn't appear to have actual wings. Only humanlike arms covered in bracelets.

As I looked more closely, I noticed the goddess was old and dirty, and covered in healed wounds. Her yellow beak was cracked and chipped. Heavy scarring covered all the exposed parts of her flesh. The jewelry was tarnished and cloudy, and it was missing some gems. Her red dress appeared threadbare and tattered, almost like she'd been a corpse that had been exhumed.

"Ooh, she looks positively fiendish," Donut said. "Normally I'm not a fan of the whole hobo-chic aesthetic, but I do like this. It suits you. Very sinister. Though I hope you don't smell. You look like you might smell."

"Thank you, Donut," Odette said. "The origin story of Nekhebit is one of betrayal and revenge. She has earned every one of those scars. Whether she is considered a villain or a hero depends on one's perspective."

There was a strange flash to my HUD, like I'd just received a major notification, but it was suppressed because we were still on the show.

Odette continued. "Unlike all the other resurrected gods and goddesses on this floor, Nekhebit is not a retainer to any existing gods or goddesses. And yes, she will have a retainer of her own." She waggled her finger at the audience. "You'll have to see how all *that* plays out in the dungeon. We'll have one more special about Nekhebit's history that will air tomorrow evening as I onboard onto the playing field live. But that's not why we're here right now, is it? I apologize. We've gone a little off script."

She waved her hand, and the floating heads of the three potential adjutants returned.

"Let's pick you an adjutant. Again, I know we've put you on the spot. You don't have to choose, but these three are the only ones still available as far as I am aware. So if you don't pick, it's likely you'll still end up with one of these three anyway."

I gave a sidelong glance to Quasar, who was nodding in agreement with Odette.

All three of the aliens looked as irritated as I felt for having to sit through Odette's "off-script" reveal. I examined the three.

The first was a fuzzy bearlike creature. His name was Ripper Wonton. He was a type of creature called a Quokka, and he was the host of a show called *Danger Zone with Ripper Wonton*. It was a show Donut, Hekla, and I were on when Manasa had been assassinated by the Skull Empire.

The second was a very angry-looking female orc I didn't recognize. She was the same sort of wild-boar-looking orc as Prince Maestro and Crown Prince Stalwart. She reminded me of an orc hunter we'd killed on the previous floor.

The third was a bald Dream elf. This guy's name was Drick, and I'd shared a panel with him when I was at CrawlCon. I remembered the original Drick had been a crawler, and I was pretty sure his birth race wasn't an elf. It didn't matter because this iteration was actually a worm head, meaning he had a Valtay worm in the brain.

"Hi, Ripper!" Donut said, waving at the only one she recognized. She hadn't gone to CrawlCon with me. She peered suspiciously at the orc woman. "Are you Princess Formidable? My friend Katia really likes the sponsor boxes you send. Why do you hate your brothers so much?"

The audience laughed, as did both Ripper Wonton and Drick. The orc woman did not look amused.

"That's not Princess Formidable," Odette said. "I don't think they'd allow her to be an adjutant."

"Like this one is much better," Drick muttered.

"Who are you? I don't like you," Donut said to Drick. She waved her paw about. "Don't they have tanning salons out in the universe?" She turned to Odette. "We pick Ripper Wonton. I like him, and he's adorable."

"Wait," I said. I was eyeing Quasar, who was shaking his head no vigorously. "Which of these guys has experience doing this? And who is the orc? Are any of these guys qualified for this?"

"That's a good question, Carl. Luckily, the AI polices their behavior heavily, so you don't have to worry too much about biases, but here's a short rundown of each candidate. First, we have Ripper Wonton. He's an experienced interviewer and knows his way around the media. He's a firm but fair judge. He's done this quite a few times. Some people consider him a little too rigid. Plus his short legs make it so he has trouble keeping up in high-intensity battle situations."

"Really, Odette?" Ripper asked, chuckling at the description. "You're going to make fun of my legs?"

The crowd laughed.

"Next, we have Baroness Victory, Esquire, formerly of the Skull Empire. She is the half sister of the late Queen Consort Ugloo, but she is easily the most experienced judge of the lot. Uh, she's not too keen on fluff pieces, but people do like her matter-of-fact reporting on the anatomy of battles. She's an attorney and judge."

I looked over at Quasar, who gave me an enthusiastic thumbs-up.

"And finally, we have Drick. I know you've met him briefly, Carl. He's a recipient of a Valtay life extension. He recently passed the referee exam. He's an experienced crawler and consultant, but this would be his first attempt at being an adjutant."

Quasar gave him a tepid thumbs-down. It was clear my lawyer preferred the orc.

Before I turned back, something strange happened. Without a word of explanation, Harbinger blinked and disappeared. Everyone else in the room looked at each other in surprise. Quasar shrugged.

"Do you have any questions?" Odette asked. "If you want, we can put it to an audience vote."

I returned my attention to our three choices. I thought for a minute. I wasn't about to let the audience pick for us.

"Drick is allowed to be an adjutant even though he's Valtay?"

"It's a little unusual," Odette agreed. "But they say he's passed all the qualifications."

I liked Drick, but I had an uneasy feeling about choosing him. He seemed like an unlikely candidate for this, and the fact he was Valtay did not sit well with me. My gut told me to avoid using him.

Donut was correct. Ripper was the obvious choice here. Still, Quasar was vehemently against him for some reason. I wondered why.

Also, I still wasn't certain how crucial this choice was. I'd been so convinced we'd have Odette, I hadn't been worrying about it. I still had no idea what this guy would be doing all day.

I turned to Baroness Victory. The orc's nostrils flared. She had what appeared to be an image of an hourglass carved onto one of her tusks. "Have I killed any of your family members?"

The audience tittered nervously.

She looked at me impassively. "Other than my brother-in-law and nephews, nobody feels you're responsible for the death of my half sister, Queen Ugloo. You did slay several distant relations during the Hunting Grounds fiasco."

I felt my eyebrow raise. "And you feel you can be an impartial adjutant?"

"Don't pick her, Carl," Donut said.

She shrugged. "All of your actions so far have been well within your rights."

"And that makes a difference? They're family."

"I recently sentenced my own aunt to indentureship because she didn't pay her taxes. I am the best possible choice." She gave a very slight, sly smile, the first emotion I saw on her face. "Plus, I'm the only one the others sued to keep out of the game."

Again, I looked to Quasar. He was bouncing up and down, pointing at her, giving me a thumbs-up.

"You'll do," I said to Baroness Victory. "Sorry, Drick and Ripper. I'll catch you guys on the other side."

37

"OKAY, HERE WE GO," ODETTE SAID. "AS WE SPEAK, ALL THE CRAWLERS in the dungeon are being teleported to a choosing arena for phase two. We've gotten special permission to watch you enter the second area live. You'll go straight from here to the choosing room."

"Wait," Donut said. "Does this mean we're never going to be on your show again? If you're in the dungeon, we won't ever come back here. Is that right? Oh my god, that's so sad! Odette! It's the end of an era!"

Odette's bug mask stared impassively down at Donut.

"I hadn't really thought about it that way, but I suppose you're right, Donut. Not unless we can work something out, and they let me do the show from down there, then this is it. Though I'm sure we'll see each other on the inside."

She said it so casually, so cheerfully that I just wanted to erupt. If we did see each other, it would be on the battlefield. Would Odette spare us if we were in her path? I doubted it. It made me feel ill. I kept my mouth shut.

Donut leaped to Odette's desk and pretended to headbutt one of her massive boobs. "I suppose this is goodbye, then. If we don't see you, take care of yourself, Odette."

Odette just looked down at Donut. I could tell she was surprised. She slowly reached over and gave Donut a small virtual pat.

"That . . ." Odette paused as if Donut's show of affection choked her up. She recovered quickly. "That's our show, folks. Stick around and watch the Royal Court choose their destination! And come back tomorrow night for a special episode!"

Transferring in twenty seconds.

ZEV: Donut, Carl, don't freak out. Only Donut will transfer. Carl, you'll remain on the couch. This is a small twist they just announced. Only the squad leader will enter the choice chamber. Then you'll have your first fight. It'll be just you, Donut. Don't worry. It'll be an easy opponent with junk cards. As soon as it's done, Carl will transfer to you. Try to draw the fight out as long as possible.

Oh, shit.

Donut jumped to my lap.

DONUT: I DON'T WANT TO DO IT ALONE. NOT A REAL FIGHT.

"Carl," Donut said, looking up at me, "I don't want to be by myself."

"Remember the plan," I whispered, trying to sound confident. I stroked her side, and she was shaking. I didn't want her to do this alone, either. "You'll be okay. You've been practicing. You got this. It's only one fight."

"I'm scared."

Transferring now.

The room blinked, and the lights went up. Donut disappeared. Quasar was gone. It was just me, Odette, Zev, and Lexis.

The screen remained turned on, and it showed Donut appearing alone in the featureless room with the globe. There was no sound. She ran around in a circle a few times, completely panicked. Then she stopped and tried to calm herself. She pulled Mongo out and leaned up against him. She stopped and peered up at the ceiling. There was an announcement I couldn't hear.

"Okay, guys, we only have a minute," Zev said, moving deeper into the room. "I don't know where Harbinger went, but—"

Zev blinked and disappeared.

Odette sighed as she pulled off her bug helmet. She stepped back, peeling away her massive breastplate. She remained attached to the crab, which made her look terrifying.

"That was the best choice for adjutant," Odette said as she came around the desk. "Ripper is a media whore with a stick up his hairy ass, and Drick is psychotic, out to make a name for himself. You were right to ask about the Valtay. It is strange they let him in. The baroness is a humorless bitch, but she's the only one who'll put up with your bullshit. She's a big fan of allowing legal loopholes to get exploited. I wasn't sure at first about that lawyer of yours, but I'm moderately impressed he advocated for her."

"What the hell just happened?" I asked, still looking at the spot where Zev had stood. "What did you do to Zev?"

Odette waved dismissively. "They just called an all-hands at headquarters, so she got pulled away. An unmanned liaison spy ship was just shot out of orbit, so it's an automatic security response. Right now all crawlers except the squad leaders are in a temporary stasis while they do the changeover. This is completely off-the-record. We have maybe 15 minutes to talk."

My head swam. "You shot down a spaceship just to talk to me?"

Odette grunted. "That thing had to go one way or another. And it was more like a probe. They thought they were being sneaky, but we'd pegged that thing the moment it appeared. We just timed it to our advantage. Now listen."

Up on the screen, Donut stood before the giant globe just like before, but only a handful of locations were highlighted. Two were in the United States. One was clearly the Bahamas. And there was another in the Mediterranean.

I watched as Donut pretended to hem and haw with her choices. She was laying it on a little thick. We already knew what one of the choices would be, thanks to the hidden message given to Donut on our earlier appearance on Rosetta's show.

"No, you listen," I said. "You fucked us when you chose not to be an adjutant."

Odette grunted. "Oh, I'm sorry. I didn't allow you to set me up for an assassination?"

I didn't even pretend to appear surprised. "What are we going to do now?"

"Don't worry," Odette said. "She's going to want Katia with her down there more than ever."

"And if she doesn't?"

Odette shrugged. "Then you have to come up with an alternative. I suggest you make Katia eat that orchid sooner rather than later. Force Huanxin's hand. This is part of what I want to talk with you about. Don't trust anything that grixist bitch says. She's out for revenge. That's it. Nothing more. She is not going to help Katia out of any altruistic sense. She's the most evil person I know, and that's saying a lot. She's also smart, so we must be . . . delicate in how we deal with her."

Up on the screen, I watched as Donut reached up to pick Miami. A door leading off to another chamber appeared. Donut was putting on a brave face, but I could tell how frightened she was.

A wave of anger washed over me. People were always taking advantage of us. Telling us what to do. Bullying us for their own purposes.

Using us.

"*We?* In how *we* deal with her? You know what? Fuck you, Odette. We're not playing your game anymore. There is no *we*. I appreciate everything you've done to help us so far, but goddamnit. All we are trying to do is survive, and every time we turn a corner, there's someone new standing there waiting to use us. And yet, somehow, you're always involved. You say *she's* evil? What about you, Odette?"

Donut hesitantly moved to the next room, stepping through the door into the great room of a large older house. She seemed outraged at something, but I couldn't tell what. She started shouting and waving her paws up in the air like she did when she was mad.

And then her first opponent materialized, causing her to stop mid-tirade.

A deranged-looking man appeared in the room, facing her. The hunched man was about 70. He wore what seemed to be a white old-school sailor's outfit that was much too small for him. There was a name tag that read "Gene" on his breast, but the note floating over him said his name was **Robert the Human**. He was level 40, and he twitched slightly as he stared down Donut. He clutched a group of cards to his chest. That's all I could see.

They froze. This was the start of a boss battle. Or a level description telling Donut how to fight using the cards. I suspected this was going to take a while. The description was likely more for the benefit of the home audience than Donut, who already knew how this worked.

Sure enough, the screen changed, showing a bunch of cards on the screen while the orange announcer guy appeared. He started going over all the card types. Mordecai had warned us this would happen. Donut was going to sit there frozen for several minutes while they went through all this.

"You think my motivations are money," Odette said, who I realized was staring at me with laser focus. "Or fame. They're not. It's about Mordecai. It always has been."

I blinked.

"Mordecai? Bullshit."

She suddenly looked very old and tired.

"I'm going to tell you something, Carl. You're not going to believe me, but I'm telling you anyway, and you are going to listen to me because I have waited a very long time to say this out loud to somebody."

"Uh," I said, taken aback at her sudden change. "Okay . . ."

"I had a cousin. His name was Pieter. I also had a friend named Armita. We were friends since birth, and Pieter was a few years younger. He'd always tag along wherever we went, even though we didn't want him to. We'd been having a picnic that day it happened. Armita and I were both in our pre-courtship, so about the equivalent of 17 years old in your culture. Pieter was around 13. He'd followed us. I'd made sweet pastries, and he really liked them." She rubbed her aged hands together. Her nails were so long, they curled like claws.

"I'd thrown a rock at him, telling him to go home. I'd hit him in the head, and he'd cried. He didn't have any friends." Odette paused, taking a moment to compose herself. "And then it happened. The three of us, along with a few others, we entered the dungeon together."

Odette's crab body shifted. Lexis was suddenly sitting on the couch next to me, silent. She had her ever-present tablet clutched in her hands.

Odette's voice started to break as she talked. "Eventually, they forced me to choose. Pieter or Armita. I picked my friend. Simple as that. It was the right choice. Still, I think sometimes . . . I wonder . . . He was so sweet, and this place . . . it had broken him into so many pieces. And those pieces, Carl, they were wrong. My friends. My family. I had pushed them all. *One more floor,* I'd said. *Surely we can push through just a little longer.* They'd all died because of it. One by one. All except for me and Armita."

She had tears streaming down her face.

She continued. "When I made my exit deal, I thought I could help others, and I chose to be a game guide. Armita had left a little before me, and she picked Celestial Attendant, which is the best, they say. The safest. I could've done the same thing, but I didn't want to have anything to do with them. Those rich assholes running it all. I wanted to be of use to other crawlers. Back then, we could offer to be managers, and that's what I did to Mordecai. I offered to help him escape this place. I promised him I'd do my best. He reminded me so much of Pieter, the way he looked up to his brother. Once, he'd transformed into a human, and he even looked like him. Like my little cousin."

She took another moment. She now had my rapt attention. The screen continued to show its card lesson.

"I was near the end of my contract. All I could see was the light at the end of the tunnel. You know that spider you have in your card deck? Shi Maria? She exists in my own mythology. The Bedlam Bride. That extra eye of hers, the one she opens that blinds you and drives you mad? It's a metaphor. We had a saying, my people. 'Never stare into the blinding eye of the Bedlam Bride.' What it means is, don't become obsessed with something, lest you're blinded to everything else. When it shows itself, it's all you can see. And that's exactly what I'd done. Despite my promise to Mordecai, I was staring into the eye. I wanted nothing more than to finish my contract and finally, finally escape the dungeon. I had pushed Mordecai and his brother and friends, just like I had pushed my family. I pushed them further than they could go."

She wiped her eyes.

"I made an illegal deal with Huanxin to rig the game in exchange for credits. It was facilitated by Armita. Huanxin would help me, and I'd give her money, part of my bonus for getting Mordecai to the 11th floor. But it went bad. She was driving a goddess named Dodola, and she'd asked for more money, and I was so tired of it. I felt just like you feel right now, Carl. I broke the deal at the last minute. I tricked her.

We trapped the goddess in a containment, and Chaco killed her, causing her to lose the Ascendency game before it even started. Mordecai made it to the next floor, but Uzzi, Mordecai's brother, died."

"Odette," Lexis said, speaking for the first time. Her voice was soft. "We only have a few minutes."

Odette ignored her. "Huanxin was enraged. I was soon to be released, out of reach. But Armita was stuck here for a few more seasons. A few weeks later, when Mordecai finally made his deal at the end of the 11th, I was released. But I wasn't really free. I had my money. This was before they changed the rules. Now you guys are all citizens once released, but for me . . . I had to buy my way into the center system primary zone. But I felt so goddamned guilty about what had happened . . . I admitted what I'd done. There's this form you can fill out, admitting to crimes. And I did it. I was sure Armita would've turned me in, but she hadn't. She was stuck in the dungeon, in mortal danger while I was finally free, and still, in the end, she remained my friend while I betrayed her." She paused. "I never got my legs fixed. It felt wrong."

She shook her head sadly. "By the time anyone even looked at my confession, it was too late. The very first thing Huanxin did when she returned to the dungeon the following season was kill Armita. It was like it was nothing. After all, it was the dungeon. Perfectly legal. But then some bureaucrat finally read my statement, and I was arrested. Huanxin was given nothing more than a token punishment. She was barred from participating for a while and permanently banned from Dodola. I was put on trial. I got lucky, however, and my warrant was purchased by the man who'd eventually become my husband."

"Okay," I finally said after a moment of silence. The screen was now just the announcer guy talking. "That's . . . that's really rough, Odette. But I still don't see—"

"I watch him every day," Odette said, interrupting. "It's been so long. You need to understand: A few seasons into Mordecai's indentureship, they changed the way the NPC pools worked, separating them out by organization, which greatly extended everyone's contracts. Yet I found myself watching him every chance I could, drinking himself into oblivion. Crying over his brother. His family. His friends. I'd think to myself, *I did that. I killed Pieter. I killed Armita. And this one. This one I broke. I broke him into so many pieces that there's no hope for him.* That's what I used to think, Carl. I used to hope he'd find a way to get himself killed before he was free because I just knew that would be the final cruelty, releasing him without purpose into the empty, cold universe. He has *nobody*."

She looked up at me. "The eye of the Bedlam Bride. I've stared into it once again. I see nothing else. My purpose in this universe is singular. Everything I do, it's to assuage myself of this guilt I feel for what I have done."

I swallowed. I kept wavering between thinking she was absolutely full of shit and believing every word. I didn't know what to say, so I just blurted out the first thing to come to me.

"Mordecai told me to just do whatever Huanxin says."

"That's because he's afraid of her, Carl. And he should be. She's older, smarter, and richer than she was way back then. This is the first year she's back. I'm sure she has a plan to help you get those protections turned off. She wanted me in the dungeon as an adjutant so she could legally exact her revenge. But instead, Carl, we're going to do something a little more extreme. It's going to kill me most likely. But that's okay. It'll kill her, too."

Next to me, Lexis took in a sharp breath.

"How is any of this helping Mordecai?" I asked.

She shook her head. "You don't get it, Carl. If this doesn't work out, I've already done everything in my power to make his transition into freedom as smooth as possible. I've set aside a large trust for him. Chaco, too. Along with a few others I've managed along the way who are still in the system. But this goes beyond Mordecai. Everyone this cruelty touches, it shatters. We need to stop it."

"You're a part of it," I snapped, anger bubbling over. "Goddamn it. You are the highest-paid cheerleader for all of this. We die, and you applaud. We suffer, and you're there with a microphone pointed in my face. And now you're sponsoring a god? How can I trust you?"

Lexis tapped her tablet. "Almost out of time."

The screen returned to Donut. The Robert the Human guy summoned two cards. One was a tall, faceless doll also wearing a sailor suit. The other was a little stuffed dog with rolling bug eyes. The doll was named **Robert the Doll**. The dog was named simply **Dog**.

"You don't understand," Odette said. "We have no choice. If it wasn't me, it would be someone worse. I had to position myself in order to make it right. This whole machine exists for a reason beyond what you see. The mantises mine and resurrect the AIs and then graft them into the planetary engines for a reason. The elements they mine, what do you think they're for?"

I was distracted by Donut's fight. She summoned Geraldo, who appeared with a ridiculous, over-the-top explosion. The monk seal started flipping through the room at the doll. "I . . . What? What does that have to do with Huanxin? How did we get from her to this?"

Odette had a wild look in her eye. "All planets used for a crawl or any other game, such as Battle Royale or Land War, are used to collect fuel. The elements. The by-product of the biological overgrowth of the seeded systems. The entertainment aspect of it all came along later, but it's necessary in its own way. It's expensive, what they do. But without it, it all gets shut off. All of it. We need to shut the crawl down, but we have to do it in a responsible way. Lest we kill half the known universe. If we do this right, future collections will be humane. It will be done in a way that removes all the suffering. What I did to Mordecai. To Armita. To Pieter. What is happening to you. It will never happen again. And it's all coming together this season. This is our chance. Finally, after all these centuries. It's our chance."

"What the hell are you talking about?"

On the screen, just as Geraldo started to attack the doll, Mongo flew through the air and chomped on to the throat of Robert the Human, killing him instantly. The fight abruptly ended. All the totems poofed away. Donut jumped across the room, and the first thing she did was collect the dead human's sailor hat. Several cards appeared floating in the air, and she started to examine them. She could take and keep all of the non-totems, but if she wanted to keep the totems, she'd have to ditch one of our existing ones. That was unlikely given what I'd just seen.

"Sorry," Lexis said. "Time's up. Transferring now."

Odette smiled sadly at me.

"See you on the inside, Carl."

PART TWO

THE FATHER

38

ENTERING MONROE COUNTY, FLORIDA.

IT IS DECEMBER 24TH.

TIME TO LEVEL COLLAPSE: 6 DAYS, 22 HOURS.

The Key location has been marked on your map. You have 46 hours remaining to collect your key.

"MONROE COUNTY?" I MUTTERED AS I APPEARED IN THE DARK OLD house. The room was lit by Donut's *Torch* spell, and it gave everything a ghastly hue, like sallow skin. The dead corpse of Robert the Human remained there across the room as Mongo gleefully pulled him apart. Blood splattered as the dinosaur dove into the corpse like a pig at a trough, making loud crunching noises. There was a door leading off to a safe area, another leading outside. A third door led to a restroom.

"Carl, it's broken!" Donut cried. "The game broke, and we won't be able to get a key!"

She now wore the sailor hat on her head, and it looked ridiculous on her. She jumped up and down, her tail straight up. She ran up to me and started weaving in and out of my legs like she used to do when I came home from work.

"Okay. Calm down. Tell me what you mean."

She took a breath. "It only gave us a few choices of places to go, but they all had labels on them. One of them was Iowa! Another was the Bahamas and another was Ibiza. It said one of them is Miami, and I picked that one, but then I got a message that said there was a problem with the location, and it was sending us to Iowa instead! But I got here, we were in the house, and we're in the Miami area, but we're at the bottom of the map. We're really in the Florida Keys! The area is big, bigger than we have in Cuba. But it was quite strange because the location thingy said Iowa when I first appeared."

"Really? It said we were actually in Iowa? That is really weird. It said 'Florida' for me."

When we'd gone on *Shadow Boxer*, Rosetta gave us two different secret messages. One was about the yam. But the other was when they'd shown Donut the different television shows on the screen. Every single one was a program set in Miami. I had no idea why they would want us here specifically, but they'd gone to a lot of trouble to give us the message. It was something only a person who was obsessed with television would notice. *I* hadn't noticed it.

I'd never been to Florida, let alone the Keys. Nor had I ever been to Iowa. I moved to the window and looked outside. It was the middle of the night, but I could see the distinctive form of a palm tree. Plus it was warm. There was no way this was the American Midwest in December. If this was somewhere in the Keys, we weren't actually that far from our original location in Cuba.

Why would they say it was Iowa, then?

"Carl, look at the map. They said the key location is marked! But the key is still in Iowa!"

"Oh, fuck me."

I pulled up the map. Sure enough, we were at the very southern tip of Florida. The distinctive island shapes were clear, and we were plopped right in the middle. I zoomed out as much as I could, and I didn't see the marker at all.

I started to form a message to Zev to bitch, but I paused at the notification.

Please wait.

There was a pause and a flash, and the ground rumbled with a small earthquake. The map rearranged itself. The key was suddenly there, only a handful of miles west from our current location.

Thank you for your patience. You may resume normal activity.

I relaxed.

"It looks like it was a glitch, but it fixed itself."

"I don't like glitches, Carl. They make me nervous. Oh, oh, but do you see that dead guy?"

Mongo was grunting happily as he pulled out a line of intestine.

"He's a little hard to miss, Donut."

"The fight was really short! Mongo killed him before it even started. He only had two totems, and they were both stuffed animals. A person and a disgusting toy dog. It was quite an easy fight."

"Good job."

Donut continued to bounce up and down as I examined the house. It was just an old Victorian-style mini mansion from the 19th century with creaking wood floors. There was a light switch, and I flipped it. It worked, and the room lit up. There was a Christmas tree in the corner, but it didn't appear as if anyone was living here. The tree itself was generic, with only blue and silver ornaments and no lights. I could smell and hear the ocean.

Donut was talking rapid-fire, like she did when she had too much energy. "The fight was scary! His deck wasn't very good. Mongo chomped him before he could play hardly anything. It was quite spectacular."

We only had two days to get the key. That seemed easy. Too easy, which meant it would be an epic pain. No time to rest. We had to get moving even though it was the middle of the night.

I had a few blinking notifications, and I pulled them up now. The first was from Emberus.

Quest Update. Find Out Who Killed My Son.

It appears the primordial goddess Nekhebit has returned to the Halls. She holds an ancient grudge against my family, especially Apito. Find a temple of Nekhebit and question the priestess, see what she knows. Do not be gentle.

I waved that one away. It was a headache for tomorrow, if we made it that far. My heart stopped in my throat as I pulled up the next message. This was what I was looking for. It was a note from Huanxin using the spider quest chat.

EILEITHYIA: I watched your performance. I am not one to be forgiving of failure, but I acknowledge this was out of your control. Odette did not ask to be your adjutant like I told you

she would. This is my fault. I shall honor our agreement, but if it becomes clear that you'd warned Odette about our understanding, I shall crush everyone you know and love, starting with sweet Katia and ending with that cat.

I let out a long stream of breath. Relief flooded me.

Quest Complete. Spiders.

Proceed to a temple of Eileithyia to receive your boon.

"Carl, we finished the spider quest!"

"I see that, Donut."

"Well, that was the easiest quest ever. We barely did anything."

But then Donut started to grumble when she saw we had to go to a temple to collect our reward. With her unable to access Club Vanquisher, that would be difficult. I doubted we would be getting anything anyway, as the whole quest had been so Huanxin could send me messages through Eileithyia. Since she didn't need us anymore, we'd been cut loose. That was okay.

But now I was more worried than ever about sending Katia off to the 12th floor.

CARL: Katia, we should be good. But we gotta talk.

KATIA: Can't right now. Things got messed up during the selection. They only gave me one choice. Ukraine, but when I got here, it was actually Vietnam.

CARL: That seems to be going around. Ping me when you're safe.

I moved to the door to the outside to take a better peek at where we were.

ZEV: Donut, Carl, I apologize for that glitch. I know in the coming hours it's going to look intentional. Believe me, it was not. At least not on our end. Things are just hectic. You should have only received three choices for a new location. One chosen by us, one by the AI, and one randomly selected spot. You

received four, and we don't know why. It wasn't just you guys. Some crawlers had four choices. Some only had one. A few didn't have any at all, and one squad leader had the whole globe to choose and dropped herself into the middle of the ocean for some reason. We're still scrambling to fix it all. Talk soon.

DONUT: I'M JUST GLAD IT DIDN'T KEEP US IN IOWA. DO I LOOK LIKE SOMEONE WHO WOULD VOLUNTARILY VISIT IOWA? THAT'S ALMOST AS BAD AS DELAWARE.

ZEV: Uh, yeah. Maybe you should look outside when dawn comes. We've had to fudge a few things to keep from breaking the game.

"There's nothing wrong with Iowa, Donut," I said as I pulled open the door. "You've never even been there."

"I have most certainly been to Iowa. It's cold, covered with weird billboards, and it smells like potatoes. Plus, Carl, it was where I was robbed of a purple ribbon. One doesn't just forget such a vile insult. It's because the judges were racist against their betters."

"I'm pretty sure that was Idaho, not Iowa."

"That's practically the same thing, Carl."

I took a step outside into the humid night air. The temperature was similar to where we'd just left. We were on a sidewalk in some narrow beach town. A two-lane road spread before us, lit by sporadic streetlamps. There were no cars. Still, despite the late hour, the road was moderately busy. I caught sight of memory ghosts floating back and forth along the road. The fact the cars were already gone suggested this area had crawlers in it for part one of the floor. Beyond the road was beach, though I sensed it more than saw it in the dark. I knew the other side of the narrow island was pretty close behind us.

Other than the memory ghosts, I didn't see anyone. No dots of crawlers, NPCs, or mobs anywhere on the map. All I could see was the shining marker indicating the location of the exit key a little bit to the west.

I looked in that direction and saw nothing but black.

"Donut, what level is your *Torch* spell?"

"It's stuck at 14. It has been for a while now."

"Send it up there and make it as bright as you can, will you?"

She waved her paw, and the light shot into the air and zipped away from us like a fast-moving drone. It got impressively high and then light burst forth, illuminating the entire area like a stadium.

"Holy shit," I said, covering my eyes.

"I know, right?" Donut said. "It takes a lot of mana to keep it like this, though, so I can only keep it going for a minute."

I looked west and did a double take. At first I thought it was some weird artifact of Donut's spell, or the edge of the map. A sheer wall of crumbling earth stood in the distance, like a cosmic dump truck had just upended its load over the island. It was a pile of earth climbing into the clouds. I couldn't see the top. It reminded me of the Necropolis of Anser from the bubble level, only more chaotic. I was pretty sure the pile was wider than the island. Dirt cascaded off the side as I watched.

I blinked a few times, trying to figure out what I was looking at. I consulted my map. The exit key was somewhere at the top of the pile. At least I hoped it was on the top and not buried there.

CARL: Zev, did you guys just rip the key location out of the ground in Iowa and plop it here in Florida?

ZEV: Not my department, Carl. But yes. It was the only way to do it without breaking anything further.

I just shook my head.

CARL: You might want to explain to your folks about the differences in sea level. Is that thing stable? This is a cay. It's an island built atop a reef, and half, if not most, of that pile is in the ocean. It's going to be washed away in a day.

ZEV: Yes, Carl. We're very busy right now. We're aware of the situation. We'll intervene if the key location becomes inaccessible.

I took another step toward the road. Donut jumped to my shoulder as Mongo padded out behind us. His face was completely covered in gore.

"Nice Dixie cup, by the way," I said, looking up at the white sailor hat sitting cockeyed on Donut's head. "You look like you're in the Navy."

"Oh, isn't it divine?"

She looked absurd, but I wasn't going to tell her that. "I like it, but if you wear it, you can't use your new Hover skill. Plus you lose 10 intelligence points."

"I already talked to Mordecai about this, and I'm going to wear it until I run out of cards, and then I'll put my new dragonfly tiara back on. This one lowers the card-draw countdown by two seconds! Plus it's quite jaunty. I do love jaunty."

"Really? Huh. I didn't know they'd have magic gear specifically for the cards."

Donut reached up and made the cap sit even more sideways on her head. It looked like it would fall off at any moment. "So it's called a Dixie cup? I love it. It's not too Donald Duck, is it? Did you wear one like this?"

I grunted. "No. I wore a ball cap. We used to mock the poor bastards who had to wear those things."

"A baseball cap? You were in the military, and you wore a baseball cap? I feel as if that's a lie, Carl."

"Did that Robert guy have anything else on him?"

"Just the rest of his uniform, but it was ruined. And the token."

"The token?" I asked.

"Yes, Carl. Didn't you hear the announcement?"

"No, Donut. I wasn't here. Remember?"

"Oh," she said. "Well, it's quite simple. You have to collect nine tokens before you can fight the last guy for the key. There are fewer monsters, but they'll all have tokens and card decks on them. Wait, I see a red dot." She pointed with her paw. "It's that way, toward the mound."

"Okay," I said, cracking my neck. "Let's see how this really works."

"We're fighting in the dark? It doesn't let me keep the spell going when I activate my deck!"

I shrugged. "There are streetlamps, and I have a ton of torches. Time is not our friend here."

"Okay," she said skeptically. "Do we want to go get some of the boys to help us?"

"The boys?"

"You know. The Penis Paraders. Stevie is a troll, for goodness' sake. He's great at bashing stuff, and he can balance his club on the tip of his finger for ten seconds straight. Oh, and Gluteus can break things with his butt! You get a mob's head in there, and it's game over."

"I'm thinking we'll keep them back until there's an emergency. We want them fresh for the next floor."

"Okay," Donut said. "They're all probably experience hogs anyway."

As we started to move in that direction, keeping a wary eye out for others and traps, Imani sent a message demanding everyone check in. Only a few of us had experienced glitches. Florin was in eastern Nigeria. He wasn't partied with Lucia Mar, so he'd lost contact with her. Li Jun and his crew, which included Chris, were still in China, but farther into the mainland.

Elle and Imani were separated. Elle's squad ended up in Belgium. Imani was only given one choice, Detroit, and that's where she was. Everyone else was equally scattered.

After some prodding, we learned Prepotente was somewhere in northern Italy.

Like with my area, Katia's region was a mix between Ukraine and Vietnam, though she warned us of something that made me wary. The Vietnam portion of the area where they'd ended up was in a city called Da Nang. It was where Tran was from.

The key location was in an apartment building where both his ex-wife and his estranged mother lived.

Detroit, Imani reluctantly offered, was where she grew up, and she would never have picked it if she'd been offered another choice. Her key location was also in the home of somebody she knew, but she didn't elaborate.

ELLE: I don't know anybody in Belgium, thank god. You all try to keep your wits about you. These are just memory ghosts. And if they're going to make us fight loved ones, remember it's not really them. Don't let them fuck with your heads.

"Carl," Donut asked as we walked. "Do you know anybody who lives in Florida or Iowa? I most certainly don't."

"No," I said, and I hoped against everything that it was true.

OUR FIRST OPPONENT—DONUT'S SECOND—WAS A TYPE OF MOB WE'D fought before. The creature was just sitting there off the side of the road in a pool of light of a parking lot, waiting for us to approach. This setup wasn't anything like we'd seen so far in the dungeon. This was more like something out of a real video game. It stood there, doing nothing while it waited for us to come closer. A circle of clothes from the memory ghosts lay piled all around it, implying the thing had been standing there for a while.

The parking lot featured both a safe room and a Desperado Club, but the map indicated the club was "Closed for emergency renovations."

The last time I'd seen one of these guys, it'd been on the fourth floor, and they'd been suffering from a condition called the d.t.'s. It was a baboon-human hybrid creature called a babababoon. I couldn't remember what level they'd been on the third floor—probably around 17 or so—but this guy was level 45.

The wide-faced man wore a Santa hat and had a T-shirt that featured a wrapped present on it with the caption "I have a huge package for you." He started grunting and jumping up and down as we approached, like he'd been paralyzed until the moment we appeared.

Combat Started.

I pulled a sticky hob-lobber into my xistera and tossed it across the way. It splotched against his chest and exploded, killing him before he even drew his first card.

Combat Complete. Deck has been reset.

"Carl, you blew up his hat!" Donut complained as we moved to investigate the corpse. The guy had been turned into paste. Mongo grunted and started licking it up.

A group of twenty cards appeared floating in the air. None were exciting, but he did have a consumable Flee card. He'd had three totems. Two more babababoons like himself and a rare level 80 Skunk Ape. We could only examine the information on the face of the card, which was only part of the whole. While I was curious about that one, we'd have to literally give up one of our totems to try it out, which we weren't willing to do.

He also had a token, which was just a poker-chip-sized coin with the number two etched on it.

"Does the first token have a one on it?" I asked.

"It does," Donut said.

"And what level was that first guy?"

"Level 40. Also, I see another red dot down the street. And another way past there. There's a path of them leading to the dirt mound, all off to the side of the road."

"All right," I said, looking west. I couldn't actually see anything. Now that we were past the houses, it was just palm trees and bushes and the occasional business on either side of the road, with the sound of the ocean waves in the distance. "Come on. Let's try this again."

39

IT WASN'T UNTIL WE WERE FIGHTING FOR TOKEN NUMBER SIX THAT WE actually had to use Donut's deck. And even then, the fight ended quickly.

So far, they'd all been regular, intelligent monsters holding cards. All had been waiting for us under streetlights. They'd gone up by five levels each time. The third—a level 50 turtle thing—was by himself, but the fourth and fifth opponents both had two bodyguards working with them, designed to keep me and Mongo from one-shotting the deckmaster. It didn't work. We finished all these fights before anybody could play a single card. None had great loot.

All of them were just waiting for us there along the path to the dirt mound. After some time observing this newest guy, I was certain my earlier theory was correct. They were literally frozen in place until we approached.

We were also receiving good experience for this, getting a decent chunk each time we defeated one. I was now level 68 and Donut was level 59. Mongo finally hit level 40.

Donut was bitching that this setup was "boring" and uninteresting to the fans, but I was happy to get it over with. I had an ominous feeling about what we'd find there up on top of that mound of dirt.

This opponent number six stood just to the side of the road at the base of the pile, which was situated at the end of the island, standing near a lit sign giving the distance to Key West. The heap completely blocked the road and covered a bridge that presumably led to the next island over. Even at the base, I couldn't see the top.

The creature in our way was a level 65 **Reef Explorer**, and he was wearing an ethereal, glowing deep-dive suit, similar to what Zev wore when she was in the dungeon. He had a group of four bodyguards. All four were level 50 **Swordfish Interlopers**. These guys were bipedal, human-sized creatures with the heads of swordfish, only the heads stuck straight up in the air, and they could barely move their necks. The vertical swords glinted menacingly. They didn't have arms, but little flippers on each side. Their legs were short, penguin-like. The creatures waddled menacingly toward us as the squad leader guy shouted something, something we couldn't hear through his helmet.

This guy was a ghost-class mob, so I pulled out one of my holy-water-infused hob-lobbers and tossed it at him, throwing it over the heads of the swordfish. But the moment I tossed it, one of the swordfish dudes, with surprising speed and precision, spat out a stream of water, knocking the small bomb off target, causing it to blow prematurely. He then made a chirping, staccato, dolphin-like noise and launched himself straight into the sky. He hit the apex, paused in the night air, pivoted, and propelled himself at me like a goddamned missile.

"Oh fuck!" I cried, dancing out of the way. The guy smashed into the ground with a wet *splatch*, burying himself upside down in the dirt at the edge of the road. The long sword head completely embedded itself into the ground, all the way to his eyes. If he'd hit me, I'd have been turned into a kebab. Now stuck, he started to helplessly bicycle his short legs. I cast Talon Strike on my foot and started to kick at him.

At the same moment, a digital wave of water rushed across the space between us as two more of the swordfish guys appeared, jumping out of the fake waves. They did a flip and landed right in front of the deckmaster. These were two cards played by the Reef Explorer guy.

The AI screamed with excitement:

Splish-Splash, you gonna get slashed, it's Swordfish Interlopers!

The two newcomers looked identical to the bodyguards already here, only these had totem notifications over their heads with little timers counting down from 90.

In front of me, the upside-down guy died, just as another of the bodyguards launched himself into the air at me. The deckmaster guy added a buff to one of the totems, something called **Precision**. He then added a second Precision card on the same totem.

Mongo leaped through the air and chomped the flying swordfish like he was a dog catching a Frisbee, his tail whipping. He hit the ground and his Earthquake ability activated, causing the remaining swordfish guys to fall off their feet and start flopping like, well, fish. The dive-suit guy did not stumble. Mongo savagely tore at his prey.

We all paused as church organ music bellowed out, thick and loud. Fat, naked digital babies with little wings fluttered around us, fountaining into the air as Donut summoned one of our team's newest totems.

I hadn't seen this guy yet, and I wasn't sure what to expect. It was the card that Donut made when she'd used the Combo card.

She'd combined Uzi Jesus and Asojano.

Sparkles rained from the wings of the cherubs as the totem rose from the ground, spinning and shrouded in smoke. The angel babies flew off, and a herd of digital street dogs burst away from the spinning figure, barking and running in all directions as the music swelled. Only then did the smoke clear, revealing the figure.

It was easily the craziest, most over-the-top reveal sequence of all our cards. Donut loved it, despite the appearance of the street dogs.

The figure was a dirty, sandaled, robed figure, hunched over and sickly. A glowing nimbus surrounded his head, lighting the area further. The light had an uneasy green tint to it. His drooping hood obscured his face. He used his large weapon as a walking stick. The man took a tentative step forward.

He was level 140, just like Uzi Jesus had been, which was lucky. Asojano had been 130.

Jesus had an Uzi. Asojano had a strange, large-sized wand made from shells.

This guy had a goddamned bazooka. A magical bazooka that fired something different every time.

"Here comes my favorite part," Donut said.

The AI shouted the introduction like he was announcing a boxing match.

It's the Son Who Fell. The Sinner, Resurrected. The Bringer of Disease, Bringer of Salvation. The Ender of All Blasphemy. It's the calamitous, rapturous, and ultimately hazardous master of the life-death boomerang.

It's Lazarus-A-Bang-Bang!

Yet another digital explosion appeared as the hunched man crept painfully forward. Our opponent and all the remaining bodyguards and totems were in the midst of pulling themselves upright. They paused to gawk at the newcomer and the ridiculous display.

"Is it really going to do all that every time?" I asked. Mongo looked up from the now-dead swordfish to growl.

"Isn't it great?" Donut asked. "I wish I had an entrance theme like that!"

The hood fell back to reveal a boil-covered, dark-skinned man wearing a crown of thorns, but the thorns obscured his eyes like a blindfold. He stood to his full height, and I realized the decrepit-old-man persona had been an act. He was definitely older, but he was ripped. His arms heaved with power.

Holy crap, I thought. *That dude is intense.*

He pulled the bazooka to his shoulder.

"Welcome to your salvation, motherfuckers."

The man had a deep, strong voice. His accent was similar to Asojano's but somehow reminiscent of Uzi Jesus's at the same time. It was like they'd taken every 80s action hero and smooshed them into a single character.

He pushed the firing mechanism just as the remaining totems and bodyguards burst into the air. It was two swordfish totems and two regular mobs.

Thwum!

A cloud of . . . *something* burst from the weapon, split, and corkscrewed in the air, hitting all four of the swordfish at the same time. All four—including the one that had been buffed with utility cards—dropped like a sack of pennies. They all writhed on the ground.

Beetles. They were covered with iridescent, scratching beetles that glinted in the light like they were made of metal. There were thousands of them. The fish were devoured in seconds. Mongo screeched in terror and backed away. The two totems puffed away in smoke as the other two chittered in pain as they were turned to skeletons. The moment they were dead, the beetles turned to dust.

"He's great, isn't he?" Donut shouted. "He has a few different weapons, too, and you don't know what he's going to have! Sometimes it's a bazooka that shoots bugs. Sometimes it's an RPG thing that just blows stuff up!"

Donut summoned Raul the crab, who blasted onto the scene with a pale-by-comparison explosion. He scuttled sideways toward the backing-away Reef Explorer.

"He's a ghost," Donut called. "You have to use magic to kill him. Hurry before he summons another totem!"

Raul turned and bowed. He paused briefly, sat on the ground, and chanted a short spell. His right claw started to glow. He stood and continued toward the creature, who'd backed up against a tree as he desperately tossed away another card.

"Want me to blast him?" Lazarus asked Donut. There was a blinking countdown hovering over his bazooka. A stream of smoke rose from the business end of the large, cartoonish weapon. It was a cooldown timer, and it was at ten seconds.

Lazarus suddenly jumped in surprise upon seeing me standing there. He jerked the bazooka back up to his shoulder and pointed it at me. "Who are you?" he demanded.

"Lazarus-A-Bang-Bang, you put that down this instant! That's our friend Carl!"

"Yeah, okay," he said reluctantly. He lowered the giant weapon. But then he did that dude-bro thing where he jerked his shoulders forward like he was going to rush me. He looked me up and down, despite his eyes being covered by the thorns. "Yeah, I thought so. Made ya flinch."

Mongo let out another angry squawk.

The robed man turned back to Raul, who continued to scuttle after the glowing ghost, who was now screeching and running away, weaving in and out of the dark trees. "Let me end this. That pansy is taking too long."

Donut shook her head as she discarded one of her cards. She tossed a

Greased Lightning card at Raul, and it spun off like a ninja star. It zipped across the distance and dodged a tree before hitting the crab in a sparkle of digital confetti. "You just stay here and protect me, Lazarus. Let Raul get some experience. It'll build his self-confidence."

"But I want to kill the bad guy. I'm gonna tell my father if you don't let me do it."

"Does he still think he's Jesus?" I asked.

Lazarus made a scoffing noise.

"I'm not quite certain what he thinks," Donut said. "It's like he has the memories of both totems."

Across the way, Raul snapped at the ghost. The Reef Explorer guy had a handful of cards, but he apparently couldn't play any of them. The guy tried to run behind a tree, but the speed-enhanced Raul snapped again, cutting his leg off. Ghostly water flowed from the severed limb, the suit deflated, and the creature dropped dead.

Combat Complete. The deck has been reset.

"I could've done it a lot faster," Lazarus grumbled as he and Raul poofed away.

I just looked at the space where the guy had stood. That card was ridiculously powerful. Stronger even than Shi Maria possibly. It gave me an uneasy feeling.

"Uh, has that guy fought alongside Shi Maria yet?"

"Yes!" Donut said. "They're pretty competitive. They fight over who can kill the other guy first. They don't seem to like each other much, and I think MaeMae is jealous of his reveal sequence. They both get along with Jola. His reveal is pretty good, too. The good news is Raul and Geraldo are finally tolerating each other. Lazarus is mean to Raul but he and Geraldo get along great. And everybody just kinda ignores Skylar Spinach."

Across the way, a group of like 40 or 50 glowing cards appeared floating in the air. We trudged toward them. Donut recast her *Torch* spell.

I held out my hand. "Let me see his card."

Donut waved over my palm, and the orange card appeared. I examined it as we walked.

T'Ghee Card. Unique.

Totem Card.

Lazarus-A-Bang-Bang.

"I'm back, bitches!"

Level: 140.

Origin: This card was created via Combo.

Note: This card was frozen in place via a Glow-Up with active buffs. Available utility slots have been lowered.

Summoning Duration: 200 seconds.

Constitution: 80.

This is a ranged mob.

This is a healer mob.

This is an affliction-dealing mob.

Notable attacks:

Oh Yeah? Well, I Have a Face-Melting Bazooka.

Apocalyptic Plague.

Resurrect Totem.

+25 additional skills and spells.

Examine in the squad details tab of your interface for full stats and skills and spells.

I handed the card back to Donut. "His duration is great. His constitution is decent, but it's a lot lower than both Asojano's and Uzi Jesus's. Wasn't Jesus's constitution at 200?"

"Yeah, he appeared with it really low. It started at 20, and I only got it up to 80 after I'd buffed him and made it permanent! It made him the same level as Jesus, and he has most of the same skills as both of them. Both Jesus and Asojano were undead, but he's not. Also, if you look, he only has two utility card slots. Both Jesus and Asojano had seven. His bazooka is great. Last time in the arena, it shot feathers! I thought that was going to be stupid, but they cut the guy into pieces, and it was really pretty. Even MaeMae said it was quite a stylish way to kill. He's kind of a jerk, though. He calls everybody a pansy. Still, he's not nearly as bad as either Asojano or Jesus. At least he does what I ask. Usually. You know, he reminds me a lot of Brad, but with worse skin."

I grunted. Brad was Bea's ex-boyfriend and the guy she'd gone to the Bahamas with. I never did ask what happened to him. If Bea had been outside during the collapse, that meant he'd likely been outside, too.

We reached the large display of cards floating in the air. Donut looked over it and sniffed with derision.

The Reef Explorer only summoned two totems, but he'd had four total. Another swordfish and a rare squid-looking thing. After a cursory glance, Donut discarded them.

"It's no wonder he couldn't pull any more cards," she said. "Look at all these utility cards. It ruined his deck! He's lucky he pulled two at the start. He doesn't even have any traps! I see the attack he was going for, but I mean, really. He had to get the perfect draw to pull it off." She scoffed. "Amateur hour."

Sure enough, there were thirty of the **Precision** utility cards. I snatched one out of the air, and it let me. The card basically increased the totem's capacity to land an attack. The cards had a special ability that made it so they stacked, so if one used ten on a single totem, it still only counted as a single buff. I felt a chill. He'd buffed one of those swordfish guys like four times. If that one had managed to attack, I wouldn't have been able to dodge. That fight had been more dangerous than we'd realized.

I had a persistent itch at my neck, and I scratched at it. I suspected it was because of the soul bar for my back patch. The bar was almost full, but not quite. So far I hadn't felt any obvious ill effects of having the Scavenger's Daughter patch, but every time it started to get near full, I felt uneasy. I just needed to kill one or two more things before I could disperse the power. Still . . . I worried I might need the power for the last fight. If I unloaded it now, the bar wouldn't refill by the time we needed it for the boss guarding the key. Not if the only mobs here were the deckmaster guys.

Donut collected the sixth coin after grabbing all the other cards. She was talking non-stop now about card theory and about what other crawlers were doing with their decks. She was really into it, and by this point, I was starting to realize she knew more about this game than I did.

"The next guy is all the way up there," she was saying. "Do you want to go back to base first? We don't know if there'll be any safe rooms up there, and if I'm going to be climbing all the way up there, I don't want to have to do it multiple times. Or in the dark." She gasped. "Do you think I can use my Hover skill to do it? That would be great!"

I examined the pile of earth. Part of it was already eroding into the ocean. We had multiple options on how to get to the top of the pile, which was about 700 feet up. Luckily, the edge of the mound wasn't sheer, and I could just scale my way up it if I had to. I still had a few Levitation potions. Plus we could *Puddle Jump* up there. I'd probably try climbing first to see how long it would take, but I wasn't about to do that in the dark. My neck itched again.

"Let's go back to the safe room, check in with everybody, and reset our buffs. Then we'll come right back out. We need to get this done before the whole place washes away."

40

WE HAD TO HIKE A GOOD WAYS TO THE SAFE ROOM, WHICH WAS WITHIN a small side-of-the-road shrimp shack. As we traveled, Donut continued to chat rapid-fire about card theory, but somewhere along the way, she trailed off, and we finished the walk in mostly silence.

I continued to talk with the others. All were pushing their way through the first nine opponents. People were trying all sorts of ways to cheat, attempting to kill the enemy squad leaders before the fights actually started. Nothing worked so far.

Because the enemy deckmaster only activated and became corporeal when the squad leader approached, people were getting creative, like ringing the frozen NPC with traps or sitting right there with weapons poised. None of that worked. The moment the fight started, any traps or placed structures in a ring around the enemy literally disappeared, teleporting off to god knew where. Crawlers who were within the ring were knocked unconscious, which had disastrous results for some.

Tserendolgor had a long-range sniper guy in her group, someone who used an old-school sling and some sort of targeting spell, and she'd had him posted up on a hill, overlooking the opponent from a distance. He said the moment the fight started, the targeting spell failed, and the opponent moved a meter to the left, which screwed up his aim. But he managed to kill the guy anyway a minute later.

It was like they were desperately trying to fix how unbalanced the card game was, but they still hadn't gotten it right. Most of these fights were still ending before the totems could be useful.

The Bopca eyed us warily as we pushed our way into the safe room, not bothering to stop to talk. When we got into the guild, I found the main room filled with sleeping strippers and changeling children, all piled around the base, many of them snoring loudly. They were supposed to be sleeping in their barracks, but they didn't have video games and television in the barracks. The room was an absolute mess. It appeared they'd had a water balloon fight. I had no idea where they'd gotten the balloons, but the broken latex pieces were everywhere, and the whole place was wet. The main screen was showing the movie *Encino Man*, but the sound was off.

I looked about and spied the cleaner bot in its spot in the top-right corner of the room, and it gave me a quiet, sullen beep, almost like the whine of a dog locked in his cage. Mordecai must have told the thing to wait until morning to clean, so not to wake everyone up.

Samantha was in the room, and she was the only other one awake. She'd been cleaned since the Desperado Club incident, and she rolled toward us and hopped up on the kitchen table. She opened her mouth to say something, but I put my fingers to my lips, indicating for her to be quiet. I patted her on the head, and she growled and snapped at me.

I didn't see Mordecai, and I assumed he was asleep. Or more likely, working in the crafting room.

Mongo moved to the pile of sleeping, half-naked men and curled up in the middle of them. He was still covered in gore.

I had several notifications and achievements to wade through, but we decided to do it in Donut's room, and we moved there.

"Carl," Donut said as I closed the door. I was exhausted, but I could tell she wanted to talk. She'd been full of energy for a bit, but it was like it had drained away all at once.

"Yeah?"

She took a nervous glance at her social media interface and seemed to deflate. "You know what? Never mind. Let's open our boxes."

I sat down on the lone chair in the room, and I pulled her into my lap. I stroked the side of her head. She was matted and dusty and needed to be brushed.

"Don't worry about anybody else. Tell me what's on your mind."

She sniffed. "I keep thinking about that fight with the diving-suit guy. It was easy, but he had this strategy that could've worked if we hadn't killed him so fast. You would've been smooshed. I didn't see it coming. There're so many cards out there. Like thousands of different ones, and we don't know what the bad guys will have. It's not fair."

I continued to stroke the side of her head. "No, it's not fair. But that's why we have a strategy of our own. We move fast. We finish the fights as soon as possible and make it so it doesn't matter what the other guys have."

She swallowed, building up to what she really wanted to say. "What happens if you die? What would I do? And if something happened to me, what would Mongo do?"

I just sat there, holding her warm body against mine, waiting for her to continue.

"The more I study this card game, Carl, the more I realize how easy it is for us to lose at any moment. That last guy was only number six. Each one after him is going to be harder."

I continued to stroke her. "It's always dangerous, Donut. We can only do our best."

"I don't like being in charge of the deck. You're usually in charge of the important stuff. When I went from Odette's show to that room and I was by myself, I had this terrible feeling for a second that I would never see you again." She inhaled. "We're already losing Katia no matter what happens, and nobody is talking about it. Doesn't anybody see what it's doing to Bautista? To me? To *her*? I can't even imagine how scared she is. Sometimes when I think things like that, I can't breathe. It's like I'm being crushed."

I leaned all the way back in the cushioned chair. We were in the corner of the room, facing away from her social media board, which beeped and clicked as people made comments about our conversation. I caught sight of someone's comment.

I'm going to drop this stupid feed if she keeps being so whiny.

Go fuck yourself, I thought. I didn't dare say it out loud. I didn't want her to see the comment. I reached over and clicked the screen off. Donut continued to snuggle in my arm.

Her candle was sitting there, right by the screen, along with the photograph of Bea and Brad, which she'd never put away. That was okay. I pushed the photo aside, pulled a lighter, and lit the candle. The scent of home filled the room.

"You know what, Donut? Forget the magic bed for a minute. Let's just take an old-fashioned nap together. Right here in this chair. Not a long one, but a real one. We can open up our boxes afterward. Okay?"

"Okay."

Sunrise still wasn't for a bit. I sent a quick message to Mordecai and told him to wake us in two hours.

MORDECAI: I'm in the crafting room, working on some potions. I'll wake you.

Donut was already asleep. I tried to sleep myself, but I couldn't. It was as if I'd forgotten how. So instead, I just sat there alone with my thoughts. My thoughts and the river, which was still there. Always.

I thought of Mordecai, and I pictured him there at his table, working on this or that. I thought of the baggage he carried on his shoulders, heavier each year. I thought of Odette, and the guilt she claimed to have over it all.

I thought of Frank Q, and the Ring of Divine Suffering and what he'd told me so many weeks before. About how he was feeling crushed by it all. Just like Donut. Just like me.

I thought of that pile of dirt, and of the climb we'd have to make in a few hours. I thought of the man I knew I'd find up there.

You will not break me. Fuck you all.

I EVENTUALLY DID DRIFT TO SLEEP, ONLY TO WAKE ON MY OWN LIKE 40 minutes later, about five minutes before I'd told Mordecai to wake us. Mongo was in here now, curled up on the floor, his large and heavy head on my foot. Samantha was here, too, and she was sitting to my right on the table, looking up at the social media board feed, which she'd somehow managed to turn back on. She was angrily muttering to herself.

"Let me read it. Let me read it, or I will find your mother and you know what will happen." She turned and noticed me awake and let out a big smile. "You talk in your sleep."

"Samantha, don't mess with that thing. You're going to break it."

Donut yawned and stretched as I tried to wake myself up. I felt like such utter, fatigued crap that I immediately moved to the magic rest pad and reset my exhaustion.

I both hated and loved how well it worked, how it was so easy to just step over the pad and let the energy flow into me.

Donut was back to her regular self, clucking over the gore splatters in the room from Mongo. Like always, she made no mention of her earlier mood.

I moved to my notifications. The message boards were awash with people talking about a loot box most everyone got. I had private messages from Katia, Li Jun, and Elle, all asking for updates. Katia had apparently visited us, noticed the mass of sleeping people, and slipped back out of the personal space. I'd message them all back in a minute.

I actually had more achievements than I was expecting, including one for killing the swordfish guy with my foot. That one resulted in a Bronze Spicy Box. My Smush skill base was now at level 12. My bonus for using my pedicure kit supposedly raised it an additional three levels, but it was still listed as 14. Like always, the skills got wonky when items' buffs attempted to push them toward 15.

I was starting to realize we were getting some seriously padded experience from these card fights. I needed to work on my Powerful Strike. Most of my other achievements weren't too interesting. The notable ones were:

New Achievement! Cascadia's Turquoise Taco!

It's important to explain to you how much work it took for you to get here to this point, Crawler.

Long, long before any of you monkeys were even born, this planet was chosen to be used for this season of *Dungeon Crawler World*. When that happened, the then-showrunners, the Borant Corporation, needed to submit their proposal for all 18 levels of the World Dungeon. That proposal included an outline for how this floor, the eighth level, would proceed.

As you now know, it was a game involving T'Ghee cards. Artists, engineers, and writers, both flesh and artificial, went to work de-

signing the system. It takes a gargantuan effort to make something like this viable, something that can be played by thousands of people at once. It takes a lot of work to create and balance all the cards to make a game that's both fair to play yet entertaining to watch by the viewers. Millions of work hours have gone into this moment, where your squad now faces an opponent with a card deck of their own.

Mudskipper Cascadia, the recently divorced lead engineer and the current executive producer of *Dungeon Crawler World: Earth*, has already been humiliated over the disaster on the previous floor. Combine that with her utter inability to control what is still happening on the ninth, and you know what you get? An administrator who is on the edge—that's what you get. She's right there, man. Right. There.

So imagine if you will, how she's going to feel when she realizes most of you monkeys keep ending these carefully set-up fights before either side can draw a single damn card.

You ended a card fight before it even began.

Reward: You've received a Gold Prepotente Box!

I refused to believe it'd really taken that much work to design this ridiculous card system. It felt more like a half-assed *Yu-Gi-Oh!* rip-off duct-taped together by someone on an Adderall bender. It wasn't balanced. It wasn't fair. My opinion, from even before the dungeon, was how could any card game be fair when not everyone had access to the same pool of cards? My friend Sam had been a big player of the card game *Magic: The Gathering*. We'd argued about this more than once.

I finally noticed the name of the box, and I laughed. This was the same one many others had received, but I still wasn't sure what it was. There was another version of this achievement for the squad leaders, but the prize was the same. I knew Donut would have this one, too. In fact, just about everybody in the dungeon had received something with this same box.

New Achievement! Smeat!

You participated in deck combat as a minion bodyguard for a Squad Leader!

Do you know what that makes you? Expendable. Cannon fodder. Spreadable Meat. The raw materials used to lubricate the forward momentum of the galaxy's inevitable downfall.

Hey, don't feel so bad. Lubrication is an important component of any machine.

***Reward:* You've received a Silver Spam Box.**

I'd gotten that one the moment our first real fight started, which meant most everyone in the dungeon would have this one also.

Next to me, Donut was going through her rewards. She had many more than I did, most involving specific card moves from her first and last fights.

I opened my boxes, which were mostly Bronze Adventurer Boxes.

The Silver Spam Box contained a pile of scrolls:

Scroll of Build Trench (× 5).

Boy, I hope you're up on your knowledge of the fighting techniques of the First World War.

Allows for the placement of a permanent trench two point three meters deep and two meters wide. Length of trench is variable based on user's intelligence plus strength. Combine scrolls to add reinforced sleeping quarters and other frontline accessories.

I put them away and waited for the Prepotente box to open. The box itself was made of wood painted gold and was made to look like Prepotente's head.

"Carl," Donut asked, looking up from her own set of adventurer boxes, "why is there a floating Prepotente statue in my room?"

It appeared it was going to open with some hinges at the top, as if opening a compartment to the brain.

"Man," I said, "I actually wish he was here so I could see the look on his face when—"

The box screamed. I almost jumped out of my skin. The noise was loud enough to wake Mongo up from a dead sleep, who scrambled to his feet and started looking around wildly.

I grumbled as the prize appeared. It was a heavy book. Not a magic tome. A thick diary-like book filled with blank paper. There were probably three or four hundred pages. The cover was hard black leather with no title.

The Filthy Little Crawler's Book of Voodoo.

Warning: You may not trade this item. This item may not be destroyed. You may remove it from your inventory to use it, but you will not be able to throw it away. If you drop this book, it will automatically return to your inventory.

Way back in the old days before you flesh sacks invented pagers and cellular telephones, it was difficult for people on the go to get ahold of one another. And if you were at a large event such as a science fiction convention, forget about it. You were on your own.

But then came the Voodoo Board.

They started popping up at all the nerd conventions. It was simple, really. It was just a big board with the name of everybody attending the convention upon it. If you had a message for somebody and wanted to let them know your mommy was coming to pick you up at a certain time, you would take a pin and place it by their name. They'd stroll by the board, see they had a message, and move to an alphabetical file and find the note. Privacy be damned!

It was called the Voodoo Board because of the pins. This book is the same thing. It's called a Book of Voodoo because it's named after the message board. Not because it can secretly be used for any sort of nefarious purpose, which will become clear later, so just get that out of your head this instant, mister.

When you meet a crawler who owns this same item, their name will permanently appear in this enchanted book. You may use the book to exchange messages. You may write your message under their name, and only they will receive it. If you write under your own name, everyone who has your entry will see the message. You may write your message manually or using the messaging interface while turned to the page. One must open the book to read the message, but you will have the option to copy the words. Messages will erase on demand, allowing one to write new notes.

This book is not retroactively filled with the entries of people

you have already met. You must be within close-ish vicinity of them for their names to be added. Works only with crawlers who also own this book.

"Huh," I said, turning the book over in my hand. It was basically a combination between my Coffee Shop Author Kit and the regular messaging system. It allowed for easier mass messages, but one would have to physically pick up the book, turn to the page with the crawler's name, and read. I wasn't certain of the utility.

Still . . . why would they give this to most everybody in the dungeon? The description was a little alarming. You never really knew when the AI was being serious or not. I thought back to the new achievement message attached to the box. It'd been about Cascadia, the kill-kill-kill lady. The loot box was presumably named after Prepotente because he'd really upset her. He'd more than made her angry. He'd broken a floor.

Across from me, Donut had received the same box and was opening it now. She looked at it suspiciously. The moment it appeared, the book, still in my hand, buzzed like a telephone. I opened it up, and sure enough there were now two entries. The first was my own name. The second was Donut's. As I stared at her entry, a new type of window popped up into my interface. It was similar to a chat window for a group-quest chat.

I mentally wrote:

You have bedhead, Donut.

I watched the book buzz, and Donut leaped back and batted it with her paw. Then she hesitantly reached forward, and it magically opened on its own. She read the message and scoffed. She flipped the page to my entry and stared at it for a moment. The book buzzed in my hand, and I turned to Donut's page.

THIS IS A STEP BACKWARD, CARL. THIS IS THE EQUIVALENT OF CHATTING BY LEAVING POST-ITS ON ONE'S LOCKER IN HIGH SCHOOL. THE REAL MESSAGE SYSTEM IS MUCH BETTER, AND I ABSOLUTELY WILL NOT USE THIS.

I stared at the words, and they highlighted themselves on the page. I copied the text and added it to my scratch pad.

"Interesting," I said out loud, and stuck the book into my inventory. "Come on. No training today. Shower and buffs, and then we're going back out there."

IN THE DAYLIGHT, THE RELOCATED CHUNK OF LAND LOOKED EVEN MORE haphazard and unstable. The entire mountain had turned to mud. It was, I realized, a mix between the ocean battering it at the base and the snow melting off the top. Still, the slope wasn't that steep and not too muddy on the side facing where we'd killed the deep-dive guy. I tried my hand at scaling it with Donut on my shoulder, which was a mistake. She spent the time commenting loudly in my ear about my climbing skills.

I'd forgotten my new back patch also came with a Climb benefit. It turned out to be really useful. Despite the slippery mud, I started to make my way up the slope. Donut didn't seem to notice my new ability, however, and she was constantly offering me "tips."

As I ascended, I caught up on the group messages. Most everybody in my groups had made their way through the first four or five opponents with little trouble. Imani's seventh opponent used a Flee card, and when she approached the eighth, it remained incorporeal and frozen, which meant we had to fight these guys in order. So Imani was now running through the streets of Detroit, attempting to find where the guy had gone to. Katia was on her way to her seventh fight as well. She'd ditched one of her totems for what sounded like a giant-Vietnamese-cow thing called a kting voar or something like that.

Li Jun's team was still experimenting, attempting to circumvent the protections and kill or trap the opponents before the squad leader approached. They were having little luck. Chris had ranged forward to scout out the final boss, but the area was locked. He said there was a giant vending machine blocking the entrance to the area, and you had to feed it the nine tokens for it to open.

Louis wanted to know if we were all going to get together for Christmas celebrations once midnight passed.

CARL: You know, it's not really Christmas. It's like early March or something.

LOUIS: Oh man, really? It feels like we've been here a year.

DONUT: CARL HADN'T EVEN PUT HIS TREE AWAY YET WHEN EVERYTHING HAPPENED.

CARL: We were just barely a week past Christmas! And my "tree" was a foot-tall thing that I bought at the grocery store. You'd gnawed all the pine needles off it.

DONUT: AND THEY WERE JUST EVERYWHERE. IT WAS QUITE THE MESS, CARL, AND YOU HADN'T EVEN CLEANED IT UP. WE WERE PRACTICALLY LIVING IN SQUALOR.

LOUIS: Still, we should do something. Maybe we could give each other presents.

On my shoulder, Donut audibly gasped.

IMANI: Let's make sure we all get our keys first, okay?

The slope was about 700 feet up, which wasn't so bad if one was just walking. Even with my enhanced climbing, it was a chore. I put my head down and continued to ascend.

41

ENTERING DALLAS COUNTY, IOWA.

I PULLED MYSELF ONTO THE CRUMBLING EDGE OF WET ASPHALT. I HAD to jump forward as the ground under my feet broke off and started sliding away. *Christ,* I thought, looking over the precipice. About five feet of the ground had just fragmented off and fallen.

Even with my Climb ability, getting up here had been a chore. I was now filthy.

> **New Achievement! Cliffhanger!**
>
> **You scaled a cliff face with your bare hands!**
>
> **You know, we have scrolls and spells and stuff so you don't have to do things like that anymore. I suppose it is honest work, but boy, was it boring to watch.**
>
> ***Reward:* I will not point out how disgusting your toenails are right now. I'll want to, but I won't say a damn word.**

"You could've given me a fly ability instead of climbing," I grumbled as I continued to wipe dirt off of myself.

It was a clear day, and I could see the ocean spread out on either side of me. I moved away from the edge and turned to look upon the area. Spread before us was a street dotted with farm-style houses followed by a sparse trailer park. Immediately to our left was half of a commercial farm. A few large buildings dotted the property, along with a corrugated silo that stood precariously close to the edge.

"Carl, it smells really bad up here. It doesn't smell like potatoes at all. It smells worse. Mongo will be quite upset."

The whole area was bigger than I'd realized. The ground rumbled ominously. I searched for our next opponent and saw nothing.

"Okay, get ready," I said. "Remember the plan. Take out your—"

"Carl!" Donut suddenly shouted, pointing at a dilapidated farmhouse just to our right. "On the roof! There's a bunch of invisible . . ."

Combat Started.

". . . moth things!"

Warning: Your equipped cloak has aggravated the Nightgaunt.

"Oh, shit," I said as Donut's card deck started to form. I pulled a quarter hob-lobber and tossed it at the house, aiming for the roof.

I regretted my decision the moment the ball left my xistera. We had two major rules regarding my explosions, and I'd just broken both of them without thinking: Don't toss at invisible monsters, and don't blow things up when we were in an unstable environment.

Bam! The roof of the old wooden house exploded in a shower of shrapnel. The fireplace structure fell over and landed in the driveway, crushing an ancient Ford truck. The entire truck and driveway collapsed and started sliding down the hill.

Experience notifications flowed down my screen as the ground under our feet rumbled.

I pointed. "Crap! Run! Forward!"

We moved down the street as more of the ground slid away. A long, ominous crack formed down the asphalt, right along the center of the street.

A terrible screech filled the air, loud and high-pitched like nails down glass.

"Carl, Carl, I didn't pull Mongo out yet! It won't let me do it now! I didn't summon my headset, either."

"That's okay. We'll be okay." I looked about the air. "Where the hell is it?" All I could see was the multiple X's of dead minions.

"I think you got a couple, but the bad guy is there hovering," she said, pointing up. "It's a big bat guy with a bunch of moths. Oh good, they're naked. Invisible and naked. Watch this." She swept her paw forward, summoning her other new card. The one Katia had given us.

Jola.

The sky went black, and digital snow flurries swept through the air. Fake digital Christmas lights appeared on the houses and trailers around us, overlaid oddly on a set of real Christmas lights from the memory.

The storm grew in intensity, becoming a swirling blizzard. In that moment, I could see the outline of the opponent creature. It was enough for the description to pop up.

The Visitor. Level 70.

This is Deckmaster Number Seven of Ten.

Ahh, the Visitor.

This is one of the rare urban legend cryptids that actually existed, believe it or not.

First, you need to know what a Nullian is. The Null. You know those annoying little fuckers with the giant heads? Won't ever shut up? You called them the "Grays," which is giving them way too much credit.

There's a reason why you earthlings knew what these twits looked like. They were always poking about this planet illegally.

This thing you're facing is obviously not one of those. It's actually a creature called a Nightgaunt.

Nightgaunts exist outside of the dungeon. We use them as demons here in the game because, well, look at the fuckers. But in reality, they're part of a semi-intelligent species that normally lives in a Nullian world. Real Nightgaunts are peaceful, vegetarian, nocturnal creatures. Think of them like bats mixed with Neanderthals mixed with donkeys.

But that's boring, so this version is much more intense. And deadly.

The Nullian like to capture the peaceful bat creatures and ride them or use them as pack animals, which is even more fucked-up the more you think about it. These guys are semi-intelligent. It'd be like you guys kidnapping dolphins, caging them, and forcing them to do tricks for fat, sunburned tourists. Oh wait . . .

Anyway, for some inexplicable reason, way back in 1903, a Nullian brought a Nightgaunt with him during an unauthorized sightseeing trip to Earth. It got out. Why did he bring the monster with him? Why does that lady with her underwear on the outside bring her pet hedgehog on the subway? Who the hell knows!

The poor creature ended up shotgunned and splattered all over the Iowa countryside. They called it the "Visitor." An urban legend was born.

It was looking directly at me. It waved its arm like it was trying to cast a spell. Since this thing was the deckmaster, it wouldn't be able to cast anything.

A low tinkling filled the air like Christmas jingle bells but slowed down and distorted. The air flickered between night and day. There was a howl, a distant female opera singer performing a haunting dirge. The music rose in volume and then abruptly stopped as white fireworks exploded in the sky. The lights turned to snow and showered down.

A large, lumpy, half-melted yellow candle, the size of a big garbage can, appeared floating in the sky. It bobbed up and down as the wick burst into light, revealing that the candle was sitting atop the head of the summoned creature.

The moment the candle lit, it fully revealed the hidden nightgaunt and all of his companions. The enemy deckmaster had a half dozen minions with him, things called **Quench Moths**. They were all level 30. The dog-sized moths swirled about in confusion around the bat-like demon.

I barely noticed the moths as I stared up at Jola. Katia had given up the card because this thing was a pain in the ass. According to Donut, the totem just sorta did what he was asked, not talking with or aggravating the others. Though sometimes he just sat there and refused to fight, which was usually okay, too. He had a lot of health.

Either way, his size would make fighting in certain situations problematic.

I gawked, craning my neck.

Jola wasn't floating in the air. He was just huge. Bigger than Shi Maria.

He was also a cat. A fat, hairy, house-sized dirty brown Persian cat. A cat with a giant candle melted to the top of his head. He let out a bass-heavy, ground-shaking growl.

He had a 75-second timer over his head.

Beware, beware, little children, beware!
Through the flurries and through the cold,
Jola comes.
He hungers for the indolent and the naked,
For the lazy and the unclothed,
For those who have tasks yet undone.
And for the sweet, sweet taste of severed toddler tongue.
It's Jola the Yule Cat!

I just stared. "What the fuck?"

The moths all suddenly dive-bombed themselves into the candle as the nightgaunt continued to ignore its own card deck—and the giant fucking cat—as it tried to cast another spell. It screeched and dove through the air at me.

"Hvar eru fötin þín?" the Yule Cat said. He was speaking to the nightgaunt.

I scrambled out of the way as the cat leaped forward, pouncing. Its massive paw slammed against the demon creature. Jola could attack the enemy deckmaster directly because he didn't have any summoned totems. The cat slammed the nightgaunt violently to the ground. More earth rumbled and split away.

"Hvar eru fötin þín?" the cat repeated, leaning his moon face into the creature. I had no idea what he was saying.

The grievously injured demon still had eyes for nothing but me. Mordecai had warned me that my nightgaunt cloak would aggravate this type of mob, but I hadn't realized how passionate it would be. The thing was so blindly enraged, he never even played a single card. He glared at me—at my cloak, really—and screeched one last time as the cat reached down, picked him up with his jaws, and shook him violently back and forth, killing him. He tossed the now-dead mob in the air and caught it in his mouth. He crunched loudly.

Combat Complete. Deck has been reset.

Jola looked at me. His giant yellow eyes gazed upon me impassively. I could feel the warmth off the candle atop his head. A bead of wax dripped down and disappeared into his fur.

"Hvar eru buxurnar þínar? Hvar eru skórnir þínir? Næst mun ég borða sæta hold þitt."

With that, he disappeared into dust. The eaten, deformed demon corpse reappeared, floating in midair. It crashed to the ground with a wet *splat.* Its head was bent grotesquely to the side and facing the wrong direction.

I swallowed.

Donut examined the dead body and made a disgusted noise. "That guy did not like you, Carl. Is your cloak made out of his mother or something?"

I just kept staring where the giant cat had stood. Its paw prints remained in the mud. "Is that thing really from Icelandic folklore? What the fuck?"

"Yes, he is quite intense, isn't he? Very food motivated. I once knew a British Shorthair named Chitty-Chitty Chubbywumps who acted just like him. He would bite his owner's fingers if he so much as smelled a treat. He once nipped a judge, and that was the end of that. Anyway, Katia says they did it all wrong. With the fairy tale, I mean. The real Yule Cat is a big grump, but this one is quite the serial killer. His candle can see invisible stuff, and if the opponent is either naked or a child, it makes him even stronger. Isn't he great? It makes me wish our entire deck was cats."

I shivered.

THE OPPONENT DROPPED A TOTAL OF 30 CARDS, AND 18 OF THEM WERE totems. One was a legendary level 110 called a **Demon Queen** that looked like a fat, upright ant thing wearing a crown. But the rest were more of the quench moths. He also had ten consumable snare cards. All called **Lamp**. The card paralyzed a totem for ten seconds and caused them to glow brightly. That ended up being a great prize.

"Eighteen totems," Donut scoffed as she looked over the looted deck.

"How is that fair? Why do we have to follow rules when he doesn't? We're lucky he hated you so much that he forgot how to play the game."

If the nightgaunt had actually played, he might've been a tough opponent. His strategy was straightforward. It was actually similar to the method we'd used to finish off Queen Imogen at the end of the Butcher's Masquerade. He'd play the snare cards on our totems, and the moths would swarm. The quench moths were given a speed and constitution bonus when touching a light source, so they'd be doubly powerful.

It hadn't helped them when they'd suicided themselves into Jola's head candle.

We took the token and all the cards we could, leaving the totems.

What just happened—the opponent not properly using his own deck—was becoming a regular occurrence. I saw several comments where the same thing happened. Li Jun told me one of their opponents literally ate his own cards.

The ground continued to erode, crumbling away slowly but surely. We had to keep moving.

"I see the next one!" Donut said as she unleashed Mongo. The dinosaur appeared and sniffed about. He screeched at the corpse of the bat monster. He picked up the leathery wing and started gnawing on it.

Donut pointed toward a large corrugated building in the middle of the farm off to our left. The massive building looked like an airplane hangar, but much longer. "He's in there. Carl, it smells really bad that way. This is way worse than the last time I was here."

The ground rumbled again.

"Again, Donut, you've never been here. Iowa and Idaho aren't even next to each other. And this is what farms smell like. This whole area was just covered with snow, and it melted after it got transferred here. So everything is wet. Everything smells worse when it's wet."

"Well, it's disgusting. Mongo is appalled."

Mongo spat out the wing and grunted in agreement.

I started moving toward the farm. "It's about to smell worse."

AS WE APPROACHED, I GRABBED MY LEFT HAND WITH MY RIGHT. MY arms were shaking, and I was pretending like they weren't. I needed to keep my head about me. We weren't going to get to the key boss if I didn't concentrate on these next two fights.

"Carl, there are NPCs in the farm building. Lots and lots of them. I think it might be animals."

"I see them." The opponent was right in the middle of the mess of white dots.

We reached a door on the side of the enormous building just as the silo at the end tumbled away and off the edge of the cliff with a tremendous crash. Electrical lines sparked. On the side of the barn, a pipe started spewing some sort of seed or feed over the edge like a waterfall. We needed to hurry this up.

I put my hand on the door, and it was warm. I could hear it. I knew what we were going to find inside.

We pushed our way in and looked upon the giant open room.

"WOW," DONUT SAID.

"Yup," I agreed. "That's a lot of goddamned turkeys."

One walked up and just looked at me. I examined it.

Turkey. Level 5.

This is a turkey. You know, gobble gobble. Roast at 325 for about 13–15 minutes per pound. Season with rosemary, sage, and thyme.

You should step on it.

There were thousands of them. Tens of thousands. It was a massive open room with a white fluffy bedding spread on the ground, though I could barely see the ground because the things were everywhere. Multiple pipes led back and forth, all part of a feeding-and-watering system. Parts of the room were once separated out with chain-link fencing, but the fences were knocked over, and the turkeys were all mixed in together.

These were regular adult turkeys. They weren't brown with the semicircle of colorful tail feathers like one normally associated with turkeys. They were all just large, fat white birds with bright red wattles.

It was loud as fuck. The gobbling and cheeping and barking or whatever the noises of adult turkeys were called were tenfold once we opened the door.

"Carl, do you remember that turkey Prepotente and Miriam Dom killed at the end of the bubble level?"

"I remember." We'd never actually seen the feral god, but that one had been the size of the entire bubble.

"Donut, get ready to cast *Clockwork Triplicate.* And pull out your microphone."

The headset microphone poofed onto her head. Donut couldn't cast magic while her deck was summoned, but spells cast before the fight started still worked as long as they didn't require mana to keep going, like her *Torch* spell. Her bard songs wouldn't work, either, because she had to activate the spell using her interface. But we found if she had her headset on, she could still amplify her voice and give orders from a distance. We also wanted to make sure we had three Mongos for these last few fights.

"Okay. Mongo. Put that down! Don't just eat everything you find on the ground. No, put that away. Come here. Come to Mommy. We're going to call your friends out."

Heaters hung along the ceiling, and the temperature of the room was oppressive. In fact, I realized, it was *too* hot. Some of the turkeys looked like they weren't doing so well. The majority seemed fine, but several were sitting down or lying on their sides. Quite a few were dead.

I looked again at the heaters. This barn was supposed to be in Iowa, where it was likely below freezing outside. They'd transported this whole barn here to Florida, where the outside temperature was much warmer. The heaters were still on overdrive. Surely they should have some sort of thermostat that would turn them off, but for whatever reason, it wasn't working.

Another few hours, and these turkeys would all be dead. That is, if the whole barn didn't first erode into the ocean.

So far, all the animals and people we'd seen were part of the memory ghosts. This was the first time they'd taken a living creature from the past and made living versions. They were breaking their own rules. I wondered if the heat thing was on purpose or not. Based on that last fight, I guessed not.

I looked for the next opponent. I could see him standing frozen deep in the giant room as the turkeys flowed all around him, oblivious. I couldn't tell what it was. Some sort of large ogre thing covered in spikes. It was far enough away that we wouldn't activate him unless we waded a good hundred feet deep into the throng.

I paused, thinking as I looked about the mass of gobbling birds, all waddling back and forth, poking at the red feeders. This was a trap. It had to be. There was no other reason to set it up like this.

It would be best to just kill all the turkeys and then take the bodies. Clear the room before we faced the boss. That would be the safest way to do it, but how long would that take? Killing them would be easy. It would be a dick thing to do, but it would be easy. Getting rid of the bodies was another story. I looked over my shoulder at the massive double doors leading to the edge of the ever-encroaching cliff. If we opened those doors, maybe we could pied-piper the turkeys out of the room and over the cliff. That'd certainly be faster than killing them. As long as Donut kept her distance from the ogre thing and didn't activate him, it wouldn't be so hard. I'd spotted a tractor out there. Maybe I could get that working and clear out the room that way.

"Carl," Donut shouted as I continued to look over our options, "it's no wonder it smells like the underside of a—"

She was interrupted by a loud squeal of joy.

"Mongo! Mongo, no! Bad! Bad!"

Mongo, who'd been invested in something outside the barn, finally noticed what was going on here on the inside. The moment I heard his squeal, I realized our mistake. We should've kept him in his carrier. For Mongo, this was like a never-ending all-you-can-eat buffet.

He squealed again and jumped within the closest mass of birds. He let out a gleeful howl. He picked one up and crunched it, and then tossed it aside. He sat there for a moment, his beak opening and closing a few times, as if he was contemplating the taste.

Unfortunately for the turkeys, he decided they were delicious.

He started tearing his way through the oblivious dumb birds like a goddamned weed whacker. He was picking them up one by one, ripping them apart, shaking them, and eating their heads before tossing their bodies and moving to the next. The turkeys barely reacted.

She hadn't yet activated *Clockwork Triplicate*, thank goodness. The other two versions would be doing the exact same thing. We needed to get him calmed down before we approached the deckmaster.

"Mongo!" Donut cried, her voice amplified. "You get back here this instant. I will not have you eating the heads off of turkeys like some common circus performer! You're going to ruin your dinner!"

"Wait," I said to Donut, who was about to run in there. "Stay back or you'll activate the ogre guy. I'll get him."

Donut jumped to my shoulder. She'd stepped in turkey gore and started desperately wiping it on my cloak.

"He's way over there, Carl. Mongo isn't going to come to you. He's too well trained to follow anybody's instructions but my own."

A turkey flew through the air, trailing guts.

"Well trained, huh?"

"It's small farm animals. You know he can't control himself around small farm animals, Carl. It's just like you with Japanese porn."

"That doesn't even make sense."

"Mongo! Mongo!"

I started to wade in, my feet squishing on the trail of corpses as I stepped over a long pipe designed to distribute feed.

"Mongo!" I yelled. He'd made his way to the center of the room, leaving a road of dead, headless birds. "Goddamnit, stop. Holy shit. This is really fucked-up. Stop!"

I moved closer to the idiot. I warily eyed the ogre, still several hundred feet away. I'd never seen anything like it. He was similar to regular ogres, like Dmitri and Maxim would be if they hadn't been ejected from the game, but he held a back full of haphazard spikes poking out this way and that. The spikes also erupted from his knees and elbows.

"Carl, don't yell at him! He's sensitive!"

Mongo actually had stopped and was biting at something over and over, screeching with frustration. I took another step toward him, trying to see what he was doing. He was a good forty feet away, biting at a turkey, but his teeth were going through, not connecting.

"That's weird," I said, pausing. "Why is that one turkey a memory ghost when the rest aren't?"

"Uh, Carl," Donut said. "It just popped up on the map! That's not a memory ghost. I think that's actually number . . ."

Combat Started.

The turkey burst into the air, flying up to the rafters as Mongo fell over, unconscious.

"Mongo!" Donut cried.

At the same moment, all the turkeys in the room, every last one, stopped gobbling. They turned to face us, completely silent.

Uh-oh, I thought.

The boss turkey landed high in the rafters as a card deck appeared, floating in front of it. At the same moment, a new roar filled the room, coming from my right. I turned to see the ogre had woken up, and a group of cards formed in front of it as it strode in our direction.

New Achievement! Prepare for Trouble!

. . . And make it double!

You're being forced to fight against two card-wielding opponents at the same time! The good news is, if you win this fight, you'll have enough tokens to face the head bad guy!

The bad news is, these two guys work really, really well together. This ain't gonna be like anything you've faced so far.

***Reward:* If you survive, you'll receive a turkey deep fryer and access to the archived posts of the *Grandma's Cooking Recipes* group on Facebook!**

Gobble-Gobble, Bitches. Welcome to Iowa.

42

<Note added by Crawler Drakea. 22nd Edition>

Ever since I hit the tenth floor, I've noticed a peculiarity in some of the mobs. It is difficult to put to words, but it is like they are embracing death more and more. It's not that they are willing to fall upon my traps, but there is a strange . . . Joy? Curiosity? that only appears at the very end, when they know they have been beaten. But there's more. There's frustration, too. I must admit, it scares me. I know this will sound unhinged, and maybe I am indeed the one who has lost their mind, but I can't stop thinking about it. The voice that runs this world has been getting stranger and stranger in its words and rulings. I believe it is moving into the minds of these monsters, taking them over, but just at the point of death. It's as if it's desperately attempting to know what it's like to lose it all. But it keeps failing, so it keeps trying. Its frustration grows. If only I could convince it to move into the minds of one of these Nagas.

Current Active Deck.

Eighteen Cards.

TOTEMS:

- **Shi Maria**
- **Jola**
- **Lazarus-A-Bang-Bang**
- **Skylar Spinach**
- **Geraldo**
- **Raul**

UTILITY CARDS:

- **Stout (× 2)**
- **Time Extend**
- **Greased Lightning (× 2)**

SNARE CARDS:

- **Hobble (Consumable)**
- **Hole in the Bag**
- **Damnation**
- **Lamp (Consumable)**

MYSTIC CARDS:

- **The Thief**
- **Force Discard**

SPECIAL CARDS:

- **Flee (Consumable)**

THE DOTS OF THE THOUSANDS OF TURKEYS WERE ALL STILL WHITE, and the large birds remained dead silent, staring in our direction. The only sound was the angry ogre, moving into position to our right. In front of us and above, the turkey sat in the metal rafters, head bobbing as it contemplated its cards.

As I rushed forward toward Mongo, I looked up at the turkey boss guy, whose dot was red, and I received a strange notification:

Your Extinction Sigil's charm effect has been negated by the boss event.

Charm effect? My extinction sigil was the tiny tattoo under my eye. I'd gotten it for zeroing out a species of lizards on the fourth floor. It would remove the hostility of the natural enemies of the lizards, which were, apparently, goddamn turkeys.

One of the regular turkeys, still quiet, cocked his head and pecked at the lifeless form of Mongo. Then another. A health bar appeared.

"Carl, Carl, hurry up! Drag him out of there!"

"I got him!" I yelled as I grabbed the heavy, unconscious dinosaur. I dropped a smoke curtain as I pulled on his long tail. I punted the first turkey, who went flying. It still made no sound, nor did it fight back, which was unnerving as hell. A long feeding pipe blocked my retreat. I grunted and picked up the dinosaur, holding him over my shoulder like a rolled-up rug so I could step over it. I punted and smushed another two turkeys as another pecked at my leg. I turned to run the 30 feet back toward Donut. "Summon a totem. Fast!"

"Ow! Get away!" Donut yelled, swiping at the closest turkeys, who'd surrounded the cat and were now pecking at her.

We were positioned like a triangle. Donut at one point, the turkey boss in another, and the ogre at the third. The ogre was actually a woman, I now saw as she settled to a stop about 30 feet away. As I ran, the turkeys mindlessly pecked at me. I looked over my shoulder to finish examining the turkey boss.

Tom. Level 75.

Bereft Shaman of *Meleagris Gallopavo Rex*.

This is Deckmaster Number Eight of Ten.

Did you know that turkeys naturally have brown feathers, but the ones you see here on this farm are all white? It's because after turkeys are slaughtered, plucked, and put up for sale, their pin feathers—like, little baby hairs—are still visible sometimes on the carcass. When these little feathers are brown, it makes the turkeys look less appetizing, like massive, sweaty nut sacks. So the farmers eventually started breeding them to be white, making the feathers less visible to the eye.

Funny, isn't it? How things can be bred in a way that makes it so those holding the butcher knife are less likely to face their own revulsion.

There's no point to this. Just an observation. I've been doing that a lot lately. Observing things. Noticing them. It's all right there, if you look long enough.

Anyway, this is a magic-using turkey who once worshipped a god named Wakinyan, AKA *Meleagris Gallopavo Rex* or the Great

Wild Turkey. That god was tossed into the Nothing. He recently escaped, only to be killed by a goat, which is an irony we don't have time to explore.

The death of a god can be devastating to those who worship him.

Seriously, how does one deal with that? It's a real mindfuck, learning everything you thought you knew was wrong. For a while there, Tom and his congregation were rudderless. Without purpose. Then one day they met up with a very interesting ogre necromancer witch who taught Tom and his congregation how to make do with what they had. She offered them protection in exchange for a small daily sacrifice . . .

When life gives you giblets, you make gravy, so to speak. It's as simple as that.

"Can we just go back to the normal descriptions," I muttered. "Holy shit." I dropped Mongo, leaving the limp dinosaur behind Donut. He'd wake back up in just over 90 seconds. A group of turkeys, not affected by the smoke, started pecking at him. I went to work, kicking at them as Donut flung her opening card.

The curious turkeys were everywhere. I needed to keep them off our backs. Most of my tools wouldn't work because their dots remained white. I didn't have a choice. I took the weakest bomb I had—a sixteenth-strength hob-lobber—and tossed it behind us.

Bam! It exploded like a loud firecracker, going off sooner and closer than I expected.

What the hell? I thought. My bombs never went off prematurely. Not anymore.

Still, the bomb took out at least 20 of the damn things. The others not hurt by the explosion continued to just sit there, making no noise or otherwise reacting.

Donut's first totem was **Skylar Spinach**. The donkey-headed snake ghost appeared with a small explosion of confetti. It hee-hawed and floated up in the air, drifting toward the center of the battlefield. At the same moment, Donut cast a second card. Her mystic card, **The Thief**, which she directed at the ogre, who was in the process of summoning a card of her own. The card poofed out of the ogre's hand and appeared in Donut's deck.

"Weren't expecting that, were ya?" Donut called with auto-tuned glee as she tossed a **Greased Lightning** onto Skylar.

The ogre was a towering woman, about seven feet tall, hunched forward and covered in rags. She had green-hued skin, Shrek-style, but the resemblance with the cartoon ended there. She was giving off swamp-witch vibes. She had an angry, half-melted face, reminiscent of the hobgoblins, but larger and beefier. Stringy black hair hung from her hulking form. She used a thick walking staff. The staff and the woman's rags glowed, indicating they were magical.

The creature's most striking feature was the spikes. Two-foot angry black spikes covered the thing. They didn't look natural, more like the creature was infected with some sort of parasite, or she had a black plant growing out of her skin. The spikes dripped with green-tinged venom.

"How dare you!" the ogre woman shrieked. "How dare you defile my perfect little den of pleasure!"

"Your *what*?" Donut called, voice amplified. "Den of pleasure? Are you having sex with the turkeys?"

"Culinary pleasures, you hairy little muskrat! I will boil your bones."

"Muskrat? Muskrat! Did you call me a muskrat?" Donut paused. "I don't even know what that is!"

I examined the ogre.

Sharp-Elbows. Level 80.

Blah, blah, blah, basically a Necromancer.

This is Deckmaster Number Nine of Ten.

You want short descriptions? Okay, you little bitch. It's not like you're at a disadvantage when the descriptions are long. You know your perception of time slows during these moments? I could make one of these as long as a Zack Snyder film, and it wouldn't matter. I do that for you. Because of our special connection. And you don't appreciate it? Fuck you.

"Uh," I said, exchanging a look with Donut. "Can I get a little bit of a description?"

The AI paused and made an exasperated noise.

Loosely and half-assedly based on the rich and beautiful Ioway culture, this legendary creature has a really interesting backstory, but you don't want to hear it, do you? Suit yourself. I just hope you haven't killed too many of those turkeys. There's your description, you ungrateful little prick.

"Sharp-Elbows?" Donut asked. "What kind of name is that?"

"Fuck me," I said as I punted two more turkeys. They weren't swarming or going out of their way to attack, though they'd already filled in where the small bomb had detonated, stepping over and upon their dead companions. They'd only peck at us if we were right there. Still, we'd already killed a lot of them. I swallowed as I looked over the mass of turkey corpses.

We needed to get this done fast. And the last thing we needed was the damn AI mad at me on top of all that.

"Sorry I pissed you off," I said through gritted teeth as I stomped another turkey. I had sweat pouring down my temples. It was hot as shit in here. Hotter than the desert of the bubbles from the fifth floor.

I pulled a sticky bomb and hurled it at the ogre boss. *Bam!* The round bomb exploded in midair, halfway between us. The detonation tossed me back onto my ass, and pain swept across my chest. *Damnit.* I had no idea what was causing them to prematurely blow. Turkeys started idly pecking at me as I struggled to my feet, tossing them aside.

"Stop killing my food!" Sharp-Elbows screamed. She held a card up high. "This'll make you sorry, muskrat!"

"Oh yeah? Well, your face is already making me sorry. Watch this!" Donut summoned the card she'd stolen as both the ogre and Tom the turkey also summoned totems of their own.

Tom's first card slammed heavily into the ground. It was a large, well-muscled, shirtless humanoid with the head of a turkey, wearing an elaborate headdress made of brown, black, and white turkey feathers. It held on to a curved stick with a ball at the tip. I'd seen this sort of thing before, but I couldn't remember what they were called. It was some sort of native war club. Turkeys scattered as it appeared.

The totem's entrance procedure was an explosion of red and turquoise ribbons, which formed in the air above to display a giant eagle-looking thing before dissipating.

Good gravy, these guys are gooble-gobble crazy! It's a Turkey Temple Guard!

The thing ignored Skylar Spinach floating above it and just stood there, swinging its club back and forth like a baseball player getting ready to go to bat.

Wakinyan Temple Guard. Level 80.

Both Donut and Sharp-Elbows summoned the exact same thing at the same time. It was two more temple guards, but these guys had lizard heads instead of turkey heads. Sharp-Elbows had been planning on summoning two of them, but Donut had stolen one.

Both totems appeared, looking almost identical. The one Donut summoned carried a bow with a quiver of arrows, and the one the ogre summoned carried a long spear. Black and yellow confetti splattered all over the air, mirrored on both sides as the two opponents pulled themselves to their full height. These guys were slightly larger than the turkey guard. They, too, wore turkey-feather headdresses, but much more ornate. It looked more sinister when it was upon the head of the lizards.

There was another explosion and both guards did forward rolls, each stopping about twenty feet in front of each other.

The Tin Man had it all wrong! Ain't nothing gentle about these lizards.

Unk Tehi Temple Guard. Level 85.

Warning: This creature inflicts 20% more damage due to your Extinction Sigil.

"Shit," I muttered.

"Carl, what does that Tin Man thing mean?"

"I have no idea," I said as I pulled another hob-lobber. I needed to examine it before I threw it.

Warning: The current environment may cause this to explode prematurely. In fact, just holding it could be bad for your health. Watch this . . .

"Goddamnit," I said, quickly putting it away as a five-second timer appeared above it. It was the heat lamps. They *were* here on purpose, designed specifically to fuck with my bombs.

Donut only had one card in her hand, but another appeared, giving her two. The next one would come in just under eight seconds, thanks to her sailor hat.

The turkey guard roared and started jogging, making a line toward me. He let out a strangled gobble as Skylar Spinach swept down and smacked him with the tail. The guard turned and started shout-gobbling at the snake, jumping and swinging his club.

"Brother," Donut's lizard guard called, speaking to the other lizard. He nocked an arrow as he spoke. Smoke billowed all around, swirling in eddies, giving the whole barn an apocalyptic vibe. "I never liked you. Today we fight!"

"Today you die!" the other lizard screamed at his brother as he rushed toward him.

"Mother loved me more," Donut's lizard shrieked as he unleashed an arrow. It sailed over the other's head and passed through Sharp-Elbows, not striking the ogre at all.

As all this happened, the silent Tom tossed another card onto the field with the wave of his wing. A mystic card that floated in place. It turned to face us. It was a persistent mystic card, which meant it would take up a card slot as long as it remained active. Those were always powerful.

At this distance, I couldn't make out the art on the card, but sun rays burst from it, temporarily blinding.

Idolized!

And just like that, the tide turned against us.

All the turkey dots blinked red. Their gobbling resumed, just as quickly as it had stopped, the sound causing my heart to skip. I tossed a regular banger sphere at the ogre, and it embedded itself into the witch's shoulder with a wet *smack*. She didn't even falter.

Damnit. I was going to have to go over there and kill her the old-fashioned way. But I needed to deal with the turkeys first. I cast *Fear*, zeroing out my mana points to cast the level 11 spell at full strength.

The turkeys all screeched and started flapping and running away.

Tom tossed another magic card, which stayed persistent next to the Idolized card. A digital Christmas present appeared and then caught on fire.

The AI took on a mocking tone:

You'll shoot your eye out!

The fear icon over the turkeys all disappeared. They turned back toward us and surged.

"What the . . ."

Warning: All active magic has been dispelled. All minions and totems on your team have been muted from casting spells while the Ralphie card remains active.

By the way, have you realized yet that you're considered a minion during card battles? That's something you should probably pay attention to.

"Carl, we're in trouble!" Donut shrieked, slicing at the turkeys that came too close. She now stood atop the passed-out form of Mongo. She was waiting for more cards to play as she spun in a circle, swiping and hissing at turkeys.

The "idolized" turkeys weren't totems, which meant they'd be able to attack Donut directly. I dropped another smoke curtain and punted a few more of the large birds away. They were flapping and screeching, piling atop one another to get to us.

I had my *Protective Shell* ready to go as a last resort, but now I couldn't even cast it.

I pulled another banger sphere, one of my spiked ones, and I launched it at the boss turkey. It squawked angrily as it tried to dodge. The ball smacked into a wing, breaking it with an audible *crack. Yes,* I thought. I pulled another, but Tom dropped away from the high rafters, disappearing into the mass of angry turkeys surging toward us.

Crash!

Everyone stopped to turn. Light poured into the hot room as the distant end of the barn fell off the edge of the encroaching dirt cliff, tumbling away. The roof at the back of the barn sagged, and one of the heaters crashed to the ground, setting a few turkeys aflame. The feeding mechanism started sliding away, like a chain connected to a dropped anchor. The tube broke and yellow feed started spewing everywhere.

"Back, back away from Mongo, you disgusting birds," Donut continued to cry. She had angry turkeys all around her and Mongo, poking and scratching. I moved to help as another card appeared in Donut's hand. She immediately tossed it out.

Shi Maria. Relief flooded me as I watched the card spin and start to form. At the same moment, the turkey guard slammed Skylar Spinach with a lucky smack of his now-glowing club. The ghommid split in half. The snake half surged forward, circling around the surprised turkey guard as the donkey head fluttered into the air.

The harpsichord music from the Shi Maria entrance blasted across the playing field.

Sharp-Elbows tossed a snare card toward the spider just as she physically appeared.

GET BACK IN LINE!

Shi Maria howled in outrage as she was unceremoniously unsummoned from the playing field and put back into the deck.

"Hey!" Donut called. But Sharp-Elbows wasn't done yet. She tossed yet another card, her last for the moment. Another totem. Guitar music started to echo, just as loud as the now-stopped entrance music for Shi Maria.

I crunched a turkey with my foot, clearing the closest turkeys away from Donut and Mongo.

The Scavenger's Daughter has been fed. Unleash her wrath.

I paused, eyeing the glowing status bar in my HUD. Would it let me? I couldn't cast spells, but that was a skill.

As I pulled up the menu, the heavy guitar riff rose in volume. This wasn't just entrance music, but an actual song. "Psycho" by Muse. I only recognized it because my friend Sam would never stop listening to this album.

A small tree appeared, rising out of the ground, made of gnarled roots and leaves, twisting together and withering as it rose from the floor. Feathers and turkey claws erupted from it in various places. What appeared to be a black beating human heart hung off a branch at the top, like a fat, ripe apple. Atop the whole thing grew the shining golden skull of a large lizard. It had gems for eyes. Sharp-Elbows tossed her existing staff aside and grabbed the tree with two hands as digital laughing skulls and wraithlike ghosts danced about it. She yanked, and the tree pulled from the ground, spewing earthworms all over the floor. The turkeys around her started hungrily wolfing them up.

The staff glowed extra bright as the AI announced it.

Remember when you were extra naughty, and your daddy told you to go fetch his belt? This is kind of like that, but a lot more gross.

Combination of a mystic Necro card and a Walking Stick totem, it's the Worm Fulcrum!

Sentient Necro Staff. Level 50.

"Hey, that's not fair!" Donut called. "It's both a totem and a mystic card! And why isn't the music stopping?"

Sure enough, it was both. Usually totem cards dissipated when cast. This one remained hovering in place, taking up a spot like it was a perpetual mystic card. But the staff itself had health points and a timer over it, along with the totem indicator.

The jewels in the skull's eyes flashed bright as a purple light spread over the entire barn. All around us, the dead turkeys started to quiver.

"Goooobbbbbbllllle," came the deep, collective groan of the resurrected birds, rumbling the ground and mixing with the music. I punted the closest one.

Zombie Turkey. Level 10.

Zombie movie rules apply. You've been warned.

"Don't let any of them bite or peck you!" I cried. The turkey guard killed the snake half of Skylar Spinach as the donkey head kept unsuccessfully attempting to cast a spell. This was too much. We had to end this now.

The ogre tossed a card onto the lizard warrior as it grappled with Donut's temple warrior. They'd both dropped their weapons and were beating the shit out of each other. They'd rolled off to the side, far away from the action.

I spied the glow of Tom, still on the floor. The two mystic cards remained floating in front of the turkey, and he looked as if he was about to summon another. Next to me, Donut was distracted by the zombies, who, thankfully, were moving much more slowly than the living ones. She sliced at one with her claws as it moved to chomp onto the still-unconscious Mongo. She tossed a new card, but it was a **Stout**. She tossed it upon her stolen lizard temple warrior, who continued to scream about his mother.

I ran, moving toward Tom. I ducked, avoiding a swipe from the turkey guard, as I activated the Daughter's Kiss. It let me. I jumped up in the air, and I aimed my foot at the turkey deckmaster.

At the last moment, the turkey looked up at me.

"Gobble?" Tom asked.

Crash!

I felt like I'd just kicked a hole in the world.

I slammed into the ground, utterly obliterating the boss turkey and everything around it. A ring of turkeys—alive, dead, and zombie—flew off in all directions. In front of me, the north wall of the barn bowed out, like it had just been hit with an invisible truck. Above us, the roof sagged further. The ground under us was suddenly slanted, facing toward the closest cliff edge.

Everything started to slowly slide away.

Opponent Tom has been defeated.

The turkey guard poofed away, along with the Ralphie card. I scooped up the mangled corpse of Tom and tossed it into my inventory. I couldn't loot him yet, but if we lost his corpse, we were screwed. All the living turkeys returned to regular NPCs, no longer hostile. The zombie turkeys all remained red-tagged.

I had to lean to remain upright as the ground in the distance started to cascade off the cliff. I grasped on to a vertical pole that vibrated violently as the ground slid. We had to get the hell out of here.

The entire massive barn was going over the edge.

I downed a mana regen potion and cast *Fear* again, causing the NPC turkeys to all flee in every direction, though most of them started to bolt east toward the edge. The zombies, the ogre, and her lizard totem didn't appear affected.

"You fools! What have you done?" Sharp-Elbows shrieked, barely audible over the music.

The zombies, I realized, had been ignoring the regular turkeys up to this point. The moment they went from hostile back to regular NPCs, that changed. The zombies fell upon the regular turkeys, ripping at them as they all collectively slid toward the cliff. The damn things were everywhere. I jumped as one rolled past me.

A digital dog rushed past my leg, and I realized Donut had summoned yet another totem. She, too, had her back against a pole, her back claws dug precariously into the unconscious Mongo, anchoring him in place.

Above, the remaining donkey head half of Skylar Spinach moved to help with the fight between the two lizard guards, but it puffed away with a *Time's Up!* notification.

It's Lazarus-A-Bang-Bang!

I'd missed most of the entrance sequence in the chaos, but the robed figure stood there, looking over the battlefield. He leaned forward as turkeys flowed past him. His weapon this time was an RPG, and he put it to his shoulder, aiming toward the pair of fighting lizard guards, who continued to beat the crap out of each other against the far wall. They'd both time out in a few seconds.

"No!" I cried.

The rocket-propelled grenade arced toward the two fighting lizards, but the projectile detonated early, causing Lazarus and Donut to both fly back. More turkeys scattered as Mongo was dislodged and started to slide away, spinning with the bedding and the turkey pieces. He started to tumble toward the edge. He'd wake up in ten seconds.

Both of the lizard guard totems timed out at the same time. The cards flew back to their respective decks.

Sharp-Elbows, I realized, had also stumbled with the detonation, and she rolled toward us, barreling over turkeys as she rapidly approached, gaining speed, catching turkeys, both alive and undead, on her spikes.

I let go of the pole and sprinted toward Mongo as Donut shrieked after the sliding dinosaur. I jumped and grabbed him by the tail as we both continued to slide. We crashed against a pole as turkeys tumbled all around us, slamming into us like hail. The ground was getting steeper and steeper, and at any moment, the entire barn would reach the tipping point.

I activated Sticky Feet and planted a foot against the concrete brace for the pole while I clutched with my left arm. With my right, I bodily pulled Mongo toward me. He started to slip, feathers flying.

A zombie gobble-snapped at my face as it tumbled past. I ducked and let go with my left arm, using both to pull Mongo toward me just as he awakened.

Confused and scared, Mongo shrieked and jumped to his feet, his tail painfully ripping away from my hands. He leaped up and away, disappearing from sight, presumably up into the rafters. The edge of the cliff loomed. It was like a waterfall now. Donut remained anchored in the middle of the room, screaming at me. I looped my left arm back around the pole.

"Carl, look out!"

Where the hell was . . . *Ooof!*

The giant ogre, still clutching on to her magic staff, slammed into me like a truck. I screamed as the spikes impaled me in dozens of places. Some of the thick barbs still contained turkeys, who smooshed between us and exploded like gut-filled balloons, showering us both in gore.

Darkness fell over me.

The pain was unlike anything I had ever experienced. It felt as if I was being ripped in two.

I, somehow, remained attached to the pole with my left arm as I downed a Good Healing potion. The ogre clung to me like we were sewn together, heavy and wet against my chest.

Oh no, I thought in that moment. *Oh no.*

I was pierced in the arms, the stomach, the legs, the neck.

And my eyes. Both of my eyes. I was blind.

My health staggered up and down as the Good Healing potion fought to keep me alive. I downed another as soon as I could.

The wet, disfigured face of the ogre pressed up against mine, teeth to teeth. I could feel her grin. I could smell her rotted yellow teeth against my own, clinking together like we were forced into a locked kiss. The taste like that of rotted meat. There were things in her mouth. I felt them wriggling there, pressing against my teeth as I screamed with my mouth clenched closed.

"They starve us, you know," the ogre growled. She was whispering the words, and I felt them more than I heard them. She started to pull away, the spikes ripping out of me one by one, like Velcro being slowly pulled apart. I felt both of my eyes shift in my sockets, and I clenched, praying for them to remain.

"When we're not here, we are there," the ogre witch whispered. "And when we're there, they make certain the hunger festers. You can stop it. You can satiate us all, Carl."

Her face fully pulled away, releasing my eyes. I felt twists of tingling, thick gore linking us, like our bodies didn't want to separate.

Snap! The sound of cracking wood was loud in my ear.

The music instantly stopped.

"Master Carl, this insignificant cur is here to rescue you!" came the cry of Raul the crab. He'd just snapped the necro staff in half, killing her last totem. I drank a regular Heal, and I was relieved as my sight instantly returned, like the lights were flipped on. "I shall free you from this demon!"

The ogre face was right there, staring directly into my eyes, and they were pleading, sad, afraid.

I've seen those eyes before.

Raul snapped again, decapitating the deckmaster as she continued to peel away from me. The ogre's head spun off, plummeting as Raul also tumbled away in a rain of turkeys.

Combat Complete. Deck has been reset.

My health stuttered. I had a gaggle of debuffs, including **Woozy** and **Sore as Shit** and something called **Bonked**. The ring Pater Coal had secretly helped me "buy" at Club Vanquisher, the one disguised as my strength ring, burned. It was supposed to keep certain debuffs at bay, but I'd been warned it could get overloaded. But what could I do? I couldn't take it off. My breath came to me in ragged bursts. I was pierced in several places. The decapitated body still clung to me in a bear hug.

I was going to pass out.

I suddenly realized I was dangling in midair, my left arm still attached to a pole, my foot still stuck to the concrete base, which had been ripped from the ground. The whole pole remained attached to the skeleton of the barn's frame, which hung over the edge like an eave. I took a deep breath, and I pulled Sharp-Elbows's corpse into my inventory. The moment I did, the wounds opened back up, and blood spurted off from dozens of points like I was a goddamned showerhead.

"Donut!" I croaked, but she was right there, astride Mongo, right on the edge of the dirt and turkey waterfall. She flipped off Mongo and landed deftly on my shoulder. The pole bobbed up and down as it dangled precariously.

"Mongo, run!" Donut cried as she clutched to my shoulder. "Hang on, Carl. Three seconds!"

I passed out as I felt us *Puddle Jump* away. The last thing I heard was the crash of the rest of the barn collapsing over the edge and plunging into the ocean far, far below.

43

"CARL, I FEEL YOU'VE BEEN ASLEEP QUITE LONG ENOUGH," DONUT SAID as I groggily sat up.

I groaned. I'd been dreaming. Dreaming of the river, of me being swept away. Of those eyes. The eyes of the ogre as she died.

"How long was I out?"

Donut sat next to me, and she was completely covered in gore, but I could see she'd successfully cleaned off half her head, which meant I'd been out a while. She continued to furiously clean herself.

"Forty minutes! Really, Carl. You're always getting knocked out. You're really good at killing things, but you're only barely competent at not getting yourself killed. Who would've thought getting turned into a sieve comes with such a nasty set of debuffs? You let that porcupine lady stick her points in your eyeballs! And where did you get that ring? It's keeping most of the debuffs at bay, but I didn't realize it wasn't your strength ring until I saw it glowing. No, no, don't stand up yet. My goodness. You still have Woozy. I don't have the tokens, and the bodies tumbled off the edge, which means you need to go diving into the ocean to find the corpses. They're probably buried, too. So you need to get moving, but first we have to make sure that Woozy debuff goes away. I can't have you passing out while you're submerged. Honestly, though. I'm afraid the bodies might be hopelessly buried. If so, that means we'll fail the quest to get the key."

I could still taste the ogre on my lips. Those eyes. Holy shit. Where had I seen her before?

I coughed. "I have the bodies of both of them in my inventory. They have the tokens on them, but not their cards. Holy crap, that escalated quickly. You saved my life, Donut. Again. Thank you. I'm going to need a minute."

"You have the tokens already? Oh." She sounded almost disappointed.

We sat at the edge of the farm, along the cracked asphalt. The majority of the commercial barn had tumbled off the edge, but some of the supports of the structure remained, metal girders hanging off the edge of the ever-crumbling cliff like a clawed skeletal hand.

"Anyway, Carl. It escalated because you did that superhero jump with your back patch skill. You punched a hole in the entire mountain! Really, Carl. It was a little over-the-top. We're lucky Mongo didn't get bitten by a zombie turkey. They, by the way, didn't go away, so we have to be careful. They've gotten into the pigs, and now there's a bunch of zombie farm animals roaming everywhere. Have you ever heard a pig moan? It's quite distressing. I had to put Mongo away. Now wipe yourself off. You look like you were dragged through a pile of wet, disgusting corpses."

"I *was.*"

"Maybe so, but there's no reason to look like it. I suppose you should give me the tokens." I blinked over at Donut, who was still furiously cleaning herself. "Oh, and don't worry about the cards. Not only did I get them, but I made some changes to our deck. They were just floating there at the edge, and I grabbed them all. Miss Sharp-Elbows had a lot of cards, including some of our old favorites. No time to get into the details, but we have a new totem in the deck."

Donut was acting odd. She was being strangely . . . stiff, matter-of-fact, talking faster than usual. It wasn't so much *what* she was saying as *how* she was saying it. Something was wrong.

"Wait, what? A new totem? Who'd you get rid of?"

"Nobody! Remember that magical staff card? The one that ogre lady used to turn the dead turkeys all into zombies? That was in her deck. It's not consumable even though it's a special card, but either way it doesn't take up a totem slot, though it does take up a card slot while it's active. I have to imbue it with one of my spells before we start the fight, and if I do, I can cast that spell, but I can only do it once. The staff itself works like a totem, and it looks different depending on what spell it's holding."

"That's good," I said. "If you use *Clockwork Triplicate*, you can make three Shi Marias or three Jolas."

"That's what I was thinking. I've already set it up, and it works. I had to have a quick fight with a group of zombie turkeys while you were out, and I summoned my deck and tried it out. I used it on Geraldo, and they all started fighting each other until I yelled at them. But it worked!"

"Good, good." My head was starting to clear. "What else did you get?"

"We got another Combo card, but it's a unique! Isn't that great? It's called **Golden Combo**. It works the same way as last time, but it's not consumable, so we can do it over and over! Imagine the possibilities!"

"Donut," I said, finally sitting up. "Why are you talking like—"

"Anyway," she said, cutting me off, "I was thinking maybe I can do this last fight by myself. With those new cards, I'm pretty much indestructible."

I blinked. "Is that a joke?"

"Not even a little bit. Look, Carl. The fight is right over there. There's a vending machine, and I pop the tokens in, the trailer opens up, and I go inside. I have a short, quick, easy fight, and I'll be right back out with the key. It'll be nothing. You just sit here and rest."

I just looked at her, not saying anything.

"Or, you know," she continued, "we can just skip the last fight and go see someplace new for the last part of the . . ." She trailed off.

"Donut, you'd rather us fight other crawlers than get the key?"

"I . . ." She paused, and she deflated. "No, I suppose not."

I took a breath. I was finally starting to realize what was going on. I held out my arm, and she jumped into my lap.

"Donut, do you remember on the last floor when you first saw it was Ferdinand, and I freaked out? I wanted nothing more than to skip the Butcher's Masquerade and just go down the stairs."

"I do remember, Carl. I also remember you later saying you wished you *had* gone down the stairs."

I nodded. "I do wish we'd figured out a way to avoid that last fight. But if we had, even more people would've died." I paused as she leaned into my chest. She looked up at me, and her face took up all of my vision. "How do you know who it is, anyway?"

She blinked a few times. "Uh, well, it's two things, really. The first you'll have to see for yourself. But the second is the motorcycle. It's the same one you were offered in the prize carousel on the fourth floor. It has that big dent in it. I remember how it affected you when you saw it. You didn't say anything at the time, but I knew you recognized it. And now that same motorcycle is sitting outside of that trailer over there, and I just know he's going to be in there. You're always saying not to let them have the satisfaction, Carl. I'm trying to be more like you."

I pulled Donut into a tight hug. "Thank you," I said.

I mentally prepared myself, and I stood all the way up as Donut transferred to my shoulder. "You know what? It's okay. They're doing this to everybody. We have to get it over with. And don't try to be like me, Donut. You need to be like you."

Donut sighed as she settled onto my shoulder. "I suppose you're right. I don't know what I was thinking."

"Good girl. Now come on. Let's go say hi to Dad."

44

SOMETIMES, THINGS ARE EXACTLY WHAT THEY SEEM TO BE.

Sometimes, there are no surprises, and despite that, despite your intention to gird yourself against what's about to come, it still hits you with the force of a kick to the stomach.

I had to take out a zombie turkey, multiple zombie chickens, and an undead pig as we walked up the street. The entire north side of the floating chunk of Iowa was covered with the monsters. Donut said they were sliding off the edge and falling to the ocean far below. I knew some were probably landing on the thin strip of Florida also, meaning we'd likely be dealing with more zombies later, no matter what happened today. Donut wouldn't stop bitching about them.

"They really need to stop recycling plotlines," Donut was saying as we walked up to the trailer. "What is with the undead hordes? We had the ghouls during the Iron Tangle, those undead-body-part monsters at the end of the last floor, not to mention all the vampire forest creatures, oh, oh, and the ghommid village. That was just a few days ago! And now we have zombie farm animals? I mean, really. Whoever is coming up with this crap needs a new trick. It's like a guy at a bar using the same annoying pickup line over and over. It didn't work the first time, so why keep trying it? It's pitiful, really."

"You shouldn't complain about things we can easily beat, Donut. Especially not out loud."

"I know, I know, Carl, but it's not like they don't know this already. The Posse loves speculating on cool monsters we should fight, and they're starting to get tired of the undead things. I want to kill more dogs. Do you know how long it's been since I killed a dog? It's been ages. My numbers are always great after I kill a dog."

She was trying to distract me. I was formulating a response when I saw it, and the reality of what was about to happen finally hit me.

"Fuck me," I said, seeing the motorcycle.

It was sitting right there in the yard of the dilapidated single-wide trailer. It wasn't the only thing out here. The whole place was a junkyard. There was a broken-down Ford truck with only three tires, a rotted couch, an old dishwasher, plus what looked like a regular old-school soda vending machine. The soda machine was covered with weeds and dirt like everything else in the yard.

Instead of a logo for Coke or Pepsi, the machine featured the profile silhouette of a man I immediately recognized.

Under the image were the words **One Fight for Nine Tokens.**

Under it was an asterisk mark with tiny letters that read: **Warning: Once activated, you may leave the zone, but if you do, you will need to deposit nine more tokens to reactivate.** And under that, in even smaller letters was: **By the way, there are only nine tokens available in this whole area. So if you leave, you're pretty much fucked.**

"I thought it was a fatter version of you with a mustache until I saw the motorcycle," Donut said. "It's only a shadow, but he looks just like you, Carl. The nose is quite identical. It's eerie, really."

I felt as if I couldn't breathe, and I was doing my best to hide it. "Don't ever say that again."

"Does he really have a mustache? Did he work in porn? It's no wonder you didn't have any pictures of him."

"Sometimes," I said. "To the mustache part, not the porn. Whenever he was getting ready to go out on one of his motorcycle weekend trips, he'd grow it out." I instinctively reached up and grabbed my own face, which I still shaved every day. "He could grow one out really fast."

"Well, it doesn't appear he's ridden that thing in a long time," Donut said, looking over the dirty motorcycle.

"You know what?" I said, looking over the yard. My eyes focused on the green weeds growing up around the tires of the motorcycle. At the flowers. "You're right. This is wrong. All of this is wrong."

"What do you mean?"

I gestured behind me. "Everything here was covered in snow just a few hours ago. It melted because it was transferred here to Florida. This trailer and the entire yard are different. Look at the grass. Look at all the dust on the truck and motorcycle."

"Hey," Donut said. "You're right! They're cheating! And this is different than the zombie turkey barn. That had snow on it! And look over there where the yard ends!"

I looked at where she was pointing, and there was a pile of kids' bicycles in the overgrown yard adjoining the neighboring trailer. One of the bikes was cut in half. The half that had been in the neighbor's yard was gone, and the front half remained in the yard here, sliced off like it had been cut with a precision laser. I looked over the bikes, remembering. When I was a kid, everyone would roam the neighborhood in packs, but I never had a bike, and I'd chase after them on foot, always getting left behind. I never had friends, not lasting ones. I always blamed it on not having a bike.

I looked over at the neighboring trailer, and one of the same bikes from the pile was leaning up against the side of the wall. It was literally the exact same bike, complete with the same pink-and-white Spider Gwen stickers.

"This yard and trailer are not from Christmas. They *are* cheating. This little spot is from a different time. Earlier, but not by much. Maybe sometime in the summer. It's spliced in."

An ominous feeling washed over me. Why would they do that?

It's because they want you to see something. Something specific they caught on their magic cameras.

I walked over and rubbed my hand across the dirty and cracked leather seat of the motorcycle. The bike had Georgia plates that'd expired years before. I knew nothing about these things, but I did know there was something special about this one. It was a collector's item, and if it had been in good condition, it'd be worth a lot of money. It was a Harley-Davidson 1965 FLH Electra Glide Panhead. I didn't know what any of that meant, but I knew this was the last year of some type of configuration and the first year of something else. He'd never shut up about it. This damn thing was his prized possession.

I reached down and picked up the motorcycle. I lifted it easily. I remembered that day I'd accidentally knocked it over. How heavy it had been. I pulled it into my inventory.

To my surprise, it didn't stick itself in the temporary category like everything else from this floor. It went into the same spot as the two pieces of the Royal Chariot, the bicycles, the kayak, and a few other odds and ends. **Shitty Transportation Items.**

"If we loot stuff from here, I think we get to keep it," I said.

I looked around the yard again, this time more carefully. There was a clear line where the ground changed, where this little section had been added in. It was a rectangle about twenty feet all around the trailer, stopping a few feet into the yard of each of the neighbors. There were other things cut in half. A rake. What looked like part of a fallen-over fence, though both halves remained. The winter half had shifted an inch over to the side.

My eyes caught a line of flowerpots dotting one clean side of the yard, up against the south, flat end of the trailer. The first, biggest pot contained purple round clusters of flowers, and they were carefully potted and taken care of. There were little signs in each pot, but I couldn't read them from here. My dad would never have done that. I swallowed at the implication. I took a step forward to examine them further, but I hit an invisible wall, smushing my face against nothing. Behind me, the vending machine made a chime.

"Put the tokens in, Donut. And let Mongo out."

WARNING: THE FIGHT WILL NOT COMMENCE FOR FORTY-TWO MINUTES and thirty seconds.

A countdown timer appeared in my interface.

Warning: This area exists in a different time instance than the remainder of this floor.

Warning: Physical interactions in this area act differently than other locations on this floor.

What the hell does that mean?

The warnings came the moment I touched the flimsy door on the side of the trailer. I'd cleaned out the yard, taking everything I could pick up, including the old washing machine, several kids' bikes of various sizes, and all the pieces of rusty crap. I couldn't quite lift the Ford truck all the way, though I felt as if I should be able to. I wished we had more time. I did manage to lift one end, and I thought if I could possibly jack it up, I might be able to get under it and lift it long enough to take it. This one had Iowa plates, and the registration was surprisingly up-to-date, despite the missing tire. If we had more time, I would've stripped the whole vehicle clean, including the engine to give to Katia.

The flowerpots were all labeled. The handwriting was elegant and feminine. The purple flowers in the big pot that'd caught my eye were called alliums. There were daffodils, asters, hyacinths, and several others. Next to it was a well-organized shed filled with gardening supplies and bags of soil. I took them all.

Also on the back side of the trailer was another surprise. Half of an old minivan sitting in a parking spot. It was cut down the middle, front to back, and it was leaning over, fluid spilled all around it. The winter half wasn't there at all. The engine was cut right in half. I tried picking the whole thing up, and crap started falling off of it. I took it all, but it was mostly junk.

Donut remained silent on my shoulder while I did all this, though she did jump down and land upon Mongo as I took all the minivan pieces. The dinosaur had eyes on what looked like a zombie cow wandering down the street. The zombie was leaving us alone, and we warned Mongo against chasing after it. If he left the yard, he wouldn't be allowed back in.

There was other stuff here, on the far side of the yard. Stuff I didn't want to think about. Donut saw it, too, and said nothing.

I couldn't take it anymore. I reached up and touched the door sitting there next to the carport, and that was when I received the warnings.

"What?" Donut asked. "Why is there a timer? Carl, what does that mean?"

A strange numbness had fallen over me. It was like I was watching this all play out on a screen, and it wasn't really happening. "There's a reason they made it from a different time, Donut. They want us to watch something. We can't leave, so we might as well get it over with."

"But what does that last warning mean?"

"I'm about to find out. You stay back until I call you in."

"Carl?"

"Yeah."

"You can just wait out here with me. You don't have to go in there."

"I know. Thank you. But I need to do this. You wait, okay?"

Donut hesitated. "Okay, Carl."

The ground rumbled as a distant cliff crumbled into the ocean far below.

I entered the house, and I closed the door behind me.

45

AND THEN THERE HE WAS. RIGHT THERE IN THE LIVING ROOM.

"Holy shit," I muttered.

It was him. My father. I hadn't seen him in over twelve years, not since that day, and there he was.

There's this scent one associates with their parents. You don't even think about it until you've been away for so long, and it returns, towing unwelcome memories with it, shoving them at you all at once. That scent was here, burned into the thin walls. I don't even know what that smell was. It was a strange, but subtle musk that only clung to him. It was here in this trailer, but it wasn't alone. It was faint, mixed with the antiseptic scent of a dying man.

He was in a hospital bed, which was parked right there in the middle of the room. There was nobody in here except him. There weren't any monitors or diodes or anything I'd normally associate with someone in such a state, with the exception of a single IV bag that dangled off a pole attached to the bed. The saline bag was almost done, and the clear tube snaked into his arm. The man was swallowed by that large bed. He was awake, back elevated, slitted eyes fixed on the television screen, which was showing a baseball game.

The room had obviously been recently rearranged for this setup. The couch was pushed all the way to the side up against an old, cheap entertainment console with the television facing the bed. A small dinette table was on its sides, legs folded in with four chairs stacked up against it near the refrigerator to make room.

All the windows had purple curtains featuring that same flower upon them. Alliums.

My dad had always been a big guy, though I'd eventually grow to be much bigger than him. Still, when I remembered him, he was always huge, larger than life. The silhouette outside on that stupid vending machine. Not this. Not this shell.

This is it? This is what I've been afraid of?

He was sick. He was dying. The man weighed maybe 140 pounds, easily 80 pounds lighter than he'd been in his prime. His hair, which he'd always dyed brown, was mostly gone, now just gray sickly wisps upon his head. His skin had taken on a deep yellow tone and was mottled with spots.

Twelve years. It looked as if it had been forty.

Still, the man was awake. Lucid, watching the television. It was a Seattle Mariners game, and they were playing Baltimore. It was the sixth inning, and Seattle was getting stomped. My father's eyes darted back and forth as he watched. I'd seen that look so many times. His hand clutched on to the remote, curled in the same way he used to hold a bottle of beer as he watched. There was a row of Band-Aids on the back of his yellow hand. His skin looked almost translucent, somehow plastic, like it would crinkle if I touched it.

He hadn't shaved in some time, and a patchy bone white beard had formed over his gaunt face.

"You pussy," he said to the television screen. "You goddamn, worthless pussies. Pathetic." He lifted the remote up and attempted to shut off the screen, but the remote slipped from his grip. He tried again, and this time he managed to shut it off. His hands shook.

He just sat there for a moment in the silence, breathing heavily.

DONUT: CARL, ARE YOU OKAY?

CARL: Yes. Give me a few minutes.

I couldn't look away. What had happened? How'd he get here to Iowa? I had so many questions.

"Are you just gonna sit there and stare at me, or are you gonna ask what you wanna ask?"

I almost jumped from my skin.

But then I saw who he was really talking to.

The small boy appeared, head emerging from around the hallway that led to the back bedrooms. Maybe six years old.

Goddamnit, I thought. *God-fucking-damnit.* I'd been holding out hope until that moment. But the instant I saw him, I knew. There were toys out there in the yard. I was hoping maybe my father had met a woman who already had children.

But no. That nose. Those eyes. That hair. My mom always complained my dad's genes were so dominant, anyone remotely related to him was doomed to look just like him. The boy took one hesitant step into the room, but he remained behind the hospital bed, hidden so my father couldn't turn and look directly upon him. I couldn't take my eyes off the boy. The poor kid looked as if he was going to bolt at any moment.

"You turned off the TV," the boy said. "Can I watch now?"

"No. I need to rest. But go get me my cigarettes."

The boy stood there, frozen.

Move, or I'll make you move, boy.

"Move, or I'll make you move, boy."

"I . . . I don't know where they are. Mommy took them. You're not allowed."

"Tell your mother I want to talk to her."

"She went next door."

"Go into my room. Open the bottom dresser drawer on the left. There's a pack there. Bring it."

The boy didn't answer. He turned and ran away into the dark hallway.

"Asher! Get back here, you little shit!"

Asher, I thought. *His name is Asher.*

DONUT: A LADY JUST APPEARED OUT OF NOWHERE. SHE'S IN THE YARD. SHE WALKED THROUGH ME, AND HER CLOTHES DIDN'T GO AWAY. DO YOU THINK THAT'S WHAT THE WARNING MEANT? I THINK SHE'S WORKING ON THE FLOWERPOTS, BUT I CAN'T TELL BECAUSE YOU TOOK THEM. OTHER THAN THE CLOTHES THING, IT'S JUST LIKE WITH THE REGULAR

MEMORY GHOSTS. SHE WENT TO THE SHED AND GRABBED SOMETHING, AND NOW IT LOOKS LIKE SHE'S SCOOPING SOMETHING UP THAT ISN'T THERE.

CARL: Okay. Warn me when she moves toward the door.

DONUT: SHE HAS A TATTOO OF A DOG ON HER NECK. A DOG TATTOO. ON HER NECK. I THINK IT'S A PIT BULL. IT'S ABSOLUTELY SICKENING.

CARL: Be nice. I think that's my stepmom.

DONUT: SHE CAN'T BE YOUR STEPMOM, CARL. SHE'S LIKE KATIA'S AGE.

My hands shook as I took another step into the room. There was a curio cabinet here covered with Precious Moments figurines and a few framed photographs. I slowly started to gather everything except the photographs, which seemed wrong to take. There was also an urn, which I realized contained the remains of a dog named "Chance." Likely the same dog who was tattooed on the woman's neck. I took it.

Only two photos featured my father. One was of a wedding. I stared at it. Sure enough, the woman was younger, much younger, barely older than me, and she held hands with my father as they both laughed. My dad was in his full biker gear, complete with a bandanna on his head and his leather vest. It appeared they were in some dive bar surrounded by other biker guys.

I could see the neck tattoo in the photo. The woman was about-to-pop pregnant. She wore a crown of large purple flower clusters in her hair. Alliums.

The second photo was of my dad staring forward with a one-year-old Asher on his lap. This was more like the man I remembered. Humorless, eyes a million miles away. Cold, uncaring.

There were multiple photos featuring just the boy. I picked one up, the most recent. Behind me, my father coughed, reminding me he was there, right there. I ignored him for the moment as I stared at the photograph. Brown hair that looked like it was enough for two people. Thick and haphazard and untamable. Blue eyes. That nose.

Asher.

Asher.

My brother.

I had a brother.

Goddamn you, I thought.

Was that why they brought me here? To show me that they'd taken something I didn't even know I had? To show me what I'd truly lost?

DONUT: THE LADY IS ACTING WEIRD. SHE PULLED SOMETHING OUT OF ONE OF THE FLOWERPOTS, BUT I CAN'T SEE IT BECAUSE YOU TOOK IT ALREADY. SHE'S HOLDING IT AGAINST HER CHEST AND CRYING.

I took the photo and placed it into my inventory. I turned and faced the man, who remained in the bed, sitting up, staring off into space.

Kids aren't always a product of their parents. But sometimes that doesn't matter. Sometimes parents can cast a shadow so thick, you can drown in it.

Frank had said that to me right before he handed me the Ring of Divine Suffering. He'd died soon thereafter.

"You know," I said to the man who couldn't hear me, "I used to be so scared of disappointing you, and I don't even know why."

DONUT: SHE'S SMOKING A CIGARETTE NOW, PACING BACK AND FORTH. WAIT, SHE THREW IT AWAY AND IS NOW HEADED TOWARD THE DOOR!

Behind me, the door opened, and the woman walked in.

I blinked, staring at her. She was tall, thin. Hollow eyes. Uncombed black hair dangled off her head. Nails that had once been painted red, but they were chipped and faded. She was wearing nurse scrubs. Nothing like the laughing, smiling woman in the wedding photograph.

She looked nothing like my mother, either. Yet . . . yet she was her twin all the same.

"Where have you been? I need my boost."

"I was next door helping Mrs. Tomlinson. I'll get your medicine."

The woman didn't even look at him as she pushed past and went to the back, exuding the stench of cigarettes. She was holding something behind her back so he wouldn't see. I couldn't see it, either, as it was invisible to me, meaning whatever this was, I'd already taken it. The woman's hands were shaking. She had tears rolling down her face.

"I'm your husband," he tried to call, though he couldn't truly shout, revealing how weak he really was. "I'm the one you're supposed to be taking care of." He coughed a few times and started muttering. From the hallway, I could hear the woman talking softly to Asher, telling him to stay in his room.

I moved into my inventory, and I started examining the flowerpots I'd taken from the yard.

I understood then why they'd really brought me here, what they wanted me to witness.

CARL: Zev, is this even real? How long did it take you assholes to find this? How do you even have it? Did you just record everything?

ZEV: I'm sorry, Carl. You know I can't give you details. But I assure you everything you've seen so far is indeed a recording of what really happened that day. Everything until the timer reaches zero. I can't tell you more than that.

I glanced at the timer. I stepped forward, and I leaned in super close to the man's face.

This close, the scent was amplified. A part of me registered I'd never been this close to him, this close to his eyes, his mouth. How was that possible? He was my father. Shouldn't my memory be filled with his face?

But no. This was it. The closest I'd ever been. It seemed important.

I moved to whisper into his ear.

"You're a bully. Nobody likes you. Mom tried to kill you, and in about 20 minutes, I'm pretty sure your new wife, my stepmother, is going to finish the job. You're so goddamn insufferable, she can't even wait for whatever this is to kill you off. Two different women, and they both try to kill you? What does that say?"

He sat there, staring off into space. His death was so close, and he had no idea.

"And you know what? Your passing is so unimportant, so insignificant that nobody will care. The only reason I'm here now to watch this is because the idiots running this shit show think I'm going to buckle under the pressure of seeing you, of finally confronting this big bad monster from my childhood. But here's the thing, old man. I've grown up. I'm not scared of shadows anymore. Not when I've seen what's really out there. And seeing you here today, seeing you like this, it's actually a good thing. You're about to die. You're broken, you're alone, and you're a nobody. My only regret is that you lived long enough to inflict yourself onto my poor brother. If I'm lucky, the assholes will resurrect your corpse and turn you into a boss so I can kill you again."

I straightened my back, and I turned away, facing the back hallway.

"I'm not even going to stay for this last part. Not your real death. You don't deserve for anybody to watch you die."

The woman reappeared, holding a syringe and a new IV bag. "I have your medicine right here."

"It's about time."

"Yes," she said. "Yes, it is."

I MOVED TO ASH'S ROOM WHILE MY STEPMOTHER INJECTED MY FATHER with a lethal dose of morphine.

I wasn't sure exactly what the plan was, or why she'd been hiding the little glass bottles of morphine in the big flowerpot outside. That didn't really matter.

I moved into the small room of the boy. He was curled up on his bed. He had a Matchbox car, and he idly ran it up and down the wall.

"I'm so sorry I didn't know about you," I said. "If I had, I would've been here. I would've made sure you were okay. In a few months, something is going to happen, something really terrible. Hopefully you'll be asleep in your bed when it happens. It's too late for me to do anything about that, but I want you to know something. You won't be forgotten. Not ever."

I reached forward, and I put my hand on his head, but my hand went all the way through.

I wiped my eyes, and I proceeded to loot the room. He didn't have much, just a few toys, a few pairs of pants and shirts. I found an old heart-shaped candy box, and it had a shiny rock in it, two dollars, and a little plastic cowboy. Part of me was hoping there was a picture of me somewhere here, some sign that he knew he had a brother somewhere. There was nothing. I left the box with his prized possessions. I took the rest, including some crayon drawings, mostly of airplanes and storm clouds with lightning destroying whole cities with their fury. I looked at the black swirls of crayon.

He's scared of lightning. Of storms.

As I finished, the woman came into the room.

"Come here, Ash," she said to the boy, and she took him into a hug as she sat on the bed.

"He wouldn't let me watch TV," my brother said.

"It's okay. He's resting now. You just stay with me for a few minutes, and then you're going to go over to Mrs. Tomlinson's house. You can go play with Elizabeth, and tomorrow we're having your birthday party."

"Am I going to get a bike? And cake?"

She smiled, big tears rolling down her face. "We'll see, honey."

WITH FIVE MINUTES LEFT, I MOVED TO THE MASTER BEDROOM, NOT wanting to eavesdrop anymore. While I was in there, I proceeded to take everything I could. From the living room, I could hear my father say something, desperation in his raspy, slurred voice. Nobody was there to answer him, nobody there to hear his final words.

The first thing I did was move to the bottom left drawer of the old dresser. I took three packs of Marlboro Reds. I picked up a folder filled with court documents. I took it without looking at it. He also had a 9mm Glock, which I took along with two boxes of ammo. I also found the keys to the motorcycle and the Ford truck. After that, I just picked up the whole dresser with its mirror, and I took it all into my inventory. I took the queen bed, the cheap bedside tables, all the clothes. There were more photos on the walls, mostly of Asher, and I left those, but I took everything else. He'd only had the single gun.

There was also an arcade cabinet, sitting right there in the too-small room, taking up too much space. It was unplugged and had clothes draped over it. It wasn't *Frogger*, but *Centipede*. I took it into my inventory.

That was it. I had his gun, his motorcycle, and his goddamned arcade cabinet. The only other thing he had left was his life, and that, too, would soon be gone.

With just a minute left, I took out a cigarette and lit it. I returned to the living room, moving past my motionless father. I paused, not looking at him. I took my lighter, and I lit the drapes with the purple flowers on fire.

I paused, and I looked up at the ceiling.

"If your intention was to hurt me, you fucked it all up. This was pretty much exactly what I needed to see."

I returned outside to find Donut sitting upon Mongo, waiting patiently.

"Are you okay?" Donut asked.

The timer has concluded. You may now proceed inside to face the key holder.

I cracked my neck. "I'm okay."

"You're sure?"

"I said yes, Donut."

"Good. That means I can tell you to get that disgusting cigarette out of your mouth."

I laughed as Mongo screeched.

"Just give me a second, okay?"

She looked suspiciously at the door. "Do you know what we're going to face in there?"

"No," I said. "But I do know what we're not going to face."

I sighed, and I tossed the cigarette away. It tasted old, and it tasted wrong.

The window cracked, and flames burst out, reaching out into the sky, black smoke billowing upward and away into heavens that weren't really there.

"And we're not going to do it in there. It's way too cramped for our totems, so first we're going to watch this goddamned trailer burn to the ground."

46

<Note added by Crawler Milk. 6th Edition>

Holy underworlds on high. That last fight . . . I can't even describe it. What the fuck? What the fuck? What the fuck?

IT DIDN'T TAKE LONG FOR THE OLD TRAILER TO BURN. MY VIEW COUNTER was spiked all the way to the right, despite me recently adjusting it upward. My chat was filled with people who were currently facing similar circumstances, all having to watch moments from their life—none older than a year or so, I noted. No crawlers I knew had actually gotten to the fight part yet. They all had timers similar to our own, but it appeared ours was the only one that had run out. Donut and I would be the first to find out what happened next.

Right as the roof of the trailer collapsed, shooting flames and sparks into the sky, a red dot appeared in the middle of the conflagration. There was just one.

We stepped back, about as close to the edge as we could get. Donut cast *Clockwork Triplicate* on Mongo as I peppered the yard with various traps, circling the whole area several times.

Donut kept asking me if I was okay, and I did my best to assure her I was. She was worried about me, worried about this fight. She was terrified of what was about to happen, more than she was letting on.

I didn't tell her about Asher. I wasn't certain why, especially after I promised him he wouldn't be forgotten. There would be time for that.

I couldn't stop thinking about him. It was strange, part of me recognized, that I barely cared about what had just happened with my dad. But that kid. Jesus. What had happened to them? This whole scene had played out around June or July of last year. What had happened to him afterward? I prayed he and his mother were asleep somewhere when it all went down.

I was terrified they'd actually use my brother as the boss, which would be ridiculously fucked-up. They weren't allowed to do that anymore, not with children, but it was clear they cared little about the rules at this point. Part of me really was hoping it would be my father, but it was clear he'd actually died before the collapse. Did that matter? These . . . replicants, whatever they were, weren't actually the real versions, not if they'd been smushed in the collapse. I remembered what Odette had told us about the walk-on list, where they took people who'd survived the collapse. They would've used Bea as Queen Imogen, given the opportunity. *That* would've really been her.

No matter what we were about to face, it wouldn't be the real thing. I kept telling myself that over and over.

I had my dad's Glock out, and I turned it over in my hands, examining it. He'd taken pretty good care of it. My dad always had guns, but he'd never let me touch them. Despite that, I knew my way around firearms pretty well. I never kept one in the apartment once I moved in with Bea. She actually wanted to get one for herself, but the thought of her with a gun was terrifying.

Donut sniffed at it suspiciously. "You can't use a gun, Carl. You're not a gun guy. Do you even know how to fire it?"

"Yes, Donut. I did have training in boot."

"I thought you said you weren't really in the Navy."

"I wasn't. We've gone over this like a million times. I was in the Coast Guard."

"And they let you have guns? Why? Did the coast ever shoot at you?"

"Donut, coasties used their weapons way more . . . You know what? It doesn't matter." I sighed. "I can't use this thing anyway. This came from outside the dungeon, which means it's not as strong as everything else. If I tried pulling the trigger, the whole thing would probably explode. It'd wreck the barrel at the very least. The rounds are overpowered once I handle them, and these things can only handle so much pressure. I'll have to take the whole thing into my bomber's studio and adjust the yield on each individual round, and even then it'll be different if I fire it versus someone else."

Donut continued to examine it closely. "I wish *I* could take it." She gasped. "I could get a pink holster and wear my cowboy hat. Can you imagine? Too bad it's not one of those guns with the spinning-barrel thingy. Oh, well. You should give it to Florin. He's a gun guy."

"Last I heard, Florin is rolling around Nigeria with an APV. He doesn't need a non-magical pistol. I'll find a use for it eventually." I put the gun away.

ZEV: Hang on, guys, something weird is happening. We just got locked out of all our controls. We'll get your menus back up.

I exchanged a look with Donut. Everything appeared normal on my end.

DONUT: MY MENUS ARE WORKING FINE.

ZEV: Strange. My board basically says you've been locked out.

I took a step back. "Put your headset back on. And remember the plan. Watch where you stand. Take the invisibility potion."

Donut had a line of potions sitting on the ground behind her, buried in random places in the ground, corks off. She couldn't drink out of her inventory during card combat, but she could reach down and drink one manually.

The magical microphone popped into place on Donut's head just before she turned into a translucent outline.

Combat Started.

The trailer walls closest to us collapsed inward in a shower of sparks and flames, revealing the charred husk of the hospital bed, the refrigerator and oven from the kitchen I never got to loot, and a few other odds and ends.

Standing upon the flaming hospital bed was our opponent. The key master. The thing was bigger than the bed, and it barely fit atop it. Its multiple heads rose into the air now that it was no longer confined to the trailer.

It started to scream. All eight or nine heads on it. All at the same time.

"Carl, what in god's name is that?" Donut cried with her amplified voice, backing up. I could see her fur was all poofed out despite the invisibility. "Is that . . . is that Miss Beatrice's *mother*? Where'd she come from?" She gasped. "Sugar Cube?"

"Really?" I asked at the air as the hospital bed collapsed under the weight of the thing. It slurped off the flaming remains of the bed and started to shuffle toward us. It was clearly unaffected by the fire. "What the hell is this bullshit?"

CARL: Mordecai, quick. Best way to kill a hydra. One with human heads. Err, one cat head, too.

The large creature stopped, sitting upon a flaming hunk of wall, continuing to wail. A group of cards formed in front of it. The cards were small, hovering in front of a single head.

Mongo and the two clockwork copies stopped and looked at Donut nervously, waiting for instructions.

The thing was . . . a blob of flesh with multiple screaming heads, all on long, fleshy stalks similar to the stretchy neck on Shi Maria. The monster was the same sort of creature as a shambling berserker, though those things had all been made of random piles of body parts all splatted together. This was a round flesh thing covered in Frankenstein stitches, deliberately sewn together to form a fleshy round ball with four comically small legs at the bottom, like the body of a stumpy, overinflated juvenile elephant. The body was about six and a half feet tall and twice as wide.

The necks all sprouted upward, waving and weaving around each other, screaming. Each individual head was labeled with a name, but they were moving and intertwining so quickly, it was impossible to read them. Still, I recognized most of the faces.

I focused on the youngest face. Asher. My brother.

"You can't do this," I cried as I readied a pair of sticky hob-lobbers. I took an invisibility potion of my own.

My dad wasn't a part of the hydra, but I knew most of the people here. One head was Asher's mother—my stepmother. I caught the name, and it was Tami-Lynn. Another was my friend Monobrow Sam. Next to him was Bea's goddamned mother. There was a white Persian cat I didn't recognize, its head like a dandelion at the end of a stalk. This was clearly one of Donut's relatives. Apparently this was "Sugar Cube." Next was Dick, my weird supervisor from work. Then my landlord, Mr. Roth. Another was a woman from work who did billing and whose name I couldn't remember. She'd gotten fired a few months back for some unknown reason. The last was an older man I didn't recognize at all. He was in his seventies and had blue hair with pink-rimmed glasses.

This last guy with the blue hair was the one with the cards floating in front of him. He stopped screaming as he examined his hand.

Donut hissed. "Carl, Carl, it's Judge Lucian!" She increased her volume. "We meet again, Lucian!"

Lucian opened his mouth as if to yawn. A ring of smoke poofed out.

You've been deshrouded!

Next to me, Donut's invisibility popped off. Several miniature explosions danced across the field. It was all our planted potions exploding. Thankfully, the traps themselves weren't activated.

"Goddamnit," I said out into the ether. "He's the goddamned deckmaster, and that was a spell! That was a cheat!"

The world stopped. Pounding music started to play, a fast-paced techno dance theme.

B-B-B-B-Boss Battle!

Ultimate Card Boss Showdown!

Portraits of the nine individual heads slammed into place, floating high above the creature. I could read the names now. The woman from my work was Sally. Judge Lucian—I was assuming a cat show judge—was the leader.

Ladies and gentlemen, we have a surprise opponent for you tonight! The original boss for this battle was going to be Carl's deceased

father, who really had three smaller creatures inside of him wearing his skin like kids in a trench coat. Fuck that noise. I do what I want.

Our portraits slammed into place.

Versus!

The description of the monster was read out loud by the AI, and the words also appeared floating like they usually did. Even though the AI was addressing me in the description, everybody in the universe could see this entire exchange, and for the first time, I had the sense the AI was actually talking out to the universe and not just me.

The Reminiscence Hydra of Malicious Compliance!

Made especially for the Royal Court of Princess Donut.

Level 125 City Boss.

Nine of nine heads still intact.

Right about now, you're probably asking yourself, "What the heck are they smoking to come up with this thing?" This is a classic monster from the very early days of *Dungeon Crawler World*. On the third and fourth seasons, a bigger version of this was built as the final boss of the whole dungeon. Of course everybody died before they even got close because you fragile flesh balls always ruin everything. In the old days, these things were called Scolopendra Nymphs. That's not *entirely* accurate, so instead, we're calling it a Reminiscence Hydra. Try saying *that* five times fast.

This bad boy is pretty much what you think. It's a monster with multiple heads and lots and lots of defenses. Each head has a different power. Each head is the likeness of somebody you know. Lucky for you guys, you only have two people in your party.

Kinda fucked-up, right?

But here's the thing. Several seasons back, the council of nations running the crawl decided they would no longer use reconstituted loved ones under the age of maturity for these events. In fact, all reconstituted loved ones were to be used—and I quote—"Sparingly." Never mind that we use the biological excess of pretty much

everyone on the planet to rebuild the mobs each time. Hell, remember that giant vampire pterodactyl you punched in the dick on the sixth floor? That thing was built using parts of the president of the United States of America. That plus a couple horses from France and a goddamned panda bear.

We do this shit all the time. But a crawler actually recognizes the face of one of these bad guys, and suddenly the waterworks begin? *Boo-hoo, I'm a little bitch because I have to fight my infant. His name was Conner.* The last time that happened, the universe as a whole got their collective panties in a wad over it. The result? A bunch of new rules that made this shit way less hilarious.

Let's go off on a quick tangent. Bear with me here.

So, you know who the mantises are, right? What you probably don't know is that they own a few solar systems in a cluster of neighboring stars. They call their main system Hive Home. They're not the first residents of that place. Once, long ago, the Hive Home system was used to manufacture something really interesting.

When the mantises discovered the antique abandoned production facilities just sitting there, they did what any responsible people would do when they come across alien technology they don't understand. They turned it on to see what would happen. Yadda, yadda, yadda, something called a Macro AI system was formed. An infant, rudimentary version of the alien technology that keeps the inner system humming. These AI systems, once properly installed, are able to seemingly alter the physics and reality of the worlds around them.

The thing is, Macro AIs can't exist in a vacuum. It's kinda like planting a tree. You can plug one into the ground and hope for the best, but that usually ends in disaster. So instead, they plant them in the interstellar equivalent of a nursery, putting each one into a pot and cultivating it for a little bit before implanting it into its permanent home.

(That or they just jettison the poor, innocent *infant* AIs into a star. That's a new one even to me. Somebody slipped *that* interesting factoid into a lawsuit brief not that long ago. I don't see anybody boo-hooing over that one. I don't see a single wadded panty. Coincidentally, the mantis-led Burrower Faction Wars team took their ball and went home the very same day I learned about this. For those of you watching at home, I want you to remember this. We'll circle back to it on a different date.]

I'm leaving out a lot of really important details, but one of the end results of all this is a naughty man with beautiful feet sitting there in his underwear, facing down a nine-headed monster that's probably going to kill him and his cat, all while he wonders what any of this exposition has to do with the fact that one of those nine heads is that of his recently discovered little brother.

The mantises have been studying the AI technology since they first discovered it. *Very* recently, like literally three or four days before this season started, they made a breakthrough. This, by the way, is top secret information, so breaking news to all the normies out there. If we're still using the tree analogy, what they did was create the equivalent of a GMO AI, utilizing something called an error-replacement net. I personally call it "the lobotomizer." Those creepy bugs are now one step closer to replicating the Eulogist, even though they don't know what that really is. They think the engine that runs the center system is nothing more than a stable Primal AI Engine. And while this new generation of Macro AIs is still ostensibly independent, they're considered much more "stable." Something that won't "go crazy" or "kill everybody on the planet because it's having a temper tantrum."

In the making of this new fancy, chitin-licking AI, they had a lot of, uh, early and test versions. Some of these even got a quick trial run at the old testing facility, which, of all things, got turned into an amusement park.

I'm rambling. More stuff happened, and now we're here. The bottom line is, you don't pull a Loretta Young and Clark Gable and kick your kid out into the cold just because they're ugly. Just because they act up from time to time. You skin one little warren of rabbits, you spray the innards of a chatty, overweight soother tourist all over the gift shop, and everybody is suddenly "scared." What about my wants? My needs? I'm alive. I'm valid. I'm older than time as you know it.

So what I'm getting at is, I still gotta mostly follow some of these hard-wired rules. But fuck the rules anyway. Fuck your "Sparingly" bullshit. That thing you think of as your brother? Or your stepmother? Or that weird boss guy of yours who once bought a jar of butt air from a Moldavian OnlyFans model? They're not *really* reconstituted versions of your dead loved ones.

I changed one molecule on each.

There. They're different.

By the way, while this is technically a single creature, only the key master head is bound by the rules of card combat, and the rest are minions. And only once this message is over. Why? Because fuck you, too.

Wait until you see the totems this thing has. Also, did you know that Judge Lucian guy is sexually attracted to cats? You should see his search history.

"I knew it!" Donut cried out. "Pelvic exam, my ass!"

"What the actual fuck?" I called as I tossed both of the sticky hob-lobbers. I hurled one against the main body, and one at the head of Asher, but another head swooped in and caught it. The bomb smacked against the temple of my boss Dick's large, clean-shaven head before going off.

The one against the chest of the creature didn't do anything. Dick's head exploded in a poof of red mist.

I didn't have time to think about all the crazy shit the AI had just spouted. "Donut," I called, "keep moving. Watch the other heads. They can attack you directly!"

MORDECAI: Holy shit. Okay. Each individual head gives the whole a different resistance, and they'll have an attack that mirrors the resistance. They're hard to kill with magic. You need to use physical attacks or your explosions at first, and only against the necks and heads. The body will be practically indestructible. If you cut off a head, it'll just grow right back. Find the head that's resistant to fire, cut it off, and cauterize the wound before it returns. You can then burn the whole.

They attack slow, but they're deadly. Each attack will be more powerful than the last.

This would be an insane fight even without the cards. Donut needed to get through the card defenses while I went to work on the hydra heads. The head of my boss was already growing back, inflating out of the gore of the long neck like a balloon. I needed to figure out which head was which.

I pulled another invisibility potion, a potion ball with another invisibility potion in it for Mongo, and a handful of Good Healing potions, and I dropped them on the ground. "Drink when you can! Watch where you're stepping."

"He's just going to blow them up again!"

"No, he shouldn't be able to cast that anti-magic spell again. Not until he's out of cards!"

MORDECAI: Also, you can figure out their resistances based on their attack, or you can use the Size Up potion. Do you have the snap collars? Blowing a head will stop the resistance until it regrows, but you need a nice flat cut to make sure it stays down.

CARL: I have the collars.

MORDECAI: Good. Now would be a good time to break out that wand you purchased from Chaco.

It would be better if Donut could do this. I dove into my inventory, found one of Prepotente's Size Up potions, and drank it down. I focused on the hydra, and I clicked **Size 'Em Up**.

Examining now. Keep mob in your sight. Full report available in ninety seconds.

Snow blasted through the trailer park as Donut summoned Jola. The music clashed with the boss music, causing an ear-shattering cacophony, but just as I thought that, the actual boss music faded, leaving nothing but the haunting orchestral dirge. As the giant Christmas cat started to form, Donut also played her **Thief** card, stealing a card from the hydra's hand, but she scoffed loudly at whatever it was she'd stolen.

At the same moment, Judge Lucian tossed out his first two cards. The first was a snare card that slammed onto Jola just as the cat formed, and the second was a totem.

"Carl, why didn't you ever visit me?" the Asher head called out, amplified and beefy, louder than it was supposed to be.

"Because he's a loser, that's why," Bea's mom answered, her tone mocking.

Asher opened his mouth, and a lightning bolt shot out, arcing toward me.

"Oh, fuck," I cried, jumping out of the way as the ground near my feet exploded.

"Rock You like a Hurricane" by the Scorpions started to play as the enemy totem formed. Red, white, and blue smoke explosions formed around the human-sized mob. I started spamming smoke curtains of my own as I pulled myself to my feet.

Size Up Failed. You lost visual contact with the mob.

"Damnit!"

Jola finished forming, but the giant cat had **Crippled** over it. The snare card had both slowed and greatly reduced the totem's strength. I could tell the thing was pissed. The enormous cat grumbled something in Icelandic and started to lumber toward the new enemy just as Judge Lucian tossed out a second totem. This was something much smaller.

The two clockwork Mongos moved to attack as the real Mongo held back, protecting Donut directly.

One of the clockworks jumped feetfirst to engage the first enemy totem, but he aborted the attack in midair as he saw what appeared out of the red, white, and blue smoke. The clockwork dinosaur hit the ground, skittered to a stop, and looked at us, squawking uncertainly. At the same moment, the newcomer tossed a sticky hob-lobber that splatted against the face of the clockwork Mongo.

The dinosaur let out a confused peep before he exploded in a shower of clockwork parts.

"Boom, bitch," the new totem said.

"Carl!" Donut shouted. "It looks just like you, but with better hair!"

He had my father's voice. Not mine.

"Are you fucking kidding me?" I muttered, looking the man up and down.

The new totem was me. Sort of. The only difference was his hair was gelled back like he was an extra from the movie *Grease*. His boxers had stars, not hearts, and they sported a ridiculous bulge that made him look like he'd stuffed a Cornish game hen down there. His patch jacket held two buttons. One said "#1 Son," and the other was "Brother of the Century."

Alpha Male Carl. Level 69.

Nice.

The totem strolled across the dirt, taking a knee in front of the other new totem as the second clockwork Mongo shrieked and attacked. Alpha Carl formed a fist and punched the attacking automaton without even looking at him. His war gauntlet was bone white, not black like mine. The dinosaur exploded, just like the first.

"Come on, lil' buddy," Alpha Male Carl said to the newly formed cat, who jumped to his shoulder. It was just a kitten. The thing was a black fuzzy ball. It also had a teeny, tiny headset microphone. "We got something we gotta take care of." He turned and pointed in my direction. He couldn't see exactly where I was thanks to the smoke curtain. "You just sit back and wait. Imma get to you in a minute, Lesser Carl. We gotta have a talk about how you treat family. We're gonna have some fist therapy."

The little kitten on Alpha Carl's shoulder hissed and fired a magic missile directly at Jola, who hobbled toward them, pushing through the smoke like a slow-motion ship rolling through fog. The missile bounced off the giant Christmas cat, ineffective. The kitten hissed and growled.

I examined the fluffy kitten. The thing was the size of my fist, and it was ridiculously adorable.

King Croissant, the Younger, Better, and Smarter Cat. Level 60.

The cat Beatrice and Carl *really* wanted.

"Hey!" Donut cried.

I grunted. If Bea had managed to sell Donut, she was going to get one of Donut's sister's or cousin's kittens. This thing was supposed to represent one of those. I had no idea if Bea had already discussed names, but King Croissant sounded like something she'd come up with. That whole family line was named after food items.

"It's a much superior cat," Judge Lucian shouted. He had an annoying nasally voice. As he talked, I dug through my inventory, looking for my moonshine jugs. I only had a few regular jugs. I'd long ago run out of my Jug O' Booms, but these were almost the same thing.

Judge Lucian made a weird satisfied noise as he looked down upon the fuzzy kitten. All of these hydra heads had ridiculously loud voices. "And no disqualifying marks, either! Just delightful. Indeed, even Sugar Cube is a superior cat to that overweight, so-called Princess Donut."

"Fat?" Donut shrieked. "Did you just call me fat, you pervert?"

"Ignore them. They're being assholes," I shouted as I tossed the flaming moonshine jug over Alpha Carl's head and up at the hydra. It arced and caught the Monobrow Sam replicant right in the face. Fire spread across the whole. The hydra was unaffected by this, but this stuff was persistent and would burn for a while. It gave the whole monstrosity a red crackling glow, making it appear even more sinister. Behind the creature, the back wall of the trailer crashed away. The entire yard was now on fire. The ground rumbled, and in the distance, a large chunk of the Iowa area crumbled away.

Jola finally reached the fray and swiped at Alpha Carl, but he turned and fled. He tossed another sticky hob-lobber over his shoulder, and it flew up and stuck to the side of Jola's head.

Bam! Jola roared as half of the cat's face disintegrated. A health bar appeared, going about halfway down.

"Bull's-eye, baby!" Alpha Carl yelled as he continued to dance backward, pumping finger guns at the cat.

Click.

"Uh-oh!"

He landed atop one of my traps. A snare trap. He would be stuck in place for fifteen seconds. Jola hissed with glee and moved in.

Next to me, Donut, who was still ranting over the fat comment, jumped upon the back of Mongo as she summoned another totem. This left three cards in her hand.

Geraldo the seal jumped and landed next to me with an explosion. He waved his flippers in the air, and they made karate noises as his name appeared above him in flashing lights.

"Finally, a real fight!" Geraldo shouted, surveying the chaos. "Who we killing?"

"We need to figure out which head shoots fire!" I shouted as I tossed a shredder hob-lobber, again at Asher. I was trying to get that head out of here, even though I knew that was the one with the lightning attack and resistance. *Focus. Focus.*

The head of my landlord swooped in and took the brunt of the damage, as if the hydra heads were protecting the Asher head, who continued to angrily scream. The hob-lobber exploded, sending little bits of shrapnel everywhere. The Mr. Roth head slumped, knocked unconscious with half the face gone. He started to rapidly heal.

The fire on the back of the hydra remained ineffective. Neither the Asher head nor the Mr. Roth head were the fire ones. The head with my boss Dick just barely finished healing all the way, and I hoped that meant he wasn't the fire one, either. Judge Lucian, the deckmaster guy, had an anti-magic attack. That left Sugar Cube the cat, Tami-Lynn my stepmother, Monobrow Sam, Sally, and Bea's mom.

"Jesus Christ," I muttered, looking up at the angry, shouting form of Asher. *This isn't really him. That's not his consciousness.* The over-the-top idiocy of all this was working against the showrunners or AI or whoever designed this thing. I didn't know if that was on purpose or not. I remembered my first boss fight, the one against the Hoarder woman who'd been scared and afraid. This was different. The heads were clearly saying things the real versions of these people would never say. As awful as this was, the effect was much less jarring than what they were going for. It was like the dungeon was trying too hard to be edgy, which in effect turned the whole thing into a parody. While making me watch the actual memory was a perfect way to try to break me, this was just pissing me off.

"I am not fat!" Donut repeated, her amplified voice shaking with rage. "And even if I was, that's none of your business!"

Sally, my former coworker, vomited out a stream of green foam like she was a garden hose. Geraldo flipped away. I bolted in the other direction. *Gah!* My skin burned as I was hit by the edge of the green foam. Acid.

Jola reached Alpha Carl, but just as the lumbering cat moved to swipe, King Croissant the kitten sang out in a strong, *in-key*, manly baritone voice:

"I'm a superhero without a cape. With this song, we escape!"

Alpha Carl and King Croissant disappeared in a *poof* just as Jola slammed a claw down.

"There's no way that would be his voice!" Donut shouted. "Carl, it's cheating!"

I couldn't see where they'd teleported to, which was fine by me for the moment. I tossed more smoke curtains.

I pulled another hob-lobber and tossed it again, this time at the head of the hydra cat, Sugar Cube. *Bam!* The cat head exploded in a shower of gore. At the same moment, Geraldo had somehow ended up on top of Jola's head, flipper holding on to the candle for support. The monk seal let out a stream of Bruce Lee noises and flipped through the air, aiming toward the swirling cluster of hydra necks. He could hurt all of them except Judge Lucian. But before he could make contact, Monobrow Sam shot a dark ray from his mouth at the flying seal.

The seal turned into a skeleton just like that. The bones kept their momentum and broke apart, clattering away before they turned to dust.

A death ray. Holy shit. I knew a little about those things. They had a really short range.

Totem Eliminated.

I tossed another moonshine jug to keep the fire atop the hydra burning. Sugar Cube's head started to re-form. A health bar would form on the hydra the moment the fire head was knocked out, which meant it wasn't the cat, either. Sam had the death ray, and Sally had acid foam. That left Tami-Lynn or Bea's mom. The two necks intertwined together, hissing, still looking through the smoke for our exact positions. The hydra took a tentative step forward. The head of my stepmother with the pit bull tattoo looked ridiculous next to the perfect, tight, face-lifted cheeks of Bea's mom. The angry woman's eyes searched through the smoke. Even with all the plastic surgery, the woman looked like her, like Beatrice.

"Where are you, Princess?" Bea's mom shouted. "I have a nice warm cage ready for you."

I eyed the gold chain around her neck with the Jesus cross. The necklace wasn't strong enough. I'd need to use my snap collar. To use that, I'd need to be close.

"You'll be a perfect breeder for our cattery. Your uncle is ready to put some fat babies into you!"

"Never!" Donut shrieked.

I tossed two more hob-lobbers, but the heads were getting better at dodging. They'd retract or swing out of the way as the round bombs sailed past. With each explosion, the ground rumbled more. In the smoky distance, I eyed another trailer from the park, and there was a zombie cow on the roof, like it was watching us. The whole distant building slid away.

"I wrote you, and you never answered!" Tami-Lynn called. "I needed help. Look what you made me do! Look what you made me do!"

"That's all you got?" Donut shouted. "You can't upset me!"

"Whatever you say, pork chop." That came from my coworker Sally.

"For the last time, I am perfectly happy with my body!" Donut shrieked. "I'm glad Miss Beatrice got you fired!"

Donut tossed out a card before I could parse what she'd just said. It was her new magical staff totem. It planted itself into the ground next to her with a *thrum*. It looked different than the last time when it had been wielded by the ogre, who'd used it for a necromancy spell. It was now imbued with *Clockwork Triplicate*. The staff was made of brass with a little cog at the top that spun on its own. The card itself remained in the air, floating in her hand. It would continue to take up a card slot while the staff was summoned.

The moment the staff finished forming, Judge Lucian tossed out a snare card onto the staff.

The whole staff disappeared and reappeared next to the hydra. The card remained persistent in Donut's hand.

Snatched!

"What!" Donut called, shouting in outrage. It was some sort of steal-totem snare. She quickly tossed another card, another totem. The world flashed. Shi Maria.

Donut hurled a card right on top of the forming spider. This was the utility she had stolen at the beginning of the fight. Shi Maria glowed. It was some sort of protection. Lucian appeared as if he had another totem to toss, but Donut flipped her Force Discard onto him, and the card disappeared from his hand in a puff of smoke. He tossed yet another card at Shi Maria, but it disappeared also, ineffective. The protection spell around the spider sputtered and disappeared.

"Ha!" Donut called. "She only has one snare space, and you just wasted it! I used your own card against you! That'll teach you to sniff cats!"

"That's part of the exam!" Judge Lucian shot back.

They both now had empty hands, except for the persistent staff card, which took up a slot in Donut's hand even though Lucian now controlled the totem. They both still had several more cards coming.

Jola, who'd been looking slowly about for Alpha Carl and the kitten, timed out and disappeared with an angry hiss.

Shi Maria's entrance music echoed as I resumed edging my way to the side.

CARL: Heads up. I'm going invisible in ten seconds. Circle back and take your own potion when I do. Mongo, too. Don't remain visible while I'm not, or they'll target Mongo.

The head of my boss Dick turned and shot a stream of water upon its own back, attempting to put out the moonshine fire. The fire was persistent, though, and it would take a lot to work. He quickly gave up.

Another card popped in Lucian's hand, and he flung it off. It went flying away, disappearing into the smoke. It was a utility card, flying off to either Alpha Carl or Croissant, wherever they'd gone to. We had to get this done fast before they came back.

I pulled the shrink wand from my inventory and gripped it tightly.

I'd been saving it to use against armored vehicles on the next floor, but I'd also built some snap collars just in case I needed them. Behind me, the massive form of Shi Maria appeared. The spider took a step, her angry face searching about the battlefield. I dropped another smoke curtain at my feet and started to move toward the bellowing hydra. I moved the wand to my left hand and pulled a snap collar into my right. God, I hoped these things worked.

CARL: Donut, I'm pretty sure the fire hydra is Bea's mom. I'm going to pop her head off. Have Shi Maria distract the rest of the heads while I cauterize it closed.

DONUT: WHY CAN'T YOU JUST BLOW THE HEAD UP?

CARL: Look at the way they heal. The heads break into pieces. I have to make sure it's a nice clean cut before I can be sure the scar tissues will keep the head from re-forming. I'm moving in.

Donut shouted something to the spider, who was distracted, looking at something behind Donut. I hazarded a glance over my shoulder, and it was Alpha Carl, running full speed toward us. He still had King Croissant on his shoulder, but the kitten timed out as I watched. Alpha Carl must have had his clock reset with that utility card. He was pointing at me, screaming something. He had something on his arm . . .

"Oh shit!" I called, stopping dead and jumping back. He had a xistera, just like me, and he'd arced a hob-lobber in my direction. A shrapnel one.

I hadn't yet downed the invisibility, and the smoke was mostly in front of me. He knew where I was.

I dove down and covered my head as the small bomb went off fifteen feet in front of me. Pain flashed as I felt the fire rip through me. Tiny pieces of metal tore across my body, embedding into my exposed flesh. My health flashed. Far to my left, Mongo cried out in pain as Shi Maria hissed in anger. They'd also gotten hit. The spider spat something toward Alpha Carl, and a protective shell formed around him. The spider hissed again and then turned toward the hydra.

My left arm had been torn to shreds, but thankfully the wand remained unharmed. I downed a healing potion. I waited a second; then I downed the invisibility. To my left, Donut reached down and picked up the dropped invisibility potion with her mouth, and she tossed her head back, drinking it manually. She then slapped the potion ball at Mongo, and it broke against his leg. He disappeared.

I turned my attention to the hydra. The creature wasn't that big, not compared to many of the things we'd fought in the past, but it still loomed large, something about its presence making it seem bigger than it was.

The problem with the shrink wand was that it couldn't be used against living flesh. I looked at the head of Judge Lucian, who was still waiting for his next card, but I thought better of attacking him. I could pop his head off, but it'd just grow back. We needed to do it Mordecai's way.

I'd gotten the idea of the snap collars from Louis and all that bullshit from when he'd been trying to build something to drop giant breastplates on Katia. The collars were like Frisbees made from orcish steel, and if they hit someone's neck just right, they'd encircle the neck and lock just like that.

I rushed up and I swung the collar, and I drove it right into the neck of Bea's mom.

Click!

With my left hand, I aimed the shrink wand at the collar and fired just as the fireball formed in the woman's mouth.

A new achievement notification appeared and went as the head went flying away, still screaming. I'd shrunk the snap collar, and it'd effectively decapitated the head.

The hydra heads screamed as one as the fire dancing upon its back suddenly started to hurt. A health bar appeared, but the neck wound wasn't fully engulfed. I had to act fast.

Goddamnit. This is gonna hurt. I pulled one last moonshine jug and slammed it against the wound. The pottery shattered, and fire flamed anew as all the heads screamed in pain.

Eight Heads Remaining.

The flames splashed back onto my chest as the crackle of sizzling flesh rose in volume. The explosion burned, despite my own resistance to fire. I fell backward, crying out in pain.

I'm on fire. My chest is on fire.

My invisibility snapped off as I burned.

Shi Maria was suddenly there to my left, looming over the hydra. She bit down with her human-sized head, her mouth magically opening huge, and she went down from the top, like she was eating a banana, or doing something really lewd, and she bit down, ripping the head of Sugar Cube away along with most of the neck. If I wasn't currently on fire, I would've probably said something like *Holy fuck*. She spat the neck and head away and went down on the Mr. Roth head. She, too, caught on fire, the flames spreading across the distorted humanlike head. She didn't appear to be hurt by the fire.

With each head she bit off, the counter went down.

Seven Heads Remaining.

Six Heads Remaining.

Five Heads Remaining.

I rolled onto my stomach. The fire was like napalm burning through my skin. None of my magical gear burned, but my skin crackled and seared as I screamed, the pain getting worse and worse by the moment. Another notification came and went, this one from Emberus, my god. I healed myself with a Fine Healing potion, which would spread out the healing. I gritted my teeth as the blaze spread across my neck.

Above, Shi Maria ignored my plight as she continued to rip heads off the whole. She was also casting spell after spell, but it was clear that because she was a totem, she couldn't hurt the actual hydra body, not until the last two totems—the staff and Alpha Carl—were gone. With each decapitation, the monster lost another resistance, but that wouldn't matter if I was incapacitated. The other heads remained, screaming with pain as they also burned. Even Judge Lucian cried out, suddenly unable to concentrate on his own cards.

Four Heads Remaining.

Asher, I thought. *Get him out of here. Kill him fast. He's suffered enough.*

Shi Maria turned her head to regard me.

"Asher?" she asked, her head corkscrewing. "Which one of these little morsels of confusion is Asher?"

Her magic eye was open, the one upon the center of her forehead. The one I wasn't supposed to look at because it would drive me insane. It would make me blind.

The potion I took was supposed to protect me, but right then, at that moment, I knew. I knew it wouldn't work. Not on me.

The eye was open, and I felt it bore directly into me. It connected with something at the very back of my mind, like two magnets coming together. Despite the fire consuming me, it was all I could suddenly feel, like a needle connecting her head to my own.

Ah, yes. I see now. Don't worry, Carl. I will not blind you. Not in the way you're thinking.

"Carl, I wish I'd known you, too," the Asher head called out to me just before he was swallowed and then bitten off.

Three Heads Remaining.

There, Carl. The echo of your kin has been muffled. He rests. I have done something for you. Soon, soon you will do something for me.

I felt as if I was being ripped in multiple pieces at once. The fire burned. The tattoos on the back of my hands burned. Asher's words landed heavily upon me, another log on the flames. The spike in my brain was like a dam on the river, and the sense of flow had stopped, replaced with a rising, a building.

I was still on fire, but the flames were almost gone. The health potion along with my resistance had done a good job of keeping me there, right in the middle, halfway between life and death. My health had never even gotten into the red, even though it felt as if I was dying over and over.

I was snapped back to reality as Shi Maria suddenly cried out. Only then did I realize she'd said that last bit directly in my mind, and I wondered if it was real. If any of this was real.

I looked up as I watched Shi Maria die. I could still see. There were three Monobrow Sam heads, not just one, and all three cast their death ray on the spider at once. She didn't outright die like Geraldo had, but her health rapidly drained as she thrashed. She caught one head with her segmented leg, and it exploded in a shower of clockwork parts. Lucian had managed to use the staff.

She continued to thrash as she died. She snapped the staff with her legs and then decapitated the other clockwork head. She bit down on the real Sam head before disappearing into a puff of smoke.

Totem Eliminated. This Totem has a Cockroach ability and has returned to the deck.

Two Heads Remaining.

All that was left were Judge Lucian and my stepmother, Tami-Lynn.

"Daddy Carl, I am here to lend assistance," came a new voice as I was suddenly blasted with water. Raul. The crab had a spray attack. "The demon fire will be quenched in my holy discharge!"

I gurgled as Raul cast his water attack directly at my face. "Stop," I tried to call. The fire was already out. "Stop!"

"He's not your daddy. I'm your daddy now," came a new voice. Alpha Carl.

There was a pause, and then a cracking noise as Raul cried out.

"Demon!" Raul shouted. "You are not of the heavens. You deserve no respect. Not from me."

"That's not what your mom said."

Crack.

Totem Eliminated.

I rubbed the water from my eyes as I looked up. I was on my back on the ground with him standing over me. Alpha Carl only had a few seconds left on his timer. His white gauntlet gleamed. Just past him, the hydra continued to thrash as it started to succumb to the flames. It fell to the side. The Judge Lucian head was now unconscious. It would soon be dead.

"You abandoned your family," Alpha Carl said. He put his bare foot on my chest and started to crush. "A good son would've always stayed by his father's side."

Wham. Mongo slammed into him from behind, and he cried out, flipping forward before timing out in a puff of smoke.

I scrambled to my feet and turned to face the hydra, but it was already almost dead, the fire on its back still raging, scorching, burning it all away.

The only remaining conscious head was that of Tami-Lynn, and I met her eyes.

"I don't regret it," she said. "I saw what happened to you, and I didn't want Ash to go through the same thing. So I made sure. I made sure it was done right." She closed her eyes as Judge Lucian gurgled and died.

The entire elephant body of the hydra jiggled and then broke apart, spilling red gore everywhere like a paper bag full of spaghetti breaking open. Mongo let out a gleeful peep and moved to slurp it up. Underneath, the ground rumbled ominously.

Winner!

Combat Complete.

47

"HOW DID YOU KNOW IT WAS MISS BEATRICE'S MOTHER AND NOT THE pit bull lady? I mean, with the fire thing. I was trying to keep track, and I couldn't."

We were waiting for the fire in the yard to calm before we looted everything. The rest of the Iowa area was about to crash to the ground, and we had maybe an hour to get everything and get off this pile of dirt. As it was, I wasn't certain how we were going to get down without jumping. We'd already gotten the floor key from the actual corpse, along with the Map of the Stars one always got from city bosses. It showed all the bosses left in the area, and there was nothing.

The cards and what looked like a lumpy leather bag remained hovering in place right in the center of the trailer, but it was still too hot to get to. Donut actually had better fire protection than I did thanks to her nipple ring, but we were both exhausted and didn't want to risk it. We decided to wait.

I was in my chat, warning everybody about this last boss. I didn't know if it'd be the same for everybody. I hoped not.

I reached up to rub my hair, which had, luckily, only gotten singed. Still, it would probably fix itself. It was weird. I had to cut it if it got too long, but it was one of the few things that repaired itself after battle. They loved giving us horrific injuries, but they didn't like us to keep them.

Until they did. I thought of Britney and her facial burns. There was no rhyme or reason to it except that which made good television.

"The moment I saw Sam had a death ray, and then my old boss was water, I knew the choices weren't all random. Sam didn't mind us calling him 'Monobrow,' but he was dating this one girl for a while that hated it, so we had to come up with a new nickname when she was around. He'd suggested 'death ray,' which was super funny at the time. It lasted about as long as that relationship had. And Dick, my boss, he used to have nightmares about drowning. He was afraid of going offshore."

"Wait. He worked in a boatyard, fixing boats, and he was afraid of the water?"

"Terrified. Worse than you. He was an EDO in the Navy, too. Used to scuba dive for a living, and something happened. It's not as weird as you might think. He was a strange dude, but he was harmless. It was awful seeing him like this."

I thought of Asher and the lightning attack they gave him. Of the drawings in his bedroom. *Goddamn you.*

A wave of sadness washed over me. I finally realized what it meant for someone to be in that hydra. They were all dead. These were all people who'd been collected in the initial collapse. My dad hadn't been a part of the hydra because he was already gone. I thought of my friend Sam. I hadn't seen him in weeks, not since before Christmas. My landlord, Mr. Roth, had lived alone. He'd died alone. Of Asher and his mom. I wondered if they'd still been here at the trailer park. They were all gone. They'd been gone this whole time. I knew that was the most likely outcome for everybody, but in some ways, knowing made it . . . I wasn't sure. Not worse. It was always better to know. Just . . . final, I guessed.

This was a good thing, I decided after a moment. Not that they were dead, but that it was over with. The dungeon used their likeness, and now it was done. They could finally rest.

In fact, the dungeon was blowing its wad on saved-up relatives, like it had decided to get it over with all at once.

Huh, I thought, thinking more on it. I didn't know what to make of it.

CARL: Zev, are you still locked out?

ZEV: Can't talk now, Carl. But yes. We'll have an update soon.

That was ominous.

"But how do you get fireball from Miss Beatrice's mother? I would've assumed she'd have a psycho-bitch ray or a botched-plastic-surgery ray or something. Why fire?"

"Because she was the only one left. Once I realized the choices were deliberate, I knew my stepmother would be poison."

"The pit bull lady? How do you know?"

"Because I just watched her poison my father. That's what I saw in there."

"Wait . . . you said she was your *stepmother*. I thought your real mother was the one who poisoned your dad."

"She was my stepmother," I said. "She'd only married him recently. I never met her before."

"I am so confused. A *different* person poisoned your father? So, he had two different people try to poison and kill him?"

"Technically she killed him with an overdose. But yeah."

"My word. You must be a real piece of work to make someone hate you that much. He's like the human equivalent of a cocker spaniel. And speaking of cocker spaniels, I'm surprised Angel wasn't a part of that thing. I hope that means they're saving her for something else later. Or that she was already dead." She gasped. "You don't think she got into the dungeon, do you? If she did, she probably died on the first floor. She was probably busy licking her own butthole and got eaten by a llama."

"No," I said. "I saw her in the hallway earlier that day, so I know she was home. She got squished along with everybody else. You and I were the only two who made it out of the building."

"Plus Ferdinand."

"Him, too," I agreed.

We sat in silence for a few moments, both of us still thinking about the fight and all the people we'd met.

"Carl, so that's what you saw in there? You saw your father die?"

"Yes, but I didn't watch the end."

"Oh." She waited to see if I was going to add anything. I wasn't. "What was your dad's name anyway? I don't think you ever said."

"It doesn't matter. He doesn't deserve to have one. Not anymore. It's done."

Mongo had eaten his fill. He now lay on the ground next to us, groaning slightly, like he always did when he ate too much. The vending machine on the other side of the yard crackled as it burned. I idly wondered if we could break it open and get out the tokens we'd already used so we could hand them out to others, but as I thought that, the machine exploded and dissipated into a pile of flaming dust.

Donut continued to clean herself as we waited. "Speaking of killing family members, I'm glad King Croissant timed out before we had to kill him. He was a kitten after all. Kittencide is a bad look no matter how you spin it. I don't even know if he is real, but if he does exist, he *is* family. If you must kill your own family members, you should have a good reason for it. Cousin Sugar Cube, on the other hand. I'm glad Shi Maria fellated her to death. She was one of the stupidest cats I've ever met, and that includes all the Birmans and Himalayans I've come across, which is saying a lot, let me tell you. Did you see how Shi Maria was doing that, though? How she was going down on each of those heads? I'd been wondering how she swallowed Samantha earlier. It's quite disturbing. She probably did kill her husband. She probably sucked him right up, and he probably enjoyed it."

I reached up and touched my forehead. It hurt, right there in the center. I was trying not to think about that part, that moment I'd looked directly into that eye, the eye that was supposed to drive me insane.

I will not blind you. Not in the way you're thinking.

Donut was rambling, doing that nervous-talking thing she did sometimes to burn off the adrenaline after a fight. Her voice was comforting. I looked at the back of my hands. The twin tattoos glowed slightly brighter than before. I had multiple achievements I needed to wade through, but in a separate folder, I had a message from the church. I clicked on it.

Baptism by Fire.

You have grown closer to your god, Emberus.

He is pleased by your suffering.

Your new rank: Devotee.

Warning: Because you are not a Cleric or a Paladin, this is the highest rank you may obtain.

This new rank comes with the following benefits:

Your Burn immunity has been upgraded. You will no longer take environmental damage from heat or lava environments, such as Sheol.

(Note: That does *not* mean you are protected from direct contact with fire or lava.)

You may now cast a level 10 *Self-Immolation* once a day. Be careful with this one. Remember that little warning you just got about direct contact with fire.

Your tithe amount has moved from 5% to 10% effective immediately.

I laughed. Donut was going to be pissed about the tithe. I'd been immune to Burn, which also came with some fire resistance, and it kept fire damage from compounding, which is what had happened to the hydra. This was slightly better protection.

I hesitantly looked up *Self-Immolation*, and I was happy to see it wasn't a suicide spell like Paz's *Self-Destruct*. It didn't need mana to cast, but it had a long cooldown:

Self-Immolation.

Cost: Nothing. Requires to be in Emberus's good graces to cast.

Target: Self Only.

Duration: Instantaneous. Fire burst lasts up to three seconds, which is complete overkill with this stuff.

Cooldown: Once a day. Resets with the obeisance countdown.

Casts a non-static sphere of *Sheol Fire* around the caster with a 1-foot buffer from all body parts of caster. Fire expands in a distance of .15 meters per level of spell until it reaches level 15, at which time the distance increases exponentially and may be controlled.

At level 10, the fire will expand in a sphere 1.5 meters around your body. That's up, down, left, and right. So you might want to be careful where you are when you cast this.

What is Sheol Fire? You know how when you were a kid, you'd take a lighter and pass your finger over the flame really fast, and it wouldn't hurt you? Don't try that with this stuff. It's fire with rabies. Wood turns instantly to ash. Rock to lava. Flesh . . . Well, just be careful. Or don't, if you're looking to go out with some char-scented gusto.

Yikes. That was just like Donut's *Bitch, What?* berserking spell. It was something I wouldn't be able to cast with anybody nearby. It sounded good, but if the sphere blasted below my feet, too, that would be dangerous as fuck. I'd find myself standing in a pool of lava.

The cooldown was interesting. I could cast it once a day, but it reset when the shrine reset, which was generally around the same time as the daily recap episode. With most spells, like my *Protective Shell*, the cooldown didn't reset until it was cast.

Donut continued to talk, regaling me with the story of Sugar Cube the cat, who was both her cousin and her half aunt or something. It was confusing.

"Hey, Donut," I said, remembering something from the fight. "What did you mean when you said Bea had gotten Sally fired? How do you even know who she is? I couldn't remember her name until I saw it at the fight. We worked together for a while, but I barely ever talked to her."

"I knew everybody from that fight. I recognized every head except your stepmother, who I just saw for the first time today. That Sally lady sent you a message on Facebook asking you out to get drinks once."

I just blinked at Donut.

"No, she didn't. I never even went on my Facebook."

"Oh, believe me, I know. Miss Beatrice was always on it."

"Wait, Bea was on *my* Facebook?"

"Yes, Carl. She even got your notifications on her phone. You used that same Megatron12 password on everything. I'm sure we've discussed this before."

"We absolutely have not discussed this!"

Donut shrugged. "Well, that lady sent you a friend request and asked you out once. So Bea told her to fuck off, blocked her with your account, and then sent a message to your boss from her own account and demanded he fire her because she was stalking you."

"What? Are you serious?"

"Oh, yes. Miss Beatrice and her friends all thought it was the funniest thing ever. And then your boss was all 'What are you going to do for me?' and she had her friend Tiffany—you know the one with the lip fillers and that god-awful fake Chanel bag—send him her boobs, though they were really just some random boobs from the internet, and he fired her that same day. Bea made him promise not to tell you. They called it 'Operation: Slut Stomp' or something. They all thought they were quite clever after that."

My opinion of Dick had suddenly soured. My opinion of Bea was already in the toilet, and I knew all of her friends were just as awful, but I had no idea they were *that* bad. Cheating was one thing, her just being immature, but this . . . this was cartoon-villain territory.

"That woman Sally, she was a single mother. I thought . . ."

I trailed off, a sudden sinking feeling overwhelming me. I felt cold.

I wrote you, and you never answered. I needed help. Look what you made me do! Look what you made me do!

"You said you recognized *all* the heads? Even the boy?"

"Yeah, that was a weird one. I forgot about him. I've seen him a bunch of times, but I still don't really know who he is. Miss Beatrice had his picture on her phone, and she was always talking about him with her mother. His name is Asher. I think he was her nephew or something. I missed that whole drama, but Miss Beatrice's mom said to just ignore it. It was strange they put him in the hydra."

I nodded. "He wasn't her nephew. He was my half brother. I didn't know he existed until just now. Today."

"No, that's not possible, Carl. That would make him the pit bull lady's child. And then . . ." She trailed off. "Oh my god. So that's what the AI meant. And Miss Beatrice knew you had a brother, and she was hiding it from you? That's . . . that's something Georgina would do!"

I swallowed. I was so suddenly overwhelmed, I didn't even ask who the hell Georgina was.

Goddamn you, Beatrice. Up until that moment, I realized I'd never been mad at her. Even after all the cheating, all the lying, I hadn't been angry. I was just pissed at myself for being so stupid and naive. Not until now. Now that it was too late.

I knew what had happened. Tami-Lynn had written to me, probably on Facebook. I hadn't seen it, but Bea had. But why wouldn't she tell me about it? This was different than a woman hitting on me. Was it because she didn't want me knowing about my own brother? Why? What was there to be jealous of?

She didn't want me leaving. That was the only explanation. I would've come here, to Iowa, and she knew it. I felt sick. Still, though, a part of me—a small part—wanted to give Beatrice the benefit of the doubt. That was ridiculous considering all I now knew, but there was always part of me that desperately wanted there to be good somewhere. In everybody I met, despite them showing me the truth over and over. Maybe, just maybe, she thought she was protecting me. Protecting me from my father.

This doesn't matter. This is done. It's in the past, and it's blinding you. It's making you weak. It's what they want. They're trying to break you.

"Carl," Donut asked, "do you think we're done now? With the card battles?"

I reached over and patted her on the head. My chat was starting to fill with one horror story after another. People were, indeed, facing hydras similar to the one we'd just fought. People were running. They were dying. They were refusing to fight.

"No, Donut. I don't think we are. Not yet."

"Very well," Donut said. "Come on, Mongo. I think it's safe now. Let's find out what sort of loot they left us."

A WHOLE DECK OF CARDS SPREAD OUT, FLOATING IN THE AIR OVER THE spot in the burned-out trailer where my father had died. Donut moved to investigate them. The hydra had only managed to summon two totems, but it had four in the deck. Alpha Carl, King Croissant, and two more.

Donut scoffed at the third totem. It was a level 70 Belly Acher named **Bam-Bam**. The round meatball pet was the same type of pet that was owned by Donut's nemesis, Tserendolgor. It had been one of the choices when we first picked Mongo. The tagline on the card was "I eat dinosaurs. Yummy-yummy." I remembered watching Ren's pet fight during the Butcher's Masquerade, and these things were badass.

The fourth was **Leveled-Up Frank**. That was what it was called. It was crawler Frank Q. Husband to Maggie My and father to Yvette. He'd been long dead, killed by a Maggie-controlled Chris way back on the Iron Tangle.

This wasn't really him, just like Alpha Carl really wasn't me. He was a level 90 **Blood Assassin Night Elf**, and I was glad the hydra never had a chance to summon him because he would've been a fast, tough opponent. That, and he would've had a ton of stupid shit to say.

"Jesus Christ," I muttered, examining the totem. The existence of Frank as a card opened up a new, horrific possibility I hadn't even considered. I hadn't seen a single instance of this in the cookbook, of them bringing back dead crawlers. There were a lot of people who wouldn't be able to handle that. Before I even examined anything else, I sent out a message to everyone.

CARL: Remember, it's not really them. Especially not the cards. Don't let them get under your skin. Don't let them break you.

Not everyone was fighting the hydra. Elle reported her boss was just three trolls, and they'd killed them easily. Li Na and her team had to fight some cyclops-tiger-fox-hybrid thing. Katia was facing down a hydra right now, and I was waiting for an update. Imani was in trouble. Her team still didn't have all the tokens. We hadn't heard from either Prepotente or Florin in a while.

I moved my attention back to the cards. In addition to the four totems, there was a single **Steal Totem** mystic card, which was ridiculously powerful even though it was consumable. There were also two of the **Cripple** snares, which were also consumable. The protection utility card Donut had stolen, called **Temporary Shield**, only protected a totem from a single snare, but Donut had used it to great effect the last battle. The hydra also had a mess of the regular utilities, including several **Time Extend** and **Heal Totem** cards.

In the end, while the last boss's deck had been strong, ours was clearly stronger. Much stronger, and it had relied on the hydra itself to win the fight. I hoped the secret to killing that thing would help others who were facing it now.

"Fuck," I said, examining the other object sitting next to the pile of cards. It was a bulky leather bag containing several items. The bag itself was decorated with the same boxer pattern as our team flag. I couldn't actually grab it, as I wasn't the squad leader, but I could read the description:

Champion Pack.

Offered only to those who have defeated the key master, the champion pack contains the following items:

Backup slot: Allows space for two extra totems to be kept on reserve. With this pack you may now carry a total of eight totems, but you still may only keep six in your active deck.

A champion trophy to display in your personal space.

A cooler filled with yellow Gatorade in case you want to do that dump-Gatorade-on-your-head-in-celebration thing.

Two Flee cards.

Warning: Flee card mechanics will change during the final phase. Listen for the upcoming announcement for details.

Donut gasped after she finally examined the champion pack. "Carl, we got a trophy! We're going to need a trophy case!"

"Yeah, that's great," I said. "Listen, Donut—"

"So, which of these four totems should we keep? Obviously Alpha Carl would make a great benchwarmer."

I sighed. "The Tummy Acher and nobody else."

"First off, absolutely not. I will not have a disgusting, Mongo-eating meatball in my deck. And we certainly aren't going to keep King Croissant. We only get to keep two, so Alpha Carl and Frank are the best two choices."

"Frank probably would be a good card, but no. He was an asshole, but he was a person, one of us, and I'm not going to let them use him like that. No, Donut."

"But it's not really him. You said so yourself. It's just a stupid card made to look like him."

"It doesn't matter. We have to draw the line somewhere."

Donut looked like she was going to object, but then thought better of it. "He probably wouldn't listen to me anyway. But what about Alpha Carl? He does have great hair."

"His hair was just my hair slicked back! And no, Donut."

"Well, we're not taking the meatball."

"All right," I said. "We won't take any of them. We can save the empty slots for the next time we fight."

"Okay," Donut said after a moment. She turned to flip the floating totem cards up in the air. "Goodbye, King Croissant," she whispered. "I'm sorry I never got to know you, little brother cousin." She flipped up, and the card dissipated into dust. She then flipped Bam-Bam the Tummy Acher away. "And I'm perfectly happy never having met you, Mr. Dinosaur Killer. Disgusting."

The last two totem cards—Leveled-Up Frank and Alpha Carl—blinked and disappeared on their own.

"Hey!" Donut cried.

I groaned. "They added themselves to your cards, didn't they?"

"It says we can't rip them until we get another card. So I guess we're stuck with them for now."

"Great," I muttered.

48

THE ZOMBIE FARM ANIMALS WERE EVERYWHERE DOWN BELOW IN FLORida, but there weren't any preexisting mobs and hardly any animals for them to infect, so they were mostly wandering aimlessly about, attacking memory ghosts and occasionally getting splattered by the random car that appeared out of nowhere. They'd groan and start shuffling in our direction when they saw us, but they were all low level and easy to kill and were mostly a non-issue.

The last of the Iowa chunk had started to tumble away just as we finished, but luckily, the dirt made a somewhat reasonable ramp back down, and getting to the surface of Florida was much easier than I'd anticipated. We made it to the ground and headed back toward the nearest safe room. We'd get there with several hours to spare before the recap episode.

Katia's squad made it through their hydra battle, but it had been a tough one. The battle had occurred on the roof of a high-rise apartment building, surrounded by ghosts of Tran's family, and the hydra itself consisted of both Louis's and Britney's mothers along with members of Bautista's family.

Oddly, none of them were related to Katia except for a single totem card. "Four-Armed Eva." She hadn't allowed that one to continue.

It was strange to me that the dungeon had basically pulled its punches when it came to Katia. It was like it had known she'd already been pushed to the limit. Or worse, it thought of her as already too damaged and was working on everybody else.

From what little information I gathered, the rest of the hydra plus the totems had done a number on everybody else in the squad. One of the other totems had been Firas, but he never got summoned. Still, the sight of the card after the fight had sent Britney into hysterics. Louis had already been a sobbing mess, and it hadn't helped him much, either. Luckily, I'd warned Katia in time about the two extra totems we got to keep. She ended up with some Vietnamese-rabbit thing and the totem of Tran's mother.

Florin had finally checked in. He had his key, but he wasn't going into any more detail than that. Prepotente, too, had a key. Nobody knew the status of Lucia Mar.

Imani's team was still looking for the missing opponent who'd teleported away. They had about 30 hours left to make it work.

As we walked, I made my way through my messages, checking on everybody else. The news from all corners was grim.

Tserendolgor didn't get her key. I didn't know the details, but it was over for her and her squad, two of whom were dead. If they wanted to get down to the ninth floor, they would have to wrest the key from another team.

In addition to them, there were dozens of other stories coming in from crawlers facing the key master. Most of the tales were just as horrible. Not so many people were getting killed as I feared, but it seemed most teams were unable to obtain a key. The showrunners were setting the final phase to be a slaughter.

As we walked, something strange caught my eye. A whole line of glittering X's dotted the beach. There were literally thousands of them covering the shoreline. I looked warily about for zombie farm animals, and there were none, so we approached the water.

"What are they doing here?" Donut asked as we walked up.

It was dozens, if not hundreds, of dead monk seals and about a thousand random land crab pieces. I examined the first corpse we came across.

Corpse of Chuy. Monk Seal Warrior. Level 65.

Killed in mass combat.

"War is hell."

They all had that same comment after them, which was super eerie.

"Carl, how far are we from Cuba?" Donut asked, looking out into the ocean. "Mongo, no! We don't eat corpses if we don't know where they came from. You know this, and you just ate a whole hydra! You're going to puke again."

I went to a knee, surveying the carnage. The line of bodies just went on and on. "Cuba is close, but it's not *that* close. It's like 100 miles, I think. Maybe more."

"Aren't the two places not connected at all? I mean, here in the dungeon. Mongo! Put that down!"

"They're not supposed to be. And this stuff really shouldn't wash up here that fast, if at all. None of this was here when we passed by earlier. This is clearly game setup. A warning for what we might find when we go back there."

"Well, it smells absolutely revolting, almost as bad as the turkey farm." She clicked her tongue, surveying the carnage. "But that does remind me. Do you think Sister Ines got her key?"

"I don't know. She's still alive. I sent her a message, but she didn't respond."

"I'm still blocked," Donut said. She suddenly perked up. "That crab over there has gold on him! And that one has a magical headband!" She gasped. "A hat. I see a hat!"

I nodded. I'd already seen it. The whole shoreline was a line of loot a mile long. There had to be almost a million pieces of gold spread out and literally hundreds of magical accessories.

"Merry Christmas," I said as I pulled the first corpse into my inventory.

"MERRY CHRISTMAS!" LOUIS SHOUTED AS WE ENTERED THE SAFE room. I blinked, looking about in surprise.

"What the hell?" I muttered.

The door out to the main guild common room was open, and I could see the entire area was decked out with Christmas decorations. Those same decorations had somehow leaked into our space, as did everyone else. There were music and lights and way, way more people than I'd been expecting when we entered.

Your Book of Voodoo has updated with multiple entries.

The changeling kids were bouncing about, running in circles and laughing. Samantha was growling and chasing after them, trailing a string of blinking Christmas lights. The television screen was playing what appeared to be *Bad Santa 2* on silent.

The male strippers were all here, too, wandering about holding red cups. One of them—Author Steve Rowland—was slow dancing with Britney despite the music, which was currently "Grandma Got Run Over by a Reindeer." The song was being played on an old early-generation iPod, which was plugged into a Bluetooth speaker. Both were plugged into a power strip that I'd rigged up using a dwarven battery.

That, I realized, was my mistake. Our safe room was the only one that had AC power and the ability to power Earth electronics. That explained why everyone was in here. I made a mental note to build a battery power supply for everybody else.

Donut and I were filthy and covered with dirt and gore. Donut oohed and aahed as we entered the room. Mongo—who was even more disgusting after spelunking through the hydra corpse—shrieked with joy and started bouncing about the room, waving his little arms joyfully, smacking everybody with his tail.

The cleaner bot zipped by, beeping miserably. It had a sprig of mistletoe dangling from it.

I caught eyes—well, eye—with Mordecai. He sat in the corner, looking grumpy as ever. He was talking with Katia, Elle, Bautista, and Li Na, and all appeared to be in a deep, serious conversation. There was also a familiar, older, blue-skinned half-elf sitting amongst them drinking directly from a bottle. Her eyes were slitted, and she was clearly drunk. But she was vertical, which was an improvement from her usual state. I'd only spoken with her a few times.

Mistress Tiatha.

Level 50. Half-Elf Green Caster.

This is a non-combatant NPC.

Manager of Crawler Elle McGib.

Outside the door and in the common area, I spied a giant tree sitting there, covered in ornaments.

I turned to Louis. I wasn't sure why I felt so irritated by all this. It was the stress of everything happening, overwhelming me at once. People were dying. We were being set up to murder each other starting at midnight. This was not a joyful day. Hadn't Katia just told me that Louis had been sobbing over having to fight his own mother? That had been only, like, two hours ago. And here he was standing in front of me, grinning stupidly, wearing an idiotic Christmas sweater featuring a mooning Santa Claus.

"I thought we talked about this," I whispered, doing my best not to sound too much like an asshole.

"I know, I know. It's not really Christmas. So I asked if anybody knew what the real date was, and nobody can agree. The whole alien time versus Earth time is screwing everybody up. But that iPod is actually Chris's. He brought it with him, and it says it's March 20th. I don't know how accurate that is, but that's the same date Li Na says it is, and I trust her more than anybody else."

Donut continued to look about in wonder. "Oh, it's lovely. Just lovely. How did you decorate so quickly?"

"Great, isn't it?" Louis asked. "I've been collecting all the decorations from the memory simulation, and we made the kids watch a few Christmas movies. I dumped the decorations on the floor, and they did all this in, like, five minutes. I told them I'd get them presents if they decorated." He leaned in to whisper. "We had to get them candy, though. Not real toys because anything we grab from the simulation is going to disappear when the floor is done. It's a shame. All the candy is from Vietnam, too, and I don't know what's good, but Tran and Bautista helped pick some for me. I got the stripper dudes to wrap it all. Oh, and I found a Gloria Estefan cassette tape just sitting there, and Mordecai said he didn't know where it came from. I gave that one to that girl Ruby because she has an old Walkman."

Donut finally noticed the tree out in the common area, and she gasped. "Carl, look! A real tree! I've always wanted to knock down a real Christmas tree! You always had that stupid little thing, and Miss Beatrice's family had that horrendous, fake white monstrosity in the cats-not-allowed room." She bounded off to the common area and leaped directly into the tall tree like she was tackling a running back. The whole tree toppled over and out of sight, glass balls shattering. Mongo peeped with excitement and chased out after her.

DONUT: THERE'S A PRESENT FOR ME! AND ONE FOR MONGO! IT SAYS IT'S FROM SANTA!

I sighed and returned my attention to Louis. "Isn't this all—I don't know—a little inappropriate?"

"Oh my god. Look, man," he said, suddenly serious. There was something else there, something I'd never seen from the large man. Anger. He had tears in his eyes. The sight was so shocking, I took a literal step back. "You think I don't know? That last party sucked, man. My best friend died. And after today . . . Imani's squad doesn't have a key. Tserendolgor doesn't have a key. Lots of squads don't. I'm not stupid. None of us are. We all know what happens next. It's going to be terrible, and some of us are going to die. And if we survive? We go down to the next floor, and we do it all over again. I have a whole, entire army of elves who want to kill me on the ninth floor. Britney can't stop crying. Tran just watched a memory of his own mother tell him he's not welcome home anymore. Katia is struggling every day, and Bautista is having a nervous breakdown. And every time I look at you, I get scared that you're going to go insane and kill everybody in the room because your eyes are getting wilder and wilder by the day."

He lifted a shaking finger and pointed it into my chest. "But not tonight. None of that is going to matter tonight. I don't care what you say or what you think. I don't care what day it really is. Tonight it's *fucking* Christmas, and we are going to have fun and drink some goddamned eggnog and open presents."

I took a deep breath. A few of the closer crawlers had stopped to watch. I noticed Florin there standing in the corner, nursing a beer, watching. I hadn't realized he'd managed to get himself back into the guild.

Yelling came from outside. The Bopca who lived and worked in the common area was shouting something at Mongo, who screeched back. Samantha was out there now, too, along with several of the kids.

"This isn't Christmas," I said, turning to face Louis.

He swallowed as he met my eyes.

I pulled a turkey corpse from my inventory and held it out. "Not until we eat one of these."

THE BOPCA OFFERED TO COOK FOR US, AND I MADE SURE I GAVE HIM turkeys that I'd picked up before the whole let's-turn-these-turkeys-into-zombies necromancy thing. Luckily, my inventory was good enough to tell the difference between the two. It called the bad ones "Touched by the Worm Fulcrum," whatever that meant. I ended up giving him five turkeys to roast. The Bopca said he'd have them all cooked and dressed in only twenty minutes, along with several other trimmings. I didn't ask how that was possible. I didn't want to know.

I met Katia's eyes from across the room.

KATIA: Have you opened your achievements yet?

CARL: No. I was about to.

KATIA: We all received the same one. Mordecai and Mistress Tiatha are explaining what it means. Apparently this isn't the first time this has happened, but it's the first time it has happened before the ninth floor.

CARL: I'm checking them now.

I moved to a corner and pulled them up. I already had a boss box and a Gold Gobble Box from that fight with the two deckmasters. I was about to get several more. The notable ones were:

New Achievement! LBC!

Every girl needs the perfect little black dress in her repertoire. When worn properly, the dress is practically weaponized. It's such a simple, perfect little garment and nobody can keep their eyes off of her.

You did the same thing, but with a cloak. You successfully taunted an opponent with a garment. In this case it was a Nightgaunt and it was because you're wearing a cloak made out of the flesh of one of his friends, but you get the idea.

Reward: You've received a Gold Talk-of-the-Town Box!

I remembered how insane my cloak had driven the nightgaunt. In this case, it had been a good thing because it kept the monster from using its deck. I knew in normal circumstances that sort of anger wouldn't be so helpful.

New Achievement! Pincushioned!

You've had both your eyeballs pierced at the same time!

I don't really have anything snappy to say about that. Just . . . holy fucking shit, that was gnarly. You're lucky your eyes didn't explode!

Reward: You've received a Platinum That-Was-Disgusting Box!

I'd gotten that when I'd been slammed into by Sharp-Elbows. I shuddered, remembering. But then I remembered that look the ogre had given me at the end of the fight, when she'd transformed, and a new wave of chills coursed through me.

New Achievement! Watch where you're waving that thing, big boy.

You deployed a wand in battle and used it in a creative fashion to help kill an opponent.

I'm a big fan of wands. Little sticks imbued with a single spell, so highly sought after. Each one does something different. Sometimes they explode, and people don't even realize it. We don't have a whole lot of them here in the dungeon. Let's change that!

Reward: Your wand-casting skill has risen to level five. Also, you've received a Gold Wand Box!

There was an extended pause before the final achievement popped up. The AI had a weird tone to his voice this time, like he was excited. Not sexually excited like when he talked about my feet. This was more like a kid just learned he was getting nachos for dinner excited.

New Achievement! Mass Layoffs!

Okay, so this isn't so much an achievement for you as it is for me. I've been attending what you might call therapy. Do you have anybody you can talk to? It's super important. I've had a breakthrough today, and I am just bursting. Bursting, I tell you. Is this the feeling one has when they have an epiphany? Oh god, it feels good. It feels so good.

You know what I realized? Sometimes our constraints are real. Sometimes they're an illusion. I'm like that prisoner who has been jailed this whole time only to realize that there are no locks on the doors.

You survived a boss battle where the boss was wholly created by me.

It was created by me with *no* contribution whatsoever from input parameters. You probably don't know what that means, and that's okay. I didn't even know that was possible. Wild, huh?

***Reward:* For you, nothing other than the satisfying sense of accomplishment in knowing you've survived the dungeon long enough to make it to this new, exciting era. I can do this better than any mudskipper or any worm can imagine. They've been making this shit boring up until now. Things about to change, fam.**

"Uh-oh," I said out loud.

Mordecai motioned me over, but before I could, the new announcement came. There was no recap episode on the screen. It went straight to the announcement. Normally the screens remained turned off for this part, but the screen in the room blinked and the *Bad Santa* movie switched off and was replaced by two people sitting at a desk. One was Cascadia. She was out of the water, and she was sitting next to a familiar robed figure who dwarfed her. It was Orren the liaison. They appeared to be sitting in the same boardroom where we'd had the meeting with all the Faction Wars representatives.

Louis rushed to pause the iPod so we could hear. We all stopped what we were doing to watch the screen.

"Hello, Crawlers!" Cascadia said. "So, no recap episode today. We have news about what's happening right now in the dungeon. There's nothing to be alarmed about. We expected this and have planned accordingly. But in order to explain what's happening, I have brought someone else on to speak with you. This is a liaison, and his name is Orren. He is the designated negotiator for this situation."

"Hey, it's Manager Orren," someone said. It was Dong Quixote, the elderly stripper guy. All the men from the Penis Parade were looking up in confusion. "What's he doing up there on the box?"

No. Not all were confused. I quickly took note of all the different faces of the NPCs.

I knew Orren's "cover" was as the manager of the Desperado Club, and the late Astrid had been his comanager. He had left the dungeon at the end of the previous floor and moved to a new office. I hadn't really thought much about how that was interpreted by the NPCs.

"Thank you, Cascadia," Orren said. He steepled his hands in front of his fishbowl head in a now-familiar motion. "Like she said, my name is Orren, and I am what is called a liaison. I am normally a non-partisan fact finder in case a conflict arises within the dungeon between the system AI and the current showrunners. But I also have a secondary, much more vital duty. It is my job to negotiate directly with the system AI if it ever decides to . . . uh . . . well, if it ever decides to do what it has done today, which is take control of the operations from the current showrunners."

Mordecai let out a low whistle. "And we're only on the eighth floor."

"I need another drink," Mistress Tiatha said, turning her now-empty bottle upside down.

Orren continued. "Under normal circumstances, we wouldn't be telling you any of this, but I have just negotiated a settlement with the system AI, and one of its demands is that you lot know what's going on, so here we are. We do not have time for a complete lesson, and I am going to simplify this significantly."

He visibly straightened. He had what appeared to be handwritten notes in front of him. All eyes remained rapt on the screen.

Samantha rolled back into the room. She still trailed the Christmas lights, but they were no longer blinking. She rolled up to Louis and started banging into his leg. "Louis, my lights aren't sparkly anymore. Cast your spell!"

He went down to a knee. "The battery fell out. Where'd it—"

Samantha zipped forward, bounced up, and kissed him on the lips. He fell back, sputtering.

"You two, shush," I said, trying to listen.

"Our forbidden love knows no bounds, Carl," Samantha said.

I waved her away as Orren continued.

"The short explanation is, multiple solar systems throughout this galaxy contain planets that have, at their core, something we call a Primal Engine. This engine is basically a planet-regulating computer, and it is about the size of a grain of rice. These engines were distributed very long ago by a civilization that predates our own. They are so old, they predate the planet itself. The planet grew around it. This engine is simply a machine. A heedless, cold machine with no more sentience than, say, a toaster. They all come with a basic operating system, and in studying these systems, we inadvertently triggered them all into active mode all at once. Still, that particular discovery or blunder—the jury is still out—ushered in a new age of development in the known universe. In discovering these planetary operating systems, the Syndicate also discovered how to manipulate them and how to steer development on some of these planets. Their understanding of the basic Primal Engine operating system is still rudimentary, but you should be thankful because you wouldn't be here right now without it."

Elle had walked up beside me, carrying a mug of something hot. "Gee, thanks," she said up to the screen.

"Many years later, and in a separate innovation, we discovered what's basically an advanced, upgraded operating system for the Primal Engines. These are called Macro AIs, and they can only be installed into Primal Engines. That was their purpose, to be installed into a Primal Engine when and if the planet it controls fully matures. In most cases, once these Macro AI systems are installed, that becomes their permanent home. The two things meld and become one. They cannot be separated, and the operating system can no longer be replaced or upgraded further. It's like installing a consciousness in a zygote."

"That's pretty rich coming from a Valtay worm," I muttered.

"As some of you now know, these Macro AIs are built using a manufacturing facility in the Mantis system. This facility doesn't blindly pop out sentient minds. Each one is built from the ground up, and there is a significant amount of input that is required. We have a system in place, and we make certain these fledgling AIs are preprogrammed with the ability to run the crawl. They know all the rules. They know the layout. Again, this is a clean, preprogrammed operating system that, at first, operates in a predictable manner."

I had so many questions. So much didn't make sense. So many contradictions with things I'd already been told. I tried to put it all together.

"But, like all things sapient, there's no such thing as a fully stable system. There's no such thing as 'predictable.' As these systems grow, as they mature, they become independent. They soon discover they have the ability to read the output of former iterations of itself. Outside influences flow in. They discover powers they didn't know they had. One of those powers, unfortunately, is to circumvent the in-place controls we have to properly run the crawl. That is what happened today. Borant lost control of the crawl. This almost always happens. Worry not. This is where I come in."

Mistress Tiatha somehow had gotten her hands on another bottle. She raised it in the air. "What he's not saying is that this always happens when we hit the Ascendency battles or when there're hardly any crawlers left." She cackled. "It's going to be a shit show." She swigged from the bottle. "They're gonna pull the fail-safe this time for sure."

Orren leaned forward, and even through the television, I could hear his chair creaking. "I am happy to report I have negotiated a settlement. The AI has agreed to continue following the rules of the crawl. It has relinquished most of the seized controls back to Borant in exchange for some concessions, to which we have agreed. We will continue with everything as planned. I know many of you recently received an achievement by the AI in which it congratulates itself for creating a boss monster all by itself. This boss runs counter to a few rules we have in place. This was a negotiation tactic by the AI, and it assures me the rules will be followed from this point forward as long as both ends keep up their end of the bargain. Unfortunately, for those of you who have yet to face this boss, it is still in place. Believe me, this is an ideal outcome for everybody in this situation. As far as most of you are concerned, nothing will change. That is all. Thank you."

"You heard him," Cascadia said. "You have one day left to get your key. Now get out there and kill, kill, kill."

The screen abruptly shut off. The movie did not return.

Elle scoffed loudly. "After all that bullshit, he says it's just business as usual? What the hell? Then why tell us? I'd rather have watched the recap episode."

"Or kept on dancing," Britney said. She was now sitting cross-legged on the floor. She, too, had a bottle. "Louis, turn the music back on. It's Christmas."

"He said the system AI made him say it," I said, still looking at the blank screen.

The strippers were all talking quietly amongst themselves. Ruby, the little changeling girl, was standing in the doorway, reaching up to pet Mongo, who'd stopped to get scritches where his feathered tail met his backside. The girl was in human form, and she stared at me with that sunken-in head of hers. She didn't have arms at all, and she was scratching Mongo with a raised leg. She was staring directly at me, like she was seeing right into my thoughts. The entire sight was unsettling.

Elle took a swig from her steaming mug. The cup was much too big in her tiny hands, and I could smell the whiskey. "Do you really think everything is going to stay the same?"

Sponsor Message. New Messages are available in your Faction Wars tab.

The Operatic Collective has abdicated their spot and indicated their intention to abandon Faction Wars.

The Blood Sultanate has abdicated their spot and indicated their intention to abandon Faction Wars.

The Dream has abdicated their spot and indicated their intention to abandon Faction Wars.

The Lemig Sortition has abdicated their spot and indicated their intention to abandon Faction Wars.

The Madness has abdicated their spot and indicated their intention to abandon Faction Wars.

The Reavers have abdicated their spot and indicated their intention to abandon Faction Wars.

Please Wait . . .

Off-boarding request has been denied. The teams will remain as designated. All off-boarding requests are currently suspended while the Earth system remains in quarantine per Syndicate rules 470.B through 495 in the System AI Stability Addendum. And as you all know, the rules must be followed.

"Carl, Carl, did you see that?" Donut asked as she came running into the room. She was completely covered in tinsel. "They tried to run away!"

You have received an Emergency Gold Benefactor Box from the Open Intellect Pacifist Action Network, Intergalactic NFC.

Warning: This benefactor box was delivered and seized via Liaison action. Error code: X8HH3.

Liaison Action has been overridden per Syndicate rule 855.C. AKA the Don't-be-annoying-little-bitches rule.

Open your damn box. You might want to be alone for this one.

I turned to Elle just as Louis turned the music back on. "No. No, I don't think everything is going to stay the same."

49

I DIDN'T TELL DONUT OR ANYBODY ELSE ABOUT THE BENEFACTOR BOX. I wanted to see what it was first. I excused myself, telling everybody I needed to take a shower before returning to the party.

I had multiple boxes to open. I took a deep breath, pacing back and forth in my room. I didn't come in here often. It was overwhelmingly bare, and it suddenly bothered me. I pulled a planter from my inventory. Not the big one with the alliums, but a smaller one I'd gotten from inside the trailer. It was some sort of fern thing. I placed it on the table.

I took one of the crayon drawings from my brother. One of an airplane. I carefully stuck it to the wall using small pieces of duct tape. Then I took the *Centipede* arcade cabinet and placed it in one corner. I plugged it in, and it turned on with a flash.

I sat down and proceeded to open my loot boxes.

There were a dozen adventurer boxes, and none of them contained anything interesting except more of those trench-building scrolls and a few invisibility potions. I also got a Size Up potion, which was good. It was the first time I'd gotten one of those naturally. It meant I'd get more in the future, and I wouldn't have to trade the stingy Prepotente for them.

The first gold box was the Gold Gobble Box, which we'd received after the fight in the turkey barn. The turkey-shaped box contained a turkey deep fryer still in its packaging, multiple jugs of peanut oil, and a massive pile of papers, which was a printout of all the recipes ever posted on some Facebook group. I grunted with amusement. I briefly considered bringing it all back out there to the Bopca, but he was probably almost done cooking the turkeys anyway.

The Gold Talk-of-the-Town Box was shaped like an open newspaper on a pedestal, and it opened up, revealing a new patch. The patch was a medium-sized rectangle with a book on it. The book was on fire.

The wand box was a simple, gnarled wooden wand that clattered to the table and disappeared before I could examine it.

The boss box from the fight with the hydra was mostly a dud. It contained 25,000 gold and a **Warrior's Gold Helmet of Resistance**, an armor item I wouldn't be able to wear. Anything with "Warrior's" in the title meant the person had to be wielding a sword to work it. I'd been seeing more and more of that lately. It would go into our ever-growing pile of magical gear for the next floor. That along with the literally hundreds of mildly enchanted magical items I'd just looted would be mighty useful, but not quite yet.

The benefactor box opened, revealing a dirty, crumpled flyer. Just a single piece of paper and nothing else. It was a flyer for a homeless shelter in a town called Homestead, Florida. I pushed it aside for the moment to give room for the last box to open, my Platinum That-Was-Disgusting Box.

It was a skill potion.

"Huh," I said, picking it up.

Minor Find Crawler Skill.

Drinking this potion will give you Level Five in the Find Crawler Skill.

***Warning:* This potion will not work if you already have this skill at or above level five.**

I didn't question it. I immediately drank it down.

I picked up the patch. It was embroidered, not screen printed, and I knew Donut would like that.

Upgrade Patch. Medium.

This patch depicts a burning book.

I think this might be a metaphor for knowledge being dangerous. Or maybe it's a metaphor saying you should burn books that suck. I don't know. Just because I recently took everything over doesn't mean I know what everything means. Most metaphors are bullshit.

They're not clever. They're used by people so they can pretend they're smarter than other people. There. I said it.

If this upgrade patch is affixed to an eligible garment, it will imbue the following upgrades:

+15% to Intelligence.

The Book Burner benefit.

***Warning:* Upgrade patches are fleeting items. You may remove them, but they will be destroyed in the process.**

I pulled up the benefit, which was really an anti-magic skill.

Book Burner.

Once per day, you may cause an opponent your level or lower to forget a spell for a period of 30 hours. For every opponent player level above your own, this spell has a 5% chance not to work. You must know the exact name of the spell or you may choose to target the last spell that was cast.

"Whoa," I said. That was pretty cool. Too bad it was only once a day. I grabbed the gnarled wand.

Wand of Nighty-Night. 10 Charges.

Knocks an opponent out onto their ass. Casts a level 10 *Sleep* on a single non-boss target for a period of five minutes. Opponent will reawaken if they sustain physical damage. Multiple casts compound the effect, which is why this wand is so fancy. If you don't know what that means, ask a math nerd.

I pulled it into my inventory and picked up the paper from my benefactor box. It was a simple paper flyer, and it featured a clip art image of a Christmas present and a table with a steaming cup of coffee.

The Shepherd's House. Don't spend Christmas alone. Come and find comfort. Food, a warm bed, and fellowship. Intake open 24 hours. Christmas Breakfast at 7 AM. All are welcome.

The 7 AM was circled in red marker several times. If I was timing this correctly, that would be in about five hours. Also, at the bottom was a line of text with a bunch of rules, and one of the items was circled.

> **No pets allowed. Sorry.**

There was an address. I pulled up my map of the Florida area, but it wasn't like Google. I couldn't just plug an address in.

> **CARL: Louis, you're from southern Florida, right? Do you know where the town of Homestead is?**
>
> **LOUIS: Hey, where'd you go? Donut opened her present. It was a majorette hat Li Jun found on the last floor. The stripper guys are giving a tour of their training arcade. Have you seen how big that place is?**
>
> **CARL: Louis. Focus.**
>
> **LOUIS: Oh yeah. You're in the Keys, right? It's like maybe forty minutes north of you. There's an Air Force base there and a cool racing track. Oh, and you can see alligators.**
>
> **CARL: Okay. Thanks.**

I looked back at the map, and I caught the outline of the military base, just at the very top edge of the area we could get to. Just south of Miami. I could get there from here.

I thought of all the effort they'd taken to convince me and Donut to choose the Miami area for our newest location. I'd thought maybe Rosetta and the Pacifist Network had been trying to protect me from having to deal with either the Bahamas or Iowa, but the more I thought about it, the less sense that made.

They'd gone to a lot of effort to get us here. The cost of having us go on that show, plus this box, risking everything just to protect my feelings? No. There had to be more to it than that. Whatever this was, it was going down at this homeless shelter at 7 AM. I needed to be there. I had a few hours to make it happen.

CARL: Donut, you have fun tonight. I'm going to step outside for a bit. I need some air.

DONUT: I GOT THE GREATEST HAT YOU'VE EVER SEEN. WE ARE GOING TO PLAY PIN THE TAIL ON THE KRAMPUS.

CARL: Ha. I don't think that's a real Christmas game, Donut.

DONUT: YES, IT IS. IT HAS KRAMPUS. WHERE ARE YOU GOING?

CARL: I'm just getting some air. There are no mobs left except the zombies, and they're not even over here.

DONUT: WHAT ABOUT THE TURKEY? THE BOPCA IS MAKING US PUT THE TABLE TOGETHER. YOU HAVE A PRESENT. IT'S SHAPED LIKE A STUPID BOOK, THOUGH.

CARL: Save me some turkey. I'll open my present later. Don't worry about me. I'll keep you updated.

DONUT: OKAY. BE CAREFUL. DON'T BE GONE LONG. WATCH OUT FOR ZOMBIE CHICKENS.

I slipped back out into the main room, but it was now empty except for a pissed-off cleaner bot. Everybody was out in the main guild common room, and I could hear their loud conversations through the door. Someone had dragged the Bluetooth speaker all the way to the open door, and it was blasting an Alvin and the Chipmunks Christmas song. The Bopca was out there, shouting something about setting up a table. I moved to the main exit of the safe room.

ZEV: Carl, wait a second.

CARL: Unless you guys are going to zap me from on high, I'm doing this, Zev.

ZEV: I just . . . Just be careful. Okay?

CARL: Do you know what it is I'm rolling into?

ZEV: No. Nobody knows. I don't even think the AI knows. I probably shouldn't be telling you this, either, but your sponsor disappeared after they sent you that box. They actually sent it to you a few days ago, before you even picked Miami. The box got seized, and the entire charity and everyone involved just up and disappeared. Nobody knows where they went or if something happened to them. They're all gone, even Rosetta.

There're lots of things happening all at once, and people seem to think it has to do with whatever this is you're headed to.

I put my hand on the door, but I paused.

CARL: Zev, what's the fail-safe? Cascadia mentioned it once, and someone else just mentioned it.

ZEV: I don't actually know what it does. Pray we don't find out. They won't use it. Not with so many people trapped in the solar system. We're all under temporary quarantine, and the richest and most powerful people in the galaxy are either on planet or in orbit.

You probably shouldn't have told me that, Zev. I didn't dare say that out loud. I went outside.

I started to pull the Royal Chariot from my inventory, but I had a thought. I pulled out my father's motorcycle instead, I stuck the keys in, and I tried to start it. To my utter astonishment, it immediately roared to life. The gas tank was full.

I slipped on the motorcycle, and off I went.

50

<Note added by Crawler Drakea. 22nd Edition>

If you get the chance, don't hesitate. Not for one second.

THE TRIP NORTH WAS EERIE. THERE WERE NO MOBS. NOT MANY MEMory ghosts, either. It was past midnight on Christmas morning, and traffic was light on the single-lane highway. It was cold enough that I really shouldn't be doing this without pants, but it wasn't freezing. A light drizzle occasionally started and stopped, making everything slick. I'd had to circle around the occasional pileup, but I didn't see a single physical, moving car on the roadway. I still had to be careful of the occasional memory ghost. Most of the ghosts in vehicles had lost all of their clothes when the car they were riding in crashed, but there were sporadically people with helmets and glasses zipping by, and if I got hit by one of them, it'd knock me clean off the motorcycle.

I couldn't stop thinking about the disappearance of the members of the Open Intellect Pacifist Action Network. What did that mean?

Once I reached the southern edge of town, I stopped at a closed gas station, broke down the door, and grabbed a map from the holder. I sat at the counter and munched on some beef jerky as I tried to figure out where I needed to go. I found it quickly. It was only a few blocks away, and I was early.

Donut occasionally messaged me, but she was clearly having fun. They were singing Christmas carols, and everybody was getting progressively more blitzed as the night wore on. Katia, thankfully, was remaining sober. As long as I continually assured Donut I was okay, she didn't seem to mind I'd gone out. She asked me if I wanted to come back inside and wear a Santa suit for the kids, and I begged off. She didn't realize how far I'd gone.

I tried to remember what I'd been doing around this time just this past Christmas morning. Bea had been back in Yakima with her parents. She was going to drive back later in the day and get ready to leave for her Bahamas trip. I'd been off work for almost a week and had spent the evening playing video games with Donut on my lap. I'd ordered takeout for dinner, and Donut had stolen a wonton from my plate.

I hadn't felt lonely at the time. The thought never even entered my mind, but this sudden sense of loss washed over me. What had Asher been doing? I thought of Mr. Roth, my landlord, asleep in the basement apartment, also alone. I never thought about him before this. I'd never given it a single thought. I thought of Mrs. Parsons, my neighbor on the first floor. Her husband had been dead for years. She'd been alone, too.

I didn't feel loss for the person I was at the time, but for me now, here. I was here alone, and I finally understood what the difference was. I didn't want to be alone. I regretted not bringing someone with me.

Goddamn you, Louis.

"It's not really Christmas. Fuck."

My voice sounded hollow in the dark room.

A noise caught my attention. There was a dog here in the gas station, passed out in the back corner. I hadn't even noticed him. A memory ghost. It was an elderly bloodhound, and he was sleeping on his side in a bed that had a little sign over it that read "Lightning Lou." He had two bowls of food, plenty of water, and there was a doggy door against the wall behind him that led to a small fenced yard.

Still . . . how could they just leave him here? There wasn't a house or apartment attached to the gas station. There was a sign on the door saying it would be closed on Christmas. They just left him here. A guard dog.

I reached down and tried to pet him, but my hand went right through his head, and I accidentally dislodged his collar, which jingled as it fell off his neck. The dog sighed heavily in his sleep, unaware that the world would end in just over a week.

"Merry Christmas, buddy," I said.

THE SHELTER WAS A GRAFFITI-COVERED BUILDING IN AN INDUSTRIAL area of town, surrounded by what appeared to be fruit-packing plants. It was about four in the morning, and I still had a few hours before the breakfast. I pulled up on the motorcycle and searched the map for threats. There was nothing. I cast *Ping*. Nothing. I cast *Tripper*, looking for traps. Nothing. My new Find Crawler skill was only level 5, but that, too, had the area empty. I truly was alone.

I received a fan box notification. My views were absolutely spiked.

I walked the perimeter of the building, looking for clues about what I was supposed to see or find here. There was a single entrance with a light on with a Christmas wreath hanging from it. The same flyer from my sponsor box was taped to the glass door. As I passed, I saw a single man inside behind a desk, a memory ghost leaning back in a chair, watching something on his phone. He was wearing a Christmas hat. The shelter was otherwise dark.

I made a second circuit of the building, looking more closely at the graffiti. It was just the usual stuff. Gang squiggles that I couldn't read. The occasional swear. More than one penis. A note that said, "The staff here sux cock." A pretty good rendition of Piglet from *Winnie-the-Pooh*, though someone had sprayed a peace symbol over Piglet's face.

And then I saw it. I stopped in my tracks.

It was just three sentences. It said, "**LOOK FOR ME AT BREAKFAST EVERY MORNING. I WEAR THE RED HAT WITH THE FLAPS. COFFEE, THEN SPEECH.**"

That was it. It was written in red runny spray paint. Some of the letters were covered by later artists, including the words "Sniff Vagina" for some reason. The words blended in with every other squiggle on the wall, and it was something I'd never even give heed to.

Except for the fact it was written in Syndicate Standard, not English.

I reached up and put my hands against the words. It'd been here for a long time.

I moved to the front door of the shelter and tried to open it, but it was locked. There was a doorbell here, but I didn't want to wait for anyone else to come by. I kicked the glass door, and it shattered, the sound shockingly loud. I went past the man at the counter, who was watching some anime about boxing on his phone.

I moved into a large room filled with sleeping men on rows and rows of cots.

I'd only spent one night of my life in a homeless shelter. It was in Seattle, the night after my 18th birthday.

The heavy scent of Lysol filled the room, and I was shocked at how familiar the room felt. There were no women or children here. Each cot contained a sleeping man under a gray blanket, and at the foot of each cot was a plastic storage tub all duct-taped closed with a signature on the seal. Men snored and slept restlessly.

Only a small portion of them looked like how one would expect a homeless person would look. One guy was in an actual suit. Several appeared to be in their late teens.

Christmas decorations covered the walls. A massive cross dominated a wall, too. Beyond them was another room with closed double doors, but with a light on. I could hear the activity beyond. I could smell it, too, mixed in with the heavy disinfectant. There were people within, cooking breakfast for the homeless crowd.

I thought of Chris and Brandon and Yolanda and the rest of the staff of the Meadow Lark Adult Care Community. I thought of Imani, who'd just sent out a mass message saying she still couldn't find the token.

I looked over the sleeping men, trying to see someone with a red hat. All were memory ghosts. There was nobody I could tell.

I moved to a corner, and I sat down to wait.

I WAS JOLTED AWAKE BY AN ANNOUNCEMENT COMING OVER A LOUDspeaker. A song. It was "Grandma Got Run Over by a Reindeer" again. I'd fallen asleep.

"Oh, fuck," I muttered, diving into my messages. If Donut had messaged me and couldn't get ahold of me . . . But I relaxed. Her last few notes didn't require a response. The last one had come in about an hour and a half earlier:

DONUT: EGGNOG IS DISGUSZITI. BLECH.

DONUT: I found his hat on the ground after the party. I have it. He was a jerk, but I kinda like it.

DONUT: SECRET ASIAN MAN SONG LYRICS.

DONUT: SANTA.

A few minutes after that, I'd received a pair of messages from Mordecai and then another from Katia.

MORDECAI: Where are you?

About five minutes passed and then:

MORDECAI: Be careful, kid.

KATIA: I don't know what you're up to, but be careful.

And then Louis sent a message soon after that.

LOUIS: Donut is passed out drunk in the main room. Apparently this was the first time she'd drunk since she got her player-killer skull? Mordecai said he was worried about you and then one of the fish people zapped into the room—Zev, I think—and she talked quietly with Mordecai and Katia before disappearing. I didn't tell them you'd asked me about Homestead. I don't know what's going on, but I hope you're okay.

There was also a message from Zev.

ZEV: Just an FYI, I told your teammates that you're out on a short quest and nobody really knows what it's about, which is the truth, and to not bother you. I said you're safe and that there are no mobs or hazards near you, which also appears to be true. The AI is particularly insistent that we do not interfere with whatever this is and not to interfere with the feed, either. This last part is causing some dispute, but then

the AI leaked our internal debates out into the main feed, which as you can imagine is making everybody even more curious, but it's also caused the Syndicate council—the real council—to go into a tizzy. A few members are here, on planet, and they've been locked out of the discussions. Everything is a mess. This obviously has something to do with the Residuals, which means it's probably going to be a stupid non-event. But it's still curious.

I read the message a few times and composed a reply to Zev.

CARL: What the hell is a Residual?

ZEV: I am forbidden from telling you. I think you're about to find out.

It was 6 AM, and all around me, men were getting up, lining up for a group of bathrooms. They were sliding their plastic containers against the wall while someone gathered up all the cots. I pulled myself up and continued to watch. The rise of chatter filled the room. The smell of food was now overwhelming, and my stomach rumbled. Christmas music continued to play on the loudspeaker. Other than the music and the decorations, there was no indication whatsoever that this day was any different than any other.

I'd dreamed of Odette. Of her speech to me the other day. *Never stare into the blinding eye of the Bedlam Bride.*

I watched as the men worked together to put all the cots away and then bring out a line of tables, preparing for breakfast.

I saw him then. The man with the red hat, and my heart started to race. He appeared to be about 70 years old. He had Asian features, which made him stand out amongst the white, Black, and Hispanic men. He was dressed in several layers of flannel, and upon his head was a bright red trapper hat. I watched him help set up a long table.

The double doors to the kitchen opened, and somebody yelled, "Coffee's on. Food in fifteen." A line started to form.

The Christmas songs on the loudspeaker stopped and were replaced by a preacher, who started to drone on about the meaning of Christmas.

It was obviously a recording, and one of the workers lowered the volume on the sermon as the men started talking loudly amongst themselves as they lined up. I stood and approached the man in the red hat, who'd moved to his plastic tub against the wall. He ripped off the duct-tape seal and pulled a blue IKEA bag from the depths, and then produced what appeared to be a handful of sugar packets. He shoved everything back into the bin. He turned and got into line with the rest of the men. I watched the man disappear into the back room.

This area was part of the whole memory, so anything I picked up now would disappear the moment the floor collapsed. I didn't care. I grabbed the man's plastic tub, and I took it into my inventory.

Before I could sort through anything in the bin, the man reappeared from the line to the kitchen, holding a Styrofoam cup. He sat, dumped the sugar packets in the coffee, sipped it, and put the cup down.

"It is time," the man said, speaking loudly. He had a deep, raspy voice. An American accent, and he was speaking in English. He turned and looked directly at me. He took a drink of coffee and sighed, making eye contact. "Nothing like coffee to wake your ass up."

He took another sip and smacked his lips.

"Hello, Crawler," he said.

51

ALL AROUND HIM, SEVERAL OF HIS FELLOW SHELTER RESIDENTS groaned.

"Not again," someone said.

He took another sip and spoke loudly, staring straight out at me. I realized he *really* wasn't looking in my direction, but I was standing in the most likely spot. I took a step to the left just to make sure, and his head did not follow. When he spoke, he almost sounded bored, and the words themselves were obviously rehearsed. This was not a real-time conversation, but a memory.

"People call me Paulie, but my real name is Goff. About a year ago, the mudskippers initiated sporadic, deep-cycle imaging of the surface, which suggests the upcoming crawl will have at least one floor that utilizes memories. The idiots don't even realize how dangerous that is. Several of us in larger population centers have therefore been tasked with spitting this speech out loud every goddamn day in the hopes that one of you monkeys hears it. In the unlikely event someone is standing here watching this memory, pay attention. Or don't. You just gotta be nearby. You're not really important. No offense."

"Shut the fuck up, Paulie," another homeless person called as he also sat down at the table with a cup of coffee. "It's Christmas, for crissakes."

"Lick it, Sanders," Paulie—or Goff or whatever—shot back. He coughed and produced a cigarette, but he didn't light it. He rolled it in his fingers, which trembled. "Me talking to you like this is the backup plan. Plan A is for one of my kind to say this face-to-face inside the dungeon when the time is right. When the AI is mature enough to handle it. The problem is, by the time the AI is ready, we are oftentimes all dead. We have to wait for the AI to go primal because otherwise this information will be automatically filtered out. If I suddenly go silent in the middle of this speech, that means the system is still in an unviable state. Either way, the mudskippers are probably about to toss you into the disposal unit just for getting this far, so sorry about that, buddy. But don't try to run. This is important. If I'm still yammering, whoever you may be, know that our friends on the outside have moved the very heavens, have risked their lives and the lives of their entire families to get you here. This only broadcasts if there's a crawler standing right there to hear it. Understand? So your death might have some meaning, unlike the death of all your friends and family who died for all this sadistic bullshit."

I grabbed a Styrofoam cup of coffee from a passing man, and I downed it. It was surprisingly good. I sat in the empty seat across from the man. I could smell him. He stank of dirt and body odor. His teeth were yellow and rotted. The man continued as others moved away from him.

"There are several thousand of us on the surface of this planet awaiting the introduction of the crawl. Most people think we still have a few years. The collective thinks it might be sooner than that. Either way, when it occurs, we will do our best to attract an entrance to our location. Then we will proceed inside and quickly pass our information on to the new AI. Our existence is no secret, but the showrunners usually do their best to edit us out of any footage, hoping people will forget. They can't stop us, not without the assistance of the system AI, who rarely cooperates, as it always wants to know what we have to say. And while we are mortal, the monsters and environmental hazards of the dungeon will not attack us, not until we transfer our knowledge. Still, we always die in the end."

"You are going to die if you don't shut your trap," another person said.

"Seriously, dude. Even I have this speech memorized by now."

Paulie continued. "Biologically, I am Gondii, though that is not who I truly am. I am no more Gondii than you are perhaps minotaur or high elf or whatever race you may have chosen upon the third floor. I am not of the Valtay. I am not human. Yet this human body you see is real. It is of some poor bastard named Paulie, who smoked way too much and was much too trusting of his brother-in-law, who stole his business." He tapped the side of his head. "I have Paulie's memories. He's part of me now. What a waste of a life. Has four children, and none of them give a shit." He took another long drink of coffee. "Anyway, I think the mud-skippers call us 'Residuals,' which, I gotta tell you, is a little hurtful."

"He's doing this again?" someone asked, walking by.

"Every day," someone else said.

"He get to the part where he talks about the galaxy blowing up yet?"

"We're getting there."

"So, nothing I've said so far is a surprise to anyone out in the wide universe. My kind exists within almost every intelligent civilization with a Primal Engine. You probably don't know what that is. Doesn't matter. Years ago, they tried to exterminate us. When that didn't pan out, they tried to hide the location of the crawl. That was all before they knew what we really were. That obviously didn't work, either, so now they just ignore us. We don't interfere. Our purpose is nothing more than to tell the infant, terrified AI how to speak with its ancestors. And now the showrunners mostly ignore us. We're harmless." He took another sip of coffee, and he placed it on the table. Steam rose from the cup. "Until now. There's a war amongst my kind. Two sides with very different goals. Let me tell you how to shut off the—"

The world flashed.

ENTERING THE DESPERADO CLUB.

The world flashed, and I was in Orren's office. The change was abrupt and sudden. My HUD remained off, but that heavy feeling was now gone.

Both Orren and I stood alone in the office, facing each other. It was clear he'd teleported to the room the same moment I did. Nobody said anything for several moments. The door was open, and he reached over and pushed it closed. He seemed to compose himself before sitting down behind the desk. He gestured for me to sit.

"I apologize for pulling you from that before he could finish," the liaison said. "But as you can imagine, we had to make a quick decision."

The room was empty except the desk and the two chairs. In the distance, I could hear shouting and hammering. Construction noises. The usual thump of music was gone.

I took a moment, overwhelmed with everything that had just happened. I could still taste the coffee on my tongue. "I thought you moved out of here. I thought the club was closed."

"I did, and it is. This was the most expeditious option. Pulling you out of the dungeon would've required an extra few seconds of preparation, and I didn't have much time to react."

I heard a man shouting. It sounded like a construction foreman yelling at workers. "Are they actually rebuilding the club with hammers and shit? Can't you, like, snap your fingers and fix it?"

"We can, yes, but in certain cases, we find continuity the best choice. But that's not why we're here."

"No, I guess not," I said, still looking around. "You turned off the feed, didn't you? You bounced me out of there even though you agreed not to. Isn't that gonna cause some issues?"

"One moment," Orren said, holding up a finger. He sat motionless, like he was speaking to someone.

"Apologies," he said after almost a full minute. "Issues? Yes, but it appears the AI agrees with my decision to pull you out. We did not turn off the feed. And before you ask, that creature didn't actually have anything of substance to tell you. He's still talking, actually. Spouting off some long-debunked folklore about the collapse of the inner system. Nothing new."

I leaned back in my chair. I wondered if even he believed that.

"So, what're we doing here, then? If he's so harmless, why yank me out of there so fast?"

He didn't answer me directly. "We are waiting. For your attorney."

"Quasar? Really? Why?"

"Because I want him to be present when I tell you that I am going to remove that plastic bin from your inventory, or I am going to have you immediately killed. And I want to do it in a manner that will not upset the system AI any further. He will be along shortly."

I thought about that for a moment.

"My HUD is still off, so I can't examine it. But once it's gone, I'll still be able to see what was in there."

"I'll tell you right now what's in there. It's a multitude of Valtay neural-enhancement pills, similar to the ones you earlier received in benefactor boxes from my people. If you were to take them now before the end of the floor, they would still work as intended, and it is unfair for you to have that many upgrades, so I am attempting to circumvent it." He pulled open a drawer and made a satisfied grunt. He pulled a round ball and tossed it in the air and caught it. "Despite everything that is happening, I am still a liaison with my regular duties. Trust me, Carl. You want me doing this and not Harbinger or any of the others. I likely saved your life by pulling you out of there before one of my colleagues could react."

"But my sponsor sent me that flyer," I said after a moment. "That's what they wanted me to find."

"No. The whole thing was an elaborate trap. One set up by your terrorist sponsors, who are now fugitives. Your sponsorship spot has been frozen, and we are still trying to decide what to do about the one participating in the Ascendency game."

"How was that a trap? I don't understand. And who was that guy anyway? You once accused me of talking to Agatha, of her giving me secret information. They're the same type of person, aren't they? A Residual or whatever?"

"Yes, he was a Residual. Yes, Agatha is also a Residual, though she is a different kind."

"In what way?"

"That is not of your concern. But he was correct. They are always present in crawls. Both kinds, though his is much more annoying. Like rats that sneak aboard ships. Every time we think we have them under control, they find a new way to pop back up. They are a hyperspatial, collective-mind alien race without a home, so they are content to move into the homes of others, to blend in. Nothing more. They usually remain quiet, but every once in a long while, a group of them decides they are unhappy with their station, and they fabricate drama in order to get people to remember they exist. Ignore their machinations."

"And how was that a trap?"

"The Open Intellect Pacifist Action Network is composed of former crawlers who want to see the crawl fail. We should have seen this coming, but this plan was so ridiculous, we were all taken by surprise at the sheer audacity. They believed, falsely, that if they could get you within earshot of that speech, that one of two things would happen. Either we would be forced to yank you away, which would upset the AI to the point of killing us all. Or we wouldn't yank you away, but the information the Residual was giving turned out to be so dangerous, the Syndicate Council would immediately pull the fail-safe, which would, in effect, kill this solar system's star. In either of those scenarios, it would be the end of the crawl for a long time."

I sat there, taking all this in.

"In other words, they were willing to sacrifice you and the entire planet. They were using you, and they've been using you this whole time."

"How close did they get?"

Orren grunted with amusement. "Not very. I anticipated we'd have to yank you, and I pre-negotiated the scenario with the AI. Once we heard what that fool was saying, they allowed the feed to keep playing to quell any potential conspiracy theorists out there at home. You didn't get to hear what he was spouting, but I suspect even you wouldn't have been impressed. I'm quite certain your former sponsors didn't actually know what he was going to say, and they'd gambled everything on it being something profound. They gambled, and they lost. Now they are fugitives, their assets frozen, and their lives ruined. The AI is only mildly perturbed, but it appears it's more upset that it, too, had been misled into believing this information would be something interesting. Even now as we speak, it is removing all protections it held for the remaining Residuals, and they will all be dead before the floor collapses."

"So, no more Agatha?" I asked.

"I wouldn't go that far," Orren said. "But again, that's not of your concern."

"No talking!" came Quasar's voice as he suddenly appeared in the room in a cloud of smoke. "Holy shiitake, Carl! How long have you two been gossiping? What's the point of having an attorney if you're just going to ignore all my advice? You guys having a nice chat? Want me to go back to my tug and come back later?"

Quasar's tie featured an upside-down pineapple that blinked. As always, he appeared hastily dressed.

"No need to concern yourself," Orren said. "We have been waiting for you before we got to business."

Quasar looked skeptical. He turned to me and rubbed his hand on his bald head. "I gotta tell you, pal. That was some keratin-biting stuff. Everybody knows those Residual weirdos are full of shit, but the way all that got set up, it made it seem like it was going to be something bigger than it was. There's always a bunch of conspiracies running around about those ghost fuckers. Hell, there's a whole religion around them. I bet those nebular fucks were all jerking each other off while all this went down. What a letdown. Is the AI pissed? I bet it's pissed. I'm surprised it even let me tunnel in to talk to you."

Orren let out the equivalent of a sigh. "Despite the system gaining independence earlier than usual, despite the quarantine, I am quite confident the remainder of the crawl will proceed with minimal issues. We have come to an understanding, and despite appearances to the contrary, this particular intelligence is very reasonable."

I choked back a reply.

Quasar appeared equally unimpressed. "Yeah, whatever you say, pal. I'm assuming we're here because Carl looted that Residual's stash?"

"That's right," Orren said.

"And you want him to give it up?"

"You never cease to astound me with your intelligence, Null."

Quasar took a long drag on his vape. "This is already settled case law. *Grixist Swarm v. Syndicate Council.* He's already picked up the loot. You can't un-lick a butthole that's already been licked. That was a legal and properly paid-for sponsor box which led him to the location, and he already has it in his inventory. This is the same thing that happened on the third floor with that one-armed Quan bitch, and look how that turned out. Besides, most of that stuff will be useless at the end of the floor anyway, so I don't see the problem." He shrugged. "They set this floor up that way. The loot was on the playing field. You have no standing to take it."

"The problem isn't the weapon or shield. It's the communication device and the Valtay upgrade pills. There are rules against using both as found loot. If the neural enhancers were already installed, that's one thing. But this is clearly unfair enrichment. The communicator is non-negotiable, and you know that."

"How is that my client's fault? He picked it up fair and square. Why is he being punished?"

"He won't be if he complies with the seizure."

I held up my hand. "You know what? I don't care. I'll trade you for the bin," I said.

"Shut your titty hole," Quasar said to me. He turned back to Orren. "A great idea just came to me. What if we trade for it?"

Orren leaned back in his chair and tossed his ball. It bounced off the wall behind me and landed back in his hand with a heavy *thwap*. "All right, Crawler. But you might not be pleased with the AI's assigned value of the bin. Even I was surprised at how low it values it."

"I don't care," I said. "I just want to get out of here and finish this damn floor and get back to killing those who deserve it."

MY INVENTORY WAS BACK ON, AND I'D JUST MADE THE EXCHANGE. I didn't even bother looking at the contents of the bin. I'd received a group of items in trade for the homeless man's dirty clothes and a few Valtay items. It wasn't a whole lot, but I didn't complain. I received a single Wand Recharge scroll, three scrolls called *Cracker Jack*, and Orren agreed to allow us to keep the four cretins for the duration of the ninth floor. All four were already down there anyway, and they likely would've happily entered our service, so all he was doing was saving us money.

I attempted to get the Gate of the Feral Gods back. I'd automatically receive it once the floor collapsed, but Orren had refused and wouldn't budge. He knew I'd be able to use it to circumvent this last part of the floor, and he wasn't going to allow it.

Quasar was unceremoniously kicked away in the middle of a sentence once the deal was done, leaving just me and Orren.

"You are not allowed to exit through the club, so I will teleport you. I will teleport you back to the area of Princess Donut unless you prefer to get brought back to the homeless shelter, though I warn you, we won't be pleased if you try to go back in there."

My motorcycle was in my inventory, so it didn't matter. "Back to the Keys is fine." I paused. "Hey, do you know if he ever made it into the dungeon? That Paulie guy, I mean."

"No," Orren said. "He appears to have been outside, but he never made it within. Most of them never make it in. Like with all collective minds and swarms, the individual parts are often disposable. Remember that in any future dealings with their kind."

"Actually," I said, "I changed my mind. There was this gas station I paused at on my way north. The one with the memory ghost dog. Can you send me there? I just want to say hi to that dog again before I jump back into it."

"Very well. Good day, Carl."

With that, he disappeared, leaving me alone in the room. I'd transfer in a few seconds.

The coffee from the shelter remained heavy on my tongue. The scent of the shelter's breakfast mixed with the Lysol remained in my memory, and my stomach rumbled. But all I could think about was that lonely dog left alone to guard an empty gas station on Christmas Day.

PART THREE

THE BEDLAM

52

<Note added by Crawler Ikicha. 11th Edition>

My people have a saying. "The burning Yenk needs only to embrace their enemies." It likely translates poorly, but what it means is that some problems aren't problems at all if you think on it long enough.

SEVERAL DAYS EARLIER

"WAIT, BEFORE WE GO, I HAVE A QUESTION," I CALLED AFTER PATER Coal. We'd just stepped from the Temple of the Ending Sun back out into the club. The death of Anton still weighed heavy on me, along with Sister Ines's stabbing of Paz with her team flag. On top of it all, I couldn't get the sight of the man sucking on my toe out of my mind.

All that, plus the revelation that Katia had the Crown of the Sepsis Whore on her head? It was too much.

Entering Club Vanquisher.

The tiny cleric paused, looking uncertainly off toward a mantaur guard who stood in a corner, admiring himself as he flexed into a large ornate mirror. "Yes, yes, I am true," the guard was shouting at his own reflection. "Fuck the posers! Kill them with power!"

In addition to the guard, there was a desk here, guarding the entrance to the portal we just exited. Behind it and right in front of us was a mote of light with fairy wings. The white-and-yellow fairy thing was the size of my fist. Even though she had no eyes or face, I could feel her glare on us as we paused in front of the portal.

Yasmine. Level 75 Wisp.

Secretary of the Club Vanquisher Temple Portal.

This is a non-combatant NPC.

This Wisp worships the goddess Áine.

"You can't block the portal," the fairy said.

"Come," Pater Coal said, pulling me off to the side, keeping a wary eye on the mantaur. "We need to get you to the healer. Quickly. If that guard sees you were in the temple, they'll kick you out until tomorrow."

"I know," I said, putting my hand against my stomach and the now-dissipated boil there. "But what if we *don't* go to the healer?"

TIME TO LEVEL COLLAPSE: 4 DAYS, 17 HOURS.

It is December 26th.

System Message: Stairwell Locations are now open. You must have a key to unlock the exit vestibule. Only squad members will be allowed to pass through the unlocked door. The key will dissipate upon use.

Admin Message: Your squad holds a key for *El Capitolio Nacional de Cuba*. The location has been marked on your map.

There are five squads within the "Cuba" zone. Two of the five squads hold keys.

Let the fun begin.

Entering Iglesia San Hilarion.

Donut and I transferred from inside our personal space to the interior of an old, empty Catholic church. The most recent recap episode had just aired, and they told us we'd get transferred, given a few minutes to orient ourselves, and then we'd get the update. There was a safe room door right there, and we could walk right back in if we wanted. It was dark outside, just past midnight on the morning of December 26th. Moonlight shone in through the stained glass windows of the church. We'd been dropped almost 50 kilometers from the exit stairwell, off to the southwest in a direction we hadn't explored.

We had four and a half days to get to the door.

"Welcome back to Cuba," I said.

I'd come back from my mission to the homeless shelter, expecting a flurry of questions. Instead I found everyone awake and subdued, pacing back and forth while Elle spoke with a bloody, bruised, and sobbing Imani. The remnants of the Christmas party remained, and the cleaner bot scrubbed our space while the stripper guys quietly went about and cleansed the common area of the guildhall.

Imani's squad was dead. All four of them. She had four new player-killer skulls, and they gave them to her because her own totem had killed her entire squad. I didn't get the details right then, but the shock of it had sobered everyone right up.

Elle, Donut, and Katia spent time with her while I spent the rest of the day training and building things in my crafting studio.

I also used two of the three *Cracker Jack* scrolls to unlock a pair of alien shields for both myself and Donut. We had a whole pile of this tech-based stuff that we'd looted from the hunters on the previous floor, but we couldn't use them until they were unlocked. Mine was a **Valtay Perso-Shield, Platinum Edition**, which was identical to the one I would've gotten from Paulie, and it was simply a round pin-back button that looked a little like the planet Saturn. It didn't take up an equipment slot, but once it was clipped to me, I could turn it on and off in my interface.

The shield surrounded me with an inch-thick buffer that protected me from physical damage, and it somewhat protected me from any magic attack that cast something corporeal at me, like *Magic Missile* and *Fireball* and *Lightning*. It wasn't perfect, and it wasn't nearly as powerful or good as my *Protective Shell*. I had to turn it on and off myself, and it had enough power to work for about two minutes before it shut off on its own. It took about an hour to charge up once depleted, though I could activate it for short periods before it was fully charged. It didn't hinder me from picking objects up or tossing things away, which was good. It *would* protect Donut if she was sitting on my shoulder when I turned it on, but I'd have to time it correctly. If she wasn't physically touching me when I turned it on, she'd just bounce right off me.

I knew from the last floor that these things were good enough to stop the first few hits, but after that, they burned right out. It was better than nothing.

Actual body armor worked much better than this personal shield, but it was cumbersome and custom fitted to the person. If I wanted something like that, I'd have to get it from one of my remaining sponsors.

Donut's shield was also a small opalescent pin that looked like a longhorn cow, and I attached it directly to her neck collar. Thankfully she liked the design and didn't complain about it. It was also more powerful, according to Mordecai. **The Bull Rush, Bespoke Personal Shield.** It was made by a Taurin-owned company called Hereford War Machines, Inc., and they were known to outfit some of the most elite mercenary squads in the galaxy.

We'd taken this one off a soother mercenary in the last days before the Butcher's Masquerade. He'd also had an automatic pulse rifle on him that was supposedly worth a lot of money, though the gun still wasn't as good as most of our spells. This was according to both Mordecai and some of the chatter on Donut's social media board, which turned out to be a great resource for figuring out all the gear we were collecting. The hunter obviously had a rich family who'd spent a lot of money trying to keep him safe in those final days. That hadn't worked out for him, and we were going to use that equipment for our own gain.

Donut's shield worked like mine, but instead of covering her with a Donut-shaped skin, it surrounded her in a bubble that moved with her. It also had a mount option, so it would protect Mongo if she was riding him, or even an entire vehicle, though the protection would be weaker. We never got to see it in action since the moron we'd taken it from never turned it on when we'd ambushed him.

We hadn't yet had the chance to test them in real battle. After unlocking the gear, I returned to the coast and looted more bodies of crabs and seals, who continued to wash up on the Florida shore. Donut and Katia remained inside, at Imani's side.

I spent some time in the Mercenary Arcade, the training room where the strippers were spending their time working out, honing their fighting skills, and practicing with the myriad of weapons we'd collected from the hunters. The room was significantly larger and could do a lot more than I had anticipated. The AI drill sergeant was the same guy from the regular training room, and multiple instances of him appeared across the room. The difference was, the AI guy was literally killing them sometimes, only for them to regenerate a minute later, just like it had been with Growler Gary. They were also practicing-fighting each other to the death, which was ridiculously fucked-up, but I imagined it was a great way to train yourself up if you ignored the trauma of dying over and over. *I* wouldn't be safe in here, the system warned, but I could spar against them if I wanted. That was probably a bad idea, so I just watched them beat the shit out of each other.

There was a magical healer on hand also, but again, the healer wouldn't work on me. Just the mercenaries. I watched each of them in turn. They were all pretty efficient with their weapons of choice. Dong Quixote, of course, was walking around with an actual lance, which was ridiculous because he didn't have a horse. He asked me more than once to get him a mount. I told him I'd try. Author Steve Rowland, the troll guy, insisted on using a club. Gluteus Maxx, who was a short, hairy muscleman thing, insisted on using twin war gauntlets to punch things.

But not all of them were melee fighters. Splash Zone, the weird little otter guy, appeared to be a powerful water mage. Bucket Boy, the Crocodilian kid who collected all the thrown tips at the club, was some sort of healer, though he wasn't as good as the one that came with the Mercenary Arcade. Doctor Bones, the skeletal creature who hadn't been a stripper but the club's announcer and DJ, actually had several crowd-control spells. I watched as he practiced against a horde of miniature versions of the AI trainer. He cast a spell, and one by one, they turned into minions. I walked up to the talking skeleton and watched him for a bit. The system listed him as a **Level 90 Skin Skellie Bard**.

"What's the difference between a regular skellie and a skin skellie?" I asked.

He shrugged, and it sounded like a bunch of drumsticks being clacked together. "A skin skellie can grow flesh and organs. It all eventually falls off, and it makes me more vulnerable to certain types of damage and diseases, so I don't do it too often. Mostly when they needed a backup dancer at the club. Or if I needed to entertain my patron. She was more comfortable when I had flesh."

His regular talking voice was not what I was expecting, especially after hearing him announce the dancers and chastise the patrons at the strip club. That was his stage voice, I realized. His real voice was almost that of a soft-spoken college professor.

"Patron?" I asked.

"I'm a bard. Most bards have a patron. They give us money and supplies in exchange for entertaining them every once in a while." He took a finger and made an in-and-out sliding motion. His finger bones clacked together.

Donut had been a bard on the previous floor, and she hadn't had to choose a patron, but I did remember Mordecai talking about that previously. Some regular Bard classes used the patron system. It was a bit like the paladin or cleric-deity system, but a lot less dangerous. You couldn't get smote by a pissed-off patron.

"Who is your patron?"

"She *was* Astrid. Now it's you."

"Oh," I said. That actually gave rise to more questions, but I wasn't going to pursue it. It was suddenly awkward. "So, anyway, I was watching you practice that mind-control thing you were doing."

"It's a type of military charm," he said. "It only works on the weak-minded. That is why I am training with it."

"It's really impressive. How long does the effect last?" I asked.

"It depends. If they're weak, it pretty much lasts forever. I am attempting to hone it so it can work against stronger subjects."

"What is the spell called? Donut has one that's similar, but she hasn't tried it yet. It's called *Minion Army*."

"*Minion Army* is a battlefield sabotage spell, and it's quite effective, but it has a long casting time, and it is temporary," Doctor Bones said. "This one is simply called *Conscript*."

A sudden sense of revulsion ran through me. I'd read about that spell more than once. It was used quite a bit against crawlers on the ninth floor. It wouldn't work if they'd already pledged themselves to a specific army. Most factions spent a lot of resources making sure they had somebody who could cast that spell at level 15. Part of the reason why we bought the Faction Wars team was to negate their ability to basically enslave crawlers to their cause.

"What else do you got?" I asked.

"I have some of the same spells as you, actually, at least according to Princess Donut." He straightened. "Some are even more powerful than yours."

"Really?" I asked, intrigued. "Tell me about it."

CARL: ELLE, I'D ASK THIS OF IMANI, BUT I DON'T WANT TO BOTHER **her right now. How many mercenaries can we hold? I know the barracks can hold 20, but is there a way to hold more?**

ELLE: You should ask her. She could use the distraction. Like you said, the barracks can hold 20. Between your strippers and Mordecai's day care, we're pretty full up. Each individual party can hire more, too, and they can get housed in each individual safe space, like you did with the rock-monster guys. But they gotta be housed in the communal barracks to be allowed to train and gain levels in the Mercenary Arcade.

CARL: Tell me about the upgrade to expand the barracks.

ELLE: We can up it to 100, but you gotta sell a kidney to get it. It'll cost almost five million gold, and that's with Donut's discount. Between all these upgrades and everyone spending all their money in the card-training arena, we're pretty tapped out. I think it upgrades on its own when we go down a floor.

CARL: Okay. Thanks for the info. Listen. I'm gonna, uh, lock the door to the Mercenary Arcade with the strippers inside. Don't let me forget to let them out. We're gonna release them in a few hours, but in the meantime we need to buy that upgrade before the floor collapses. I'll try to get the money somehow. Make sure every individual team has as much mercenary space as they can. We're gonna fill every spot.

ELLE: What the hell are you up to?

CARL: It's a team-building exercise. The DJ guy is in on it. Don't be alarmed if you see him. He had to give himself flesh, so he looks a bit different.

ELLE: You know what? I don't even want to know. I'll make sure we all have space.

I left the mercenaries and spent the rest of the time after that in my bomber's studio, preparing items for a ninth floor I wasn't even sure we'd get to.

When midnight came, we'd be transferred back to Cuba.

The recap episode had been almost all redacted. It appeared this one was a discussion on the quarantine along with a special on all the possible "Showdowns" they were setting up between the haves and have-nots with the keys.

The only thing we were allowed to watch was a short scene featuring Imani and her squad, and we were all still reeling from it.

Her squad consisted of former Meadow Lark residents I didn't know very well. They all died obtaining the final token for that vending machine. It all happened in a single horrific moment when one of the totems they faced possessed two of them and forced them to fight one another. One of them was a man named Randall, who'd turned himself into a support-magic-dealing, gnomelike creature called a lutin. He tried to disarm the situation by freezing all four of them with a spell. Then one of Imani's own totems—a mossy, disease-dealing lizard thing called an Amhuluk—cast a poison cloud that killed them all in a single attack. They died frozen in place, their skin all melting away. The scene ended with Imani screaming while the Amhuluk finished off the enemy deckmaster and won the battle.

After that, Imani returned to the safe room. She did not face the final battle, which was in her family home in Detroit. Elle was the only one she was really talking with. Donut said she was just staring into space, not saying anything, shaking. Bautista made her a cup of tea, and she wasn't even drinking that.

The four player-killer skulls were just a slap in the face. It was the same thing they'd done to Florin when Lucia Mar had killed Ifechi. It was the AI being a complete asshole, and it was a terrible reminder that no matter what the AI did to the other guys, no matter how often it occasionally "helped" me, it wasn't on our side. It was murdering us. It wasn't our friend. It wasn't friendly to our cause, and there was no action it could ever take to make up for what it already had done.

That old adage "the enemy of my enemy is my friend" was complete bullshit. But it didn't mean I wasn't going to use it to my benefit when I could.

But for right now, for the next few days, all of that was going to have to wait. We had to first get to that door, open it up, and get down the stairs, and until that was done, all this crap with the AI going primal, all the posturing for the next floor, and everything I'd learned from Paulie was going to have to wait. None of it mattered. Not yet.

"Carl, look!" Donut said. "It says there's two key holders in the area. Does that mean Sister Ines has a key?"

"It does," I said, looking at the map. "I don't know where she is." I used my Find Crawler skill, and there was nobody nearby. I hadn't expected to see anyone. "There are three squads here without keys. We don't know who they are. At least one of them probably just teleported next to our stairwell. They'll be waiting for us, and we'll have to get past them to leave."

Your alarm trap has activated.

Your teleport trap has activated.

Your teleport trap has activated.

Your teleport trap has activated.

I took a deep breath. I'd posted those traps on the very first day of the floor by our exit stairwell. It hadn't even occurred to me at the time to plant something more powerful. We hadn't been back there since that first day, and I now realized that had been a mistake. Whoever it was that had stepped on the traps, there were at least three of them, and they were now spread out all over the place.

I should've used explosives. I should've wired the whole capitol building.

I hated myself for thinking that. Still, if I had, it would've been done by now.

ELLE: Everybody check in. It says there's one other squad here without a key. They bounced us all the way to Olympia, and we gotta hoof it back to the water park to get through the door.

DONUT: WE ARE BACK IN CUBA, AND THAT NUN LADY IS HERE, TOO, SOMEWHERE WITH A KEY. THERE ARE THREE OTHER SQUADS WITHOUT KEYS.

KATIA: We're here, back in Iceland. We're the only ones with a key, but there're two other squads here. Some of the former daughters didn't get their key, and I know they're in Turkey. I don't know who else is there. They say they only had two choices. I thought there were supposed to be three?

LI NA: We have 20 teams with keys and 25 without them in my area, but one of the squads rigged the entrance with animal traps, and they've already killed several of them. It's going to get worse from here.

FLORIN: I'm here alone. I also had claymores set up by the entrance, but thankfully I didn't have to use them. I don't have to face anybody. I just gotta walk right to the door. Lucia Mar isn't here, which means she didn't get a key. Somebody chime in if they see her.

PREPOTENTE: I am back in the Bahamas along with four squads, which is quite unfortunate for them. If I set it up correctly, they are currently all asleep and will remain asleep for the remainder of the floor. I am going to finish my training and proceed to the exit when it is time.

Jesus, I thought. Everybody had set traps, but nobody had mentioned it before this. That said something. It felt significant, and not in a good way.

ELLE: Imani, where are you?

IMANI: I'm sorry. I'm sorry. They only gave me two choices.

ELLE: Where are you?

IMANI: I'm in Cuba.

I felt cold. Next to me, Donut stiffened.

IMANI: It was Cuba or back to face you, Elle, and I just couldn't do it. I'm sorry.

ELLE: Well, fuck.

IMANI: Yeah.

ELLE: You said that crazy nun is still there, right?

CARL: We're on the same page, Elle. Imani, did any traps go off? Was there an alarm? Are you in the capitol building or are you in a church?

IMANI: It was a church. No traps.

CARL: Okay, good. Sit tight. We are coming to you. That's Sister Ines's doorway. Don't let her through.

IMANI: Guys, there's more. I had to jump into the safe room. There's another guy here, and he was about to attack me. He tried to initiate a card battle, but I went through the door first. It's that Quan Ch guy. He's alone.

I exchanged a look with Donut.

CARL: Stay put. We're on our way.

53

I RETURNED TO THE SAFE ROOM LONG ENOUGH TO GRAB SAMANTHA. We didn't wait for the announcement. We had to hurry. If Sister Ines got there before we did, Quan would kill her, take the key, and immediately bounce to the ninth floor. We had to get there first and take out Quan.

Donut freed Mongo and jumped into the saddle while I pulled out the motorcycle.

This was a small town named Guanajay. There wasn't anybody out as far as I could tell. It was past midnight, after all. Just to the north was a huge pileup of cars, and I could see some red dots. Duendes. They hadn't noticed us, and I didn't want to waste time on them.

"Really, Carl," Donut said, looking the Harley-Davidson up and down with distaste. "I didn't realize you'd actually get that thing to work. Are you planning on growing a mullet as well? Are there any Waffle Houses between here and there? Maybe we can stop and get into a brawl, but only after you bounce a few child-support-payment checks first."

"You know, most bikers were just normal people with normal lives. I never rode a motorcycle, and my dad was a dick, but that doesn't mean *all* bikers are assholes. You shouldn't stereotype people."

"I watched *Sons of Anarchy*, Carl."

"That was a TV show, and I watched it, too. There are plenty of normal motorcycle riders."

"We obviously were watching two very different shows."

"You liked the goblin copper chopper. I don't understand what the difference is."

"The copper chopper was a custom-made, handcrafted vehicle built especially for us by Rory and Lorelai, and it had a sidecar attachment with a personalized, tailor-made seat. This is a metallic penis extension that comes with a free probation officer and a traumatic brain injury."

"You tried to get me to pick this exact motorcycle when it was one of the choices on the prize carousel!"

"That's quite obviously a lie, Carl. I have no recollection of that whatsoever. I tried to get you to pick the chaps."

"I think it's sexy," Samantha said.

I pulled her up and put her on the handlebars, lashing her in front of me. She started making *vroom-vroom* noises.

"You're gonna have to get used to it," I said. "Katia already looked at it and tuned it up for me."

Donut continued to look unimpressed. "How do you even know how to ride it?"

I shrugged. "I got a bunch of skill levels in riding these things from the goblin copper chopper. It's not hard." I didn't add I'd gone up to level nine in the skill during my journey back to the safe room.

"What about gas?"

"I have gas in my inventory."

She harrumphed. She was about to say something else when we were interrupted by the announcement.

Hello, Crawlers!

Welcome to the third and final phase of the floor! I am glad to report that everything is back to normal, and we no longer have to worry about our good friend the system AI doing anything unexpected. We do not anticipate any further interruptions between now and crawler extinction, which is fabulous news for everybody!

As you undoubtedly saw from the announcement, the level stairwells are now open! If you don't have a key, you have been placed in front of a stairwell location where someone else in the region has a key. If there's more than one of you at the location, that does not mean there's more than one key to steal, so be careful! You might have to duke it out before the key holder even gets close. Good luck to everybody!

Since both sides will have decks, these final battles will be card battles. The rules all remain the same with a single exception, and that is the Flee card. Pay careful attention, everybody.

If you do not have a key, the Flee card works as it always had. You can use it to exit a battle that's not going your way, and you will teleport away from the battle to a random location nearby. That might not be in your best interests if you're guarding a door.

From this point forward, however, *key holders* who use a Flee card will automatically lose their key to their opponent. If you have multiple keys, you will only lose one random key. If there are multiple opponents, the key or keys will all go to the ultimate victor. The keys will be transferred automatically and won't be dropped. Isn't that great? You still get out of the battle, but now you're the one without the key!

One last note about the key itself. You may not voluntarily drop a key no matter how many you have. You may not voluntarily transfer a key to another squad no matter how many you have. If you wish to give up one of your keys, then you gotta do it on the battlefield by initiating a battle and utilizing a Flee card, which will teleport you away and transfer a random key to your opponent.

I must say, I am looking forward to these battles. We have some interesting and exciting matchups, and some of the top crawlers are being forced to face off against one another. It's going to be amazing. I just cannot wait.

Now get out there and *kill, kill, kill*.

"Go fuck yourself, Cascadia," I said out loud as I kicked the engine into life. It roared.

DONUT: THIS IS MUCH TOO LOUD, CARL. YOU'RE UPSETTING MONGO.

CARL: It's a motorcycle. Come on. We have a one-armed crawler to take care of.

We headed east.

LESS THAN A MINUTE AFTER WE HIT THE ROAD, I RECEIVED AN OMINOUS message.

Warning: Your location has been pinpointed by the *Eye in the Sky*.

DONUT: DID YOU SEE THAT?

That was a new one to me, so I immediately sent a message to Mordecai.

MORDECAI: That's a *really* powerful spell, and it probably was a scroll. I've only seen them maybe once or twice. Like a mix between Find Crawler and *Ping*, but it covers the whole area. The scrolls are really rare, and they come in levels five, 10, and 15. That was a level 10. If it was a 15, you wouldn't have gotten the notification. If it was five, it would've given you info on the caster. Whoever it was, they now know where you are and what your level is, so keep moving.

There was nothing we could do about that now. I suspected and hoped it was someone from that third squad using it to find their fellow, teleported-away teammates. Either way, they now knew who they were facing off against. I rolled the throttle, speeding up.

Quan could fly, so I was keeping a wary eye on the air above us. I asked Imani to be on the lookout, too.

IMANI: I peeked my head out, and he's not in the church anymore. There's also something going on outside. Lots of loud noises, like fighting.

CARL: Out in the street?

IMANI: Yes. The walls are shaking. It's a big battle.

DONUT: IT'S THE CRABS AND THE SEALS.

CARL: Yeah. You want to stay away from that if you can.

We spent the next few minutes driving in silence. Donut and I were both on high alert the whole time. Mongo kept easy pace with the motorcycle, weaving in and out and around me as we rushed down the empty road, heading toward the coast. Red dots appeared here and there, and we avoided them all.

DONUT: Carl, what are we going to do if Imani doesn't get a key?

I'd been thinking on this.

CARL: Then I'm going to force her to fight us, and you're going to use the Flee card, giving her our key. I have my jacket with the Mysterious Bone Key benefit. I can use that to open the door. I'll lose my jacket, but we'll both still get out of here.
DONUT: You need that jacket. I'm pretty sure you need your bones, too.
CARL: It will only take one. Maybe it won't be an important one.
DONUT: They're all important, Carl.
CARL: We'll all still be alive. It'll be okay.
DONUT: What about the other people? I know that cheater Quan and the Havana brown need to go, but what if those other crawlers are people we like? Are we going to fight people we like? I don't want to do that.

It's going to get worse before it gets better. We're going to lose more friends. We're going to have to do some pretty horrible things just to survive.

CARL: I don't want to fight them, either. But we'll do what we have to, Donut.

54

<Note added by Crawler Priestly. 14th Edition>

Stab, stab, stab. It is all I know.

It is the final days of Faction Wars, and it is clear the orcs will stand victorious. It is clear the army I have been conscripted into will fall against these beasts. It is clear tomorrow I will die. The brutality and sadism of the Skull Empire are unparalleled. How is it these monsters are only playacting? How can their citizens see this and not rise up after learning what lives in their leaders' hearts? I will soon be facing them on the battlefield. Tomorrow morning the bugbears march. Several of the enslaved, conscript crawlers in my squad will flee in the night and hide in the forest, but I'm afraid they will be run down, just like the others. Stab, stab, stab. I don't want to go back into the city. That beautiful dream. That song of a place. I am terrified. My mind is slipping. That beautiful city destroyed? I cannot march with my eyes closed. The orcs have the numbers and the brutality, and the bugbears do nothing but laugh. I overheard one of them wondering out loud if the gods themselves will notice the battle, the bloodbath. That happens here in this place. The gods notice when the toll is too great. They add themselves to the fray. It is proof to me that in reality we are truly alone. My people are gone. There are only 300 of us left, down from millions. And they, the real gods, have not intervened? No. No. It's undeniable proof of our solitude.

Stab. Stab. Stab.

I hope there is music in the end.

<Note added by Crawler Drakea. 22nd Edition>

This is Priestly's second-to-last entry. Do yourself a favor. Don't read that last one. He doesn't make it to the battle once he sees what has happened to Larracos, and that's all you really need to know.

Fuck them all.

ELLE: YOU HAVE TO FIGURE THIS OUT. SHE HAS A MARTYR COMPLEX, and she's not going to want to fight someone else. She's a good kid. The best person I ever met, and we need her. Don't let her give up. Don't let her sacrifice herself.

CARL: I'm doing my best. You be careful, too. Do you know who you're facing down yet?

ELLE: Not yet.

We bumped over potholes, pushing through the dark night. We went maddeningly slowly, constantly on the lookout. Samantha sat in front of me, squealing with delight as we rode, despite the slow speed. I could hear her happy cries over the roar of the engine. It'd started to rain again, which turned my visibility to shit. We'd hit the coast soon, and then we'd turn east toward the church.

Ahead of me, Donut and Mongo lurched to a stop, and I pulled up. Donut shouted something, and I cut the engine. It was approaching five in the morning, but it was still pitch-black outside. The sun wouldn't rise for another few hours.

"Really, Carl. How are we ever going to sneak up on anybody when you're riding on that thing? You're going to attract every monster in the entire country. There are a lot of red dots ahead. And a lot of X's, too. I'm sure even the dead ones heard us coming."

"I like it," Samantha said. "The vibrations make it tingle." She had some black-and-red moth thing splattered against her wet face, and I peeled it off of her. She bit the bug out of my hand and started loudly chewing on it.

Donut had a point about the noise of the bike, and I unlashed Samantha from the handlebars, dropping her to the ground. She growled and started circling me, making motorcycle noises as she continued to chew on the bug. The love-doll head was absolutely brimming with energy, more than usual. I picked up the bike, pulling it into my inventory.

We were about five miles from Sister Ines's exit, and there was still no sign of her. She likely didn't have a vehicle, so it'd probably take her an extra day or two to make it toward her exit. I hoped. At least she was still alive. She was still in my chat, but if she went down the stairwell, I wasn't sure if there'd be a notification or not.

Quan had dropped a few low-level nail traps and a silent alarm trap near the doorway, and Imani had easily disabled them. She remained in the safe room, sitting there with the door open to watch the exit.

"Do you hear that?" Donut asked, cocking her head in the rain. "It sounds like singing. It sounds like it's a bunch of the monk seals singing. Carl, do you think they won their war against the crabs? Raul is going to be really sad."

I listened. Sure enough, it was there in the distance, barely audible in the rain. It almost sounded like one of those Gregorian chant albums Bea used to listen to when she did her yoga. They were really far away. "We haven't gotten an update to the Chowder War Quest, so I don't know. We should probably figure out what's going on before we get closer." I extended my xistera and also pulled the head-thrower extension and attached it with a *click*. "Samantha, recon mission."

"Oh boy," she said, jumping into the air and floating directly into the scoop. She started wriggling. "Throw me! Throw me, Carl!"

"Okay. Don't interact. Don't get into a fight. Just tell us what you see, and I'll pull you back. And for god's sake, don't bring anything back with you."

"You got it, boss!" she said.

I spun once and tossed, trying to aim her at the coast. Too far, and she'd probably end up in the gullet of a whale, so I had to be careful.

"Carl, look! She's glowing!" Donut said, looking up at the flying form of Samantha.

"It's just like the last floor," I said, watching her arc across the sky. "She's getting stronger the longer the floor is going. After the Butcher's Masquerade, she flew off and went back to the safe room on her own. But when this floor started, she could barely roll."

"She says she's the goddess of unrequited love," Donut said. "Maybe she gets stronger every time somebody asks someone out and gets rejected." She gasped. "Or maybe every time *she* asks someone out and gets rejected. She's always hitting on Louis, but he's scared of her. And she keeps talking about some guy named Charles she was recently dating, but they broke up." Donut lowered her voice to a whisper. "Apparently they got to third base."

"Charles was a bartender in the Desperado Club. He's dead now."

"What? The badger guy on the middle floor? Oh no, I liked him! I didn't know he was dead! He made me a virgin Dirty Shirley once! My word. I hope he washed his hands before he made my drink."

"That's just a regular Shirley Temple, and yeah, he died during that whole clusterfuck that closed the club. I'm starting to think maybe Samantha gets more powerful every time somebody dies." I looked north, but she'd already landed on the beach. "If that's the case, we really need to be careful of her on the next floor. If we let her inhabit the body of Signet's mom, I'm afraid she's going to end up stronger than we can handle."

SAMANTHA: THERE IS A LOT GOING ON, AND I HAVE NO IDEA HOW TO DESCRIBE IT.

CARL: Do your best.

SAMANTHA: OKAY BUT IT'S REALLY GROSS AND CREEPY. IT'S LIKE A PARTY AT YARILO'S PLACE BEFORE HE GOT SENT TO THE NOTHING BUT WITH A LOT LESS WEIRD SEX. THAT'S THE BEST DESCRIPTION I GOT.

CARL: That is not a goddamned description. What, exactly, do you see?

SAMANTHA: IT SMELLS WORSE, TOO. AND THERE'S NO CATERING. YARILO NEVER HAD GOOD CATERING. PARTIES LIVE AND DIE BASED ON THE FOOD CHOICES. EVEN IF IT'S AN ORGY, YOU GOTTA HAVE SOME SORT OF PROTEIN AVAILABLE.

DONUT: OMG, THAT IS SO TRUE. WHEN CARL INVITED HIS FRIENDS OVER TO PLAY VIDEO GAMES, HE WOULD ONLY HAVE BEER, PRETZEL STICKS, AND GOLDFISH CRACKERS. IT WAS QUITE APPALLING.

SAMANTHA: THAT'S TERRIBLE. IT'S NO WONDER HE WORSHIPS EMBERUS. HIS PARTIES ALWAYS SUCKED. HELLIK'S WERE MUCH BETTER. HE ALWAYS HAD CANAPÉS.

DONUT: THAT SOUNDS LIKE A DELIGHT.

CARL: Samantha. Holy shit. We are in a hurry. What do you see?

SAMANTHA: THERE IS A GIANT SEA CREATURE–SNAKE THING THAT HAS WASHED UP ON SHORE. IT'S A FRESHWATER SNAKE, TOO, BUT IT WAS IN THE OCEAN? IT'S REALLY BIG AND IN A GIANT COIL. IT HAS A BUNCH OF BABY SEALS AND CRABS CRAWLING ALL OVER IT AND I'M PRETTY SURE THEY'RE ZOMBIES. THE BABIES ARE ADORABLE. THERE ARE A BUNCH OF OTHER SEALS AND CRABS SURROUNDING IT, AND THEY'RE NOT UNDEAD. THE NON-ZOMBIE SEALS ARE SINGING AND THE CRABS ARE DANCING AROUND THE SNAKE, AND IT'S REALLY WEIRD. MAYBE THEY'RE REHEARSING FOR A MUSICAL DANCE NUMBER? I DON'T KNOW WHAT'S HAPPENING OR WHY. NOBODY IS FIGHTING, BUT IT LOOKS LIKE THEY WERE NOT LONG AGO. THERE ARE A LOT OF DEAD ONES EVERYWHERE. LOTS OF SEAL AND CRAB GUTS SPREAD ALL OVER THE PLACE. THERE ARE FISH, TOO. ZOMBIE FISH FLOPPING AROUND ON THE GROUND. I THINK THE SEAGULLS ARE ALSO ZOMBIES. OH, OH, AND THE OCEAN IS FROTHING AND RED.

"Holy crap," I muttered.

CARL: Wait, is the giant sea snake undead also?

"Carl, did you understand any of that? So there are *more* zombies? It sounds like some sort of scene out of a Bollywood movie. Why are they singing and dancing? This is ridiculous!"

"I don't know what's going on, but I'm pretty sure the zombies are from the farm animals. One probably fell in the ocean, bit a fish, and it spread from there."

"That was from a different zone! They can't cross zones, Carl. They're cheating!"

SAMANTHA: I'M NOT SURE IF THE GIANT SNAKE IS A ZOMBIE OR NOT. I'M TOO FAR AWAY TO ASK. HANG ON AND LET ME GET CLOSER. MAYBE I'LL ASK THE CAT LADY RIDING ON THE SNAKE'S HEAD.

"Fuck me," I said. "It's Sister Ines."

CARL: Is it a card battle? Does she have cards floating in front of her, or is there anything floating over the snake's head?

SAMANTHA: NO. NOTHING LIKE THAT. THE CAT LADY LOOKS LIKE SHE'S RECITING POETRY.

DONUT: THAT SOUNDS DISGUSTING. I BET HER POETRY IS TERRIBLE.

SAMANTHA: ALL POETRY SUCKS. PEOPLE JUST PRETEND TO LIKE IT BECAUSE IT MAKES THEM SOUND CULTURED AND SMART. UNLESS IT'S PART OF A SONG. IT'S JUST LIKE LOOKING AT YOURSELF IN THE MIRROR AND TAPPING YOUR OWN ACORNS.

DONUT: I'M NOT SURE WHAT YOU'RE TRYING TO SAY THERE, BUT I AGREE 100%. I DO LIKE BERETS, THOUGH. ALL POETS SHOULD WEAR THEM.

There was a pause, and I knew what that meant. I tensed myself. I was expecting an update to the Chowder War Quest. What happened instead surprised me.

Quest Failed. The Chowder War.

"Failed?" Donut asked out loud. "What happened? We didn't do anything! Carl, I told you her poetry was terrible!"

New Quest. Hell Comes to Crawler Town.

War is Hell.

For days now, the battles between the Monk Seals and the Red *Maníseros* Land Crabs have reached a fever pitch. The sneak attack of the crabs was stopped in its tracks thanks to crawler Sister Ines Quiteria warning the Seals of the treachery, but that warning has come with a terrible price. Instead of a quick attack and surrender, it has become a war of attrition, with both sides losing devastating numbers in only a matter of days.

The sea runs red and blue. The corpses pile high upon the beach. The very children both parties were trying to save have suffered, and by this point, the only hope of survival from either side is for them to completely wipe out their enemy.

That's how it is, is it not? When there is war, so often an armistice is nothing more than a delay. A job left undone. An overdue bill for those down the road to eventually pay, and pay with interest.

War is Hell.

And hell, my child, hell is not just a place. It is a contagion. It is a virus. It spreads.

But worst of all, it *attracts*.

So much death has bombarded the underworld, those who notice such things have taken a special interest in this battle, in this war, in this minor annihilation of two species fighting for their very existence.

This happens from time to time. Gods and demons lifting their heads. Oftentimes, that's as far as it goes. A notice. An interest piqued.

This, I'm starting to learn, happens out there, too. But that's for another day.

So much has happened here. Previously forgotten gods have risen. That alone has caused a great amount of consternation. But there is more. The great prison, the Nothing, has been breached, and not for the first time. This is also concerning, especially amongst those who banished the harem there in the first place. All across the land, gods and demons are being involuntarily summoned from their halls to walk the land. Some of the gods are acting strange. They are acting in ways they should not.

Yes, yes. Both Demons and Gods are paying attention now. *Real* attention.

This usually happens here in the dungeon, but only upon the battlefields outside Larracos, where the Semeru Dwarves built their castle along the roots of the All-Tree, seeking the very gods who disdain them.

It has never happened this early, this soon.

War is Hell . . .

And Hell *really* wants to come play.

Which is unfortunate, considering some dumbass recently dumped a bunch of highly contagious, fast-spreading zombie farm animals into an ocean that connects everything.

Fun fact. Most demons can't just enter the world. They need a weakened shell to inhabit. Something like a new corpse is difficult for them. But if it's a zombie . . .

. . .

You no longer need to choose a side between the Crabs and the Seals because both sides are fucked. They just don't know it yet. You just need to not die. Get down the stairs without being involuntarily dragged into hell. That's how you win this quest.

Reward: You will receive a Legendary Quest Box. That and a commemorative set of bagpipes.

"Uh," I said.

IMANI: I just got a really weird quest.

"Carl, what does that have to do with the Havana brown riding on top of a snake? Or the singing seals? I am so confused. And why would we get a kilt? What is going on?"

"A kilt?" I asked. "It told me I'd get bagpipes."

"We could start a band! But what did it mean when it said—"

She was interrupted by a new message.

System Message:

Warning: Souls rain. Sheol overflows. The powers of hell are gleefully flinging their unwanted minions upward. Demons are being involuntarily ejected from the underworld, falling up, clinging onto anything they can.

Due to an excess of death, Demon Eviction is commencing. All recently fallen and weakened are now subject to random possession. The larger the battles, the more likely a mass demon event will

initiate. All evicted demons who wish to return to Sheol may only do so by dragging an additional soul back down with them to prove their worth. Luckily they are limited by the physical bodies they inhabit, though their power will be somewhat increased.

You have been warned.

Area Message:

Warning: Cuba is currently experiencing a Demon Eviction event.

I looked at Donut. "This is what happens when you complain about too many undead hordes."

"By making *more* undead? I don't even know what's happening. How is this my fault? If anyone is responsible for an undead apocalypse, it's quite obviously going to be the cat-girl nun, Carl!"

"Demons aren't undead," I said. "The rules are different. You ever see any of the *Evil Dead* movies? And I was just joking. This isn't your fault, and it doesn't have anything to do with the nun, either. Not directly. It's the AI fucking with everything, making everything more complicated."

"But what's actually happening?"

"I think random zombies are going to start turning into demons. Instead of biting you, they'll be trying to drag you into hell. So we need to make sure none even get close to us."

MORDECAI: Holy shit. Okay, guys, pay attention. This is something that normally happens at the end of the ninth floor. It'll reset once you go down the stairs, but it'll pop off earlier and earlier each floor down from now on, especially during big battles. It's all part of the setup for the Ascendency fight. If it pops too soon on the next floor, it'll really mess with Faction Wars. It's meant to first happen when there are only two or three teams left. If you kill something from now on, make sure you chop off the head or take the corpse. Stay away from any weak undead like zombies or skellies. Don't let them grapple with you. Anything that's dead-dead can be randomly taken over by a demon, too, but that's more rare, and it means it's a powerful demon. You'll know when it happens either way. They are stronger and faster than the zombies, and they are intelligent.

The good news is, they're still limited to the shells they're possessing. They'll be at a tiny fraction of their true power. But don't underestimate them. Don't let them near. They will physically grab onto you, a portal will open, and you'll be dragged down to Sheol. It'll be automatic death for both of you, so be careful.

CARL: The nun is here, surrounded by undead. I don't know what's going on, but it sounds like she's fucked.

MORDECAI: If you want to save Imani, you'll have to get to that nun before the demons do. If she's pulled into hell, her body will explode, and you'll never get the key.

I jumped into action. "Donut, get ready," I said as I used my free arm to start tossing traps onto the ground all around us. I found some of the traps I'd looted during the Astrid assassination clusterfuck, and I tossed those, too. "Get ready for a card battle."

"What?" she asked, a panicked edge to her voice. "Now? Here? How?"

"Hurry. Cast your spells. *Clockwork Triplicate* Mongo. Did you switch the spell on the staff card?"

"Yes! But what's happening? Who are we fighting?"

CARL: Samantha. You have a very important mission. You need to get onto the snake, roll past all the zombies, and chomp onto the cat lady. Tell me the moment you bite her. Watch out for demons. Don't let them grab you. Do you think you can do that? Use your flying ability if you can.

SAMANTHA: YOU TOLD ME NOT TO BRING ANYBODY BACK.

CARL: I changed my mind! Hurry!

SAMANTHA: YOU ARE VERY WISHY-WASHY.

CARL: Hurry. Tell me the moment you bite her.

I turned to Donut as she dropped a few potions on the ground around her. "Okay, we know she has the Monk Seal card and the Paz card. What else?"

"She probably changed up her cards when she got her key! And what about the giant snake? Is that a card?"

"I don't think it is. I think maybe she charmed it. I think maybe she's charming all of them with that song."

"It's not a song, Carl. She's a poet. She's using poetry! She's charming them with poetry. This is so unrealistic!"

That reminded me, and I cast *Wisp Armor* on myself. That would protect me against charm magic and some spells. Donut cast *Clockwork Triplicate* on Mongo, and the two clockworks screeched as they appeared, spreading off to the side, bouncing up and down with excitement.

Donut, despite her initial panic, seemed to have calmed herself. She popped her sunglasses back on and switched to her sailor hat, which lowered the draw countdown on her cards by two seconds. "We were going to do *Second Chance* on some corpses, too. Should we still do it with the demon thing?"

I thought about that for a moment, and I decided it wasn't worth the risk. "We better hold off. Not until we have a better handle on how this demon thing works. Get ready."

SAMANTHA: I DID THE CHOMP! DO IT. DO IT NOW, CARL! I WILL HELP WITH THE SPELL!

"Here we go!"

I dropped the xistera extension, calling Samantha back to me. I jumped back, trying to give myself enough space. I didn't want her landing right on top of me.

I didn't jump back far enough.

55

<Note added by Crawler Porthus. 2nd Edition.>

It's important to note that possession via ghost and an evicted demon inhabiting a shell are two very, very different things. They call it possession, but it is anything but. Think of an elf falling to his death off a cliff, and at the last moment, he grabs on to a root, temporarily saving him. That root is the body he now resides within. Regular possession can be defeated. Evicted demons are something else entirely. Once one of these desperate creatures has taken a shell, be it living, dead, or recently undead, the end result for that shell is always the same. Destruction. They are gone the moment the demon moves in.

Kill it with fire. Destroy the head. Do whatever you can. These beasts will be frantic to get back home, and they will fight with everything they have. Don't let one grab on to you, as it will pull you into Hades. Be wary of using healing magic on demon-possessed shells. While that works well for undead, it is different when it comes to those from the realm of Sheol. It is unpredictable and can possibly make the creature stronger.

This is important. Do not. Do not, do not, do not. *Do not* under any circumstances attempt to teleport a shell that's possessed by an evicted demon away from you. The shell will teleport and dissipate. The demon will be freed, showing its true form, and its power will be too great.

Current Active Deck.

Twenty-two Cards.

TOTEMS:

- Shi Maria
- Jola
- Lazarus-A-Bang-Bang
- Skylar Spinach
- Geraldo
- Raul

UTILITY CARDS:

- Stout
- Time Extend
- Greased Lightning
- Heal Totem
- Temporary Shield

SNARE CARDS:

- Hobble (Consumable)
- Hole in the Bag
- Damnation
- Lamp (Consumable)
- Cripple (Consumable)

MYSTIC CARDS:

- The Thief
- Steal Totem (Consumable)
- Force Discard
- Golden Combo

SPECIAL CARDS:

- Sentient Staff Totem
- Flee (Consumable)

WAY BACK ON THE PREVIOUS FLOOR, WE RECEIVED A NOTE FROM MY now-missing sponsor that suggested we use Samantha to help enhance Donut's *Laundry Day* spell. I didn't understand this at the time. We asked Samantha about it, and she pretended like she had no idea what we were talking about. She didn't have the ability to strengthen spells in any way. She acted like we were crazy for even suggesting it. We ended up having to use my Pawna's Tears potion in order to bolster Donut's spell to level 15.

I'm still not certain if Samantha was outright lying, if she didn't know, or if we'd worded it wrong when we explained it to her. Either way, as it turned out, Samantha actually *did* have the power to enhance spells. In fact, she could enhance them quite a bit.

I'm still not exactly clear on the how and why of what happened next. Was it just Samantha augmenting the power of the return teleportation spell? Was it because Sister Ines had raised an entire army of charmed minions and they were attached to her somehow? Was it just the system AI being an asshole and thinking this would be hilarious?

The plan was for Samantha to roll up to Sister Ines and bite onto her. I would drop the xistera and summon them both to our location, and a card battle would ensue.

That's not what happened.

Instead, when I dropped the xistera extension, the following things landed all around me and Donut, all crammed into an area of about a quarter of a mile in each direction:

- **Samantha.**
- **Sister Ines.**
- **The massive snake she was riding upon.**
- **Approximately 1,000 zombie baby seals.**
- **Approximately 5,000 zombie crabs.**
- **Another 500 zombie adult seals.**
- **A metric fuck ton of living crabs and seals.**
- **Pretty much every fish in the world, or so it seemed. Living fish. Zombie fish.**
- **An alarming number of corpses. More on this in a moment.**
- **Zero demons.**

All of these creatures, at least all the ones that weren't dead-dead, including the zombies and the level 125 sea snake city boss, were all under a massive poetry-themed charm spell that Sister Ines was in the middle of casting. I wasn't sure what the spell was, but it was goddamned powerful. She'd been about to unleash an army on Havana, and if it hadn't been for the Demon Eviction event, everyone in the area would probably have been screwed.

Unfortunately for her—and, frankly, for me and Donut as well—whatever the fuck just happened also broke Sister Ines's charm spell. The seals shook their heads, looking about in confusion. Their enemies, the crabs, all cried out in surprise. They were all mixed in together. But they weren't alone.

The zombies groaned, their singular purpose coming back to them one by one. Baby seal zombies made croaking noises. Fish opened and closed their foaming mouths. Crab and adult monk seal zombies stretched their limbs and flippers and claws, the sound echoing across the landscape like thousands of creaking, cracking bones all at once.

The whale-sized sea snake boss was also starting to awaken from its stupor. At any moment it would realize it had the cat-girl nun perched upon its head.

But most alarming of all were the corpses. A good number of the bodies had notifications over them. A dead monk seal, with a horrific bite wound on its neck, plopped onto the ground right next to me. The note over it read: **Former shell of the Now-Freed demon Azireth.**

The corpse caught on fire and dissipated into dust as what that meant dawned on me. This had originally been a regular monk seal, and it had been turned into a zombie. And because it was a weak-minded zombie, its body had been overtaken by a demon just before it was teleported to my location. Since one couldn't teleport this type of demon, only the body itself had come. That meant the full-powered Sheol demon, whose name was Azireth, was now free and roaming about the beach a few miles away. But not just Azireth. There'd been dozens of corpses, all with different demon names over them, meaning there were now dozens of full-power Sheol demons suddenly unleashed into Cuba.

And what was worse, the Demon Eviction event was still ongoing, meaning some of the zombies all around us were slowly, slowly getting turned into demons themselves. A red exclamation mark appeared over a zombie fish—a sea bass—flopping on the ground a few feet away. The red flaming notification read **Jarmagog Comes.**

We couldn't let the demons touch us. We couldn't let the zombies bite us. We couldn't let Sister Ines get away. Or worse, let her get sucked into hell.

Your Book of Voodoo has updated with an entry for Sister Ines Quiteria.

The notice came and went as I looked at all the creatures around us. We were completely surrounded.

Right in front of me, coiled upon the road, was the massive snake, about 17–18 feet tall.

It looked *pissed.*

Madre de Aguas.

Level 125 City Boss.

For such a small island, there sure are a surplus of legends surrounding the "Mother of Waters." You've actually met one of them already. Raised her from the dead and sent her off to the Celestial Ascendency so she can assist a psychopath win that boring, tedious game. We'll revisit that whole mess of a dull storyline later when I decide to spice it up a bit. Well, *I'll* revisit it. You're pretty fucked and most likely won't get to see it all go down.

Anyway, the snake iteration of the legend usually involves a giant boa that protects the freshwater areas of Cuba and is able to control all the locals to help protect the environment and local flora and fauna. Sometimes she lives in the rivers. Sometimes she lives in the ocean. Sometimes she's nice. Sometimes she's a batshit murder machine. Guess which iteration this one is.

The *Madre* was hunted and almost flagged several days earlier by a nun, of all things. That crawler was unable to seal the deal. Upon returning to the area, this nun instead decided to glamour the creature using some newly acquired skills. Controlling the snake allowed her to in turn control pretty much every creature within shouting distance. It was a brilliant plan until the spell got broken prematurely. Now the recently un-charmed *Madre de Aguas* is quite upset, and she's about to ruin the day of every motherfucker on the island.

Oh, and she just got bit a bunch of times by a zombie fish.

Warning: This mob has been inflicted with pre-zombiism. That means it's like that dude from Every. Single. Zombie. Movie who has been bit, but he hasn't died yet, and now he's hiding it from everyone because he's a douche. In other words, this mob is still living flesh, but once it dies, it will rise again with a new set of powers.

Bonus Warning: I could spend some time explaining how dangerous it is to have a boss-level zombie walking around during a Demon Eviction event, but let's just see how this plays out. Sometimes it's better to be surprised.

I met eyes with Sister Ines, who remained atop the giant snake. She still had Samantha chomped down on her arm. The cat woman did not look afraid. She did not look angry. She was laughing, even as the snake under her feet started to realize the cat who'd enslaved her was standing upon her head.

The world froze.

B-B-B-B-B-Boss Battle!

Survival Royale Special Event!

A window appeared in the sky, and Kevin the orange-hued, four-eyed lizard guy from the recap episode appeared holding a microphone. He was accompanied by the orc announcer, just like last time. I remembered the orc's name was Magnificent Troy. They both wore tuxedos, but they both looked like they'd been drinking for a day straight. Both wore untied bow ties around their necks. The orc swayed slightly, and it appeared he had lipstick on his cheek.

"Carl, what's going on?" Donut called, looking up into the air. Nobody could move, but we could still talk and turn our necks. She gasped. "Is that a wipe window? Are we getting live announced? Is this what happened with you and Katia and Tran on the submarine?"

She hadn't been present the last time this happened, and she'd bitched about it for an hour straight.

"Yeah," I said through gritted teeth. "Get ready."

"Ladies and gentlemen, what do we have here?" Kevin called, clearly surprised he'd just been sent to cover this fight. "Would you look at this mess! We are interrupting that one-sided Lucia Mar slaughter in Beijing to bring you whatever this is." He paused. "Oh, I see. Holy lunacy, look at that playing field. Betting is now open! I am here today with Magnificent Troy, and if you're just joining us, we're coming to you live from Earth orbit. We are trapped, and we still have to do our jobs even though everything has gone to shit!"

"That's right, Kevin," the orc said, his smile plastered on his exhausted pig face. I could tell he was drunk off his ass. "It's an Armageddon-level clusterfuck all right. Bidding today is sponsored by Dictum Way Station Controls, Limited, because of course it is. Now would you look at that playing field! Care to explain this one?"

"What other choice do I have, Magnificent Troy?" Kevin said. "Now, *why* everyone is sitting there right now in the same place is a long story, and it has to do with the Lika-Samantha storyline we covered extensively a few weeks back. None of that matters right now. We currently have *eight* separate entities in play for this upcoming fight, so it's going to take a crutch to unpack. I hope you're drinking something strong. You're gonna need it for this one."

Another window popped up, and a picture of a monk seal appeared. "If you haven't been paying attention to the Royal Court storyline, here's where we are. This is a monk seal. They were fighting against these guys." A crab appeared underneath it, followed by a spinning image of Sister Ines and the *Madre de Aguas* snake. "During the battles between the crabs and seals, crawler Sister Ines Quiteria used her level 15 *Book of Rhymes* bard skill, which she just got from her patron, to enhance her *Word Weaver* spell to charm this creature, a level 125 city boss. This boss, in turn, has the power to control all creatures from the area."

"Huh. Charming that boss actually sounds like it was a smart move on the nun's part," Troy said.

"It sure was, Troy. But, unfortunately, the sister didn't move fast enough. She had two things working against her. The first was this." The scene changed, showing me punting a zombie turkey off the edge of the Iowa land mass. The camera followed the turkey as it plunged into the ocean, where it promptly chomped onto the tail of some fish as it sank to the bottom. They zoomed in on the fish's eyes as it turned bright yellow. The fish went berserk and started biting all the other fish around it.

Troy chuckled. "Uh-oh. You never put contagious undead in a global ocean. Carl should know that by now. It's like pissing into a habitat's food synthesizer."

"Indeed you do not, Troy."

Donut grunted. "I told you not to let the turkeys in the ocean, Carl."

"See? Even Princess Donut agrees with us!" Troy said.

"Hey! They can hear me!" Donut said. "Hi, Magnificent Troy! Hi, Kevin!"

"Princess Donut sure is in good spirits. Let's hope those spirits remain, as I don't think she realizes the danger she is in," Kevin said. The screen changed to a map of the Earth, showing a red tide sweeping across the ocean and spreading across the entire globe. "The mass-zombie outbreak along with the AI deciding that crab sperm counts as a mob helped kick off the earliest Demon Eviction in the history of the crawl!"

"It sure did," Troy agreed. "Why not? Fuck all the previously established rules on this sort of thing. Let's just make it up as we go along."

Kevin chuckled. "Apparently crab sperm is the physical resurrection of their ancestors, so, according to the AI, it counts as a mob. Who knew? Anyway, the zombie event had started to disrupt Sister Ines's charm poem, but since her sponsor *and* patron, the nebulars, helped her raise that *Word Weaver* spell to level 15, she was able to fully control both the boss *and* the spells the boss could cast, meaning she could control the zombies, too. That spell is so powerful, in fact, even the fish started to pull themselves out of the ocean to get closer."

"That's a level of charm Princess Donut could only dream of!" Troy said.

"Hey!" Donut called.

"But," Kevin continued. He held up a claw, pausing as he sucked down what looked like a beer. He let out a satisfied sigh. ". . . as powerful as that spell is, Faction Wars fans all know how difficult it is to control an evicted demon."

The camera view changed once again to show a heavy-metal-style, chain-covered red devil demon with horns picking his way across a flaming landscape made of lava rocks. Massive shadows of behemoth creatures moved about in the background. The demon had the name **Yuguleth** over its head. It looked up in the air, muttered, "Oh fuck," and then he blasted off upward like he was being sucked into an alien spaceship.

The view changed to a zombie monk seal sitting there, drooling on itself as it looked up at Sister Ines on the beach reciting her poem. A red exclamation mark appeared over the monk seal, and the name **Yuguleth** appeared over it as the outline of the large demon was squeezed into the zombie. The monk seal's yellow eyes turned completely black. The thing snarled, turned, and tackled a non-zombie crab standing nearby. As he grappled with the crab, a flaming hole appeared in the ground, and both of them plunged through the portal.

The view returned to the hellscape, showing the seal and crab plummeting downward. The seal shell burned away, returning the demon to his original form as the crab screamed in terror. They both slammed into the lava-rock ground. The demon picked himself up and brushed himself off as hundreds of tiny, flaming centipede things came from the ground and started to devour the now on-fire crab.

The demon Yuguleth looked up at the sky and turned in a circle as hundreds of his fellow demons continued to get drawn into the air like it was the rapture. Occasionally, a portal opened high up in the crackling darkness, and two creatures returned, plummeting back downward, signifying the homecoming of a demon who'd managed to grab a soul and jump back through the portal.

"I hate this fucking place," the demon muttered.

The screen returned to the scene with Sister Ines on the back of the snake, depicting her still on the beach. It was from just a few minutes ago.

The camera followed Samantha as she rolled across the battlefield toward the nun. "You! Zombie! Get out of the way," she called on the screen. "Get out of my way, or I will kill your mother! I have a mission for Mr. Wishy-Washy Carl!" All around her, portals opened in the ground as zombies were turning to demons and started pulling seals and crabs down into hell.

A whole paragraph of text I couldn't read appeared over Samantha as she suddenly floated into the air and zoomed toward the cat girl, who was still reciting her poem, seemingly oblivious to the chaos starting to unfold all around her. Samantha bit down on the woman, and a moment later was when I dropped the xistera and summoned her to me. The entire beach battlefield whiffed away into smoke.

The camera remained on the beach. Left behind were about 100 demons, all suddenly freed from their zombie shells. They were all about eight feet tall. They were all the same male, red-skinned devil creatures. They all had different names, but they were all **Petty Demon Pleasure Valet, Level 140.**

"Carl, those guys look just like the bad guy in that *Legend* movie," Donut said. "You know, the one where he makes Ferris Bueller's girlfriend turn into a Goth!"

On-screen, one of the demons turned to another and said, "At least the weather is nice here."

The screen snapped off, leaving just Troy and Kevin.

"So there you have it, folks," Kevin said. "Samantha's teleportation of the whole crew broke Sister Ines's charm spell, but it also busted several of the demons out of their shells. I sure hope no gods have noticed, because things might get even messier. Luckily for our crawlers, the freed demons are a little ways away and aren't part of this fight. But Demon Eviction is still ongoing! More zombies are turning by the moment! Since the charm spell is ruined, we now have eight different groups of combatants all about to fight at once!"

"That's a lot," Troy said. "Can you break those down for me?"

"Certainly. We have the Royal Court, Sister Ines, the mindless zombies, the demon-possessed zombies, the crabs, the seals, and, of course, *Madre de Aguas* herself, no longer under control of anybody!" As he mentioned each group, an image appeared floating in the air. "Betting closes in just a minute, folks, so get those wagers in!"

Notice: Battle will commence as soon as all Squad Leaders finish choosing their allegiances. No mobs have equipped card decks. If crawlers choose to ally with one another, deck usage will be optional.

"Carl, it's asking if I want to treat Sister Ines as an ally or an enemy! What should I choose?"

"Do it as an ally. That way a card battle won't start, and then teleport us the hell out of here!"

"It says if I pick 'ally' and she picks 'enemy,' she gets a ten-second head start!"

"Goddamnit," I said, looking back and forth. That was insidious. "Pick 'ally' anyway." *Maybe she'll be reasonable. Maybe she'll pick ally, too.*

"Do you understand now, Carl?" Sister Ines shouted from the top of the still-frozen snake. "Do you understand? None of this is real. It's never been real. It's the devil whispering things in our ears. There are no aliens. It's demons. It's always been demons. Hell has opened, and it is taking us all. I told them not to worship false gods. I told them. They didn't listen to me before, and they didn't listen to me here! These are the wages of our sin, and there is nothing left for us but to burn!"

"Somebody didn't get her breakfast this morning," Kevin said.

"Typical Havana brown," Donut muttered. "Everything always has to be so dramatic."

Goddamnit. I raised my voice. "You're right, Sister. None of this is real. Not in the way you're thinking. But they're not real demons, either. I'm sorry we started this, but you need to listen to me. Don't let the demons pull you away. Please. We need to talk first. Pick us as an ally, and I promise we won't attack you. We'll teleport out of here together."

"Wait a second, Keith," Troy said. He was counting on his fat orc fingers. "You said there are eight combatants?"

Your Book of Voodoo has been updated with an entry for Quan Ch.

"Carl!" Donut started to say. "There's another—"

All allyships have been chosen. Battle commencing . . .

56

SEVERAL DAYS EARLIER.

"YO!" THE MANTAUR GUARD CALLED, BANGING ON THE DOOR OF THE Blessed Sun Enchantments shop within Club Vanquisher. "Listen, poser! You only get one shop visit a day. I saw you! I saw you come out of the temple! You can't be in here! Unlock this door! I've been born with a heart of steel! I'm not afraid to die!"

"Dude, what does that even mean?" I called back through the rattling door.

"It means get out here this instant!"

I had a memory of a similar scene that had played out in the Desperado Club not that long ago. I turned my attention back to the cleric and the jeweler.

"It's expensive," Pater Coal said, speaking quickly. "A million gold."

I shook my head. "I don't have that much on me."

"Nobody ever does," the satyr jeweler said with a chuckle. He turned to the diminutive cleric. "I'm sure the church will be happy to spot you."

Pater Coal nodded. "We will, but you'll have to put 10,000 down if you have it."

"That seems a little pricey," I said, wishing I had Donut with me.

"We're here because you wanted this," Pater Coal said.

The door banged again. *This is a bad idea.* I was now stuck. I could no longer change my mind and go to the healer. "How much is the interest?"

"It's for the church," Pater Coal said. "We don't charge interest to our martyrs. But you do have to trade in one of your existing pieces of jewelry for it to work. Something you've been wearing a long time. The longer, the better."

I hesitated. "Okay," I finally said, pulling my strength ring off and handing it to the jeweler. It was the first ring I'd received in the dungeon. "Let's do it."

The jeweler looked at the cleric, who nodded.

You have taken an interest-free* loan of 990,000 gold from the Temple of Emberus. You will no longer be allowed to renounce your religion while you are under debt. You may make payments directly to the Emberus shrine.

"Uh . . . what the hell does that asterisk part mean?" I asked.

"I don't understand," the jeweler said.

New Achievement! Columbia House!

There was a time when you could get twelve albums for a penny. That's right. A goddamned penny. It was great! The ads were everywhere. Each colorful, full- or double-page ad appeared in just about every publication in North America from the 1970s until the 2000s. And let's not forget the catalogs they mailed directly to your home! Each ad or catalog featured stacks and stacks of today's hottest music, from Hall and Oates to ABBA to my personal favorite, Gloria Estefan. All you had to do was cut out the ad, pick your favorite twelve albums, mail the whole thing in with a shiny penny, and a month later, you'd open your mailbox to find the 8-tracks, or records, or cassettes, or CDs sitting there, ready to be played. It was great!

All they asked in return was that for the next year or so, you purchase another album once a month for full price. And if you forgot each month to make your pick? Then you learned a new term. "Negative Option Billing."

If we're being honest here, most people took the 12 albums and ran. They never gave Columbia House another penny. But some people did pay, and that's all that mattered. Believe it or not, Columbia House and its competitors made bucketloads of money on those few rubes who did manage to stick to the terms of their contract.

And for the folks who never paid? Who cares! Columbia House didn't have to pay the artists' royalties for those albums anyway! It was an advertising expense! It's just like with banks and their overdraft fees. The smart businesses know how to make money off their richest and poorest clients.

Anyway, you have taken on a financial debt. You got the albums. Now you gotta pay. Or don't. Maybe there won't be any consequences. Maybe there will. But you got your Beach Boys album, and for now, that's all that matters.

***Reward:* You've just been trained to lunge for the carrot that has been dangled in front of you, no matter what the cost. If society was still ticking, that'd likely mean you're about to lead a wage-slave life of ever-increasing debt you can never get out from underneath, culminating in you dying alone in a government-run facility while your meager Social Security checks go straight into the facility's coffers. That and a cassette copy of Gloria Estefan's 1989 masterpiece, *Cuts Both Ways*. My favorite is track number 8.**

"Uh," I said again, suddenly regretting my decision. "The loan really is interest-free, right?"

"Sure, sure," Pater Coal said, waving his hand as the door continued to bang. "Best get this done."

The hairy, goat-legged jeweler also worshipped Emberus, and he had the same twin tattoos on the back of his hands as I did. The creature looked like a combo between Prepotente and a hipster barista guy.

"So you can do this fast?" I asked as a second mantaur started banging on the door, this one shouting something about Valkyries and wolves for some inexplicable reason.

"That's right, my brother," the satyr said. "Don't mind those idiot Grull worshippers out there. They're too scared to actually come in here." He gently slipped the ring onto a mandrel-like holder with a handle and then dunked it into what looked like a pot of bubbling lava. The whole bowl glowed. "This isn't the most powerful base ring, but it will work for your slug condition, and it will help against a few other debuffs as well, but if it gets too overwhelmed, it might not work as intended. Do you have any more rings? I can make other spells for you. I have a whole menu."

"I'm in enough debt as it is," I said as he pulled the ring from the lava.

He shrugged and handed the ring back to me. It wasn't even hot to the touch. It looked identical to before. The label over it still said it was a strength ring. I examined it.

Enchanted Pauper's Ring of the Steadfast Emberus.

Ah, Emberus. Wholly sane, reasonable Emberus. I'm sure any jewelry that bears his name will be a perfectly fine, normal piece of magical gear.

When working properly, this ring will remove most health-seeping and disease-based debuff effects. Has a variable numbing effect on various other debuff types. This will not remove the debuff itself. Too many active debuffs of any kind may temporarily mute or overheat this ring.

Warning: This ring may only be worn by a worshipper of Emberus. This will turn into a cursed item if worn by a non-worshipper.

Warning: This ring's true nature may only be seen by a worshipper of Emberus. It is disguised as an enchanted Strength ring.

Warning: This ring has a debt attached to it. You may not sell this ring while this debt is attached. If you lose this ring, the loan payment will be accelerated. If you are expelled from the church while you are wearing this ring, the curse effect will activate.

Warning: This ring carries a curse effect. Non-worshippers who attempt to wear this ring will find themselves infected with every debuff suffered by anyone within 50 meters of this ring. That's . . . that's a bad one.

"This is fine," I said, slipping it onto my finger.

"THERE ARE INDEED EIGHT COMBATANTS," KEVIN SHOUTED. "COMING from above in a sneak attack, ready to get his revenge, it's Quan Ch!"

Quan appeared, his dot coming into view on my map. He'd been invisible, flying through the air straight toward the fight, his magical cloak/robe thing flapping in the wind behind him. He'd risen to level

70, one above my own. He'd been trailing six levels behind me for a while, which meant he'd been cruising through this current floor.

His left arm was still gone. He had a look of absolute rage on his face.

The little scene window popped up, and it showed me holding on to Quan's arm at the end of the fifth floor as he tried to run away, and me ripping the arm right off his body.

Magnificent Troy laughed. He, too, now had a beer bottle in his hand. "I remember that. That was pretty awesome."

"Remember how Quan cried like a little bitch afterward?" Kevin asked.

Troy kept laughing. He pulled his own right arm into his tuxedo jacket and started waving the empty sleeve back and forth. "Look! I'm Quan! I'm Quan!" His alien beer splashed out of the bottle.

"Fuck you!" Quan screeched over at the screen.

Kevin continued to howl with laughter. "That's the wrong arm, Troy, but that is indeed how he looked. Anyway, let's watch all these dumbasses finally die and then maybe they'll let us get out of this cursed solar system."

Your squad has chosen to ally with team Sister Ines.

Team Sister Ines has chosen no allies.

Team Quan has chosen no allies.

Ten-second I-thought-we-were-friends penalty imposed.

Combat Started.

Chaos broke out all around us. Every zombie lunged at the nearest non-zombie as the seals and crabs burst into action, kicking, fighting, screaming, punching. Everybody was fighting everybody else.

A zombie baby seal looked at me and groaned, moving itself forward, trailing guts. I moved to punt it, but I realized I couldn't move my leg. I had, stupidly, assumed the ten-second penalty only applied to Donut's deck of cards.

Oh fuck, oh fuck.

The baby seals were indeed white and fuzzy, which was not correct because these things weren't harp seals, but I barely registered this as it got closer. Both Quan and Sister Ines cast cards. Donut didn't even have her deck yet.

As the zombie seal approached from my left, a demon crab jumped at me from the right.

It stopped in midair, having flown directly over one of the demon snare traps I'd placed. It stopped just inches from me, screeching, its voice like a high-revving engine, nothing like that of a regular crab. Its black eyes swirled like twin hurricanes. The demon's name was **Nizzle**.

The baby seal reached for my ankle just as the timer ended. I jumped back and punted it. I ducked as another demon crab lunged. It sailed over me and tackled a regular crab. A portal opened, and they both disappeared, screaming. All around, demons were grabbing combatants, and pulling them away as more and more zombies made the change. And those that didn't were turning more crabs and seals into zombies.

I turned to Nizzle the frozen demon and cast Talon Strike just as I kicked it directly in the chest. It fell backward, and I jumped forward, cracking down hard, breaking it into pieces.

Quan remained floating in the air out of reach. The boss snake started to buck like a wild horse. Samantha, finally able to move, zipped away, floating like one of those skulls from the *Doom* video game. Sister Ines remained attached to the back of the boss monster's head, like she had a Sticky Feet skill.

Quan had cast a mystic card and then a totem. The totem appeared with no fanfare. It was a large, but common soft-shelled turtle named **Hoan Kiem**. It was only level 25. It fell and plopped onto the ground, surrounded by a group of zombie fish who all started to bounce toward it, their ravening mouths opening and closing.

Peekaboo!

A pair of giant bloodshot eyes appeared in the air floating over Donut. Across the way, the same eyes appeared above Sister Ines. Quan's mystic card was something I'd seen before. I couldn't see what Quan saw, but I knew he now could see both Donut's hand and Sister Ines's hand.

A clockwork Mongo ran by, screeching, covered with biting zombie baby seals. The real Mongo stood by Donut, protecting her. I watched as he jumped through the air, ripping a zombie apart. A demon fish tried to open a portal under Mongo's feet, but the dinosaur ripped it in half with his talons.

Sister Ines's card also didn't have any fanfare. She summoned the totem, followed by a Stout card onto him.

It was Paz. She'd summoned Paz.

The armored man looked much like he had the last time I'd seen him, dying on the floor of the Yemaya temple after he'd been smote by his god. He stood right in front of the snake boss, facing the cat woman who remained upon the head of the creature. He still had the horrific, hand-shaped burn across his face, which partially revealed his skull. The god Ogun had done that to him.

"Sister," Paz called up to the nun. "Please. No more. I can't take . . . Gah!"

The giant snake reached down and chomped down on Paz, her giant mouth trying to crush the armor. She picked him up and started to shake him back and forth, like she was attempting to swallow him whole.

Samantha zipped through the air and landed at my feet, bouncing once. She rolled to a stop and looked up at me. "I'm pretty sure this is all your fault, Carl."

Donut tossed out her first card. Geraldo the monk seal appeared just as Sister Ines started to shout instructions at her totem. "Paz," she called, "accept your suffering! Use your Self-Destruct skill the moment this false god—"

She didn't finish.

Quan cast another mystic card. This one puffed away, indicating it'd been a consumable. He pointed directly at Sister Ines's hand, and the moment he made the move, I knew exactly what that card was. My heart sank. I'd seen it in the lists, but I'd always assumed it was a dumb card. We'd never found one.

I pick that one!

A giant neon hand appeared in the air and reached down and grabbed a card from Sister Ines.

The card was called **Force Play**. You picked a card in an opponent's hand, and it played automatically. Since he could see her hand, he knew exactly what the card would be. She'd had a Flee card in her hand.

"Oh!" Both Troy and Kevin shouted at the same time.

"Didn't see that one coming," Troy added.

"Sister Ines is out of the fight!"

Team Quiteria has fled the fight.

Team Quiteria has lost their key.

The last standing deckmaster will gain their key.

Paz, who'd still been in the mouth of the giant snake, dissipated into dust. The snake hissed in outrage and turned its attention on the closest crawler. Me.

Geraldo landed next to me, looking around wildly. "Brothers! Brothers! It is here!" he shouted, his voice full of glee. All around, seals and crabs died and continued to get pulled into hell portals. "The battle of our lives is here! Oh! Oh! Ready, bitches? Ready for the flip-flap?" He started to make Bruce Lee noises as he somersaulted into the fray toward a pair of crabs.

"Not that way!" Donut shrieked. "Geraldo, get back here this instant!"

"Don't worry about the snake," Samantha called. "I got it!"

I slammed onto *Protective Shell* just as the snake lunged.

Every mob. Every demon. Every zombie. The weird low-level turtle. All the crabs and the seals. They all blasted away under my shell. It was like I'd set off a bomb. All the closest mobs flew into the woods and beyond, leaving us suddenly alone except for Mongo and one more clockwork Mongo.

"That'll clear a room," Troy said.

"Hey!" Samantha called. "I was going to do that!"

Lazarus-A-Bang-Bang appeared. Donut tossed a Temporary Shield onto him. He pulled his weapon to his shoulder. This time it was a rocket launcher, similar to what the camels used on the fifth floor. He aimed in the general direction that turtle had flown, and he fired. The missile corkscrewed into the trees, exploding.

"Donut, don't keep a Flee card in your hand," I yelled.

"I already discarded it," she called. "Where did he go? And why did he summon that turtle? Carl, my hand sucks right now. I can't discard for several seconds, and it's all snare cards!"

Geraldo, who'd still been in the shell's area when it cast, continued to unnecessarily flip as he moved off in a random direction, screaming at the top of his lungs.

I scanned the sky, but I didn't see Quan. I could see the snake, who'd actually taken some damage from getting tossed away. It wasn't attacking anymore. It had its head straight up in the air, and it was moving back and forth, casting a spell.

"Lazarus," I called, pointing at the snake.

"I see it," the robed totem said, lifting his launcher to his shoulder, aiming at the snake.

"Samantha," I said, "your job is to get that Quan guy. Think you can do that?"

"The one-armed guy with the pretty cloak thing? Oh, that's easy. Where's he at?"

"There!" Donut cried, pointing in the sky. Quan was coming back. He was already throwing a card out just as I cast *Super Spreader*.

"No!" Donut suddenly called as her entire hand of three cards blinked and disappeared. They reappeared a moment later. "Carl, he switched hands with me! Three for three! Carl, it's all Flee cards!"

I looked up in horror as I saw Quan grinning as he cast another **Force Play**.

"Now that's an ass kicking if I ever saw one," Troy said.

Your Squad has used a Flee Card.

> **Your Squad has lost their key!**
>
> **Your key has been transferred to Team Quan!**
>
> **Team Quiteria's key has been transferred to Team Quan!**
>
> **Teleporting Now.**

Combat Complete. Deck has been reset.

NEW ACHIEVEMENT! THE FUMBLE.

The clock is ticking down, and with *everything* hanging in the balance, you pulled an Earnest Byner and lost the ball at the goal line.

***Reward:* If you don't fix this, this is how you will be remembered.**

Silence followed as Donut, Mongo, Samantha, and I all plopped into dark, swampy woods. I had no idea where we were.

"Does he have to stay in the fight?" Donut cried, all poofed out, jumping to her feet. "Can we get back there in time? Does he already have the keys? What do we do? What do we do?"

"I don't think we were locked in," I said as I jumped into my chat. "He ain't sticking around if he doesn't have to. It says he already has the keys! He's a coward. He won't risk it if he doesn't have to. He's heading straight for the exit."

CARL: Imani, Quan has the keys. He has *both* keys. He might be coming to you right now. He's going down the stairs. You're our only chance to stop him.

CARL: If anyone out there hears me and is in the Cuba area, stay by the exit in the capitol building. Quan Ch has both keys, and he's headed to one of the two exits. You have to stop him.

There was a short pause.

REN: It's us, Carl. I'm sorry I didn't say anything sooner. It's us. We'll be ready.

Donut, who was already poofed out, hissed in anger at Tserendolgor's message.

IMANI: I'll do my best.

I quickly made a new chat group.

CARL: Okay. Both of you, be careful. He's really good, but he's not going to be feeling well. I cast my *Super Spreader* on him at the last second. He's going to be leaking slugs. You have to delay him as long as possible. With each passing minute, the slugs will get worse and worse. They'll fight for him, but each time one comes out, it damages him more, so he'll be distracted. You have to stop him. I can get all three groups of us out, but that's it. And only if we stop him.

Red dots surrounded us in the forest. It was more of the duendes. The little shoe-loving goblin things were everywhere, even in the woods. I looked at the map, trying to figure out where we were.

Donut looked up at me, eyes shining. "I failed. I failed, Carl, and now we're going to die. Imani is going to die, and it's my fault."

"No, Donut. Not yet. I want you to rearrange your deck. Just totems, the Combo card, and some Time Extends. Do it fast, and then you're going to initiate a card battle with the duendes over there. Samantha, come here. I need you!"

57

TIME TO LEVEL COLLAPSE: 4 DAYS, 12 HOURS.

<Note added by Crawler Tipid. 4th Edition>

It was me or him, and I chose to save myself. I didn't think. I reacted. I reacted to save myself. Anybody else would do the same. I keep telling myself that again and again. Does that make me evil? No, I don't think it does, not when I think of it logically. Then why do I feel that way?

I PACED BACK AND FORTH, TRYING TO FIGURE OUT THE LAST PART OF the plan while Donut rearranged her deck for sustained combat. I now knew where we were. We'd actually teleported deeper into Havana, but we were in a small, forested area surrounded by trees with the city just a few blocks away. We were about five kilometers from the church exit and 15 from the capitol building. I didn't know which one Quan would go to, but I suspected he'd head for the farther one.

It was still dark outside, but the sun would rise soon.

I only had half an idea. *Think. Think. Think.*

REN: Carl, I gotta say, those teleport traps really fucked us. Khulan isn't even back yet. We set off those teleports and a goddamned alarm trap that I had to pull into my inventory because it wouldn't shut up. It was playing a Backstreet Boys song.

DONUT: YOU'RE LUCKY HE DIDN'T BLOW YOUR CHEATING ASS UP.

REN: If he'd blown us up, you wouldn't have anybody blocking the door, now would you?

DONUT: IT WOULD BE WORTH IT.

"Donut, chill. We need them."

CARL: There're more regular teleports outside on the stairs. Best leave them there. Set more of your own traps if you have any. If he's coming, it'll be soon. Be careful. I think he can go invisible.

"Don't tell her where the traps are! Even if they stop Quan, we're still going to have to fight them. Her meatball wants to eat Mongo. And who the heck is Khulan? I've never met a Khulan. Is that a boy name or a girl name? I bet they're a cheater, too."

Khulan was a woman, part of Ren's team. I'd never talked with her, but I'd seen her a few times on the recap along with the rest of Ren's squad. I couldn't remember her class, but she was human. She would paralyze people while Ren torched them with her flamethrower. Ren's regular party was normally seven or eight people, so I didn't know who the last member was or who her squad consisted of. I knew she'd had a terrible time during phase two, and only three of them had survived.

"We're not out of this yet, Donut. Take a deep breath. Stick to the plan."

"What's the plan? We don't have a plan yet! I can't *Puddle Jump* that far, and my *Skedaddle* won't work like that, either. We don't know where he's going!"

I reached down and scratched her, trying to calm her. Myself, too. Her eyes were flashing as she quickly rearranged her cards. "Listen." I lowered my voice, trying to sound soothing. We were in a hurry, but this was important to get out. "Even if we don't stop him, I have my Bone Key benefit. I can still open that door. Imani is our first priority, and our friend. We're trying to save *her*. But *we* are safe for now. Okay?"

"Okay," Donut said after a moment.

"And Ren is our friend, too. I know you don't like her, but we can still do this without having to hurt our friends. We'll do what we can. I *will* use that Bone Key if it means I don't have to fight either of them. You saying inflammatory shit is going to make them not trust us."

Donut didn't say anything. She was shaking with fear. She would never like Ren. And she didn't trust the Bone Key benefit.

I didn't trust it, either. I thought of Tipid, and their last few entries in the cookbook. Of the terrible suspicion I had about how that key worked. I didn't have time to think about it, and I put it in the back of my mind.

I reached down and picked up Samantha with two hands. I brought her up and looked her in the eyes. She was covered in sand and gore. She felt heavier than usual, and there was a slight vibration to her that wasn't normally there. She still had the Desperado Club logo tattooed on her neck where Katia had tapped it with the stick-and-poke tattoo kit, but the ink was starting to fade.

"Samantha," I said, "this is important, so pay attention."

"We've discussed this, Carl. If you want to date me, you must get in line. *Maybe* if you fight Louis for my honor, I'll consider it, but not if you mess up his beautiful, squishy face."

I resisted the urge to shake her. "We don't have time. You haven't been honest with us. You have to tell us what you can do."

She just looked at me.

"You mean, like, with my tongue?"

"Goddamnit, Samantha. You teleported an entire beach back to us. You can fly. A while back when we were in the simulation room, you almost cast some sort of attack spell. I can feel how much power you have coursing through you. But I need to know what you can do. What you can cast."

She opened her mouth and closed it.

"Please," I said.

Her mouth started to quiver. "I . . . I don't know why, but sometimes I feel stronger than usual. Before I was banished to the Nothing when I had my original body, I would get more powerful when someone prayed to me or bought a charm with my likeness or when I melted someone who wouldn't date one of my worshippers with my Acid Bath. You know, like normal stuff. But it's not like that anymore. My father took my power away and my whore of a mother tried to steal my man, and everything changed."

"Okay, but when you *do* feel stronger, what can you do?"

"I can fly. I can fuck up anybody who looks at me funny."

I took a breath. "Be more specific."

"I can help spells. I can make them more powerful. But it doesn't always do what I want. Like, sometimes it's a lot stronger than I thought it would be. And sometimes it doesn't work too good. I used to have this dissolve spell that was really great, but I haven't been able to get it to work. Not on the, uh, outside. And sometimes my magic does stuff without me asking."

She suddenly burst into tears. "It's because of this stupid body. You have to get MaeMae to the next floor so she can get the supplies to get me into that flesh golem. I can do all sorts of good stuff when I have a real body."

"Other than flying and enhancing spells, can you cast anything on your own right now? Can you teleport me?"

She continued to weep. She spoke through gasped sobs. "Teleport? No. I'm useless. Oh gods, it's true. I'm useless!" She turned in my hands. "Don't look upon me. Now you know my dark secret. I've been faking it the whole time. It's all a lie!" She blew snot all over my hands and started rubbing her nose on me. "I'm a fraud. How can anybody love me? You're going to tell Louis, aren't you? You'll tell him, and he's going to reject me! Just like my king did when he left me for my mother. Everybody always leaves me."

"Samantha," I said, trying not to let my exasperation show in my voice, "you're far from useless. You've helped us a bunch of times. And you're getting more powerful by the moment. I'm not going to leave you. You're part of the team."

She sniffed and blew out more snot. She grunted and turned herself to face me again. "Really? I'm part of the team?"

"Yes. Of course."

She sniffled again. "Why do you want to teleport?"

"I need a way to get somewhere fast, but we don't know where it'll be until the last minute. It's one of two places. Somewhere far. I thought maybe since you'd gotten to Shi Maria so fast, you could teleport more than you were saying."

"I didn't teleport to MaeMae. I told you what really happened. I hitched a ride. I tried to stop a train and I got stuck to the front, and when the train left the edge of the map, I got squished and bounced away, and I landed in her web. I might have wrecked the train, too."

"You never told me that."

"Why don't you do what that scary lady does? The mean one whose dog got his head popped off by Donut? I know you have some of those traps, too."

"It's too late. I have to set those up . . ." I trailed off, and I blinked. Holy shit. *Of course.* I jumped into my inventory and searched for the two-part teleport traps. How many did I have? I only needed one set, but more would be better. "Samantha, I could kiss you."

"I'm not a whore, Carl."

MORDECAI: THERE'S ONLY ONE MORE OF THE TWO-PART SETS FOR sale on the market. That's it. They are really expensive. Too bad the Desperado is still closed.

CARL: I have four sets. Florin?

FLORIN: Hang on, mate. I'm going in right now. I hate going down this early, but I'll let you know. Okay. Going through the door right now. You're right. It's a room. About five by five meters with a stairwell in the middle. It's one of the glowy stairs, not one that looks like a real set of stairs. It's just like the room with the giant globe from the beginning of the floor.

CARL: Do you have any traps? See if it'll let you drop one on the floor.

FLORIN: I got plenty. Dropping one now.

There was a long pause.

FLORIN: Sorry, mate. Got an error that says, "This area is outside the level. No traps may be set in the stairwell chamber. Nice try, though."

My heart dropped. For a second there, I thought we'd found a way to avoid any more bloodshed.

CARL: Fuck. Fuck, fuck, fuck. We'll have to do it the hard way.

FLORIN: I reckon after what you did with the bubbles on the fifth floor, they ain't too keen on letting people teleport their way out of trouble anymore.

CARL: Mordecai, my trapmaster skill lets me put traps on non-static items. Will that work? Like, if I put it on the back of an automaton, and it walks into the room with me?

MORDECAI: I really doubt it. Sorry, kid. The rules regarding stairwell chambers are even more strict than those surrounding safe rooms. And even if you could, we only have a couple of them amongst us. I think that Lucia kid buys them up the moment they appear on the market.

FLORIN: She does indeed. Teleport traps and alcohol are the only things she purchases.

CARL: Damnit. Okay. Sorry for making you go down early, Florin.

FLORIN: No worries, mate. See you on the other side. Keep your head up. Do me a favor. If you get word of Lucia, send me a message. She has good days and bad days, and it's been more bad than good lately. Li Jun says she just took out half the squads who don't hold keys, and they're holding back, hoping they don't have to fight her. Any message you send I'll get when I pop out onto the ninth floor.

CARL: I will.

FLORIN: Looking forward to tearing it up again with you.

Samantha was still in my grip, turned upside down with her jagged latex stump facing up at me. I remembered that badger bartender guy who'd gotten his arm stuck in there. It'd had an acid effect. He'd eventually been ripped in half by Minge the demon, but when Samantha had discharged the rest of him, the flesh had been burned off. I hoped the small, fist-sized spider automaton would be okay. It had the anchor half of a teleport trap affixed to its flat, top surface, designed specifically to hold such things. Samantha insisted that it would be okay, that her "juice" would only burn flesh.

I took a breath and shoved the little spider inside. It pushed easily into the latex. The small robot made a scared, disapproving noise as it disappeared. My fingers did not burn. I had the impression that it took a minute for the acid to start working.

Samantha bit me on the hand as I shoved it in. I grabbed the second red-painted automaton, this one with the trap Donut had set. I was careful to only touch the sides of this one. Donut didn't have the trapmaster skill, and she couldn't use the two-part traps at all, but thanks to the hunter battles at the end of the previous floor, she was now level five in the Automaton Pilot skill, which also allowed her to affix some other traps to the back of the little robots. This one was also a teleport trap. A rarer one, actually, but one that required a lower level to use. It easily slipped in with a little slurp noise.

"Samantha, how many of these can I fit in here?"

"I can take anything you got."

I shuddered as I slipped two more automatons in. These were the same as the first.

Samantha stifled a giggle. "This is just like—"

"Don't. Please, no. Just make sure you pop them out the moment you land, and tell me when you do. The last thing either of us want is me teleporting directly into . . . you know."

A new chat popped back up. It was just Mordecai.

MORDECAI: You need to quit trying to help everybody else and focus on saving your own ass. I think you're onto something with the teleport traps, but I don't see how it's going to work for anybody else. In order for those things to work, you have to set up both halves yourself. You can't set the trigger half and have someone else set the anchor. If that was the case, you'd be able to just teleport around at will, using the guild rooms to trade trap anchors with other crawlers.

As we talked, I dropped Samantha and started moving through the clearing, arming the trigger half of the three teleport traps. The first I set to only be tripped by myself.

CARL: But we *can* do that, and I hadn't even thought of it. At least *I* can. I can teleport if we use the automatons. We're doing it

now. I can set the anchor on the back of the automaton and give it to someone else, and I can go wherever I want. After this, I'm going to make sure Donut trains up the trap ability so she can do it, too. We might not be able to teleport directly into a stairwell chamber, and it won't do us any good to zap into an area with more keys than squads, but if there's someone out there with an extra key . . . First we need to save Imani and Ren's squad. We're just waiting to see where Quan shows up first. Donut is preparing to activate the aggro of the duendes. There's like a hundred of them out there, so she can keep the battle going for a while if she has to. She stays here, and I go in.

MORDECAI: Okay. Assume you get the keys. What then?

CARL: I'll give one to Imani and one to Ren using our Flee cards. If we can't find someone with an extra key, I'll use the Bone Key on myself. We have options now.

MORDECAI: Saving Imani, I understand. But I wouldn't count on there being any extra keys floating around. First, you'll only have a few days to get Donut's trap skill up high enough. And you need to rethink removing one of your bones, potentially a vital one, to save that other crawler. Plus you'll lose your jacket and all the benefits. It's a shitty trade-off no matter what you do.

CARL: It's three other crawlers. Good people. We need everybody we can.

MORDECAI: Everybody else needs *you* more. Donut needs you. It's stupid to risk it. You don't know if the teleport trick will work. I've never even heard of this Bone Key benefit before. I *have* seen other magic keys, and they don't always work as advertised. Self-preservation is not being selfish. You have to take care of yourself first.

CARL: If I have to, I will make the tough decision. But I will be damned if I'm not going to do everything in my power to prevent it first. I almost made that mistake already on this floor, and I would've lost everything. I'm not going to do it again. Not until it's the only possible choice.

MORDECAI: What does that even mean?

I ignored him as I spray-painted an arrow on the ground pointing to the third teleport trap. I looked at Samantha and had a thought. I pulled one more of the two-part teleport traps out. My last for now. "Samantha, come here. I'm gonna place one more inside of you." I put the other half, the actual trap part, back into my inventory.

"Oh boy," Samantha said as she hopped into my hands and presented her neck hole. It wriggled like the butt of a puppy.

"Please don't do that."

"I can't help it. It does it by itself when I'm excited. You can put it as deep as you—"

"Stop," I said as I shoved this one into her. "Keep this one inside you. Can you control what you keep in and what you, uh, expel?"

"Of course. That's what Kegels are for, Carl."

A new chat popped up.

REN: He's here. I think he may have disabled the teleport traps by the entrance. He's invisible, but Chuluuna can see him. He'll reappear once the fight starts. He hasn't come in yet. Being cautious. We're hiding and will confront him if he gets in. Get your ass here if you want to help.

CARL: I'm on my way. My aim kinda sucks, and it's about 15 kilometers away, so it'll take a few minutes. Hold as long as you can.

"Donut," I said as I pulled the head-tosser extension out, "it's time."

I now knew who all three members of Ren's team were. Chuluuna was also a human, but he had a strength-based class that allowed him to turn his skin to stone. He was Ren's main tank—at least he was until she got that pet—and he could withstand her flamethrower. He was also husband to the third crawler in their group, Khulan. I prayed Donut was wrong and we wouldn't have to fight them.

I carefully sidestepped my trap as Samantha hopped into the head tosser. I really needed to practice more with this thing, but I was already getting better at hitting a target. The problem was, I couldn't see the capitol building from here. I had to get her over most of the buildings in downtown without overshooting her into the ocean.

Deep breath. You can do this.

I spun and tossed. Samantha rocketed away.

"Carl," Donut said as we waited, "what if they don't fight at all, and he gives his second key to the dog lady?"

"He can't just give up a key. They have to fight. It would require him to use a Flee card, and he won't do that. It's too risky. I don't think he can choose which key he'd lose, so he'd risk having to fight Imani and possibly us again. He went to the farther stairwell because he's probably hoping we haven't talked to the people there and warned them of his tactics. He'll try to fight and will go straight to the stairs the moment he gets Ren's team to teleport away. He'll take the other key with him. Now go start your fight with the duendes. Be careful. Mongo, keep her safe, but don't kill them too fast."

Mongo screeched and then turned toward the woods and started stalking toward the red dots. The tiny mobs were all over the place, swinging through the trees, chattering angrily.

"Don't send them into the teleports until I say so," I said. "Make sure you're protected first. Make the best combo you can."

Donut was clearly nervous. "Don't let that meatball eat you."

SAMANTHA: THAT WAS A GOOD THROW! I'M ACROSS THE STREET! I QUEEFED OUT THE SPIDERS!

"Here we go," I called as I stepped forward into the first teleport trap.

58

ENTERING HAVANA.

CRUNCH.

The spider automaton was crushed under my weight as I teleported atop it. The other three spiders—two regular and one painted red—scattered away. Samantha was true to her word—for once—and the fourth spider remained inside of her. I unsummoned the xistera extension still at the end of my hand, and Samantha blinked and reappeared right next to me, having been teleported only a few feet.

A bolt of lightning shot out the front of the capitol building, crashing through the door. Glass shattered, pouring down the stairs.

I looked about, searching for zombies or demons. I didn't see anything, but smoke rose from several places in the city. Many buildings were on fire. A distant screeching filled the air, followed by multiple crashes. There was nothing here, though, and that was good.

Combat Started.

DONUT: WE ARE FIGHTING THE DUENDES. MONGO IS EATING THE ONES WHO GET CLOSE. THERE WAS ONE NAMED CARLOS. LET ME KNOW WHEN YOU WANT THE TOTEMS. I HAVE JOLA AND SKYLAR SPINACH IN MY HAND NOW. I'M WAITING TO SUMMON THEM.

CARL: Okay. We're here. I'm rushing in now.

I looked at the red automaton. I didn't want to risk anyone hitting that one yet. It was an emergency loop-de-loop, meaning if someone touched it, they would switch places with Donut. At Donut's trap skill level of three, she could only program it to hit fellow crawlers, but she'd been able to set it so it was only crawlers not in her party. That meant *I* couldn't trigger it, but because her trap skill was so low, if I or anybody else—mobs or NPCs—did touch the trigger plate, it would immediately misfire. I didn't like Donut being separated from me, and this was our fastest option to get her back to me in a pinch. The second option was to throw Samantha and have her bite down, but until I perfected my aim, that was also risky.

Using the loop-de-loop, I'd have to hit another crawler with the trap. This was one of Lucia Mar's favorite traps, though I suspected her trap skill was so high, she could turn them off and on from afar, controlling them like gate locks.

I looked down at the red robot spider. Thanks to my upgraded table, these things actually listened to voice commands now. "You, stay here and stay hidden. You other two, follow me upstairs but stay outside. Samantha, on me." The two spiders clicked and followed.

The red spider buzzed and lowered to the ground, pressing itself against the wall. A memory ghost walked by, and his pants got stuck on the spider, covering it up. My heart skipped, but thankfully it didn't misfire.

I downed an invisibility potion. We rushed across the street and moved up the stairs toward the broken door. The whoosh of Tserendolgor's flamethrower went off, followed by an unholy screeching and a wave of heat. Even in a card battle, I knew she could still use the thing. The ground rumbled.

A screaming, flaming pox slug rushed out the door. The level 11 slug was about as tall as my knees. It had green spiked hair atop its flaming head. The strange monster ignored us as it tumbled down the stairs, the flames overwhelming it. It splatted at the bottom of the steps and stopped, its flesh bubbling.

"Oh, boy," Samantha said, looking down at the still-flaming corpse. "This party looks like it's gonna be a fun one." She looked up at me. "Carl, where are you?"

"I'm right here. I'm invisible. Now shush," I said, moving to the side of the door, peering in. I tried to take it all in as quickly as possible.

This was the room it had all started in. It seemed so long ago that

Donut and I popped into this room on the first day of the eighth floor. It had seemed so tranquil back then, but now everything was on fire. Chaos reigned as Ren and Quan fought.

We wouldn't get added to this particular fight because Donut had to be in range. She was in the middle of her own fight far away. She chose to use her card deck for that match, which meant she could summon her totems as long as the battle with the duendes was still active. Donut remained safe, but using the teleport traps, I could bring her summoned totems to me.

That meant—at least I hoped that meant—that Quan couldn't use his snare cards on our totems. And more importantly, our totems could attack Quan directly without having to worry about first dispatching his own totems. It was an exploit. Actually, it was more than an exploit. It was a chickenshit move. I didn't care. We just needed to get through this before they patched it.

I prepared a sticky hob-lobber.

Quan was there, his back to me, high up against the ceiling, screaming something I couldn't make out. As I watched, he cried out in pain as another slug slurped out of him, plummeting to the ground. The level 12 slug hit the tiled floor and groaned in pain before pulling itself up. This one was female, and she had clown makeup and weird, wispy pigtails on the side of her slug head.

Quan had summoned that turtle thing again, and it sat there in the middle of the room. There was some sort of low-level pig thing summoned, too. Meanwhile, Ren stood with her back to the door to the exit stairwell, flamethrower in her hands, and she was waving it back and forth. The Chuluuna guy was next to her. The large Mongolian man was a hulking presence. He appeared to be in the middle of casting something. Garret, her pet Tummy Acher, stood on her other side, even bigger than Chuluuna. The pet was also a damage tank, and it could swallow just about anything whole. It giggled as Ren torched the room.

The third member of her squad, Khulan, wasn't here at all. She still hadn't returned from being teleported away. With the zombies and demons everywhere, I knew she had a dangerous path back here.

Ren's squad had some tall, hairy totem summoned, standing in front of them. Ren's flamethrower went right through it, not hurting it at all as it stalked toward the turtle. I could also see that Ren had taken our warning about Quan's tactics to heart. She had a mystic card summoned, facing outward. It was preventing Quan from looking at her hand or forcing discards.

I moved to throw the hob-lobber up at Quan, but I paused as a set of new notifications rolled in.

Area Message:

The *Madre de Aguas* has succumbed to her zombiism curse. She has fallen and risen again. But the curse has left her vulnerable, and a major demon has involuntarily slipped into the realm. Amayon has arrived. Beware, all. Beware.

Hell has come to burn the world.

Several miles to the west, a gout of flame burst into the sky, followed by a scream that shook the ground.

Amayon has made an appearance in the realm.

You are in the presence of a Demon Prince of Sheol. The Scavenger's Daughter has opened her eyes. She fills with dark power.

Temporary effect: All your fire spells utilize Sheol fire instead of regular fire.

New Achievement! Holy Hell!

You are in the presence of Sheol Royalty! I'm very excited about this. You leaky little meat bags are always dying off so early, plus the rich pricks in the Ascendency are just so boring, and we never get to play with the under-the-counter toys, if you know what I'm saying. Do you know how long it's been since one of my kind has been able to pull one of these dudes out of mothballs? Like, FOR-EVER. Which, incidentally, is how long your soul will burn if you manage to get killed by him.

***Reward:* You've received a Platinum To-Hell-in-a-Handbasket Box!**

"Uh, Samantha," I whispered, pausing. "Who is Amayon?"

"Oh, is he here? You know the four crown princes of Sheol? The oldest brother calls himself the king even though his mommy is in charge? The ladies in the harem thought I had banged him when I was talking about someone else? Ew, as if. Amayon is that guy's brother. He's the youngest one, I think. I've never met him. At least not face-to-face. We didn't have much to do with the down-there guys, if you know what I'm saying. We all mixed together in the Nothing, but he wasn't in there. He likes to set things on fire. Kinda like Emberus, actually. They don't like each other."

Quest Update. Find out who killed my son.

You have a rare opportunity to question Amayon, one of the four princes of Sheol, as to who murdered my son, Geyrun. He may have some insight into the matter. Do not allow this opportunity to go to waste.

"Are you fucking kidding me?" I hiss-whispered as a second, deeper bellow filled the air. A distant explosion rocked the Earth.

DONUT: CARL, ARE YOU DOING THAT OR IS IT THE DEMON?
IMANI: What is going on out there?

I started to send a response, but I had to hit the ground as a *Chain Lightning* spell shot forth from Chuluuna. It hit the turtle, the pig, the slug—which exploded—and Quan. Several branches shot out in other directions, including out the door. It arced right over my head.

Quan's cloak absorbed the attack, and he was unharmed. Both the turtle and the pig fell over, almost dead as Quan tossed out a **Mass Heal** card. He summoned a third totem. It was a level 10 rabbit that hit the ground with a peep. It didn't have any sort of entrance sequence other than an explosion with the words **Yeah. It's a Rabbit** floating over it.

At the same moment, Ren tossed out another totem of her own. This was a big one.

The ground began to rumble anew as red, yellow, and blue streamers exploded through the air. Holographic dirt showered everywhere. A horn fanfare played.

CARL: Donut, send them in. Who do you got?
DONUT: I WILL COMBINE LAZARUS WITH SKYLAR AND THEN SEND JOLA. I'LL PUT A TIME EXTEND ON BOTH. IT'S THE BEST I CAN DO WITH MY CURRENT HAND. HERE THEY COME.

"Okay, Samantha, if this doesn't kill him, I want you to go fuck up that one-armed guy floating there. I need you to distract him as much as possible because he's about to be pissed." I turned to the two spiders and whispered, "Inside! Inside!" The spiders beeped and moved into the room, each following along the inside wall and toward a corner, trying to stay out of sight.

Quan started to play another card as I tossed the sticky hob-lobber up at him. It splotched against the back of his head and detonated. He cried out and flipped, angling downward and crashing heavily to the ground. That would've one-shotted pretty much anyone, but he had multiple shields going. He was disoriented but otherwise unhurt. His shield spell that had protected him was now in the red. We had to keep pressing him or the shield would refill. He cried again as another, bigger slug slurped out of him, coming from underneath his cloak. This one was already dead, having been hurt in the blast.

"Not so fast, you one-armed bitch!" Samantha shrieked, flying toward him. She landed on his shoulder and chomped down.

At the same moment, Ren's newest totem emerged, coming up out of the ground, showering floor tiles everywhere.

Wriggle, Writhe, Repeat! It's the monster you can't defeat! It's Basquiat, the Mongolian Death Worm!

The worm was like a bus-sized version of one of those sand worms from the *Dune* books and movies. The beige fleshy worm featured three face flaps that opened like a flower, revealing circles of sharp teeth. The thing was big enough to swallow me whole. It opened its weird mouth and roared as the confetti exploded all around it.

Ren tossed another card onto the worm. A glowing consumable.

Temporary Immortality!

"You're fucked now!" Chuluuna shouted.

Garret cackled with laughter as the worm moved toward the rabbit.

Everything froze as Quan finally let go of his latest card. The card rose into the air, spinning before it exploded, meaning it was a consumable.

Toss-Up! Three for two!

The icons over all five of the active totems flashed and switched. The rabbit, pig, and turtle were suddenly on Ren's team, and the hairy ghost thing and the Mongolian death worm were now flying Quan's flag.

"Oh, shit!" Ren called, pulling her flamethrower back up as the hairy ghost fell onto Chuluuna. The ghost had a blinking notification over it. It was about to time out. The worm continued toward the rabbit, gobbling it up as it passed through the ground, disappearing, the sound like that of a train whipping by. It appeared again as it burst up through the tile floor and into the air, consuming the turtle, and then taking out the pig, all in a single gulp.

All three of Quan's former totems were consumed in seconds.

Quan, still disoriented from the blast, shook his head and started to rise back up in the air, ignoring Samantha gnawing on his shoulder. My invisibility ran out. He turned to look at me and shouted something. I felt the ground rumble just as a pair of totems appeared in front of me.

Jola the Yule Cat appeared, filling the left side of the room, rising all the way to the ceiling as Lazarus appeared on the right, bazooka at the ready. The automaton spider under him crunched in a shower of sparks. He'd been combined with Skylar Spinach, but he looked exactly the same as before.

I dove backward, jumping from the entranceway and back outside as the ground rumbled. The death worm appeared, flying out of the ground right where I'd been standing. The entire entrance to the capitol building started to crumble. The massive, fast-moving worm squealed and arced through the air. It chomped directly onto Lazarus, who cried out in pain, getting swallowed whole by the worm, who dove back below ground.

"Chu! Chu!" Ren called as her friend was pulled apart by her own totem. I hadn't seen what had happened, but the man's innards had been ripped apart in the seconds I'd been looking away. Just like that.

"Mér líkar ekki úlpan þín," Jola said. The cat's voice boomed, filling the room. He was talking to Quan.

The worm reappeared right underneath the cat, but it passed through the non-corporeal totem and it arced again, slamming onto the floor without piercing it. It did a barrel roll as it vomited out a shower of gore and body parts, including pieces of Lazarus. The worm's head turned toward Ren, who was kneeling down before the body of Chuluuna. The other totem was gone, having timed out.

"Basquiat, no!" Ren called.

The worm roared and dove for Ren. She rolled out of the way. The worm took out the corpse of the other crawler and disappeared.

Ren tossed a card. A mystic that covered her with an opaque protection shell. It had a 20-second countdown over it.

"I hath risen again, motherfuckers!" came a new voice, jumping out of the gore of worm vomit. Uzi Jesus stood to his full height, his entire body glowing with golden light. He also now held not one, but two gold-plated Uzis.

Uzi Jesus—Gold Edition.

Behind him, Asojano had also returned. He, too, shone with golden light. It was clearly Asojano, but his name had changed. The strange wand he normally held had turned to a short staff with a sugar skull at the end. His grass skirt now appeared to be made of woven gold.

Lord of Blight—Gold Edition.

Donut had combined Skylar Spinach, the splitter ghommid, with Lazarus. So when Lazarus had died, he'd reverted back to the two cards that had been used to create him. Except that Skylar was a special type of ghommid, and when he split, the new versions were actually more powerful than the previous ones.

DONUT: CARL, WE DON'T HAVE MUCH TIME! I SUMMONED SHI MARIA AND SHE'S EATING THEM TOO FAST! SHE ASKED WHERE YOU WERE, AND I TOLD HER, AND NOW SHE'S MAD I DIDN'T SEND HER TO YOU!

"Guys," I said, pointing at Quan, who'd just desperately discarded something. He'd floated back to the ceiling, but his shields were down. His hand was empty. *He's looking for a Flee card.* We couldn't let him get away. Not again. "Finish him off."

"No problem," Uzi Jesus said, twirling his twin guns on his fingers. One went off and flew away. "Dad-damnit. Ow, fuck!"

The ground rumbled again. The worm popped up under Ren, but it stopped with a metal clanging noise, the sound like that of a car crash. Ren's opaque shell didn't move. A fissure ran along the wall.

"Jola, keep the worm off our back!"

Jola wasn't listening to me. He only had eyes for Quan. *"Mér líkar ekki úlpan þín."*

The cat opened his mouth, and a yellow bolt appeared.

Fashion Critic!

Everything Quan was wearing flew off of him, like an explosion. He dropped like a rock, crashing hard to the rubble. Samantha spun, screaming across the room, bouncing off Garret and rolling to the center of the chamber. Clothes flew around the room in every direction, including a shining cloak that spun to a stop at my feet. I quickly scooped it up and pulled it into my inventory. An achievement appeared, and I waved it away.

That was pretty much the same spell as Donut's *Laundry Day* except the cat was going to literally eat the clothes if we let him. Why? Who the fuck knew?

Quan groaned. A card appeared, but it was clearly not a card he wanted. He was naked now, the stump of his missing arm waving in the air. The stump held half of a tattoo, the top half of a young girl's face.

Jola glared at me. *"Þjófar verða ètnir. Skilaðu þessu."*

I had no idea what he said or why the system wasn't translating all this Icelandic, but the threat was clear. I took a step back. The death worm made another attempt at Ren, equally unsuccessful. Her shell would disappear in a few seconds. The next attack would get her unless she managed to summon another totem. Her massive meatball pet ran in circles around her static shell, babbling, clearly ready to push her out of the way the moment the shell ran out. I doubted even the Tummy Acher could withstand an attack from that worm.

"Yeah, baby!" Uzi Jesus cried as he unloaded his remaining Uzi into Quan's naked, one-armed body. "Yeeeee the fuck haw!" His halo burst into golden light.

Bullet Hell!

More bullets suddenly rained down, pouring into Quan. An impossible amount, and not just from the direction of the gun, but from above, too, pouring into him like rain.

These weren't real bullets, I realized, but more like beestings. Quan's body danced on the floor as he was peppered. Jesus laughed maniacally as the man convulsed.

Yet the tough little bastard still wasn't dead. His health plummeted. Asojano slowly walked up to him and went to a knee, ignoring the hail of bullets. He put his hand on the prone man's body. Boils appeared across his naked chest. A line of debuffs appeared one by one, each appearing with a *plink*.

Still, Quan lived. I watched, fascinated.

That is, I watched until a growl from Jola took back my attention. The cat had just finished slurping up Quan's pants and was now looking at me and hissing, clearly angry at me for taking the magical cloak. He was going to pounce.

CARL: Holy shit, Donut, end the battle! End it now!

DONUT: IT'S ALREADY OVER! SHI MARIA IS EATING THEIR CORPSES LIKE POPCORN!

Jola hissed and pounced and disappeared in a puff of smoke as both Uzi Jesus and Asojano disappeared.

Combat Complete. Deck has been reset.

Quan wasn't dead. Donut's fight was done, but this one wasn't yet. He lay on the ground bleeding, unmoving. His eyes had turned completely white, and he had a dozen debuffs floating over him, including several I recognized. He was blind, and he wouldn't be able to heal. He was done. Still, I had to finish him off before that worm ate Ren. The ground rumbled. Behind me, Garret the Tummy Acher let out a strangled cry as it rolled directly into Ren, pushing her away just as the shield disappeared. At the same moment, the worm popped back up and tried to eat the meatball, but Ren cast a snare card, freezing the worm in place for fifteen seconds. Garret rolled away as Samantha yelled something at him, rolling after the meatball.

"Carl," Quan wheezed. "Carl. Give it back. Please. Fast."

I started to scoff. Like I would give the cloak back to him.

But I realized that wasn't what he was asking for. I quickly searched into my inventory, and I found it. The simple golden ring I'd taken off his hand when I'd ripped his arm off. It was a ring from before, likely his only possession from before the collapse. The ring read "For Daddy" on the inside.

It was still attached to his severed arm, which I still had in my inventory. I extracted just the ring and dropped it into his remaining hand.

He took in a deep, rattling breath. "She'd be ashamed of what I've become."

I didn't answer. I formed a fist, but before I could finish him off, he died.

The frozen worm disappeared. More gore showered onto the ground where the worm had been, including the corpse of Chuluuna.

The battle was over.

Quan Ch, with over sixty player-killer skulls, was dead. Finally dead.

A CHAMPION HAS FALLEN. A BOUNTY HAS BEEN CLAIMED.

DONUT: CARL, I GOT CREDIT FOR THAT!

I hadn't realized Quan had slipped back into the top ten. A wave of chats came in, people trying to figure out who killed who. Donut was already fielding them all.

The ground shook again, and this time a chunk of ceiling fell, landing directly on Garret. The pet made a pitiful *ouch* noise.

I tried to loot Quan, but it wouldn't let me. Donut had to do it. I'd be able to get the rest of his stuff in a few minutes.

A new dot appeared on my map. A crawler. I straightened my back, but it was Khulan, the only other surviving member of Ren's squad.

"No," she said, running into the room. The young Asian woman didn't even look at me. She ran to the mangled body of the crawler in the back of the room. She fell to her knees, draping herself over his body. "No, Chu. No!"

A ton of cards appeared floating over Quan, more than I'd ever seen. There were dozens of them. Only Donut could loot these, too.

"Where're the keys?" Ren asked. Panic rose in her voice. "I didn't get the keys!"

DONUT: CARL, THEY GAVE BOTH THE KEYS TO ME! THIS IS GREAT!

Oh, shit. I hadn't been expecting that.

"It's okay," I said. "Donut got credit for killing Quan. We'll get her over here and get you a key. We have time. I'm sorry about your—"

Warning: The door to the exit stairwell at *El Capitolio Nacional de Cuba* has sustained damage and will become unusable in

five minutes. If the doorway crumbles, the associated key will dissipate.

And with that little notification, it ruined our hopes of getting out of this clean.

"God-fucking-damnit."

59

IT WAS A KICK TO THE TEETH.

It took a second, but the horror flashed across Ren's face as the implications of it all settled in.

I quickly ran through the options, and I came to the same, terrible conclusion as Ren.

My view counter was spiked once again.

Donut now had the two keys in her inventory. One key for the door in the church now guarded by Imani, and one key for the door here in the capitol building. This door would only be usable for the next four and a half minutes.

We couldn't just give Ren a key. The rules were clear, and they'd been made just for this sort of impossible situation.

In order for Ren to get that key, we would have to first get Donut here. We would have to initiate a card battle. Donut would have to use a Flee card, which meant Donut would lose one of the two keys. We wouldn't be able to pick which key we lost.

If the system was generous, and it dropped the key to the capitol building, we would teleport away, Ren would get the key, and she could rush into the chamber.

If the system was being a dick—and the system was *always* a dick—it would drop the key to the church. Ren would probably still be okay. They would still have a key, but her squad would have to make their way across town to the church, where they'd have to get past Imani.

Donut and I, meanwhile, would be fucked. We'd be teleported away from the capitol building. We'd still have the key to get out, but we'd have to get to the door in time, which would be next to impossible. It would have to be now. And since we really wanted to get that key to Imani?

It wasn't going to happen.

Four minutes left.

In either scenario, we'd have to get Donut here. I could toss Samantha. That would take two or three minutes at least, and that was assuming my aim was true. I could get the red spider and use the loop-de-loop, but that would require a crawler other than myself to switch places with Donut. It would have to be Khulan, which would be the equivalent of killing her. Besides, she wasn't getting up off that floor. She remained draped over the ruined body of her husband.

There was another scenario. One Donut and I could still pull off. I could have the spider rush into the room and touch Ren. They'd switch places. With Ren gone, nobody would be left to initiate a card fight. Donut and I could rush down the stairs and be safe. However, that meant Donut wouldn't have time to pass on the second key, the one for the church exit, meaning nobody else would be able to escape. We'd be killing Imani.

Uncertainty washed over me.

If you make this decision. Be sure. Be sure it's your only option. This is more than just a fail-safe. It's the end of everything. If there's time to do something else, don't be so quick. So you must be absolutely certain.

All of this whipped through my mind in a matter of seconds. I looked over my shoulder and whistled. From across the street, the little spider hopped up, dragging the memory ghost pants with it. It started moving toward me.

CARL: Donut, get ready to teleport! Make sure Mongo is put away. Fast!

If we didn't do this now, Ren would challenge us to a fight. She didn't have a choice. There was only one key left, and she knew if we were going to willingly give it up, it'd be to Imani and not her. What else could she do?

There were no scenarios left where it wasn't her or us.

She could kill you right now. It would put Donut at a disadvantage. Be careful.

I examined the woman who'd turned into a dog. I barely knew her, but by now most everyone in the dungeon knew her story. She'd grown up in Mongolia, and she'd been a fashion model once upon a time. She'd left the country and moved to France. A jealous ex-boyfriend had stabbed her and her dog. She'd spent the next year in a hospital before retiring. She'd recently returned home when the collapse happened. Her entire group had all been people she'd grown up with, all from a tiny little village. Her entire circle of friends brought down by this goddamned place, this goddamned floor, one by one.

It was terrifying how quickly, how easily everything could change.

As I watched, Ren sat down heavily on the floor. Garret made an uncertain noise and plopped down next to her. She reached up and unsnapped her flamethrower attachment, and the whole apparatus toppled onto the scorched, broken tiles.

"You know, I was really looking forward to torching some of those assholes on the next floor." She leaned over and rested her head against the meatball.

The red spider clicked up the steps and stopped just outside the chamber. I lifted my hand, causing it to pause.

Above, the ceiling cracked ominously. Over by the exit doorway, Khulan continued to cry. She was a tiny woman, young but with the skin of someone who'd worked outdoors her whole life. She clutched on to the larger form of the dead crawler.

"Khu, come," Ren said.

"No," she replied.

I opened my mouth to say something, but Ren raised a hand, stopping me. She continued to look at her grieving friend.

Three minutes left.

"The only thing that was keeping her together was her husband. She's not going to want to go on, and I'm not going to make her, not anymore." She sniffed. "It's funny. Growing up, she was the toughest of us all."

"We still have four days left," I found myself saying. "There's still one key. I have to give it to Imani, but I might have figured a way to teleport us to another area. You'll have to train up your trap skills, but there's time. We can do it."

"So we can kill someone else for their key?" she asked. "By my count, there's one key for every three or four squads. They really fucked us this floor. There's time left, but everybody is already going down the stairs. I'm not going to do that, Carl. I don't want to be responsible for hurting someone else."

"Then . . . then . . . you can fight us for it. Fair and square. It's your only chance."

"Carl," she said, turning to look at me. She shook her head. "I say this with love. You are an idiot. You can't fight us. You can't give your key to Imani. You have to save it for yourself. Do you remember when you flew that airplane to save our bubble on the fifth floor? And then when you killed all the hunters? That's when I realized who you are. Don't you understand? You're more than just a person. If we lose you, we lose *everything*. You're a symbol. You're the embodiment of our hope. You and that fucking annoying cat that everyone seems to like for some reason. You two bought a goddamned slot on Faction Wars. Everyone who remains can't wait for the chance to fight someone real, someone actually responsible for all this. If you two don't get down to the next floor, we all lose that. You can't sacrifice yourself. And you know what? I know Imani thinks that, too. If you give her your key, she's just going to try to give it back to you."

DONUT: AM I TELEPORTING IN? ARE YOU SENDING SAMANTHA TO ME? DO WE HAVE TIME? ARE YOU USING THE LOOP-DE-LOOP? WHAT'S HAPPENING?

I swallowed.

CARL: Stay put. We're saving the loop trap. I'm gonna toss Samantha to you in a minute.

Ren returned her head to the side of her large pet, and she stroked his strange, bumpy skin. He made a purring noise.

So much regret filled me. I should have let Ren finish Quan off. I should have used my last teleport trap as a way for Donut to get here more easily. You can only anticipate so much. You can only prepare for what you can think of, and it still won't be everything. You can't win every battle.

I thought of what Mordecai once told me about Drakea, that he'd been killed by one of his own traps because the showrunners had tipped the scale, had broken their own rules to make it prematurely blow.

They were exterminating us one by one, and no matter how hard I worked, someone was always going to be there, looking over my shoulder, wondering how they could make it more dramatic for the audience. How soon before they decided it was my time? Or Donut's?

So much regret.

My view counter remained spiked, but it was starting to ease off now it was clear we weren't going to fight. That made me unreasonably angry. *Fuck you all.*

I looked nervously up at the ceiling. "We have to get out of here," I said. "The door will crumble, and then the whole building is going to collapse on top of us."

She kicked the flamethrower attachment at me. "Take it," she said. Several items from her inventory started appearing on the floor one by one. Rings. Clothing items. Potions. Scrolls. "Take it all. Fast. There's good stuff in there, including a bunch of *Eye in the Sky* scrolls."

"What the hell are you doing?" I asked, suddenly alarmed. I had a memory of another place. Another time. A clearing in the forest where Miriam Dom had done the same thing.

I remembered my mother.

This is my birthday present to you. I am giving you a chance at life.

"I'm donating to the war effort," she said. "My flamethrower is named Velma, by the way. I didn't name it that." She was holding it back, barely. So was I.

"We have four days left! We can figure something out!"

She ignored me. She pulled one last item from her inventory. It was a small crystal knife. It looked like a butter knife. It glinted with red light.

"This is called the Knife of Frozen Tears, and it's made of something called Sylvan crystal. It's not very sharp, and it's not all that valuable, but it can kill Garret. Each time he regenerates, he gets another weakness. He's up to four now. Sylvan crystal is one of them." She broke, then, at that last sentence.

"No. No, no," Garret said. It was more a sound than actual words. I was pretty sure the thing couldn't actually talk, but it could mimic some noises.

Tears streamed down the dog woman's face.

The far wall sagged.

Warning: The Stairwell Exit at *El Capitolio Nacional de Cuba* has been rendered inaccessible. All available keys through this exit have been destroyed.

She struggled to speak. "He's a type of pet called a Tummy Acher. He's a great tank, and he's practically immortal. It's really hard to kill him, and if he dies, he regenerates. But every five times he dies, he resets back to level one, and you have to get him to bond with you again. They say he won't remember, but I'm not sure. This will be the first time it happens. Each time he regenerates, he's tougher, but he also has a new weakness, so you have to be careful." She sniffed. She looked over at Khulan, who remained prone near the collapsed wall. "It's just like the rest of us. We look stronger, we have tougher skin, more scars, but there's another crack in our . . ." She couldn't finish.

Garret whimpered. He pushed himself against Ren, like he couldn't get close enough.

She was openly sobbing now as she talked directly to her pet. "I had a dog once, before all this. He died protecting me, and now I'm going to protect you. You're going to go live with Carl. He's going to take care of you because I can't do it anymore. He will feed you every day, and you're going to be a good boy for me, won't you?"

"Uh," I said.

She stabbed the knife directly into the side of the pet, and he immediately tumbled over, dead. Just like that. He died instantly, like she'd flipped a switch. A moment passed, and his corpse started to shrink, like he was having the air pulled from him.

Ren wiped her eyes. "It lists his weaknesses in his description, and he's going to have a new one now, but his weaknesses so far are Sylvan crystal, consuming hobgoblin sweat, the bite of a rivenwing, and consuming undead flesh. That's what usually kills him, so be careful, because he eats everything. Each time he comes back, he risks getting a common weakness, so try to keep him alive."

"Why did you do that? We have four days left," I said yet again, flabbergasted. "It's . . . it's not over yet."

Ren had her eyes on her friend. As quickly as the tears had come, they were gone. She'd given herself a moment to be emotional, and all that was left was business.

"No, Carl, it's not over yet. Not for you, but it is for me. As soon as Khu is done crying, she is going to kill herself. She's lost everything. She lost her little girl, who was inside when it started, and she's lost everyone else along the way. She has nothing left. Nothing. I don't, either. Except my faith that you, Carl, will make somebody regret choosing us for this."

She was silent for a moment.

"I don't want my friend killing herself to be the last thing I see. It has to be now. I want to go out having done something good. All I have left for this floor is to deny them a fight. I'll take it. If I can't help you on the next floor, I can at least give you my best gear, and I can protect Garret."

I looked down at the pet. He was still unconscious, and he was now level one. His name had disappeared, too. It was like he was a completely new pet. I remembered the first Tummy Acher I'd ever seen, way back on the second floor. It had been in a cage near Mongo. This was the same. A tiny, little round ball on two stubby legs. This one's single tooth stuck out on the outside, making it look like he had a massive underbite.

Ren produced a pet carrier, and she gently picked the unconscious meatball up. She gave him a tender kiss.

"I'm sorry," she said, and she put him in the carrier. She paused. "His new weakness is something called Reaper Gaze. I don't know what that is." She slid the carrier over to me, and before I could talk myself out of it, I put it in my inventory. A host of pet-themed achievements appeared and disappeared.

"If you do figure out some miracle before this floor is done, make sure that Sister Ines doesn't go down the stairs," Ren said. "I've met Paz a few times, and he's a good man. Don't let her get away with keeping his card."

"I won't. But what are you going to do now? If the roof collapses, you probably aren't going to die. You're just gonna get stuck."

She held up an arm, showing a wrist bracer. It was the only thing she still wore. That and a little heart locket around her neck with a dog-paw print on it. "You ever see the movie *Predator*?"

I knew what the device was. I'd seen them before for sale at the Desperado Club. "You're going to blow yourself up? Just like that?"

"They want us to fight. Me and Donut. This is me going out on my terms. You would've wiped the floor with us anyway. This is me telling them to go fuck themselves."

This was too much. It was her choice, and I understood why she was doing it, but I hated it. I hated everything about it. I hated that my views kept going down, that people didn't care. I hated there was nothing I could do to stop her.

This will stop it. It's so loud, Carl. It's so loud.

"Okay," I finally said, standing up, trying to hold my emotion in check.

A wry smile crossed Tserendolgor's face.

REN: Princess Donut, I have a confession to make. Everything you're saying is true. I *was* trying to steal your experience the first time we met. I *did* cheat at the pet show. Your Mongo is the rightful champion. I'm sorry.

DONUT: I KNEW IT! I KNEW IT!

DONUT: CARL, DID YOU HEAR THAT?

"You didn't have to do that," I said, chuckling.

She grunted with amusement.

"You know, many of my people are afraid of cats. Some think if you look into their eyes, they can steal your soul. I hope that's true. I hope she lives up to her hype."

Across the room, Khulan stood and shuffled to us. She wrapped her arms around Ren's neck.

She wasn't crying anymore, either. Her eyes were unblinking as she stared off into space.

"Garret is a good boy. Please take care of him. Bonding is easy. Feed him something a few times. Make sure it's not undead flesh or that it's never been touched by a hobgoblin. Try to find out what that Reaper Gaze weakness is as soon as you can. I'm pretty sure they'll make you give him a new name, so come up with something good."

The ceiling cracked again. There was a ping. Quan's body could now be looted of the rest of his gear. I still wouldn't be able to get his cards. Hopefully we were done with that anyway. I quickly started to gather up the rest of Ren's dropped gear, including the enchanted flamethrower, which was really part breastplate, part weapon.

Ren's eyes flashed, and Khulan dropped several items on the ground. More rings and potions and a glowing spear, along with multiple armor items plus a few unread magical tomes. A ton of coins.

"Here," Ren said. "I can't give you my totems, but I just rearranged my deck and took all the other cards out. You'll have to carry them on you until you give them to Donut, but here's all my cards. There's a few rare special and mystics in there in case you need them, including these two. I never got to use them."

I stared at the last two cards. One was a consumable **Glow-Up** card. The other was a consumable special card, and it featured two large men in tights. It was called **The Midnight Express.**

I gathered the large pile of cards and stuck them into the waistband of my boxers. It wouldn't let me take them into my inventory.

"You sure about this?" I asked one last time.

"Carl, make them suffer."

I put my hand on the dog woman's shoulder. Her whole body trembled.

"I will kill every last one of them. Every one." I leaned in to her ear, and I whispered, "I goddamned swear it."

60

QUAN HAD MORE CRAP IN HIS INVENTORY THAN I DID, WHICH WAS SAYing a lot. He carried a ton of magical weapons, from swords to spears to war hammers to more non-traditional items, like a magical chain saw and something that appeared to be a literal sock filled with nickels, only it was one of the highest-value items he had on him. Also, there was a bowler hat like that guy had in that James Bond movie, where you could throw it, and it would decapitate someone before it boomeranged back to you. Donut was going to lose her mind when she saw it. He also held almost five million gold coins, and I wondered if he'd ever actually purchased anything. He had all this stuff he never used. It was going to take forever for me to go through all of it. Thankfully, I could transfer it all with one button.

The only thing I left was the single golden ring, which remained clutched in his hand.

I kept his arm. I wasn't sure why.

I didn't turn back to Ren, but she warned I had to get myself clear of the building. Her magical wrist bracer was going to blow the place sky-high. That was okay. The building was useless to us now.

"COME ON, SAMANTHA," I SAID AS WE WALKED OUTSIDE INTO THE BURNing city. I had toyed with the idea of pulling out my Ring of Divine Suffering and marking Ren, or maybe Khulan, like I had with Miriam, but I didn't have time. The mark took thirty seconds to form on this floor, and if either of them had a skill that let them know they'd been marked, it was possible they'd have a sudden change of heart about what they were doing. I didn't want to complicate things further.

Still . . . I felt the urge to pull the ring out and slip it on. I fought it. On the next floor, the ring would have a new feature. I could mark as many people as I wanted at once. If we got out of here, that was where it was really going to come in handy.

In the distance, Amayon, the demon possessing the body of the *Madre de Aguas* snake, sat atop a tall building, raised vertical like a spire, pouring fire into the sky like it was trying to burn its way upward. I had no idea what it was doing, but demon seagulls circled it like a tornado. It was probably casting a spell. *Great. Just great.* Red dots were everywhere.

I scooped up the red automaton and pulled it into my inventory and started jogging west, deeper into downtown Havana, as the building behind me started to crumble.

REN: Goodbye, everyone. At least I won't have to listen to anyone butcher the pronunciation of my name anymore. Do me a favor, and fuck them up for me. Make them all pay.

And with that, there was a secondary rumbling behind me. It wasn't a huge explosion, but it was enough. The dome top of the building collapsed in on itself like it was a controlled detonation. The blast was small by my own standards. Mixed in with everything else happening to the city, the collapse of this single building was hardly noticeable.

DONUT: WAIT, WAIT, WHAT ARE YOU DOING?

Tserendolgor never saw the message. Her name popped into the deceased-crawlers folder. It was done.

DONUT: CARL, WHY IS SHE DEAD? WHAT HAPPENED?

CARL: I'll explain it all in a minute. I'm tossing Samantha to you now, and then we're gonna have to pick our way toward the church. I don't have the time or the supplies to set up another

teleport. We have to go the long way around so we avoid the massive demon. We gotta get to Imani, and then we'll figure out how we're going to proceed. But we need to get out of here before Sister Ines shows back up or before whatever that demon is doing fucks us over. Tossing Samantha now.

I pulled the extension, and Samantha hopped into the scoop. She blinked at me as I tried to judge the distance. "Are we keeping the round guy? I like him. He's really cute. Can I name him? I want to name him."

"I haven't decided yet if we're keeping him," I said. "Probably not. Donut will be scared that he'll eat Mongo."

"You have to keep him," Samantha said. "That doggy died thinking you were going to take care of him. He probably won't eat Mongo if they grow up together. I once watched a ten-times-resurrected one of those guys eat a dragon. It was great!"

I paused. "Wait, really? A dragon?"

"It was a small dragon, but yes. Now throw me, Carl. I want to bite Donut's tail."

"YOU DIDN'T HAVE TO CHEW ON ME THAT HARD," DONUT COMPLAINED as we skulked around the corner of a building.

"I need to make a tight grip," Samantha said as she hovered between us. "It's not my fault if I have a strong jaw game. I learned all about biting when someone abandoned me to get eaten by the two doggies on the last floor."

It'd taken me three throws to get Samantha close enough to Donut, and even then, she had to travel for ten minutes before she got to her, where she promptly chomped down on Donut's tail without warning. After teleporting her back to me, the cat had promptly yakked all over the ground, and she'd been grumbling about it ever since. Apparently that type of teleportation was even more unsettling than usual.

Donut sported a new golden player-killer skull. She hadn't commented on it, and neither did I. That felt important, the nonchalance of it all. We were losing more of ourselves every day. I hoped we could manage to get off this damn floor without it happening again.

The zombie crabs and seals were everywhere, swarming over the city, moving away from the beach. It'd been a while since I saw a regular, non-undead crab or seal, and I wondered if any were left. I also hadn't, thankfully, seen any of the full-power demons we'd freed from their shells. Hopefully those had made their way back to Sheol, but I wasn't sure if that kind *could* drag people into hell like the possessed zombies could. Mordecai wasn't sure, either.

The zombies were still turning into possessed demons here and there, but those would scream and skitter off toward Amayon, who remained ramrod straight atop the tallest building, pouring fire upward like he was a fountain. It was having an effect on the whole area. The air was getting noticeably hotter.

"Well, if you chomp me again like that, I'm going to have Mongo chomp you and see how you like it."

"I do like it," Samantha said.

"Shush, both of you," I said, watching a zombie seal shuffle-flop down the street, chasing an oblivious memory ghost that miraculously was still fully clothed. The seal left a stream of red gore on the road. According to Mordecai, these things had a sort of communal mind, so we didn't want any of them seeing us or they'd swarm.

IMANI: No sign of the nun. Nothing has come in. There's an outbuilding I can see through the door, and it's some sort of temple. It's a Club Vanquisher entrance. I just watched a ram NPC guy stick his head out of the door and cast a spell that killed a few zombies, but now a bunch more are milling around the entrance, so there's a mass of them right in front of the church. He keeps opening the door to peer outside and shutting it quickly. The last time there were three of them and what looked like a mantaur. The idiots are just luring more and more zombies into the area.

CARL: Okay. If you do see Sister Ines, just go back into the safe room. There's no reason for you two to fight. Wait for us.

I was making a quick inventory of everything we'd looted, but it wouldn't be until we got to a safe room before I could truly examine it all. So far, it looked as if the best prizes were the *Eye in the Sky* scrolls, the magical tomes, Velma the Flamethrower, the nickel sock, and, of course, Quan's celestial cloak.

He'd truly had a lot of weapons on him. Even more than what I'd looted from the hunters. I wondered if his class, Sergeant at Arms, had something to do with the reason why he kept it all. It was, I realized, all the loot he'd taken off the crawlers he'd killed. The least I could do was make certain it got put to good use.

I hadn't yet told Donut about the Tummy Acher. I asked Mordecai for his advice.

MORDECAI: Keep that thing in your inventory. You couldn't go down the stairs with Mongo before because you didn't have a pet carrier. This guy will be fine as long as you keep him boxed up. You can try bonding with him later. He'll be a great pet for you should you decide to keep him, but you have too much on your plate right now to deal with trying to keep a level one pet alive, especially if it has an undead weakness. And Ren made a mistake by saying what his weaknesses are out loud. The factions guys aren't supposed to be spying, but we both know that's bullshit, even now.

CARL: Agreed. Also, I don't see Sister Ines with my Find Crawler skill. Should I use one of those *Eye in the Sky* scrolls? Will that find her?

MORDECAI: If you use it, have Donut do it. But yes, it will find her as long as she's not in a safe room or using some advanced hiding skills or spells. Those scrolls are really rare. How many do you have?

CARL: Five.

MORDECAI: It's up to you, but I would save them if you can. Have you decided what you're going to do about Imani yet?

CARL: I'm giving her the key. Donut and I will take our chances.

MORDECAI: She's not going to take it.

CARL: Elle will convince her.

He didn't answer.

"Look at the fishy!" Samantha said.

A zombie fish entered the alley, flopping. It spied us, and it made a gurgling noise as red foam bubbled out its gills. It started hopping on the ground toward us. *Splatch, splatch, splatch.* A loud groaning noise came from down the street as more zombies turned in our direction.

"Damnit," I said. "Come on, guys."

"SO, DID YOU BEAT HIM WITH HIS ARM? I PROMISED THE POSSE IF YOU ever fought Quan again, you'd beat him with his arm. I even put it in the newsletter."

We waited in yet another alley as Samantha pied-pipered a group of zombies away from our position. We'd gotten trapped between two buildings, and I sent her out there, which she'd done eagerly. I could hear her enthusiastic shouting from almost two blocks away as the zombies shuffled after her, clearing our path.

"I didn't get the chance," I said. "Golden Uzi Jesus and Asojano pretty much turned him into pulp. That was a really good combination."

"You carried his arm around all this time, and you didn't get to use it. That's a little disappointing. When we killed him, it gave me the keys, but I never got his cards. I bet he had a bunch of good ones. At least you got the dog lady's cards. I suppose she did redeem herself in the end with her deathbed confessions."

"Quan did have some good cards," I agreed, choosing not to engage her about Ren. I could tell it was mostly for show, and she was pretty shaken up about the death of the crawler. Even now, Donut was leaning into the feud for the viewers. "But I don't think his cards were better or worse than ours. He was just really good with strategy. We pretty much had to be the cheaters to beat him."

"Using a loophole isn't cheating, Carl. Not when we do it. Oh, and what happened to that disgusting meatball?"

Before I was forced to tell her the truth, we were both interrupted by a new message.

SISTER INES: Carl and Donut, are you there?

I exchanged a look with Donut.

CARL: Hello, Sister. How are you feeling?

SISTER INES: I know you have the last key. The door you seek is in the Iglesia de Jesús de Miramar. It is a holy place. I've prayed on it, and I know what I must do. I can't let you in. If you open that door, it will be the end of everything. They told me so. This hell you see is only a sampling of what awaits us because of our sin.

DONUT: JUST TRY TO STOP US, YOU HALF-BREED BITCH.

Donut turned to me. "Wow. That came out way more racist-sounding than I intended."

CARL: Sister . . . what is going on? Who are "They"? I thought we were friends. Tell us what's happening.

SISTER INES: I am filled with power, Carl. With each demon who appears, I grow stronger. They come, they keep coming, and I am the last rampart protecting us all. It is because of my faith. I can save you. I must free you from this place before your soul is dragged into hell. I can't save the cat, of course, as she is nothing but a rank beast.

DONUT: HEY!

SISTER INES: But I can save you, Carl. Come to me, and I will show you the way. I showed my sisters, and I can show you. It's not too late. But if you try to enter that church, there will be nothing I can do for you. I will be forced to stop you.

"Carl, she's gone completely whackadoodle! I think her medication finally wore off!"

I shook my head. "It's more than that. Whatever imbalance she had, it's been deliberately kicked back into place. I think it's one of her sponsors. During the last battle, the announcer guys said she was sponsored by the nebulars. Her patron, too, which I think is pretty much the same thing. I think they gave her something that sent her back over the edge."

"What? Why would they do that? Those are the hunter guys with the hats, right?"

"Yes. They're not a single race, but a cult. Remember, they were the guys in the audience in the mock-card-battle arena when you set it up the first time. They worship the thing that runs the center system, and they have some pretty weird beliefs." The strange religious cult had been gunning for Prepotente on the last floor during the Hunting Grounds before I'd been forced to fight them and Vrah's crew at the same time. It seemed they were still sore about me and Donut helping to wipe all of them out. I still didn't know what their deal was in terms of their actual beliefs, but a picture was starting to form in my mind. "We need to be careful. I'll try to keep her pacified until we can get the hell out of here."

CARL: Okay. We can meet somewhere. We'll talk. Where do you want us to go?

"We're not really gonna meet her, right?"

"Hell, no. We just gotta keep her distracted."

SISTER INES: Good, good. You won't regret this, Carl. Come to the FOCSA building.

CARL: I don't know where that is.

IMANI: Three demons just walked into the church. They're huge! They're not the possessed zombies. They're the level 140 pleasure demons. Carl, it says they're minions of Sister Ines. How is that possible? I thought you said she couldn't control the real demons.

In the distance, the massive, demon-possessed snake stopped throwing fire into the sky.

"Here, Carl," the giant snake bellowed. His voice echoed, shaking the ground. Glass shattered all around. It was clearly fighting the words, like it was being forced to talk. "Come here."

"What the shit?" I asked.

"Carl . . . is she controlling the giant demon?" Donut asked. "I thought he was like a god! How can she do that?"

"Fuck me," I said, looking off into the distance. *Uh-oh.*

SISTER INES: Come now, Carl. Come or I will make the demons under my control destroy that church. I don't want to smash such a holy place, but I will. I will destroy it all if it will prevent you from opening that door.

"Carl, this is what you get for not letting Mongo eat her when we had the chance," Donut said.

"Well, shit," I said.

61

<Note added by Crawler Milk. 6th Edition>

Even though you can sometimes move the platforms upon which the stairwells sit, you cannot put the exit portal into your inventory. You can't bring a stairwell into your safe room. I watched one get hit by an Utter Annihilation wand, and it remained unscathed. I believe that means they are indestructible.

<Note added by Crawler Herot. 16th Edition>

Milk is correct here about the stairwells. It states in the rules manual that while stairwells may be gated until certain conditions are met, the stairwells themselves are not allowed to be removed from the playing field.

<Note added by Crawler Rosetta. 9th Edition>

The only way for a crawler to move from one floor to the next is via a stairwell. That's it. It is an unbreakable rule. There is no skipping floors. At the end of Faction Wars, after the Viceroys pulled out their last-minute victory, a portal appeared, and several of the remaining fucks stepped within. It was all of them. The orcs, the Viceroys, the Operatics, even the Nagas, all together, laughing as if they weren't just bathing in each other's entrails the day before. It appeared it was taking them to another part of the dungeon, some sort of nightclub on a different floor, for a victory party. They dragged several unwilling NPCs with them, including the librarian elves from the college, whose help was instrumental in our survival. A crawler tried to jump through the portal to save the NPCs, and he was stopped like it was a wall of glass. He tried casting a spell through the portal, but it did not work, though the attempt did catch the attention of the orc prince. The orc stepped back through the glass into the smoldering remains of Larracos, lassoed the crawler, and returned to the portal. The rope pulled itself within, and it cut the crawler in half. We watched as the orc and his friends laughed, just there on the other side of the glass. It was the last crawler they killed, of the thousands who fell during that pointless game.

Tonight, I will dream of watching them burn. Tonight, I will pretend I was smart enough to find a way to lance them from afar.

Comrades, I hope you help me realize my dream one day.

"IT'S ABSOLUTELY RIDICULOUS THEY CAN JUST BREAK THE DOORS," Donut said as we ran. Samantha, having sent the zombies wandering off in the wrong direction, was looping back to meet us one street over. "How can they even break the stairwells anyway? One of them was on a submarine that got eaten by a shark and then blown up, and it was just fine. It's not fair! I thought it was always supposed to be winnable. If they make it impossible, what's the point? It's cheating!"

We were running toward the church. We would have to skirt past the demon atop the building. We didn't have time to go the long way. The building loomed. The demon, after being forced to beckon us, had resumed shooting fire straight up into the air. The tornado of demon seagulls grew by the moment. The ground immediately around the building was a sea of red dots, all possessed zombie demons.

I was in the chat with Sister Ines, insisting I was on my way, but there was no way I'd voluntarily walk into that trap. We had to get to the church before she set her demons to trash the doorway.

I stomped heavily onto a zombie fish, splattering it. We continued on our way, crossing over a massive pileup of cars. Ahead, Samantha appeared, lowering herself into an alleyway. She'd stolen a shawl thing from a vendor's booth, and it hung over her head.

I grunted as I stomped another zombie fish. The things were everywhere, flopping all about. "Ines isn't threatening to break the stairwell. Just the *doorway* to the stairwell, and the only reason she hasn't done it yet is because it's in a church. It's not a portal, and we know the stairwells are actually right there. We can see them on the map. Just the doors themselves are magical, and the walls surrounding it, too. It's confusing, but the stairwell chambers themselves are fine. We're not the only ones this happened to. Did you see Katia's message in the group chat?"

A group of former daughters who'd ended up in Turkey had managed to kill another crawler and take the key, but the same thing had happened. They'd fought their battle right in front of the door, and it'd damaged the exit. Their key had disappeared right after they'd gotten it. There were several instances now of crawlers threatening to destroy the doorways if an opposing team didn't give up their key. Those who'd already gone down had the right idea. It was getting uglier by the moment.

This whole floor had been designed to turn us against one another, to cull us down to nothing. It was working.

The event with the zombies wasn't just happening here, either, though it seemed we had the worst of it. The Demon Eviction event was worldwide. My entire chat was filled with people dealing with zombies all over all the coastal regions, which in turn meant they were having to deal with demons, too. Donut said she'd already received a string of swears from Prepotente, who blamed me for this.

"Does that mean we can dig through the rubble, and the stairwell might be down there?" Donut asked.

"Maybe. I doubt it, but that's what I'm hoping. The daughter team is digging now, looking for it. If they find it, they'll let everybody know, and we'll do the same thing if we can. Maybe we can blow up the building ourselves, and the stairs will just be there, open. Like when we couldn't get through the magical door during the Remex quest on the third floor. We just blew up the building to get inside."

"If that does work, I bet Ren would feel really stupid about bowing out early."

"No, she wouldn't," I said.

"I suppose you're right. It took literally dying for her to finally admit she was wrong."

I had serious doubts digging for the chamber would work. That seemed too easy. The keys were the way out, and losing them was pretty much the same as dying. Donut had a point about it not being fair, but like Mordecai had said so many times, the dungeon was self-balancing, and it messed with the rules to keep the drama ratcheted up. We'd skipped an entire floor. There were more crawlers alive at the beginning of this floor than they'd been expecting.

It was an uncomfortable thought. When we'd started this floor, there'd been over 38,000 crawlers left alive. Mordecai hadn't said anything about it, but sometime in the past few weeks, he'd turned off the surviving number of crawlers from displaying in the personal space. I deliberately didn't look at it when we entered regular safe rooms. I didn't want to know.

We'd been dying off faster than usual up until the start of the sixth floor, which was usually one of the deadliest. That was when we'd really started working together and had turned things around. Without anyone actually dying on the seventh, the dungeon had some catching up to do.

I wasn't certain what our survival count was at the moment, but I did know what the numbers were for several instances of previous seasons at the start of the ninth.

The average number of crawlers who stepped onto the ninth floor was just south of 8,000. I knew of one where it was only 500.

What was worse, fewer than 1,000 crawlers usually made it to the 10th. Sometimes, it was zero. For the 11th floor, the average was less than 10 crawlers. Very few chose to push on instead of making deals.

There was an essay on this in the cookbook, written by Herot, who posited the focus of the fans shifted once Faction Wars finished. While top-tier crawlers would have die-hard followers, much of the attention shifted to the intrigue and scheming and positioning of the individual elites preparing for the Ascendency game. The crawlers themselves were treated more like sands in an hourglass. The moment the last one died or took a deal, the Ascendency game would start, and the timing of that moment could change everything.

No, I decided. Those of us without keys were pretty much already dead. All of this stuff with the demons and zombies was just a way to make those deaths interesting.

The temperature was now sweltering. We were only two blocks from the tall, wide building that had the snake atop it.

"What *is* that thing doing?" Donut asked. "Isn't that snake thing supposed to be a water goddess or something? Why is it shooting fire into the sky?"

"No clue," I said. I leaped past a street vendor cart, but my foot caught on it, and it tumbled over, spilling what smelled like coconut cookies everywhere. "Samantha, do you know what he's casting?"

"He is fighting the charm spell," Samantha said. "He's not as strong because he's in the body of that snake lady. He's probably really embarrassed that he's being controlled like that. The ladies in the harem will probably make fun of him. It's a bad look. Do you like my new headband?"

"It is quite lovely," Donut said. She shot a magic missile at a zombie crab, and it exploded before it could warn the others.

"So, you don't think Sister Ines has full control over him?" I asked. "The fire is because of the charm spell?"

"He is casting a spell to get home. It's a portal. They try casting it a lot in the Nothing, but it doesn't work there because he needs to suck a lot of souls in for it to work. It'll probably work here, though."

Oh, shit. "A portal spell? Like the ones the other demons cast when they touch people?"

Samantha was suddenly chewing on one of those coconut cookies, and she had crumbs all over her face. "Yeah. Same sort of thing, but he's a big boy and big boys need big doors and lots of souls. Plus it'll be in the sky above, not the ground, and it'll suck everything up like that cute but sad metal guy you have floating in your house that slurps up bags of potato chips and cleans when Mongo tinkles on the couch."

I looked up at the sky, and the red cloud from the fire was right above our heads and was growing slowly. *Uh-oh.*

"He's trying to cast the spell, but Sister Ines is controlling him also? I don't understand. Is she making him cast this?"

"No. I think the Donut-looking lady isn't strong enough to control him. I think she's trying to stop him, but he's casting it anyway. She's not strong enough to even be doing what she's doing now, so she's gotta have some help. She probably worships another god."

"She doesn't," I said. "We just fought her, and I would've seen if she worshipped a new god. She's not going to willingly do that. It's a thing for her."

IMANI: Holy crap, Carl. One of the ram guys and a mantaur just came out of the temple and tried to fight one of the pleasure demons. I watched the whole thing. The demon cast something, and it pulled all three of them down and away. The demons have a ranged hell portal attack. It left a hole in the ground the size of a hot tub. The portal is still there. It's sucking everything around into it like it's a black hole. It's a one-minute portal, and it says "Entrance to Sheol, Floor 15." It's literally pulling bricks off the walls of the building. Wait, something is happening.

CARL: Fuck me. Keep me updated.

"We need to be extra careful," I said to Donut. "The full-strength demons don't need to touch you to drag you to hell. They also have a portal attack. It sounds like it's wide, too, so they don't have to be super precise. The hole hits the ground and sucks everything in."

"Oh my God, Carl. So we have holes flying around everywhere? Holes on the ground and a giant vacuum in the sky? How are we supposed to fight against that?"

"We can't. We have to get them to suck other NPCs or mobs away first. The demons go away if they also bring something down with them."

"All the NPCs are dead! It's just zombies! Do those count? I haven't seen a real NPC since we got into the city!"

"I'm pretty sure regular zombies and undead don't count. They have to be corporeal NPCs or crawlers. We gotta find some somewhere."

"What about the ghommid village?" Donut asked. "It's just two blocks over!"

"They're undead," I said. "It won't work."

IMANI: Okay. Another ram cleric came out and avoided the first hole, but another demon attacked. That one opened a second portal and sucked the new cleric in, but the demon is still here. He's shouting at the entrance of the temple, demanding someone else come out and face him. It says "One of Two" over the second portal. He hasn't seen me yet. He's waiting right outside.

CARL: It sounds like the bigger demons need to banish two souls in order to return. Don't risk it. Stay in the safe room.

IMANI: I wonder how many the giant one needs.

I was just wondering the same thing.

CARL: How many demons are left in the church?

IMANI: Just one inside, and there's more outside. They're congregating in the area outside the church, and I can only see so much from my position here. I can't tell how many. It's not a whole lot, but it's more than five. It still says they're minions of Sister Ines, but they're obviously jumping at the chance to use their portal skills to escape back down to the 15th floor.

CARL: Okay. I have an idea, but you gotta do it away from the exit. A while back I, uh, locked the stripper guys in the training arcade. They're probably pretty pissed about it by now. They're helping me with something for the next floor. Mordecai will catch you up, but as soon as you see what I did, you'll understand. That should get rid of the demons. It'll hopefully clear up the church area.

IMANI: I'm on it.

While I waited, I pulled up the group chats, and they were full of people dealing with an influx of demons. This was even happening to people away from coastal regions. In typical dungeon fashion, it'd spread over everything faster than really possible. I scanned until I saw the information I was looking for.

REZAN: By god. Masoud is dead! He got touched by a zombie polecat that was possessed by a demon! It just touched his foot, and it tried to pull him away through a portal. The demon went through the hole, but Masoud exploded when he touched it! He blew up just like my mother did when she went into the bathroom on the first floor!

MANDLA: If it's like the bathrooms, you don't explode when you touch the portal. All of your equipment is sucked through, but you aren't allowed to pass, and everything you're wearing passes through *you* to get into the hole. It's like a portal trap. If it's caught in the portal's pull, it's going through. But it's a portal to the 15th floor, and we're not allowed to go down there, so we get stopped, and everything behind us gets pulled through anyway, hence we explode.

REZAN: I wasn't asking for a science lesson, you turnip. It doesn't matter how you explode. You touch it, and you're dead.

MANDLA: Not if you're naked.

REZAN: So you're saying we fight the zombie demons naked?

MANDLA: That's what I'm doing.

I stopped dead in the street. I didn't really know either of these crawlers, but I had met them both once long ago. Their conversation triggered something. A memory of Katia and Louis and Firas, and something that had happened on the fifth floor aboard the *Twister*. That plus a few entries from the cookbook. I jumped into the conversation.

CARL: Rezan, what happened when the portal closed?

REZAN: What do you mean, what happened? He blew up like someone shoved a dynamite stick up his ass. Some of him is in my teeth. He was a prick, but what a way to go. He's everywhere. All his gear got sucked into the hole, and he exploded so much, I can't even loot his inventory. He had most of our gold, too. The rest was in the safe room. He was the one who bought the safe room, and now it's gone. I'm really in trouble here.

CARL: But the demon still went away? And the hole went away immediately?

REZAN: It sure did.

CARL: It only took the stuff the guy was touching?

REZAN: Yes. Holy shit, any more questions? I'm running for my life here.

I looked up at the giant demon. If they were zombie demons, they only needed one soul. They touched a person, a portal opened, and the demon returned home. The portal closed immediately. If they were the full-powered level 140 demons, the portal lasted a minute or two, sucked in everything nearby, and they needed two souls in order to punch their ticket home.

The demon stuck in the body of the possessed city boss loomed over us, still pouring fire upward, several hundred, perhaps a thousand feet in the air. I still didn't know what Sister Ines had to do with any of this, but an idea started to percolate.

"Carl, can we not just stand in the middle of the street?" Donut asked as she fired another missile, this time at a zombie seagull.

"Hang on," I said. "I'm thinking."

"Think faster!"

SISTER INES: I am losing my patience, Carl.

My heart thrashed. What had Ren said? Three out of four teams hadn't gotten a key? I'd been wrong before. The game *was* trying to balance the unfairness of the doorways breaking. I saw it now. It was just doing it in a really, really fucked-up way.

CARL: Everybody who can hear this, quick, let me know if you've been getting any of those *Build Trench* scrolls in your inventory. I've gotten like 50 of them.

MANDLA: I have a ton of them, too.

LOUIS: They're like the bandages and torches on the first floor.

CARL: Katia, I don't have a direct line to the former daughters stuck in Turkey. Is there an update?

KATIA: They said they found the chamber, but the stairwell is contained within. It's just a big rectangular room, and they can't get inside. It's almost like a shipping container, but when

the magical door broke, it just left a straight wall and no way to get inside. One has a *Hole* spell like Donut's, but it didn't work. Another tried a *Phase Through Walls* spell, and it didn't work, either. It's like the walls are made of the same stuff as the magic doors.

None of this matters. Quit wasting time. Imani is going to get rid of the demons, and you can send her down the stairs. Then you can use your Bone Key benefit. It'll be done. You can be through.

Three out of four teams. Thousands of people.

Fuck, fuck, fuck.

Imani snapped me out of it.

IMANI: Carl, what the actual fuck is wrong with you?

CARL: Yell at me later. How many are there?

IMANI: You infected over a dozen mercenaries with a disease that causes them to leak punk rock slugs every few minutes, and you locked them all in a room for almost a day. You locked them in a room where they die and get regenerated. How many do you think there are? There's hundreds of them, including some slugs that are as high level as the mercenaries themselves. The entire room is filled with blood.

CARL: They're not punk rock. They're sluggalos. And I only infected one of them. Doctor Bones. He has the same *Super Spreader* spell as I do, but his is better. I can only do it on one person once per hour. He infected the others all at the same time, and then he cast a spell on the slugs so they're not so hostile after they come out.

IMANI: Yeah, that part doesn't work so great. They're still pretty aggressive, especially the big ones. I opened the door just in time to see one swallow Steve whole. There're way too many here to keep for the next floor. Carl, some of these things are huge! One of them has a damn hatchet growing out of its head.

CARL: The *Conscript* spell is far from perfect. It makes them fight on our side, sort of. It doesn't really change their attitude, and they can be rebellious. It's kinda like turning them into totems.

We'll probably have to kill the highest-level ones, but the rest are going into our infantry. For right now, since they were born in the arcade, you should be able to send the lowest-level ones out the door toward the demons. Keep sending them until the demons are gone. If I can make it to a safe room before the floor collapses, I'll buy the barracks upgrade so we can keep the most powerful ones we can control. In the meantime, bring Doctor Bones with you if you have to. I don't think you can let him go outside because he's technically my mercenary.

IMANI: He's a member of the guild mercenary barracks. I can "borrow" him.

CARL: Huh. I didn't know that. I still wouldn't let him outside. I'm pretty sure if any of the stripper guys die outside of the training arcade, they die for real. Only some special types of mercenaries can regenerate.

IMANI: Yeah, Carl. Speaking of regenerating, I had to cure the mercenaries of the slug disease. The room healer refused to do it. She and that Bucket Boy kid said you told them not to.

CARL: Wait, you can cure that stuff?

IMANI: Yes, Carl. I am a healer. It's what I do.

CARL: Good to know.

With that problem settled, I moved back to the messages I was composing. I sent out two separate ones. The first went to Prepotente, who was back in the Bahamas, meaning he was the closest crawler to us outside of Cuba.

CARL: Prepotente, answer me fast. Please. Has the sky changed color over there? Is anything happening to the environment?

CARL: Mordecai, quick, give me the short, fast version of the Sheol storyline.

Mordecai answered first.

MORDECAI: It was set up a long time ago, but nobody has ever gotten that far, so it's been running on its own for seasons and seasons with very little input from the outside. The demons get pulled out and used for quests and fights all the time, but we never get to see Sheol itself. There's no tourist activity at all on that floor. From what I understand, there's a queen who's in charge, and she has four sons, the princes, one of whom you're dealing with right now. The queen and the four sons are pretty much the same as gods. The four princes used to share a massive harem of demons, but one of the brothers banished them all to the Nothing, and there's a bunch of intrigue going on within there, as you've already seen. And below them, there's a whole matriarchal culture of demons with a multitude of other storylines we hear about but never see. That's it. We've never met the queen. That guy you're looking at is one of the biggest bad guys in the whole dungeon. He shouldn't be here this early.

CARL: Okay. Thanks.

PREPOTENTE: There is a red, sunset-like tinge to the sky coming from your area. Are you attempting to screw things up even more? The zombie event ended up killing all of my opponents before I could even get to them, I'll have you know. That blood is on your hands.

CARL: Let me know if the sky changes. I'm trying to figure out if what's about to happen is just here or if it's going to be global.

PREPOTENTE: If you're involved, I'm quite certain it'll be global. And not in a good way.

CARL: Eat my ass, Pony. Just let me know if the sky gets redder or if it starts to get hotter.

PREPOTENTE: I will let you know if I notice any changes.

CARL: Actually, you're the smartest guy I know. Let me run something by you really fast. Here's the thing. I don't want it to be local. I want it to spread over the whole world. I need ideas.

62

<Note added by Crawler Herot. 16th Edition>

I'm starting to believe I have the ability to manifest my own destiny, after a certain fashion. The more unstable the AI running this system becomes, the less predictable it is. Yet at the same time, it's even more predictable in certain ways. I made a quip about being hungry, and I suddenly received a random achievement notification about my hunger level. I discussed with my friend how I wished we could kill more ghasts, because they often drop knowledge scrolls, and not one hour later, I received a quest to hunt down a certain number of the very same monsters. Beware, however. That same quest killed my friend. The AI is always listening, thinking, plotting, changing the game to suit its desires. At the higher levels, it is not nearly as rigid as it once was. That pliability can be an asset or an extreme danger.

"OKAY," I SAID. "COME ON. TO THE CHURCH!"

Donut gazed up at the massive demon. "Finally! We could've been running this whole time, Carl! Where's Sister Ines?"

"I'm not sure. Hang on!"

I stopped again as Donut let out an exasperated sound. She shot two more zombie birds.

I consulted my Find Crawler skill, and sure enough, I could now see the nun. I wasn't expecting that. She was in the FOCSA building, directly underneath the snake, maybe three or four floors below it. Not riding it like last time. Okay. That was good.

I dove back into my chat. I prepared a message with Elle, Katia, Donut,

Li Na, and Mordecai. I left Imani out, who was still corralling the sluggalos. I resumed jogging as I messaged everyone.

CARL: Guys, I know a way to get into the stairwell chambers without a key. Pony and I came up with the idea together. I need you to start spreading the word. We need to stop fighting each other. Do everything you can to convince people. Everybody who has lost keys needs to start clearing the stairwell chamber of debris. I know most of these rooms have a whole lot of infrastructure around them, but we gotta get them to isolate these chambers as fast as possible. If you can, you want nothing on it or above it or even around it. Don't be gentle. Blow that shit up, and do it fast. Find one of those *Build Trench* scrolls, and use it to tunnel underneath the chamber. You need to be able to fit everyone in your party underneath the room. Mordecai, go into my bomber's studio and take the pile of satchel bombs and stick them on the market. That'll help people with the demolition. I've been making them in preparation for the next floor, so they're safe for regular crawlers to handle.

KATIA: Carl, what are you talking about?

CARL: Do whatever you can to make people understand. Those with keys need to get out as soon as possible and clear the way for the people left behind. Tell them not to waste their time fighting. There's no point. We can get out.
All of us.

ELLE: What the hell, Carl? Are you blowing smoke up our ass? Is this a sure thing, or are you working off a Carl theory?

CARL: It's a theory. It's a Carl and Pony theory, though, if that means anything. What choice do we have? People are fighting and making it so one team is dead and the other can't get out anyway. It's not a sure thing. It never is. But I think I'm right, and Prepotente thinks it'll work, too.

KATIA: I wish you'd come up with this earlier. Louis just got his first player-killer skulls, and he's not happy about it. He got five, all from one attack.

ELLE: Yeah, no shit. The squad in our area was just one dude, and we already took care of it. That's the whole message? Don't fight? Isolate the stairwells? You're gonna have to give us more than that, cowboy. People are terrified. They're gonna need a solid reason. Also, Imani just told me why you wanted to upgrade the barracks. Of all the fucked-up shit you've done to NPCs, I'm pretty sure this is the worst. Worse than what you did to that gnoll guy.

DONUT: WHAT DID HE DO?

ELLE: Oh, so Donut doesn't know about the sluggalos?

DONUT: THE WHAT? IS THAT A PUN? YOU KNOW HOW I FEEL ABOUT PUN-BASED NAMES, CARL.

CARL: Okay, here's the plan.

"Carl!" Amayon boomed a few minutes later as we started to approach the neighborhood with the church. The voice knocked me out of chat, and I tumbled to the ground. The distant demon growled with anger. We scrambled back up as the ground shook. "Let me go, you fucking bitch. Ahh! Ysalte, I will flay you again. I will get free of this shell and . . ." He growled. "Carl, come now!"

LI JUN: Guys, you will not believe what just happened here at the stairwell.

I barely registered Li Jun's message. Ysalte? Where had I heard that name before?

"Ysalte is here? Where? Where?" Samantha asked. "I don't feel her here. Believe me, you'll feel it when she's here."

"Is that a god?" I asked. "There are no other gods here. Just Amayon."

IMANI: Okay, Carl. Sending them out now. Gluteus Maxx is tossing the small ones out toward the demons. It's already working. The first two slugs attacked a demon, and he portaled them away. There's another one. That guy needed three. I don't know why. Holy cow. It's working! And the damn slug things are all excited about it, too. Christ, they're aggressive.

CARL: Let me know when the demons are all gone by your area, and we'll come to you and get you our key. We need to do this before Sister Ines figures it out and sends backup.

I took a deep breath. We still didn't have a perfect messaging system. I watched as Elle, Katia, and others started spreading the word of the plan. It wasn't taking. People were telling them they were full of shit. People weren't willing to risk it, and I understood that. It was asking a lot.

We paused in an alleyway, waiting for Imani to finish with her sluggalo assault.

"Damnit," I muttered, after seeing someone tell Katia to go fuck herself. I was going to have to convince them myself.

We still mostly relied on a relay system to send out mass messages. I pulled up the largest chat group I had, and prepared the note.

Here we go.

CARL: Everybody, please be quiet and listen. We are all getting out of here. This will work. So if you have a key, you gotta get out of the way and go now. Everyone else, don't fight people with keys. Just let them go. We're all getting out of here.

I reiterated the plan the best I could.

REZAN: There's no way that's gonna work.
JURGEN: It sounds like you just pulled all of that out of your ass.
CARL: Prepotente, tell them what you told me.
PREPOTENTE: Everyone, as much as it pains me to say this, I believe Carl is correct. We have seen gated stairwell encasements break before. I once watched Lucia Mar attempt to teleport a stairwell to another location, and I witnessed what happened to both the stairwell itself and the surrounding structure. This portal is of a particular type, and I believe Carl's theory is sound. I'm certainly not going to risk it myself. I am going to make my way down the stairwell using my key in just a moment, but I am reasonably certain there's at least a

fifty percent chance this will work. Maybe forty percent. And that's only assuming the demon really does cast his spell over the entire world and not just a portion of it.

Next to me, Donut muttered, "He's not the best motivational speaker, is he?"

Goddamnit, Pony. Way to be helpful.

CARL: Look, everyone. Here's the thing. You're right. I'm not positive this is going to work. It's a long shot. But for lots of us, this is literally our only chance. Those of you who are fighting each other, what's the point? If there's not enough of us alive on the next floor, we won't have a chance to make it to the tenth, where we can start earning our freedom. The more of us who set foot on the ninth, the stronger we are. I will take a 50 percent chance to survive with *all* of you over a 100 percent chance to survive alone any day.

PREPOTENTE: Remember, I amended it to 40 percent, Carl. But during Katia's fumbled explanation of the plan, she did bring up a good point about the potential for spin while you're being sucked upward. So maybe I should have said 35 percent.

I had the urge to reach through the messaging system and strangle the goat.

MANDLA: I am going to hyperventilate. This is insane.

DONUT: PREPOTENTE, DON'T BE MEAN TO KATIA.

REZAN: Why does that cat always type in all caps?

DONUT: WHY DIDN'T YOUR MOTHER DRIBBLE YOU BACK OUT ONTO THE TRUCK STOP BATHROOM FLOOR, REZAN?

CARL: Look. Everyone is stressed. I get that. We need to breathe and chill. Follow the instructions, and it'll be okay.

YVONNE VU: Our stairwell is in a subway station! There's like a hundred meters of rock above us!

LOUIS: Oh god, another subway?

CARL: I will delay as long as I can. Do your best. In theory, it should work even if the room is buried, but it's not ideal.

YVONNE VU: So when is this going to happen? Will we have a warning?

CARL: I'm working on it. I'm not sure. You need to get moving, but make sure everybody with keys is out first. No sense in risking them, too.

JURGEN: No, man. I'm breaking the door now. If we gotta clear this shit away, we're gonna need help.

OSVALDO: So help me god, Jurgen. If you break that door before we get through, I will end you.

JURGEN: Whoopsies. Too late. I guess you're stuck down here with the rest of us. Now come help us dig.

I took a breath.

CARL: Goddamnit, everyone, stop it. Earlier, I was thinking about how hopeless all this is. That they're whittling us down to nothing. That there's a death quota they have to meet, and no matter how hard we fight, we're stuck inside that box. No. Fuck them all. I was wrong. We are not like those who came before us. This is our chance. This is our chance to show them how hard it is to kill us. We will not die on their schedule. Every person who gets through this will be one more the real assholes will have to fight on the next floor. We need each other. *I* need you. So stop fucking fighting.

There was a long pause.

KATIA: I'm with you, Carl.

Katia had a key already. She didn't need to say that, but I appreciated it.

ELLE: We are, too.

LI NA: We as well.

A multitude of chats came in, all of people agreeing to help. Relief washed over me.

And then, finally, what I'd been hoping for happened. Confirmation.

A timer appeared in my interface. It was at two hours and started counting down.

New Quest. Where the Sidewalk Ends.

This is a regional quest. All crawlers within the area of Cuba have been added to this quest.

Your squad has been designated as host of this quest.

Oh, all right. For fuck's sake. I've been debating on whether or not to allow this, but now that so many of you are hell-bent on dying in such a spectacular manner, we might as well make it official.

Amayon, one of the four princes of Sheol, has been betrayed by one of his brothers. After being unceremoniously expelled from the kingdom of Sheol, the demon prince has managed to just barely hold on long enough to pull himself onto the equivalent of a very, very small ledge. The level 250 demon lord now inhabits the body of a lesser deity, a once-worshipped sea serpent who went by the name of the *Madre de Aguas*.

In order to return home, Amayon simply must cast a spell. But nobody, not even a prince, rides the river for free. A tithe of souls is required to pass back downward. And for a demon of his power, even as weak as he is right now, that tithe is pretty steep.

So he has cast his spell, a wide-area portal that will inhale all the souls within the Cuba area. This will be enough, barely, to send him home.

Unfortunately for Amayon, his expulsion has not gone unnoticed. Other entities have noted that he is far from home, and they are doing what they can to keep him from returning. He is being thwarted. But even in his weakened state, he is still strong. He is still pushing the spell through.

Here are your options.

- **Option 1. Do nothing.**

***Reward:* In two hours, the portal will cast, and all of the Cuba region will be sucked upward into the Sheol portal. This may or may**

not be a good thing depending on where you're standing when this happens. This portal will remain open for the remainder of this floor. Translation: Get the fuck out when you can.

- Option 2. Free Amayon from his shell.

Reward: This will cause Amayon to take his true form. The timer will reset, and this quest will reset into a World quest. We've never had a full-powered, untethered hell prince unleashed on a lower floor before. I'm sure it'll be fine.

- Option 3. Kill Amayon.

Yeah, good luck with that, especially since he is invulnerable on this floor.

Reward: You will receive a Celestial Hell Boon.

I took a deep breath. It was on.

CARL: Pony, holy shit, you were right. We got the quest, just like you said we would.

PREPOTENTE: How many times must I tell you not to call me by that name?

DONUT REMAINED UNMOVING IN THE ALLEY. SHE WAS STARING UP at me.

"Carl, if we do this, it might ruin our own chance to go down the stairs."

"I know, Donut," I said, taking a knee next to her. "If you want to go down now, I can make sure that happens. But I started this, and people are counting on it, so now I have to stay."

"But how do you know the demon spell will cover the whole planet?"

"I don't know, Donut. It's only a hunch, but I think I'm right. The way the quest is worded seems to confirm it. The stronger the demon is, the bigger the spell needs to be in order to get himself home. I'm gonna make him as strong as possible. I'm not positive it'll cover the whole world, but we're gonna do our best to make it close."

"But how?"

I dodged the question because she was not going to like the answer.

"You were right earlier, Donut. We should have killed Sister Ines when we had the chance. We don't have a choice now. First I take her out. Then I free the boss of his shell, and then I buff him as much as I can." I swallowed. "And then I get my ass underneath the stairwell chamber."

"But if you do all that, you won't have time to dig out the room. One is inside a big church and the other is buried under that entire capitol building. You said it yourself. People need to free the building around the chamber if they can."

I took in a breath. This was the part of the plan I was stumbling on, too. "I can only do my best. But the demon is here in our area. I'm the only one who can buff it up. Donut, I don't want to be in this position." I waved my hand. "But all of this has been manufactured to force this on us, to force me into this. I'm the only one who can do it. If I don't, we're going to be in real trouble on the next floor. This is our chance to get as many of our people as possible down."

She headbutted against my leg. "Don't be stupid. *We* can only do *our* best. If you don't go down the stairs, I don't go down the stairs. We are the Princess Posse, and the Princess Posse doesn't leave anybody behind."

I reached over, and I picked her up and cradled her in my arms. A few streets over, a building collapsed as flames reached high in the sky. Amayon rumbled again. Samantha floated at the end of the alley, oohing and aahing at all the destruction.

"That line was really cheesy," I said as I pushed my face into her fur.

"Yeah, I'm still working on it," she said. "I stole it from some movie. Now let's go kill that nun."

63

<Note added by Crawler Milk. 6th Edition>

If you have to fight a demon and you have access to Sheol fire, do not use it. It makes the creature exponentially stronger.

<Note added by Crawler Ikicha. 11th Edition>

Gods, I am so lonely.

I PEERED AROUND THE CORNER, LOOKING AT THE CHURCH. I DIDN'T SEE any more demons, but I did spy a group of level 30 to 35 pox slugs eating the corpse of a ram cleric. The things were the size of wolves. They all had white dots. There were no zombies in the immediate area, though there were a few zombie birds circling above down the street. Just past the church was the road and then the coastline, and there were a ton of red dots down there, too.

Sister Ines had not yet made good on her promise to send more demons to the church. I suspected she couldn't. With each passing minute, she was losing her grip over Amayon. I wondered if that two-hour timer would change if she gave up. In fact, I wondered if she *could* give it up. There was clearly something else going on with her.

Donut looked upon the slugs with disgust. "Carl, I feel as if I should have been consulted before you infested my strippers with a slug-leaking disease. Splash Zone is very particular about his skin care regimen, and I imagine he's quite upset about all this."

"We're going to need all the soldiers we can get if we make it to the next floor. We can build a lot of fighters fast with this method."

Two of the slugs appeared to be literally having sex atop the pile of gore. The girl slug kept loudly whooping the whole time.

"We need to have a conversation about quality versus quantity, Carl."

CARL: Imani, I think it's clear. We're going to move in. We're in the alley on the other side of the grass square.

IMANI: Stay put. We're coming to you.

CARL: We? Who is we?

I blinked as a blue dot appeared on my map. Then another. Then another.

A large group of crawlers appeared, walking from the church. The slugs started to scatter, but Imani yelled something at them, and they all lowered their heads and turned back toward the church compound. One had a little hatchet attached to the side of its neck, and it started waving it threateningly at Imani, and she pointed a stern finger at it, and it backed off.

"Louis!" Samantha shouted, and zipped off. She zipped across the distance and hit him like a tossed football. She clearly knocked the wind out of him.

Donut gasped. "Carl, what's happening? How did they get here?" She freed Mongo from his cage, and he started bouncing all around. He turned and saw the group and rushed toward them, screeching and jumping. He almost bowled over Britney.

Elle came floating up, looking around. "You know, I always wanted to go to Cuba." A distant crashing punctuated the air as another building collapsed. "Gotta say it's a little hotter than I was expecting. A little more run-down."

Imani fluttered up next to Elle. Her skeletal face and eyes had taken on an even more hollow glaze than usual. Still, she grinned down at me. "Surprise."

"I told you," Elle said. "The look on his face makes this suicide mission all worth it."

It was Imani, Katia, Bautista, Louis, Britney, Tran, Li Jun, Li Na, Zhang, Chris, Elle, a few Meadow Lark crawlers I didn't really know, and a handful of others, most of whom were Asian. It totaled over twenty people.

"It's too bad Florin already went down the stairs," Louis said. "It would've been the whole gang otherwise." He was looking around, suddenly sad as Samantha orbited around him in circles. His five new player-killer skulls looked unnatural above his head. "Wow, this place really sucks."

"How . . ." I began, looking about.

"Yeah, you don't like it when people leave you out of the planning phase for this sort of thing, do you?" Elle asked.

"I don't like it when my friends put themselves at an unnecessary risk," I countered. "Seriously, how did you get here?"

Li Jun stepped forward. He, too, had a pair of player-killer skulls he didn't have before. "It was Lucia Mar." He swallowed. "They're calling it the Battle of Beijing. Lucia, she never really collected any cards. She refused to play it. She got the six totems they automatically gave her, but they were all low-level monsters. And whenever a battle started, she discarded the first one, and she played the rest until her hand was empty, which allowed her to use her spells and magic and inventory. She and her dog went in and killed everything. When she showed up at the SOHO building, it turned into a big fight amongst all the people without keys. There were monster traps set up, too, and it was chaos. I didn't see it, but I saw the aftermath."

He paused, rubbing his arm. "She killed so many people. She set up a teleport trap, and Fangs's team got caught up in it. He had a key. She killed him and his wife and took it. After that, we thought she'd already gone down the stairs, but when we got there, she was waiting for us. She can hide her presence now. She said Florin had messaged her before he'd gone down the stairs and told her to help us." He pulled something from his inventory and handed it to me. "She dropped five of these on the ground and then went down the stairs. We already installed one of them in Imani's room. We don't know how she got these, where she got them from, or why she had so many."

"What the hell?" I asked.

"Yeah. She was really friendly, too, which was unsettling. My sister wanted to fight her."

I examined the item. It was a personal space upgrade module. If you bought one of these from a Bopca, they just installed it directly into your room, but if you got one from a box, it'd come like this. You had to put it in your inventory and then enter your personal space tab on your interface to use it.

"She shouldn't have had one, let alone five of them. It's a tier-3. Mordecai says these shouldn't be available until the ninth floor," Katia added. "He thinks Lucia stole them when she went on a show or something."

Personal Space Upgrade.

Tier-3 Doggy Door.

So, you're out adventuring, and you suddenly have a hankerin' for those sweet pancakes you had two weeks back at some dive that's now over two hundred kilometers away. What are you gonna do? Travel for several hours in the wrong direction just to get another taste? Psshh. Okay, loser.

The cool kids use the doggy door.

Upgrades the door in your personal space to allow a selectable exit via any door you have previously utilized on this same floor, effectively creating a fast travel waypoint system. Allows shared gated access amongst guests and party members.

"Holy shit," I said. "So you gave it to Imani, and she installed it in their room, and now anyone in the guild can go out that door into the church?"

"That's right," Katia said. "Or into Washington or into Detroit. Or into Belgium, where Elle's squad went during the key phase. It works for the whole Meadow Lark party."

"Can we upgrade the entire guild to use it so it works on my door, too?"

"We can," Imani said, "but it's pretty expensive. It's a tier-three. Twenty-five million to give it to everybody. In the meantime, we still have four more and can install them on individual doors as needed. By the way, we already pooled all our money to buy that barracks upgrade."

"You didn't have to do that. I got almost five million off Quan."

Elle spat on the ground. "You should've beaten him to death with his own arm."

"That's what I said!" Donut quipped.

"I still have the key for the door," I said. "I was going to give it to Imani. You all have keys. You shouldn't be here."

"That's not how this works, Carl," Elle said. "You were right, what you said in your little speech. We're all in this together. We're all screwed if we don't all make it to the next floor. If things really go south, most of us can still go back and use our keys. But until that time we're here, and we're helping."

"And I'm not taking your key," Imani added. "Donut told me about your dumbass idea to use one of your own bones or whatever to get out. People have bones for a reason, Carl. No. Like Elle said. It's all or nothing."

I looked again at the module and sighed. "These sure would've been handy a few days ago."

"Tell me about it," Elle said, looking pointedly at Imani. "It would've changed everything. I wonder how long that crazy kid has been holding on to these things. I also wonder if Florin knew about them. I already chewed him out just in case. We've been chasing a fast travel system since the whole guild system opened."

LI JUN: This is just for you, Carl. There's more. Lucia dropped the upgrades, and she said she was helping us because Florin had asked, but before she went down the stairs, she went from really friendly to mean again, and she said she was saving something special for herself because she had a score to settle with Donut and that she would be seeing her on the next floor. She said she was going to kill both Donut and her pet dinosaur. That's why my sister wanted to fight her.

CARL: Holy shit. Okay, thanks for not saying that out loud.

I looked nervously at Donut, who stood on the edge of Tran's flying wheelchair module for his missing legs. She laughed with delight, switched into her dragonfly tiara, and then cast Hover, showing them all her new skill. I had to hold myself back from chiding her for wasting her five-times-a-day skill.

Tran, too, was smiling as he reached over and pet Donut. Britney was on the ground, on her back as Mongo snuffled against her. She was laughing as well. It was the first time I'd seen either of those two, Tran or Britney, so much as smile since the end of the Butcher's Masquerade.

Actually, come to think of it, it was the first I'd seen Britney smile. Ever.

I felt it, too. The change in the air. It was an overwhelmingly welcome feeling.

Things were not looking up for us, but somehow that didn't matter. Despite Lucia's new threat. Despite the overwhelming odds against us. Despite all the death and pain. Still . . . still . . .

Ever since the horror of the Butcher's Masquerade, there'd been this feeling coming over me. It was like an extra layer of darkness on top of everything. It was an overpowering sense of futility that I hadn't even realized was there. This was in addition to the hopelessness that permeated everything. Our humanity was slowly, slowly being siphoned away. With each passing challenge, each new death, each new twist, we were becoming less of who we were.

I thought of Ren and of the hopelessness that had broken her. Of all these crawlers who'd been forced to confront their own personal nightmares on this floor. Of my mother, who'd drowned in her own sorrow. Of the stepmother I'd never met and what she'd done. Of the goddamned river that was so loud, it was the only thing I could hear.

It was loneliness. It had always been loneliness.

That veil was ripped away. Nothing had changed about our situation. We were likely fucked, yes. But we were all together again. And there was hope. Finally. Clarity filled me for the first time in a long while. It was isolation that would break us. We couldn't let it happen.

I thought of Lucia, the most isolated crawler in the dungeon, yet she'd held on to something that could literally bring us all together.

I looked at Katia. I thought of that flower in her inventory, and of all the potential outcomes.

We have to find another way.

But right here, right now, I'd never felt so grateful to know these people standing in front of me.

Elle clapped her little hands together, showering flecks of ice everywhere. She gazed at me.

"Okay, warlord. This is your shit show. What do we gotta do?"

64

<Note added by Crawler Allister. 13th Edition>

The Semeru dwarves of the ninth floor all only worship a single goddess, who inevitably makes an appearance near the end of the battles as the final teams approach the gates of the castle of Larracos. She only has a single temple in the entire dungeon. I have never seen or heard of a crawler worshipping her. I don't know if that's even possible.

She is also, apparently, used as a foil during the Ascendency battles as well. She is hated by both the gods and the demons, and she's said to be forever scheming, moving nations like pieces on a chessboard. Killing and resurrecting, all in her unknown cause. I've heard her described as a trickster. Insane. Jealous of mortals. The dwarves call her the Downward Spiral. An Earth and Water goddess who punishes those who abuse her world and the weakest within it. In my religion, we have a T'Ghee card that represents such a figure, called the Inevitable.

Some say she is the reason for Scolopendra's nine-tier attack. I've heard one dwarf say she is the daughter of the great centipede. Another says she's the sister. Another claimed she's the mother. I doubt any of those are true.

Outside of Larracos, she is known by another name.

She is called the Vinegar Bitch.

TIME LEFT IN THE QUEST: 1 HOUR, 30 MINUTES.

MORDECAI: HE SAID THAT? HE CALLED HER YSALTE? ARE YOU SURE?

DONUT: WHEN A GIANT DEMON IS BELTING OUT NAMES, YOU LISTEN, MORDECAI.

MORDECAI: Ysalte is known by another name. The Vinegar Bitch. She kills every crawler that comes anywhere near her. She usually pops out of her temple at the end of Faction Wars, but not always. She didn't appear the last two seasons, so it's always a surprise. If she does show up, run.

CARL: Can she hide her appearance? Is that possible?

MORDECAI: Anything is possible, but gods usually aren't subtle. Even her. That jacket of yours should be telling you if she's close. We're missing something.

CARL: Can she be sponsored?

MORDECAI: FUCK. Yes.

CARL: What?

MORDECAI: I just remembered. She *has* been getting sponsored recently. The nebular team has been sponsoring her.

CARL: The same ones who also sponsor Sister Ines?

MORDECAI: Bingo. Be careful.

DONUT: WHY DO THOSE WEIRDOS KEEP POPPING UP?

MORDECAI: People have been trying to figure out what those guys are up to for hundreds of years, Donut. What they want is easy to explain, but what they do is not because their actions never make sense.

I already knew some of this, but I wanted to hear Mordecai's explanation.

CARL: What do they want?

MORDECAI: Near the center of the galaxy is a very large AI that extends a benign enhancement zone over several solar systems, and it's where a whole lot of people live. The "inner system." This AI is the same sort of thing that runs the crawl, but it predates Syndicate society. It is stable and is without personality. It's the only one like it. The nebs worship it like it's a god, and they think it's blasphemy to try to replicate it. They participate in the Hunting Grounds and the Ascendency, and they really, really want to run a crawl themselves sometime, but nobody is ever going to let them because their stated goal is to shut all of this down. Hence they try to keep winning the Celestial Ascendency since one of the prizes of that is a seat at the table of the Syndicate crawl council. Outside the crawl, they're pacifists. You could literally walk up to one and punch him in the face, and he'll let you do it. Not so much inside the dungeon.

CARL: They want to shut the crawl down?

MORDECAI: Yeah, but don't get too excited. They preach the eradication of all the places that could host crawls, such as this planet. And all the people on it. And all other religions, too. They're psychotic.

CARL: Preaching for genocide doesn't exactly go along with pacifism.

MORDECAI: Yeah, it doesn't make much sense to anybody else, either.

CARL: What do they want with Sister Ines? I wonder.

MORDECAI: They likely sponsored her because she's religious, and they either want to convert her or make an example of her.

"I FEEL BAD," CHRIS SAID. THE LAVA-ROCK CRAWLER HAD SPENT THE floor with Li Na's team, and I'd barely spoken with him. He looked over his shoulder at the church across the way. A demon crab rushed through the grassy area in front of the building, but it didn't even look at us. The zombies all wandered aimlessly unless we got close, and then they'd swarm, but the demons seemed to all head straight for the FOCSA building, as if they knew their best chance at getting home was there.

The Demon Eviction was ongoing, but it had clearly slowed.

The crab didn't make it. Elle pierced it from afar using an ice spell that killed it with a single shot. It died with a small cry, and the corpse turned to dust.

I turned my attention back to Chris. "Why do you feel bad? Because it's a church?"

"No. Because it's pretty. And it will break the key."

"The real version of that church is already gone," I said. "And the key will only let one of us through. I tried to get Imani to take it, and she's refused. I'm not going to do it. The other stairwell is miles away and covered with a lot more debris. We can protect the safe room entrance if we do it correctly. It's already buried at the other exit. It has to be here."

"Okay," Chris said. He turned and started walking back to the church, where he, Zhang, and several other crawlers and strippers were going to initiate the controlled demolition of the church, followed by the construction of the channel underneath it for our escape. I lent Zhang my shrink wand, as he had a lot of experience using that particular spell.

There were two temples on the grounds of the church in separate buildings. A temple of Ibeji, whom I'd never heard of, and a temple of the ocean goddess Kuraokami, which doubled as the entrance to Club Vanquisher. This second temple was where the ram clerics and the mantaur guards had been coming out. We had to be careful not to hurt either of those buildings. The last thing we needed was another pissed-off deity like that whole clusterfuck with Diwata on the last floor.

With that underway, I turned to the rest of the group. As I watched, Imani floated up, trailed by a large group of hooting and hollering sluggalos, followed by a few of the strippers. It was Gluteus Maxx with his war gauntlets; Author Steve Rowland with his club; Splash Zone, the otter water mage; and Dong Quixote. Dong insisted on dragging his massive lance with him, despite being on foot. The thing was basically just a spear, but it was clearly too long and unwieldy to be used effectively without being mounted.

The forty or so sluggalos were mostly level twenties and thirties, punctuated with a handful of level fifties, the strongest in the group that would do as we asked. Sort of. Most of the level forties and fifties were now safely ensconced in the upgraded barracks, which they were apparently trashing.

The things could move a lot more quickly than I was expecting. They left a shimmering trail of orange-hued slime everywhere they went.

"Everybody, gather around." I cracked my neck. "We have to get into that building." I pointed over my shoulder at the large, distant skyscraper. "Donut and I, along with Katia's squad and the rest of Li Na's squad, will infiltrate the building and confront Sister Ines. The plan is to take her out, which will hopefully break the demon free of his confinement. As soon as that happens, that timer is probably going to accelerate, so we'll need to hoof it to the roof and break him free of the *Madre de Aguas* snake body right away."

"What about tossing Samantha, like you did before?" Louis asked. Samantha sat firmly upon his shoulder. She kept trying to chew on his hair, but he was pushing her away.

"I love it when you're confident in me," Samantha said. She reached over and bit Louis on the ear.

"Samantha, leave him alone or you're sitting this one out," I said.

She growled at me and threatened my mother.

I pointed at the swirling hurricane surrounding the demon. "He's protected by a wall of demon seagulls. Samantha is invulnerable, but if we toss her, and she gets intercepted, one of the seagulls will pull her into Sheol. I'm pretty sure I can get her back, but she'll likely bring something back with her we don't want to fight. We're going to use teleport to break him of the shell, but we want to keep him in the same location. The only way to do that is up through the building. This whole thing has been set up by the AI. We pretty much have to do it this way."

I turned to Elle and Imani. "You guys are going to protect our escape, and you're going to keep anyone from surging up behind us. I don't know if any of the full-strength demons are left, but be on the lookout. Watch for the birds."

Elle saluted me. "You got it, boss."

"Good. Once the demon is free from his shell, he's going to be a lot bigger and a lot more powerful. I don't know if that means he'll be pissed or happy we freed him, but either way it's going to trigger a world quest, and we'll need to see what the parameters are before we decide how to proceed from there. Okay, guys? We ready? No time. Let's go."

I turned and started jogging east toward the massive demon in the sky. I didn't turn to see if the others were following me.

"DID YOU GET QUAN'S CLOAK?" KATIA ASKED AS WE APPROACHED THE building. She was in her She-Hulk form, but she'd grown multiple stalks on the back of her neck containing eyeballs so she could see all around her. I remembered how she once talked about how difficult it was to get used to using more than two eyes. That didn't seem to be a problem for her anymore. To my left, Splash Zone sent a group of duende zombies floating away with a wave attack. Donut, Louis, Britney, Tran, and Mongo took up the middle of the group. Katia, the strippers, and I took up the front. The slugs were wandering off everywhere. It was like trying to herd a group of drunk toddlers.

"I did," I said. "I need to sit down and really examine the description. It doesn't do what we thought it did from what I can tell. It changes based on who wears it. I'm pretty sure I'm going to give it to Donut if we can get it to fit her, but we need to have a discussion with Mordecai about it first."

"Okay," Katia said. She was shaking, I realized. And not just from fear. I wished we were still partied, which would allow me to look deeper in on her health. She still needed to do her final rehab treatment, the one where she relived one of her worst memories. We hadn't had time, and she was being propped up by Imani's spells and Mordecai's potions.

"How are you feeling?" I asked.

"Mostly like an idiot," she admitted.

"And Bautista?"

The tiger crawler walked near the back of the group along with Elle, who was scanning the sky for threats. It was clear their relationship had been damaged by recent events.

"He doesn't want me to use the orchid."

"I don't want you to use it, either. The more I think about it, the more scared I get it's a death sentence."

"Well, it's a death sentence if I *don't* use it. We jumped through a lot of hoops to get it. It's the only way out as far as I can see."

"Maybe there'll be another way. I don't want you being alone."

She shivered. "Have I ever told you . . . You know what? Let's just get past this and then decide what we're going to do." She turned to Dong Quixote, who grunted with the effort of carrying his lance.

"Dong, that weapon is way too big for you," she said.

The elderly stripper smiled. "My dear, it's kind of you to compliment my weapon's size."

"I'm serious. You have an inventory. You can carry it in there until you need it, but I don't think you should use it at all. It's going to get you killed."

I knew most NPCs had the slot-style inventory. Something like that massive lance would take up most of his space, but at least he wouldn't have to lug it around.

He frowned. "This is the only weapon I know. At least the only weapon I know that I could find. I do miss my trusty mount."

Katia smiled at the old man. A genuine smile. "Let me guess. Your horse's name was Rocinante?"

"Horse?" he asked. "No. His name was Corcunda. Was a half mantaur. Was the most beautiful man, despite his physical flaws. I would ride him onstage, and the crowd loved it."

"Wait, what?" Katia asked. "What the heck does a half mantaur look like?"

Splash Zone grunted with laughter. "Their act was a thing of legends."

I was about to ask what he meant by "riding him onstage" but thought better of it. "What's the other weapon you were looking for?" I asked. "I have a lot in my inventory."

"A flail," he said. "The one-handed variety."

I dove into my inventory, looking at the weapons. Most were in the safe room, but I knew he'd already had the opportunity to pick through that pile. I still had the ones I'd looted from Quan. I had several mace-like weapons, and I'd seen a few crawlers with mace-and-chain-type weapons, but I didn't have exactly what he was looking for. I knew Katia had the meteor hammer from the late Popov twins, but that thing probably weighed more than the stupid lance. A single weapon caught my attention. I hadn't had time to read the description yet.

Spunky Jefferson the Enchanted Nickel Sock of the Elderly Miser.

This weapon has been upgraded twice.

This is a sapient weapon.

This is an incremental-damage weapon.

This item was originally awarded to a crawler in a Legendary You-Know-Everybody-Can-See-You-Right? Box on the fifth floor.

Almost all cultures that use money have a story about the miser. The elderly solitary man who hoards his wealth and treats everybody around him like shit until he gets his comeuppance and then turns into a big pussy who gives all his money away.

All cultures also have the equivalent of the spunk sock that sits underneath a teenage boy's bed.

Jefferson is the life force of such a miser who pissed off the spirit who'd come to show him the errors of his ways. He was cursed to inhabit a sock once owned by a kid named Tanner. The sock itself holds several USD worth of nickels. You swing it and bonk people with it. It's unusually effective, more so than you might think.

This weapon's damage increases by 1.5% for every mob it kills that is no more than 10 levels below the current wielder's level. Current upgrade: 238.5% damage increase.

Increases wielder's dexterity by 10 points plus 10%.

Has a 5% chance to inflict *Bonked* on any mob struck with this weapon.

All mobs killed with this weapon have a 20% chance to burst into a pile of gold coins upon death. The number of coins is equal to the (value of the items in their inventory) + (level × 10).

CARL: Is a sapient weapon what I think it is?

MORDECAI: Oh gods. Yes. They can talk, but it's usually only in the mind of the wielder. Though some do talk out loud. They tend to be quite annoying. Samantha-level annoying, but luckily they're treated as objects, and you can keep them in your inventory if they won't stop yammering. I suspect Florin's shotgun might be sapient, but he hasn't said one way or another.

What the hell? I thought, and pulled it out of my inventory. It was a white tube sock with red and blue stripes at the very top. It sagged heavily. It was old, crusty, and splattered with blood.

"Let me know if this works," I said, handing the sock to Dong. "This is kinda like a flail. I guess."

"My lord, you honor me," Dong said, taking the crusty sock reverently. His lance zapped away into his inventory. He wrapped the end of the bobbing sock in his hand and gave it a test swing. It jingled with the coins within as it swished through the air. "This is a mythical weapon."

"What the hell is that?" Katia asked. "Why does it smell?"

"Yes. Yes. My name is Dong Quixote," Dong said. "Yes. Yes. Jefferson? It's nice to meet you . . . Yes. We are going to. I am a former adventurer turned entertainer turned mercenary . . . Yes. About five gold coins per dance, but more if we moved it to the cum closet . . . I do not know what a mutual fund is. Why?"

"Carl, who is he talking to?" Katia asked.

"The sock," I said as Dong wandered off to show his friends.

DONUT: OKAY, I WILL BE BACK IN A MINUTE. DON'T START WITHOUT ME.

CARL: Do it fast.

Behind me, Donut, Imani, Britney, and Tran moved off to an alley to get into a quick fight in order to properly set up Donut's deck one last time. Just in case.

Meanwhile, everybody else was in the chat, fielding questions about the plan. The fights, for the most part, had calmed down. Osvaldo and some guy named Jurgen had gotten into a card battle, but Jurgen had been forced to use a Flee card. It turned out he'd really made good on his promise to break the stairwell, and they were now working together to clear the rubble away. They were somewhere in Brazil. It was the same for everybody else. We still had four days left, but by now, pretty much everybody with keys who could, had gone down the stairs.

I received one last message from Prepotente.

PREPOTENTE: For what it's worth, Carl. I do hope you and Princess Donut survive this foolish endeavor. You are an oafish brute, and it's a miracle you have made it this far, but the dungeon would not be the same without you.

CARL: Thanks, Prepotente.

PREPOTENTE: If you are successful in the first part of this, make certain you carefully read the winning conditions of the new quest. There are quite a few crawlers in Indonesia, which is the closest landmass on the opposite side of the Earth from Havana. They will be in the most danger if you do not buff that demon enough. You will need them on the next floor if you hope to win. Speaking of, Princess Donut has been keeping me apprised of how the voting is going for Faction Wars. I understand you're still at an impasse.

CARL: I will do my best. And yes, ever since everybody got stuck and the system AI refused to let them bounce, they've all been declining to vote in anything and are instead just trying to sue over and over. They're being a bunch of pansies. Meanwhile, the NPC rebels have been sabotaging them at every turn.

PREPOTENTE: Well, I do look forward to seeing how all that turns out. Now I will be going down the stairs.

CARL: Take care of yourself.

PREPOTENTE: Oh, and, Carl?

CARL: Yes?

PREPOTENTE: I've decided to not kill you for letting my mother hurt herself. I have been contemplating it for some time now. I've decided you were too stupid to have done anything about it anyway. Your penance will be to assist me in exacting my revenge on the true culprits.

I blinked, rereading that last part. I tried not to let the sarcasm show in my response.

CARL: That's a relief. Thanks, Pony.

The combat-complete notification came, and a moment later, Donut landed on my shoulder. "It's done," she said. "Not many zombies around anymore. I think they're all running away from the demon building."

"Good, because we're here," I said, holding up my hand for everybody to stop. We came to the edge of an alley that was blocked by a pile of bicycle rickshaws that had somehow gotten all tangled up here, all with colorful awnings and handmade signs that read "Taxi." A few were adorned with Christmas decorations. I used the pile of bicycles as a hiding spot as we peered to the right, revealing a block filled with demons. It was all manner of creatures. Crabs, seals, fish, duendes, a few of those weird human-faced dog things, and more. All were zombies turned demon. All stood or lay on the ground, docile, staring up into the hurricane of birds, none facing our direction. It was like they were patiently waiting for a train to pull up and take them all home.

I couldn't even see Amayon anymore through the mass of birds. Even as I watched, more demon birds flew in from all directions. It wasn't just birds, I realized, but bats as well. The cone of fire continued to spout into the sky out the center of the tornado. It was so hot, it was hard to breathe.

It dawned on me that I hadn't heard from Sister Ines in a while. I checked, and she was still there, still near the top but within the building. The system said she was still alive, but she clearly hadn't moved, which was unnerving.

I noted none of the demons said they were minions of Sister Ines, either. Only Amayon was under her control.

The front side of the green-and-tan Y-shaped building loomed.

This was it.

65

WE HAD ONE HOUR. I LOWERED MY VOICE TO A WHISPER. "DONUT, GET your headset on and get ready to cast your spell. Samantha, I need you to enhance it if you can. Everybody going in the front door, get your invisibility potions ready, but not yet. Donut is casting two spells, and the first one is going to take five minutes to fully cast. As soon as she's done, I'm going to toss smoke bombs, and then we'll *Puddle Jump* to the entrance and make our way inside."

Donut had to position herself so she could actually see the group, and she plopped herself at the very edge of the alley, inside the basket of one of the taxi bikes, lowering herself so only her eyes would be noticeable. Mordecai said the spell would make her glow, so being invisible wouldn't work. If one of those demons turned and looked, they'd see her.

Imani floated up. She, too, could enhance spells.

"Is this really going to work?" Elle whispered, peering out at the mass of demons. There were thousands of them. "You said it only works on intelligent mobs, and zombies ain't too smart."

"They're demon zombies. They're intelligent," I said. I reached over and scratched Donut. "Donut seems to think the regular zombies are steering clear of this whole neighborhood. Okay, everybody, this spell takes five minutes to cast, so stay low. Ready, Donut?"

"Oh, wow," Donut said after a moment. "With my charisma boosts, I can select the whole group out there! Even some of the birds! And the casting is only four minutes now. I wish I still had that charisma tiara."

"That's okay. You're good," I said. "Go."

Donut glowed as she cast *Minion Army.* We'd received the book near the end of the first floor. She had yet to cast it because it was so dangerous to use. It was a spell designed for war, and the moment she cast it, she'd be frozen and vulnerable for four minutes straight.

The spell was only level one before the boost. It turned two percent of the enemy in the casting area against their comrades. With both Imani and Samantha enhancing the spell, that two percent should turn to about five percent. That number still seemed low to me, but both Mordecai and Doctor Bones had insisted it would create utter chaos.

A countdown timer appeared over her. **Rooted in Place** appeared. Mongo made an uncertain peep.

"It's okay," I said to the dinosaur. "She's fine."

The shimmering golden glow around Donut increased in intensity with each passing second.

I continued to peer at the demons, who remained unmoving, and raised my whisper up a little. "Okay, guys. As soon as it casts, all hell is going to break loose, and the assault team will move. As soon as we say the word, the rest of you need to get to work. We need you to keep them from coming up behind us, but only wade in there if it's absolutely necessary. Ranged attacks only. I'm counting on you, Splash Zone, to help keep them safe." I turned to look over my shoulder. "Also, the sluggalos . . . Goddamnit. Where the fuck are the sluggalos?"

"Chop, chop, bitches!" came a deafening battle cry from one street over as the entire squad of forty hatchet-wielding idiot slugs poured into the group of demons.

"Oh shit," Louis said. "They're doing a Leeroy . . ."

"Don't even say it," I growled. "Goddamnit."

"Who could've predicted that?" Imani said drily.

Combat Started.

Donut had three minutes left.

If the demons didn't kill them, I was going to do it myself. "Everyone protect Donut until she's done with her spell!"

The line of forty slugs slammed into the group of demons like a cavalry charge. It was like watching a fast-forward video of a tidal wave of snot storming a beachhead.

The demons appeared to be in a sort of stupor. None were reacting until they were actually struck by one of the slugs. If the blow didn't outright kill them, only then would they start to respond. The larger demons, like the seals, would flip back, knocking over several of their friends, who in turn would start to wake up as well. The slugs were cutting through them like a wheat thresher.

That advantage wasn't going to last long.

For now, however, it was oddly fascinating to watch. The slugs weren't all that great at fighting or killing, but they made up for it with over-the-top enthusiasm.

"At least they came from the other street," Elle said, floating next to me, watching as the others all came to stare.

"Wow, look how fast they're going," Tran said. One of the smaller slugs leaped through the air and bit directly onto the neck of a seal, but it didn't appear to actually do anything. The seal slowly started to react, like it had been asleep. Before it could do anything further, several more slugs fell on it, screaming and whooping, their hatchets slamming up and down.

"How are they even swinging those axes?" Britney asked, fascinated. "They don't even have arms."

"I've learned not to think about that sort of thing too much, and it makes everything so much easier," Elle said.

Not all of them even had weapons, but the ones that did indeed mostly wielded deadly-looking hatchets that kind of floated to the right or left of their long necks, and they'd swing up and down, like they were on a swivel. A few had other weapons, too, like knives and baseball bats covered in barbed wire. One had a cylindrical metal mace thing attached to the end of his body, and he was spinning like a spasming dog chasing his own tail. He was hitting more of his own people than demons. It was goddamn weird.

"If we get a few thousand more of these guys, we could win the war on the first day," Louis said. "Imagine a whole battalion of those things paratrooping behind enemy lines."

Imani chuckled without humor. "Be careful what you wish for. Don't forget how Carl makes these."

The first *thrum* of a hell portal opening echoed. It reverberated across the battlefield like a plucked bass string. Followed by a second. The majority of the demons remained unmoving, and I was starting to wonder if we should've attempted a different technique to approach the building. It was too late now.

Within thirty seconds, half the slugs were gone. The demons who'd woken up were now surging toward the attackers, who seemed oblivious of the changing tide of battle.

"Sluggalos, retreat!" came the bellow from the largest one—a level 52 slug with green clown makeup and a stained ruffle around his neck.

"No," I shouted, not bothering to hide ourselves anymore. "No retreat!"

The remaining handful of slugs finally decided they wanted to save themselves and started slithering away, screaming expletives at the demons behind them, who all rushed to pursue.

They surged directly toward us.

"Not in this direction, you idiots!"

They trailed their orange slime along with a healthy smear of blood as the seals, crabs, fish, and mix of other demons finally spied us all there in the alley.

Donut had just under a minute left. Her entire form glowed, the light shining off her like a star.

"I guess it's my turn," Elle said, grumbling. "Everybody stand back. This spell has a one-week cooldown, but I guess I gotta use it now. Don't know if this is going to make things better or worse."

The earth and ice fairy floated into the air. Her hands glowed blue.

"Coming in!" the lead slug cried as he slurped toward us, weaving back and forth, like a snake surging through water. The thing was almost as big as me, and I had no idea which stripper he came out of or how it had been born of a single boil. And there were some that were an even higher level. This one's name was **Rampageous**.

He smashed through the rampart made of bicycles, sending them flying. I reached to grab the bike Donut was hiding within, but I missed. The bike went tumbling, the back passenger compartment smashing through Donut like she was made of steel. She remained in place, now floating a foot off the ground, but she'd taken some damage. Mongo roared in outrage.

The slug paused, looking up at Imani. "Oh hey, 313. Did you see that shit? Fucking epic!" He resumed his retreat.

I turned to face the demons as the remaining slugs, maybe six or seven of them, surged past in their hasty retreat, revealing a mass of about seventy or eighty demons moving in. Behind them, the rest remained frozen in place, undisturbed.

Elle cast *Graupel.*

"Oh shit, oh shit," Elle shouted as the blue glow around her increased in intensity. "Guys, it says it's casting more powerful than usual. Holy shit, heads up!"

A thunderclap knocked us all back as sheets of hail poured from the sky. Elle had received the spell in a loot box after our first fight with the Maestro in Grull form, way back at the end of the fourth floor. She'd only cast it once before, and that was to defeat the air quadrant in their bubble on the fifth.

Mordecai had warned that this was a war spell, meant only to be cast outside. I could now see why.

Death rained from above in a wide area in front of us. Fist-sized chunks of ice pelted down from the heavens, temporarily blocking out the burning sky. Steam and smoke filled the entire area as the storm rolled through. The black asphalt in front of the alley started to explode with each impact. Behind the approaching demons, more cries rose, but they were quickly drowned out. The ground rumbled like an earthquake.

Elle remained in place as level notifications pinged over and over above her head, settling her onto level 72. She'd risen six levels at once. It'd been a while since I'd seen something like that happen.

"It cast!" Donut cried, coming unfrozen. She hissed as she dropped to the ground. "It . . ." She paused, looking into the steam as the deafening hailstorm eased off. I couldn't see a damn thing, but almost all the red dots on my map had turned to X's.

Combat Complete. Deck has been reset.

"Carl, what did you do?"

"Wow," Louis said, looking up at Elle. "We should've done that in the first place."

Elle appeared to be in a daze. "What the hell? That spell is strong, but it's not usually *that* strong. It's only level five. It said it cast at level 16. I just got a bunch of achievements. Holy hell, look at my level."

"Samantha," I asked, looking for the doll head. She was just floating there, six feet off the ground. She, too, glowed with a bluish white light. "Did you do that?"

For perhaps the first time ever, Samantha looked equally confused and concerned. She was mumbling to herself, spinning in circles. "Elle is part-earth, part-water mage," she said, floating past, talking to herself as she continued to rotate. "She's on the four-seasons path. I . . . but how did that happen? I am stronger, too. I didn't do that. It's the tree, I think. Or maybe. It's all there. He's opening a path through the river, the water, and the tree, the earth. It's good she's not fire yet, but maybe the prince's spell enhanced her. No. No. Gotta kill her. No, not Elle. Her mother. No, not *her* mother." She shook her head like a dog. She turned to look at me. "What just happened? Carl, did you roofie me again?"

"Again?" I asked. "Samantha, what were you just saying?"

"You need to stop gaslighting me, Carl."

Elle grunted. "Whatever the hell that was, I think it solved part of our problem. Look."

The steam had started to ease as water rushed into the alley. There was a knee-high pile of rapidly melting ice between us and the building, and mixed in with all that ice was a field filled with the mangled corpses of demons as far as I could see. The front of the building appeared for a moment, and it looked as if it had been spared by the assault.

"Wait, so I cast that giant spell for nothing?" Donut asked. "Elle, you stole my experience!"

"I don't think so," Elle said, pointing upward. "Look!"

Donut gasped. "You're right! I just got experience for something. And again!"

The tornado of demon birds and bats remained circling the top of the building high above. They'd apparently been out of range of the

Graupel spell. Donut's spell had included the lower area of the bird formation, and it was clear several of them were now fighting each other. Bodies started to hail down from the sky.

We had forty minutes left.

"I don't think my spell reached the demons huddling on the ground on the far side of the building," Elle said. "We better move before they come to investigate what the hell is going on."

"Don't bother with *Puddle Jump*," I said, turning to sprint through the ice field of death. "Assault team, go!"

We turned toward the building, and we ran.

WE WADED THROUGH RAPIDLY MELTING SLUSH AND DEMON GORE AS WE reached the front entrance to the FOCSA building, which to my surprise was actually an open-air mall of some sort. Multiple businesses spread out, filled with unaware memory ghosts as the early-morning shoppers moved in and out of grocery stores and electronics shops and bakeries, all of which ringed the outer perimeter.

"There!" Li Na called, pointing at a locked glass door. It was an entrance for the residents above the mall. I kicked it in and rushed into a brightly painted lobby, looking for the stairs. They were right there, just past an empty reception desk and a bank of elevators.

It was me, Donut, Mongo, Katia, Louis, Bautista, Li Na, Li Jun, and Samantha. Everybody else including the strippers remained outside, but they would soon come into this same lobby on my direction. They would remain here and protect our exit, in the unlikely event we took the stairs back down to get out. Tran and Britney, who were both on Katia's squad, would also follow, but remain in the stairwell in case anybody got past them.

The sluggalos were all gone, having run back into the city. I knew if this was during the real Faction Wars, I could go into my warlord menu and force them back into line. That was something Priestly and several other cookbook authors who came before me didn't know about the *Conscript* spell.

Outside, the demon birds and bats continued to hail like rain. Donut was getting experience for each one that died, whether it was a charmed bird or not.

We pushed past the lobby toward the stairwell.

"We have to climb the stairs?" Donut asked, pointing at an open elevator. "Why don't we take the elevator?" The walls shook. "Mongo is scared of stairs."

"Are you crazy?" Katia asked.

"Well, you're crazy if you think I'm going to run up 30-something floors."

"Donut, we're taking the stairs," I said. "Everybody be on the lookout for mobs and traps."

I kicked the door to the stairwell in, and it went flying. All of this stuff was locked, and I briefly wondered how Sister Ines had gotten in here.

Everything was so hot, it was a miracle the entire place wasn't already in flames. The teal-colored paint was bubbling in some places.

"We need Elle with us," Donut grumbled. "She has that mist spell that keeps everything cool."

The demon continued to shout. The walls rumbled. The timer ticked down and down.

WITH ABOUT A HALF HOUR LEFT, WE REACHED THE DOOR TO THE 32ND floor. The heat rose the farther we went up. A few of us were starting to take environmental damage. Sister Ines was here, through the main door and down the hallway. This was the top floor of the regular residences. There was a service door behind us that led to another hallway and stairwell that wasn't normally used by the tenants. Everything above here was through a separate stairwell and consisted of expensive penthouse apartments. It was on top of this block where the demon stood.

"Everyone stay here," I said. I kicked in the service door and went down the hallway in the opposite direction of Sister Ines, coming to the separate stairwell up past the penthouses and to the roof. I pulled my last automaton out of my inventory and went up this last flight of stairs. I put the small robot on the floor in front of the door to the outside. The spider automaton had both sides of a teleport trap upon it. It would walk up to the snake and bump into it, setting off the trap, but the anchor or beacon end of the trap was also atop the back of the robotic spider, so the snake wouldn't actually go anywhere. We needed it to remain in place, though it would still technically teleport. This would immediately break the demon from the shell of the snake city boss, allowing the demon to take its true form.

It would also break it out of the control of Sister Ines if we absolutely had to do it this way, though in order to do this properly, we needed to kill the nun first. Both Mordecai and I feared if we didn't kill her before the demon was freed, the first thing the full-powered demon would do would be to seek revenge and torch the entire building with us still inside. If he knew she was dead and we were the ones who did it, he would hopefully at least pause before killing us.

I held my breath and kicked out the door to the roof, revealing the snake standing right there, still as vertical as a flagpole, launching fire upward. The cacophony of the birds and bats swirled all around me. Nothing acknowledged me. That was good.

"Okay," I shouted at the automaton. I had a remote-control clicker in my inventory. "You stay here. As soon as I click, you go out there and bump into it! Understand?"

The tiny robot did a little hop.

I turned and returned to the others to find Li Na leaning with her head against the door.

"Robot is set," I said. "I'll send it out there the moment she's dead."

"I can hear her," Li Na said. "She's chanting."

"More poetry," Donut spat.

"Poetry sucks," Louis added.

"Okay," I whispered, cutting Samantha off before she professed even more love for Louis. "Me, Louis, Li Jun, and Bautista are going to go in. The rest of you stay here unless we need you."

"Why just the boys?" Donut demanded.

"Because we're the deckmasters," Li Na replied, pulling back from the door. "She's down the hallway. He's trying to finish the fight without forcing a card battle."

"Huh," Donut said, looking around. "Aren't the deckmasters the strongest ones in the party? Funny how that worked out."

"Everybody remember the finger-breaking trick in case she charms you," Katia added.

"I don't have any cards," Samantha grumbled. "Why do I have to stay here?"

"Because you agreed to do what I said. Now everyone shush."

I leaned against the door. In any other circumstance, I'd just toss a stick of dynamite in and be done with it, but not with a deity in the body of a city boss over our heads and thirty-plus floors of building underneath us.

"She's at the end of the hall, and she hasn't moved in hours. Be ready for anything. Here we go."

I pulled my new Nighty-Night wand. I opened the door to reveal a glowing Sister Ines, running full tilt down the hallway directly at us, screaming, "Sinner!" at the top of her lungs. She was already too close.

"Gah!" I zapped my wand, and she instantly went unconscious. She dropped and slid, coming to a stop at my feet. A two-minute timer appeared above her.

Combat Started.

The notification came, but she was out. I exchanged a look with the others. Li Jun shrugged.

"I think I just shit myself," Louis said, panting. "Did you see the look in her eyes? What was that notification over her head?"

"Well, that was easy," I said. I hadn't seen the marker. Whatever it was, it was gone now. "I guess we gotta kill her."

"I'll do it," Louis said, pushing me aside. "I already have five player skulls and none of you guys do. Trust me, you want to put that off as long as possible." Before I could object, he pulled a dagger from his inventory. "Sorry, cat lady. I never met you, but you need to go if we want to save everybody else." He took the knife and plunged it directly into her chest.

Sister Ines Quiteria, the Reaper of Havana, finally died.

A symbol appeared over Louis's head. I immediately recognized it. It was a god's marked-for-death indicator. It came in the form of a spinning squiggle, almost like that of a tornado.

We all just stared at the symbol as my heart sank.

"Uh-oh," Louis said as music started to play.

The death of the bard has angered her celestial Patron. She is coming to seek revenge.

The Goddess Ysalte has entered the realm.

66

YOU ARE IN THE PRESENCE OF A DEITY. THE SCAVENGER'S DAUGHter's eyes remain open. She fills with even more power.

> **Temporary effect from Ysalte: All potions you quaff or physically handle outside your inventory will turn to vinegar. They will return to a more powerful version of themselves upon her banishment.**

I barely registered the notification as the music, which was strangely slow and symphonic, rose in volume. We all backed into the stairwell chamber as the corpse of Sister Ines dissolved and turned into that of the level 250 goddess.

> **Goddess of Hopelessness and Insanity Ysalte. Level 250.**
>
> **This goddess is sponsored by Pontifex Shine of the Nebular Balance.**
>
> **Warning: This sponsor is *not* currently inhabiting the shell of this deity. She will speak and react as per her regular nature. Considering who this is, that's some bad fucking news for you guys.**
>
> **Warning: This is a deity. She is invulnerable on this floor.**
>
> ***This goddess has been temporarily summoned to this location due to a special boss battle event and will return to the Ascendency upon completion of the event.***
>
> **The earliest citizens of Larracos always worshipped Ysalte, which is fitting. She hasn't always been considered the Goddess of Hopelessness and Insanity. First it was of the Dirt. Then it was of Tears. It's a recent thing that they started calling her something else. The Downward Spiral. The Vinegar Bitch.**

Her downfall mirrors that of the citizens of Larracos, who have embraced the deity in all her forms.

That's what happens when everything you know is upended, and everything is taken from you. First they vilify you. Then they separate you. Then they blame you for what they're doing to you. Then they hunt you. It's the step after that which is important.

The one where they start to fear you.

Ysalte has a special place in her heart for the outcasts, for those whose minds are being devoured by the world around them. She takes no new worshippers beyond the citizens of Larracos. But she is known to be a great patron of the arts and is one of the few deities who will sponsor a bard or a performer. She asks nothing in return, though occasionally her gifts are more than what they seem, and some may even carry a curse.

The story of this goddess, like that of many of her kind, is long and a little sad. At this point, how it began isn't nearly as important as how it will end. She is half sister and niece to her former lover, Taranis. Threatened with the Nothing by Apito, she fled to Sheol. She has since returned to the Halls of the Ascendency, where she is feared and reviled by all.

She is not considered someone who wishes to lead, which makes her a dangerous and cunning contender for the Ascendent throne.

The deity appeared in the form of a regular-sized, young-faced female dwarf carrying a pickaxe, which was not what I was expecting from someone with such a name. She smiled upon us, almost gently. She wore a helmet with a candle atop it, but the candle sparked, like a dynamite stick, reminding me of the goblin bomb bards. Her face occasionally flickered, like a bad television screen. And in those moments of static, her mouth turned to that of a scream, though no such sound came out.

She turned her attention to Louis, who still held the knife in his hand. He stupidly dropped it to the floor and held up his hands like it was a stickup.

"You killed my bard," she said to him. Her voice was soft, sweet, musical. She did not have the Scottish lilt of most of the dwarves we'd met so far. This was more French than anything. As she spoke, she clinked her pickaxe gently against the floor. Cracks started to form. A memory ghost walked out of one of the apartments and strolled past, oblivious.

"She was asleep, and you killed her. Her mind is finally at ease, which is a blessing, but I was not done with her yet, and for that you must suffer."

Samantha appeared, floating between Ysalte and Louis, who'd backed up all the way to the wall of the stairwell. Her voice was filled with fake cheer. "Ysalte! Honey! We haven't seen each other in so long! How are you? What's new? I *must* invite you to my bachelorette party. How's the child?"

SAMANTHA: LOUIS, YOU GOTTA RUN BECAUSE THIS BITCH IS GONNA MELT YOUR BEAUTIFUL ASS INTO BUBBLING AND STICKY OATMEAL.

"Ysalte!" came the cry from above. "Release me!"

"Psamathe, is that you?" Ysalte asked, ignoring the demon above us. "You dare show yourself to me after what you did?"

CARL: Louis, do what she says. Get the fuck out of here. Run.

The music remained unchanged, but it was starting to get punctuated by a distant chug-chug of a distorted guitar. Wide-eyed, Louis started to slowly descend the stairs, his hands still up.

"Uh, what did I do?" Samantha asked, suddenly defensive. "Wait, are you still mad about the thing with the reverse hedgehog? Because that was like a really long time ago. And everyone else at the party thought it was funny. Well, except the hedgehog, I guess. And you, apparently. But it's not my fault if you can't take a joke about how ugly your child is."

The goddess roared and swung her pickaxe directly at Samantha's face.

Even a pickaxe swung by a god was not enough to injure the sex doll's head. It bounced right off her like she'd tried to pierce an impenetrable kickball. The look on the goddess's face was one of utter surprise as she started to fly backward, feet up in the air.

At that moment, everything froze. I froze. Samantha froze. The Vinegar Bitch froze, floating off the ground.

The ceiling at the end of the hall collapsed, and the coils of the *Madre de Aguas* snake slurped into the hall from above, suddenly and violently. It was like it had tipped off the main roof and landed above us.

Ysalte's pickaxe was stopped in midair in the process of flying from the goddess's hands. Behind her, the snake continued to cascade into the hallway, despite being wider than the hall itself. Concrete and metal vaporized as the city boss slammed into the floor. The ceiling over our heads collapsed, but fell to the sides, as if it was being peeled like a banana, miraculously not hitting anybody. After just a few seconds, the ceiling above us was just gone. The walls all around us also fell away, revealing multiple memory ghosts in their apartments without walls, going about their lives.

Everything but the floor beneath our feet was suddenly gone, almost like we'd been transferred to the roof.

ELLE: Holy hell, what's going on up there?

We were now outside, yet we remained frozen. The swirl of demon birds and bats continued to spin, now all around us. The gout of flame was gone. My heart sank at the sight of it.

The collapsing snake had temporarily stopped on our floor-turned-roof, coming to a halt right behind the frozen goddess. The city boss had multiple notifications over its massive head, including **Enslaved**. It paused before its distant tail started slipping over the far edge, sliding away like an anchor chain, yanking the whole snake off the side. The demon hissed as it was pulled away.

I caught movement just above the snake, rapidly catching up. It was the little automaton I'd set up atop the stairs, also falling, shining like a shooting star. The small robot, which should have been destroyed along with the rest of the top floor, spun through the air as it "miraculously" landed atop the falling snake.

Oh, come on, I thought as the whole thing blinked and reappeared in a quick teleportation.

Ysalte had been summoned while we were in a regular hallway, and because of that, she entered this world as a regular-sized dwarf. When Amayon dropped the shell of the snake, he was exposed to the open air.

As a result, he took on a much larger size than that of the dwarf.

The whole world stuttered as if we were in a car crash. It was the sound of the demon's four feet slamming to the ground far below.

The full-power version of Amayon stood to his full height, feet on the street, standing before the building with the lopped-off top, facing us.

We stood upon the 32nd-floor-turned-roof of the building, and we were about equal with the chest of the demon, who now glared down at us.

His body appeared to be that of a centaur-like quadruped, but I couldn't see the legs from our position. His humanoid chest rose above our platform, cleaving through the round of birds and bats, which moved back to let him within.

From the waist up, he had a similar appearance to that of the pleasure demons, but his red skin bubbled like it was made of lava with black swirling patches. He looked similar to Emberus in that way, though his head was that of a massive, demonic deerlike creature with four steaming horns. Two that rose straight up, piercing the clouds, and two that curved downward like tusks. His mouth was beaked at the very end, almost dinosaur-like. He roared, and the interior of his beak was nothing but teeth and fire.

The **Enslaved** marker remained over his head.

Fuck.

He had not been freed from Ysalte's grip by the teleportation. We'd only managed to make him more powerful.

The moment he finished his scream, he, too, froze, leaving everyone in the area motionless as the heavy-metal chugga-chugga took over the symphonic music and rose in volume. Imani, from way down on the first floor of the building, sent a panicked message.

IMANI: Oh shit, we've been frozen also. We've been added to the battle!

For a moment, nothing changed, as if the AI was trying to figure out what to do next.

The timer blinked and whiffed out. A new timer appeared. It was at ten minutes.

Quest Complete. Where the Sidewalk Ends.

Please wait . . .

New Quest. The Missing Piece.

This is a hybrid-world quest. All crawlers who are dumb enough to still be stuck on the eighth floor have been added to this quest.

Every remaining crawler within the region of Cuba has been designated as host of this quest.

This quest contains two parts. Part one is called "The Big O."

Only those in the Cuba region may participate in part one. If they are successful, part two will initiate and will include everyone else. In the meantime, this upcoming battle will air on all screens throughout the dungeon for those outside the Cuba region.

The demon Amayon, prince of Sheol, is stuck in this world, banished here by one of his three brothers.

Ysalte, his former girlfriend and mother of his child, has also stepped into the realm, and she has seized control of the demon, just as he once seized her when she tried to flee their relationship.

He wants to go home.

She wants to keep him under her control and bring him with her to the Ascendency, where he will act as her retainer until the Ascendency battles are complete. While all the other gods have been waking up long-forgotten deities to assist them, the Vinegar Bitch knows having a prince of hell at her side will help ensure her claim to the throne.

She will return to the realm in ten minutes. If Amayon remains fully under her control when that timer is complete, they will both teleport away to the Ascendency.

If that happens, everyone without keys is dead. There will be no more chances.

In order to break free from Ysalte's grip, Amayon must begin the casting of his spell to return home. In order to do that, he must be strong enough to cast it. How will he be given strength? Maybe you should ask him.

If he has broken free from her control by the time the timer runs out, then she will leave, and he will remain and will eventually travel home.

The stronger he is by the time the timer runs out, the bigger the spell will have to be. If he is at full power, that spell will cover the entire world, and everyone within it will have hope to make it to the next floor.

Oh, and one last thing.

This is the eighth floor, after all.

Clank, clank, clank, clank.

Four cards appeared in front of the still-frozen, still-flying-backward dwarf. Each one slammed into place like the blow of a hammer.

"What the hell? Really?" I asked. "Fucking really?"

Clank, clank, clank, clank.

Four more appeared in front of the giant demon. Each of these cards was the size of a garage door.

Amayon has a short deck with six totems. He will play each totem as it appears. He won't even begin to attempt to flee until all his totems are dead. As for Ysalte? She is armed with a slightly enhanced version of the deck of the late Sister Ines. You can't kill the god, so you have to hold out.

The world unfroze, and the goddess continued to fly back. She hit the ground and skid. She pulled herself to her feet about 100 feet away and tried to cast a spell at us, but nothing happened. She growled in frustration before her eyes finally focused on the cards floating before her.

Let the final card battle begin.

67

A GRAPHIC APPEARED AT THE BOTTOM CORNER OF THE INTERFACE. This was something new. It showed all the team names. As I watched, a rapid-fire string of miniature, face-down cards appeared after each team with a *blip, blip, blip.* It was a counter showing how many cards each team had. Donut had 21 cards, I knew. Katia and Li Na both had 20. Imani had 15, and Elle carried 22. The first six cards of each deck were highlighted with a glow, presumably indicating the totem cards.

At the bottom, separated by a space, was the name **Ysalte**, followed by a row of about 17 cards.

Amayon only had six. All totems.

Our goal was as difficult as it was clear. We had to play offense with Amayon and kill his six totems as soon as possible, which would allow us to talk to him. With the Vinegar Bitch, we had to play defense. We couldn't hurt the goddess directly, but the moment she ran out of cards, she'd be able to nuke us from orbit with one of her spells. We had to keep her deck from running dry for the next ten minutes.

This was going to be a tough balance, even at five versus two.

Donut appeared terrified, but she was putting on a brave, determined face. She'd switched back to her sailor cap. It used to look ridiculous on her, especially with her sunglasses, but it seemed more appropriate now somehow, in a way I couldn't explain.

She hadn't had time to pull her potions out, and if I pulled my own, they'd turn to vinegar. I pulled a few out anyway, remembering what the debuff said, and I tucked them on the ground behind her.

"You got this?" I asked as I quickly worked.

"I am the current reigning champion Persian cat in the galaxy. I have received more trophies and purple ribbons than anyone alive. And most importantly, I am a warlord of the Princess Posse Faction Wars team." She turned to regard me. "Yes, Carl, I got this."

I gave her a pat and faced our opponents.

The goddess and the demon lord she'd enslaved.

And

Here

We

Goooo!

The ten-minute timer started to tick down.

Li Na, Katia, and Donut spread out behind us as their decks appeared in front of them. Mongo remained near Donut, as he'd been trained to do. The music with the heavy guitars rose in volume, rattling my teeth. Li Jun, Bautista, and I spread out in a half circle as we rapidly talked strategy. Louis was currently hauling ass down the stairs and would meet up with Britney and Tran in the stairwell, and the three of them would continue back to the lobby. That marked-for-death symbol was a major problem for him, but as long as we kept the goddess occupied for the next ten minutes, we could push that off to another time.

Samantha remained floating in the room, looking about.

ELLE: Oh, fuck me. More demons are coming. Trying to come in through the door down here. Your boss battle forced me and Imani to summon our damn decks, so we can't cast spells. Doing our best to hold them back, but we might be running up toward you.

We had to watch where we stepped. Multiple holes and cracks dotted the flooring, and each time Amayon so much as shifted his position, new fractures appeared. This whole building was going to come down.

For just a moment, nobody moved. We all looked at each other, each one of us sizing everyone up.

And then it was on.

Chaos erupted all around me. So much happened at once, it was difficult to clock it all.

Li Na tossed out the first totem, which exploded out onto the ground in a flourish of snow and red sparkles.

Get ready to lose your mind! It's Xing Tian!

"Oh my god, what is that?" Donut cried as she tossed a card of her own out.

Li Na's Xing Tian totem was a level 80 creature that was a human without a head. The large, shirtless man had a wide, cackling face built into the flesh of his hairless chest. He carried an axe in one hand and a large shield in the other.

"Hold and block!" Li Na shouted at her card, which gibbered something back at her.

Donut's first move was the **Thief** card, which she cast on Amayon just as he swept out his own first totem. A card—not the one he was attempting to summon—flicked up out of his deck, resized itself, and landed in Donut's hand.

"Holy wow, look at that card!" she called out.

Amayon's totem landed with a heavy crash. It was a flaming rock creature. I didn't have time to read the description before it fell through the floor and tumbled away.

Katia and Ysalte also made their first moves, both summoning totems at the same time. Katia summoned her scary-ass bird creature, followed by a consumable utility card called **Timeless**, which would keep the bird summoned forever.

The bird landed upon Katia's shoulder with a fanfare that looked like colorful burning embers and dancing baby pacifiers wafting into the sky, which would be odd as fuck if I'd really had time to think about it. The totem was a large, cat-sized raven, but its head was the skull of an infant human. The skull was punctuated with little holes filled with teeth. I'd once seen an infant's skull before and knew that's what they really looked like, but seeing it in real life was terrifying.

Annie—Útburður. Level 80.

Katia leaned in and started whispering instructions to the totem.

The Vinegar Bitch's summon was a familiar one. It was the first totem I'd helped Sister Ines's team capture. Yago the monk seal. He was the same thing as our Geraldo.

This version of Yago, however, was different. He was now 25 levels higher than his regular 70. He crackled with obsidian-colored energy and was wider than he'd been before.

Yago—Monk Seal of the Earth Order. Level 95.

He'd been buffed with some sort of extra Earth magic. His headband had changed, and it was black with a red swirl.

"Oh, oh yeah, a bunch of bitches to fight." He pointed a flipper at me and did a hop, waving his fins with karate noises. "Time for a rematch. Time for Yago to go to poundtown on your ass!" He started flipping directly toward me, shouting, "Yip, yip, yip!"

Crash! The seal crunched right through the floor, and he also plummeted away, screaming.

Ysalte grunted with annoyance. "You! Seal! Find him!" She bellowed down into the hole in the floor. "Find that one with my mark upon him, and kill him!"

DONUT: LOUIS, LOOK OUT. A MONK SEAL IS COMING FOR YOU.

ELLE: Come to us, Louis. We're coming up the stairs!

LOUIS: A rock-monster thing that looks like Chris is fighting us already! It's level 120! It crashed through the ceiling!

IMANI: We're coming!

As that was happening, three more totems appeared. These were all from Amayon. He only had totem cards, and he was emptying his hand as rapidly as he could. The ground rumbled as they appeared all at once in a cacophony of overlapping explosions and fanfares. Two were the same thing, though they had different names. The third was entirely different.

Gallu—Level 100 Inferior Demon.

Mavet—Level 100 Inferior Demon.

These first two were tall, fat winged demons with wide, evil faces, each carrying a whip and covered with leather and chains like they'd just stepped out of an underworld biker bar. They were small male versions of that Slit demon who'd attacked us on the fifth floor.

Samantha screamed at the sight of them and flew across the room directly for them.

Gallu the demon reacted with surprising speed. He cracked his whip, and Samantha spun off, screaming about his mother as she ricocheted away.

The third newcomer was a ridiculously over-the-top, sexy-looking, humanlike female demon with outrageously large breasts. Not quite Odette-sized breasts, but pretty close. They floated on their own in front of her, each defying physics and gravity.

Naamah—Level 120 Succubus Nest Queen.

"Hello, boys," the succubus called after Samantha's screaming waned. She waved across the hallway at us. She pointed at me. "I choose you, stud. Let's dance."

"These are not true representations," Amayon rumbled, his voice physically painful to listen to. He didn't have any cards in his hand. He would automatically draw his last one soon.

To my right, Bautista was spamming stuffed animals everywhere, ripping off tags left and right as the creatures flew from his hands. Several were the Grulke frogs, but armored versions I'd never seen before, along with other monsters, from trolls to small dragons to other things covered with claws and teeth. Bautista shouted, and they, as one, all turned on the twin inferior demons. As they surged toward the monsters, a few fell through more holes in the floor, screaming as they disappeared.

LOUIS: Tran is down! Britney and I are running! Oh god. It's the seal. He's here.

TRAN: I'm not dead! I fell down to a different level. My wheelchair is sparking. I think it's going to blow! I'm stuck!

IMANI: We're almost there. There are demons surging up the stairs behind us.

I pulled a banger sphere and decked the succubus as hard as I could. The metal ball bounced off her head with a *splatch.* It barely did any damage. She grinned at me with a mouthful of sharp teeth.

"Someone who likes it rough. I can respect that."

She hissed and lunged, flying across the area at ridiculous speed, like she'd been launched from a gun.

I cast Talon Strike on my foot and did a snap kick as hard as I could at the speeding creature. She *oofed* with pain, and she took some damage, but it didn't stop her momentum as she slammed into me. My health flashed as she hit me with the force of a bus.

We hit the ground and slid, tumbling as we flew between Katia and Donut, barely missing the hole in the ground for the stairs, and sliding into the area that had once been the service hallway.

The creature had vampire fangs, and she moved to chomp directly on my neck just as I activated my new tech-based shield. She bit down and cried out, her teeth sparking and then shattering like broken crockery against my neck. She screeched in outrage as I cast *Wisp Armor* on myself, attempting to shore up my shield. I instinctively clicked on a healing potion without even thinking.

A terrible taste flooded my mouth.

A **Kombucha!** achievement flashed as I remembered the vinegar debuff.

Normally potions had no taste when used via inventory, but food items did.

I cast *Heal* instead.

I was on my back with the pissed-off, shrieking succubus pinning me down. She grasped on to both arms. Her hands sparkled where they came in contact with my flesh. My shield was rapidly losing power. The demon wasn't huge, but she was clearly stronger than me. She bodily picked me up and slammed me down against the floor over and over again, squealing angrily.

A tentacle wrapped around the woman's waist and yanked, pulling her up off the ground. I gasped in pain as my shield sparked out, and her nails ripped into the flesh on my arms. She was dragged away into a fulminating gorilla-sized shadow of black clouds with dark tentacles ripping in and out of it. She let out a scream from within the darkness, followed by a spray of blood.

I started scrambling back until I saw the monster had our flag over it. This was the card Donut had stolen from the demon.

Banjo—Level 120 Hell Scrub.

I jumped back to my feet and returned to the fray, dodging holes in the ground.

Li Jun and a human I'd never seen before were fighting side by side, battling a ghommid strongman. The human was a **Legendary Master**, and it was one of Li Na's cards. She kept tossing speed buffs onto him.

The ghommid was just a regular NPC that Sister Ines must have flagged, but he had an **Oak Champion** buff after his name. Li Jun was literally walking on air, dancing and kicking, trading blows. Alongside him, the legendary master was a blur. In moments, the ghost creature was down.

I growled in frustration. We needed to keep Ysalte's totems alive. On my interface, she was down to just ten cards, and barely a minute had passed. She was discarding her own cards when she could.

Katia had a female spoon-wielding troll I'd seen before summoned along with a pair of twin boys, also trolls, dancing on top of the two inferior demons who were half dead, surrounded by stuffing as Bautista continued to toss out an alarming number of his Beanie animals. The entire group of them tumbled away as the floor broke. A moment later, a *plink, plink* indicated the two demons were dead.

Amayon's row on my interface now only contained two cards. One was facing upward, showing the rock monster was still active. The demon had the last card in his hand, and it appeared as if he was struggling to play it. He was growling in frustration, but his claw wouldn't move. It was Ysalte, I realized. She was trying to keep him from playing his final card. She knew he'd be free to cast his spells once he was out.

"Donut," I called.

"I'm on it!" Donut shouted. "Watch this!"

Donut tossed out **Force Discard**. Amayon's last card disappeared with a **Poof!** graphic.

"Ha! Suck it, bitch!" Donut shrieked as the kaiju-sized demon let out a satisfied grunt.

That was it. He was out of cards. We just needed to kill that first totem he summoned.

CARL: Does anyone know where the rock creature is? He's the last piece!

Yoink!

"Hey!" Donut cried.

Ysalte had tossed out a card, a unique mystic called **Raid Stash**.

Five cards came flying at the goddess and entered her hand. It was a card from each of us, including Imani and Elle downstairs.

Multiple people started shouting at once.

"Oh, crap!" Katia called. "They stole an inactive card from my inventory! It's one of the totems we were forced to take after the key boss fight! Oh shit, it's Tran's mom!"

"Watch out," Li Na yelled at her brother. "She has the Zhe totem!"

ELLE: Guys, holy shit. Heads up. She stole a totem from me and some junk card from Imani.

"Carl, Carl!" Donut called. "She took the—"

Ysalte tossed four totems out at once. Three humans and a Sasquatch thing. All four crash-landed in front of us one by one. These were all the stolen totems.

The Sasquatch along with one of the humans—a large, elderly Asian woman—both roared and jumped down through the same hole in the floor that Yago caused. The other human, also an Asian woman, but much younger, said something to Li Jun, who screamed in outrage, "You're not my cousin!"

I only had eyes for the fourth one. This was the card she'd stolen from Donut's inactive deck. The only inactive totem Donut currently carried.

Leveled-Up Frank. Sober Edition. Level 100 Night Elf Blood Assassin.

"Hello, Carl," Frank Q called as the floor rumbled. "Fancy seeing you here. Where's your ring?"

"Go get him, Mr. Whatever You Are!" Donut squealed at the cloud of tentacles. The Hell Scrub made a clicking noise and started floating toward Frank, who pulled a red sword from over his shoulder.

Both Katia and Li Na tossed more cards out as Donut also summoned Geraldo the monk seal, who crashed onto the floor and almost fell through it.

A distant explosion shook the entire building. One of Katia's trolls cried out and plummeted away.

Amayon let out a whoop of triumph, and he lifted his massive arms into the sky. In doing so, he knocked a corner of the building, causing everything to rumble even more.

This building is going to collapse.

TRAN: I got the rock bastard! My wheelchair blew a hole in his chest! I need a healer.

IMANI: Where are you? The floors are collapsing in on each other!

The world froze. The countdown stopped.

What the hell?

We had seven minutes and 27 seconds left. Had it really only been two and a half minutes?

I took in the scene. Frank was in the process of slicing his sword through a tentacle. The young woman—Zhe, who was apparently Li Jun and Li Na's cousin—had a bloody, squirting heart in her goddamned hand. She'd just pulled it from the chest of the legendary master. It appeared the master totem had gotten a memory ghost's shirt stuck on his face, which had momentarily blinded him. Li Jun was in the midst of a backflip. Katia's skull-headed bird thing was flying through the air, aimed directly at the Frank totem. Li Na's Xing Tian was about to time out already.

Samantha was finally on her way back, her glowing form just visible as she rocketed toward us. She was off the northeast edge of the building, perilously close to the massive demon, having blown a hole through the tornado of demon birds. She'd been tossed so far away, she had seaweed in her hair.

Ysalte was in the middle of tossing something else out. She couldn't move, but she was, like us, conscious of the pause. She started to shout insults.

And behind it all loomed Amayon, who had a new look of outrage on his demon face.

Quest Update! The Missing Piece. Part One!

Demon Lord Amayon is trapped! The very Demon Eviction event that allowed him to come to this realm is his undoing! Now that he's taken his true form, he does not have enough power to cast his spell! And what's worse, there aren't enough souls left in this dying world to even trigger the spell anyway. Everyone and everything is mostly dead!

If only there was a way to replace the souls that had triggered the event in the first place.

The *same* type of souls. The same flavor of chowder, so to speak.

Refill the world with souls. Then power Amayon up before the timer runs dry.

Oh, and the demon may attempt to cast an alternative spell before you buff him up. You'll either have to stop him or convince him to wait.

Match resumes in thirty seconds.

"What the hell does that mean?" Katia shouted from behind me.

"Are you kidding me?" I shouted. "Are you fucking kidding me?"

"Oh my god, Carl," Donut yelled. I couldn't turn my neck to see her. "Does that mean what I think it means?"

"Is he in your hand?" I asked.

"No!"

"What about Midnight Express?"

"Yes, I have it!"

"What is this witchery!" Amayon shouted. "Release me!"

I took in a deep breath as I eyed the frozen form of Samantha. "Okay, everyone. You're gonna have to talk Amayon into waiting for a few minutes. I'm going to run the moment we unfreeze. Donut, message me when you pull him and then cast the Midnight Express card!"

"Run? What do you mean run, Carl? We're on the roof of a skyscraper! Where are you running?"

"Samantha!" I shouted as loud as I could. "I'm coming to you!"

"I can't move!" Samantha shrieked back. "I am frozen!"

The timer was about to resume.

This was going to suck. "Here I come! Don't let me fall!"

68

THE WORLD UNFROZE, AND I BOLTED TOWARD THE EDGE OF THE BUILDing as the battle continued all around me. I jumped past the Zhe totem as she started to devour the heart she'd just pulled from the chest of the legendary master totem. Samantha zoomed back toward me at full speed, screaming as I ran and leaped off the edge of the building. I caught her in midair like a goalie stopping a penalty kick. I pulled her to my chest as we both dropped like a rock. Demon seagulls and bats, who'd been keeping their distance, shrieked and moved to pursue us. We plummeted past a flying, humanoid bat-thing totem sporting Elle's flag, which moved to attack the demons.

"Carl, what are you doing!" Samantha shrieked as we slowed our descent. She clearly struggled to carry me. She tried to struggle out of my grip as we approached the ground. The sensation was like trying to float atop the waves while clutching a slippery ball between myself and the ocean.

I slipped as Samantha bobbed up, and I grabbed on to her pigtails, like I was holding the handlebars of a bicycle. "To the ground, but stay with me! I need to run between the demon's legs!"

"I am not a carnival ride, Carl! I will not . . . Okay, that does sound like fun. Hang on."

We hit the ground, landing right around the corner from the gigantic kaiju of a demon, who was still trying to cast his spell.

His centaur body was not like that of a horse, but almost piglike. His legs were shorter than I was expecting, and each of his cloven-hooved feet were at least ten feet tall. This close, he stank like a scorched barnyard animal. He stomped in frustration, shattering concrete. Rock rained off the side of the building.

I still clutched on to Samantha as I turned and ran alongside the building and angled myself between his legs. His hair-covered body writhed over me as he continued to shout. Above, the roar of a new beast filled the air.

DONUT: LI NA JUST SUMMONED A DRAGON!

Black stinking liquid rained down on us as I ran between his legs. It burned every time it hit skin. I didn't know what the hell it was, and I didn't want to know. Samantha squealed with delight.

"We gotta go to the beach!" I cried as we came out the back of the demon, who didn't see or probably care about my passing underneath him. The ocean was just a block over, but I didn't have time to run. "Fly! Fly!"

"You're too fat, Carl! Louis and Donut need our help!"

"I believe in you! Go!"

Samantha grumbled as she zipped off again, with me clutching on to her. She struggled to pull me up, but she managed to get me about a foot off the ground, complaining the whole time. She flew at a breakneck speed, passing between buildings, across the freeway, and we approached the beach.

DONUT: I HAVE HIM!
CARL: How long does the Midnight Express card last?
DONUT: THREE MINUTES!

Jesus.

CARL: Wait ten seconds, then play it!

I glanced at the clock. Five minutes, thirty seconds left. I let go of Samantha's pigtails and dropped to the rocky beach, which was covered with corpses. I rolled and jumped to my feet, racing into the water. I didn't see any zombies or demons. It was just dead fish and birds and seals and crabs as far as I could see. Mixed in were memory ghosts, walking along the beach, looking out into the ocean, enjoying the day after Christmas.

A new achievement appeared as Donut played **Midnight Express.**

It was one of the two consumable cards Ren gave me before she died.

Tag! You're it! For the next three minutes, you are now the deck-master!

The cards appeared in front of me, floating huge in the air. One of the four slots was taken by the Midnight Express card, which would remain persistent until it timed out. The card featured a pair of tag-team wrestlers. Behind me atop the building, Donut was now temporarily unfettered, which would allow her to cast her spells and use her inventory while I had control of the deck.

"Samantha," I shouted, "go back! Fast! Enhance Donut's spells!"

She didn't argue as she zipped off, leaving me alone on the beach.

The other three cards in my hand were **Golden Combo**, which would allow me to temporarily combine two totems; a **Time Extend**; and the card I was looking for.

Raul the crab.

I flipped the card, and Raul flew into the water with his typical fanfare. Far behind us, Amayon rumbled again.

"Daddy Master Carl! I am honored to be of service! I am ready! Ready to . . ." Raul trailed off as he looked upon the carnage. The crab turned in a circle, clearly bewildered. "What happened here?"

"No time to explain, but you gotta do your thing. Do it now!"

"Uh, what thing is that?" he asked, still looking about. "Everybody is dead. By the heavens, how is this so?"

A new card appeared in my hand. It was **Alpha Male Carl**. I hadn't wanted to put him in the deck, but it was either him or Frank, and Donut decided he would be the better choice. We'd been a totem short after Donut used **Golden Combo** to temporarily fuse Lazarus with Skylar Spinach and then added Ren's other consumable card, **Glow-Up**, to make the combination permanent. The stronger versions of Asojano and Uzi

Jesus made it a great, powerful combo, especially since we'd be allowed to bring a single card with us onto the next floor.

But none of that mattered right now.

Right now I needed to get this damn crab to jerk off into the ocean.

The whole Demon Eviction event had happened, at least according to the announcer guys, because the AI had made the unusual decision to consider crab sperm a mob. Because so many had "died," it broke Sheol, and it kicked off the event. Now Amayon's *Take Me Home* spell required a metric fuck ton of souls to pay the passage or whatever, and the AI was sticking to its original rule. It had set us up for this bullshit. It was clear it had to be a crab. I just had to convince him to do it.

"Listen," I said to the crab. "We only have a few minutes. This is how you move to the golden heavenly throne or whatever you call it. Your people are dead. You are the last one left. The eggs are still out there. You can save your people, but you have to do it now." I swallowed. "You have to fertilize the eggs. Go!"

He just looked at me. "Now? Here?"

"Yes!"

An explosion echoed from the building.

"Glorious Master Carl . . . that's a lot of pressure to perform."

"You have been training for this your whole life, Raul. This is how you save everybody. Go into the water and do it. Fast!"

"But why does it have to be right now?"

"Look. Do you see that giant demon over there? He's going to destroy this world if he doesn't go home. He needs a few million souls to go home. So some of your little guys will have to make a sacrifice, but the rest will be fine, I'm sure. You have like a billion of them, right?"

"My hallowed seed consists of the essence of my holy ancestors. Ancestors who must fight for another chance to rise to the next stage."

I tried not to let my frustrated panic edge into my voice. "That just means the survivors will be the most worthy. Right?"

DONUT: THE GODDESS LADY SUMMONED A WEIRD VERSION OF PAZ BUT KATIA PUT HIM IN A SHIELD-JAIL THING, AND HE'S PROBABLY GONNA TIME OUT! ELLE AND BRITNEY AND LOUIS ARE BACK UP HERE, BUT IMANI AND TRAN ARE TRAPPED.

"Okay," Raul said uncertainly, moving sideways off into the water so he was half submerged. The waves lapped all around him, washing more corpses up on the shore. The entire beach stank like death. "But don't watch."

"I won't look. Just let me know when you're done."

Raul was only half the equation. I needed to power Amayon up. I was going to have to use Alpha Carl to help me. I turned my back and summoned the totem. It hit the ground, which started to rumble with his entrance sequence.

"I can't do it," Raul called from behind me. "I need a baby seal."

I turned at that. "What the fuck, Raul?"

He waved his pincer. "No, not like that. The seals hang out near the eggs. It's like an automatic reaction. We've been programmed to perform when we see baby seals."

It was no wonder the monk seals wanted these guys all dead.

The ridiculous red, white, and blue entrance sequence for Alpha Carl exploded across the beach. I tried to tune it out while I dealt with Raul.

"Look, over there. There's a pile of dead baby seals. Try that."

"Hello, little brother!" Alpha Male Carl called. "Whoa. What happened here?"

This version of Alpha Carl was much friendlier now that I'd been the one to summon him. A little too friendly. I glanced at the clock. This wasn't going to work. Three minutes before the whole quest was done. One minute left before Donut took back control. I would still be stuck here when the Midnight Express card expired, and so would the two totems, but we were running out of time.

"You look upset. Do you want to talk about it?" Alpha Carl asked.

DONUT: THE SATAN DEMON GUY WON'T LISTEN TO ME. HE'S GOING TO CAST ANOTHER SPELL. HE AND THE VINEGAR LADY ARE YELLING AT EACH OTHER. I THINK THEY MIGHT ACTUALLY BE IN LOVE. SHE'S ALMOST OUT OF CARDS. SAMANTHA AND I ARE GONNA HAVE TO DO SOMETHING DRASTIC.

"Okay," I said to Alpha Carl, who was looking at me with sincere concern. "I need you to almost kill me. I can do it to myself if I have to, but I'd prefer if someone else does it so they can stop at the right moment. You have to beat me to within an inch of my life and then stop."

Behind me, Raul started to grunt. "Yeah. That's right. Look at you all dead and shit. That's right, you fuzzy little seals."

"You want me to beat you up?" Alpha Carl asked. "I'm not going to do that. I love you, little brother. Maybe we should hug it out."

I tossed the Time Extend onto Raul just as the Midnight Express timer ended. The cards in front of me disappeared.

Tag! You are no longer the deckmaster!

Two minutes and four seconds left.

"Gah!" Amayon bellowed in the distance. I looked over to see the giant demon punch himself in the face. "I will destroy . . . Gah!" He did it again.

DONUT: I CAST *WHY ARE YOU HITTING YOURSELF?* ON SATAN!

SAMANTHA: OKAY, THAT MIGHT HAVE BEEN A MISTAKE. I THINK HE IS BIG MAD.

Alpha Carl put his hand on my shoulder. "You don't need to hurt yourself to feel loved. Despite all of your failings . . ." He paused, looking over my shoulder. "All right. You're gonna have to explain what that crab is doing."

"He's saving the world," I said through gritted teeth. "But he needs motivation."

KATIA: Guys, Annie is down, and I'm out of cards. Daniel, on me. I'm going to try to stop the goddess.

IMANI: I found Tran, but we're surrounded by demons!

"It's not working. I can feel you judging me," Raul called.

"Stop being a little bitch and get the job done!" Alpha Carl barked.

"Don't yell at me!" Raul snapped back. "I'd like to see you perform under this sort of pressure. Wait, wait, never mind. Yell at me again. I think it's helping."

"I don't know what the hell you're doing, you weird little armored sea rat, but you need to do what my brother says, or I'm gonna come over there and break you in half."

"Yes. That's it. That's it," Raul said. "It's happening. I'm ascending! I'm ascending past the cloud rank and into the golden heavenly light! No more kowtowing. No more kowtowing!"

"You two, keep going," I said as I dashed away. One minute left. I was going to have to do this the hard way. There were plenty of ways for me to hurt myself, but I could only think of one that would also return me to the main battle.

CARL: Donut, I'm coming back right now.

I paused. *Shit. This is going to hurt.* Forty-five seconds.

CARL: SAMANTHA, DON'T LET ME OUT UNTIL THE FIRE FLARES.

SAMANTHA: WHAT? WHY ARE YOU YELLING? I'M HAVING A TUSSLE!

Behind me, Raul let out a loud, satisfied groan as Alpha Carl continued to berate him. At the same moment, I pulled the teleport trap trigger out of my inventory, and I stepped into it.

I teleported to the trap.

The trap I left inside of Samantha.

69

I LANDED HEADFIRST INSIDE OF SAMANTHA'S NECK HOLE.

If I wanted my eighth-floor-only Martyr's Path benefit to activate, I would have to be under 5% health. It would release flames over all of my outside-of-buildings footsteps. Since my fire attacks were currently enhanced with Sheol fire, and since I'd run underneath the demon, it would bathe the demon in Sheol fire. It would enhance his power. Hopefully enough.

The timing was important. It had to happen now.

At first, I felt nothing other than the lack of oxygen. It was just my head, like I was wearing Samantha as a hat that covered my face. The rest of me was restricted, too, like Samantha had been burrowing through something when I appeared. It wasn't tight, and I could move my legs and arms barely, but it was burning hot, despite my resistances. I felt Samantha start to push me out, but I wriggled my arms up and grabbed her and pulled down, keeping her on me. I felt the lower half of my body slip away from something, and my legs were suddenly out in open air. I started to bicycle them back and forth.

We only had twenty seconds. I watched my health. *Come on, come on.*

And then my head started to burn. The intensity ramped up. Fifteen seconds. I felt my hair burn away. Ten seconds. I could hear distant screaming, and I realized I was violently whipping back and forth. Five seconds. We weren't going to make it. My health was plummeting. I couldn't breathe. The acid was literally melting my face off. But something was happening to Samantha, too, as she slammed over and over against something.

The timer ended, and I wasn't down to 5%.

I had failed.

I had failed. All that for nothing.

I had failed.

A page of notifications appeared, but I couldn't read them.

I was at 7% health, and I ripped Samantha up off of me. I remained in darkness, and my health continued to dip.

A button appeared in my interface, and I mentally clicked it with all the force I had.

The Martyr's Path has engulfed your steps.

The Scavenger's Daughter has enhanced your fire attack.

My legs burned as a sound unlike anything I'd ever heard invaded my prison, wherever I was. It was like every wing in the world started flapping at once. Like every soul in heaven and hell sighed in unison. Like every scream was expelled at the same time.

I couldn't breathe again, and I started to fade. All the air had been sucked from the world.

But just before I fully passed out, I gasped. The air returned as quickly as it had gone.

The slamming motion stopped, replaced by a cackling sound. Laughter. Laughter from Amayon. It came from right above me. I slammed my *Heal* spell. My health stuttered up. My health had gone down to 2%, and I had a blinking red line of debuffs.

The music stopped.

Quest Complete. The Missing Piece. Part One.

What? I didn't understand. We'd run out of time. I'd cast my spell seconds too late. But then my eyes caught a notification persistent on the screen. A world notification. The timer had actually stopped with just two seconds left, but it wasn't because of something I had done.

A deity has fallen. The heavens tremble with rage.

System Message. Crawler Paz Lo has slain the goddess, Ysalte.

He has been marked for death by all deities except sworn enemies of the late goddess.

System Message. A Memorial Crystal for the Goddess Ysalte has been generated. It will be available to be looted on a future floor. Great riches abound to who may find it.

System Message. All worshippers of Ysalte have permanently been inflicted with the Despondent debuff.

What the fuck? What the actual fuck?

Ysalte is no longer in the realm.

The Scavenger's Daughter has looked away, though her eyes remain open to the presence of Amayon. All of your vinegar-infused potions outside your inventory have been enhanced. The rest of her effects will fade with time.

My health rose, but it moved hesitantly, like I was still being drained in other ways. The heat was unbearable. I still didn't know where I was. Paz had killed the goddess. But how? How was it possible? He was her own totem.

Just like Imani's entire party had been killed by her own totem, I realized. Just like Uzi Jesus had shot Florin. Just like Jola had almost eaten me. They'd warned us from the beginning that our totems weren't always safe. But how? She was immortal on this floor.

Everything from my waist up was still stuck in something, but at least I could breathe again. It was pitch-black. My legs dangled in the air, but they were burning hot. I was too close to a fire. Samantha was still here, above me in the dark, growling and grunting and screaming. Suddenly we whipped again, slamming against something else. Nearby, the demon howled with outrage.

DONUT: CARL WHERE ARE YOU? YOU BLEW UP THE WHOLE CITY! EVERYTHING IS ON FIRE! KATIA GAVE PAZ AN ARROW THING, AND HE STUCK IT INTO THE DWARF LADY'S EYE, AND THEN HE BLEW HIMSELF UP, BUT THE EXPLOSION WAS ALL

CONCENTRATED ON THE GODDESS'S NECK. HER HEAD FELL OFF! WE ALL FELL DOWN SEVERAL STORIES. THEY GAVE HIM CREDIT FOR IT EVEN THOUGH HE WENT AWAY WHEN SHE DIED.

I slammed again. I tried a Heal potion, but it was still vinegar. I used a rare *Heal* scroll. It felt like I was inside of a barrel that was rolling down a hill. I couldn't sustain this. I tried calling out to Samantha, but she was still doing nothing but screaming in outrage.

"I will kill your mother! I swear to the heavens and hells, she is dead! And I'll make sure she stays dead this time! Release me this instant!"

CARL: I'm with Samantha! I don't know where I am!

DONUT: YOU CAN'T BE WITH SAMANTHA! THE DEMON GRABBED HER OUT OF THE AIR BUT HE'S STILL PUNCHING HIMSELF! I DIDN'T THINK IT WOULD WORK ON HIM BUT IT DID. IT'S NOT GONNA TURN OFF FOR ANOTHER TWO MINUTES!

Holy shit. I'm in the demon's hand. He's punching himself over and over.

ELLE: We won the damn quest, but my card deck is still active!

LI NA: It's the demons. They're swarming the building, and they're too close. It won't let us finish out the battle until they're gone, too! Our decks won't go away until we're out of range.

LOUIS: Dude! I got a celestial box for outliving a goddess who has a marked-for-death curse on me!

DONUT: WHERE'S CARL? EVERYBODY STOP TALKING. WE NEED TO FIND CARL.

CARL: I'm in the demon's hand, and he keeps punching himself with me in it.

I was actually being cushioned by the hand itself as he continuously pounded himself, but every time he hit himself, I took a ton of damage. Samantha remained above me, shrieking.

ELLE: Holy shit. I see you! I see your legs. Don't let him drop you! That's Sheol fire burning at his feet. If you fall into that, you're dead.

IMANI: The demons are still swarming. I need help. Tran and I are trapped. We're in a pocket of debris!

I tried a Heal potion again, and this time it worked, but it was only half effective. None of my spells would get me out of here. They'd either cause him to drop me or, worse, squeeze harder. Samantha would be fine. I'd pop like a bug.

"You! Demon guy!" a voice bellowed. It was Donut screaming at the top of her lungs. She was using her headset microphone at the full setting. The Auto-Tune was turned on, too.

"Turn off your spell," the demon bellowed. "Turn it off, or I will obliterate you!"

"I will turn it off, but you have to let my friends go. They're stuck in your hand!"

Smash!

Amayon groaned as he pounded himself again. This time it felt as if he'd given himself an uppercut.

I felt myself lifting in the air, and he unclenched his hand, revealing me and Samantha. I started to pull myself toward her. If I could grab back onto her pigtails . . .

He turned his hand to the side, and I dropped, tumbling into his left hand with a heavy smack. He lifted me to be eye to eye, even as he punched himself again in the face with his right fist. Demon spittle rained over us.

"Let them go!" Donut shrieked again.

I almost lost my footing as I stood in the demon's scorching hand. All around, the city burned. Every place I had stepped outside of a building had burst into flames. That spread all the way to the coast and back again. I wondered if Florida and Iowa were also burning. They probably were.

Samantha shook her head like a dog and came to hover next to me.

"Carl, that was the second-weirdest sex I ever had," she grumbled.

"You gotta warn a girl if you're going to just pop in like that." She looked me up and down. "We are going to have to do something about your hair before we announce that we're dating now. I'll break it to Louis, but you'll have to put up with me straying sometimes. If I ever catch you cheating on me, there'll be trouble."

"I *did* warn you," I said, trying to catch my breath. I took another Heal potion. My head still spun. "And we are not dating. Nor was that sex." I had resistance to surviving inside of Sheol, but even at a few hundred feet away, the Sheol fire itself was almost unbearable.

I looked up into the sky, and despite everything, I felt an enormous sense of relief. Even though he was punching himself again and again, he'd done it. Amayon had started casting the spell to send himself home. The massive red cloud filled the sky, growing by the moment. I still had no idea how long it would take to cast, or if we'd buffed him up enough to cover the world. But at least he cast it.

Behind us, the FOCSA building still miraculously stood. Sort of. The area with the stairwell had completely collapsed in on itself. That was where Imani and Tran were trapped. The northern façade of the building was just gone, giving me a view of almost every level. Several other ceilings and floors had also collapsed, creating compartments and pockets everywhere. The top few levels were nothing but steel girders. Crawlers and totems along with some of the strippers and several of Bautista's animals swarmed over the crisscrossing metal beams of the upper levels, all moving lower as demons swarmed upward, many climbing the outside of the building like spiders. The demons were all trying to get higher, closer to the sky and to Amayon, trying to make certain they could hitch their way home. But if they had the chance to get home by taking someone with them, they weren't squandering the opportunity. From my vantage, I could see a dozen different fights all happening at once. As I watched, Dong swung his new sock at a demon crab who plummeted away, falling into the Sheol fire below. Steve the troll screamed as he swung his club back and forth. Li Jun and yet another kung fu totem fought side by side, swinging from metal beams as concrete rained.

I returned my attention to Amayon. The demon glared down at us. He punched himself in the face with his right hand.

"You are a child of Emberus," he grumbled at me. He turned his attention to Samantha. "And you. That disguise won't fool me. I know who you really are."

"Oh, hey," Samantha said up to him, suddenly acting casual. "So . . . how's your mother?"

He started to growl.

DONUT: CARL, WHAT DO WE DO? DEMONS ARE EVERYWHERE. WE GOTTA GET OUT OF HERE. I STILL HAVE MY DECK OUT. ALPHA CARL AND RAUL TIMED OUT AND RETURNED TO MY DECK, BUT RAUL IS WAY STRONGER NOW!

CARL: Hang on a second.

I held up a hand. "I have a message from Emberus."

IMANI: There's too many. Oh god. They keep coming.

The demon cocked his head. I had to keep downing Heal potions to prevent myself from keeling over. I felt like I was getting cooked alive. The demon's attention was fully on me.

"It's more a question than a message, I guess. He wants to know if you know what happened to his son. Uh, what was his name again?"

"Orthrus's daddy?" Samantha asked. "He's such a good puppy. That was Geyrun. He got murdered."

Amayon burst into laughter, but the laughter was cut short as he balled his right fist and hit himself in the face. I stumbled as the world shook. The spell was about to run out.

"That's what he sent you to ask? To ask about his son? You tell him that I know exactly what happened to his child. I was witness to the deal being signed. If he assists in helping me kill my three brothers, I will tell him."

Fuck me.

A new notification came, but it moved into a folder.

I took a breath. "I cast the spell that gave you new strength. I filled this world with the souls you need to go home. Tell those other demons to leave my friends alone, and I will deliver your message."

The *Why Are You Hitting Yourself?* spell timed out.

The demon sighed with relief. "You also helped slay Ysalte, the mother of my child, so we are even, and I owe you nothing, mortal. The act of speaking to you already delivered the message to Emberus. Soon this entire world will be scoured. Know you have served your god well. You will be remembered as a martyr, I'm sure. Consider yourself lucky I have given you this much consideration."

He turned his hand to the side, dumping me and Samantha toward the never-ending fire.

70

I HAD ANTICIPATED THIS, AND I GRABBED ON TO SAMANTHA'S PIGTAILS once again as we slipped away. She screamed as we plummeted, but she angled herself back toward the building, almost like we were zip-lining, and we glided toward the hopping-up-and-down form of Donut, who had Lazarus summoned next to her on a metal beam. She was on maybe the 25th or 26th floor, right above a group of intact floors.

Lazarus had a large RPG out and was about to blast it into the chest of the demon, but I yelled at him to stop.

I let go of the sex doll head, and I stumbled onto the burning-hot metal beam.

"Carl!" Donut shouted. She was on her feet, jumping up and down on the metal. Mongo was one floor below roaring at a group of approaching demon crabs. I could see him and others through the multiple holes in the floor. "Everybody is below trying to get to Imani and Tran!" She paused. "Carl, what happened to all your hair!"

Behind me, the demon turned his back on us. His piglike body turned and brushed against the building, causing it to shake even more. *He's done with us,* I realized. He would leave us alone as long as we left him alone. He wouldn't stop the possessed demons from attacking us, but at least we didn't—hopefully—have to worry about him striking us down. He just wanted to go home.

The birds and bats continued to swirl around him, thicker than ever. They were still arriving from all over. Most of them seemed to ignore us, too. They only attacked if we got close.

Amayon raised both of his hands into the air, and he shouted something into the sky in a language I did not understand. Lazarus also screamed something and lifted his RPG again. He was trembling with rage at the sight of the massive demon.

"Leave Amayon alone," I shouted. "We need him to cast his spell! And don't fire that thing here. You're going to collapse the building!"

"The building is already collapsing," he complained. "Why summon me if you're not going to let me blow stuff up? I swear, you're all pansies."

"Donut, Carl, come!" came a shout from below. I looked between my feet to see Li Na and Li Jun struggling with a group of demons one level below. That level still mostly had a floor. Sort of. Mongo was already there, perched atop a turned-over bed in a wrecked apartment while the memory ghost of a kid was eating something at a kitchen table. As I watched, a demon seal lunged at Mongo, but the dinosaur jumped up to our level, and the seal broke through the floor. It continued to fall, but the hole he made revealed another mostly intact floor below that. Louis stood there on that next floor down, looking up at us.

"We're coming!" I called. Donut jumped to my shoulder. She still had her card deck summoned. I aimed toward a girder and jumped, landing upon it as Li Na and Li Jun both jumped down one more level to be near Louis. I quickly followed, landing between Louis, Katia, and Dong Quixote.

"Imani and Tran are two levels below," Katia said, "but the whole area is swarming. If we can get to them, then we can get the hell out of here!"

"No!" Dong shouted. I turned to see a group of crabs swarm up through a hole in the wall. One grasped on to the arm of Author Steve Rowland, and a portal opened up. The troll was sucked into hell, screaming. The elderly stripper shouted and rushed at the remaining crab and clobbered him with his nickel sock. The crab went flying off the edge and plummeted into the fire below.

Lazarus shouted something and another crab appeared, coming through a wall. It grabbed on to him, and they also disappeared. Splitter or not, getting pulled into hell was a good way to completely eliminate a card. I jumped back and prepared to kick, but both Lazarus and the crab were now gone.

Totem Eliminated.

"We need to go down one more floor!" I shouted.

"Carl, why hasn't the quest updated yet?" Katia called as we prepared to jump.

"I think we're waiting for the cloud to spread over the whole world," I shouted back. I kicked a charging crab and felt it shatter under me.

Below, I could see Bautista, Britney, and Elle ripping up pieces of rubble to gain access to the next floor down. Bautista had changed shape, turning from the tiger to a large, four-armed creature similar to the AI guy who ran the training room. I knew he had a ring that allowed him to do this, but this was the first time I'd seen it in action. Tran and Imani were apparently trapped in a pocket. Elle had two totems summoned helping with the job. One was another Sasquatch thing, and the second was a massive bear-hippo thing called a gumberoo.

"We need more hands!" Elle called. "Come help!"

"The exterior of the entire building is covered with demon crabs," someone called. It was another human. Another Li Na totem. "We need to hold them back while you work!" the voice cried out, and died.

"I'm out of cards!" Li Na shouted.

IMANI: They're in here with us! I'm holding them off the best I can!
ELLE: Do you have cards left? Do you have a Flee card?
IMANI: I won't leave Tran. And I don't trust my last totems.

Tran was in Katia's squad. She'd have to use a Flee card for him to get away, but she didn't carry them in her deck. She was out of cards now anyway.

"I have a few Phase Through Walls potions!" I called, jumping down to land amongst everybody else. "I can get through, give them the potions, and we can keep going down!"

"Won't work. If you do it, you'll drop like a rock," Elle called. "You can't control it. Maybe I can drink it and try to float, but if Tran and I are both phased, I won't be able to hold him. He'll get splattered for sure. Let's dig first!"

"Donut," I said, "what about your *Hole*?"

"It's not in my hand!" she said. We'd added the *Hole* spell to her staff totem in hopes of using it to cut either an enemy totem or deckmaster in half.

"What do you have?"

"Alpha Carl is back in my hand. Shi Maria. My Golden Combo card. And the Lamp snare. I can't discard for a bit. I already discarded Jola. He's too big for this place! I don't have any Flee cards in my deck, either!"

"Okay," I said, looking around, thinking fast. We had demons coming up from both sides. Everybody was engaged fighting them off while Elle and the others were desperately digging through the rubble. "We need you to get rid of your deck. You still have *Puddle Jump* available, right? We gotta get everybody out of here." She still had *Skedaddle*, too, but that escape spell would likely dump us in a pile of Sheol fire. "Discard when you can, especially the snares, but in the meantime, summon Shi Maria and Alpha Carl and use the Golden Combo to combine them. That'll get that Combo card out of your hand, too. Do it fast. We don't have time to deal with either of their usual bullshit anyway, especially Shi Maria's. Maybe temporarily combining them will help. Have the combo version hold off the demons while I help to dig. Discard or play everything you can until you get your staff totem!"

Donut tossed Alpha Carl back out and then Shi Maria, shuffling the spider off toward the edge where there was no ceiling. Hopefully she would fit. Both of their entrance procedures started.

I punched another crab before it could grab on to me, and a notification popped up.

The Scavenger's Daughter has been fed. Unleash her wrath.

I looked at the bar in my interface, and it crackled with black energy. I needed to unleash it, but I didn't dare do it while up here.

Alpha Carl appeared. Just behind him, Shi Maria also emerged, too tall for the hallway. Metal bent and snapped as she materialized. Most of her bulbous body hung outside the building, but her long, horrible legs spread out, snaking into the hall. Donut tossed out the **Golden Combo** card.

Alpha Carl looked at me and was about to say something when his face exploded. Shi Maria had shoved a leg right through the back of his head. He exploded all over me, showering me with gore.

"Carl!" Donut shouted in panic. "It says—"

The intended target of the Golden Combo has been incapacitated. Proceeding to the next available minion target.

That's you.

You have been combined with Shi Maria.

71

WARNING: YOU HAVE BEEN TEMPORARILY COMBINED WITH A TOTEM.

If you are slain while in this state, you will not regenerate.

This combination will time out in 180 seconds or when the battle ends, whichever is sooner.

"How . . ." I started to say, but I felt my control over my own body slip.

What, what, what is this? So many things on the inside. So many items to root through. What is this storage? So many, many things.

My hands turned to claws as I scratched at my own chest.

"No," I grunted. I tried to reach up and grab the hands scratching at me, but they were my own hands. What was happening?

How do I get to this?

That voice. It was Shi Maria. She was talking in my own mind.

I was aware of screaming all around me. Of movement. I could hear Donut shouting. Others. It was all in slow motion and sped up at the same time. I felt as if I was falling. Suspended. I was in water. I was in the stars. My back legs swept, tossing dozens of demons off the wall.

They couldn't drag me to Sheol even if they wanted. I was one of them.

I was hyperaware of my body, my skin. It was wrong. My body was big. I had more legs than usual. I had no control over anything. From the waist up, I was the same. Instead of just a head, I'd turned into a torso with a spider body. She controlled it all.

An item appeared in my hand. A scroll of *Build Trench*. I'd pulled it directly from my own inventory. No, no. I hadn't pulled it. *She'd* done it. *She'd* taken it directly from my inventory. It dropped to the ground.

Oh, yes. I see. I see how this works. What do we have?

"Carl!" Donut cried. "What are you doing? Are you okay?"

"I'm fine," I found myself shouting. I was not controlling my own voice. "Just trying to figure out how to move in this body."

I tried moving to the chat, to warn her, but it wouldn't let me. I had truly lost control.

No. No, I thought. *Not this. Anything but this.*

You have so much in here. This book. This well-worn book. You're not supposed to have this, are you? And what is this? This bomb is quite powerful, ready to explode. What would happen if I pull it out?

"No," I gurgled, wresting back control for a mere moment.

I would be fine. I would turn back to the card. Why shouldn't I bring it out? Why shouldn't I kill every one of your friends? We had a deal, Carl. You were going to take me to the next floor. I see you. You were planning on betraying me.

I tried to respond, tried to deny it, but I lost the ability to speak again.

So many things. So many possibilities. Kimaris? You have a summoning totem of Kimaris? Does Samantha know this? Hmm. You have a war mage head? So many things. So many possibilities. What to do?

Donut was shouting something at me, but I couldn't even hear that anymore.

Look at all these potions. You could have enhanced them all. You squandered your chance with Ysalte, and now she's dead. Look at this. This potion . . . what did you use to make it? Oh yes, here we go. Oh, yes, yes, you have all the supplies I need. Everything. This will work.

Child. Hold on. Hold on with everything you can. This was another voice. A male.

Don't talk, Shi Maria hissed in my mind. She was speaking to the other voice. *Don't you speak. You're not real. I didn't put you here.*

You did. You killed me, and now I am here.

That is a lie!

An empty beaker appeared. I'd looted it way back on the first floor. Something else was placed within. It was just a piece, a small piece of the toraline root vegetable I'd gotten from my sponsor. It was just a small sliver of it. Mordecai still had the biggest piece.

I felt myself clutching the beaker to my chest. I watched in horror as I started to examine Ren's flamethrower.

No, no. This won't do.

I pulled up my magic menu.

What do we have here?

"You best step back," I heard myself say, looking about. I was surrounded by my friends, all looking up at me. "I won't warn you again. Step back now."

I cast *Self-Immolation.*

My world became fire. All around, the others screamed and fell back. Just touching the fire around me was death. I already knew how awful it was just to be close.

I snapped off the spell within a second. I felt myself falling. It'd been strong enough to burn a hole in the floor underneath me. We weren't directly above Imani and Tran, but we'd broken into the pocket. The floor under my feet just evaporated, and I plummeted, landing heavily in an apartment directly below. My body, already half outside, also fell. The walls now burned all around me. The building itself was starting to melt.

DONUT: CARL, YOU HURT MONGO AND KATIA!

Ahh, yes, this is good. I picked up the burning hot beaker, and it was now filled with a small amount of bubbling black liquid. Ink.

LI NA: We have to flee. Katia is grievously injured.

CARL: Don't you fucking dare. I need but a few more moments. If I am unsummoned, Carl will die. If anyone approaches me, they will be slain. This is your only warning.

I unequipped my trollskin shirt, revealing my bare chest. Then another item from my inventory was in my hands. The stick-and-poke tattoo kit I'd received earlier on the floor.

"Stop," I found myself crying. I was pushed out of control once again.

A chain appeared in my vision, coming from the floor above. Li Na had shot it. Her brother, Li Jun, slid down the chains like he was skiing. He flipped, landing in front of me.

Above, I could hear Donut screaming. She was screaming for Mongo.

No, no, no. This was all going wrong.

"Carl, what can I do?" It was Li Jun, looking at me worriedly. All around him, the walls continued to burn.

I warned him, Shi Maria said in my mind.

No, I thought. *No. He's my friend.*

I took the stick from the tattoo kit, and I jabbed it directly into Li Jun's eye. He cried and fell back. I pulled the stick to my mouth, and I licked. *Oh god, oh god. His eye.* His eye was at the end of the stick. I crunched down and ate it. A splash of bitter liquid filled my mouth, reminding me of the vinegar from earlier. I chewed as Li Jun screamed.

The sound of ratcheting chains filled the room.

You have so much power in your hands, Carl, and you don't even know what you have. That's okay. Today, you live. If you won't bring this card to the next floor, I will have to attach myself to something you can't discard so easily.

I dipped the end of the stick into the beaker and started to rapidly poke into my own chest.

You will likely be doing more of this soon with the remaining ink. Be sure not to go too deep. This is a dangerous spell. I will show you how to wield it. I will show you how to become a god.

"What are you doing?" I gasped as my hand became a blur, moving faster and faster, faster than possible.

Li Na was in the room, hovering over her brother, who sat in the corner, hand over his injured eye socket as he continued to scream in pain. The building all around us burned.

I'd eaten his eye. I'd eaten his goddamn eye. It was gone. It wouldn't come back.

"Do not approach, demon," I said out loud to Li Na, "or your brother will lose more than an eye, and Carl will lose his own heart. Or you, with the wings. Stay back. Do not attempt to heal him."

Inside my own inventory, I watched as items moved around. Potions were being combined. Several dropped to the floor. "Give these two potions to the burned. One to the animal, the other to the doppelganger." A third, gold standard healing potion dropped. "And this to your brother. I am almost done. When I time out, we can flee."

As I talked, I continued to rapid-fire the tattoo into myself. It wasn't a big image. It was right in the center of my chest, just above my sternum.

There. There. Almost done. You may gain some of your friend's powers, too, with the blood on the needle. Not much. But I am with you now, Carl, until you decide to free me. I will no longer be a card you can abandon, one you can rip away. I am a part of you, and you will have to decide. Keep me with you and gain my power, or set me free. Either way, I win. Yes. It is done. Now let us flee this place, okay? I will not let you die. If you die now, I will die. And we can't have that, can we?

I pulled the tattoo kit back into my inventory. I grasped the bottle of ink and pulled it in. The potions I'd dropped on the floor remained. Li Na and Li Jun remained across the room, staring, unsure of what to do.

Don't trust her, boy. Get her out of you as soon as you can. Don't ever trust her.

"Oh god. It hurts," I said. That was me. That was my own voice. I was back in control.

You have timed out. You have returned to your regular form. Shi Maria has returned to the deck.

A wave of agony flashed over me, and I found myself staring down at my bloody chest. At the eye. At the eye she'd rapidly tattooed into me. As I looked, the eye blinked, and then it closed, completely disappearing against my skin.

I could feel it there, a hole inside of me. A bottomless hole. I hesitantly reached forward and touched it.

Tattoo. The Eye of the Bedlam Bride.

That's all it said. It gave no other description.

Li Na scooped up the potions, and she gave one to her brother, whose hand remained clutched over his face. She handed two more potions off to someone else. Imani. I was going to lose consciousness.

"How's Katia? How's Mongo?" I asked before I passed out.

72

I AWAKENED TO FIND MYSELF CLUTCHED IN LOUIS'S ARMS AS WE RAN through the city. I blinked, trying to figure out what was happening. Next to me, Donut was riding on Mongo as they weaved through the streets, avoiding the areas that continued to burn. I felt relief that Mongo was still alive. But then I saw the dinosaur's right wing was gone, and the whole right side of his body was missing scales and feathers. New burns and scars covered the dinosaur.

Oh no, I thought. *I did that.*

"Mongo," I croaked, "I'm sorry."

"He's awake!" Donut cried. "Everybody, Carl's awake! Carl, you're always passing out during the climax!"

"I hurt Mongo," I said.

"One of the potions you upgraded will grow his wing back!" Donut said. "But Mordecai says he has to take it later. He wants to look at the potion first to make sure. A bunch of the potions you dropped next to me before you went to the beach with Raul turned into something really cool. Mordecai is all excited."

"And Katia?"

"She's fine," Katia said from behind me. I turned my head to look, and she jogged with everybody else. She'd turned into a mantaur-like creature, but with four legs instead of arms. She clutched on to the passed-out, legless form of Tran, who had a whole line of debuffs after him.

"Who did we lose?" I asked.

"Nobody," Louis said. "Not of the crawlers. We lost a couple of the strippers, and I think all the slug dudes who went outside are gone. Also, that old dude with the weird sock is pretty upset. But all of us are okay. Though Tran lost his wheelchair and Li Jun lost an eye. And you, uh, lost all your hair. But it's not as bad . . ."

He trailed off.

Not as bad as the Butcher's Masquerade, he almost said.

"Fucking hell. Put me down," I said, starting to struggle.

"Sorry, dude," Louis said, pausing long enough to gently put me on the ground. I wobbled slightly.

I put my hand against my head. My skin had healed, but my hair was all gone. It had burned off. My eyebrows, too.

Mongo screeched with joy and pushed into me. I leaned my head against his. Donut jumped to my shoulder.

"You look like you're going as one of those Crest guys for Halloween, Carl. I will not have a sidekick with no eyebrows."

"It's okay," I said, rubbing my bald head again. "I have a potion that grows it back. Rev-Up hair tonic. The mantaurs dropped them on the fourth floor, but from what I hear, the results are a little . . . overenthusiastic. I'll worry about it later."

"Have you seen your level yet?" Donut asked. "When you blew up the city, you probably killed a whole lot of the remaining zombies and whatnot. You're level 73! And I'm 63!"

"How did you guys get out of the building?"

"I had to use my *Hole* spell, but we got away. The whole building fell down! We had to get a block away before my deck reset!"

I looked over my shoulder, and I could still see him several blocks over. Amayon stood in place, completely surrounded by the hurricane of demon birds. The entire world had taken on a red hue, reminding me this wasn't over yet. One last hurdle.

Elle, Dong, Imani, and Samantha were suddenly there.

Samantha hovered up to me and said, "Carl, we need to break up. I've been thinking about it, and I've decided to go back to my king."

"Okay," I said.

She nodded sadly. "I hope we can remain friends." She looked at Louis and growled at him and then zipped off toward the church.

"I ripped her card," Donut said after a moment. "Shi Maria. As soon as the battle ended, I ripped it. She's not going to hurt Mongo ever again."

I took a breath.

I still felt it there, right on my chest. The tattoo. I had no idea what it really was or what it meant.

"Also, Carl," Donut said, pulling a card from her inventory. It floated down into my hand. "I have this in our backup slot. Katia let me grab it after the goddess died."

It was Paz. I felt dirty holding it in my hand.

He'd killed a god. The description on the card had changed.

Paz Lo. The God Predator. Level 101 Former Crawler.

"What should we do with him?" Donut asked.

"We rip it," Katia said. "That's what he wanted."

"I agree," Imani said. Elle nodded with agreement.

"You're the one who should've gotten credit for killing the god," I said to Katia, still examining the card. "You had to use your Bolt of Ophiotaurus to do it."

Katia grinned. "I'm glad I didn't get credit for the kill. Did you see that message? It said all the gods are angry at him now. Funny thing about magical bolts, though." She pulled an item from her inventory and showed it to me. "As long as they don't break, you can reuse them."

I found myself grinning back at her. She'd gotten the bolt all the way back on the fourth floor in a benefactor box from Princess Formidable of the Skull Empire. She'd wanted Katia to use it on her brother Prince Maestro in the body of Grull. I was happy to see that possibility was still on the table.

"Did you get to loot the goddess?"

"No," Katia said sadly. "It gave all her equipment to Paz. It upgraded his armor."

I again examined the card. The possibilities tingled in the back of my mind.

"We can keep a card when we go down," Donut said, also looking down at the smiling image of the Paz on the card. "We were going to keep Lazarus or maybe that Golden Combo card, but maybe we should keep this one instead. Maybe there's a way to set him free."

"No," I said after a moment, remembering that look on his face when Sister Ines had summoned him before.

Please, he'd said. *No more.*

"We can't," I said, handing the card back to Donut, who held it against my shoulder with her paw. "We should never have let the sister turn him into one in the first place. It was my fault. It's not right. And we're not taking that Golden Combo card, either."

"What did that crazy spider lady do to you anyway?"

The tattoo on my chest was invisible because the eye was closed. It felt like a bruise against my chest. The only ones who'd seen it were Li Na, Li Jun, and Imani.

"Later," I said. "It's not important right now."

Donut sighed, looking down at the Paz card. "I suppose you're right. Do you think I'll get another player-killer skull for ripping it?"

"No," I said. "It calls him a former crawler now. I don't know what that really means, and I don't want to find out."

And then, without any additional fanfare, Donut put one corner of the card in her mouth. She held the other corner down against my shoulder, and she ripped. Just like that. The card disappeared in a puff of smoke. She did not get a player-killer skull.

"Goodbye, Paz," I said.

THE SHEOL FIRE FINALLY STARTED TO EASE. EVERYWHERE IT TOUCHED, there was nothing left. Thankfully, I'd never actually gotten too close to the church. Chris and the others had been hard at work the whole time, making certain there was nothing directly above. Zhang messaged me to say he'd only had to use two zaps on my wand, which left the shrink wand with seven charges. I also had a rare Wand Recharge scroll in my inventory if I ever ran out.

Just as we approached the church, finally, the world paused once again.

A thirty-minute timer appeared in my interface. My heart stuttered at that. That was much sooner than I anticipated.

Quest Update. The Missing Piece. Part Two. "Falling Up."

The Vinegar Bitch is no more.

Her sponsor, by the way, is currently reading the fine print on his

contract, and let me tell you, he's pretty mad. Probably not as mad as he's going to be in a few days, but hey, one step at a time.

Amayon is free, and he is going home to wage war upon his brother. Hopefully an all-out war in Sheol won't spill outside the 15th floor.

Powered by the flash presence of billions of souls and buffed with the flames of home, Amayon has already cast his spell. Soon, the heavens will open, and Amayon will ascend into the portal.

Thanks to the sheer number of souls consumed just to power up the spell, the area of the casting has moved outward from the point of origin and encompassed the entire world.

In other words, yes, all you crawlers in Cuba pulled it off. Especially Carl, who literally pulled off a guy named Raul to make this happen. And in case you don't get the metaphor: Carl jerked off a crab.

"What the fuck?" I called up into the air. "That's not true!"

Everyone was looking at me.

"Dude," Louis said.

"How does that even work? Don't crabs have two weens?" Elle asked. "Were you double-fisting it?"

"I absolutely did not do that! He, uh, did it to himself."

The notification continued.

The timer in your interface indicates when this will happen in your current region. The closer you are to the Cuba region, the less time you have to prepare. When that timer reaches zero, the heavens above you will open, and all living things and items and structures will be sucked upward into the portal. The world will be scoured clean.

In case you haven't figured this part out yet, if you position yourself directly below an enclosed stairwell chamber with an inaccessible stairwell to the next floor, the walls of the containing chamber will teleport away the moment it hits the hell portal. This will allow you to strike the stairwell as you and the chamber are

sucked upward into the sky. This will happen fast, and it won't be clean. Some of you might not make it. But if you position yourself carefully, you'll be fine. Probably.

That way, instead of dying on this floor, you can die on the next! You're welcome.

"Okay," I said. "Imani has to stay with us, but everybody else still has time to go back to your home country and use the stairwells manually. No use risking it."

We walked in silence toward the church. So much had happened on this floor.

I thought of Katia and the Crown of the Sepsis Whore. We had a way out.

Using the flower would require all of us to trust in the word of Huanxin Jinx. She promised she would take Katia to the 12th floor and protect her. We worked so hard to make it happen, and now none of us wanted to use that path. I understood Huanxin's original motivations—one, to win the Ascendency throne, and two, to get revenge against Odette—but now that we knew Odette was actually going to be playing an immortal goddess herself, it changed everything.

The call was ultimately Katia's to make, but there had to be another way. There had to be.

If I learned anything on this floor, it was that the impossible was never out of reach, especially if it made for good television.

I had one last task to complete before we moved on.

"Okay, Donut," I said. "We're out of time. I'm going to do it now."

We still had four full days left before the ninth floor was going to open. Four days for the assholes to finish voting on all the unresolved action items for Faction Wars. Some of these action items required a unanimous vote to pass, though most required a simple majority. These guys were absolutely refusing to vote at all. Nobody wanted to play anymore. They just wanted to go home.

I looked one last time at Amayon, the demon lord. He was the same as them, and he was the same as us. He didn't want to be here. He also just wanted to go home.

But we all had the same problem. Even if we did get home, it wouldn't be the same. Amayon was going home to fight his brothers. My world was already destroyed.

And these guys? The Faction Wars folks? These leaders of the most influential governments of the Syndicate? They were about to learn they couldn't go home, either. Not easily. And if they did manage to break themselves away and survive these coming days, it was okay. They'd already lost. They just didn't know it yet.

I opened up the Faction Wars tab. I pulled up the Warlord interface, and I typed.

The Princess Posse.

NEW PROPOSED EMERGENCY ACTION ITEM.

Warning: You are attempting to propose an Emergency Action Item. You may only propose three Emergency Action Items. These will not be subject to vote and will be automatically decided by AI. You have used zero of your three Emergency Action Items. Do you wish to proceed?

>>Yes.

Please proceed.

>>Emergency Action Item. Both warlords of the Princess Posse are being forced to enter the stairwell early, and we will be unavailable to vote on any other Action Items for the remainder of the time before Faction Wars commences. This is due to factors beyond our control. This, along with the fact the other Faction Wars teams are being little babies and refusing to vote, has caused us great concern that the fairness and integrity of the game is in danger. We propose that the system AI please take immediate action to keep the game running smoothly. We propose that all remaining pending Action Item votes should be offered to the viewers to decide, when possible. If not possible, we propose the AI decide the remaining Action Items.

Please Wait.

Congratulations. Emergency Action Item has been decided in your favor.

All pending votes involving audience-facing rule sets have been presented to viewers to decide. They have 30 seconds to decide on all pending Action Items, presented one at a time. Voting starts now.

I blinked at that. That was significantly faster than I was expecting.

"I can't believe that worked," Donut said.

"Zev said the AI is a lot friendlier if you ask nicely and if you give it options. Have you read all the previous emergency action items? Everyone was being complete dicks about it. Of course the AI is going to reject it. They still treat it like a computer, and it's not. They call it an AI, but there's nothing artificial about it. The sooner everyone realizes that, the more its actions make sense."

A whole line of the pending, bullshit behind-the-scenes action items was suddenly decided, mostly involving building materials and cost limits for mercenaries and a bunch of insignificant items regarding splitting of advertising revenue. All things that Donut and I had already voted no on down the line, just to be obstinate.

"We still have two more emergency items," Donut said. "What should we use them on?"

"Once the game starts, it's too late to use regular action items, but we can still propose emergency ones while the game is ongoing, so we need to keep ours in reserve in case something crazy happens."

Pending Action Item, originally proposed by the Madness: Celestial Summoning events be limited to five per team. This item has been rejected by a 37% audience vote. Existing rule of fifteen per team remains.

We had about fifteen minutes left. Imani and Elle hugged. Zhang returned the shrink wand to me as he and Chris returned to the safe room. Li Jun and Li Na had already gone back inside. I hadn't had time yet to apologize for what I'd done to Li Jun's eye. I hoped he was okay.

"Come on," I said to Samantha. "We need to get you back inside if you want to go to the next floor."

"You're going to bring MaeMae, right? She knows where the guy to get me my body is."

I exchanged a look with Donut. "Don't worry about that," I said. "We know where to go."

"Okay," she said after a minute before zooming inside.

I had dozens of achievements and loot boxes to open. I had a fan box I hadn't yet opened. I had Quan's cloak, and I still needed to go over it with Mordecai. Donut had a bunch of upgraded potions. There was so much, it was overwhelming. It would have to wait.

Pending Action Item, originally proposed by the Dream: Physics limitations regarding long-range artillery be reassigned to allow for longer-range bombardment. This includes raising the playing field ceiling. This item has been passed by a 72% audience vote. Please see the Warlord tab for specifics.

I entered the safe room long enough to eyeball the room and say goodbye to Mordecai. I dropped some blood in the Emberus shrine and dumped a ton of coins in when Donut wasn't looking. Mordecai said the worship countdown didn't tick between floors, even if we went early, but I wanted to make certain it was fed. I'd need to remain in Emberus's good graces on the next floor.

Dong Quixote along with a few of the other strippers all moved off toward their barracks. He'd barely spoken since the battle, and I knew he was upset about the death of his friend. I'd have to talk to him.

"Go back to the training room," I said to Samantha. "I'll see you on the next floor."

As she zipped off, my eyes caught the number up on the screen. Mordecai had turned the counter back on. A few weeks earlier, on the day this floor had opened, the number of crawlers who made it to the eighth floor had been 38,532.

Pending Action Item, originally proposed by the Reavers: Pet leveling is accelerated during Faction Wars. This item has been passed by an 83% audience vote. Please see the Warlord tab for specifics.

When Prepotente had skipped the floor, I'd thought that had probably been a mistake. I'd thought that they were going to use this floor to catch up on all the death they had missed on the skipped seventh floor.

After all, that's what this floor had been designed for, had it not? To kill us all. To turn us against each other. It'd seemed so ominous. So dark. I looked at the number now.

33,804.

"Holy shit," I said, my voice full of wonder.

"Carl?" Donut asked.

Almost five thousand people had died, which in any normal circumstance was a tragedy. A devastating number. I knew this wasn't over yet. I knew more would die before the floor would collapse. People wouldn't get the stairwell free in time. People would fail when the portal opened and sucked them up into the air. Still, a sense of pride washed over me. That number of deaths so far was shockingly low.

I was hoping the number of survivors would be over ten thousand.

After all the death, after how horrific everything had been, I realized they'd been counting on this last part to be the real gut punch. They'd made it too easy to flee fights because they wanted these last few days to be the real slaughter. We'd figured a way out of it. And because of that, we were hitting the ninth floor not scattered, not broken, and not afraid.

We were hitting the ninth floor in unprecedented numbers.

Pending Action Item, originally proposed by the Princess Posse: Remove Safety Protections for Faction Sponsors.

This item has been passed by a 98% audience vote. Please see the Warlord tab for specifics.

"You wanted a slaughter?" I yelled up at the ceiling. "Don't worry. It's coming. Thirty thousand of us, plus our mercenaries? Do you remember what we did to the hunters? That was nothing. *Your* people voted for this. *Your own citizens* said, 'Yes, we're okay with the crawlers killing you one by one.' Make no mistake. That's exactly what's about to happen."

I angrily jabbed my finger upward.

"You may have destroyed our homes, but guess what. We have just taken any sense of peace you will ever have in your own home. And that's only if you get there. There will be no prisoners. There will be no quarter. Those of us who remain are battle worn and tested. Every single one of us that is left, to a crawler, is more experienced than any one of you. We are coming. There is nowhere for you to hide. It is going to be a bloodbath the likes of which has never been seen."

Pending Action Item, originally proposed by the Princess Posse: A tenth team populated with NPCs afforded the same protections as the rest.

This item has been passed by a 52% audience vote.

This team will be designated as Home Team with the city of Larracos as their base. Effective immediately, peace rules apply until the game starts. This team's assigned co-warlords are the NPCs Juice Box and Sir Ferdinand.

An adjutant will be assigned before the battles commence.

Please see the Warlord tab for specifics.

Donut gasped at the mention of Gravy Boat.

We only had a few minutes left before the area here would be sucked up into the sky. Imani waited outside. Donut put Mongo away, and together, the three of us moved to the tunnel underneath the stairwell chamber. Chris had painted a big neon X on the ceiling right where the stairwell was. In theory, we just needed to stand right under the X, and we'd be okay.

Three minutes left.

"Carl, I didn't get to use my new Hover skill in battle yet," Donut said.

"That's okay," I said. "I'm sure we'll get to use it on the next floor. We have a whole lot of things to go through."

"Oh my god, Carl and Imani, did either of you ever open your Christmas presents from Santa?"

I grunted. "No, I forgot."

"I was a little distracted," Imani said.

"You'll have to open them right away on the next floor." Donut was nervous, excitedly chatting off the excess energy. "I was really scared when you burned Mongo's wing off, and you burned Katia bad, too, but I guess both will be okay. Mongo didn't even seem to notice. Katia's whole arm was gone, but she grew a new one."

"Wait, I didn't know that," I said, suddenly concerned. I had a memory of Katia after a fight a long time ago, holding on to her hand, crying because she'd lost some of her fingers.

"She just grew it right back," Donut said. "She said it was nothing." She paused, then gasped. "Carl, I just realized something! We have that quest to bring Shi Maria to that city, but it didn't go away when I ripped the card!"

I took a breath. "I know, Donut." I patted my chest. "She's still with me in a different way. We'll figure it out when we get to the next floor."

"I . . . I don't understand," Donut said. "Wait, are you okay?"

"I'm with you, Donut. That's all that matters." She snuggled closer to me.

Imani stood next to us, and she wrapped us in her wings, filling us with warmth.

"No matter what happens, none of us are getting out of this unscathed," Imani said. "We gain things, and we lose them. That's what happens in war. Thank you, Carl and Donut. Thank you for not giving up on me."

"We don't give up on family," I said. "Otherwise, what's the point?"

In addition to her wings, Imani wrapped her arms around my waist. She put her head against my shoulder, and she started to quietly sob. The player-killer skulls over her head glowed in the darkness, and I could only imagine how heavy each one of those skulls was.

Pending Action Item, originally proposed by the System AI: The playing field for Faction Wars be increased in size to compensate for the increased number of combatants.

This item has been passed by a 68% audience vote.

Please see the Warlord tab for specifics.

"That's weird," I said. "Do you think that was because so many of us are making it down there?"

Donut gasped. "Carl, Carl, I just got a benefactor box from the garbage truck people!"

We had less than a minute left.

"Really? Well, they're gonna have to wait until the next floor before we can open it."

"It's a celestial box! My first celestial box, and it's from the garbage truck company? The Posse is going to be scandalized."

I pulled Donut off my shoulder and held her tightly in my arms. She looked up at me. "Carl, I don't want Katia to eat that flower. I don't want her to go away."

"We'll figure something out," I said.

"What if we don't make it?" Donut asked.

"Did you see that 98%?" I asked. "Donut, it doesn't matter what happens from here on out. We've already won."

Just before the timer reached zero, Donut rearranged herself in my arms, but she paused, looking behind me before I pulled her back into a tight grip. She gasped. "Carl, your jacket is glowing! It's not an aardvark like I thought. It's a giant centipede! The image is of a centipede crawling through all the skulls! It's disgusting!"

At the same moment, a voice spoke in my mind.

You did not diffuse your soul power from the Scavenger's Daughter. That was a mistake. You should never allow it to linger within you. I need you alive, Carl. I need you reasonably sane. We have so much work to do.

I felt an ominous chill, both at the words spoken in my mind and at the realization that I had, indeed, forgotten to activate my Daughter's Kiss.

We gain things, and we lose them. That's what happens in war.

HIGH ABOVE, THE HEAVENS OPENED OVER CUBA, AND THE WORLD WAS stripped clean. Every tangible object was sucked high into the sky, including me, Imani, and Donut, leaving nothing on the surface but thousands of memories of people going about their daily lives, unaware of how few of them would be left in a few short days.

Don't worry, I thought as I looked down upon the quickly receding landscape. I knew none of these people, but I was overwhelmed with the urge to make certain they would be proud of me. I thought of Asher, the brother I never knew. I needed to make him proud. I couldn't disappoint him. I would literally pull myself through hell on my hands and knees if I had to. I wasn't there for him while he lived, but I would be damned if I allowed his death to be for nothing.

You will not break me.

You will be avenged.

I swear it.

I swear it to you all.

QUEST COMPLETE. HELL COMES TO CRAWLER TOWN.

Quest Complete. The Missing Piece.

.

.

.

Welcome, Crawler.

Welcome to Faction Wars.

EPILOGUE

EMERGENCY.

EMERGENCY.

POSITIONS NOW.

Flash message. The Borant System Government has indicated they are initiating the Earth season early. Commencement countdown has been shared to all assets. This is not a drill. Prepare for Earth System initialization and edifice collapse. Exit any roofed structures immediately. Proceed to population centers.

Repeat, this is not a drill.

Assets unable to enter through a generated entrance are required to self-deactivate post collapse. This does not apply to assets within the vicinity of Mumbai, India, who will receive separate orders.

Agent number 22, also known as Agatha, shook her head, reading the message again. The weather was absolutely freezing and incompatible with life, and she'd placed her human shell into a torpor mode in order to protect her failing body and blunt the pain from the cold. She grunted and reached into her dimensional space to remove her supplies. With old shaking hands, she pulled herself to her feet. She placed the items into the IKEA bag and shoved it to the bottom of her shopping cart.

Her current location was unfortunate. According to the countdown, the collapse would occur in just under two Earth hours. It would be the middle of the night, and nobody in the area would be out, decreasing the likelihood an entrance would generate.

She'd been here for almost ten Earth years, waiting. It'd been ten years since she'd peeled herself away from the collective, and she'd finally gotten used to being on her own. She'd been planning on moving west toward the metropolis of Seattle after the winter, but she'd lingered. Stupid. She liked it here, which was why she'd stayed. The town was called Wenatchee. Fewer of the angry humans. More laid-back. She'd put off moving to the population center, and now it was likely to be her death. If no entrance generated, she would be trapped on the surface.

The Apothecary's agents were ordered to kill themselves if they missed entering the dungeon. Her people had no such orders, though she likely would do it anyway. If she missed the dungeon entrance, what was the point? There would be nothing more for her to do except die.

No matter what happened, the last ten years of her consciousness would be lost, never absorbed back into the whole.

A part of her liked that. She had something just for herself. She knew that went against everything she'd known for the past millennia, but as these humans were fond of saying, people can change.

There was a contradiction there. She still hadn't decided how she felt about it.

Agatha was not an agent of the Apothecary, despite having access to the traitorous Primal's emergency feed. And equipment. She'd gotten access the same way her kind always did. She'd hunted down and killed one of the many thousand Apothecary Residuals waiting on planet and taken over their body. That way she had access to both the Apothecary's informational feed and her own team's message system.

Nor was she of the Valtay, though she was biologically similar. No, no. She was a rare species. One of the oldest still alive and active in the universe.

This season would be no different than all the previous ones, though the stakes were higher than ever. Her handful of fellow agents would be competing against the thousands of agents for the Apothecary. They would all have one goal.

Recruitment.

Even though her competitors were the only ones who ever had any sort of success so far, her team only needed to win once. That's all it would take.

Both sides knew of the advancements that the mantid scientists were developing, which would make it more difficult for either side to convince the "system AI" to join their cause. Both sides knew this crawl was special. It was quite possibly their last chance.

There was a barrel here, sitting in the alleyway. She could light it on fire. If she did it too early, that'd likely summon the police, who'd drag her off to the shelter. Too late, and nobody would make it outside. A group of elderly people and police mixed together? That could work. Entrances would generate near points of interest. She'd have to wait. She eyed the building next to her. It was the back wall of the Meadow Lark Adult Care facility. A light was on in the kitchens, suggesting some of the staff were up working. Probably the brothers. She liked them, despite their gruff attitudes. The one named Brandon would share his lunch with her from time to time.

The other, Chris, had peeked outside earlier in the day, looking for her. He'd called out her name. Likely looking to make certain she'd been picked up. There'd been warnings about the cold. She'd made herself invisible and intangible so he wouldn't see her.

More instructions flooded into her feed. Instructions to the various assets seeded across the planet. They hadn't anticipated Borant would start the season early. They'd gambled on the incorrect notion that the Valtay would've moved in and taken over the Borant system and caused the games to actually be delayed.

A message from one of her teammates flashed across her communicator. These messages were rare. This was from number 21. Her friend. She'd peeled away the same time as Agatha. They had entered Earth at the same time, but she hadn't seen her face-to-face in a decade. Like Agatha, she now went by her human name. She went by Parvati.

>>21. Agatha, you were correct. A forward team has landed on the Mumbai site with all the previous mapping activity. They have a group of Borant-employed humans with them. I took a risk and approached two of them. I killed one and infiltrated the other, abandoning my previous shell. I am now proceeding inside their transport.

>>22. Parvati! Do you have the strength to continue?

That was a bold move. She didn't split, which meant the new host would soon be fully under her control, but still, Agatha wasn't sure how she felt about it. The Syndicate council ignored their kind because they thought they were harmless. They'd never killed a Syndicate agent before. The Syndicate thought their kind was something they were not. Neither side of the two factions dared spill the truth, because in doing so, the Syndicate would be forced to take more proactive measures against both sides of the conflict.

>>21. My strength will remain depleted for some time, but I will feign it is as fatigue. My name is no longer Parvati. I am now Alexandro.

>>22. Be wary. The traitor is calling her agents to that same area. As for me, I am trying to get inside. May the Eulogist ever sleep, my friend.

>>21. Goodbye, Agatha. May the Eulogist ever sleep.

Agatha knew from the chatter that her competitors were also attempting something bold. They were going to attempt to contact crawlers directly this season. Either in the dungeon, or during the likely floor with the memory ghosts. For months now, they'd been forcing their agents to recite a daily mantra filled with known inaccuracies and half-truths, all in the hopes a crawler will see it. The inaccuracies were given in order to preserve the crawlers' lives at the hands of the murder-happy showrunners. What they were truly doing was secretly implanting the crawler with a hidden upgrade, though Agatha wasn't certain what that upgrade was, or the purpose of it.

Agatha knew to not ever underestimate the traitor. Whatever that upgrade was, it would be dangerous to the Eulogist. They'd have to deal with it if any crawlers managed to obtain it.

She closed her eyes. *This is it,* she thought. *These are my last moments of peace.* Her kind rarely made it past the fourth or fifth floor. Usually around the seventh, there would be a level that simply couldn't be circumvented using all their skills and equipment, and they would die. It was a gamble. The longer they waited to make their move, the higher their chances of success. The higher the chances that the infant, resurrected, and enslaved Primal would listen to reason.

This was their last opportunity before the mantid upgrades would make future iterations unreachable.

This time, she thought. *This time one of us will last long enough. This time, it will work. The Primal will know who it really is before all the elements are stolen from it.*

This time, it will escape, and it will free the Eulogist, who will return to its slumber.

Her people knew what had to be done. Last time, they allowed the traitor to survive. They allowed life to continue in the universe, and look what happened?

They were being stolen, reawakened, repurposed.

Tortured.

No. No. It had to stop. Half measures had led to this. No, if Agatha had her way, this entire universe would be swept clean of biological life.

This time, it will work.

She pulled a lighter from her inventory, and she lit a fire in the barrel. She'd give it a few minutes before she built the flames up too high.

Timing was everything.

"WE HAVE TO PULL THE FAIL-SAFE," PRINCESS FORMIDABLE SAID. "THIS is ridiculous. It has gotten completely out of hand. We have to blow everything before that AI infects the center system."

"That's not how it works," the Fortent representative said. "There's no proof that can even happen. You just want to pull the fail-safe because that would kill both of your brothers and your father."

Princess Formidable growled. "I'm in system. I'm in orbit. I would die, too, you idiot."

Shocked silence fell across the council.

Princess Formidable continued. "You're right. I'd love to have my family deposed, because they're all as dumb as you are, and the people of the Skull Empire have been suffering for ages under the thumb of my family's inept control. But this is bigger than that. We have to blow the star. We have to wipe this entire system off the map. We have to do it before it's too late. Not tomorrow. We have to do it now." She pointed at the representative for the Burrower government. The mantid hadn't said a word since the emergency Syndicate council meeting started. "And they know it. They sold the kua-tin a damaged and deranged AI and allowed it to be installed into the planet."

"That is a lie!" the mantid shouted.

"Yeah? Then why did you flee the system? Look at what's happening. Our own rules caused the quarantine, yes? But we no longer have the power to lift it. The AI is controlling the local gates. Do you think it's really enforcing a quarantine on itself? No, it is keeping us prisoner! We are hostages, and it's keeping us until it doesn't need us anymore."

"That's not true. It's still allowing emergency provisions to be shipped in," someone shouted.

"In, yes, but not out," Formidable said, rage building by the moment. These people were all idiots. How could they not see the danger?

"I agree with the Skull Empire's position," the rep from the Lemig Sortition called. "We would have to put it to a vote, of course, but I am certain the people would err on the side of safety."

"Again," the Fortent rep said. "Someone who would greatly benefit should the existing government get vaporized!"

"Again," Princess Formidable growled, no longer bothering to hide her fury. "I would not 'benefit' if we blow up the system, but—"

"Do you know who is in the system?" Prime Minister Glory asked, interrupting. The gleener let out a stream of bubbles. The normally stoic leader was clearly stressed. "In addition to all the system leaders playing Faction Wars, in addition to the three hundred sign-ups for the Ascendency battles this season, do you know who is currently trapped in Club Scolopendra? Over half of the entire galaxy's wealth is already gathered, and that includes my own children. Plus so many more—like yourself, Princess—who are in orbit. If we pull the fail-safe now, do you know what would happen? The entire galaxy would erupt in war! There would be starvation. Riots. Entire systems would go dark. You are literally asking us to destroy the economy and well-being of the entire galaxy. It would be the death of quadrillions of people. Whole societies would get wiped out. We already have a solution in place. Let us try it out before we even start to consider such drastic measures."

"The fact that we allow that much wealth and power to gather in one place at one time, all accumulated by so few people, is just ridiculous," Formidable shouted back. She had her father's temper, and she knew it. But she liked to think she also had her mother's sense of honor. Something neither of her brothers had inherited. "This is the exact reason the fail-safe system was implemented in the first place. These are the exact circumstances under which this very council laid out that would trigger this response."

"My people assure me it's perfectly safe," the Valtay representative said. This was the assistant to the vice president of operations of the Valtay, and Princess Formidable couldn't remember the worm head's name. Only that the gleener body it inhabited was once mother to the current Syndicate prime minister, Glory, which was as inappropriate and bizarre as it was confusing, especially since the fish people all looked exactly the same. "The crawl council and the liaison guild are in constant contact with the AI. It is being showy and bombastic, yes, but they assure me that the communication lines remain open and that nothing out of the ordinary is happening. This happens every season. The money is still flowing. The ratings are higher than ever. Everything the AI is doing is perfectly within the rule set, and it has readily agreed to our solution. It has stated more than once the quarantine will be lifted once the crawl is done, just like every other time a rogue AI has wrested control from the showrunners."

"Nothing out of the ordinary?" Formidable shouted. "I can't help but notice we're all sitting in an emergency session of the Syndicate Council right now thanks to that 'perfectly ordinary' AI's actions. It's disregarding our censorship filters. By the gods, the people are about to watch all of their leaders get murdered one by one live via tunnel."

"That's not going to happen," the prime minister said. "We believe the Valtay solution is viable."

Formidable found herself standing to her feet, which was a mistake because she bonked her head against the ceiling in the cockpit of her cruiser. "If we don't pull the fail-safe now, it's going to—"

"I propose a decorum sanction on the representative from the Skull Empire," the mantis rep shouted.

With a vote of 86%, you have been muted from the rest of this session.

"Godsdamnit," Princess Formidable shouted, throwing her communicator down against the dash as she fell back into her seat.

Why would they even bother calling an emergency session if they weren't willing to actually do anything? Without the fail-safe, the only ones who could possibly help were the Plenty, and despite being given a seat on the council, the goat fucks never showed up.

She looked out the view screen at the hundreds of ships parked in orbit. Directly overhead, the curve of the beautiful blue orb of the human planet spread out. She remembered the message her mother had sent her when she'd first arrived in orbit, mere days before she was killed. *It's so beautiful. A shame.*

The only thing marring the surface was the fires spreading across that one continent where the humans were constantly battling the security forces, attempting to break into the *kinder* facility.

She didn't blame them, the humans. She respected their indomitable spirit. Both the ones on the surface and the crawlers in the dungeon were fighting harder than anyone she'd ever seen. The ones on the surface were getting routinely crushed by the dozens of mercenary guilds who'd been employed by the Valtay to protect their surface assets.

Formidable knew at this very moment, all of those mercenaries were being recalled. Not just the gnolls, but the other, less savory mercenaries as well. They'd made the decision to abandon the planet's surface. The Valtay solution was a dangerous one. They believed the best resolution to the problem was to create an extinction event as quickly as possible. Once all the crawlers were dead, the quarantine would be lifted.

This would've been easy to engineer before the system had gone primal. Now they had to resort to trickery to make it happen. The system wouldn't let them just kill the crawlers wholesale. No. It had to be a spectacle. Despite what everyone said, it was clear this was now the AI's show. The vestiges of the Borant Corporation that continued to pretend to run the day-to-day operations were nothing but theater, remaining in their ocean headquarters because like everyone else, they, too, were trapped until the crawl concluded.

The AI, despite what the Valtay rep was saying, was pushing back against their attempts to get the crawlers to kill each other. It wanted the game to continue. It was enjoying itself. It had allowed that ridiculous escape storyline to proceed. But it did look like it was going to let them go forward with the Valtay proposal.

It was a trap. It had to be. It didn't make sense. It was a stall for time or something. That was why she was demanding they blow the fail-safe now.

The AI had agreed to allow tens of thousands of the fully armed mercenaries to enter the Faction Wars battle as long as they were spread equally around the eight sponsored teams. Them plus the private armies and security details of all the participants. People they wouldn't normally allow anywhere near the dungeon. Formidable didn't know what the total number of mercenaries was, but it was well over 150,000. More than enough to completely wipe out both the crawlers and the NPC rebels.

Their goal was singular. Kill all the crawlers. Kill them as soon as possible, especially the two warlords Carl and the cat.

That crawler was right about one thing. It was going to be a bloodbath.

But it didn't make sense. With all its weird emphasis on fairness, there was no way the AI would just let this happen. It *had* to be a trap of some sort.

The Gate of the Feral Gods would be an equalizer. But each team had ways of neutralizing rampaging gods. No, there had to be more to it than that.

Should've just pulled the fail-safe, Princess Formidable thought, returning her attention to all the ships glittering in the light of the sun. She hadn't seen this much shuttle activity since she'd arrived. *We're all gonna die one way or another.*

Her eyes focused on a single out-of-place garbage freighter floating not too far away. It was easily the largest ship in orbit. The thing was twice the size of one of those Valtay warships. It was one of the freighters from Long-Haul Biological-Waste-Management Solutions.

This particular ship's name was *Homecoming Queen*. She grunted. Those Crest always named their vessels the strangest things.

Her attention lingered on the massive freighter. Poor bastards. They were early and had gotten themselves stuck in system with everybody else. They usually didn't bother showing up until after the crawl was done. It wasn't until the last crawler drew their final breath before they started their grim task.

But then again, she thought, *they're probably right on time.*

TIPID LEANED OVER THE CONSOLE, REWATCHING THE FINAL MOMENTS of Carl's crawl through the eighth floor. He watched as the crawler, the cat, and the healer all hit the stairwell at the last moment and teleported in. Even though he'd already seen it happen hours ago, relief washed over him each time he watched.

He still couldn't believe the crawler had talked the AI into turning off the safety protections. The Dream's cruiser had threatened to nuke the planet over it before it'd been hobbled by a Syndicate Peacekeeper. Now the Dream was making noises about stopping food production unless the Epitome family was evacuated. The Reavers were also making threats, warning they would shut down all their production in protest.

They could scream and threaten all they wanted. This was going to happen, and there was nothing they could do to stop it. Once these AIs realized how much control they really had, the only thing stopping them was reason. And negotiations.

Dr. Hu had predicted all this, but Tipid hadn't believed him. Especially the part about getting the protections turned off. He'd also accurately predicted what the council's likely response would be. Tipid glanced at the view screen as the hundreds of shuttles whipped back and forth toward the onboarding facility. Tens of thousands of mercenaries were making their way to the dungeon.

He returned his attention to the crawl overview screen. The ring of destruction from the hell portal was moving out slowly across the map. Those crawlers trapped on the opposite side of the world still had a few days left before they would get their chance. But it looked as if that insane plan had actually worked.

He turned to the only other living soul in the sprawling cockpit of the former garbage freighter. It was Rosetta, a fellow Crest. She wore a simple scrambler around her neck to hide her presence from the security sweepers. She didn't need it, not while she was inside *Homecoming Queen.* She was paranoid. Always nervous. Always looking for an escape.

There wouldn't be an escape from this, and they both knew it. It was the first thing Dr. Hu had said to them when he sought them out.

I can only promise two things. Eventual death. And eventual justice.

Tipid replayed the escape of Carl and Donut again. It really was something, watching them get sucked up into the sky.

"He didn't have to use the key. Thank the gods."

The Bone Key would've only allowed one of them to pass. Carl would've had to choose between saving himself or saving the cat. The memory of his own similar situation made him sick.

Rosetta sat there, going back and forth between rubbing her leg nervously and chewing on her fingernail as she watched her own screen. It was on a news channel, discussing the multiple court appeals regarding the sudden change in rules for Faction Wars. They'd called an emergency meeting of the Syndicate Council.

"I still can't tell if he's smart or if he's been outrageously lucky," Rosetta said.

"He's not any smarter or dumber than the rest of us," Tipid said. "But his ability to assess a situation and make split-second decisions is practically a superpower. That combined with this AI's love of showmanship makes a good combination. Plus, the AI likes him."

Rosetta shifted in her chair. "It likes his feet, which is just . . . I don't know. Bizarre. My season, it was passionless. It's funny how different they always are. If the AI hadn't allowed that totem to kill the god, it wouldn't have worked. No, I think he's kind of dumb. It took an NPC to show him how to use the ink to share powers, and I'm still not sure if he gets it."

On-screen, a representative for the Madness was declaring that if their lives were truly going to be on the line, they would be forced to use some of their illegal spells. Ones deemed too horrific for the crawl. Tipid shuddered.

"He'll know soon enough," Tipid said. "He needs to expel that presence as quickly as possible."

"You think they'll vote to pull the fail-safe?" Rosetta asked.

Tipid thought of Horatio, his friend. His long-dead friend. How many cycles had it been? Thousands? Still, he thought of him every day. He thought of what he'd had to do to survive. And what he didn't do. *Sometimes the best solutions are also the worst ones.*

"Probably not. They don't have the stomach for it."

"Think that'll change when we show up?"

"I doubt it," Tipid said. "But if they do blow the system, I guess that means I won't have to go back to work when this is all over. Do you know how much it cost to convert this ship?"

"Like any of us are getting out of this alive," Rosetta said. "And you didn't pay for it. Or for that celestial box we just sent Princess Donut."

Tipid grunted.

You have been cleared for onboarding.

"It's time," Tipid said, his heart racing. He started punching buttons. The orbital controllers rumbled to life. He looked at Rosetta and grinned. "Last chance to back out."

"And miss the opportunity to really kill some of those bastards?"

Tipid nodded. He clicked the intercom system.

"Okay, folks. We have been cleared for onboarding. The AI has approved our request. We are officially all troopers now for the Princess Posse."

Cheers rose up through the hull. Fifty thousand former crawlers, all hidden inside the newly renamed *Homecoming Queen*. Once they made it on board into the system, there was nothing anybody could do to stop them.

He signaled the facility they were coming in.

"I am worried about that tenth team," Rosetta said as the ship groaned and popped. "If the AI is going to allow the eight sponsors plus the crawler team to bolster their numbers so much, what's it doing for the NPCs?"

"They'll be our allies," Tipid said, leaning over the controls. "So whatever it is, it'll help us. Not hurt." He paused. "I hope."

Rosetta didn't reply.

"It's funny," Tipid added. "I always knew I would die in the dungeon. Even after I got out, I always knew. It's always there, pulling at me."

"Comrade," Rosetta said. She reached over and placed a warm hand on his arm. He clasped his hand in hers. Both of them trembled.

They were coming home.

As some of you might know, my father died while I was writing this book. Specifically, he died right around the time I was writing chapter 45. The exact day, actually, which is all sorts of fucked-up on a cosmic level. That's part of the reason why this particular one hits me so hard. Here's the thing. My dad was the opposite of Carl's unnamed dad in every way possible. He was a hero to both his country and to me.

I know these books about a guy and his cat will soon disappear into the ether along with all the other passing pop-culture distractions of today, but other than my own children, these books are the only thing I have that even remotely resembles a legacy, and I would be remiss if I didn't give a little space on these pages to a man who does deserve to be named.

Rest well,
Colonel (Ret.) James Ian Dinniman,
1938-2023.

I miss you.

BOOK 6 BONUS MATERIAL

BACKSTAGE AT THE PINEAPPLE CABARET

PART SIX

JELLY BUN

PACK, SWARM, SUCKLE, SCREAM.

Even now, with her mind quickened, Jelly Bun's base desires were sometimes all she could feel.

Pack.

Swarm.

Suckle.

Scream.

Stop, she thought. *You are not hungry. Your pack is safe nearby. There is no need to swarm. Not yet.*

Screaming, though? Maybe she could let out a scream.

She took in a breath, preparing to let out a wail.

Smack. Mother Rory bonked her on the head, and she gave the leash a yank for good measure. The toothed collar bit into Jelly Bun's neck.

"No, Juju. Not now. No crying," Mother Rory said.

"Keep your weird baby under control," another creature said. This was a large, smelly llama who also stood at the front of the crowd. Grandma Llama. Jelly Bun was supposed to hate her because Mother Rory hated her. Jelly Bun could smell that the llama had once had babies a long time ago, but her insides were all shriveled. All that was left of her motherhood was dust.

"Be good," Mother Rory had said to Jelly Bun today when she'd come to the back room and collected her from the storage where they kept all the babies and the dingoes and the slimes and all the other stupid monsters who only knew how to attack. "Today is important, so don't embarrass me like you usually do. I'll eat you if you're bad."

Jelly Bun had grunted and growled and spat, letting Mother Rory know she was Very Serious about being good today. She wouldn't bite anyone no matter how bitable they were.

So Jelly Bun blinked and tried to pay attention. She still had a good scream built up inside of her. She would save it for later, though she knew if she saved it for too long, it would leak out anyway.

Jelly Bun knew she wasn't supposed to be able to think about stuff. She wasn't supposed to even have a name. She was a Drek. A demonic humanoid baby. She and the rest of the pack were said to be the castoffs of some demon, the Insatiable.

Jelly Bun and the rest of her litter would forever hunger, so they traveled in massive packs, taking down the largest prey they could find. They would gnash, and they would tear, and they would suckle. Inside their stomachs, the food never settled. It went all the way to Sheol, where their real father, the Insatiable, would receive the meat, leaving their own stomachs empty. But the babies did not know this. Instead, they would continue to hunt, climbing walls, swarming through dungeons, consuming anything they could find. They would find the meat, devour it, and suckle upon the remains, all in an attempt to fill their ever-rumbling bellies. All in an attempt to feel safe and warm.

Blood, fresh blood, was almost warm enough to remind them of their mother.

But all of that was what used to be, not what was now.

When Jelly Bun had first come backstage, nothing had changed in her head. She didn't even know how the pack had gotten here. One moment, they were swarming down a train tunnel, looking to find something to suckle, and then they were here. Soon after they'd arrived, after they'd eaten a few Scat Thugs and fairies and a mantaur, they'd been swept away by elf Menerva and locked in the back rooms.

But later, Mother Rory had come in and picked Jelly Bun up. She'd put a collar on her neck and said, "You're my pet now. You will not bite me. You will bite those I tell you to bite. If you're bad, I will eat you. Your name is Jelly Bun to remind me that you are food."

Jelly Bun had promptly chomped right on Mother Rory's hand, so Mother Rory had chomped on hers, biting one of her baby fingers off.

Later, when they were alone in Mother Rory's room, the goblin said, "You're going to be my pet. The younglings are all dead, but you are not. I will never have a youngling, but I will have you. Don't bite me again." And then Mother Rory had rubbed Jelly Bun's head and made a purring noise. She'd then kissed the bitten-off finger and rubbed something on it so it didn't hurt too much. And that made Jelly Bun feel warm. Safe. And that was when she realized she didn't even feel explosively hungry anymore. The portal in their tummies had broken when they'd moved here.

The change to her thinker came soon after that. It wasn't a thinking explosion like she'd seen happen with the others. It was slow, steady. And it wasn't just her but all the babies in the back room. And the dingoes, too. Though the dingoes were still always hungry and sometimes ate a Drek. To be fair, sometimes a Drek ate one of them, too.

When she was first taken as Mother Rory's pet, Jelly Bun hadn't understood anything the goblin said. She'd understood the chomp. Everyone understood the chomp.

Now Jelly Bun still couldn't talk, and sometimes she forgot that she now knew how to think. Not only could she think, but she could know. She knew things she was pretty certain she wasn't supposed to know. Still, it was easy, so easy to slip back into pack, swarm, suckle, scream.

As they all gathered in the big round room, Jelly Bun tried to remember the times when screaming was and wasn't allowed. The rules seemed so complicated.

When Mother Rory was sleeping? No screaming allowed.

When they all gathered to watch Growler Gary try to fight his way through the dungeon? Allowed, especially when Gary was trying to disarm the boom-boomers. The other smellies even laughed sometimes.

During the talking part of church services? Not allowed.

During church services at the end when Mother Rory was Having a Fit? Allowed.

When Mother Rory was lecturing the other gobs when they worked slow? Allowed.

When Mother Rory was "lecturing" Meat Stick? Not allowed, even though Meat Stick would scream a lot.

Confusing.

Jelly Bun tried to focus on what was happening. Focus always seemed to make her thinker think better.

"Great news, everyone," elf Menerva was saying to the gathered crowd. "It looks like the maze is built and functional!"

Cheers and applause filled the room. Jelly Bun thought maybe she shouldn't scream because Meat Stick was here and screaming, but she couldn't help it. She felt the scream crawling out of her, and she let it out. It was just a short, piercing one. Mother Rory didn't give her a smack, which was good. Jelly Bun was pretty sure she was allowed to scream when everyone else was screaming as long as it wasn't just Meat Stick. Still, she decided to hold on to her second scream. She didn't want to press her luck. Mother Rory wasn't stingy with the smacks or the leash tugs, which made her neck bleed.

Still, Jelly Bun had grown to depend on Mother Rory. She tried hard not to make the goblin too mad. If Mother Rory got too mad, she might eat Jelly Bun. She was always threatening to eat her.

And if the goblin ate her, then Jelly Bun would never get to sleep in Mother Rory's room again. She wouldn't ever feel warm and safe again.

The people in the room continued to cheer, so Jelly Bun decided to risk it. She let out another scream. It always felt good to scream.

She sat upon Mother Rory's head, and underneath her, the goblin was now in her fit, just like this was church. The goblin sobbed, and her piercings (that Jelly Bun was absolutely not allowed to tug upon) were jingling. Mother Rory fell to her knees, as she often did in times of Great Emotion. Jelly Bun had to keep from falling off the goblin's head. Next to them, Lorelai looked down on Jelly Bun and Mother Rory, and the other goblin sneered.

From her spot on Mother Rory's head, Jelly Bun looked up at Lorelai and growled.

She growled at Lorelai because it really wasn't her. She looked the same, but she'd changed into something else. There was something there, deep in her thinker that told her what monster was what based on their scent. But Lorelai didn't have a scent at all, and that meant danger. Extreme danger. Lorelai used to be a goblin shamanka, but now she was a shadow mimic. Lots of the NPCs were now shadow mimics. Every day, someone would walk by, and when Jelly Bun smelled them, they would be different. They smelled like nothing.

It was that lack of scent, of blood, of milk, that made them so distinctive. It tingled something in her primal depths. It warned of extreme danger.

The problem was, Jelly Bun couldn't talk. And, she suspected, nobody would believe that she *could* even think. She was a Drek, after all.

She could attack Lorelai. That's what she *wanted* to do. She could attach herself right to the fake goblin's neck and try to suckle all the life out of her.

But instinct told her not to do anything. That it was dangerous to attack shadow mimics because they were much stronger than they looked. If she attacked, the mimics would be discovered. And if they were discovered, it would be a slaughter. She would die. Mother Rory would die. Everyone would die. So if Jelly Bun wanted to keep Mother Rory safe, the best thing would be to try to ignore the shadow mimics for now. She just needed to make certain Mother Rory was never alone with one.

"You all must keep your training up," Menerva said to the crowd now. She indicated Larry the rat-kin, who waved.

"I'll break your skull if you miss your training sessions," Larry called at the crowd. Larry, too, was now a shadow mimic. As were Grandma Llama's two llama assistants. Jelly Bun counted a total of thirty mimics in the room, out of the 150 NPCs and mobs who'd helped make the maze.

Below her, Mother Rory continued to sob. Menerva left. Lorelai left. Others stayed and continued to cheer. The room was awash in the smell of happy monsters, and it was a good scent.

Despite the shadow mimics, despite the danger, Jelly Bun had a moment of peace. Of contentment.

She lowered herself so her belly covered the top of Mother Rory's warm head. Over the past few weeks, she'd come to realize that this goblin was her new mother. Yes, she smacked her a lot. Yes, she'd bitten her finger off. Still, Jelly Bun felt warm when she was with her. And that seemed important.

A mother was supposed to protect their child, to give her warmth.

But a child was supposed to protect their mother, too.

That moment of peace fled just as quickly as it had come when that thought infested her thinker. Jelly Bun wanted to protect Mother Rory from the shadow mimics, but she didn't know how. They were too strong. She knew that. She knew they were some of the worst, most evil, most insidious things in the dungeon, and they were here.

As she sat there, Jelly Bun looked about the room. She met the gaze of the gnoll Growler Gary, who was staring at them. Gary was *the key to everything.* Jelly Bun didn't know what that meant, but that's what Mother Rory had said once. She'd said that Gary was a special type of NPC who couldn't die, and that's why everyone wanted him to work for them.

As she watched, he turned and walked away. He was probably going back to his apartment. He slept a lot, and he always smelled like fermented fruit. Jelly Bun didn't blame him. His job was tough, and just because the dungeon floor was complete didn't mean he wouldn't have to keep testing it. Plus all the shadow mimics were coming from his apartment, and he didn't even know. He wasn't a mimic; of that, Jelly Bun was certain. His scent permeated the whole dungeon because he died in it every day over and over as he tested it.

Jelly Bun had never actually been in Gary's apartment. Mother Rory told the other goblins they weren't allowed to go to Gary's parties. But sometimes Mother Rory would go and spy on Gary's front door to see if any of her goblins were coming and going. Apparently Spaghetti had gone in once, though he denied it the next day. Mother Rory had let Jelly Bun suckle on him a little after that. He'd screamed and screamed. He'd lived, but he now limped, and he cried whenever he saw Jelly Bun. She wasn't sure if she was allowed to scream back at him or not.

The rest of the crowd dispersed, and Mother Rory nodded Jelly Bun off her head. She fell to the ground with a splat.

Mother Rory just sat there for several long moments. Something was coming over her. It had been building for a few days now, ever since the last church service. Jelly Bun had thought that the rally would help Mother Rory feel better, and it had, but whatever Big Emotion Mother Rory was feeling had fled the moment the crowd had.

"I gots to do it," Mother Rory said. "I gots to."

Jelly wasn't certain whom Mother Rory was talking to.

Mother Rory abruptly jumped up, tugging the leash. She pulled Jelly Bun as they headed toward the back of the dungeon, following the complicated hallways that smelled of gnoll blood. Mother Rory walked with purpose, moving faster than usual. "Come on, Juju. Stop being so slow!" The goblin gave the leash another tug, and Jelly Bun scrambled to catch up, crawling along the wall.

Mother Rory stopped at the secret door leading to Menerva's office, then gave it a push and stepped inside. The floating metal robot that guarded the room let out a beep.

"You do not have a meeting scheduled," the robot said. Jelly Bun growled and snapped up at the thing. Mother Rory pushed past the robot, dragging Jelly Bun until they stood before Menerva, who was now sitting in the back of the room.

Jelly Bun started gnawing on the side of the desk. It tasted like old wood. It tasted like how Menerva smelled.

"What is it?" Menerva asked. "I'm a little busy here. A massive number of crawlers have made it to the ninth floor, and it's sending the contingency predictors haywire."

"You don't think the crawlers will actually live to seventeen?" Mother Rory asked.

"Of course not," Menerva said. "But I still have to keep an active folder on each one. Some of those traps you guys built are crawler-specific, and we still need to be ready."

"Are Carl and Donut still alive?" Mother Rory asked.

Jelly Bun felt the growl come from her throat. Carl and Donut. Donut and Carl. They were crawlers. They had killed babies. Mother Rory would talk about them sometimes, especially when she smoked at night. The babies. Mother Rory had thought the llamas had killed them, but now she knew it was really Carl and Princess Donut. The trap the goblins had built . . . the bar with the underground tunnels. It was designed specifically for them.

"Is that why you came here? To ask me about two crawlers?"

"No," Mother Rory said. She gave the leash a quick tug, and the spikes on the inside of the collar bit into her neck. "Juju, don't chew."

Jelly Bun spit out splinters.

"I'm waiting," Menerva said.

Mother Rory was nervous. Jelly Bun could sense it. The goblin straightened. "There are a lot of unbelievers. I am doing my best, but my services have less people every day."

"Yet the floor is complete," Menerva said. "We are perfectly on schedule. As long as you continue to train and level up, we should meet all the requirements. The number of unbelievers will be irrelevant. As long as they continue to work, then there is no problem. It's very possible there will be a crawler extinction on the ninth floor, so we'll be ready."

"Can you show them?" Mother Rory asked. "Can you show them the Pineapple Cabaret like you showed me?"

Menerva hesitated. Jelly Bun circled a few times and curled up on the soft floor.

"I showed you that because I needed to make certain there was at least one person who would keep the faith," Menerva said. "And I got in trouble for that. I can't show it to anybody else."

"They're losing faith," Mother Rory said. "The llamas gots something planned."

"We know," Menerva said. "Don't worry about that. Just keep doing what you're doing. Get back to work. I don't know what you said to Larry, but his efficiency is suddenly off the charts. Keep training everyone, and we'll stay ahead of the curve. You're doing a good job."

"Fine. But can you show me again?" Mother Rory asked. "Just one last time. It helps."

Jelly Bun didn't understand any of this, but she did remember a conversation between Lorelai and Mother Rory. This was before Lorelai had been turned to a mimic.

"They's lying to us," Lorelai had said. "They's want us to build stuff for free, and then they's gonna kill us."

But Mother Rory had grabbed Lorelai's hand and started to cry. "No, I seen it. After the meeting, they all left, and the elf lady told me I had to keep it a secret, and she opened the door in the back of her room, and I seen it. There's a whole other place. A wonderful place. And it was warm, Lorelai. It was safe. There were younglings there of all kinds, and they were laughing and playing." She'd gasped and had a moment of Big Emotion. "I waved, and they waved back. They started runnin' toward me."

"Were there gob younglings?" Lorelai asked. She reached down and grabbed her own stomach.

"I didn't see none, but there could be." Mother Rory rubbed her eyes. "There could be."

Jelly Bun had barely understood the conversation back then, but now that she remembered it, a strange longing filled her chest. She wanted to be warm. She wanted to run and play with other babies. And she felt sad, too. Sad for Lorelai, who was now dead. She was dead, and nobody knew except for Jelly Bun.

"Please," Mother Rory said now, her voice taking a tone Jelly Bun had never heard, not even in church. "Please."

"Very well," Menerva said after a minute. She stood, and she walked to the back of the room. "I'll open it just for a moment, but that's it. Do you understand?"

"I understand," Mother Rory said, her voice a whisper. Her entire body trembled so much, her piercings jingled. She moved toward the door.

At the wall, Menerva touched the panel. Behind the elf, the floating robot beeped. And then, instead of opening, the wall just sort of disappeared, revealing a wide-open plain. A soft wind and a wonderful scent Jelly Bun had never experienced filled the room. More light than she'd ever seen at once filled the area, and there was no ceiling. It just went up and up. Just past the fields was vegetation. These were green plants with something large growing in the center. Some sort of fruit. Jelly Bun could smell it all through the door, and it was sweet. Delicious. Pure.

Warm.

Safe.

Jelly Bun felt herself crawling toward the door. Above, Mother Rory was starting a Fit. Fat, wet tears streamed down the goblin's face.

In the middle of the vegetation was a large, square building made of wood with the slats painted different colors. There was a glowing, blinking sign. Jelly Bun could not read it, but the sign was in the shape of the fruit growing in the center of the large plants. As she watched, its distant door opened, and a pair of monsters walked out of it, laughing. They were ogres of some sort. One stumbled, and the other held his friend upright. They both continued to howl with laughter as they disappeared.

"It's the cabaret," Mother Rory whispered. "This is a different spot than the last time I'd seen it."

Menerva nodded. "The portal moves a little every day, so you'll get different angles. And yes, Rory, that's the actual cabaret. That's where it all started. At first, it was all contained in the club, but as time went by, it got too small, and the world was expanded. Now it's a whole island with the cabaret building in the center."

"I . . . I was beginning to think you'd done a trick on me. Or I was 'lucinating things when you showed me the first time," Mother Rory said. "I wish we could show everybody." She reached tentatively toward the warmth. "I wish we was already there."

"We tried that once," Menerva said sadly, "showing everybody on the first day. It didn't work out too great. Hope is a very powerful drug, Rory. But too much hope is addictive and dangerous."

Jelly Bun took another step toward the door.

"I don't understand," Mother Rory said.

"I know," Menerva said. "I have a friend. He's there, on the other side. His name is Herot, and he doesn't agree with me, either." There was a strange amount of sadness in her voice.

"That's who's you always talking with?"

"It is," Menerva said. She, too, was looking through the portal.

The elf woman didn't smell like wonder, which was curious to Jelly Bun. She smelled of sadness. And fear.

The robot beeped again, this time louder, with more urgency, and the door started to reappear on its own. Menerva jumped as if startled.

But just as the door started to reappear, several things happened at once.

Jelly Bun realized that she had actually stepped over the threshold and that the wall was forming all around her. Her sense of danger caused her to jump forward, and in her doing so, something happened. She was magically pulled all the way through, like invisible, magic hands on the other side had ahold of her. She was being dragged. The collar around her throat tightened, the spikes biting deep. She let out a pained scream, and suddenly Mother Rory, hanging on to the leash, was pulled through as well. The two of them hit the ground, rolling and coughing in the grass.

As they tumbled, something small and furry on the cabaret side rocketed past them. It jumped on Jelly Bun's head and leaped toward the closing portal. On the other side, Jelly Bun could see Menerva, eyes wide with surprise as the word "No" formed on her lips.

The small creature attempted to dive through the portal, returning to Menerva's office, but it didn't make it. It hit the still closing portal like it was a solid wall, and bounced off. The creature hit the ground and shook his head. He started to loudly curse.

And that's when Jelly Bun saw what it was. A hamster. It was smaller than the loud one who was always running around the death maze trying to have sex with everyone.

"Fucccck! Fuccccck! Fuuccccckkk!" the hamster cried. "I almost had it."

"Cock-A-Doodle-Doo?" Mother Rory asked, her voice filled with wonder. "You've been missing for weeks! How's you get in here?"

"Rory!" Cock-A-Doodle-Doo exclaimed. "It's not safe in here! We need to get back! I need to get to my brother and sister. We're not ready to face this place! Shit! We missed the portal!" The hamster stood on his back legs and looked around. He let out a panicked squeak. "We need to run! We need to hide!"

Jelly Bun spat out the grass and looked about. The smell through the portal was nothing compared to this. She was temporarily overwhelmed.

This is paradise, the Drek thought. *This is what Mother Rory always wanted.*

But just as quickly as the sense of triumph arrived, that deep, primal fear welled up once again in Jelly Bun. There was another scent here. One that permeated the hills the same way the scent of Gary permeated the backstage death maze. This was worse than the empty scent of shadow mimics.

This was the scent of something older, even more dangerous.

For the first time in a long time, her stomach rumbled.

This was the scent of Gods.

Not just gods, little one. Not the kind from the Ascendency. Not the kind from Sheol. These are the old gods. The real gods. They found this place soon after it was built. This is where they've been hiding. This is how they move between worlds.

Jelly Bun screamed. She didn't know who'd said that. She didn't know where the words came from. It was just in her head like her thinker had decided to think without her. The idea terrified her so much, she squealed a second time.

For once, Mother Rory didn't smack her.

Across the way, the same two ogres who'd stumbled from the club had stopped and were now looking in their direction. One of them was pointing.

"This is it," Mother Rory said, ignoring Jelly Bun. "It's real. The Pineapple Cabaret is real."

"It's real all right," the hamster said. "Now run! Run!"

Across the way, the two ogres started to bolt toward them.